THE
MOGHUL

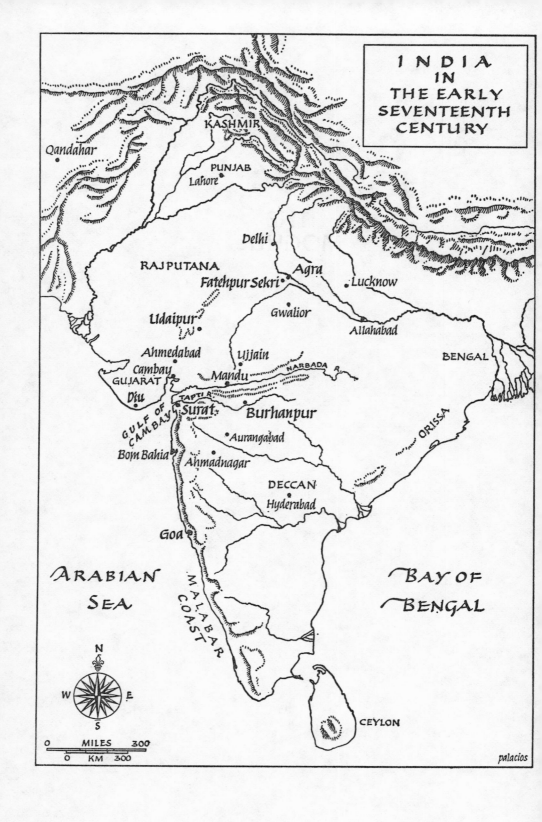

INDIA
IN
THE EARLY
SEVENTEENTH
CENTURY

Qandahar

KASHMIR

PUNJAB
Lahore

Delhi

RAJPUTANA

Agra

Fatehpur Sekri

Lucknow

Udaipur

Gwalior

Allahabad

Ahmedabad

Ujjain

BENGAL

Cambay
GUJARAT

Mandu

NARBADA R.

Diu

TAPTI R.

GULF OF
CAMBAY

Surat

Burhanpur

ORISSA

Aurangabad

Bom Bahia

Ahmadnagar

DECCAN

Hyderabad

Goa

ARABIAN
SEA

MALABAR
COAST

BAY OF
BENGAL

N
W E
S

CEYLON

0   MILES   300
0   KM   300

palacios

THOMAS HOOVER

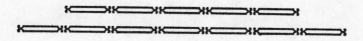

THE MOGHUL

Doubleday & Company, Inc.
Garden City, New York
1983

Also by Thomas Hoover

ZEN CULTURE

THE ZEN EXPERIENCE

Library of Congress Cataloging in Publication Data

Hoover, Thomas, 1941–
  The Moghul.

  1. East India Company—History—Fiction.
2. India—History—1500–1765—Fiction. I. Title.
PS3558.O6337M6 1983   813'.54
ISBN 0-385-17576-0
Library of Congress Catalog Card Number 82–45146

AUTHOR'S NOTE

This tale is offered to the memory of one William Hawkins (1575–1613), a brandy-drinking, Turkish-speaking seaman and adventurer who was the first Englishman to reach the court of Jahangir, the *Great Moghul* of India. There he delivered gifts from the new East India Company and a letter from King James proposing direct trade, then a zealously protected monopoly of Portugal. As he gradually adopted Indian ways, Hawkins became a court favorite of the *Moghul*, who made him a knightly khan and eventually tried to keep him in India. After several Portuguese-instigated attempts to murder him, Hawkins attached himself for safety to a certain willful Indian woman. The end of their story eventually became a minor legend throughout the early East India Company.

As astonishing as some of the elements in the historical landscape described here may seem today, they are all by and large fictional re-creations of actual events, practices, people—drawn from diaries of seventeenth-century European travelers and from Indian historical materials. Aside from the names, only the clocks in this remote world have been knowingly altered. Years in historical time have become months in these pages, months have become days. Several vicious naval engagements between English frigates and Portuguese galleons, several major land battles between Indian armies, have each been compressed into one.

But the major occurrences in this faraway saga all happened. While Shakespeare wrote of commoners and kings, while colonists hewed log cabins from the wilds of the New World, a land ruled by violent intrigue, powerful drugs, and sensual beauty lay hidden in that legendary place known as Moghul India.

BOOK ONE

LANDFALL

CHAPTER ONE

He watched from the quarterdeck as the chain fed through the whitecaps of the bay, its staccato clatter muffled, hollow in the midday heat. Then he sensed the anchor grab and felt an uneasy tremor pass along the hull as the links snapped taut against the tide. The cannon were already run in and cooling, but vagrant threads of smoke still traced skyward through the scuttles and open hatch, curling ringlets over two draped bodies by the mainmast. Along the main deck scurvy-blotched seamen, haggard and shirtless to the sun, eased the wounded toward the shade of the fo'c'sle.

He drew the last swallow of brandy from his hooped wooden tankard and instinctively shifted his gaze aloft, squinting against the midday sun to watch as two bosun's mates edged along the yards to furl the mainsail. Then he turned to inspect the triangular lateen sail behind him, parted into shreds by the first Portuguese cannon salvo, its canvas now strewn among the mizzenmast shrouds.

A round of cheers told him the last two casks of salt pork had finally emerged from the smoky hold, and he moved to the railing to watch as they were rolled toward the cauldron boiling on deck. As he surveyed the faces of the gathering men, he asked himself how many could still chew the briny meat he had hoarded so carefully for this final morning of the voyage.

The crowd parted as he moved down the companionway steps and onto the deck. He was tall, with lines of fatigue etched down his angular face and smoke residue laced through his unkempt hair and short beard. His doublet was plain canvas, and his breeches and boots scarcely differed from those of a common seaman. His only adornment was a small gold ring in his left ear. Today he also wore a bloodstained binding around his thigh, where a musket shot from a Portuguese maintop had furrowed the skin.

He was Brian Hawksworth, captain of the five-hundred-ton English frigate *Discovery* and Captain-General of the Third Voyage of England's new East India Company. His commission, assigned in London over seven months past, was to take two armed trading frigates around the Cape of Good Hope, up the eastern coast of Africa, and then through the Arabian Sea to the northwest coast of India. The Company had twice before sailed eastward from the Cape, to the equatorial islands of the Indies. No English vessel in history had ever sailed north for India.

The destination of this, the first English voyage to challenge Lisbon's control of the India trade, was the port of Surat, twelve leagues inland up the Tapti River, largest of the only two harbors on the Indian subcontinent not controlled by Portugal.

He reached for the second tankard of brandy that had been brought and squinted again toward the mouth of the Tapti, where four armed Portuguese galleons had been anchored earlier that morning.

Damn the Company. No one planned on galleons at the river mouth. Not now, not this early in the season. Did the Portugals somehow learn our destination? . . . And if they knew that, do they know the rest of the Company's plan?

Since the Tapti had been badly silted for decades, navigable only by cargo barge or small craft, he and the merchants must travel upriver to Surat by pinnace, the twenty-foot sailboat lashed amidships on the *Discovery*'s main deck. There the merchants would try to negotiate England's first direct trade with India. And Brian Hawksworth would undertake a separate mission, one the East India Company hoped might someday change the course of trade throughout the Indies.

He remounted the steps to the quarterdeck and paused to study the green shoreline circling their inlet. The low-lying hills undulated in the sun's heat, washing the *Discovery* in the dense perfume of land. Already India beckoned, the lure even stronger than all the legends told. He smiled to himself and drank again, this time a toast to the first English captain *ever* to hoist colors off the coast of India.

Then with a weary hand he reached for the telescope, an expensive new Dutch invention, and trained it on his second frigate, the *Resolve*, anchored a musket shot away. Like the *Discovery*, she rode easily at anchor, bearing to lee. He noted with relief that her ship's carpenter had finally sealed a patch of oakum and sail in the gash along her portside bow. For a few hours now, the men on the pumps could retire from the sweltering hold.

Finally, he directed the glass toward the remains of two Portuguese galleons aground in the sandy shallows off his starboard quarter, black smoke still streaming from gaps in their planking where explosions had ripped through the hull. And for an instant his stomach tightened, just as it had earlier that morning, when one of those same galleons had laid deep shadows across the *Discovery*'s decks, so close he could almost read the eyes of the infantry poised with grapples to swing down and board. The Portugals will be back, he told himself, and soon. With fireships.

He scanned the river mouth once more. It was deserted now. Even the fishing craft had fled. But upriver would be another matter. Portuguese long-boats, launched with boarding parties of infantry, had been stranded when the two galleons were lost. Together they had carried easily a hundred, perhaps two hundred musketmen.

They made for the Tapti, he thought grimly, and they'll be upriver waiting. We have to launch before they can set a blockade. Tonight. On the tide.

He revolved to find Giles Mackintosh, quartermaster of the *Discovery*, waiting mutely by his side.

"Mackintosh, start outfitting the pinnace. We launch at sunset, before the last dog watch."

The quartermaster pulled at his matted red curls in silence as he studied the tree-lined river mouth. Then he turned abruptly to Hawksworth. "Takin' the pinnace upriver'll be a death sentence, Cap'n, I warrant you. Portugals'll be layin' for us, thicker'n whores at a Tyburn hangin'." He paused deliberately and knotted the string holding back hair from his smoke-darkened cheeks. "I say we weigh at the tide and ease the frigates straight up their hell-bound river. She's wide as the Thames at Woolwich. We'll run out the guns and hand the pox-rotted Papists another taste o' English courtesy."

"Can you navigate the sandbars?"

"I've seen nae sign of bars."

"The Indian pilot we took on yesterday claims there's shallows upriver."

"All the more reason to sail. By my thinkin' the pilot's a full-bred Moor. An' they're all the same, Indian or Turk." Mackintosh blew his nose over the railing, punctuating his disgust. "Show me one that's na a liar, a thief, or a damned Sodomite. Nae honest Christian'll credit the word of a Moor."

"There's risk either way." Hawksworth drew slowly on the brandy, appearing to weigh the Scotsman's views. "But there's the cargo to think of. Taken for all, it's got to be the pinnace. And this Moorish pilot's not like the Turks. I should know."

"Aye, Cap'n, as you will." Mackintosh nodded with seeming reluctance, admiring how Hawksworth had retained mastery of their old game. Even after two years apart. "But I'll be watchin' the bastard, e'ery move he makes."

Hawksworth turned and slowly descended the quarterdeck steps. As he entered the passageway leading aft to the Great Cabin and the merchants' cabins, he saw the silhouette of George Elkington. The Chief Merchant of the voyage was standing by the quarter gallery railing, drawing on a long clay pipe as he urinated into the swells. When he spotted Hawksworth, he whirled and marched heavily down the corridor, perfunctorily securing the single remaining button of his breeches.

Elkington's once-pink jowls were slack and pasty, and his grease-stained doublet sagged over what had been, seven months past, a luxuriant belly. Sweat trickled down from the sides of his large hat, streaming oily rivulets across his cheeks.

"Hawksworth, did I hear you order the pinnace launch'd tonight? E'en before we've made safe anchorage for the cargo?"

"The sooner the better. The Portugals know we'll have to go upriver. By tomorrow they'll be ready."

"Your first obligation, sirrah, is the goods. Every shilling the Company subscrib'd is cargo'd in these two damn'd merchantmen. A fine fortune in wool broadcloth, Devonshire kersey, pig iron, tin, quicksilver. I've a good ten thousand pound of my own accounts invest'd. And you'd leave it all hove to in this piss crock of a bay, whilst the Portugals are doubtless crewin' up a dozen two-deckers down the coast in Goa. 'Tis sure they'll be laid full about this anchorage inside a fortnight."

Hawksworth inspected Elkington with loathing, musing what he disliked about him most—his grating voice, or his small lifeless eyes.

And what you probably *don't* realize is they'll be back next time with trained gunners. Not like today, when their gun crews clearly were Lisbon dockside rabble, private traders who'd earned passage out to the Indies on the easy claim they were gunners, half not knowing a linstock from a lamppost.

"Elkington, I'll tell you as much of our plans as befits your place." Hawksworth moved past him toward the door of the Great Cabin. "We're taking the pinnace upriver tonight on the tide. And you'll be in it, along with your coxcomb clerk. Captain Kerridge of the *Resolve* will take command of the ships. I've already prepared orders to move both frigates to a new anchorage."

"I demand to know what damn'd fool scheme you've hatch'd."

"There's no reason you have to know. Right now the fewer who know the better, particularly the men going upriver."

"Well, I know this much, Hawksworth. This voyage to India may well be the East India Company's last chance to trade in the Indies. If we fail three voyages in a row, we'd as well close down the Company and just buy pepper and spice outright from the damn'd Hollanders. England's got no goods that'll trade in the Spice Islands south o' here. Remember Lancaster cargo'd wool down to the islands on the first two Company voyages, thinkin' to swap it for pepper, and discover'd for himself what I'd guess'd all along—a tribe of heathens sweatin' in the sun have no call for woolen breeches. So either we trade up here in the north, where they'll take wool, or we're finish'd."

"The anchorage I've found should keep the cargo—and the men—safe till we make Surat. With luck you'll have your cargo aland before the Portugals locate us." Hawksworth pushed open the heavy oak door of the Great

Cabin and entered, stranding Elkington in the passageway. "And now I wish you good day."

The cabin's dark overhead beams were musty from the heat and its air still dense with smoke from the cannon. The stern windows were partly blocked now by the two bronze demi-culverin that had been run out aft, "stern-chaser" cannon that could spit a nine-pound ball with deadly accuracy —their lighter bronze permitting longer barrels than those of the cast-iron guns below decks. He strode directly to the oil lantern swaying over the great center desk and turned up the wick. The cabin brightened slightly, but the face of the English lute wedged in the corner seemed suddenly to come alive, shining gold over the cramped quarters like a full moon. He stared at it wistfully for a moment, then shook his head and settled himself behind the large oak desk. And asked himself once more why he had ever agreed to the voyage.

To prove something? To the Company? To himself?

He reflected again on how it had come about, and why he had finally accepted the Company's offer.

It had been a dull morning in late October, the kind of day when all London seems trapped in an icy gloom creeping up from the Thames. His weekly lodgings were frigid as always, and his mind was still numb from the previous night's tavern brandy. Back from Tunis scarcely a month, he already had nothing left to pawn. Two years before, he had been leading a convoy of merchantmen through the Mediterranean when their ships and cargo were seized by Turkish corsairs, galleys owned by the notorious *dey* of Tunis. He had finally managed to get back to London, but now he was a captain without a ship. In years past this might have been small matter to remedy. But no longer. England, he discovered, had changed.

The change was apparent mainly to seamen. The lower house of Parliament was still preoccupied fighting King James's new proposal that Scotland be joined to England, viewed by most Englishmen as a sufferance of proud beggars and ruffians upon a nation of uniformly upright taxpayers; in London idle crowds still swarmed the bear gardens to wager on the huge mastiffs pitted against the chained bears; rioting tenant farmers continued to outrage propertied men by tearing down enclosures and grazing their flocks on the gentry's private hunting estates; and the new Puritans increasingly harassed everyone they disapproved of, from clerics who wore vestments to women who wore cosmetics to children who would play ball on Sunday.

Around London more talk turned on which handsome young courtier was the latest favorite of their effeminate new king than on His Majesty's enforcement of his new and strict decree forbidding privateering—the staple occupation of English seamen for the last three decades of Elizabeth's reign. King James had cravenly signed a treaty of peace with Spain, and by that act brought ruin to half a hundred thousand English "sea dogs." They awoke to discover their historic livelihood, legally plundering the shipping of Spain and Portugal under wartime letters of marque, had become a criminal offense.

For a captain without a ship, another commission by a trading company seemed out of the question, and especially now, with experienced seamen standing idle the length of London. Worst of all, the woman he had hoped to return to, red-haired Maggie Tyne of Billingsgate, had disappeared from her old lodgings and haunts leaving no trace. Rumor had her married—some said to the master of a Newcastle coal barge, others to a gentleman. London seemed empty now, and he passed the vacant days with brandy and his lute, and thoughts of quitting the sea—to do he knew not what.

Then in that cold early dawn appeared the letter, requesting his immediate appearance at the Director's Office of the East India Company, should this coincide with his convenience. He found its tone ominous. Was some merchant planning to have him jailed for his loss of cargo to the Turks? But he'd been sailing for the Levant Company, not the East India Company. He debated with himself all morning, and finally decided to go. And face the mercantile bastards.

The new offices of the Company already seemed embalmed in the smell of lamp oil and sweat, their freshly painted wood timbers masked in dull soot. A stale odor of ink, paper, and arid commerce assailed his senses as he was announced and ushered through the heavy oak door of the Director's suite.

And he was astonished by what awaited. Standing hard by the Director's desk—was Maggie. He'd searched the length of London in vain for her, and here she was. But he almost didn't recognize her. Their two years apart had brought a change beyond anything he could have imagined.

No one would have guessed what she once had been, a dockside girl happiest at the Southwark bear gardens, or in a goose-down bed. And somehow she had always managed to turn a shilling at both—wagering with a practiced eye on the snarling dogs brought in to bloody the bears, or taking her pleasure only after deftly extracting some loan, to allay an urgent need she inevitably remembered the moment she entered his lodgings.

That morning, however, she reigned like an exotic flower, flourishing amid the mercantile gloom. She was dressed and painted in the very latest upper-class style—her red hair now bleached deep yellow, sprinkled thick with gold dust, and buried under a feathered hat; her crushed-velvet bodice low-necked, cut fashionably just below the nipples, then tied at the neck with a silk lace ruff; her once-ruddy breasts now painted pale, with blue veins penciled in; and her face carefully powdered lead-white, save the red dye on her lips and cheeks and the glued-on beauty patches of stars and half-moons. His dockside girl had become a completely modern lady of fashion. He watched in disbelief as she curtsied to him, awkwardly.

Then he noticed Sir Randolph Spencer, Director of the Company.

"Captain Hawksworth. So you're the man we've heard so much about? Understand you escaped from Tunis under the very nose of the damned Turks." He extended a manicured hand while he braced himself on the silver knob of his cane. Although Spencer's flowing hair was pure white, his face still clung tenuously to youth. His doublet was expensive, and in the new longer waist-length style Hawksworth remembered seeing on young men-about-town. " 'Tis indeed a pleasure. Nay, 'tis an honor." The tone was practiced and polite, a transparent attempt at sincerity rendered difficult by Hawksworth's ragged appearance. He had listened to Spencer mutely, suddenly realizing his loss of cargo had been forgotten. He was being congratulated for coming back alive.

" 'Twas the wife, Margaret here, set me thinkin' about you. Says you two were lightly acquainted in younger years. Pity I never knew her then myself." Spencer motioned him toward a carved wooden chair facing the desk. "She ask'd to be here today to help me welcome you. Uncommonly winsome lady, what say?"

Hawksworth looked at Maggie's gloating eyes and felt his heart turn. It was obvious enough she'd found her price. At last she had what she'd always really wanted, a rich widower. But why trouble to flaunt it?

He suspected he already knew. She simply couldn't resist.

"Now I pride myself on being a sound judge of humanity, Hawksworth, and I've made sufficient inquiry to know you can work a ship with the best. So I'll come right to it. I suppose 'tis common talk the Company's dispatchin' another voyage down to the Indies this comin' spring. Soon as our new frigate, the *Discovery*, is out of the yard. And this time our first port of call's to be India." Spencer caught Hawksworth's look, without realizing it was directed past him, at Maggie. "Aye, I know. We all know. The damned Portugals've been there a hundred year, thick as flies on pudding. But by Jesus we've no choice but to try openin' India to English trade."

Spencer had paused and examined Hawksworth skeptically. A process of sizing up seemed underway, of pondering whether this shipless captain with the bloodshot eyes and gold earring was really the man. He looked down and inspected his manicured nails for a long moment, then continued.

"Now what I'm about to tell you mustn't go past this room. But first let me ask you. Is everything I've heard about you true? 'Tis said the *dey* of Tunis held you there after he took your merchantmen, in hopes you'd teach his damned Turks how to use the English cannon you had on board."

"He's started building sailing bottoms now, thinking he'll replace the galleys his Turkish pirates have used for so long. His shipwrights are some English privateers who've relocated in Tunis to escape prison here. And he was planning to outfit his new sailing ships with my cannon. He claims English cast-iron culverin are the best in the world."

"God damn the Barbary Turks. And the Englishmen who've started helping them." Spencer bristled. "Next thing and they'll be out past Gibraltar, pillaging our shipping right up the Thames. But I understand you revised his plans."

"The Turks don't have any more cannon now than they had two years ago. When I refused to help them, they put me in prison, under guard. But one night I managed to knife two of the guards and slip down to the yard. I worked till dawn and had the guns spiked before anybody realized I was gone."

"And I hear you next stole a single-masted shallop and sail'd the length of the Barbary coast alone, right up to Gibraltar, where you hailed an English merchantman?"

"Didn't seem much point in staying on after that."

"You're the man all right. Now, 'tis said you learn'd the language of the Turks while you were in Tunis. Well, sirrah, answer me now, can you speak it or no?"

"For two years I scarcely heard a word of English. But what's that to do with trade in India? From what I know, you'll need a few merchants who speak Portuguese. And plenty of English . . ."

"Hear me out, sir. If all I wanted was to anchor a cargo of English goods and pull off some trade for a season, I'd not be needin' a man like you. But let me tell you a thing or so about India. The rulers there now are named Moghuls. They used to be called Mongols, Turkish-Afghans from Turkistan, before they took over India about a hundred years back, and their king, the one they call the *Great Moghul*, still speaks some Turki, the language of the Central Asian steppes. Now I'm told this Turki bears fair resemblance to the language of the damned Turks in the Mediterranean." Spencer assumed a conspiratorial smile. "I've a plan in mind, but it needs a man who speaks this *Great Moghul's* language."

Hawksworth suddenly realized Maggie must have somehow convinced Spencer he was the only seaman in England who knew Turkish. It could scarcely be true.

"Now I ask you, Hawksworth, what's the purpose of the East India Company? Well, 'tis to trade wool for pepper and spice, simple as that. To find a market for English commodity, mainly wool. And to ship home with cheap pepper. Now we can buy all the pepper we like down in Java and Sumatra, but they'll not take wool in trade. And if we keep on buying there with gold, there'll never be a farthing's profit in our voyages to the Indies. By the same token, we're sure these Moghuls in North India will take wool. They already buy it from the damned Portugals. But they don't grow pepper." Spencer leaned forward and his look darkened slightly. "The hard fact is the East India Company's not done nearly as well as our subscribers hoped. But now the idea's come along—I hate to admit 'twas George Elkington first thought of it—that we try swappin' wool for the cotton goods they produce in North India, then ship these south and trade for pepper and spice. Indian traders have sold their cotton calicoes in the Spice Islands for years. Do you follow the strategy?"

Spencer had scrutinized Hawksworth for a moment, puzzling at his flash of anger when Elkington's name was mentioned, then pressed forward.

"Overall not a bad idea, considerin' it came from Elkington." Then Spencer dropped his voice to just above a whisper. "But what he doesn't understand is if we're goin' to start tradin' in India, we'll need a real treaty, like the Hollanders have down in some of the islands. Because once you've got a treaty, you can settle a permanent trading station, what we call a 'factory,' and bargain year round. Buy when prices are best."

Hawksworth sensed the interview would not be short, and he settled uneasily into the chair. Maggie still stood erect and formal, affecting a dignity more studied than natural. As Spencer warmed to his subject he seemed to have forgotten her.

"Now, sir, once we have a factory we can start sending in a few cannon —to 'protect our merchants,' like the Hollanders do in the islands—and soon enough we've got the locals edgy. Handle it right and pretty soon they'll sign over exclusive trade. No more competition." Spencer smiled again in private satisfaction. "Are you startin' to follow my thinkin'?"

"What you've described is the very arrangement the Portugals have in India now." Hawksworth tried to appear attentive, but he couldn't keep his eyes off Maggie, who stood behind Spencer wearing a triumphant smile. "And they've got plenty of cannon and sail to make *sure* their trade's exclusive."

"We know all about the Portugals' fleet of warships, *and* their shipyards in Goa, *and* all the rest. But these things always take time. Took the Portugals many a year to get their hooks into India's ports. But their days are numbered there, Hawksworth. The whole Eastern empire of the Portugals is rotten. I can almost smell it. But if we dally about, the damned Hollanders are sure to move in." Spencer had become increasingly excited, and Hawksworth watched as he began pacing about the room.

"Well, if you're saying you want a treaty, why not just send an ambassador to the *Great Moghul's* court?"

"Damn me, Hawksworth, it's not that easy. We send some dandified gentry who doesn't know the language, and he'll end up havin' to do all his talkin' through court interpreters. And who might they be? Well let me just show you, sirrah." Spencer began to shuffle impatiently through the papers on his desk. "They're Jesuits. Damned Jesuits. Papists straight out o' Lisbon. We know for a fact they do all the translatin' for the court in Agra." He paused as he rummaged the stacks in front of him. "We've just got hold of some Jesuit letters. Sent out from the Moghul capital at Agra, through Goa, intended for Lisbon. They'll tell you plain enough what the Company's up against." His search became increasingly frenetic. "Damn me, they were here." He rose and shuffled toward the door, waving his cane in nervous agitation. "Hold a minute."

Hawksworth had watched him disappear through the doorway, then looked back to see Maggie laughing. She retrieved a leather-bound packet from the mantel and tossed it carelessly onto the desk. He found himself watching her in admiration, realizing some things never change.

"What the hell's this about?"

She smiled and her voice was like always. "Methinks 'tis plain enough."

"You want me gone from London this badly?"

"He takes care o' me. At least he loves me. Something you were ne'er capable of."

"And what were you capable of? All you wanted was . . ."

"I . . ." She looked away. "I know he'll give me what you ne'er would. At least he has feelin' for me. More than *you* e'er did. Or could." Then she turned back and looked at him for a long moment. "Say you'll go. Knowin' you're still . . ."

"Damn it all!" Spencer burst back through the doorway. Then he spied the leather packet. "That's it." He seized the bundle and thrust it toward Hawksworth. "Read these through, sirrah, and you'll see clear enough what we're up against. There's absolutely no point whatever in postin' a real ambassador now." He hesitated for a moment, as though unsure how to phrase his next point. "The most amazing thing is what they say about the *Great Moghul* himself, the one they call Arangbar. The Jesuits claim the man's scarcely ever sober. Seems he lives on some kind of poppy sap they call opium, and on wine. He's a Moor sure enough, but he drinks like a Christian, downs a full gallon of wine a day. E'en holds audiences with a flagon in his hand. From the letters I can sense the Jesuits all marvel how the damned heathen does it, but they swear 'tis true. No, sirrah, we can't send some fancy-titled ambassador now. That's later. We want a man of quality, it goes without sayin', but he's got to be able to drink with that damned Moor and parlay with him in his cups. No Jesuit interpreters."

Hawksworth steadied his hand on the carved arm of the chair, still amazed by Maggie. "What will your subscribers think about sending the captain of a merchantman to the court of Moghul India?"

"Never you mind the subscribers. Just tell me if you'd consider it. 'Twill be a hard voyage, and a perilous trip inland once you make landfall. But you sail'd the Mediterranean half a decade, and you know enough about the Turks." Spencer tapped his fingers impatiently on his ink-stained blotter. "And lest you're worried, have no doubt the Company knows how to reward success."

Hawksworth looked again at Maggie. Her blue eyes were mute as stone.

"To tell the truth, I'm not sure I'm interested in a voyage to India. George Elkington might be able to tell you the reason why. Have you told me all of it?"

"Damn Elkington. What's he to do with this?" Spencer stopped in front of the desk and fixed Hawksworth's gaze. "Aye, there's more. But what I'm about to tell you now absolutely has to remain between us. So have I your word?"

Hawksworth found himself nodding.

"Very well, sir. Then I'll give you the rest. His Majesty, King James, is sending a personal letter to be delivered to this *Great Moghul*. And gifts. All the usual diplomatic falderal these potentates expect. You'd deliver the whole affair. Now the letter'll offer full and free trade between England and India, nothing more. Won't mention the Portugals. That'll come later. This is just the beginning. For now all we want is a treaty to trade alongside the damned Papists. Break their monopoly."

"But why all the secrecy?"

"'Tis plain as a pikestaff, sirrah. The fewer know what we're plannin', the less chance of word gettin' out to the Portugals, or the Hollanders. Let the Papists and the Butterboxes look to their affairs *after* we have a treaty. Remember the Portugals are swarmin' about the *Moghul's* court, audiences every day. Not to mention a fleet of warships holdin' the entire coast. And if they spy your colors, they're not apt to welcome you aland for roast capon and grog."

"Who else knows about this?"

"Nobody. Least of all that windbag Elkington, who'd have it talk'd the length of Cheapside in a fortnight. He'll be on the voyage, I regret to say, but just as Chief Merchant. Which is all he's fit for, though I'd warrant he presumes otherwise."

"I'd like a few days to think about it." Hawksworth looked again at Maggie, still disbelieving. "First I'd like to see the *Discovery*. And I'd also like to see your navigation charts for the Indian Ocean. I've seen plenty of logs down to the Cape, and east, but nothing north from there."

"And with good reason. We've *got* no rutters north of the Cape. No English sea dog's ever sail'd it. But I've made some inquiries, and I think I've located a salt here who shipp'd it once, a long time past. A Dutchman named Huyghen. The truth is he was born and rais'd right here in London. He started out a Papist and when things got a bit hot in England back around time of the Armada he left for Holland. E'en took a Dutch name. Next he mov'd on down to Portugal thinkin' to be a Jesuit, then shipp'd out to Goa and round the Indies. But he got a bellyful of popery soon enough, and came back to Amsterdam. Some years later he help'd out their merchants by tellin' them exactly how the Portugals navigate the passage round the Cape and out. The Hollanders say hadn't been for the maps he drew up, they'd never have been able to double the Cape in the first place. But he's back in London now, and we've track'd him down. I understand he may've gone a bit daft, but perhaps 'twould do no harm if you spoke to him."

"And what about the *Discovery*? I want to see her too."

"That you will, sir. She's in our shipyard down at Deptford. Might be well if I just had Huyghen see you there. By all means look her over." He beamed. "And a lovelier sight you're ne'er like to meet." Then, remembering himself, he quickly turned aside. "Unless, of course, 'twould be my Margaret here."

As agreed, Hawksworth was taken to Deptford the next day, the Company's carriage inching through London's teeming streets for what seemed a lifetime. His first sight of the shipyard was a confused tangle of planking, ropes, and workmen, but he knew at a glance the *Discovery* was destined to be handsome. The keel had been laid weeks before, and he could already tell her fo'c'sle would be low and rakish. She was a hundred and thirty feet from the red lion of her beakhead to the taffrail at her stern—where gilding already was being applied to the ornate quarter galleries. She was five hundred tons burden, each ton some six hundred cubic feet of cargo space, and she would carry a hundred and twenty men when fully crewed. Over her swarmed an army of carpenters, painters, coopers, riggers, and joiners, while skilled artisans were busy attaching newly gilded sculptures to her bow and stern.

That day they were completing the installation of the hull chain-plates that would secure deadeyes for the shrouds, and he moved closer to watch. Stories had circulated the docks that less than a month into the Company's last voyage the mainmast yard of a vessel had split, and the shipbuilder, William Benten, and his foreman, Edward Chandler, had narrowly escaped charges of lining their pockets by substituting cheap, uncured wood.

He noticed that barrels of beer had been stationed around the yard for the workmen, to blunt the lure of nearby alehouses, and as he stood watching he saw Chandler seize a grizzled old bystander who had helped himself to a tot of beer and begin forcibly evicting him from the yard. As they passed, he heard the old man—clad in a worn leather jerkin, his face ravaged by decades of salt wind and hard drink—reviling the Company.

"What does the rottin' East India Company know o' the Indies. You'll ne'er double the Cape in that pissin' shallop. 'Twould scarce serve to ferry the Thames." The old man struggled weakly to loosen Chandler's grasp on his jerkin. "But I can tell you th' Portugals've got carracks that'll do it full easy, thousand-ton bottoms that'd hold this skiff in the orlop deck and leave air for a hundred barrel o' biscuit. An' I've shipped 'em. By all the saints, where's the man standin' that knows the Indies better?"

Hawksworth realized he must be Huyghen. He intercepted him at the edge of the yard and invited him to a tavern, but the old Englishman-turned-Dutchman bitterly declined.

"I'll ha' none o' your fancy taverns, lad, aswarm wi' pox-faced gentry fingerin' their meat pies. They'll ne'er take in the likes o' me." Then he examined Hawksworth and flashed a toothless grin. "But there's an alehouse right down the way where a man wi' salt in his veins can still taste a drop in peace."

They went and Hawksworth had ordered the first round. When the tankards arrived, Huyghen attacked his thirstily, maintaining a cynical silence as Hawksworth began describing the Company's planned voyage, then asked him what he knew of the passage east and north of the Cape. As soon as his first tankard was dry, the old man spoke.

"Aye, I made the passage once, wi' Portugals. Back in '83. To Goa. An' I've been to the Indies many a time since, wi' Dutchmen. But ne'er again to that pissin' sinkhole."

"But what about the passage north, through the Indian Ocean?"

"I'll tell you this, lad, 'tis a sight different from shootin' down to Java, like the Company's done before. 'Tis the roughest passage you're e'er like to ship. Portugals post bottoms twice the burden o' the Company's damn'd little frigates and still lose a hundred men e'ery voyage out. When scurvy don't take 'em all. E'en the Dutchmen are scared o' it."

Then Huyghen returned to his stories of Goa. Something in the experience seemed to preoccupy his mind. Hawksworth found the digression irritating, and he impatiently pressed forward.

"But what about the passage? How do they steer north from the Cape? The Company has no charts, no rutters by pilots who've made the passage."

"An' how could they?" Huyghen evaluated Hawksworth's purse lying on the wooden table and discreetly signaled another round. "The Portugals know the trick, lad, but you'll ne'er find one o' the whoremasters who'll give it out."

"But is there a trade wind you can ride? Like the westerly to the Americas?"

"Nothin' o' the sort, lad. But there's a wind sure enough. Only she shifts about month by month. Give me that chart an' I'll show you." Huyghen stretched for the parchment Hawksworth had brought, the new Map of the World published by John Davis in 1600. He spread it over the table, oblivious to the grease and encrusted ale, and stared at it for a moment in groggy disbelief. Then he turned on Hawksworth. "Who drew up this map?"

"It was assembled by an English navigator, from charts he made on his voyages."

"He's the lyin' son of a Spaniard's whore. I made this chart o' the Indies wi' my own hand, years ago, for the Dutchmen. But what's the difference?

He copied it right." Huyghen spat on the floor and then stabbed the east coast of Africa with a stubby finger. "Now you come out o' the Mozambique Channel and into the Indian Ocean too early in the summer, and you'll be the only bottom fool enough to be out o' port. The monsoon'll batter you to plankin'. Get there too late, say past the middle o' September, and you're fightin' a head wind all the way. She's already turn'd on you. But come north round by Sokatra near the end o' August and you'll ride a steady gale right into North India. That's the tail o' the monsoon, lad, just before the winds switch about. Two weeks, three at most, that's all you'll get. But steer it true an' you'll make landfall just as India's ports reopen for the autumn tradin' season."

Huyghen's voice trailed off as he morosely inspected the bottom of his tankard. Hawksworth motioned for a third round, and as the old man drew on the ale his eyes mellowed.

"Aye, you might make it. There's a look about you tells me you can work a ship. But why would you want to be goin'? 'Twill swallow you up, lad. I've only been to Goa, mind you, down on India's west coastline, but that was near enough. I ne'er saw a man come back once he went in India proper. Somethin' about it keeps 'em there. Portugals say she always changes a man. He loses touch wi' what he was. Nothin' we know about counts for anything there, lad."

"What do you mean? How different could it be? I saw plenty of Moors in Tunis."

Huyghen laughed bitterly. "If you're thinkin' 'tis the same as Tunis, then you're e'en a bigger fool than I took you for. Nay, lad, the Moor part's the very least o' it." He drew on his tankard slowly, deliberately. "I've thought on't a considerable time, an' I think I've decipher'd what 'tis. But 'tis not a thing easy to spell out."

Huyghen was beginning to drift now, his eyes glazed in warm forgetfulness from the ale. But still he continued. "You know, lad, I actually saw some Englishmen go into India once before. Back in '83. Year I was in Goa. An' they were ne'er heard from since."

Hawksworth stared at the old man a moment, and suddenly the name clicked, and the date—1583. Huyghen must have been the Dutch Catholic, the one said to speak fluent English, who'd intervened for the English scouting party imprisoned in Goa that year by the Portuguese. He tried to still his pulse.

"Do you remember the Englishmen's names?"

"Seem to recall they were led by a man nam'd Symmes. But 'twas a long time past, lad. Aye, Goa was quite the place then. Lucky I escap'd when I did. E'en there, you stay awhile an' somethin' starts to hold you. Too much o' India about the place. After a while all this"—Huyghen gestured fondly about the alehouse, where sweat-soaked laborers and seamen were drinking, quarreling, swearing as they bargained with a scattering of weary prostitutes in dirty, tattered shifts—"all this seems . . ." He took a deep draft of ale, attempting vainly to formulate his thoughts. "I've ne'er been one wi' words. But don't do it, lad. You go in, go all the way in to India, an' I'll wager you'll ne'er be heard from more. I've seen it happen."

Hawksworth listened as Huyghen continued, his stories of the Indies a mixture of ale and dreams. After a time he signaled another round for them both. It was many empty tankards later when they parted.

But Huyghen's words stayed. And that night Brian Hawksworth walked alone on the quay beside the Thames, bundled against the wet autumn wind, and watched the ferry lanterns ply through the fog and heard the muffled harangues of streetwalkers and cabmen from the muddy street above. He thought about Huyghen, and about the man named Roger Symmes, and about the voyage to India.

And he thought too about Maggie, who wanted him out of London before her rich widower discovered the truth. Or before she admitted the truth to herself. But either way it no longer seemed to matter.

That night he decided to accept the commission.

The *Discovery* rolled heavily and Hawksworth glanced instinctively toward the pulley lines that secured the two bronze cannon. Then he remembered why he had left the quarterdeck, and he unlocked the top drawer of the desk and removed the ship's log. He leafed one more time through its pages, admiring his own script—strong but with an occasional flourish.

Someday this could be the most valuable book in England, he told himself. If we return. This will be the first log in England to describe what the voyage to India is *really* like. The Company will have a full account of the weather and sea, recorded by estimated longitude, the distance traveled east.

He congratulated himself again on the care with which he had taken their daily speed and used it to estimate longitude every morning since the Cape, the last location where it was known exactly. And as he studied the pages of the log, he realized how exact Huyghen's prediction had been. The old man had been eerily correct about the winds and the sea. They had caught the "tail o' the monsoon" precisely.

"*August 27*. Course N.E. ½ E.; The wind at W.S.W., with gusts and rain. Made 36 leagues today. Estimated longitude from the Cape 42°50' E.

"*August 28*. Course N.E.; The wind at west, a fresh gale, with gusts and rain this 24 hours. Leagues 35. Estimated longitude from the Cape, 44°10' E."

The late August westerly Huyghen had foretold was carrying them a good hundred land miles a day. They rode the monsoon's tail, and it was still angry, but there was no longer a question that English frigates could weather the passage.

As August drew to a close, however, scurvy had finally grown epidemic on his sister ship, the *Resolve*. The men's teeth loosened, their gums bled, and they began to complain of aching and burning in their limbs. It was all the more tragic for the fact that this timeless scourge of ocean travelers might at long last be preventable. Lancaster, on the very first voyage of the East India Company, had stumbled onto a historic discovery. As a test, he'd shipped bottles of the juice of lemons on his flagship and ordered every seaman to take three spoonfuls a day. And his had been the only vessel of the three to withstand scurvy.

Hawksworth had argued with Captain Kerridge of the *Resolve*, insisting they both stow lemon juice as a preventative. But Kerridge had always resented Lancaster, particularly the fact he'd been knighted on return from a voyage that showed almost no profit. He refused to credit Lancaster's findings.

"No connection. By my thinkin' Lancaster just had a run o' sea-dog luck. Then he goes about claimin' salt meat brings on the scurvy. A pack o' damn'd foolishness. I say salt meat's fine for the lads. Boil it up with a mess o' dried peas and I'll have it myself. The *Resolve*'ll be provision'd like always. Sea biscuit, salt pork, Hollander cheese. Any fool knows scurvy comes from men sleepin' in the night dews off the sea. Secure your gunports by night and you'll ne'er see the damn'd scurvy."

Hawksworth had suspected Kerridge's real reason was the cost: lemon juice was imported and expensive. When the Company rejected his own request for an allowance, he had provisioned the *Discovery* out of his own advance. Kerridge had called him a fool. And when they sailed in late February, the *Resolve* was unprovided.

Just as Hawksworth had feared, the *Resolve*'s crew had been plagued by scurvy throughout the voyage, even though both vessels had put in for fresh provisions at Zanzibar in late June. Six weeks ago, he had had no choice but to order half his own remaining store of lemon juice transferred to the sister ship, even though this meant reducing the *Discovery*'s ration to a spoon a day, not enough.

By the first week of September, they were so near India they could almost smell land, but he dared not try for landfall. Not yet. Not without an Indian pilot to guide them past the notorious sandbars and shoals that lined the coast like giant submerged claws. The monsoon winds were dying. Indian shipping surely would begin soon. So they hove to, waiting.

And as they waited, they watched the last kegs of water choke with green slime, the wax candles melt in the heat, and the remaining biscuit all but disappear to weevils. Hungry seamen set a price on the rats that ran the shrouds. How long could they last?

Hawksworth reached the last entry in the log. Yesterday. The day they had waited for.

"*Sept. 12.* Laid by the lee. Estimated longitude from the Cape, 50°10′ E. Latitude observed 20°30′. At 7 in the morning we command a large ship from the country to heave to, by shooting four pieces across her bow. Took from this ship an Indian pilot, paying in Spanish rials of eight. First offered English gold sovereigns, but these refused as unknown coin. Also purchased 6 casks water, some baskets lemons, melons, plantains."

The provisions had scarcely lasted out the day, spread over twice a hundred hungry seamen. But with a pilot they could at last make landfall.

And landfall they had made, at a terrible price. Yet even this anchorage could not be kept. It was too exposed and vulnerable. He had expected it to be so, and he had been right. But he also knew where they might find safety.

The previous night he had ordered the Indian pilot to sketch a chart of the coastline on both sides of the Tapti River delta. He did not tell him why. And on the map he had spotted a cove five leagues to the north, called Swalley, that looked to be shallow and was also shielded by hills screening it from the sea. Even if the Portuguese discovered them, the deep draft of Portuguese galleons would hold them at sea. The most they could do would be send boarding parties by pinnace, or fireships. The cove would buy time, time to replenish stores, perhaps even to set the men ashore and attend the sick. The longer the anchorage could be kept secret, the better their chances. He had already prepared sealed orders for Captain Kerridge, directing him to steer both frigates there after dark, when their movement could not be followed by the hidden eyes along the coast.

He took a deep breath and flipped forward to a blank page in the log.

And realized this was the moment he had been dreading, been postponing: the last entry for the voyage out. Perhaps his last ever—if events in India turned against him. He swabbed more sweat from his face and glanced one last time at the glistening face of the lute, wondering what he would be doing now, at this moment, if he still were in London, penniless but on his own.

Then he wiped off the quill lying neatly alongside the leatherbound volume, inked it, and shoved back the sleeve of his doublet to write.

CHAPTER TWO

The events of that morning were almost too improbable to be described. After taking on the Indian pilot, Hawksworth's plan had been to make landfall immediately, then launch a pinnace for Surat, there to negotiate trade for their goods and safe conduct to the capital at Agra for himself. If things went as planned, the goods would be exchanged and he would be on his way to the Moghul capital long before word of their arrival could reach Goa and the Portuguese.

The pilot's worth was never in question. A practiced seaman, he had steered them easily through the uncharted currents and hidden shallows of the bay. They had plotted a course directly east-north-east, running with top-gallants on the night breeze, to make dawn anchorage at the mouth of the Tapti River. Through the night the *Resolve* had stayed with them handily, steering by their stern lantern.

When the first light broke in the east, hard and sudden, there it lay—the coast of India, the landfall, the sight they had waited for the long seven months. Amid the cheers he had ordered their colors hoisted—the red cross, bordered in white, on a field of blue—the first English flag ever to fly off India's coast.

But as the flag snapped its way along the poop staff, and the men struck up a hornpipe on deck, their triumph suddenly was severed by a cry from the maintop.

"Sails off the starboard quarter."

In the sudden hush that rolled across the ship like a shroud, freezing the tumult of voice and foot, Hawksworth had charged up the companionway ladder to the quarterdeck. And there, while the masts tuned a melancholy dirge, he had studied the ships in disbelief with his glass.

Four galleons anchored at the river mouth. Portuguese men-of-war. Each easily a thousand ton, twice the size of the *Discovery*.

He had sorted quickly through his options. Strike sail and heave to, on the odds they may leave? It was too late. Run up Portuguese colors, the old privateers' ruse, and possibly catch them by surprise? Unlikely. Come about and run for open sea? Never. That's never an English seadog's way. No, keep to windward and engage. Here in the bay.

"Mackintosh!" Hawksworth turned to see the quartermaster already poised expectantly on the main deck. "Order Malloyre to draw up the gunports. Have the sails wet down and see the cookroom fire is out."

"Aye, sir. This'll be a bloody one."

"What counts is who bleeds most. Get every able man on station."

As Hawksworth turned to check the whipstaff, the long wooden lever that guided the ship's rudder, he passingly noted that curious conflict of body sensation he remembered from two encounters in years past: once, when on the Amsterdam run he had seen privateers suddenly loom off the coast of Scotland, and then on his last voyage through the Mediterranean, when his convoy first spotted the Turkish pirate galleys. While his mind calculated the elements of a strategy, coolly refining each individual detail, his stomach belied his rational facade and knotted in instinctive, primal fear. And he had asked himself whether this day his mind or his body would prevail. The odds were very bad, even if they could keep the wind. And if the Portuguese had trained gun crews . . .

Then he spotted the Indian pilot, leaning casually against the steering house, his face expressionless. He wore a tiny moustache and long, trimmed sideburns. And unlike the English seamen, all barefoot and naked to the waist, he was still dressed formally, just as when he came aboard. A fresh turban of white cotton, embroidered in a delicate brown, was secured neatly about the crown of his head, exposing his long ears and small, jeweled earrings. A spotless yellow cloak covered the waist of his tightly tailored blue trousers.

Damn him. Did he somehow know? Did he steer us into a trap?

Seeming to read Hawksworth's thoughts, the pilot broke the silence between them, his Turki heavily accented with his native Gujarati.

"This is your first test. Officers of the *Moghul's* army are doubtless at the shore, observing. What will you do?"

"What do you think we'll do? We'll stand the bastards. And with Malloyre's gunners I think we can . . ."

"Then permit me an observation. A modest thought, but possibly useful. Do you see, there"—he pulled erect and pointed toward the shore—"hard by the galleons, there where the seabirds swirl in a dark cloud? That is the river mouth. And on either side are many sandbars, borne there from the river's delta. Along the coast beyond these, though you cannot see them now, are channels, too shallow for the draft of a galleon but perhaps safe for these frigates. Reach them and you will be beyond range of all Portuguese ordnance save their stern demi-culverin. Then they will be forced to try boarding you by longboat, something their infantry does poorly and with great reluctance."

"Are there channels on both sides of the river mouth? To windward and to leeward?"

"Certainly, my *feringhi* captain." He examined Hawksworth with a puzzled stare. "But only a fool would not hold to port, to windward."

Hawksworth studied the shoreline with the glass, and an audacious gamble began to take form in his mind. Why try to keep *both* frigates to windward? That's what they'll expect, and any moment now they'll weigh and beat to windward also. And from their position, they'll probably gain the weather gage, forcing us to leeward, downwind where we can't maneuver. That means an open fight—when the *Resolve* can barely muster a watch. How can she crew the gun deck *and* man the sheets? But maybe she won't have to. Maybe there's another way.

"Mackintosh." The quartermaster was mounting the quarterdeck companionway. "Order the mains'l and fores'l reefed. And the tops'ls shortened. We'll heave to while we run out the guns. And signal the *Resolve* while I prepare orders for Kerridge."

The grizzled Scotsman stood listening in dismay, and Hawksworth read his thoughts precisely in his eyes. There's nae time to heave to. And for wha'? We strike an inch o' canvas an' the fornicatin' Portugals'll take the weather gage sure. Ha' you nae stomach for a fight? Why na just haul down colors and ha' done with it?

But he said nothing. He turned automatically and bellowed orders aloft.

Hawksworth felt out the morning breeze, tasting its cut, while he watched the seamen begin swinging themselves up the shrouds, warming the morning air with oaths as the *Discovery* pitched and heeled in the chop. And then he turned and strode down the quarterdeck companionway toward the Great Cabin to prepare orders for the *Resolve*. As he passed along the main deck, half a dozen crewmen were already unlashing the longboat from its berth amidships.

And when he emerged again on deck with the oilskin-wrapped dispatch, after what seemed only moments, the longboat was already launched, oarsmen at station. He passed the packet to Mackintosh without a word, then mounted the companionway ladder back to the quarterdeck.

The Indian pilot stood against the banister, shaded by the lateen sail, calmly studying the galleons.

"Three of these I know very well." His accented Turki was almost lost in a roll of spray off the stern. "They are the *St. Sebastian*, the *Bon Jesus*, and the *Bon Ventura*. They arrived new from Lisbon last year, after the monsoon, to patrol our shipping lanes, to enforce the regulation that all Indian vessels purchase a trading license from authorities in Goa."

"And what of the fourth?"

"It is said she berthed in Goa only this spring. I do not know her name. There were rumors she brought the new Viceroy, but early, before his four-year term began. I have never before seen her north, in these waters."

My God. Hawksworth looked at the warships in dismay. Is this the course of the Company's fortune? A voyage depending on secrecy blunders across a fleet bearing the incoming Viceroy of Goa. The most powerful Portuguese in the Indies.

"They are invincible," the pilot continued, his voice still matter-of-fact. "The galleons own our waters. They have two decks of guns. No Indian vessel, even the reckless corsairs along our southern coast of Malabar, dare meet them in the open sea. Owners who refuse to submit and buy a Portuguese trading license must sail hundreds of leagues off course to avoid their patrol."

"And what do you propose? That we heave to and strike our colors? Without even a fight?" Hawksworth was astonished by the pilot's casual unconcern. Is he owned by the Portugals too?

"You may act as you choose. I have witnessed many vain boasts of English bravery during my brief service aboard your ship. But an Indian captain would choose prudence at such a time. Strike colors and offer to pay for a license. Otherwise you will be handled as a pirate."

"No Englishman will ever pay a Portugal or a Spaniard for a license to trade. Or a permit to piss." Hawksworth turned away, trying to ignore the cold sweat beading on his chest. "We never have. We never will."

The pilot watched him for a moment, and then smiled.

"You are in the seas off India now, Captain. Here the Portuguese have been masters for a hundred years." His voice betrayed a trace of annoyance at Hawksworth's seeming preoccupation, and he moved closer. "You would do well to hear me out. We know the Portuguese very well. Better perhaps than you. Their cruelties here began a full century ago, when the barbarous captain Vasco da Gama first discovered our Malabar Coast, near the southern tip of India. He had the Portuguese nose for others' wealth, and when he returned again with twenty ships, our merchants rose against him. But he butchered their fleet, and took prisoners by the thousand. He did not, however, simply execute them. First he cut away their ears, noses, and hands and sent these to the local raja, recommending he make a curry. Next a Portuguese captain named Albuquerque came with more warships to ravage our trade in the north, that on the Red Sea. And when servants of Islam again rose up to defend what is ours, Allah the Merciful once more chose to turn his face from them, leaving all to defeat. Soon the infidel Portuguese came with many fleets, and in a span no more than a male child reaching manhood, had seized our ocean and stolen our trade."

The pilot's face remained blandly expressionless as he continued, but he reached out and caught Hawksworth's sleeve. "Next they needed a Portuguese trading station, so they bribed pirates to help storm our coastal fortress at Goa, an island citadel with a deep port. And this place they made the collection point for all the pepper, spices, jewels, dyes, silver, and gold they have plundered from us. They lacked the courage to invade India herself, as the Moghuls did soon after, so they made our sea their infidel empire. It is theirs, from the coast of Africa, to the Gulf of Persia, to the Molucca Islands. And they seek not merely conquest, or enforced commerce, but also our conversion to their religion of cruelty. They have flooded our ports with ignorant priests. To them this is a crusade against Islam, against the one True Faith, a crusade that has triumphed—for a time—where barbarous Christian land assaults on our holy Mecca have always failed."

Then the pilot turned directly to Hawksworth and a smile flickered momentarily across his lips. "And now you English have come to challenge them by sea. You must pardon me if I smile. Even if you prevail today, which I must tell you I doubt, and even if one day more of your warships follow and drive them from our seas entirely—even if all this should take place, you will find your victory hollow. As theirs has been. For we have already destroyed them. The way India consumes all who come with arms. The ancient way. They have robbed our wealth, but in return we have consumed their spirit. Until at last they are left with nothing but empty commodity. It will be no different for you, English captain. You will never have India. It is India who will have you."

He paused and looked again toward the galleons, their sails swelling on the horizon. "But today I think the Portuguese will spare us the trouble."

Hawksworth examined the pilot, struggling to decipher his words. "Let me tell you something about England. All we ask is trade, for you and for us, and we don't have any priests to send. Only Catholic traders do that. And if you think we'll not stand well today, you know even less about the English. The thing we do best is fight at sea. Our sea dogs destroyed the entire navy of Spain twenty years ago, when they sent their Armada to invade England, and even to this day the Spaniards and Portugals have never understood our simple strategy. They still think a warship's merely a land fortress afloat. All they know to do is throw infantry against a ship and try to board her. The English know sea battles are won with cannon and maneuverability, not soldiers."

Hawksworth directed the pilot's gaze down the *Discovery*. The ship was of the new English "race-built" class, low in the water and swift. Absent were the bulky superstructures on bow and stern that weighed down a galleon, the "castles" that Spanish and Portuguese commanders used to stage infantry for boarding an enemy vessel. A full thirty years before, the English seaman and explorer John Hawkins had scoffed at these, as had Francis Drake and Walter Raleigh. They saw clearly that the galleons' towering bow and stern, their forecastle and poop, slow them, since the bluff beamy hull needed to support their weight wouldn't bite the water. A superstructure above decks serves only to spoil a warship's handling in a breeze, they declared, and to lend a better target to an English gunner.

"Your ships assuredly are smaller than Portuguese galleons, I agree," the pilot volunteered after a pause, "but I see no advantage in this."

"You'll see soon enough. The *Discovery* may be low, but she'll sail within six points of the wind, and she's quicker on the helm than anything afloat."

Hawksworth raised the glass and studied the galleons again. As he expected they were beating to windward, laboring under a full head of canvas.

Good. Now the *Resolve* can make her move.

The longboat was returning, its prow biting the trough of each swell, while on the *Resolve* seamen swarmed the shrouds and rigging. Hawksworth watched with satisfaction as his sister ship's main course swiveled precisely into the breeze and her sprits'l bellied for a run down the wind. Her orders were to steer to leeward, skirting the edge of the galleons' cannon range.

And if I know the Portugals, he told himself, they'll be impatient enough to start loosing round after round of shot at her, even from a quarter mile off. It takes courage to hold fire till you're under an enemy's guns, but only then do you have accuracy. Noise and smoke are battle enough for most Portugals, but the main result is to overheat and immobilize their cannon.

As the *Discovery* lay hove to, biding time, the *Resolve* cut directly down the leeward side of the galleons, laboring under full press of sail, masts straining against the load. The Indian pilot watched the frigate in growing astonishment, then turned to Hawksworth.

"Your English frigates may be swift, but your English strategy is unworthy of a common *mahout,* who commands an old she-elephant with greater cunning. Your sister frigate has now forfeited the windward position. Why give over your only advantage?"

Even as he spoke the four Portuguese warships, caught beating to windward, began to shorten sail and pay off to leeward to intercept the *Resolve,* their bows slowly crossing the wind as they turned.

"I've made a gamble, something a Portugal would never do," Hawksworth replied. "And now I have to do something no Englishman would ever do. Unless outgunned and forced to." Before the pilot could respond, Hawksworth was gone, heading for the gun deck.

The ring of his boots on the oak ladder leading to the lower deck was lost in the grind of wooden trucks, as seamen threw their weight against the heavy ropes and tackles, slowly hauling out the guns. The *Discovery* was armed with two rows of truck-mounted cast-iron culverin, and she had sailed with twenty-two barrels of powder and almost four hundred round shot. Hawksworth had also stowed a supply of crossbar shot and deadly langrel— thin casings filled with iron fragments—for use against enemy rigging and sail at close quarters.

Shafts of dusty light from the gunports and overhead scuttles relieved the lantern-lit gloom, illuminating the massive beams supporting the decks above. Sleeping hammocks were lashed away, but the space was airless, already sultry from the morning sun, and the rancid tang of sweat mixed with fresh saltpeter from the gunpowder caught in Hawksworth's mouth, bittersweet.

He walked down the deck, alert to the details that could spell victory or loss. First he checked the wooden tubs of vinegared urine and the long swabs stationed between the cannon, used for cleaning burning fragments of metal from the smoking barrels after each round. Fail to swab a barrel and there could be an unplanned detonation when the next powder charge was tamped into place. Then he counted the budge-barrels of powder, now swathed in water-soaked blankets to fend off sparks, and watched as Edward Malloyre, the man some called the best master gunner in England, inspected each cannon's touchhole as its lead plate was removed, assuring himself it had not corroded from the gases expelled during their last gunnery practice, in the Mozambique Channel.

"Master Malloyre."

"Aye, sir, all's in order. We'll hand the Spanish bastards a taste o' English iron." Malloyre, who had never troubled to differentiate Portugal from Spain, was built like a bear, with short bowed legs and a tree-stump frame. He drew himself erect, his balding pate easily clearing the rugged overhead beams, and searched the gloom. "The Worshipful Company may ha' signed on a sorry lot o' pimpin' apple squires, but, by Jesus, I've made Englishmen o' them. My sovereign to your shilling we hole the pox-rotted Papists wi' the first round."

"I'll stand the wager, Malloyre, and add the last keg of brandy. But you'll earn it. I want the portside battery loaded with crossbar forward, and langrel aft. And set the langrel for the decks, not the sail."

Malloyre stared at him incredulously. The command told him immediately that this would be a battle with no quarter. The use of langrel against personnel left no room for truce. Then suddenly the true implications of Hawksworth's command hit him like a blow in the chest. "That shot's for close quarters. We lay alongside, and the bastards'll grapple and board us sure. Swarm us like curs on a bitch."

"That's the order, Malloyre. Be quick on it. Set the starboard round first. And light the linstocks." Hawksworth turned to count the shot and absently picked up one of the linstocks lying on deck—an iron-plated staff used to set off a cannon—fingering the oil-soaked match rope at its tip and inhaling its dank musk. And the smell awoke again the memory of that last day two years before in the Mediterranean, with Turkish pirate galleys fore and aft, when there had been no quarter, and no hope . . .

"Beggin' your pardon, sir." Malloyre's voice was urgent, bringing him back. "What's the firin' orders?"

"Just fire the starboard round as a broadside, and set for the lower gun deck."

"Aye aye, sir." He paused. "And Lord Jesus pray we'll live to swab out."

Malloyre's parting words would have followed him up the ladder to the main deck, but they were swallowed in the muffled roll of cannon fire sounding over the bay. The galleons were spreading, circling the *Resolve* as they bore down upon her, and they had begun to vomit round after round, throwing jets of water randomly around the frigate as she plunged toward the shallows and safety. Any minute now, Hawksworth told himself, and she'll be in the shallows. If she doesn't run aground on a bar.

Then he saw the *Resolve* begin to come about, reefing and furling her sails. She's made the shallows. And the Portugals' guns have quieted.

"Permission to set sail, sir. The bleedin' Portugals'll be on her in a trice." Mackintosh stood on the quarterdeck by the steering house. And he made no attempt to disguise the anxiety in his eyes.

"Give the Portugals time, Mackintosh, and you'll see their second fatal mistake. The first was overheating the cannon on their upper decks. The second will be to short-hand their crews. They're out of cannon range now, so they'll launch longboats, and assign half the watch as oarsmen. Here, take the glass. Tell me what you see."

Mackintosh studied the shallows with the telescope, while a smile slowly grew on his hard face. "I'm a motherless Dutchman. An' there's a king's guard o' Portugal musketmen loadin' in. Wearin' their damn'd silver helmets."

They haven't changed in thirty years, Hawksworth smiled to himself. The Portugals still think their infantry is too dignified to row, so they assign their crews to the oars and leave their warships shorthanded. But they won't find it easy to board the *Resolve* from longboats. Not with English musketmen in her maintop. And that should give us just enough time . . .

"Are all the longboats out yet, Mackintosh?"

"Aye, sir." The quartermaster steadied the glass against the roll of the ship. "And making for the *Resolve* like they was runnin' from hell itself."

"Then bear full sail. Two points to windward of the bastard on the left. Full press, and hoist the spritsail. Keep the wind and pay her room till we're in range."

With an exultant whoop Mackintosh jabbed the sweat-soaked telescope toward Hawksworth, and began bellowing orders to the mates. Within moments sails unfurled and snapped in the wind, sending the *Discovery*'s bow biting into the chop and hurtling spray over the bulwarks. Hawksworth kept to the quarterdeck, studying the nearest warship with the glass. The galleon's forecastle towered above the horizon now like some Gothic fortress, and with the glass he could make out pennants blazoned from all her yardarms. Then he turned toward the Indian pilot, whose gaze was riveted on the Portuguese warships.

"What's the name of the galleon on the left, the large one?" Hawksworth pointed toward the vessel he had been observing with the glass. "I can't read it from this distance."

"That one is the *Bon Ventura*. We know her to be heavily armed."

"I'd say she's over a thousand tons burden. I wonder how handy she'll be with her best men out in the longboats?"

"She'll meet you soon enough, with her full bounty. It is said that last year she caught and sank a twenty-gun Dutch frigate trading in the Moluccas."

"She'll still have to come about into the wind." Hawksworth seemed not to hear the pilot now, so absorbed was he in the looming battle.

As though in answer to his thoughts, the *Bon Ventura* started to heel slowly about, like an angered bull. But the *Discovery* now had the windward position secure, and the Portuguese ship would have to tack laboriously into the wind. Her canvas was close-hauled and she would be slow. We've got the weather gage now, Hawksworth told himself, and we'll hold it. Then he noticed that the second galleon in the row, the *St. Sebastian*, had also begun wearing around, bringing her stern across the wind as she too turned to meet the *Discovery*.

"They've deciphered our plan," Hawksworth said quietly to himself, "and now it's two of the bastards we'll face. But with luck we'll engage the *Bon Ventura* before the *St. Sebastian* can beat to range. And the *Bon Ventura* is drawing away from the fleet. That bit of bravado will cost her."

The *Discovery* was closing rapidly on the *Bon Ventura*. In minutes they would be within range. Mackintosh was at the whipstaff now, holding their course, his senses alert to every twist in the wind. He involuntarily clenched and unclenched his teeth, while his knuckles were bloodless white from his grip on the hardwood steering lever. Hawksworth raised the glass again, knowing what he hoped to see.

"The Portugals have just made their third mistake, Mackintosh." He tried to mask his excitement. "They've sealed the lower gunports to shut out water while they're tacking. So after they get position they'll still have to run out the lower guns."

"Aye. That's why two-deckers won't buy a whore's chastity on a day like this. But they'll have the upper guns on us soon enough."

"Wait and see, Mackintosh. I'll warrant their upper guns are overheated by now. They'll think twice about trying to prime them just yet. They'll have to wait a bit. Perhaps just long enough for us to get alongside. Then the upper guns'll touch nothing but our rigging."

The breeze freshened even more, driving the *Discovery* rapidly toward her target. Mackintosh eyed the galleon nervously, knowing the frigate was heavily outgunned. Finally he could bear the tension no longer.

"We've got range now. Permission to bring her about."

"Steady as she goes. They're slow on the helm." Hawksworth glanced at the line of seamen along the port side, untying bundles of musket arrows and lighting the linstock. "Bosun! Are the men at stations?"

"Aye, sir." A gravel voice sounded through the din. "Stocks were a bit damp, but I warrant the hellish sun's dryin' 'em out. We'll give the fornicators a fine English salute."

Hawksworth gauged the galleon's course, estimating her speed and her ability to maneuver. Then he saw her start coming about in the water, turning to position the starboard battery for a broadside. Gunports on the lower deck flipped up and cannon began slowly to emerge, like hard black fangs. Nervous sweat began to bead on Mackintosh's brow as the *Discovery* held her course directly down the galleon's windward side.

The *Bon Ventura*'s broadside battery was not yet set, but a sudden burst of black smoke from her starboard bow-chaser sent a ball smashing through the *Discovery*'s quarter gallery, removing much of its ornate embellishment. Then came another flare of smoke and flame, hurtling a second ball through the lateen sail above Mackintosh's head. The quartermaster went pale, and looked imploringly at Hawksworth.

"Steady as she goes, Mackintosh, they still haven't fully set their guns." The knot in Hawksworth's stomach was like a searing ball of fire. God, for a brandy. But we've got to hold till we've got sure range. To come about now would keep our distance, and mean a classic battle. One we're sure to lose.

He pushed away the realization of the immense chance they were taking. But now there was no turning back, even if he wanted. Finally he could bear it no longer. God make it right.

"Now, Mackintosh! Bring her hard about!"

The quartermaster threw his weight against the whipstaff, shouting orders to the two seamen on the deck below to haul the tackles on the tiller, helping him flip the rudder. Then he turned and bellowed commands to the mates.

"Hands to the braces. Bring her hard about."

The seamen poised incredulously in the maintop and foretop cheered as they began to haul in the ropes securing the yards, and in moments the sails swiveled off the wind. The *Discovery* careened in the chopping sea, responding readily to the shift in rudder and canvas. By this time Hawksworth was standing over the scuttle above the gun deck, shouting to Malloyre.

"Coming about. Prepare to fire the starboard battery when your guns bear."

The *Discovery* had wheeled a sharp arc in the water, laying herself broadside to the galleon, hardly fifty yards away. The English seamen aloft stared mutely at the towering forecastle of the Portuguese warship, most never before having seen a galleon at close range. Although the guns on her upper deck were still silent, had they spoken now they would have touched nothing but the frigate's tops'ls. But as the galleon turned, the cannon on her lower deck were coming into final position. In moments she would lay the *Discovery* with a broadside. Hawksworth watched her carefully, calculating, and then the knot in his stomach dissolved like ice in the sun. The *Discovery* would be in position seconds ahead.

Malloyre's command to fire cut the awe-stricken silence. The next instant a low roar seemed to emanate from all the timbers of the English frigate, while red-tipped flame tongued from her starboard side. The ship heeled dangerously sideways, while black smoke, acrid and searing, boiled up through the scuttles and hatch, as though propelled on its way by the round of cheers from below decks, the traditional salute of ship's gunners. Hawksworth later remembered noting that the battery had fired in perfect unison, not losing the set of a single gun by the ship's recoil.

A medley of screams came first, piercing the blackened air. Then the smoke drifted downwind, over the side of the *Bon Ventura*, revealing a savage incision where her lower gun deck had once been. Cannon were thrown askew, and the mangled forms of Portuguese gunners, many with limbs shattered or missing, could be seen through the splintered hull. But Hawksworth did not pause to inspect the damage; he was already yelling the next orders to Mackintosh, hoping to be heard above the din. The advantage of surprise would be short-lived.

"Pay off the helm! Bring her hard about!"

Again the rudder swiveled in its locks, while seamen aloft hauled the sheets and braces, but this time the *Discovery* came about easily, using the wind to advantage. As he turned to check the whipstaff, Hawksworth heard a high-pitched ricochet off the steering house and sensed a sudden dry numbness in his thigh. Only then did he look up to see the line of Portuguese musketmen on the decks of the *Bon Ventura*, firing sporadically at the English seamen on decks and aloft.

Damn. A lucky shot by some Lisbon recruit. He seized a handful of coarse salt from a bucket by the binnacle and pressed it against the blood. A flash of pain passed briefly through his consciousness and then was forgotten. The *Discovery*'s stern had crossed the wind. There was no time to lose. He moved down the companionway to again shout orders to Malloyre on the gun deck. "Set for the fo'c'sle and rigging. Fire as your guns bear."

The *Bon Ventura* still lay immobile, so unexpected had been the broadside. But a boarding party of Portuguese infantry was poised on the galleon's forecastle superstructure, armed with swords and pikes, ready to fling grapples and swing aboard the frigate. The Portuguese had watched in helpless amazement as the *Discovery* completely came about and again was broadside. Suddenly the captain of the infantry realized what was in store and yelled frantically at his men to take cover. But his last command was lost in the roar of the *Discovery*'s guns.

This time flames and smoke erupted from the *Discovery*'s portside battery, but now it spewed knife-edged chunks of metal and twisting crossbars. Again the screams came first, as the musketmen and infantry on the fo'c'sle were swept across the decks in the deadly rain. Crossbars chewed through the galleon's mainsail, parting it into two flapping remnants, while the rigging on the foremast was blown by the boards, tangling and taking with it a party of musketmen stationed in the foretop. Now the galleon bobbed helpless in the water, as the last seamen remaining on the shrouds plunged for the decks and safety.

"When you're ready, Mackintosh."

The quartermaster signaled the bosun, and a line of seamen along the port gunwales touched musket arrows to the lighted linstock and took aim. Streaks of flame forked into the tattered rigging of the *Bon Ventura*, and in moments her canvas billowed red. Again the Portuguese were caught unaware, and only a few manned water buckets to extinguish the burning shreds of canvas drifting to the deck.

They were almost alongside now, but no Portuguese infantry would pour down the side of the forecastle onto their decks. The galleon's decks were a hemorrhage of the wounded and dying.

"By Jesus, 'tis a sight for English eyes." Edward Malloyre's blackened face, streaked with sweat, bobbed up through the hatch over the gun deck, and he surveyed the wreckage of the *Bon Ventura*. "Had to give 'er a look, Cap'n. See if my lads earn'd their biscuit." He beamed with open pride.

"Malloyre, how does it stand below decks?" Hawksworth yelled from the quarterdeck.

"Starboard side's swabbed out. How shall we load 'em, sir?" Malloyre leaned backward to gain a better look at the galleon, which now towered above them.

"Round shot, and run them out fast as you can."

"Aye, sir. An' no more close quarters if you please. Ne'er want to be this close to one o' the bastards again." Malloyre started to retreat through the hatch, but then he turned, paused for a second, and yelled at Hawksworth. "Beggin' your pardon, Cap'n. I knew all along 'twas best to pull alongside and lay 'em wi' crossbar. Just wanted to give the lads a bit o' a scare. Keep 'em jumpin'."

Hawksworth waved his hand and watched as Malloyre's pudgy frame dropped through the gun-deck hatch like a rabbit diving for its warren.

Mackintosh was standing on the main deck, his tangled red mane blackened with smoke, watching as the *Discovery* drifted slowly toward the side of the bobbing galleon. Then, when they were only feet away, he signaled the bosun, and a line of English seamen lit the waiting fuses and began to loft clay powder pots across the waist of the *Bon Ventura*, now almost above their heads. When they had finished, he passed orders and the *Discovery* began to pull away, before her sails could ignite. Then one by one the powder pots started to explode, spewing burning sulphur over the Portuguese vessel's decks.

Hawksworth watched the carnage, and asked himself if he had been right to do what he'd done. They'd have sunk us. Cut down the men and taken the officers and merchants to a Goa prison. And then what? We couldn't have sunk them with cannon in a week. The only choice was fire.

Then he turned to see the *St. Sebastian* making toward them. Her cannon were already run out, and at any moment she would start coming about for a broadside. Again he felt the throb in his thigh, and it triggered a wave of fear that swept upward from his stomach. The Indian pilot stood next to him, also watching the approaching galleon.

"I have seen a miracle, Captain. Allah the Compassionate has watched over you today." The pilot's face showed none of the strain of battle. And his clothes were still spotless, oddly immune from the oily smoke that blackened all the English seamen. "But I fear there cannot be two miracles on the same morning. You are about to pay for your fortune. Perhaps there is still time to strike your colors and save the lives of your men."

"We surrender now and we'll rot in a Goa prison forever. Or be pulled apart on the *strappado*." Hawksworth glared back. "And I seem to recall the Quran says 'Do not falter when you've gained the upper hand.'"

"You do not have the upper hand, my Captain, and the Holy Quran speaks only of those who trust in Allah, the Merciful . . ." His voice trailed off as he turned to stare at Hawksworth. "It is not common for a *feringhi* to know the Holy Quran. How is it you . . . ?"

"I just spent two years in a Turkish prison, and I heard little else." Hawksworth turned and was testing the wind, weighing his options. The *St. Sebastian* was almost on them. Her cannon were already run out, and at any moment she would start coming about for a broadside. He could still hear the trucks of the cannon below decks, as the starboard battery was being run out, and he knew the portside crews were only now beginning to swab the last glowing shreds of metal from the cannon barrels.

Good God, there's no time to set the ordnance. They'll blow us to hell. He deliberated for a long moment, weighing his options. As he watched, the *St. Sebastian* began to shorten sail, preparing to come about and fire. Only minutes remained. Then he noticed that the wind on the burning *Bon Ventura*'s superstructure was drifting her in the direction of the approaching *St. Sebastian*, and he hit on another gamble. They've shortened sail in order to come about, which means they're vulnerable. Now if I can make them try to take their bow across the wind, with their sails shortened . . .

"Mackintosh, take her hard about! Set the courses for a port tack."

Once again the *Discovery* heeled in the water, her stern deftly crossing the wind, and then she was back under full sail, still to windward of the burning galleon. The sudden tack had left the burning *Bon Ventura* directly between the English frigate and the approaching galleon. The *Discovery* pulled away, keeping the wind, forcing the galleon to tack also if she would engage them. Hawksworth watched, holding his breath as Portuguese seamen began to man the sheets, bringing the *St. Sebastian*'s bow into the wind.

It was fatal. The approaching galleon had shortened too much sail in preparation to come about for the broadside, and now she lacked the momentum to cross the wind. Instead the sluggish, top-heavy warship hung in stays, her sails slack, her bulky bow fighting the wind, refusing to pay off onto the opposite tack. All the while the *Bon Ventura* was drifting inexorably toward her, flaming. I was right, Hawksworth thought. She didn't have the speed to bring her bow around. With his glass he watched the galleon's captain order her back to the original tack. But time had run out.

Blinding explosions suddenly illuminated the gunports of the burning *Bon Ventura*, as powder barrels on the gun decks ignited, first the upper and then the lower. In only moments the fire found the powder room aft of the orlop deck, and as the English seamen looked on spellbound the galleon seemed to erupt in a single cloud of fire, rocketing burning timbers and spars across the sea's surface. The mainmast, flaming like a giant taper, snapped and heaved slowly into the fo'c'sle. Then the superstructure on the stern folded and dropped through the main deck, throwing a plume of sparks high into the morning air.

Although the *St. Sebastian* had righted herself, she still had not regained speed, for now the sails had lost their luff and sagged to leeward. Why isn't she underway, Hawksworth asked himself, surely she'll circle and engage us? He looked again with the glass and the reason became clear. The Portuguese crewmen on the *St. Sebastian* had begun throwing themselves into the sea, terrified at the sight of the *Bon Ventura*'s blazing hull drifting slowly across their bow. The wind had freshened again and was pushing the burning galleon rapidly now. The blaze had become an inferno, fueled by casks of coconut oil stored below decks on the galleon, and Hawksworth involuntarily shielded his eyes and face from the heat that, even at their distance, seared the *Discovery*. As he watched, the drifting *Bon Ventura* suddenly lurched crazily sideways, and then came the sound of a coarse, grinding impact, as her burning timbers sprayed across the decks of the *St. Sebastian*. In moments the second galleon was also an abandoned inferno, her crew long since afloat in the safety of the sea, clinging to debris and making for shore.

"Allah has been merciful twice to you in one morning, Captain. I had never before known the extent of His bounty. You are a man most fortunate." The pilot's words, spoken softly and with pronounced gravity, were almost drowned in the cheers that engulfed the decks and rigging of the *Discovery*.

"The battle's just begun. Boarding parties are at the *Resolve*, and there are two more galleons." Hawksworth reached for the glass resting by the binnacle.

"No, Captain, I doubt very much the Portuguese will trouble you further. Your luck has been too exceptional. But they will return another day." The pilot squinted toward the shore, as though confirming something he knew should be there.

Hawksworth trained his glass on the two galleons that still held the *Resolve* pinned in the shallows. They were heeling about, preparing to run southward on the wind under full press of sail. He also realized their longboats had been abandoned. Some were following futilely after the retreating

galleons, while others were already rowing toward the river mouth. The English frigate had been forgotten. Then he noted that although pennants no
longer flew from the yardarms of the galleons, the large, unnamed vessel had
run out a brilliant red ensign on her poop staff. He studied it carefully, then
turned to the pilot, extending the glass.

"Take a look and tell me what the colors are on the large man-of-war.
I've never seen them before."

The pilot waved away the telescope with a smile. "I need no Christian
device to tell you that. We all know it. With all your fortune, you have
failed to understand the most important thing that happened today."

"And what is that?"

"Those are the colors of the Viceroy of Goa, flown only when he is
aboard his flagship. You have humiliated him today. The colors speak his
defiance. His promise to you."

As the pilot spoke, Mackintosh came bounding up the companionway
to the quarterdeck, his soot-covered face beaming. "What a bleedin' day!
What a *bleedin'* day!" Then his eyes dimmed for an instant. "But a man'd
be called a liar who told the story."

"How many dead and wounded, Mackintosh?"

"Two maintopmen killed by musket fire. And a bosun's mate took a
splinter in the side, very bad, when the bastards laid us wi' the first bow-
chasers. A few other lads took musket fire, but the surgeon'll sew 'em up
fine."

"Then break out the last keg of brandy. And see that Malloyre's men
get the first tot . . . but don't forget to send a tankard to the quarterdeck."

Mackintosh broke an appreciative grin and headed down the companionway ladder. The sun was baking the decks now, and a swarm of locusts
had appeared from nowhere to buzz about the maintop. The wind was beginning to slacken in the heat, and silence slowly settled over the *Discovery*.
Hawksworth turned his glass one last time to the large galleon. He could still
make out the ensign over the crests of surf, blood red in the sun.

CHAPTER THREE

The bells sounded ending the afternoon watch and calling the first dog
watch. Only four hours since noon, but already the morning's carnage
seemed a memory from a distant lifetime. Sultry tropic air, motionless and
stifling, immersed the *Discovery* as the gaunt-faced seamen labored to finish
securing the mast of the pinnace. Mackintosh had ordered the pinnace's sail
unrolled on deck, and as he inspected the stitches for rot he alternately reviled
the men, the heat, the Company. Hawksworth had completed the log and
stood in the companionway outside the Great Cabin to watch the prepara-

tions, take the air, and exercise his leg. All the previous night he had stood on the quarterdeck, keeping the helm and translating for the pilot. And tonight again there would be no sleep. There's time for a rest now, his weary mind urged, till the first bell of this watch, half an hour. Then he cursed himself for his weakness, his readiness to yield, and shoved open the door of the Great Cabin.

The oil lamp swayed with each roll of the ship, punctuating the rhythmic creak of the wood paneling and adding to the sweltering heat. He locked the door, then strode aft to push ajar the two stern windows. But the stolid air lay inert, refusing to lift. He would have to prepare the chest in suffocating misery. So be it.

Brushing the hair back from his eyes, he unlocked a bronzed sea chest and began to extract one by one the articles entrusted to the Company by King James. First was the letter, in English with a formal copy in diplomatic Spanish, both scribed on parchment and sealed in a leather case secured with His Majesty's impression in red wax. The seal, set in London over seven months before, was soft in the heat now, pliant to his touch. He surveyed the room for a moment and then his eye hit on the pair of formal thigh-length stockings the Company had insisted he pack. Perfect. He bound his hose around the king's letter, knotted it protectively over the seal, and tossed the bundle into the smaller wooden chest he would take ashore.

Then he began to transfer the royal presents: a brace of gold-plated pistols, a half dozen silver-handled swords, a small silver-trimmed saddle, a set of delicate Norwich crystal, jeweled rings, a leatherbound mirror, a silver whistle studded with emeralds, a large cocked hat trimmed in silk, a miniature portrait of King James, and finally, a dozen bottles of fine English sack. He checked each item for damage and then packed them tightly into the small chest. Finally he inserted a tightly fitting false bottom and covered it with a coarse woolen rug.

Then the second packing began. He started with more gifts, these for port officials, mainly silver-trimmed knives and rings set with small inexpensive pearls. He also enclosed several boxed sets of English gold sovereigns, which the Company had requested be distributed as widely as possible, in hopes they would begin to be accepted.

Finally he looked about the room for personal goods. First he folded in a new leather jerkin, then next to it packed a new pair of leather boots. He stared at the boots for a moment, and then removed them while he carefully wrapped two primed pistols and slid one deep into each hollow toe. Next to the boots he packed a case of Spanish brandy he had been saving, for personal use aland. Lastly he took his glistening English lute from its corner berth, held it for a moment, and tested the strings. He adjusted the tuning on one string, then wrapped the lute's melon-shaped body in a silk cloth, and nestled it next to the brandy.

As he secured the lock on the chest and pocketed the large brass key, he suddenly asked himself how he would get the chest into India without its being searched. I'm not a genuine ambassador. I'm the captain of a merchantman, with no diplomatic standing. The Company, for all its mercantile wisdom, neglected to consider that small difficulty.

So I'll just have to *sound* like an ambassador. That shouldn't be so hard. Just be impressed with your own importance. And find nothing, food or lodgings, sufficiently extravagant.

Then he drew himself erect and unlocked the door of the Great Cabin. Only one thing remained.

"Mackintosh!" The quartermaster was in the pinnace now, fitting the tiller, and he glanced up in irritation. "Send the pilot to my cabin."

Hawksworth had scarcely seated himself behind the great oak table before the tall chestnut-skinned man appeared in the doorway. Hawksworth examined the face again, expressionless and secure, asking himself its years. Is he thirty; is he fifty? The features seemed cast from an ageless mold, hard and seamless, immune to time.

"May I be of service?"

"Repeat your name for me." Hawksworth spoke in Turkish. "And tell me again the business of your vessel."

"My name is Karim Hasan Ali." The reply came smoothly, but almost too rapidly for Hawksworth to follow. "My ship was the *Rahimi*, a pilgrim vessel on her return voyage from Mecca, by way of Aden, to our northern port of Diu. We carry Muslim pilgrims outbound from India in the spring, and return after the monsoon. As you assuredly must know, for a thousand years Mecca has been the shrine all followers of Islam must visit once in their life. Our cabins are always full."

Hawksworth recalled the vessel, and his astonishment at her size. She had had five masts and was easily twelve hundred tons, over twice the burden of the *Discovery* and greater than anything he had ever seen before, even the most ambitious Spanish carrack. But when they spotted her, tacking eastward across the Bay of Cambay, she was unarmed and hove to almost before they had fired across her bow. Why unarmed, he had asked himself then, and why strike so readily? Now he understood.

"And you were the pilot for the *Rahimi*?"

"I am called the *musallim*." A note of formality entered the Indian's voice and he instinctively drew himself more erect.

"Is that the pilot?"

"Yes, but more. Perhaps it is like your first mate. But I am in full charge of navigation for the *nakuda*, the owner. To you he would be captain."

"And what was your salary for the voyage?"

"I received two hundred rupees for the trip to Aden, and am allowed two extra cabins of goods for personal trade."

Hawksworth smiled resignedly to himself, remembering he had unquestioningly delivered to the *nakuda* a bag of Spanish rials of eight equivalent to five hundred Indian rupees to buy out the pilot's contract. Then he spoke.

"Tonight, we go upriver to Surat. You're still in my service and you'll be pilot."

"I had expected it. I know the river well."

"Will there be any Portugal traders on the river?" Hawksworth searched his eyes hoping to monitor their truthfulness.

"I would not expect it. Although this year's monsoons are past and the river has returned to normal, there are new sandbanks. Every season they shift, becoming more treacherous. Only those of us who know the river well understand the moods of her sands. I have never seen *topiwallah* traders in Surat this early in the season." Karim paused, following Hawksworth's puzzled expression, then continued, with an air of condescension, "*Topiwallah* is our word meaning 'men who wear hats.' We call Christian traders *topiwallahs*." He fixed Hawksworth squarely. "And we have other names for their priests."

"Call Christians what you will, but just remember England is not Portugal." Hawksworth's tone stiffened. "England has rid herself of the popery that still rules the Spaniards and Portugals. Along with their fear-mongering Jesuits and their damned Inquisition. It's now treason to practice Catholic rites in England."

"I have heard something of your petty European squabbles, your Christian rivalries. Is it your intention now to spread them to India as well?"

"All England wants is trade. Nothing else." Hawksworth shifted his leg, leaning forward to tighten the bandage. "I'm here as an ambassador. To convey the friendship of my king, and his offer of free and open trade."

"And after you begin this trade, what then? Will you next try to drive the Portuguese from our ports? So that *you* can steal away shipping from our own merchantmen, as they have done, and demand we pay *you* for a license to ply our own seas?"

"I told you we only want trade. England has no use for sailing licenses, or priests. Our only enemies here are the Portugals. And the damned Hollanders if they start trying to interfere."

Karim studied Hawksworth in silence, fingering his jeweled earring in thought as he recalled the morning's battle. Two small English merchant frigates had prevailed over four Portuguese warships, galleons. Never before, he told himself, have the Portuguese been humiliated before our eyes. Pigeons must already be winging word of this incredible encounter to Agra. Separately, no doubt, to the *Moghul* and to the queen. But Queen Janahara will know first. As always. And she will know her Portuguese profits are no longer secure.

And what about Prince Jadar? Yes, the prince will already have heard, hours ago. What will Prince Jadar decide to do? *That's* the most important question now.

"Just tell me about the navigation of the river," Hawksworth continued, unable to decipher Karim's distant expression. "How long will it take for our pinnace to reach Surat? We cast off at sunset."

"The tide will be running in tonight, and that will aid your oarsmen." Karim instantly became businesslike. "There will also be a night breeze off the sea. But the Portuguese have no authority on our river. Once you are inland you are under the rule of the governor of Surat . . . and, of course, Prince Jadar, whom the *Moghul* has appointed to administrate this province."

Hawksworth heard the first bell and walked to the stern windows to monitor the slant of the dying sun and to inhale the fresh evening air. Then he wheeled and examined Karim, the pilot's face shadowed in the half light.

"And who are these officials? This governor and prince?"

Karim smiled and carefully secured the fold of his turban. "The governor administers the port of Surat. He collects trading duties of the *Moghul's* court in Agra. Prince Jadar is the son of the *Moghul* and the military ruler of Gujarat, this province."

"Then who will I meet in Surat?" Hawksworth groped for a pattern. "The governor or the prince?"

Again Karim paused, wondering how much to tell, before continuing evenly, "Neither of these need concern you now. The first official you must satisfy will be the Shahbandar, what the Moghuls call the *mutasaddi*. The Shahbandar controls the customs house, the portal for all who would enter the *Moghul's* domain. His power over the port is absolute."

Hawksworth slapped one of the bronze cannon to punctuate his dismay.

In India also! Good Jesus, every Muslim port in the world must have this same petty official. I've heard that Shahbandar is Persian for "Lord of the Haven," and if that's true the office is named perfectly. Every one I've known has had the right to refuse entry to anyone, at his whim, if bribes are insufficient and no more powerful official intervenes.

"Who does the Shahbandar here answer to? The governor? The prince? The *Moghul* himself? Or somebody *else* you haven't told me about yet?" Hawksworth tried to push back his rising anxiety.

"Captain, you have, in your guileless *feringhi* way, raised a question it is wiser not to pursue. I can only assure you the Shahbandar is a man of importance in Surat, and in India."

"But who should I seek out when we reach Surat?"

At that moment two bells sounded on the quarterdeck, and with them a ray from the fading sun pierced the stern window, glancing off the oak boards of the table. A twilight silence seemed to settle uneasily over the *Discovery*, amplifying the creaking of her boards.

"Captain, I have already told you more than most foreigners know. You would be wise to prepare now to meet the Shahbandar." Karim rose abruptly and bowed, palms together, hands at his brow. "You must forgive me. In Islam we pray at sunset."

Hawksworth stared after him in perplexity as Karim turned and vanished into the darkened companionway.

Not yet even aland, and already I sense trouble. He fears the Shahbandar, that's clear enough, but I'm not sure it's for the usual reasons. Is there some intrigue underway that we're about to be drawn into, God help us?

He took a deep breath and, fighting the ache in his leg, made his way out to the quarter gallery on the stern. A lone flying fish, marooned in the bay from its home in the open sea, burst from the almost placid waters, glinting the orange sun off its body and settling with a splash, annoying the seabirds that squabbled over galley scraps along the port side. Seamen carrying rations of salt pork and biscuit were clambering down the companionway and through the hatch leading to the lower deck and their hammocks. Hawksworth listened to them curse the close, humid air below, and then he turned to inhale again the land breeze, permeated with a green perfume of almost palpable intensity.

Following the direction of the sweetened air, he turned and examined the darkening shore one last time. India now seemed vaguely obscured, as through a light mist. Or was it merely encroaching darkness? And through this veil the land seemed somehow to brood? Or did it beckon?

It's my imagination, he told himself. India is there all right, solid ground, and scarcely a cannon shot away. India, the place of fable and mystery to Englishmen for centuries. And also the place where a certain party of English travelers disappeared so many years ago.

That should have been a warning, he told himself. It's almost too ironic that you're the next man to try to go in. You, of all the men in England. Are you destined to repeat their tragedy?

He recalled again the story he knew all too well. The man financing those English travelers almost three decades past had been none other than Peter Elkington, father of George Elkington, Chief Merchant on this voyage. Like his son, Peter Elkington was a swearing, drinking, whoring merchant, a big-bellied giant of a man who many people claimed looked more and more like King Harry the older and fatter he got. It was Peter Elkington's original idea those many years back to send Englishmen to India.

The time was before England met and obliterated the Armada of Spain, and long before she could hope to challenge the oceanic trade networks of the Catholic countries—Spain to the New World, Portugal to the East. In

those days the only possible road to India for England and the rest of
Europe still was overland, the centuries-old caravan trail that long preceded
Portugal's secret new sea route around the Cape.

The idea of an English mission overland to India had grown out of
Peter Elkington's Levant Company, franchised by Queen Elizabeth to
exploit her new treaty with the Ottoman Turks, controllers of the caravan
trade between India and the Mediterranean. Through the Levant Company,
English traders could at last buy spices directly at Tripoli from overland caravans traveling the Persian Gulf and across Arabia, thereby circumventing
the greedy Venetian brokers who for centuries had served as middlemen for
Europe's pepper and spices.

But Peter Elkington wanted more. Why buy expensive spices at the
shores of the Mediterranean? Why not extend England's own trade lines all
the way to India and buy directly?

To gain intelligence for this daring trade expansion, he decided to
finance a secret expedition to scout the road to India, to send a party of English traders through the Mediterranean to Tripoli, and on from there in disguise across Arabia to the Persian Gulf, where they would hire passage on a
native trader all the way to the western shore of India. Their ultimate destination was the *Great Moghul*'s court, deep in India, and hidden in their
bags would be a letter from Queen Elizabeth, proposing direct trade.

Eventually three adventurous traders were recruited to go, led by Roger
Symmes of the Levant Company. But Peter Elkington wanted a fourth, for
protection, and he eventually persuaded a young army captain of some reputation to join the party. The captain—originally a painter, who had later
turned soldier after the death of his wife—was vigorous, spirited, and a
deadly marksman. Peter Elkington promised him a nobleman's fortune if
they succeeded. And he promised to take responsibility for Captain Hawksworth's eight-year-old son, Brian, if they failed.

Peter Elkington himself came down to the Thames that cold, gray February dawn they set sail, bringing along his own son, George—a pudgy, pam-
pered adolescent in a silk doublet. Young George Elkington regally ignored
Brian Hawksworth, a snub only one of the two still remembered. As the sails
slowly dissolved into the icy mist, Brian climbed atop his uncle's shoulders to
catch a long last glimpse. No one dreamed that only one of the four would
ever see London again.

Letters smuggled back in cipher kept the Levant Company informed of
progress. The party reached Tripoli without incident, made their way successfully overland through Arabia, and then hired passage on an Arab trader
for the trip down the Persian Gulf. The plan seemed to be working perfectly.

Then came a final letter, from the Portuguese fortress of Hormuz, a salt-
covered island peopled by traders, overlooking the straits between the Per-

sian Gulf and the Gulf of Oman, gateway to the Arabian Sea and India's ports. While waiting at Hormuz for passage on to India, the English party had been betrayed by a suspicious Venetian and accused of being spies. The Portuguese governor of Hormuz had nervously imprisoned them and decreed they be shipped to Goa for trial.

After waiting a few more months for further word, Peter Elkington finally summoned Brian Hawksworth to the offices of the Levant Company and read him this last letter. He then proceeded to curse the contract with Captain Hawksworth that rendered the Levant Company responsible for Brian's education should the expedition meet disaster.

Peter Elkington admitted his plan had failed, and with that admission, the Levant Company quietly abandoned its vision of direct trade with India.

But Brian Hawksworth now had a private tutor, engaged by the Levant Company, a tousle-haired young apostate recently dismissed from his post at Eton for his anti-religious views.

This new tutor scorned as dogmatic the accepted subjects of Latin, rhetoric, and Hebrew—all intended to help Elizabethan scholars fathom abstruse theological disputations—and insisted instead on mathematics, and the new subject of science. His anti-clerical outlook also meant he would teach none of the German in fashion with the Puritans, or the French and Spanish favored by Catholics. For him all that mattered was classical Greek: the language of logic, pure philosophy, mathematics, and science. The end result was that the commoner Brian Hawksworth received an education far different from, if not better than, that of most gentlemen, and one that greatly surpassed the hornbook alphabet and numbers that passed for learning among others of his own class.

To no one's surprise, Brian Hawksworth was his father's son, and he took naturally to marksmanship and fencing. But his first love came to be the English lute, his escape from the world of his tutor's hard numbers and theorems.

It lasted until the day he was fourteen, the day the Levant Company's responsibility expired. The next morning Brian Hawksworth found himself apprenticed to a Thames waterman and placed in service on one of the mud-encrusted ferryboats that plied London's main artery. After three months of misery and ill pay, he slipped away to take a berth on a North Sea merchantman. There he sensed at once his calling was the sea, and he also discovered his knowledge of mathematics gave him an understanding of navigation few other seamen enjoyed. By then he scarcely remembered his father, or the luckless expedition to India.

Until the day Roger Symmes appeared alone back in London, almost ten years after that icy morning the Levant Company's expedition had sailed.

The *Discovery* groaned, and Hawksworth sensed the wind freshen as it whipped through the stern quarter gallery and noticed the increasingly brisk swirl of the tide. Almost time to cast off. As he made his way back to the Great Cabin for a last check, his thoughts returned again to London, those many years ago.

He had found Symmes at the offices of the Levant Company, nursing a tankard of ale as he sat very close to their large roaring fireplace. He bore little resemblance to the jaunty adventurer Hawksworth remembered from that long-ago morning on the Thames. Now he was an incongruous figure, costumed in a tight-fitting new silk doublet and wearing several large gold rings, yet with a face that was haggard beyond anything Hawksworth had ever seen. His vacant eyes seemed unable to focus as he glanced up briefly and then returned his stare to the crackling logs in the hearth. But he needed no prompting to begin his story.

"Aye, 'tis a tale to make the blood run ice." Symmes eased open a button of his ornate doublet and shakily loosened his new ruff collar. "After the Venetian rogue gets us arrest'd with his damnable lie, the bastard Portugals clap us in the hold of a coastin' barge makin' for Goa, in company with near a hundred Arab horses. When we finally make port, they haul us out of that stink hole and slam us in another, this time the Viceroy's dungeon. We took ourselves for dead men."

"But what happened to my father?" Hawksworth blinked the sweat from his eyes, wanting the story but wanting almost more to escape the overheated, timbered offices that loomed so alien.

"That's the horrible part o' the story. It happen'd the next mornin', poor luckless bastard. We're all march'd into this big stone-floor'd room where they keep the *strappado*."

"What's that?"

"'Tis a kindly little invention o' the Portugals, lad. First they bind your hands behind your back and run the rope up over a hangin' pulley block. Then they hoist you up in the air and set to givin' it little tugs, makin' you hop like you're dancin' the French lavolta. When they tire o' the sport, or they're due to go say their rosary beads, they just give it a good strong heave and pop your arms out o' your shoulders. Jesuits claim 'twould make a Moor pray to the pope."

Hawksworth found himself watching Symmes's wild eyes as he recounted the story, and wondering how he could remember every detail of events a decade past.

"Then this young captain comes in, struttin' bastard, hardly a good twenty year on him. Later I made a point to learn his name—Vaijantes, Miguel Vaijantes."

"What did he do?"

"Had to see him, lad. Eyes black and hard as onyx. An' he sports this sword he's had made up with rubies in the handle. Ne'er saw the likes o' it, before or since, e'en in India. But he's a Portugal, tho', through an' through. No doubt on that one."

"But what did he do?"

"Why, he has the guards sling Hawksworth up in the *strappado*, lad, seein' he's the strongest one o' us. Figur'd he'd last longer, I suppose, make more sport."

"Vaijantes had them torture my father?"

"Aye. Think's he'll squeeze a confession and be a hero. But ol' Hawksworth ne'er said a word. All day. By nightfall Vaijantes has pull'd his arms right out. They carried him out of the room a dead man."

Hawksworth still remembered how his stomach turned at that moment, with the final knowledge that his father was not merely missing, or away—as he had told himself, and others—but had been coldly murdered. He had checked his tears, lest Symmes see, and pressed on.

"What happened to you, and to the others? Did he torture you next?"

"Would have, not a doubt on't. We all wonder'd who'd be the next one. Then that night they post a Jesuit down to our cell, a turncoat Dutchman by the name of Huyghen, who spoke perfect English, thinkin' he'd cozen us into confessin'. But he hates the Portugals e'en more'n we do. An' he tells us we'd most likely go free if we'd pretend to turn Papist. So the next day we blurt out we're actually a band o' wealthy adventurers in disguise, rich lads out to taste the world, but we've seen the error o' our ways an' we've decided to foreswear the flesh and turn Jesuits ourselves. Thinkin' of donatin' everything we own to their holy order." Symmes paused and nervously drew a small sip from his tankard of spiced ale. "Vicious Papist bastards."

"Did they really believe you?"

"Guess the Dutchman must've convinc'd 'em somehow. Anyway, our story look'd square enough to get us out on bail, there bein' no evidence for the charge o' spyin' in any case. But we'd hardly took a breath of air before our old friend the Hollander comes runnin' with news the Viceroy's council just voted to ship us back to Lisbon for trial. That happens and we're dead men. No question. We had to look to it."

Symmes seemed to find concentration increasingly difficult, but he extracted a long-stemmed pipe and began stuffing black strands into it with a trembling hand while he composed himself. Finally he continued. "Had to leave Goa that very night. What else could we do? So we traded what little we had for diamonds, sew'd 'em up in our clothes, and waded the river into India. By dawn we're beyond reach o' the Portugals. In India. An' then, lad, is when it began."

"What happened?"

" 'Twould take a year to tell it all. Somehow we eventually got to the *Great Moghul's* court. I think he was named Akman. An' we start livin' like I never thought I'd see. Should've seen his city, lad, made London look like a Shropshire village. He had a big red marble palace called Fatehpur Sekri, with jewels common as rocks, an' gold e'erywhere, an' gardens filled with fountains, an' mystical music like I'd ne'er heard, an' dancin' women that look'd like angels . . ."

His voice trailed off. "Ah, lad, the women there."

Symmes suddenly remembered himself and turned to examine Hawksworth with his glassy eyes. "But I fancy you're a bit young to appreciate that part o' it, lad." Then his gaze returned to the fire and he rambled on, warming to his own voice. "An' there was poets readin' Persian, and painters drawin' pictures that took days to do one the size of a book page. An' the banquets, feasts you're ne'er like to see this side o' Judgment Day."

Symmes paused to draw on his pipe for a moment, his hand still shaking, and then he plunged ahead. "But it was the Drugs that did it, lad, what they call'd *affion* and *bhang*, made out o' poppy flowers and some kind of hemp. Take enough of them and the world around you starts to get lost. After a while you ne'er want to come back. It kill'd the others, lad. God only knows how I escap'd."

Then Symmes took up his well-rehearsed monologue about the wealth he'd witnessed, stories of potential trade that had earned him a place at many a merchant's table. His tale expanded, becoming ever more fantastic, until it was impossible to tell where fact ended and wishful fabrication began.

Although Symmes had never actually met any Indian officials, and though the letter from Queen Elizabeth had been lost en route, his astonishing story of India's riches inspired the greed of all England's merchants. Excitement swelled throughout London's Cheapside, as traders began to clamor for England to challenge Portugal's monopoly of the sea passage around the Cape. Symmes, by his inflated, half-imaginary account, had unwittingly sown the first seeds of the East India Company.

Only young Brian Hawksworth, who nourished no mercantile fantasies, seemed to realize that Roger Symmes had returned from India quite completely mad.

CHAPTER FOUR

"Pinnace is afloat, Cap'n. I'm thinkin' we should stow the goods and be underway. If we're goin'." Mackintosh's silhouette was framed in the doorway of the Great Cabin, his eyes gaunt in the lantern light. Dark had dropped suddenly over the *Discovery*, bringing with it a cooling respite from the inferno of day.

"We'll cast off before the watch is out. Start loading the cloth and ironwork"—Hawksworth turned and pointed toward his own locked sea chest— "and send for the purser."

Mackintosh backed through the doorway and turned automatically to leave. But then he paused, his body suspended in uncertainty for a long moment. Finally he revolved again to Hawksworth.

"Have to tell you, I've a feelin' we'll na be sailin' out o' this piss-hole alive." He squinted across the semi-dark of the cabin. "It's my nose tellin' me, sir, and she's always right."

"The Company's sailed to the Indies twice before, Mackintosh."

"Aye, but na to India. The bleedin' Company ne'er dropped anchor in this nest o' Portugals. 'Twas down to Java before. With nothin' but a few Dutchmen to trouble o'er. India's na the Indies, Cap'n. The Indies is down in the Spice Islands, where seas are open. The ports o' India belong to the Portugals, sure as England owns the Straits o' Dover. So beggin' your pardon, Cap'n, this is na the Indies. This might well be Lisbon harbor."

"We'll have a secure anchorage. And once we're inland the Portugals can't touch us." Hawksworth tried to hold a tone of confidence in his voice. "The pilot says he can take us upriver tonight. Under cover of dark."

"No Christian can trust a bleedin' Moor, Cap'n. An' this one's got a curious look. Somethin' in his eyes. Can't tell if he's lookin' at you or na."

Hawksworth wanted to agree, but he stopped himself.

"Moors just have their own ways, Mackintosh. Their mind works differently. But I can already tell this one's not like the Turks." Hawksworth still had not decided what he thought about the pilot. It scarcely matters now, he told himself, we've no choice but to trust him. "Whatever he's thinking, he'll have no room to play us false."

"Maybe na, but he keeps lookin' toward the shore. Like he's expectin' somethin'. The bastard's na tellin' us what he knows. I smell it. The nose, Cap'n."

"We'll have muskets, Mackintosh. And the cover of dark. Now load the pinnace and let's be on with it."

Mackintosh stared at the boards, shifting and tightening his belt. He started to argue more, but Hawksworth's voice stopped him.

"And, Mackintosh, order the muskets primed with pistol shot." Hawksworth recalled a trick his father had once told him about, many long years past. "If anybody ventures to surprise us, we'll hand them a surprise in turn. A musket ball's useless in the dark of night, clump of pistol shot at close quarters is another story."

The prospect of a fight seemed to transform Mackintosh. With a grin he snapped alert, whirled, and stalked down the companionway toward the main deck.

Moments later the balding purser appeared, a lifelong seaman with an

unctuous smile and rapacious eyes who had dispensed stores on many a pros-
perous merchantman, and grown rich on a career of bribes. He mechanically
logged Hawksworth's chest in his account book and then signaled the bosun
to stow the heavy wooden trunk into the pinnace.

Hawksworth watched the proceedings absently as he checked the edge
on his sword. Then he slipped the belt over his shoulder and secured its large
brass buckle. Finally he locked the stern windows and surveyed the darkened
cabin one last time.

The *Discovery*. May God defend her and see us all home safe. Every
man.

Then without looking back he firmly closed the heavy oak door, latched
it, and headed down the companionway toward the main deck.

Rolls of broadcloth lay stacked along the waist of the ship, and beside
them were muskets and a keg of powder. George Elkington was checking
off samples of cloth as they were loaded into the pinnace, noting his selec-
tion in a book of accounts.

Standing next to him, watching idly, was Humphrey Spencer, youngest
son of Sir Randolph Spencer. He had shipped the voyage as the assistant to
Elkington, but his real motivation was not commerce but adventure, and a
stock of tales to spin out in taverns when he returned. His face of twenty
had suffered little from the voyage, for a stream of bribes to the knowing
purser had reserved for him the choice provisions, including virtually all the
honey and raisins.

Humphrey Spencer had donned a tall, brimmed hat, a feather protruding from its beaver band, and his fresh doublet of green taffeta fairly glowed
in the lantern's rays. His new thigh-length hose were an immaculate tan and
his ruff collar pure silk. A bouquet of perfume hovered about him like an invisible cloud.

Spencer turned and began to pace the deck in distraught agitation,
oblivious to his interference as weary seamen worked around him to drag rolls
of broadcloth next to the gunwales, stacking them for others to hoist and
stow in the pinnace. Then he spotted Hawksworth, and his eyes brightened.

"Captain, at last you're here. Your bosun is an arrant knave, my life
on't. He'll not have these rogues stow my chest."

"There's no room in the pinnace for your chest, Spencer."

"But how'm I to conduct affairs 'mongst the Moors without a gentleman's fittings?" He reviewed Hawksworth's leather jerkin and seaboots with
disdain.

Before Hawksworth could reply, Elkington was pulling himself erect,
wincing at the gout as his eyes blazed. "Spencer, you've enough to do just
mindin' the accounts, which thus far you've shown scant aptness for." He
turned and spat into the scuppers. "Your father'd have me make you a mer-

chant, but methinks I'd sooner school an ape to sing. 'Tis tradin' we're here for, not to preen like a damn'd coxcomb. Now look to it."

"You'll accompany us, Spencer, as is your charge." Hawksworth walked past the young clerk, headed for the fo'c'sle. "The only 'fittings' you'll need are a sword and musket, which I dearly hope you know enough to use. Now prepare to board."

As Hawksworth passed the mainmast, bosun's mate John Garway dropped the bundle he was holding and stepped forward, beaming a toothless smile.

"Beggin' your pardon, Cap'n. Might I be havin' a word?"

"What is it, Garway."

"Would you ask the heathen, sir, for the men? We've been wonderin' if there's like to be an alehouse or such in this place we're goin'. An' a few o' the kindly sex what might be friendly disposed, if you follow my reckonin', sir."

Hawksworth looked up and saw Karim waiting by the fo'c'sle, his effects rolled in a small woven tapestry under his arm. When the question was translated, the pilot laid aside the bundle and stepped toward the group of waiting seamen, who had all stopped work to listen. He studied them for a moment—ragged and rank with sweat, their faces blotched with scurvy and their hair matted with grease and lice—and smiled with expressionless eyes.

"Your men will find they can purchase *arak*, a local liquor as potent as any I have seen from Europe. And the public women of Surat are masters of all refinements of the senses. They are exquisite, worthy even of the *Moghul* himself. Accomplished women of pleasure have been brought here from all civilized parts of the world, even Egypt and Persia. I'm sure your seamen will find the accommodations of Surat worthy of their expectations."

Hawksworth translated the reply and a cheer rose from the men.

"Hear that, mates?" Master's mate Thomas Davies turned to the crowd, his face a haggard leer. "Let the rottin' Portugals swab cannon in hell. I'll be aswim in grog an' snuffin' my wick with a willin' wench. Heathen or no, all the same, what say?"

A confirming hurrah lifted from the decks and the men resumed their labor with spirits noticeably replenished.

Hawksworth turned and ascended the companionway ladder to the quarterdeck, leaving behind the tense bravado. As he surveyed the deck below from his new vantage, he suddenly sensed an eerie light enveloping the ship, a curious glow that seemed almost to heighten the pensive lament of the boards and the lulling melody of wind through the rigging. Then he realized why.

The moon!

I'd forgotten. Or was I too tired to think? But now . . . it's almost like daylight. God help us, we've lost the last of our luck.

"Ready to cast off." Mackintosh mounted the companionway to the quarterdeck, his face now drawn deep with fatigue. "Shall I board the men?"

Hawksworth turned with a nod, and followed him down to the main deck.

Oarsmen began scrambling down the side of the *Discovery*, a motley host, shoeless and clad only in powder-smudged breeches. Though a rope ladder dangled from the gunwales, the seamen preferred to grasp the deadeyes, easing themselves onto the raised gunport lids, and from there dropping the last few feet into the pinnace. They were followed by George Elkington, who lowered himself down the swaying ladder, breathing oaths. Hawksworth lingered by the railing, searching the moonlit horizon and the darkened coast. His senses quickened as he probed for some clue that would trigger an advance alert. But the moonlit water's edge lay barren, deserted save for an occasional beached fishing skiff, its sisal nets exposed on poles to dry. Why the emptiness? During the day there were people.

Then he sensed Karim standing beside him, also intent on the empty shore. The pilot's back was to the lantern that swung from the mainmast and his face was shrouded in shadow. Abruptly, he addressed Hawksworth in Turki.

"The face of India glories in the moonlight, do you agree? It is beautiful, and lies at peace."

"You're right about the beauty. It could almost be the coast of Wales." Hawksworth thought he sensed a powerful presence about Karim now, something he could not explain, only detect with a troubled intuition. Then the pilot spoke again.

"Have you prepared yourself to meet the Shahbandar?"

"We're ready. We have samples of English goods. And I'm an ambassador from King James. There's no reason to deny us entry . . ."

"I told you he is a man of importance. And he already knows, as all who matter will soon know, of your exceptional fortune today. Do you really think today's battle will go unnoticed in India?"

"I think the Portugals noticed. And I know they'll be back. But with luck we'll manage." Hawksworth felt the muscles in his throat tighten involuntarily, knowing a fleet of warships from Goa would probably be headed north within a fortnight.

"No, Captain, again you miss my meaning." Karim turned to draw closer to Hawksworth, flashing a joyless smile. "I speak of India. Not the Portuguese. They are nothing. Yes, they trouble our seas, but they are nothing. They do not rule India. Do you understand?"

Hawksworth stiffened, unsure how to respond. "I know the *Moghul* rules India. And that he'll have to wonder if the damned Portugals are still master of his seas."

"Surely you realize, Captain, that the Portuguese profits are staggering.

Are you also aware these profits are shared with certain persons of importance in India?"

"You mean the Portugals have bribed officials?" That's nothing new,
Hawksworth thought. "Who? The Shahbandar?"

"Let us say they often give commissions." Karim waved his hand as
though administering a dispensation. "But there are others whom they allow
to invest directly in their trade. The profits give these persons power they
often do not use wisely."

"Are you telling me the *Moghul* himself invests with the damned Portugals?" Hawksworth's hopes plummeted.

"On the contrary. His Majesty is an honorable man, and a simple man
who knows but little of what some do in his name. But do you understand
there must be one in his realm who will someday have his place? Remember
he is mortal. He rules like a god, but he is mortal."

"What does this have to do with the Shahbandar? Surely he'd not challenge the *Moghul*. And I know the *Moghul* has sons . . ."

"Of course, he is not the one." Karim's smile was gentle. "But do not
forget the Shahbandar is powerful, more powerful than most realize. He
knows all that happens in India, for his many friends repay their obligation
to him with knowledge. As for you, if he judges your wisdom worthy of your
fortune today, he may choose to aid you. Your journey to Agra will not be
without peril. There are already those in India who will not wish you there.
Perhaps the Shahbandar can give you guidance. It will be for him to decide."

Hawksworth studied Karim incredulously. How could he know? "Whatever I may find necessary to do, it will not involve a port official like the
Shahbandar. And a trip to Agra surely would not require *his* approval."

"But you must find your way." Karim examined Hawksworth with a
quick sidelong glance, realizing he had guessed correctly. "My friend, your
defeat of the Portuguese today may have implications you do not realize.
But at times you talk as a fool, even more than the Portuguese. You will
need a guide on your journey. Believe me when I tell you."

Karim paused for a moment to examine Hawksworth, as though wondering how to couch his next words. "Perhaps you should let the stars guide
you. In the Holy Quran the Prophet has said of Allah, 'And he hath set for
you the stars . . .' "

" 'That you may guide your course by them.' " Hawksworth picked up
the verse, " 'Amid the dark of land and sea.' Yes, I learned that verse in
Tunis. And I knew already a seaman steers by the stars. But I don't understand what bearing that has on a journey to Agra."

"Just as I begin to think you have wisdom, again you cease to listen. But
I think now you will remember what I have said."

"Hawksworth!" Elkington's voice boomed from the pinnace below.

"Have we sail'd a blessed seven month to this nest o' heathens so's to idle about and palaver?"

Hawksworth turned to see Humphrey Spencer gingerly lowering himself down the ladder into the pinnace, the feather in his hatband whipping in the night wind. The oarsmen were at their stations, ready.

"One thing more, Captain." Karim pressed a hand against Hawksworth's arm, holding him back. "One thing more I will tell you. Many feringhi, foreigners, who come to India are very unwise. Because our women keep the veil, and dwell indoors, foreigners assume they have no power, no influence. Do not act as other foolish feringhi and make this mistake. In Surat . . ."

"What women do you mean? The wives of officials?"

"Please, listen. When you reach Surat, remember one last admonition from the Quran. There it is written, 'As for women from whom you fear rebellion, admonish them and banish them to beds apart.' But sometimes a woman too can be strong-willed. She can be the one who banishes her husband, denying him his rights. If she is important, there is nothing he can do. Remember . . ."

"Damn it to hell," Elkington's voice roared again, "I'm not likin' these moonlight ventures. 'Tis full risk aplenty when you can see who's holdin' a knife to your throat. But if we're goin', I say let's be done with it and have off."

Hawksworth turned back to Karim, but he was gone, swinging himself lightly over the side of the Discovery and into the pinnace.

Across the moonlight-drenched swells the Resolve lay quiet, her stern lantern reassuringly aglow, ready to hoist sail for the cove. And on the Discovery seamen were at station, poised to follow. Hawksworth looked once more toward the abandoned shore, troubled, and then dropped quickly down the side into the pinnace. There was no sound now, only the cadence of the boards as the Discovery's anchor chain argued against the tide. And then a dull thud as the mooring line dropped onto the floor planking of the pinnace.

Hawksworth ordered Mackintosh to row with the tide until they reached the shelter of the river mouth, and then to ship the oars and hoist sail if the breeze held. He had picked the ablest men as oarsmen, those not wounded and least touched by scurvy, and next to each lay a heavy cutlass. He watched Mackintosh in admiration as the quartermaster effortlessly maneuvered the tiller with one hand and directed the oarsmen with the other. The moon was even more alive now, glinting off the Scotsman's red hair.

As the hypnotic rhythm of the oars lulled Hawksworth's mind, he felt a growing tiredness begin to beg at his senses. Against his will he started to drift, to follow the moonlight's dancing, prismatic tinge on the moving crests of waves. And to puzzle over what lay ahead.

Half-dozing, he found his thoughts drawn to the Shahbandar who waited in Surat, almost like a gatekeeper who held the keys to India. He mulled Karim's words again, the hints of what would unlock that doorway, and slowly his waking mind drifted out of reach. He passed unknowing into that dreamlike state where deepest truth so often lies waiting, unknown to rationality. And there, somehow, the pilot's words made perfect sense . . .

"Permission to hoist the sail." Mackintosh cut the pinnace into the river mouth, holding to the center of the channel. Hawksworth startled momentarily at the voice, then forced himself alert and scanned the dark riverbanks. There was still nothing. He nodded to Mackintosh and watched as the sail slipped quietly up the mast. Soon the wind and tide were carrying them swiftly, silently. As he watched the run of the tide against the hull, he suddenly noticed a group of round objects, deep red, bobbing past.

"Karim." Hawksworth drew his sword and pointed toward one of the balls. "What are those?"

"A fruit of our country, Captain. The *topiwallahs* call them coconuts." Karim's voice was scarcely above a whisper, and his eyes left the shore for only a moment. "They are the last remains of the August festival."

"What festival is that?"

"The celebration of the Hindu traders. Marking the end of the monsoon and the opening of the Tapti River to trade. Hindus at Surat smear coconuts with vermilion and cast them into the Tapti, believing this will appease the angry life-force of the sea. They also cover barges with flowers and span them across the harbor. If you were there, you would hear them play their music and chant songs to their heathen gods."

"And the coconuts eventually float out to sea?"

"A few, yes. But mostly they are stolen by wicked boys, who swim after them. These few perhaps their gods saved for themselves."

Hawksworth examined the bobbing balls anew. The coconut was yet another legend of the Indies. Stories passed that a man could live for days on the liquor sealed within its straw-matted shell.

The moon chased random clouds, but still the riverbank was illuminated like day. The damp air was still, amplifying the music of the night—the buzz of gnats, the call of night birds, even the occasional trumpet of a distant elephant, pierced the solid wood line on either side of the narrowing river. Hawksworth tasted the dark, alert, troubled. Where are the human sounds? Where are the barges I saw plying the river mouth during the day? I sense an uneasiness in the pilot, an alarm he does not wish me to see. Damn the moon. If only we had dark.

"Karim." Hawksworth spoke softly, his eyes never long from the dense rampart of trees along the riverbank.

"What do you wish, Captain?"

"Have you ever traveled up the river before by moonlight?"

"Once, yes, many years ago. When I was young and burning for a woman after our ship had dropped anchor in the bay. I was only a *karwa* then, a common seaman, and I thought I would not be missed. I was wrong. The *nakuda* discovered me in Surat and reclaimed my wage for the entire voyage. It was a very hungry time."

"Was the river quiet then, as it is now?"

"Yes, Captain, just the same." Though Karim looked at him directly, the darkness still guarded his eyes.

"Mackintosh." Hawksworth's voice cut the silence. "Issue the muskets." His eyes swept along the shore, and then to the narrow bend they were fast approaching. Karim is lying, he told himself; at last the pilot has begun to play false with us. Why? What does he fear?

"Aye aye, Cap'n." Mackintosh was instantly alert. "What do you see?"

The sudden voices startled Elkington awake, and his nodding head snapped erect. "The damn'd Moors have settl'd in for the night. If you'd hold your peace, I could join 'em. I'll need the full o' my wits for hagglin' with that subtle lot o' thieves come the morrow. There's no Portugals. E'en the night birds are quiet as mice."

"Precisely," Hawksworth shot back. "And I would thank you to take a musket, and note its flintlock is full-cocked and the flashpan dry." Then he continued, "Mackintosh, strike the sail. And, Karim, take the tiller."

The pinnace was a sudden burst of activity, as seamen quickly hauled in the sail and began to check the prime on their matchlocks. With the sail lashed, their view was unobstructed in all directions. The tide rushing through the narrows of the approaching bend carried the pinnace ever more rapidly, and now only occasional help was needed from the oarsmen to keep it aright.

A cloud drifted over the moon, and for an instant the river turned black. Hawksworth searched the darkness ahead, silent, waiting. Then he saw it.

"On the boards!"

A blaze of musket fire spanned the river ahead, illuminating the blockade of longboats. Balls sang into the water around them while others splattered off the side of the pinnace or hissed past the mast. Then the returning moon glinted off the silver helmets of the Portuguese infantry.

As Karim instinctively cut the pinnace toward the shore, Portuguese longboats maneuvered easily toward them, muskets spewing sporadic flame. The English oarsmen positioned themselves to return the fire, but Hawksworth stopped them.

Not yet, he told himself, we'll have no chance to reload. The first round has to count. And damn my thoughtlessness, for not bringing pikes. We could have . . .

The pinnace lurched crazily and careened sideways, hurtling around broadside to the longboats.

A sandbar. We've struck a damned sandbar. But we've got to face them with the prow. Otherwise . . .

As though sensing Hawksworth's thoughts, Karim seized an oar and began to pole the pinnace's stern off the bar. Slowly it eased around, coming about to face the approaching longboats. No sooner had the pinnace righted itself than the first longboat glanced off the side of the bow, and a grapple caught their gunwale.

Then the first Portuguese soldier leaped aboard—and doubled in a flame of sparks as Mackintosh shoved a musket into his belly and pulled the trigger. As the other English muskets spoke out in a spray of pistol shot, several Portuguese in the longboat pitched forward, writhing.

Mackintosh began to bark commands for reloading.

"Half-cock your muskets. Wipe your pans. Handle your primers. Cast about to charge . . ."

But time had run out. Two more longboats bracketed each side of the bow. And now Portuguese were piling aboard.

"Damn the muskets," Hawksworth yelled. "Take your swords."

The night air came alive with the sound of steel against steel, while each side taunted the other with unintelligible obscenities. The English were outnumbered many to one, and slowly they found themselves being driven to the stern of the pinnace. Still more Portuguese poured aboard now, as the pinnace groaned against the sand.

Hawksworth kept to the front of his men, matching the poorly trained Portuguese infantry easily. Thank God there's no more foot room, he thought, we can almost stand them man for man . . .

At that moment two Portuguese pinned Hawksworth's sword against the mast, allowing a third to gain footing and lunge. As Hawksworth swerved to avoid the thrust, his foot crashed through the thin planking covering the keel, bringing him down. Mackintosh yelled a warning and leaped forward, slashing the first soldier through the waist and sending him to the bottom of the pinnace, moaning. Then the quartermaster seized the other man by the throat and, lunging like a bull, whipped him against the mast, snapping his neck.

Hawksworth groped blindly for his sword and watched as the third soldier poised for a mortal sweep. Where is it? Good God, he'll cut me in half.

Suddenly he felt a cold metal object pressed against his hand, and above the din he caught Humphrey Spencer's high-pitched voice, urging. It was a pocket pistol.

Did he prime it? Does he know how?

As the Portuguese soldier began his swing, Hawksworth raised the pistol and squeezed. There was a dull snap, a hiss, and then a blaze that melted the soldier's face into red.

He flung the pistol aside and seized the dying Portuguese's sword. He was armed again, but there was little advantage left. Slowly the English were crowded into a huddle in the stern. Cornered, abaft the mast, they no longer had room to parry. Hawksworth watched in horror as a burly Portuguese, his silver helmet askew, braced himself against the mast and drew back his sword to send a swath through the English. Hawksworth tried to set a parry, but his arms were pinned.

He'll kill half the men. The bastard will . . .

A bemused expression unexpectedly illuminated the soldier's face, a smile with no mirth. In an instant it transmuted to disbelief, while his raised sword clattered to the planking. As Hawksworth watched, the Portuguese's hand began to work mechanically at his chest. Then his helmet tumbled away, and he slumped forward, motionless but still erect. He stood limp, head cocked sideways, as though distracted during prayer.

Why doesn't he move? Was this all some bizarre, senseless jest?

Then Hawksworth saw the arrows. A neat row of thin bamboo shafts had pierced the soldier's Portuguese armor, riveting him to the mast.

A low-pitched hum swallowed the sudden silence, as volleys of bamboo arrows sang from the darkness of the shore. Measured, deadly. Hawksworth watched in disbelief as one by one the Portuguese soldiers around them crumpled, a few firing wildly into the night. In what seemed only moments it was over, the air a cacophony of screams and moaning death.

Hawksworth turned to Karim, noting fright in the pilot's eyes for the very first time.

'The arrows." He finally found his voice. "Whose are they?"

"I can probably tell you." The pilot stepped forward and deftly broke away the feathered tip on one of the shafts still holding the Portuguese to the mast. As he did so, the other arrows snapped and the Portuguese slumped against the gunwale, then slipped over the side and into the dark water. Karim watched him disappear, then raised the arrow to the moonlight. For an instant Hawksworth thought he saw a quizzical look enter the pilot's eyes.

Before he could speak, lines of fire shot across the surface of the water, as fire arrows came, slamming into the longboats as they drifted away on the tide. Streak after streak found the hulls and in moments they were torches. In the flickering light, Hawksworth could make out what seemed to be grapples, flashing from the shore, pulling the floating bodies of the dead and dying to anonymity. He watched spellbound for a moment, then turned again toward the stern.

"Karim, I asked whose arrows . . ."

The pilot was gone. Only the English seamen remained, dazed and uncomprehending.

Then the night fell suddenly silent once more, save for the slap of the running tide against the hull.

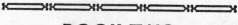

BOOK TWO
SURAT — THE THRESHOLD

CHAPTER FIVE

The room was musty and close, as though the rainy season had not passed, and the floor was hard mud. Through crude wooden shutters they could glimpse the early sun stoking anew for the day's inferno, but now it merely washed the earthen walls in stripes of golden light.

Hawksworth stood by the window examining the grassy square that spanned out toward the river. The porters, in whose lodge they were confined, milled about the open area, chanting and sweating as they unloaded large bales of cotton from the two-wheeled bullock carts that continually rolled into the square. He steadied himself against the heavy wooden frame of the window and wondered if his land legs would return before the day was out.

"God curse all Moors." Mackintosh stooped over the tray resting on the grease-smudged center carpet and pulled a lid from one of the earthen bowls. He stared critically at the dense, milky liquid inside, then gingerly dipped in a finger and took a portion to his lips. He tested the substance—tangy curds smelling faintly of spice—and his face hardened.

"'Tis damned spoilt milk." He spat fiercely onto the carpet and seized a piece of fried bread to purge the taste. "Fitter for swine than men."

"What'd they do with the samples?" Elkington sprawled heavily in the corner, his eyes bloodshot from the all-night vigil upriver. "With no guards the heathens'll be thievin' the lot." He squinted toward the window, but made no effort to move. His exhaustion and despair were total.

"The goods are still where they unloaded them." Hawksworth revolved toward the room. "They say nothing happens till the Shahbandar arrives."

"What'd they say about him?" Elkington slowly drew himself to his feet.

"They said he arrives at midmorning, verifies his seal on the customs house door, and then orders it opened. They also said that all traders must be searched personally by his officers. He imposes duty on everything, right down to the shillings in your pocket."

"Damn'd if I'll pay duty. Not for samples."

"That's what I said. And they ignored me. It seems to be law." Hawksworth noticed that the gold was dissolving from the dawn sky, surrendering to a brilliant azure. He turned, scooped a portion of curds onto a piece of fried bread, and silently chewed as he puzzled over the morning. And the night before.

Who had saved them? And why? Did someone in India hate the Portuguese so much they would defend the English before even knowing who they were? No one in India could know about King James's letter, about the East India Company's plans. No one. Even George Elkington did not know everything. Yet someone in India already wanted the English alive. He had wrestled with the question for the rest of the trip upriver, and he could think of no answers. They had been saved for a reason, a reason he did not know, and that worried him even more than the Portuguese.

Without a pilot they had had to probe upriver slowly, sounding for sandbars with an oar. Finally, when they were near exhaustion, the river suddenly curved and widened. Then, in the first dim light of morning, they caught the unmistakable outlines of a harbor. It had to be Surat. The river lay north-south now, with the main city sprawled along its eastern shore. The tide began to fall back, depleted, and he realized they had timed its flow perfectly.

As they waited for dawn, the port slowly revealed itself in the eastern glow. Long stone steps emerged directly from the Tapti River and broadened into a wide, airy square flanked on three sides by massive stone buildings. The structure on the downriver side was obviously a fortress, built square with a large turret at each corner, and along the top of walls Hawksworth could see the muzzles of cannon—they looked to be eight-inchers—trained directly on the water. And in the waning dark he spotted tiny points of light, spaced regularly along the top of the fortress walls. That could only mean one thing.

"Mackintosh, ship the oars and drop anchor. We can't dock until daylight."

"Aye, Cap'n, but why not take her in now? We can see to make a landin'."

"And they can see us well enough to position their cannon. Look carefully along there." Hawksworth directed his gaze toward the top of the fortress. "They've lighted linstocks for the guns."

"Mother of God! Do they think we're goin' to storm their bleedin' harbor with a pinnace?"

"Probably a standard precaution. But if we hold here, at least we'll keep at the edge of their range. And we'd better put all weapons out of sight. I want them to see a pinnace of friendly traders at sunup."

The dawn opened quickly, and as they watched, the square blossomed to life. Large two-wheeled carts appeared through the half-dark, drawn by muscular black oxen, some of whose horns had been tipped in silver. One by one the oxen lumbered into the square, urged forward by the shouts and beatings of turbaned drivers who wore folded white skirts instead of breeches. Small fires were kindled by some of the men, and the unmistakable scent of glowing dung chips savored the dark clouds of smoke that drifted out across the river's surface.

Then Hawksworth first noticed the bathers that had appeared along the shore on either side of the stone steps: brown men stripped to loincloths and women in brilliantly colored head-to-toe wraps were easing themselves cere-moniously into the chilled, mud-colored water, some bowing repeatedly in the direction of the rising sun. Only the waters fronting the stairway remained unobstructed.

When the dawn sky had lightened to a muted red, Hawksworth decided to start their move. He surveyed the men crowded in the pinnace one last time, and read in some faces expectation and in others fear. But in all there was bone-deep fatigue. Only Elkington seemed fully absorbed in the vision that lay before them.

Even from their distance the Chief Merchant was already assessing the goods being unloaded from the carts: rolls of brown cloth, bundles of indigo, and bales of combed cotton fiber. He would point, then turn and gesture excitedly as he lectured Spencer.

The young clerk was now a bedraggled remnant of fashion in the powder-smudged remains of his new doublet. The plumed hat he had worn as they cast off had been lost in the attack downriver, and now he crouched in the bottom of the pinnace, humiliated and morose, his eyes vacant.

"Mackintosh, weigh anchor. We'll row to the steps. Slowly."

The men bobbed alert as they hoisted the chain into the prow of the pinnace. Oars were slipped noisily into their rowlocks and Mackintosh signaled to get underway.

As they approached the stairway, alarmed cries suddenly arose from the sentinels stationed on stone platforms flanking either side of the steps. In moments a crowd collected along the river, with turbaned men shouting in a language Hawksworth could not place and gesturing the pinnace away from the dock. What could they want, he asked himself? Who are they? They're not armed. They don't look hostile. Just upset.

"Permission to land." Hawksworth shouted to them in Turkish, his voice slicing through the din and throwing a sudden silence over the crowd.

"The customs house does not open until two hours before midday," a tall, bearded man shouted back. Then he squinted toward the pinnace. "Who are you? Portuguese?"

"No, we're English." So that's it, Hawksworth thought. They assumed we were Portugals with a boatload of booty. Here for a bit of private trade.

The man examined the pinnace in confusion. Then he shouted again over the waters.

"You are not Portuguese?"

"I told you we're English."

"Only Portuguese *topiwallahs* are allowed to trade." The man was now scrutinizing the pinnace in open perplexity.

"We've no goods for trade. Only samples." Hawksworth tried to think of a way to confound the bureaucratic mind. "We only want food and drink."

"You cannot land at this hour."

"In name of Allah, the Merciful." Hawksworth stretched for his final ploy, invocation of that hospitality underlying all Islamic life. Demands can be ignored. A traveler's need, never. "Food and drink for my men."

Miraculously, it seemed to work. The bearded man stopped short and examined them again closely. Then he turned and dictated rapidly to the group of waiting porters. In moments the men had plunged into the chilled morning water, calling for the mooring line of the pinnace. As they towed the pinnace into the shallows near the steps, other porters swarmed about the boat and gestured to indicate the English should climb over the gunwales and be carried ashore.

They caught hold of George Elkington first. He clung futilely to the gunwales as he was dragged cursing from the bobbing pinnace and hoisted on the backs of two small Indian men. Arms flailing, he toppled himself from their grasp and splashed backward into the muddy Tapti. After he floated to the surface, sputtering, he was dragged bodily from the water and up the steps. Then the others were carried ashore, and only Mackintosh tried to protest.

The last to leave the pinnace, Hawksworth hoisted himself off the prow and onto the back of a wiry Indian whose thin limbs belied their strength. The man's turban smelled faintly of sweat, but his well-worn shirt was spotless. His dark eyes assessed Hawksworth with a practiced sidelong glance, evaluating his attire, his importance, and the approximate cash value of his sword in a single sweep.

Only after the porters had deposited them on the stone steps did Hawksworth finally realize that India's best port had no wharf, that human backs served as the loading platform for all men and goods. As he looked around, he also noticed they had been surrounded by a crowd of men, not identified by turbans as were the porters but uniformed more expensively and wielding long, heavy canes. Wordlessly, automatically, the men aligned themselves in two rows to create a protected pathway leading up the steps and into the square. Hawksworth watched as they beat back the gathering crowd of onlookers with their canes, and he suddenly understood this was how the port prevented traders from passing valuables to an accomplice in the crowd and circumventing customs.

Then the tall bearded man approached Hawksworth, smiled professionally, and bowed in the manner of Karim, hands together at the brow. "You are welcome in the name of the Shahbandar, as a guest only, not as a trader."

Without further greeting he directed them across the open square toward a small stone building. "You will wait in the porters' lodge until the customs house opens." As he ordered the heavy wooden door opened, he curtly added, "The Shahbandar will rule whether your presence here is permitted."

He had watched them enter, and then he was gone. Shortly after, the food had appeared.

Hawksworth examined the room once more, its close air still damp with the chill of dawn. The walls were squared, and the ceiling high and arched. In a back corner a niche had been created, and in it rested a small round stone pillar, presumably a religious object but one Hawksworth did not recognize. Who would venerate a column of stone, he mused, particularly one which seems almost like a man's organ? It can't be the Muslims. They worship their own organs like no other race, but they generally honor their law against icons. So it must be for the gentiles, the Hindus. Which means that the porters are Hindus and their overseers Moors. That's the privilege of conquerors. Just like every other land the Moors have seized by the sword.

He glanced again at the tray and noted that the food had been completely devoured, consumed by ravenous seamen who would have scorned to touch milk curds six months before. After a moment's consideration, Hawksworth turned and seated himself on the edge of the carpet. There's nothing to be done. We may as well rest while we have the chance.

George Elkington had rolled himself in a corner of the carpet and now he dozed fitfully. Humphrey Spencer fought sleep as he worked vainly to brush away the powder smudges from his doublet. Mackintosh had finished whetting his seaman's knife and now sat absorbed in searching his hair for lice. Bosun's mate John Garway lounged against a side wall, idly scratching his codpiece and dreaming of the women he would soon have, his toothless smile fixed in sleepy anticipation. The master's mate, Thomas Davies, dozed in a heap by the door, his narrow face depleted and aged with scurvy. In a back corner dice and a pile of coins had miraculously appeared, and the other seamen sprawled about them on the floor, bloodshot eyes focused on

the chance numbers that would spell the longest splurge in port. Hawksworth stretched his wounded leg once more, leaned stiffly against the front
wall, and forced his mind to drift again into needed rest.

Hawksworth was suddenly alert, his senses troubled. The sun had
reached midmorning now, and it washed the mud floor in brilliant yellow
light. He sensed that a heavy shadow had passed through its beam. He had
not specifically seen it, but somehow, intuitively, he knew. Without a word
he edged to the side of the heavy wooden door, his hand close to his sword
handle. All the others except Mackintosh were by now asleep. Only the
quartermaster had noticed it. He quickly moved to the side of the door opposite Hawksworth and casually drew his heavy, bone-handled knife.

Without warning the door swung outward.

Facing them was the same bearded man who had invited them ashore.
The square behind him was bright now with the glare of late morning, and
in the light Hawksworth realized he was wearing an immaculate white turban, a long blue skirt over tightly fitting white breeches, and ornate leather
shoes, turned up at the toe in a curved point. This time, however, he no
longer bore welcome.

"Where have you anchored your ships?" The Turki was accented and
abrupt.

News travels fast, Hawksworth thought, as he tried to shove the haze
from his mind. "Where is the Shahbandar?"

"Your merchantmen were not in the bay this morning. Where are they
now?" The man seemed to ignore Hawksworth's question.

"I demand to see the Shahbandar. And I'll answer no questions till I
do."

"You do not demand of the Shahbandar." The man's black beard
worked nervously, even when he paused. "You and all your men are to be
brought to the customs house, together with your goods."

"Where is he now?"

"He is here."

"Where?"

The Indian turned and gestured quickly across the *maidan*, the square,
toward the large windowless stone building that sat on the water's edge opposite the fortress. Hawksworth looked at the cluster of armed guards and realized this must be the mint. This was the building, he now remembered
Karim telling him, where foreign money was "exchanged." All foreign coins,
even Spanish rials of eight, were required to be melted down and reminted
into rupees before they could be used for purchase. Supposedly a protection
against counterfeit or base coin, this requirement produced months of delay.
The Shahbandar gave only one alternative to traders in a hurry: borrow
ready-made rupees at exorbitant interest.

"After he has authorized the beginning of today's work at the mint, he will verify the seal on the door of the customs house"—he pointed to the squat building adjoining their lodge—"and open it for today. All goods must be taxed and receive his *chapp* or seal before they can enter or leave India."

The men had begun to stir, and Hawksworth turned to translate. The English assembled warily, and the air came alive with an almost palpable apprehension as Hawksworth led them into the bustling square.

"We must wait." The tall Indian suddenly paused near the center of the *maidan*, just as a group of guards emerged from the mint. Each wore a heavy sword, and they were escorting a large closed palanquin carried on the shoulders of four bearers dressed only in white skirts folded about their waist. The guards cleared a path through the crowd of merchants, and made their way slowly to the door of the customs house. The crowd surged in behind them, blocking the view, but moments later the tall doors of the customs house were seen to swing open, and the crowd funneled in, behind the palanquin and the guards. Then the Indian motioned for them to follow.

The interior of the customs house smelled of sweat, mingled with spice and the dusty fragrance of indigo. As oil lamps were lighted and attached to the side walls, the milling crowd grew visible. Through the semi-dark porters were already bearing the English goods in from the *maidan* and piling them in one of the allotted stalls.

The tall guide turned to Hawksworth. "You and all your men must now be searched, here in the counting room."

"I'll not allow it." Hawksworth motioned the English back. "I told you I demand to see the Shahbandar."

"He'll receive you when he will. He has not granted an audience."

"Then we'll not be searched. Tell him that. Now."

The Indian paused for a moment, then reluctantly turned and made his way toward a door at the rear of the large room. Elkington pressed forward, his face strained.

"Tell the bleedin' heathen we're English. We'll not be treated like this rabble." He motioned around the room, a bedlam of Arab, Persian, and Indian traders who eyed the English warily as they shouted for the attention of customs inspectors and competed to bribe porters.

"Just hold quiet. I think they know exactly who we are. And they know about the ships."

As they waited, Hawksworth wondered what he should tell the Shahbandar, and he again puzzled over the words of Karim. Think. What can you tell him that he hasn't already heard? I'll wager he knows full well we were attacked by Portugals in the bay. That we burned and sank two galleons. Will he now hold us responsible for warfare in Indian waters? I'll even wager he knows we were attacked on the river. And who saved us.

The large Indian was returning, striding through the center aisle accompanied by four of the Shahbandar's guards. He motioned for Hawksworth to follow, alone.

The door of the rear chamber was sheathed in bronze, with heavy ornate hinges and an immense hasp. It seemed to swing open of itself as they approached.

And they were in the chamber of the Shahbandar.

As he entered, Hawksworth was momentarily blinded by the blaze of oil lamps that lined the walls of the room. Unlike the simple plaster walls and pillars of the outer receiving area, this inner chamber was forbiddingly ornate, with gilded ceilings almost thirty feet high. The room was already bustling with clerks straightening piles of account books and readying themselves for the day's affairs.

The room fell silent and a way suddenly cleared through the center, as the Hindu clerks fell back along the walls. They all wore tight, neat headdresses and formal cotton top shirts, and Hawksworth felt a sudden consciousness of his own clothes—muddy boots and powder-smeared jerkin and breeches. For the first time since they arrived he found himself in a room with no other Europeans. The isolation felt sudden and complete.

Then he saw the Shahbandar.

On a raised dais at the rear of the room, beneath a canopy of gold-embroidered cloth, sat the chief port official of India. He rested stiffly on a four-legged couch strewn with cushions, and he wore a turban of blue silk, narrow-patterned trousers, and an embroidered tan robe that crossed to the right over his plump belly and was secured with a row of what appeared to be rubies. He seemed oblivious to Hawksworth as he cursed and drew on the end of a tube being held to his mouth by an attending clerk. The clerk's other hand worked a burning taper over the open top of a long-necked clay pot. The tube being held to the Shahbandar's mouth was attached to a spout on the side. Suddenly Hawksworth heard a gurgle from the pot and saw the Shahbandar inhale a mouthful of dark smoke.

"Tobacco is the only thing the *topiwallahs* ever brought to India that she did not already have. Even then we still had to devise the *hookah* to smoke it properly." He inhaled appreciatively. "It is forbidden during this month of Ramadan, but no man was made to fast during daylight and also forgo tobacco. The morning sun still rose in the east, and thus it is written the gate of repentance remains open to God's servants."

The Shahbandar examined Hawksworth with curiosity. His face recalled hard desert nomad blood, but now it was softened with ease, plump and moustachioed. He wore gold earrings, and he was barefoot.

"Favor me by coming closer. I must see this *feringhi* captain who brings such turmoil to our waters." He turned and cursed the servant as the *hookah* continued to gurgle inconclusively. Then a roll of smoke burst through the tube and the Shahbandar's eyes mellowed as he drew it deeply into his lungs.

He held the smoke for a moment while he gazed quizzically at Hawksworth, squinting as though the air between them were opaque.

"They tell me you are English. May I have the pleasure to know your name?"

"I'm Brian Hawksworth, captain of the frigate *Discovery*. May I also have the privilege of an introduction."

"I will stand before Allah as Mirza Nuruddin." He again drew deeply on the *hookah*. "But here I am the Shahbandar." He exhaled a cloud and examined Hawksworth. "Your ship and another were in our bay yesterday. I am told they weighed anchor at nightfall. Do English vessels customarily sail without their captain?"

"When they have reason to do so." Hawksworth fixed him squarely, wondering if he was really almost blind or if he merely wanted to appear so.

"And what, Captain . . . Hawksworth, brings you and your contentious warships to our port? It is not often our friends the Portuguese permit their fellow Christians to visit us."

"Our ships are traders of England's East India Company."

"Do not squander my time telling what I already know." The Shahbandar suddenly seemed to erupt. "They have never before come to India. Why are you here now?"

Hawksworth sensed suddenly that the Shahbandar had been merely toying with him. That he knew full well why they had come and had already decided what to do. He recalled the words of Karim, declaring the Shahbandar had his own private system of spies.

"We are here for the same reason we have visited the islands. To trade the goods of Europe."

"But we already *do* trade with Europeans. The Portuguese. Who also protect our seas."

"Have you found profit in it?"

"Enough. But it is not your place to question me, Captain Hawksworth."

"Then you may wish to profit through English trade as well."

"And your merchants, I assume, also expect to profit here."

"That's the normal basis of trade." Hawksworth shifted, easing his leg.

The Shahbandar glanced downward, but without removing his lips from the tube of the *hookah*. "I notice you have a wound, Captain Hawksworth. Yours would seem a perilous profession."

"It's sometimes even more perilous for our enemies."

"I presume you mean the Portuguese." The Shahbandar cursed the servant anew and called for a new taper to fire the *hookah*. "But their perils are over. Yours have only begun. Surely you do not expect they will allow you to trade here."

"Trade here is a matter between England and India. It does not involve the Portugals."

The Shahbandar smiled. "But we have a trade agreement with the Portuguese, a *firman* signed by His Majesty, the *Moghul* of India, allowing them free access to our ports. We have no such agreement with England."

"Then we were mistaken. We believed the port of Surat belonged to India, not to the Portugals." Hawksworth felt his palms moisten at the growing game of nerves. "India, you would say, has no ports of her own. No authority to trade with whom she will."

"You come to our door with warfare and insolence, Captain Hawksworth. Perhaps I would have been surprised if you had done otherwise." The Shahbandar paused to draw thoughtfully on the smoking mouthpiece. "Why should I expect this? Although you would not ask, let me assume you have. The reputation of English sea dogs is not unknown in the Indies."

"And I can easily guess who brought you these libelous reports of England. Perhaps you should examine their motives."

"We have received guidance in our judgment from those we have trusted for many years." The Shahbandar waved aside the *hookah* and fixed Hawksworth with a hard gaze.

Hawksworth returned the unblinking stare for a moment while an idea formed in his mind. "I believe it once was written, 'There are those who purchase error at the price of guidance, so their commerce does not prosper. Neither are they guided.'"

A sudden hush enveloped the room as the Shahbandar examined Hawksworth with uncharacteristic surprise. For a moment his eyes seemed lost in concentration, then they quickly regained their focus. "The Holy Quran—Surah II, if I have not lost the lessons of my youth." He stopped and smiled in disbelief. "It's impossible a *topiwallah* should know the words of the Merciful Prophet, on whom be peace. You are a man of curious parts, English captain." Again he paused. "And you dissemble with all the guile of a mullah."

"I merely speak the truth."

"Then speak the truth to me now, Captain Hawksworth. Is it not true the English are a notorious nation of pirates? That your merchants live off the commerce of others, pillaging where they see fit. Should I not inquire, therefore, whether you intrude into our waters for the same purpose?"

"England has warred in years past on her rightful enemies. But our wars are over. The East India Company was founded for peaceful trade. And the Company is here for no purpose but to trade peacefully with merchants in Surat." Hawksworth dutifully pressed forward. "Our two merchantmen bring a rich store of English goods—woolens, ironwork, lead . . ."

"While you war with the Portuguese, in sight of our very shores. Will you next make war on our own merchants? I'm told it is your historic livelihood."

As he studied Hawksworth, the Shahbandar found himself reflecting on the previous evening. The sun had set and the Ramadan meal was already underway when Father Manoel Pinheiro, the second-ranked Portuguese Jesuit in India, had appeared at his gates demanding an audience.

For two tiresome hours he had endured the Jesuit's pained excuses for Portugal's latest humiliation at sea. And his boasts that the English would never survive a trip upriver. And for the first time Mirza Nuruddin could remember, he had smelled fear.

Mirza Nuruddin had sensed no fear in the Portuguese eight years before, when an English captain named Lancaster had attacked and pillaged a Portuguese galleon in the seas off Java. Then the Viceroy of Goa brayed he would know retribution, although nothing was ever done. And a mere five years ago the Viceroy himself led a fleet of twelve warships to Malacca boasting to burn the eleven Dutch merchantmen lading there. And the Dutch sank almost his entire fleet. Now the pirates of Malabar daily harassed Indian shipping the length of the western coast and the Portuguese patrols seemed powerless to control them. In one short decade, he told himself, the Portuguese have shown themselves unable to stop the growing Dutch spice trade in the islands, unable to rid India's coasts of pirates, and now . . . now unable to keep other Europeans from India's own doorstep.

He studied Hawksworth again and asked himself why the English had come. And why the two small English vessels had challenged four armed galleons, instead of turning and making for open sea? To trade a cargo of wool? No cargo was worth the risk they had taken. There had to be another reason. And that reason, or whatever lay behind it, terrified the Portuguese. For the first time ever.

"We defend ourselves when attacked. That's all." Hawksworth found himself wanting to end the questions, to escape the smoky room and the Shahbandar's intense gaze. "That has no bearing on our request to trade in this port."

"I will take your request under advisement. In the meantime you and your men will be searched and your goods taxed, in keeping with our law."

"You may search the men if you wish. But I am here as representative of the king of England. And as his representative I will not allow my personal chest to be searched, no more than His Majesty, King James of England, would submit to such an indignity." Hawksworth decided to reach for all the authority his ragged appearance would allow.

"All *feringhi*, except ambassadors, must be searched. Do you claim that immunity?"

"I am an ambassador, and I will be traveling to Agra to represent my king."

"Permission for *feringhi* to travel in India must come from the *Moghul* himself." The Shahbandar's face remained impassive but his mind raced. The stakes of the English game were not wool, he suddenly realized, but India. The English king was challenging Portugal for the trade of India. Their audacity was astonishing. "A request can be sent to Agra by the governor of this province."

"Then I must see him to ask that a message be sent to Agra. For now, I demand that my personal effects be released from the customs house. And that no duty be levied on our goods, which are samples and not for sale."

"If your goods are not taxed, they will remain in the customs house. That is the law. Because you claim to represent your king, I will forgo my obligation to search your person. All of your men, however, will be searched down to their boots, and any goods or coin they bring through this port will be taxed according to the prevailing rate. Two and one-half percent of value."

"Our Chief Merchant wishes to display his samples to your traders."

"I have told you I will consider your request for trade. There are many considerations." He signaled for the *hookah* to be lighted again. The interview seemed to be ended.

Hawksworth bowed with what formality he could muster and turned toward the counting-room door.

"Captain Hawksworth. You will not be returning to your men. I have made other arrangements for your lodging."

Hawksworth revolved to see four porters waiting by an open door at the Shahbandar's left.

I must be tired. I hadn't noticed the door until now.

Then he realized it had been concealed in the decorations on the wall. When he did not move, the porters surrounded him.

No, they're not porters. They're the guards who held back the crowds from the steps. And they're armed now.

"I think you will find your lodgings suitable." The Shahbandar watched Hawksworth's body tense. "My men will escort you. Your chest will remain here under my care."

The Shahbandar returned again to his gurgling *hookah*.

"My chest will not be subject to search. If it is to be searched, I will return now to my ship." Hawksworth still did not move. "Your officials will respect my king, and his honor."

"It is in my care." The Shahbandar waved Hawksworth toward the door. He did not look up from his pipe.

As Hawksworth passed into the midday sunshine, he saw the Shahbandar's own palanquin waiting by the door. Directly ahead spread the city's teeming horse and cattle bazaar, while on his right, under a dense banyan tree, a dark-eyed beggar sat on a pallet, clothed only in a white loincloth and wearing ashes in his braided hair and curious white and red marks on his forehead. His eyes were burning and intense, and he inspected the new *feringhi* as though he'd just seen the person of the devil.

Why should I travel hidden from view, Hawksworth puzzled?

But there was no time to ponder an answer. The cloth covering was lifted and he found himself urged into the cramped conveyance, made even more comfortless and hot by its heavy carpet lining and bolster seat. In moments the street had disappeared into jolting darkness.

CHAPTER SIX

He felt the palanquin drop roughly onto a hard surface, and when the curtains were pulled aside he looked down to see the stone mosaic of a garden courtyard. They had traveled uphill at least part of the time, with what seemed many unnecessary turns and windings, and now they were hidden from the streets by the high walls of a garden enclosure. Tall slender palms lined the inside of the garden's white plaster wall, and denser trees shaded a central two-story building, decorated around its entry with raised Arabic lettering in ornate plasterwork. The guards motioned him through the large wooden portico of the house, which he began to suspect might be the residence of a wealthy merchant. After a long hallway, they entered a spacious room with clean white walls and a thick center carpet over a floor of patterned marble inlay. Large pillows lay strewn about the carpet, and the air hung heavy with the stale scent of spice.

It's the house of a rich merchant or official, all right. What else can it be? The decorated panels on the doors and the large brass knobs all indicate wealth. But what's the room for? For guests? No. It's too empty. There's almost no furniture. No bed. No . . .

Then suddenly he understood. A banquet room.

He realized he had never seen a more sumptuous private dining hall, even among the aristocracy in London. The guards closed the heavy wooden doors, but there was no sound of their footsteps retreating.

Who are they protecting me from?

A servant, with skin the color of ebony and a white turban that seemed to enclose a large part of his braided and folded-up beard, pushed open an interior door to deposit a silver tray. More fried bread and a bowl of curds.

"Where am I? Whose house . . . ?"

The man bowed, made hand signs pleading incomprehension, and retreated without a word.

As Hawksworth started to reach for a piece of the bread, the outer door opened, and one of the guards stepped briskly to the tray and stopped his hand. He said nothing, merely signaled to wait. Moments later another guard also entered, and with him was a woman. She was unveiled, with dark skin and heavy gold bangles about her ankles. She stared at Hawksworth with frightened eyes. Brisk words passed in an alien language, and then the woman pointed to Hawksworth and raised her voice as she replied to the guard. He said nothing, but simply lifted a long, sheathed knife from his waist and pointed it toward the tray, his gesture signifying all. After a moment's pause, the woman edged forward and gingerly sampled the curds with her fingers, first sniffing and then reluctantly tasting. More words passed, after which the guards bowed to Hawksworth almost imperceptibly and escorted the woman from the room, closing the door.

Hawksworth watched in dismay and then turned again to examine the dishes.

If they're *that* worried, food can wait. Who was she? Probably a slave. Of the Shahbandar?

He removed his boots, tossed them in the corner, and eased himself onto the bolsters piled at one end of the central carpet. The wound in his leg had become a dull ache.

Jesus help me, I'm tired. What does the Shahbandar really want? Why was Karim so fearful of him? And what's the role of the governor in all this? Will all these requests and permissions and permits end up delaying us so long the Portugals will find our anchorage? And what will the *governor* want out of me?

He tried to focus his mind on the governor, on a figure he sculpted in his imagination. A fat, repugnant, pompous bureaucrat. But the figure slowly began to transform, and in time it became the Turk who had imprisoned Hawksworth in Tunis, with a braided fez and a jeweled dagger at his waist. The fat Turk was not listening, he was issuing a decree. You will stay. Only then will I have what I want. What I must have. Next a veiled woman entered the room, and her eyes were like Maggie's. She seized his hand and guided him toward the women's apartments, past the frowning guards, who raised large scimitars in interdiction until she waved them aside. Then she led him to the center of a brilliantly lighted room, until they stood before a large stone pillar, a pillar like the one in the porters' lodge except it was immense, taller than his head. You belong to me now, her eyes seemed to say, and she began to bind him to the pillar with silken cords. He struggled to free himself, but the grasp on his wrists only became stronger. In panic he struck out and yelled through the haze of incense.

"Let . . . !"

"I'm only trying to wake you, Captain." A voice cut through the nightmare. "His Eminence, the Shahbandar, has requested that I attend your wound."

Hawksworth startled awake and was reaching for his sword before he saw the swarthy little man, incongruous in a white swath of a skirt and a

Portuguese doublet, nervously shaking his arm. The man pulled back in momentary surprise, then dropped his cloth medicine bag on the floor and began to carefully fold a large red umbrella. Hawksworth noted he wore no shoes on his dusty feet.

"Allow me to introduce myself." He bowed ceremoniously. "My name is Mukarjee. It is my honor to attend the celebrated new *feringhi*." His Turki was halting and strongly accented.

He knelt and deftly cut away the wrapping on Hawksworth's leg. "And who applied this?" With transparent disdain he began uncoiling the muddy bandage. "The Christian *topiwallahs* constantly astound me. Even though my daughter is married to one." One eyebrow twitched nervously as he worked.

Hawksworth stared at him through a groggy haze, marveling at the dexterity of his chestnut-brown hands. Then he glanced nervously at the vials of colored liquid and jars of paste the man was methodically extracting from his cloth bag.

"It was our ship's physician. He swathed this after attending a dozen men with like wounds or worse."

"No explanations are necessary. *Feringhi* methods are always unmistakable. In Goa, where I lived for many years after leaving Bengal, I once served in a hospital built by Christian priests."

"You worked in a Jesuit hospital?"

"I did indeed." He began to scrape away the oily powder residue from the wound. Hawksworth's leg jerked involuntarily from the flash of pain. "Please do not move. Yes, I served there until I could abide it no more. It was a very exclusive hospital. Only *feringhi* were allowed to go there to be bled."

He began to wash the wound, superficial but already festering, with a solution from one of the vials. "Yes, we Indians were denied that almost certain entry into Christian paradise represented by its portals. But it was usually the first stop for arriving Portuguese, after the brothels."

"But why do so many Portuguese sicken after they reach Goa?" Hawksworth watched Mukarjee begin to knead a paste that smelled strongly of sandalwood spice.

"It's well that you ask, Captain Hawksworth." Mukarjee tested the consistency of the sandalwood paste with his finger and then placed it aside, apparently to thicken. "You appear to be a strong man, but after many months at sea you may not be as virile as you assume."

He absently extracted a large, dark green leaf from the pocket of his doublet and dabbed it in a paste he kept in a crumpled paper. Then he rolled it around the cracked pieces of a small brown nut, popped it into his mouth, and began to chew. Suddenly remembering himself, he stopped and produced another leaf from his pocket.

"Would you care to try betel, what they call *pan* here in Surat? It's very healthy for the teeth. And the digestion."

"What is it?"

"A delicious leaf. I find I cannot live without it, so perhaps it's a true addiction. It's slightly bitter by itself, but if you roll it around an areca nut and dip it in a bit of lime—which we make from mollusk shells—it is perfectly exquisite."

Hawksworth shook his head in wary dissent, whereupon Mukarjee continued, settling himself on his haunches and sucking contentedly on the rolled leaf as he spoke. "You ask why I question your well-being, Captain? Because a large number of the *feringhis* who come to Goa, and India, are doomed to die."

"You already said that. From what? Poison in their food?"

Mukarjee examined him quizzically for a moment as he concentrated on the rolled leaf, savoring the taste, and Hawksworth noticed a red trickle emerge from the corner of his mouth and slide slowly off his chin. He turned and discharged a mouthful of juice into a small brass container, clearing his mouth to speak.

"The most common illness for Europeans here is called the bloody flux." Mukarjee tested the paste again with his finger, and then began to stir it vigorously with a wooden spatula. "For four or five days the body burns with intense heat, and then either it is gone or you are dead."

"Are there no medicines?" Hawksworth watched as he began to spread the paste over the wound.

"Of course there are medicines." Mukarjee chuckled resignedly. "But the Portuguese scorn to use them."

"Probably wisely," Hawksworth reflected. "It's said the flux is caused by an excess of humors in the blood. Bleeding is the only real remedy."

"I see." Mukarjee began to apply the paste and then to bind Hawksworth's leg with a swath of white cloth. "Yes, my friend, that is what the Portuguese do—you must hold still—and I have personally observed how effective it is in terminating illness."

"The damned Jesuits are the best physicians in Europe."

"So I have often been told. Most frequently at funerals." Mukarjee quickly tied a knot in the binding and spat another mouthful of red juice. "Your wound is really nothing more than a scratch. But you would have been dead in a fortnight. By this, if not by exertion."

"What do you mean?" Hawksworth rose and tested his leg, amazed that the pain seemed to have vanished.

"The greatest scourge of all for newly arrived Europeans here seems to be our women. It is inevitable, and my greatest source of amusement." He spat the exhausted betel leaf toward the corner of the room and paused dramatically while he prepared another.

"Explain what you mean about the women."

"Let me give you an example from Goa." Mukarjee squatted again. "The Portuguese soldiers arriving from Lisbon each year tumble from their ships more dead than alive, weak from months at sea and the inevitable scurvy. They are in need of proper food, but they pay no attention to this, for they are even more starved for the company of women. . . . By the way, how is your wound?" Mukarjee made no attempt to suppress a smile at Hawksworth's astonished testing of his leg.

"The pain seems to be gone." He tried squatting in Indian style, like Mukarjee, and found that this posture, too, brought no discomfort.

"Well, these scurvy-weakened soldiers immediately avail themselves of Goa's many well-staffed brothels—which, I note, Christians seem to frequent with greater devotion than their fine churches. What uneven test of skill and vigor transpires I would not speculate, but many of these *feringhis* soon find the only beds suited for them are in the Jesuit's Kings Hospital, where few ever leave. I watched some five hundred Portuguese a year tread this path of folly." Mukarjee's lips were now the hue of the rose.

"And what happens to those who do live?"

"They eventually wed one of our women, or one of their own, and embrace the life of sensuality that marks the Portuguese in Goa. With twenty, sometimes even thirty slaves to supply their wants and pleasure. And after a time they develop stones in the kidney, or gout, or some other affliction of excess."

"What do their wives die of? The same thing?"

"Some, yes, but I have also seen many charged with adultery by their fat Portuguese husbands—a suspicion rarely without grounds, for they really have nothing more to do on hot afternoons than chew betel and intrigue with the lusty young soldiers—and executed. The women are said to deem it an honorable martyrdom, vowing they die for love."

Mukarjee rose and began meticulously replacing the vials in his cloth bag. "I may be allowed to visit you again if you wish, but I think there's no need. Only forgo the company of our women for a time, my friend. Practice prudence before pleasure."

A shaft of light from the hallway cut across the room, as the door opened without warning. A guard stood in the passageway, wearing a uniform Hawksworth had not seen before.

"I must be leaving now." Mukarjee's voice rose to public volume as he nervously scooped up his umbrella and his bag, without pausing to secure the knot at its top. Then he bent toward Hawksworth with a quick whisper. "Captain, the Shahbandar has sent his Rajputs. You must take care."

He deftly slipped past the guard in the doorway and was gone.

Hawksworth examined the Rajputs warily. They wore leather helmets secured with a colored headband, knee-length tunics over heavy tight-fitting trousers, and a broad cloth belt. A large round leather shield hung at each man's side, suspended from a shoulder strap, and each guard wore an ornate quiver at his waist from which protruded a heavy horn bow and bamboo arrows. All were intent and unsmiling. Their leader, his face framed in a thicket of coarse black hair, stepped through the doorway and addressed Hawksworth in halting Turki.

"The Shahbandar has requested your presence at the customs house. I am to inform you he has completed all formalities for admission of your personal chest and has approved it with his *chapp*."

The palanquin was nowhere to be seen when they entered the street, but now Hawksworth was surrounded. As they began walking he noticed the pain in his leg was gone. The street was lined by plaster walls and the cool evening air bore the scent of flowers from their concealed gardens. The houses behind the walls were partially shielded by tall trees, but he could tell they were several stories high, with flat roofs on which women clustered, watching.

These must all be homes of rich Muslim merchants. Palaces for the princes of commerce. And the streets are filled with dark-skinned, slow-walking poor. Probably servants, or slaves, in no hurry to end the errand that freed them from their drudgery inside.

Then as they started downhill, toward the river, they began to pass tile-roofed, plaster-walled homes he guessed were owned by Hindu merchants, since they were without gardens or the high walls Muslims used to hide their women. As they neared the river the air started to grow sultry, and they began passing the clay-walled huts of shopkeepers and clerks, roofed in palm leaves with latticework grills for windows. Finally they reached the bazaar of Surat, its rows of palm trees deserted now, with silence where earlier he had heard a tumult of hawkers and strident women's voices. Next to the bazaar stood the stables, and Hawksworth noticed flocks of small boys, naked save for a loincloth, scavenging to find any dung cakes that had been overlooked by the women who collected fuel. The air was dense and smelled of earth, and its taste overwhelmed his lingering memory of the wind off the sea.

The streets of Surat converged like the spokes of a wheel, with the customs house and port as its hub. Just like every port town in the world, Hawksworth smiled to himself: all roads lead to the sea.

Except here all roads lead to the customs house and the Shahbandar.

Then, as they approached the last turn in the road, just outside the enclosure of the customs house, they were suddenly confronted by a band of mounted horsemen, armed with long-barreled muskets. The horsemen spanned the roadway and were probably twenty in all, well outnumbering the Rajputs. The horsemen made no effort to move aside as Hawksworth and his guards approached.

Hawksworth noticed the Rajputs stiffen slightly and their hands drop loosely to the horn bows protruding from their quivers, but they did not break their pace.

My God, they're not going to halt. There'll be bloodshed. And we're sure to lose.

Without warning a hand threw Hawksworth sprawling against the thick plaster side of a building, and a large, round rhino-hide buckler suddenly was covering his body, shielding him entirely from the horsemen.

Next came a melee of shouts, and he peered out to see the Rajputs encircling him, crouched in a firing pose, each bow aimed on a horseman and taut with its first arrow. The musket-bearing horsemen fumbled with their still uncocked weapons. In lightning moves of only seconds, the Rajputs had seized the advantage.

Not only are their bows more accurate than muskets, Hawksworth thought, they're also handier. They can loose half a dozen arrows before a musket can be reprimed. But what was the signal? I saw nothing, heard nothing. Yet they acted as one. I've never before seen such speed, such discipline.

Then more shouting. Hawksworth did not recognize the language, but he guessed it might be Urdu, the mixture of imported Persian and native Hindi Karim had said was used in the *Moghul's* army as a compromise between the language of its Persian-speaking officers and the Hindi-speaking infantry. The Rajputs did not move as the horseman in the lead withdrew a rolled paper from his waist and contemptuously tossed it onto the ground in front of them.

While the others covered him with their bows, the leader of the Rajputs advanced and retrieved the roll from the dust. Hawksworth watched as he unscrolled it and examined in silence. At the bottom Hawksworth could make out the red mark of a *chapp*, like the one he had seen on bundles in the customs house. The paper was passed among the Rajputs, each studying it in turn, particularly the seal. Then there were more shouts, and finally resolution. The dark-bearded leader of Hawksworth's guard approached him and bowed. Then he spoke in Turki, his voice betraying none of the emotion Hawksworth had witnessed moments before.

"They are guards of the governor, Mukarrab Khan. They have shown us orders by the Shahbandar, bearing his seal, instructing that you be transferred to their care. You will go with them."

Then he dropped his bow casually into his quiver and led the other men off in the direction of the customs house, all still marching, as though they knew no other pace.

"Captain Hawksworth, please be tolerant of our Hindu friends. They are single-minded soldiers of fortune, and a trifle old-fashioned in their manners." The leader of the guard smiled and pointed to a riderless saddled horse being held by one of the riders. "We have a mount for you. Will you kindly join us?"

Hawksworth looked at the horse, a spirited Arabian mare, and then at the saddle, a heavy round tapestry embroidered in silver thread with tassels front and back, held by a thick girth also of tapestry. The stirrups were small triangles of iron held by a leather strap attached to a ring at the top of the girth. A second tapestry band around the mare's neck secured the saddle near the mane. The mane itself had been woven with decorations of beads and small feathers. The horse's neck was held in a permanent arch by a leather checkrein extending from the base of the bridle through the chest strap, and secured to the lower girth. The mare pranced in anticipation, while her coat sparkled in the waning sun. She was a thing of pure beauty.

"Where are we going?"

"But of course. The governor, Mukarrab Khan, has staged a small celebration this afternoon and would be honored if you could join him. Today is the final day of Ramadan, our month-long Muslim fast. He's at the *chaugan* field. But come, patience is not his most enduring quality."

Hawksworth did not move.

"Why did the Shahbandar change his order? We were going to the customs house to fetch my chest."

"The governor is a persuasive man. It was his pleasure that you join him this afternoon. But please mount. He is waiting." The man stroked his moustache with a manicured hand as he nodded toward the waiting mount. "His Excellency sent one of his finest horses. I think he has a surprise for you."

Hawksworth swung himself into the saddle, and immediately his mare tossed her head in anticipation. She was lanky and spirited, nothing like the lumbering mount his father had once taught him to ride at the army's camp outside London so many, many years ago.

Without another word the men wheeled their horses and started off in a direction parallel to the river. Then the one who had spoken abruptly halted the entire party.

"Please forgive me, but did I introduce myself? I am the secretary to His Excellency, Mukarrab Khan. We were cast from the civilized comforts of Agra onto this dung heap port of Surat together. Perhaps it was our stars."

Hawksworth was only half-listening to the man. He turned and looked back over his shoulder in time to see the Rajputs entering into the compound of the customs house. The leader of the horsemen caught his glance and smiled.

"Let me apologize again for our friends of the Rajput guard. You do understand they have no official standing. They serve whomever they are paid to serve. If that thief, the Shahbandar, discharged them tomorrow and then another hired them to kill him, they would do so without a word. Rajputs are professional mercenaries, who do battle as coldly as the tiger hunts game." He turned his horse onto a wide avenue that paralleled the river. The sunlight was now filtered through the haze of evening smoke from cooking fires that was enveloping the city.

"Do Rajputs also serve the governor?"

The man laughed broadly and smoothed the braided mane of his horse as he twisted sideways in the saddle and repeated Hawksworth's question for the other riders. A peal of amusement cut the quiet of the evening streets.

"My dear English captain, he might wish to hang them, but he would never *hire* them. His Excellency has the pick of the Moghul infantry and cavalry in this district, men of lineage and breeding. Why should he need Hindus?"

Hawksworth monitored the riders carefully out of the corner of his eye and thought he detected a trace of nervousness in their mirth. Yes, he told himself, why use Hindus—except the Shahbandar's Hindu mercenaries got the advantage of you in only seconds. While you and your pick of the Moghul cavalry were fiddling with your uncocked muskets. Perhaps there's a good reason the Shahbandar doesn't hire men of lineage and breeding.

Hawksworth noticed they were paralleling a wall of the city, a high brick barrier with iron pikes set along its capstone. Abruptly the wall curved across the road they were traveling and they were facing a massive wooden gate that spanned the width of the street. Suddenly guards appeared, each in uniform and holding a pike. They hurriedly swung wide the gate as the procession approached, then snapped crisply to attention along the roadside.

"This is the Abidjan Gate." The secretary nodded in response to the salute of the guards. "You can just see the field from here." He pointed ahead, then urged his horse to a gallop. A cooling dampness was invading the evening air, and now the sun had entirely disappeared into the cloud of dense cooking smoke that boiled above the city, layering a dark mantle over the landscape. Again Hawksworth felt his apprehension rising. What's the purpose of bringing me to a field outside the city, with dark approaching? He instinctively fingered the cool handle of his sword, but its feel did nothing to ease his mind.

Then he heard cheers from the field ahead, and saw a burning ball fly across the evening sky. Ahead was a large green, and on it horsemen raced back and forth, shouting and cursing in several languages, their horses jostling recklessly. Other mounted horsemen watched from the side of the green and bellowed encouragement.

As they approached the edge of the field, Hawksworth saw one of the players capture the burning ball, guiding it along the green with a long stick whose end appeared to be curved. He spurred his mottled gray mount to-

ward two tall posts stationed at one end of the green. Another player was
hard in chase, and his horse, a dark stallion, was closing rapidly toward the
rolling ball. As the first player swept upward with his stick, lofting the burning ball toward the posts, the second player passed him and—in a maneuver
that seemed dazzling to Hawksworth—circled his own stick over his head
and captured the ball in midair, deflecting it toward the edge of the green
where Hawksworth and his guards waited. Cheers went up from some of the
players and spectators, and the horsemen all dashed for the edge of the green
in chase of the ball, which rolled in among Hawksworth's entourage and out
of play. The horseman on the dark stallion suddenly noticed Hawksworth
and, with a shout to the other players, whipped his steed toward the arriving
group.

As he approached, Hawksworth studied his face carefully. He was pudgy
but still athletic, with a short, well-trimmed moustache and a tightly wound
turban secured with a large red stone that looked like a ruby. He carried
himself erect, with a confidence only full vigor could impart, yet his face was
incongruously debauched, almost ravaged, and his eyes deeply weary. There
was no hint of either triumph or pleasure in those eyes or in his languorous
mouth, although he had just executed a sensational block of an almost certain score. He reined his wheezing mount only when directly in front of
Hawksworth, sending up a cloud of dust.

"Are you the English captain?" The voice was loud, with an impatient
tone indicating long years of authority.

"I command the frigates of the East India Company." Hawksworth
tried to keep his gaze steady. What sort of man can this be, he asked himself? Is *this* the one who can demand the Shahbandar's signature and seal
whenever he wishes?

"Then I welcome you, Captain." The dark stallion reared suddenly for
no apparent reason, in a display of exuberance. The man expertly reined him
in, never removing his gaze from Hawksworth, and continued in an even
voice. "I've been most eager to meet the man who is suddenly so interesting
to our Portuguese friends. Although I have a personal rule never to dabble in
the affairs of Europeans, as a sportsman I must congratulate you on your victory. A pity I missed the encounter."

"I accept your congratulations on behalf of the East India Company."
Hawksworth watched him for some sign of his attitude toward the Portuguese, but he could detect nothing but smooth diplomacy.

"Yes, the East India Company. I suppose this company of yours wants
something from India, and I can easily imagine it might be profit. Perhaps I
should tell you straightaway that such matters bore me not a little." The
man glanced impatiently back toward the field. "But come, it's growing
darker as we talk. I'd hoped you might join us in our little game. It's elementary. Should be child's play for a man who commands at sea." He turned to

one of the men standing by the side of the field. "Ahmed, prepare a stick for Captain . . . by the way, I wasn't given your name."

"Hawksworth."

"Yes. Prepare a stick for Captain Hawksworth. He'll be joining us."

Hawksworth stared at the man, trying to gauge his impulsiveness.

"You, I presume, are the governor."

"Forgive me. I so rarely find introductions required. Mukarrab Khan, your humble servant. Yes, it's my fate to be governor of Surat, but only because there's no outpost less interesting. But come, we lose precious time." He pivoted his pawing mount about and signaled for a new ball to be ignited.

"You'll find our game very simple, Captain Hawksworth. The object is to take the ball between the posts you see there, what we call the *hal*. There are two teams of five players, but we normally rotate players every twenty minutes." His horse reared again in anticipation as the new ball was brought onto the field. "Years ago we played only during the hours of day, but then our *Moghul's* father, the great Akman, introduced the burning ball, so he could play at night. It's *palas* wood, very light and slow-burning."

Hawksworth felt a nudge on his hand and looked down to see a stick being passed upward by one of the attendants. The handle was sheathed in silver, and the stick itself was over six feet long, with a flattened curve at the bottom, like a distorted shepherd's crook. Hawksworth lifted it gingerly, testing its weight, and was surprised at its lightness.

"You will be playing on the team of Abul Hasan." He nodded toward a middle-aged man with a youthful face and no moustache. "He is a *qazi* here in Surat, a judge who interprets and dispenses law, and when he's not busy abusing the powers of his office, he presumes to challenge me at *chaugan*." The official bowed slightly but did not smile. His dappled gray mare was sniffing at the governor's stallion. "He thinks he has me at a disadvantage, since in Agra we played with only one goal, whereas here they use two, but *chaugan* is a test of skill, not rules. He leads the white turbans." Only then did Hawksworth notice that the governor's team all wore red turbans.

The governor waved to his attendant. "A clean turban for the English captain."

"I'd prefer to play as I am." Hawksworth saw a flash of disbelief in the governor's eyes. It was obvious he was never contradicted. "I never wear a hat, though it seems in India I'm still called a *topiwallah*."

"Very well, Captain Hawksworth. The *topiwallah* wears no turban." He seemed to smile as he turned to the other players and signaled for play to start. "Abul Hasan's team is composed of Surat officials, Captain. You will notice, however, that I am teamed with some of our merchants—Muslim, of course, not Hindus—something I must do to ensure challenging opponents. The mere presence of merchants here today should give you some idea how very tedious I find living in Surat. In Agra no merchant would be allowed near a *chaugan* field. But here my officials enjoy winning their money so much that I am forced to relent." And he laughed warmly.

The burning ball was slammed toward the middle of the field, and the players spurred their horses after it in lunging pursuit. Hawksworth gripped the *chaugan* stick in his right hand and the reins in the other as his mount galloped after the others, obviously eager to begin. The red turbans reached the ball first, with the governor in the lead. He caught the ball on a bounce and, wielding his stick in a graceful arc, whipped it under the neck of the dark stallion and directly toward the *hal*, while in the same motion reining in his mount sharply to follow its trajectory.

But a white turban had anticipated his shot and was already in position to intercept the ball. He cut directly in front of the governor's path and with a practiced swipe bulleted the ball back toward the center of the field, knocking a spray of sparks across the face of the governor's horse. Mukarrab Khan's stallion seemed scarcely to notice as he reared, whirled, and flew in chase.

The shot had passed over the heads of the three other white turbans and bounced off the grass a few feet behind Hawksworth, still well to the rear. Hawksworth reined his mount about and bore down on the ball, beginning to feel some of the exhilaration of the play. He reached the ball on its second bounce and with a rigid arc of his arm swung the *chaugan* stick.

The impact recoiled a dizzying shock through the wood and up his right shoulder. He dimly heard the cheers of his teammates, seeming to congratulate him on his stroke. But where's the ball? he wondered as he scanned the darkened, empty expanse down the field. Then he realized he had only deflected it, back toward the three white turbans in the center of the field. The last white turban in the row snared the ball with his stick, deflecting it again, but now in the direction of the reds.

Dust was boiling from the surface of the field, increasingly obscuring the players and the play. The darkened arena had become a jostling mob, friend scarcely distinguishable from foe, and all in pursuit of the only certain object, the still-glowing ball. Hawksworth's eyes seared and his throat choked as he raced after the others—always, it seemed, bringing up the rear, while his mount took her head and rarely acknowledged his awkward attempts at command. He clung to the iron ring of his saddle, content merely to stay astride.

Give me a quarterdeck any day.

The red turbans again had command of the ball, and Hawksworth watched as the governor now raced to the lead, urged on by his teammates. He snared the ball effortlessly and with a powerful swing sent it arcing back toward his own *hal*.

The other red turbans rushed in pursuit, but a white turban was already at the *hal*, waiting to deflect the play. He snared the ball in the crook of his stick and flung it back toward the center. The reds seemed to anticipate this, for they reined as one man and dashed back. But now a white had control, and he guided the ball alone across the grassy expanse, while a phalanx of other whites rode guard. Hawksworth was still lagging in front of his own *hal* when suddenly he saw the ball lofting toward him, a flaming mortar in the darkened sky.

It slammed to earth near his horse's flank, spewing sparks. He cut his mare sharply to the left and galloped in pursuit. Above the shouts he only dimly heard the reds thundering behind him, closing in as he reached the ball and caught it in the curve of his stick.

Roll it, he told himself, keep it on the ground . . .

The reds were on him. In what seemed a swing for the ball, Abul Hasan brought his stick in a wide arc, its hardened crook accurately intersecting Hawksworth's directly in the middle. Hawksworth felt an uneven shudder pulse through his arm and heard his own stick shatter. The lower half flew to his right, and he watched in dismay as it sailed across the path of Mukarrab Khan's mount, just as the governor cut inward to block Hawksworth. The hard wood caught the dark stallion directly across its front shins, and the horse stumbled awkwardly. Hawksworth stared at horse and rider dumbly for a moment, as the stallion lost its stride, and he suddenly realized the governor's horse would fall. And when it did, Mukarrab Khan would be thrown directly below the horses thundering behind them.

He cut his mount sharply to the right and deliberately slammed into the governor's stallion. Mukarrab Khan's dazed eyes flashed understanding and he stretched for the center ring of Hawksworth's saddle during the fractional second their horses were in collision. At the same instant, he disengaged himself from his own stirrups and pulled himself across the neck of Hawksworth's mare.

Two alert reds pulled their mounts alongside Hawksworth and grabbed the reins of his mare. The dark stallion collapsed in the dust behind them with a pitiful neigh. Then it rose and limped painfully toward the edge of the field, its left foreleg dangling shattered and useless. Mukarrab Khan lowered himself to the ground with an elaborate oath.

A cheer sounded as the whites scored the ball unmolested.

Hawksworth was still watching the governor when one of the attendants rushed from the sidelines, seized the silver-topped fragment of his broken stick, and thrust it toward him.

"The silver is yours to keep, Sahib. It is the custom that one whose *chaugan* stick is broken in play may keep its silver tip. As a token of bravery. For you it is especially deserved." He was short, swarthy, and dressed in a dust-covered white shirt. He bowed slightly, while his eyes gleamed their admiration in the darkness.

"Take it, Captain. It is an honor." Abul Hasan rode up stiffly, brushing the dust from the mane of his horse. "No *feringhi*, to my knowledge, has ever before attempted *chaugan*, and certainly none has earned a silver knob."

"Captain Hawksworth, you rode well." Mukarrab Khan had commandeered a mount and also drew alongside. There was a light scratch along the right side of his face, and the whimsical look had vanished from his eyes as he searched the faces clustered around. "A very curious accident. It has never happened before." He stared directly at Hawksworth. "How was your stick broken?"

"The *feringhi* made an unfortunate swing, Excellency," Abul Hasan interjected. "He played superbly, for a beginner, but he has still to fully master the stroke."

"Obviously. But he compensated by his luck—my luck—in saving me from a fall. He rides well enough, no matter how uncertain his stroke." The governor examined them both skeptically.

Hawksworth watched the exchange in incredulous silence. The *qazi* may be covering for his own accident. Or perhaps it wasn't an accident. And if not, then he tried to kill the Mukarrab Khan in a way that would look like it was *my* responsibility.

"I still maintain it was most curious." Mukarrab Khan turned to watch as the stable-keepers prepared to shoot his favorite horse. "But tell me now what you think of *chaugan*, Captain Hawksworth?"

"It's exhilarating. And dangerous. A seaman might say it's like taking the whipstaff all alone in a gale, without a safety line." Hawksworth tried unsuccessfully to decipher Mukarrab Khan's thoughts.

"A quaint analogy, but doubtless apt." He tried to smile. "You know, Captain, there are those who mistakenly regard *chaugan* as merely a game, whereas it is actually much, much more. It's a crucible of courage. It sharpens one's quickness of mind, tests one's powers of decision. The great Akman believed the same, and for that reason he encouraged it years ago among his officials. Of course it requires horsemanship, but in the last count it's a flawless test of manhood. You did not entirely disappoint me. I suspect you English could one day be worthy of our little game."

A shot rang out, and the governor's face went pale for an instant, his eyes glossed with sadness. Then he turned again to Hawksworth.

"Deplorable waste. To think I bought him just last year especially for *chaugan*. From a grasping Arab, a confirmed thief who sensed I fancied that stallion and absolutely refused to bargain." The voice was calmer now, the official facade returning. "But enough. Perhaps I could interest you in a drink?"

He signaled toward the edge of the field, and a waiting groom ran toward them, bearing a black clay pot with a long spout.

"The sun has set. Ramadan is finished for this year. So I will join you.

Let me show you how we drink on horseback." He lifted the pot above his head, tilted the spout toward him, and caught the stream effortlessly in his mouth. Then he passed it to Hawksworth. "It's called *sharbat*. The *topiwallahs* all seem to like it and mispronounce it 'sherbet.'"

The water was sugar sweet and tangy with bits of lemon. God, Hawksworth thought, would we had barrels of this for the voyage home. As he drank, drenching his beard, he first noticed the icy stars, a splendor of cold fire in an overhead canopy. The town's smoke had been banished by the freshening wind, and a placid silence now mantled the field. The players were preparing to leave, and the grooms were harnessing the remaining horses to lead them home.

"Tonight we feast to mark the end of Ramadan, Captain, our month of fasting during daylight hours. It's an evening celebrating the return of sensual pleasure." Mukarrab Khan stared at Hawksworth for a moment. "By the looks of you, I'd suspect you're no Jesuit. I would be honored if you could join me." He forced a blithe cheerfulness his weary eyes belied.

As Hawksworth listened, he realized he very much wanted to go. To lose himself for a time. And suddenly the words of Huyghen, and of Roger Symmes, flashed through his mind. Of the India you would not want to leave. Until you would not be able to leave.

As they rode toward the town, Mukarrab Khan fell silent. And Abul Hasan, too, seemed lost in his own thoughts. Hawksworth slowly let his horse draw to the rear in order to count the governor's personal retinue of guards. Thirty men, with quivers of arrows beside their saddle, pikes at their right stirrup, and a matchlock musket. As they rode, the other horsemen eyed Hawksworth warily, keeping to themselves and making no effort to talk. Hawksworth thought he sensed an underlying hostility lurking through the crowd, but whether it was between the merchants and officials, or toward him, he could not discern.

Then a presumptuous thought passed through his mind.

Could this entire scene have been staged by Mukarrab Khan to somehow test me? But to what purpose? What could he want to find out?

Whatever it was, I think he just may have found it.

Then he leaned back in the saddle, pushed aside his misgivings, and sampled the perfumed evening air.

CHAPTER SEVEN

They were deep within the center of Surat, nearing the river, when suddenly the street opened onto a wide stone-paved plaza. The first thing Hawksworth saw through the torchlight was a high iron fence, sentries posted with bucklers and pikes along its perimeter, and an ornate iron gate. Then, as they neared, he realized the fence was the outer perimeter of an immense pink sandstone fortress, with high turrets and a wide, arched entryway. Finally he spotted the water-filled moat that lay between the fence and the fortress walls. The moat was spanned by a single wooden bridge, and Hawksworth noted that when the bridge was drawn inward it neatly sealed the entry of the fortress.

As they approached the iron outer gate, the party of *chaugan* players began to disperse; after formal and minimal farewells the merchants and officials turned and disappeared into the night. Soon only Hawksworth and Mukarrab Khan were left, together with the governor's private grooms and guards. Hawksworth studied the departing players with curiosity. What sway does Mukarrab Khan hold over them? Respect? Fear?

Then the iron gate swung wide and their horses clattered across the wooden drawbridge. Hawksworth looked about and began to understand that the governor's palace guards were not merely ceremonial. Lining both sides of the drawbridge were uniformed infantrymen armed with pikes. Then as they passed under the stone archway leading into the fortress, Hawksworth turned to see even more armed guards, poised just inside, pikes in formal salute. And farther back he saw two armored animals, gigantic, many times larger than the biggest horse, with massive ears and a snout several feet in length.

That must be what a war elephant looks like. So they really *do* exist. But why so many guards? It's virtually a private army.

Then he felt a groom tug the reins of his horse and signal for him to dismount. They were now inside the palace grounds. Ahead, through an intricate formal garden, stood the residence of the governor of Surat. The elaborate carvings of its pink sandstone decoration reflected hard red in the torchlight.

Mukarrab Khan directed him through a marble entryway, ornately rounded at the top like the turret of a mosque. They had entered some form of reception hallway, and Hawksworth noticed that the marble floor was decorated with a complex geometry of colored stone.

Above his head were galleries of white plasterwork supported by delicate arches, and along the sides were ornate, curtained recesses. Hanging oil lamps brilliantly illuminated the glistening walls, while rows of servants dressed in matching white turbans lined the sides in welcome.

As they approached the end of the reception hallway, Hawksworth studied the door ahead. It was massive, and thick enough to withstand any war machine that could be brought into the hallway, and yet its protective function was concealed from obvious notice by a decoration of intricate carvings and a flawless polish. The servants slowly revolved it outward on its heavy brass hinges and Mukarrab Khan led them into a vast open courtyard surrounded by a veranda, with columns supporting balconies of marble filigree. It seemed a vast reception hall set in the open air, an elegant plaza whose roof was stars, and whose centerpiece was a canopied pavilion, under which stood a raised couch of juniper wood lined with red satin—not unlike an English four-poster bed, save the posts were delicately thin and polished to a burnished ebony. Large bronze lanterns along the balconies furnished a flickering vision of the complex interworking of paths, flower beds, and fountains surrounding the central pavilion.

Waiting on the veranda, just inside the entryway, were six tall figures, three on either side of the doorway. They were turbaned, exquisitely robed, and wore conspicuous jewels that gleamed against their dark skin. As they bowed to the governor, Hawksworth examined them for a brief moment and then his recognition clicked.

Eunuchs. They must be Mukarrab Khan's private guards, since they can go anywhere, even the women's apartments.

"Captain Hawksworth, perhaps you should meet my household officials. They are Bengalis—slaves actually—whom I bought young and trained years ago in Agra. One must, regrettably, employ eunuchs to maintain a household such as this. One's palace women can never be trusted, and one's intriguing wives least of all. I named them in the Arab fashion, after their position in the palace, so I need not trouble to remember their names, merely what they do. This is Nahir, who is in charge of my accounts." He gestured toward a pudgy face now glaring out from beneath a deep blue headdress, a tall conical turban tied in place with a wrap of white silk that circled his bloated throat. The eunuch's open jacket was a heavy brocade and it heaved as he breathed, betraying the sagging fat around his nipples.

"The one next to him selects my wardrobe." The second eunuch gazed at Hawksworth impassively, his puffed, indulgent lips red with betel juice. "That one selects the clothes for my spendthrift women, and the one on his left is responsible for all their jewels. The one over there takes care of the household linens and oversees the servants. And the one behind him is in charge of the kitchen. You will be asked to endure his handiwork tonight."

The eunuchs examined Hawksworth's ragged appearance with transparent contempt, and they seemed to melt around him as he walked through the doorway—two ahead, two behind, and one on either side. None spoke a greeting. Hawksworth examined them carefully, wondering which was in charge of the women's apartments. That's the most powerful position, he smiled to himself, nothing else really counts.

A servant came down the veranda bearing a tray and brought it directly to the governor. Then he kneeled and offered it. It was of beaten silver and on it were two large crystal goblets of a pastel green liquid.

"Captain, would you care to refresh yourself with a glass of *tundhi*. It's the traditional way we break the fast of Ramadan." He directed the servant toward Hawksworth. "It's prepared in the women's apartments during the day, as an excuse for something to do."

Hawksworth touched the drink lightly with his tongue. It was a mixture of sweet and tang quite unlike anything he had ever known. Perhaps the closest was a brisk mug of spiced ale, pungent with clove and cinnamon. But this spiced drink was mysteriously subtle. Puzzling, he turned to Mukarrab Khan.

"What is this? It tastes like the air in a garden."

"This? I've never paid any notice, although the women down it by the basinful after sunset." As he received his own goblet he turned to one of the eunuchs. "Nahir, how do the women prepare *tundhi?*"

"With seeds, Khan Sahib. Seeds of melon, cucumber, lettuce, and coriander are pounded, and then blended with rosewater, pomegranate essence, and juice of the aloe flower. But the secret is to strain it properly, and I find I must carefully oversee the work."

"Doubtless." Mukarrab Khan's voice was curt. "I suspect you should attend the accounts more and the women's apartments less." He turned to another eunuch.

"Is my bath ready?"

"As always, Khan Sahib." As the eunuch bowed he examined Hawksworth's dust-covered face and hair discreetly. "Will the distinguished *feringhi* also require a bath?"

"He was on the *chaugan* field this afternoon, just as I was."

Hawksworth groaned inwardly. What English host would have the effrontery to suggest a guest needed a bath? For that matter, what Englishman would even consider bathing more than twice a year? It's known well enough King James *never* bathes, that he never even washes his hands, only brushes them with a moist napkin at mealtime. Yet this Moor wants a full bath before a meal, merely to remove a bit of dust.

"I would be content to rinse my hands."

Mukarrab Khan examined him for a moment and then broke into a wide smile. "I always forget *feringhi* are positively afraid of water." He spoke quickly to one of the eunuchs, who turned and barked orders to the servants in a language Hawksworth did not understand.

"The servants will provide whatever you require." Mukarrab Khan bowed perfunctorily to Hawksworth and disappeared through one of the arched doorways leading off the courtyard, followed by the eunuchs. Then Hawksworth turned to see a dark-skinned man bearing a large silver basin down the veranda. Behind him a second man carried a red velvet cushion, shaped like a long cylinder, and placed it on a stool next to the canopied pavilion, gesturing for Hawksworth to sit.

As Hawksworth seated himself and turned toward the basin the servant held waiting, he caught the fresh aroma of a full bouquet, as though the fragrances of some tropic Eden had been distilled into the water. He looked down to see flower petals floating on its shimmering, oil-covered surface. How curious, he thought. English countrywomen sometimes distill toilet water from the flowers in their gardens, but never in such quantities that it can be used merely to wash hands. And while English toilet waters are cloying and sweet, violets and gilliflowers, this aroma is light and delicate.

War elephants and perfumed waters, in the same palace. It's incredible.

He gingerly splashed his hands, and looked up to find a steaming towel being proffered. He sponged away the remaining mud of the playing field and watched as one by one the servants began to melt into the darkened recesses of the marble galleries. The last was an old withered gamekeeper, who wandered through the garden berating a sullen peacock toward its roost. And then the courtyard fell austerely quiet.

Illuminated now only by lanterns and pale moonlight, it became a fairyland almost outside of time. He smiled as he thought of where he had been only the previous night—fending off an attack by Portuguese infantry. And now, this.

His thoughts began to drift randomly, to float in and among the marble latticework of the veranda. And he thought once more of Roger Symmes and his bizarre stories of India.

He was right. It's a heaven on earth. But with an undertow of violence just beneath the serene, polished surface. All this beauty, and yet it's guarded with war elephants and a moat. It's a world that's . . . artificial. It's carved of marble and jewels, and then locked away. Now I'm beginning to understand why he found it so enticing. And frightening. God, for a brandy. Now.

"Khan Sahib awaits you." Hawksworth looked up to see the eunuch standing directly in front of him, freshly attired in a long robe of patterned silk. As he rose, startled from his reveries, a pudgy hand shot out and seized his arm.

"Your sword is not permitted in the banquet room."

Hawksworth froze. Then he remembered the knife strapped inside the top of his boot and the thought gave him comfort.

He unbuckled his sword slowly, deliberately, pausing to meet the eunuch's defiant stare as he passed it over.

The eunuch seemed to ignore Hawksworth's look as he continued.

"You will also remove your boots. It is against custom to wear them in the banquet room."

Hawksworth moved to protest, then sadly concluded there would be no point. Of course the room would be filled with carpets. And *that* must be the reason everyone I've seen here wears open shoes with the backs folded down: they're constantly being removed at doorways.

He bent over and unbuckled his boots. The eunuch stiffened momentarily when he saw the glint of the knife handle in the lamplight, but he said nothing, merely swept up the boots with his other hand.

As they walked slowly down the marble hallway toward the bronzed door of the banquet room, Hawksworth tried to rehearse what he would say to Mukarrab Khan.

He has to petition the court in Agra to grant safe conduct for the trip. He just has to send one letter. How can he possibly refuse? Remember, you're an ambassador . . .

The eunuch shoved wide the bronzed door, and Hawksworth was astonished by what he saw.

The governor of Surat lounged against a purple velvet bolster at the far end of a long room whose walls were a cool expanse of flawless white and whose marble floor was softened with an enormous carpet in the thick Persian style. His skin glistened with light oil, and he had donned a fresh turban, patterned in brown and white, tied in intricate swirls, and bound with a strand of dark jewels. A single large pearl hung over his forehead, and two tassels, each also suspending a pearl, brushed his shoulders. He wore a tight-fitting patterned shirt in pale brown, and over this a heavy green vest lined in white satin and embroidered in gold. It was bound with a woven cinch decorated with brocade. Around his neck were two strings of pearls, the shorter suspending a large ruby from its center. He had put on heavy bracelets, and intricate rings circled the first and fourth fingers of both hands. Hawksworth also noticed for the first time that he wore earrings, each a tiny green emerald.

The eunuchs stood behind him, and around the sides of the room servants and slaves stood waiting. Along a back wall two men sat silently poised, one behind a pair of small drums and the other holding an ornate stringed instrument, its polished body glistening in the light. The only women in the room mingled among the servers.

"Captain Hawksworth, our fare tonight will be simple and unworthy, but please honor my table by your indulgence." Mukarrab Khan smiled warmly and motioned Hawksworth to enter. "At least we can talk freely."

"Is this an official meeting?" Hawksworth did not move, but stood as officiously as he could muster.

"If you wish. Our meeting can be considered formal, even if we are not."

"Then as ambassador of His Majesty, King James of England, I must insist that you rise to receive me." Hawksworth tried to suppress the feeling that he looked vaguely foolish as a barefoot ambassador. But no one else in the room wore shoes either. "A governor is still his king's subject. I represent my king's person."

"I was not informed you were an ambassador." Mukarrab Khan's face sobered noticeably, but he did not move. "You are Captain-General of two merchant vessels."

"I'm here in the name of the king of England, with authority to speak for him in all matters regarding trade." Hawksworth recalled the effect this had had on the Shahbandar. "I'm entrusted with his personal letter to the *Moghul*."

Mukarrab Khan examined Hawksworth for a long moment, seeming to collect and assemble a number of thoughts.

"Your request would be proper for an ambassador. Let us say I comply in the interest of mutual good will." He rose and bowed formally, if only sightly, more a nod. "The governor of Surat welcomes you, a representative of the English king."

"And I convey my king's acknowledgment of your welcome." Hawksworth entered and seated himself facing Mukarrab Khan, against a large velvet bolster already positioned for him.

"And what is this letter your English king sends to His Majesty?" Mukarrab Khan reclined back on his own bolster and arched his fingertips together.

"That is a concern between King James and the *Moghul*." Hawksworth caught the quickly suppressed flash of anger in Mukarrab Khan's eyes. "I only ask that you petition the court in Agra for permission to travel there. It would also be helpful if you would order the Shahbandar to allow our merchants to trade their goods at the port of Surat."

"Yes, I understand you had the pleasure of meeting our Shahbandar. I regret deeply having to tell you I have virtually no influence over that notorious man. He was appointed by the *Moghul*'s son, Prince Jadar, who is in charge of administering this province. He acts very much as he pleases."

Lie number one, Hawksworth thought: you forced him to order my transfer here.

"Surely you're aware," Mukarrab Khan continued evenly, "that no other Europeans besides the Portuguese have ever before landed cargo on the shores of India. Arabs, Persians, even Turks are a common sight, but no other Europeans. Not even your Dutch, who, I'm told, consort with some of our southeastern neighbors. In fact, the *Moghul*'s trade agreement with the Portuguese is intended to exclude all other Europeans." Mukarrab Khan stirred on his bolster and signaled one of the eunuchs to prepare the carpet for dining. "Although frankly he has little choice, since they control the seas. In fact, it might be said that *they* allow *our* merchants to trade. Indian cargo vessels must all acquire a license from Portuguese officials in Goa before leaving port."

"The Portugals control India's trade because you've allowed them to. Your territorial waters belong to India, or should."

Mukarrab Khan seemed to ignore Hawksworth as he watched the servants spread a large covering of tooled leather across the carpet in front of them. After a moment his concentration reappeared, and he turned abruptly.

"Ambassador Hawksworth, we do not need to be advised by you how India should manage her own affairs. But perhaps I will advise *you* that His Excellency, the Portuguese Viceroy, has already sent notice by messenger that he intends to lodge charges of piracy against your two ships. He has requested that they be confiscated and that you, your merchants, and your crews be transferred to Goa for trial."

Hawksworth's heart stopped and he examined Mukarrab Khan in dismay. So the *chaugan* match had merely been an excuse to take him into confinement. After a moment he stiffened and drew himself erect. "And I say the Portugals were the ones acting as pirates. Their attack on our English merchantmen was in violation of the treaty of peace that now exists between England and Spain, and by extension to the craven Portugals, who are now nothing more than a vassal of the Spanish king."

"Yes, I've heard rumors of this treaty. We in India are not entirely ignorant of Europe. But His Excellency denies there's any such treaty extending to our shores. As I recall he characterized England as an island of stinking fishermen, who should remain content to fish their own sea."

"The treaty between England and Spain exists." Hawksworth decided to ignore the insult. "We have exchanged ambassadors and it is honored by both our kings. It ended almost two decades of war."

"I will grant you such a treaty may indeed exist. Whether it applies here I do not know. Nor, frankly, do I particularly care. What I do know, English ambassador, is that you are very far from the law courts of Europe. The Portuguese still control the seas off India, as they have done for a hundred years. And unenforceable treaties have little bearing on the rule of might."

"We showed you the 'might' of the Portugals yesterday."

Mukarrab Khan laughed heartily, and when he glanced toward his eunuchs, they returned obsequious grins. "You are truly more naïve than I ever imagined, English Captain Hawksworth. What effect can one small engagement have on the fleet of warships at Goa? If you want protection at sea, you will have to provide it yourself. Is *that* what your king hopes to gain from the *Moghul*, or from me?"

"I told you I have only two requests. One is your message to Agra requesting permission for my journey. The other is your approval to trade the cargo we've brought."

"Yes, so you have said. Unfortunately, what you ask may not be all that easy to grant. Your unhappy engagement with the Portuguese Viceroy's fleet has made my situation more than a trifle awkward." He leaned back and spoke rapidly in Persian to the eunuchs standing behind him. Then he turned back to Hawksworth. "But as one of our Agra poets, a Sufi rascal named Samad, once penned, 'The thread of life is all too short; the soul tastes wine and passes on.' Before we explore these tiresome concerns further, let us taste some wine."

The eunuchs were already dictating orders to the servants. A silver chalice of fresh fruit appeared beside Hawksworth, brimming with mangoes, oranges larger than he had ever before seen, slices of melon, and other unknown fruits of varied colors. A similar bowl was placed beside Mukarrab Khan, who seemed to ignore it. Then as Hawksworth watched, the servants began spreading a white linen cloth over the red leather coverlet that had been placed on the carpet in front of them.

"A host is expected, Ambassador, to apologize for the meal he offers. I will take the occasion to do that now." Mukarrab Khan flashed a sprightly smile. "But perhaps after your months at sea, you will be lenient. For my own part, I have fasted today, and there's an Arab proverb that hunger is the best spice. Still, I prefer leisurely gratification. I concur with our Hindu sensualists that pleasure prolonged is pleasure enhanced. All pleasure. Perhaps this evening you will see their wisdom."

Before Hawksworth could respond, two heavy doors at the back of the room slowly opened, glinting the lamplight off their elaborate filigree of gold and bronze, and the first trays appeared, covered with silver lids and borne by young men from the kitchen. Uniformed servants preceded them into the room. One by one the trays were passed to the eunuchs, who removed their lids and carefully inspected the contents of each dish. After a brief consultation, the eunuchs ordered several of the dishes returned to the kitchen.

Hawksworth suddenly realized he was ravenous, and he watched the departing dishes in dismay. Did they somehow fail the eunuchs' exacting standards? Sweet Jesus, who cares? It all looks delicious.

After final approval by the eunuchs, the silver serving bowls were passed to servants waiting along the sides of the room, who in turn arrayed them across the linen cloth between Hawksworth and Mukarrab Khan. A chief server then knelt behind the dishes, while several stacks of porcelain plates were placed next to him. Hawksworth tried to count the silver serving bowls, but stopped after twenty.

One by one the server ceremoniously removed the silver lids from the bowls. Beneath them the contents of the dishes had been arrayed in the colors of a rainbow. On beds of rice that ranged from white to saffron to green, and even purple, was an overwhelming array of meats, fish, and birds of all sizes. There were carved baked fruits; tiny balls of meat flaked with spice and coconut; fried vegetables surrounded by silver cups of a pastel green sauce; large flat fish encased in dark baking shells flecked with red and green spices; and a virtual aviary of wild fowl, from small game birds to plump pea hens.

The server dished hearty helpings from each bowl onto separate porcelain plates, together with mounds of almond rice and jellied fruits. As he started to pass the first plate to Hawksworth, Mukarrab Khan roughly arrested his hand. "This ill-bred kitchen *wallah* will serve in the stables after tonight." He seized the serving spoons and, with a flourish of traditional Moghul etiquette, personally laded extra portions from each of the dishes onto Hawksworth's plates. The server beamed a knowing smile.

Hawksworth stared at the food for a moment, dazzled, and then he gingerly sampled a meatball. The taste was delicate, yet hardy, and he caught the musky flavor of lamb, lightened and transmuted by a bouquet of spice. He next pulled away the side of a fish and wolfed it, before realizing the red and green flecks on its surface were some incendiary garnish. He surveyed the room in agony, praying for a mug of ale, till an alert eunuch signaled a servant to pass a dish of yogurt. To his amazement, the tangy, ice cold liquid seemed to instantly dissolve the fire on his tongue.

He plunged back into the dishes. He had never eaten like this before, even in England. He suddenly recalled with a smile an episode six months into the voyage. After Zanzibar, when he had become so weary of stale salt pork and biscuit he thought he could not bear to see it again, he had locked the door of the Great Cabin and composed a full English banquet in his mind—roast capon, next a pigeon pie larded in bacon fat, then a dripping red side of roast mutton, followed by oysters on the shell spiced with grilled eel, and finally a thick goose pudding on honeyed ham. And to wash it down, a bottle of sack to begin and a sweet muscadel, mulled even sweeter with sugar, to end. But this! No luscious pork fat, and not nearly cloying enough for a true Englishman. Yet it worked poetry. Symmes was right. This was heaven.

With both hands he ripped the leg off a huge bird that had been basted to a glistening red and, to the visible horror of the server, dipped it directly into one of the silver bowls of saffron sauce meant for pigeon eggs. Hawksworth looked up in time to catch the server's look.

Does he think I don't like the food?

To demonstrate appreciation, he hoisted a goblet of wine to toast the server, while he stretched for a piece of lamb with his other hand. But instead of acknowledging the compliment, the server went pale.

"It's customary, Ambassador, to use only one's right hand when eating." Mukarrab Khan forced a polite smile. "The left is normally reserved for . . . attending to other functions."

Hawksworth then noticed how Mukarrab Khan was dining. He, too, ate with his fingers, just as you would in England, but somehow he managed to lift his food gracefully with balls of rice, the sauce never soiling his fingertips.

A breeze lightly touched Hawksworth's cheek, and he turned to see a servant standing behind him, banishing the occasional fly with a large whisk fashioned from stiff horsehair attached to a long stick. Another servant stood opposite, politely but unnecessarily cooling him with a large fan made of red leather stretched over a frame.

"As I said, Ambassador, your requests present a number of difficulties." Mukarrab Khan looked up and took a goblet of fruit nectar from a waiting servant. "You ask certain things from me, things not entirely in my power to grant, while there are others who make entirely different requests."

"You mean the Portugals."

"Yes, the Portuguese Viceroy, who maintains you have acted illegally, in violation of his law and ours, and should be brought to account."

"And I accuse *them* of acting illegally. As I told you, there's been a Spanish ambassador in London ever since the war ended, and when we return I assure you the East India Company will . . ."

"This is India, Captain Hawksworth, not London. Please understand I must consider Portuguese demands. But we are pragmatic. I urge you to tell me a bit more about your king's intentions. Your king's letter. Surely you must know what it contains."

Mukarrab Khan paused to dip a fried mango into a shimmering orange sauce, asking himself what he should do. He had, of course, posted pigeons to Agra at sunrise, but he suspected already what the reply would be. He had received a full account of the battle, and the attack on the river, before the early, pre-sun Ramadan meal. And it was only shortly afterward that Father Manoel Pinheiro had appeared, frantic and bathed in sweat. Was it a sign of Portuguese contempt, he often wondered, that they would assign such an incompetent to India? Throughout their entire Society of Jesus, could there possibly be any priest more ill-bred? The Jesuit had repeated facts already known throughout the palace, and Mukarrab Khan had listened politely, masking his amusement. How often did a smug Portuguese find himself explaining a naval disaster? Four Portuguese warships, galleons with two gundecks, humiliated by two small English frigates. How, Mukarrab Khan had wondered aloud, could this have happened?

"There were reasons, Excellency. We have learned the English captain fired langrel into our infantry, shredded metal, a most flagrant violation of the unwritten ethics of warfare."

"Are there really supposed to be ethics in warfare? Then I suppose you should have sent only two of your warships against him. Instead you sent four, and still he prevailed. Today he has no need for excuses. And tell me again what happened when your infantry assaulted the English traders on the river?" Mukarrab Khan had monitored the Jesuit's eyes in secret glee, watching him mentally writhe in humiliation. "Am I to understand you could not even capture a pinnace?"

"No one knows, Excellency. The men sent apparently disappeared without a trace. Perhaps the English had set a trap." Father Pinheiro had swabbed his greasy brow with the sleeve of his cassock. His dark eyes showed none of the haughty disdain he usually brought to their meetings. "I would ask you not to speak of it outside the palace. It was, after all, a special mission."

"You would prefer the court in Agra not know?"

"There is no reason to trouble the *Moghul*, Excellency." The Jesuit paused carefully. "Or Her Majesty, the queen. This really concerns the Viceroy alone." The Jesuit's Persian was grammatically flawless, if heavily accented, and he awkwardly tried to leaven it with the polite complexities he had been taught in Goa. "Still less is there any need for Prince Jadar to know."

"As you wish." Mukarrab Khan had nodded gravely, knowing the news had already reached half of India, and most certainly Prince Jadar. "How, then, may I assist?"

"The English pirate and his merchants must be delayed here at least four weeks. Until the fleet of galleons now unlading in Goa, those of the spring voyage just arrived from Lisbon, can be outfitted to meet him."

"But surely he and his merchants will sail when they choose. And sooner if we deny them trade. Do you suggest that I approve this trade?"

"You must act as you see fit, Excellency. You know the Viceroy has always been of service to Queen Janahara." Pinheiro had paused slyly. "Just as you have been."

The cynicism of Pinheiro's flaunting his knowledge had galled Mukarrab Khan most of all. If this Jesuit knew, who else must know? That the governor of Surat was bound inescapably to the queen. That on any matter involving Portuguese trade he must always send a formal message to the *Moghul* and a secret one to the queen, and then wait while she dictated the ruling Arangbar would give. Did this Jesuit know also *why* Mukarrab Khan had been exiled from Agra? To the wilderness of provincial Surat? That it was on orders of the queen, to marry and take with him a woman becoming dangerous, the *zenana* favorite of the *Moghul*, before the woman's influence outweighed that even of Janahara. And now this female viper was in his palace forever, could not be removed or divorced, because she was still a favorite of the *Moghul's*.

"So you tell me I must make them rich before you can destroy them. That seems to be Christian wisdom at its most incisive." Mukarrab Khan had summoned a tray of rolled betel leaves, signifying that the interview was ended. "It is always a pleasure to see you, Father. You will have my reply when Allah wills."

The Jesuit had departed as awkwardly as he had come, and it was then that Mukarrab Khan decided to meet the Englishman for himself. While there was still time. How long, he wondered, before the Shahbandar realized the obvious? And the prince?

In the banquet room the air was now dense with the aroma of spice. Hawksworth realized he had so gorged he could scarcely breathe. And he was having increasing difficulty deflecting Mukarrab Khan's probing questions. The governor was skillfully angling for information he properly did not need, and he did not seem a man given to aimless curiosity.

"What do you mean when you ask about the 'intentions' of England?"

"If the *Moghul* should approve a trade agreement with your East India Company, what volume of goods would you bring through our port here in Surat?" Mukarrab Khan smiled disarmingly. "Is the Company's fleet extensive?"

"That's a matter better addressed to the merchants of the Company." Hawksworth monitored Mukarrab Khan's expression, searching for a clue to his thoughts. "Right now the Company merely wishes to trade the goods in our two merchantmen. English wool for Indian cotton."

"Yes, I am aware that was the first of your two requests." Mukarrab Khan motioned away the silver trays. "Incidentally, I hope you are fond of lamb."

The bronzed doors opened again and a single large tray was borne in by the dark-skinned, unsmiling servants. It supported a huge cooking vessel, still steaming from the oven. The lid was decorated with lifelike silver castings of various birds and animals. After two eunuchs examined it, the servants delivered it to the center of the linen serving cloth.

"Tonight to signify the end of Ramadan I instructed my cooks to prepare my special *biryani*. I hope you will not be disappointed. My kitchen here is scandalous by Agra standards, but I've succeeded in teaching them a few things."

The lid was lifted from the pot and a bouquet of saffron burst over the room. Inside, covering a flawless white crust, was a second menagerie of birds and animals, wrought from silver the thinness of paper. The server spooned impossible portions from the pot onto silver plates, one for Hawksworth and one for Mukarrab Khan. The silver-foil menagerie was distributed around the sides of each plate.

"Actually I once bribed a cook in the *Moghul*'s own kitchen to give me this recipe. You will taste nothing like it here in Surat."

Hawksworth watched as he assembled a ball of the rice-and-meat mélange with his fingers and reverently popped it into his mouth.

"Please try it, Ambassador. I think you'll find it remarkable. It requires the preparation of two sauces, and seems to occupy half my incompetent kitchen staff." The governor smiled appreciatively. Hawksworth watched dumbfounded as he next chewed up and swallowed one of the silver-foil animals.

Hawksworth tried to construct a ball of the mixture but finally despaired and simply scooped up a handful. It was rich but light, and seemed to hint of every spice in the Indies.

"There are times," Mukarrab Khan continued, "when I positively yearn for the so-called deprivation of Ramadan. When the appetite is whetted day long, the nightly indulgence is all the more gratifying."

Hawksworth took another mouthful of the savory mixture. After the many long months of salt meat and biscuit, he found his taste confused and overwhelmed by its complexity. Its spices were all assertive, yet he could not specifically identify a single one. They had been blended, it seemed, to enhance one another, to create a pattern from many parts, much as the marble inlays of the floor, in which there were many colors, yet the overall effect was that of a single design, not its components.

"I've never tasted anything quite like this, even in the Levant. Could you prepare instructions for our ship's cook?"

"It would be my pleasure, Ambassador, but I doubt very much a *feringhi* cook could reproduce this dish. It's far too complex. First my kitchen prepares a *masala*, a blend of nuts and spices such as almonds, turmeric, and ginger. The bits of lamb are cooked in this and in *ghee*, which we make by boiling and clarifying butter. Next a second sauce is prepared, this a lighter mixture—curds seasoned with mint, clove, and many other spices I'm sure you know nothing of. This is blended with the lamb, and then layered in the pot you see there together with rice cooked in milk and saffron. Finally it's covered with a crust of wheat flour and baked in a special clay oven. Is this really something a ship's cook could do?"

Hawksworth smiled resignedly and took another mouthful.

Whoever thought there could be so many uses for spice. We use spice in England, to be sure—clove, cinnamon, pepper, even ginger and cardamom —but they're intended mainly to disguise the taste of meat past its prime. But here spices are essential ingredients.

"Let us return to your requests, Captain Hawksworth. I'm afraid neither of these is entirely within my power to bestow. In the matter of trading privileges for your cargo, I'll see what can be done. Yours is an unusual request, in the sense that no Europeans have ever come here to war with the Portuguese, then asked to compete with them in trade."

"It seems simple enough. We merely exchange our goods for some of the cotton cloth I saw arriving at the customs house this morning. The Shahbandar stated you have the power to authorize this trade."

"Yes, I enjoy some modest influence. And I really don't expect that Prince Jadar would object."

"He's the *Moghul's* son?"

"Correct. He has full authority over this province, but he's frequently on campaign and difficult to reach. His other duties include responsibility for

military conscription here, and maintaining order. These are somewhat uneasy times, especially in the Deccan, southeast of here."

"When will we learn your decision, or his decision? There are other
markets for our goods."

"You will learn the decision when it is decided." Mukarrab Khan
shoved aside his plate and a servant whisked it from the carpet. "Concerning
your second request, that I petition Agra to authorize your travel there, I
will see what can be done. But it will require time."

"I would ask the request be sent immediately."

"Naturally." Mukarrab Khan watched absently as more brimming trays
were brought in, these piled with candied fruits and sweetmeats. A *hookah*
water pipe appeared and was placed beside Hawksworth.

"Do you enjoy the new *feringhi* custom of smoking tobacco, Captain
Hawksworth? It was introduced recently, and already it's become fashionable. So much so the *Moghul* just issued a decree denouncing it."

"King James has denounced it too, claiming it destroys health. But it's
also the fashion in London. Personally, I think it ruins the taste of brandy,
and wine."

"Overall I'm inclined to agree. But tell me now, what's your opinion of
the wine you're drinking? It's Persian."

"Better than the French. Though frankly it could be sweeter."

Mukarrab Khan laughed. "A common complaint from *topiwallahs*.
Some actually add sugar to our wine. Abominable." He paused. "So I gather
then you only use spirits?"

"What do you mean?"

"There are many subtle pleasures in the world, Ambassador. Liquors admittedly enhance one's dining, but they do little for one's appreciation of
art."

As Hawksworth watched him, puzzling, he turned and spoke quietly to
one of the eunuchs hovering behind him. Moments later a small golden cab-
inet, encrusted with jewels, was placed between them. Mukarrab Khan
opened a tiny drawer on the side of the box and extracted a small brown
ball.

"May I suggest a ball of *ghola?*" He offered it to Hawksworth. It
carried a strange, alien fragrance.

"What's *ghola?*"

"A preparation of opium and spice, Ambassador. I think it might help
you better experience this evening's entertainment." He nodded lightly in
the direction of the rear wall.

The snap of a drum exploded behind Hawksworth, and he whirled to
see the two musicians begin tuning to perform. The drummer sat before
two foot-high drums, each nestled in a circular roll of fabric. Next to him
was a wizened old man in a black Muslim skullcap tuning a large six-

stringed instrument made of two hollowed-out gourds, both lacquered and polished, connected by a long teakwood fingerboard. About a dozen curved brass frets were tied to the fingerboard with silk cords, and as Hawksworth watched, the player began shifting the location of two frets, sliding them an inch or so along the neck to create a new musical scale. Then he began adjusting the tension on a row of fine wires that lay directly against the teakwood fingerboard, sympathetic strings that passed beneath those to be plucked. These he seemed to be tuning to match the notes in the new scale he had created by moving the frets.

When the sitarist had completed his tuning, he settled back and the room fell totally silent. He paused a moment, as though in meditation, then struck the first note of a somber melody Hawksworth at first found almost totally rootless. Using a wire plectrum attached to his right forefinger, he seemed to be waving sounds from the air above the fingerboard. A note would shimmer into existence from some undefined starting point, then glide through the scale via a subtle arabesque as he stretched the playing string diagonally against a fret, manipulating its tension. Finally the sound would dissolve meltingly into its own silence. Each note of the alien melody, if melody it could be called, was first lovingly explored for its own character, approached from both above and below as though a glistening prize on display. Only after the note was suitably embroidered was it allowed to enter the melody—as though the song were a necklace that had to be strung one pearl at a time, and only after each pearl had been carefully polished. The tension of some vague melodic quest began to grow, with no hint of a resolution. In the emotional intensity of his haunting search, the passage of time had suddenly ceased to exist.

Finally, as though satisfied with his chosen scale, he returned to the very first note he had started from and actually began a song, deftly tying together the musical strands he had so painstakingly evolved. The sought-for resolution had never come, only the sense that the first note was the one he had been looking for the entire time.

This must be the mystical music Symmes spoke of, Hawksworth thought, and he was right. It's unlike anything I've ever heard. Where's the harmony, the chords of thirds and fifths? Whatever's going on, I don't think opium is going to help me understand it.

Hawksworth turned, still puzzling, back to Mukarrab Khan and waved away the brown ball—which the governor immediately washed down himself with fruit nectar.

"Is our music a bit difficult for you to grasp, Ambassador?" Mukarrab Khan leaned back on his bolster with an easy smile. "Pity, for there's truly little else in this backwater port worth the bother. The cuisine is abominable, the classical dancers despicable. In desperation I've even had to train my own musicians, although I did manage to steal one Ustad, a grand master, away from Agra." He impulsively reached for the water pipe and absorbed a deep draw, his eyes misting.

"I confess I do find it hard to follow." Hawksworth took a draft of wine from the fresh cup that had been placed beside him on the carpet.

"It demands a connoisseur's taste, Ambassador, not unlike an appreciation of fine wine."

The room grew ominously still for a moment, and then the drums suddenly exploded in a torrent of rhythm, wild and exciting yet unmistakably disciplined by some rigorous underlying structure. The rhythm soared in a cycle, returning again and again, after each elaborate interlocking of time and its divisions, back to a forceful crescendo.

Hawksworth watched Mukarrab Khan in fascination as he leaned back and closed his eyes in wistful anticipation. And at that moment the instrumentalist began a lightning-fast ascent of the scale, quavering each note in erotic suggestiveness for the fraction of a second it was fingered. The governor seemed absorbed in some intuitive communication with the sound, a reaction to music Hawksworth had never before witnessed. His entire body would perceptibly tense as the drummer began a cycle, then it would pulse and relax the instant the cycle thudded to a resolution. Hawksworth was struck by the sensuality inherent in the music, the almost sexual sense of tension and release.

Then he noticed two eunuchs leading a young boy into the room. The youth appeared to be hovering at the age of puberty, with still no trace of a beard. He wore a small but elaborately tied pastel turban, pearl earrings, and a large sapphire on a chain around his pale throat. His elaborate ensemble included a transparent blouse through which his delicate skin glistened in the lamplight, a long quilted sash at his waist, and tight-fitting trousers beneath light gauze pajamas that clung to his thighs as he moved. His lips were lightly red, and his perfume a mixture of flowers and musk. The boy reached for a ball of spiced opium and settled back against a quilted gold bolster next to Mukarrab Khan. The governor studied him momentarily and then returned to the music. And his thoughts.

He reflected again on Abul Hasan's blundering "accident" on the *chaugan* field, and what it must signify. If it were true the *qazi* had been bought by the Shahbandar, as some whispered, then it meant Mirza Nuruddin must be alarmed to the point of imprudence. Fearful of what could happen if the English were detained long enough for the Portuguese warships to prepare. Which meant that somewhere behind it all lay the hand of Prince Jadar.

He examined Hawksworth again, wondering how this English captain could have savaged the Viceroy's fleet with such embarrassing ease. What, he asked himself again, will the queen order done?

"I'm sorry you don't find our music more congenial, Ambassador.

Perhaps I too would be wiser if I loved it less. The passion for classical music has cost many a great warrior his kingdom in India over the last centuries. For example, when the great Moghul patriarch Akman conquered Baz Bahadur, once the proud ruler of Malwa, it was because that prince was a better patron of music than of the arts of war." He smiled reflectively. "Admittedly, the great Akman himself also flooded his court with musicians, but then he had the wit to study arms as well. Regrettably, I find myself lacking his strength of character."

He paused to take a sip of nectar, then shrugged. "But enough. Tell me now what you really think of my Ustad, my master sitarist. There are those in Agra who will never forgive me for stealing him away."

"I'm not sure what I think. I've never heard a composition quite like the one he's playing."

"What do you mean by 'composition'?" Mukarrab Khan's tone was puzzled.

"That's how a piece of music is written out."

Mukarrab Khan paused and examined him skeptically for a long moment. "Written out? You write down your music? But whatever for? Does that mean your musicians play the same song again and again, precisely the same way?"

"If they're good they do. A composer writes a piece of music and musicians try to play it."

"How utterly tiresome." Mukarrab Khan sighed and leaned back on his bolster. "Music is a living art, Ambassador. It's meant to illuminate the emotions of the one who gives it life. How can written music have any feeling? My Ustad would never play a raga the same way twice. Indeed, I doubt he would be physically capable of such a boorish feat."

"You mean he creates a new composition each time he plays?"

"Not precisely. But his handling of the specific notes of a raga must speak to his mood, *my* mood. These vary, why not his art?"

"But what is a raga then, if not a song?"

"That's always difficult to explain. At some rudimentary level you might say it's simply a melody form, a fixed series of notes around which a musician improvises. But although a raga has a rigorously prescribed ascending and descending note sequence and specific melodic motifs, it also has its own mood, 'flavor.' What we call its *rasa*. How could one possibly write down a mood?"

"I guess I see your point. But it's still confusing." Hawksworth took another sip of wine. "How many ragas are there?"

"There are seventy-two primary scales on which ragas are based. But some scales have more than one raga. There are ragas for morning, for evening, for late at night. My Ustad is playing a late evening raga now. Although he uses only the notes and motifs peculiar to this raga, what he does with them is entirely governed by his feeling tonight."

"But why is there no harmony?"

"I don't understand what you mean by 'harmony.'"

"Striking several notes together, so they blend to produce a chord."

Mukarrab Khan studied him, uncomprehending, and Hawksworth continued.

"If I had my lute I'd show you how harmony and chords are used in an English song." Hawksworth thought again of his instrument, and of the difficulty he'd had protecting it during the voyage. He knew all along it was foolish to bring it, but he often told himself every man had the right to one folly.

"Then by all means." The governor's curiosity seemed to rouse him instantly from the opium. "Would you believe I've never met a *feringhi* who could play an instrument, any instrument?"

"But my lute was detained, along with all my belongings, at the customs house. I was going to retrieve my chest from the Shahbandar when you intercepted his men."

"Ambassador, please believe I had good reason. But I thought I told you arrangements have been made." He turned and dictated rapidly to one of the eunuchs. There was an expressionless bow, and the man left the room. Moments later he returned through the bronze entry doors, followed by two dark-skinned servants carrying Hawksworth's chest, one at each end.

"I ordered your belongings sent from the customs house this afternoon. You would honor me by staying here as my guest." Mukarrab Khan smiled warmly. "And now I would hear you play this English instrument."

Hawksworth was momentarily startled, wondering why his safety was suddenly of such great interest to Mukarrab Khan. But he pushed aside the question and turned to examine the large brass lock on his chest. Although it had been newly polished to a high sheen, as had the entire chest, there was no visible evidence it had been opened. He extracted the key from his doublet, slipped it into the lock, and turned it twice. It revolved smoothly, opening with a soft click.

The lute rested precisely where he had left it. Its body was shaped like a huge pear cut in half lengthwise, with the back a glistening melon of curved cedar staves and the face a polished cherry. The neck was broad, and the head, where the strings were wound to their pegs, angled sharply back. He admired it for a moment, already eager for the touch of its dark frets. During the voyage it had been wrapped in heavy cloth, sealed in oilskins, and stored deep in his cabin chest. Not till landfall at Zanzibar had he dared expose it to the sea air.

Of all English music, he still loved the galliards of Dowland best. He was only a boy when Dowland's first book of galliards was published, but he had been made to learn them all by heart, because his exacting tutor had despised popular ballads and street songs.

Mukarrab Khan called for the instrument and slowly turned it in the lamplight, its polished cedar shining like a great jewel. He then passed it to his two musicians, and a brief discussion in Persian ensued, as brows were wrinkled and grave points adjudicated. After its appearance was agreed upon, the instrumentalist gingerly plucked a gut string with the wire plectrum attached to his forefinger and studied its sound with a distant expression. The torrent of Persian began anew, as each string was plucked in turn and its particular quality debated. Then the governor revolved to Hawksworth.

"I congratulate your wisdom, Ambassador, in not hazarding a truly fine instrument on a sea voyage. It would have been a waste of real workmanship."

Hawksworth stared at him dumbfounded.

"There's not a finer lute in London." He seized it back. "I had it specially crafted several years ago by a master, a man once lute-maker to the queen. It's one of the last he made."

"You must pardon me then, but why no embellishment? No ivory inlay, no carved decoration? Compare, if you will, Ustad Qasim's sitar. It's a work of fine art. A full year was spent on its decoration. Note the head has been carved as the body of a swan, the neck and pegs inlaid with finest ivory, the face decorated with mother-of-pearl and lapis lazuli. Your lute has absolutely no decoration whatsoever."

"The beauty of an instrument is in its tone."

"Yes, that's a separate point. But perhaps we should hear it played by one skilled in its use. I must confess we are all curious what can be done with so simple an instrument." Mukarrab Khan shifted on his bolster, while the young man next to him toyed with a jewel, not troubling to disguise his boredom.

Hawksworth tuned the strings quickly and meticulously. Then he settled himself on the carpet and took a deep breath. His fingers were stiff, his mind groggy with wine, but he would play a song he knew well. A galliard Dowland had written when Queen Elizabeth was still alive, in honor of a Cornwall sea captain named Piper, whom she'd given a letter of marque to attack the Spanish, but who instead turned an uncontrollable pirate, pillaging the shipping of any flag convenient. He'd become an official outlaw but a genuine English folk hero, and Dowland had honored his memory with a rousing composition—"Piper's Galliard."

A full chord, followed by a run of crisp notes, cut the close air. The theme was somber, a plaintive query in a minor mode followed by a melodic but defiant reply. Just the answer Piper would have given to the charges, Hawksworth thought.

The servants had all gathered to listen, and the eunuchs had stopped gossiping. Then Hawksworth glanced toward the musicians, who had shifted themselves onto the carpet to watch. Both the sitarist and his drummer still eyed the instrument skeptically, no hint of appreciation in their look.

Hawksworth had expected it.

Wait till they hear this.

He crouched over the lute and attacked the strings with all four fingers, producing a dense toccata, with three melodic lines advancing at once, two in the treble and one in the base. His hand flew over the frets until it seemed every fingertip commanded a string, each embellishing a theme another had begun. Then he brought the galliard to a rousing crescendo with a flourish that spanned two entire octaves.

A polite silence seemed to grip the room. Mukarrab Khan sipped thoughtfully from his cup for a moment, his jeweled rings refracting the lamplight, then summoned a eunuch and whispered briefly in his ear. As the eunuch passed the order to a hovering servant, Mukarrab Khan turned to Hawksworth.

"Your English music is interesting, Ambassador, if somewhat simple." He cleared his throat as an excuse to pause. "But frankly I must tell you it touched only my mind. Not my heart. Although I heard it, I did not *feel* it. Do you understand the difference? I sensed nothing of its *rasa*, the emotion and desire one should taste at a moment like this, the merging of sound and spirit. Your English music seems to stand aloof, unapproachable." Mukarrab Khan searched for words. "It inhabits its own world admirably, but it did not enter mine."

Servants suddenly appeared bearing two silver trays, on which were crystal cups of green, frothy liquid. As the servant placed Hawksworth's tray on the patterned carpet, he bowed, beaming. Mukarrab Khan ignored his own tray and instead summoned the sitarist, Bahram Qasim, to whisper brief instructions in his ear. Then the governor turned to Hawksworth.

"Perhaps I can show you what I mean. This may be difficult for you, so first I would urge you try a cup of *bhang*. It has the remarkable effect of opening one's heart."

Hawksworth tested the beverage warily. Its underlying bitterness had been obscured with sweet yogurt and potent spices. It was actually very palatable. He drank again, this time thirstily.

"What did you call this? *Bhang?*"

"Yes, it's made from the leaves of hemp. Unlike wine, which only dulls the spirit, *bhang* hones the senses. Now I've arranged a demonstration for you."

He signaled the sitarist, and Bahram Qasim began the unmistakable theme of "Piper's Galliard." The song was drawn out slowly, languorously, as each individual note was introduced, lovingly explored for its own pure

sound, and then framed with microtone embellishment and a sensual
vibrato. The clear, simple notes of the lute were transmuted into an almost
orchestral richness by an undertone of harmonic density from the sitar's sympathetic strings, the second row of wires beneath those being plucked, tuned
to match the notes of the song and respond without being touched. Dowland's harmonies were absent, but now the entire room resonated with a
single majestic chord underlying each note. Gradually the sitarist accelerated
the tempo, while also beginning to insert his own melodic variations over the
original notes of the theme.

Hawksworth took another sip of *bhang* and suddenly noticed the notes
seemed to be weaving a tapestry in his mind, evolving an elaborate pattern
that enveloped the room with shapes as colored as the geometries of the Persian carpet.

Next the drummer casually introduced a rhythmic underpinning, his
lithe fingers touring easily over and around the taut drumheads as he dis-
sected, then restructured the simple meter of Dowland's music. He seemed
to regard the original meter as merely a frame, a skeleton on which the real
artistry had yet to be applied. He knowingly subdivided Dowland's meter
into minuscule elements of time, and with these devised elaborate new in-
terlockings of sound and silence. Yet each new structure always resolved to
its perfect culmination at the close of a musical phrase. Then as he punctuated his transient edifice with a thud of the larger drum—much as an artist
might sign a painting with an elaborate flourish—he would catch Hawksworth's incredulous gaze and wink, his eyes twinkling in triumph.

Meanwhile, the sitarist structured Dowland's spirited theme to the
drummer's frame, adding microtones Dowland had never imagined, and
matching the ornate tempo of the drum as they blended together to become
a single racing heartbeat.

Hawksworth realized suddenly that he was no longer merely hearing the
music, that instead he seemed to be absorbing it.

How curious . . .

The music soared on to a final crescendo, a simultaneous climax of sitar
and drum, and then the English song seemed to dissolve slowly into the incense around them. After only a moment's pause, the musicians immediately
took up a sensuous late evening raga.

Hawksworth looked about and noticed for the first time that the lamps
in the room had been lowered, settling a semi-darkness about the musicians
and the moving figures around him. He felt for his glass of *bhang* and saw
that it was dry, and that another had been placed beside it. He drank again
to clear his mind.

What's going on? Damned if I'll stay here. My God, it's impossible to
think. I'm tired. No, not tired. It's just . . . just that my mind is . . . like I'd
swilled a cask of ale. But I'm still in perfect control. And where's Mukarrab

Khan? Now there are screens where he was sitting. Covered with peacocks that strut obscenely from one screen to the other. And the eunuchs are all watching. Bastards. I'll take back my sword. Jesus, where is it? I've never felt so adrift. But I'm not staying. I'll take the chest and damn his eunuchs. And his guards. He can't hold me here. Not even on charges. There are no charges. I'm leaving. I'll find the men. . . .

He pulled himself defiantly to his feet. And collapsed.

CHAPTER EIGHT

The dream was more vivid than reality, intensely colored and astir with vague forms that drifted through his mind's ken, appearing then fading. The room seemed airless, a musk-filled cell of gilded blue panels and gold brocade. Guarded faces hovered around and above, their eyes intense yet unseeing, distant as stained-glass masks of cathedral sinner and saint.

A fingertip brushed his cheek, and with its touch the room gloried in a powerful fragrance of saffron. Then a hand, floating unattached, gently removed his doublet; another slid away his mud-smeared breeches.

He was naked.

He looked down as though from afar at the texture of chest and thigh, and he wondered dimly if they were his own. Then other hands . . . and suddenly he was immersed in a sea whose shores were white marble, whose surface sheened with oil of the rose. Translucent petals drifted randomly atop the crests. Hands toured his frame, discovering every tightened nerve, while powdered sandalwood enveloped his hair and beard until he seemed lost in a fragrant forest.

As suddenly as the sea had come it drew away, but now there were steaming wraps tingling with astringent orange and clove, and he drifted through a land of aloe balm and amber.

The room dissolved into semi-darkness, until at last only a single face remained, a woman with eyes round and moist and coldly dark. Her lips were the deep red of betel, while her hair was coal and braided in a skein of jeweled tresses. A faceted stone sparkled on her left nostril, and heavy gold rings swung gently from each ear. Henna-red nipples pressed erect against her diaphanous blouse, and between her breasts clung a garland of pearls. The heavy bracelets on her wrists and her upper arms glistened gold in the flickering candlelight.

As he studied her eyes, they seemed locked into his own, and betrayed no notice of his body. He sent his voice through the dream's carpeted chambers, but his words were swallowed in dark air that drew out their sound and washed it to thin silence. In a final, awkward futility he struggled to free himself from the velvet bolster.

But gently she pressed him back.

"What would you have, my love? Sweet *bhang* from my hand?"

A cup found his lips, and before he knew he had taken more of the incendiary green confection. Its warmth grew slowly into a pale light that shimmered off the gilded panels and then coalesced into the rainbow now pivoting pendulum-like above him, a glistening fan of peacock feathers swayed by a faceless, amber-skinned woman.

His gaze returned to the eyes, and again he searched for sound. Then came a voice he recognized as his own.

"Who are you?"

"You may call me Kali. Others do. It's a name you would not understand. But can you understand that love is surrender?" The words coiled about his head, coruscating and empty of meaning. He shook them away and watched as she brushed a strand of hair from his face. With that simple motion, her nipples traced twin heliotrope arcs across the gossamer screen of her blouse. He examined her in disbelief, unable to find words.

"When my lover lies silent, I do as I choose."

Deftly she uncoiled the white silk sash from around her waist and in a single practiced motion bound it over his eyes. The room vanished. In the dream's sudden night he grew intensely aware of touch and smell.

Commands came in an alien tongue, and he felt his breast and thighs brushed lightly by a new, pungent fragrance.

"We have cloaked you in petals of spikenard, to banish the sight of your unshaven body. A *feringhi* knows so little of what pleases a woman."

He felt a light brush across his parted lips, and then her eyelashes, stiffened dark with antimony, trilled a path downward over his skin, to his nipples. The hardened lashes stroked each nipple in turn with rapid flutters, until the skin tightened almost to bursting. An excruciating sensitivity burned through him, but still the lashes fluttered, determinedly, almost unendurably, until his aroused tips touched the aching portals of pain. Then he sensed a tongue circle each nipple in turn, searching out the one most ripe.

He felt her kneel above him, surrounding him with open thighs that clasped his chest. The room fell expectantly silent. Then, as an unknown syllable sounded somewhere above him, he felt the nipple of his right breast seized in the lock of a warm, moist grasp. The surrounding thighs rocked gently at first, but slowly increased their rhythm in time with the sound of breath. Suddenly he felt her body twist lightly and another tip, hardened as that on his chest, began to trace the nipple's swollen point. Her thighs were smooth and moist as she pressed in with spiraling, ever more rapid intensity. He found himself deeply conscious of her rhythms and the hard cadence of breath. He reached for the strength to rip the silk from his eyes, to end the dream's tantalizing dark. But strength was not there. Or time.

Before he could stir, he sensed the hardened tip shudder. Again a grasp took his nipple and worked it with measured spasms, until the room's austere silence was cut by her sharp intake of breath, timed to match a single insistent contraction that seemed to envelop the whole of his breast. He felt her seize his hands in her own, and although he could see nothing, in his mind there grew a vision of her eyes at that moment. Then there came a sound, partially stifled in her throat, but not before it had found the gilded walls and returned, annealed to a glassy relic of release.

He felt her slowly withdraw, but then her mouth took his breast, till it had drawn away the musk. At last, perhaps to signify repletion, she lightly brushed his lips with the tip of her tongue.

"You have pleased me." Her voice was quiet now, almost a whisper. "Now we will please each other."

A hand worked at his loins, methodically applying a viscous, harshly scented oil.

"Would you could see with my eyes. The lingam of the fabled Shiva was never garlanded such as this, or anointed so lovingly."

Then her voice turned harsh as she spoke short, staccato commands in an unknown tongue. Bangles sounded and silk rustled as the room emptied. Now he caught a new scent, the harsh smell he remembered from the box the governor had offered.

"I will tell you my secret." She whispered close to his ear. "There is no more exciting way to experience the ecstasy of love than with *affion*, the essence of the poppy. But I have a way to receive it no one else knows. It is like the burst of a lightning stroke. Its power envelops the senses."

He felt her smooth a thick paste along the sides of his phallus, and sensed a tingle as she clasped it carefully with both hands. Again she moved above him, but curiously there was no touch of her body. Only the presence of her scent.

A tight ring seemed to circle his flesh, and he felt the weight of her rounded buttocks slide down onto his thighs.

He startled upward in shock and disbelief. Never will I . . .

"You must lie still, my love. In your surrender, only I may have my will."

She began at once to move above his thighs, and again muted sounds struggled stillborn in her throat. With deliberate regularity her rhythm mounted, while an overwhelming sensation spread upward through his body. Slowly he felt his new resolve slipping from him.

The convulsions started in his lower thighs, as muscles tightened involuntarily. And then the precipice grew near and he was at its edge and he was falling. He felt the surge, as though drawn out by the twist of her buttocks. Then again and again, each spasm matched by her own as she worked to envelop him completely. He was scarcely aware of her nails fixed in his breasts. At that instant he seemed to drift apart from his body and observe mutely as it was consumed by its own sensations. Until numbness washed over him, stilling his sense.

As he lay in exhaustion his mind sorted through her words, and in the dream's darkness he vowed to take her again. The next time, it's you who'll surrender, woman called Kali. To my will. And you'll find out the meaning of surrender.

But his thoughts were lost among the gilded panels as she pulled the silk from his eyes and quietly whispered something he did not understand. In that instant he thought he saw where a tear had stained a path across one cheek. She looked at him longingly, then touched his lips with her own for a long moment before slipping quietly into the dark.

The dream dissolved in sleep. And she was gone.

Hawksworth was suddenly awake. The chill of early dawn penetrated his face and hands, and his hair sparkled with light jewels of dew. His leather couch was moist and glistening, while the pale sky above was blocked by a tapestried canopy. Only in the east, above the white railing of the rooftop, could he see the glitter of a waning Venus, her brief reign soon to dissolve in the red wash of early sun. He looked about his white brick enclosure and saw only a light wooden door leading into a second-floor apartment.

He had no sooner drawn himself up to inhale the flower-scented dawn than two smiling men were standing over him, bowing. Both wore turbans, pastel-colored jackets, and a white wrap about their lower torso. Squinting into their eyes, Hawksworth remembered them from the evening before. They had brought the basin of water in which he had first washed.

As he pulled the embroidered coverlet closer about him he noticed a strange numbness in his body. And his mind ached as he tried to remember what precisely had happened.

There was a game on horseback with the governor, and then a banquet, with an argument in which Mukarrab Khan threatened to betray us to the Portugals, a curious evening of music. And then dreams . . .

Pulling himself up off the couch, he started unsteadily across the hard flat tile of the roof. Immediately a servant was beside him, producing a heavy silk wrap and swathing it around his shoulders and waist. Then the man bowed again and spoke in accented Turki.

"May Allah prosper you today, Sahib. May your fortunes answer the prayers of the poor." The man's expression softened to match his own compliment. "Should it please the Sahib, his morning bath is waiting."

Without thinking, without, even, hearing the words, he allowed himself to be led through the doorway into the second-floor apartment. There, in the center of the room, was his chest, its lock intact. He examined it with a quick glance, then followed the servants down a set of stone stairs to the ground-floor veranda—where a steaming marble tub waited.

Good Jesus, not again! How can I make them understand? Bathing weakens a man.

He started to turn, but suddenly two eunuchs appeared out of nowhere and were guiding him up the two marble steps to a stone platform, where they seated him on a filigreed wooden stool. Silently the servants stripped away his light wrap and began to knead his body and his hair with a fragrant powder, a blend of wood bark and some astringent fruit. The scent was mild, pleasant, and as their hands traveled over him he felt the pores of his skin open to divulge their residual rankness.

This is better, he thought. Cleaning without water. With only some sort of powder. I feel refreshed already.

His muscles loosened as the men vigorously worked the mixture into his skin and then carefully cleansed it away with bulky cotton towels. Next they turned to his hair, combing and massaging more of the powder through it strand by strand. At last they signaled for him to rise and enter the tub. Its surface glistened with a perfumed oil, and the rising steam smelled faintly of clove. Before he could protest, the eunuchs guided him down the marble steps.

As he settled into the steam again he was surrounded by waiting servants, who sprinkled more oil over the water and massaged the emulsion into his hair and skin.

I'm being bathed in oil, he smiled, marveling. It's absurd, yet here it seems perfectly right.

The men worked devotedly, as though he were an inanimate utensil whose purity was their lifelong obligation. His body now glistened with a reddish tint of the oil, matching the early glow of the sun that penetrated the half-shuttered windows. As they motioned for him to leave the bath, he discovered to his amazement that he would have been perfectly content to stay. Forever. But again hands were there, guiding him, this time toward a low wooden bench covered with thick woven tapestries.

What now? What else can they do? I'm cleaner than the day I was born. What more . . .

He was prostrate on the couch. A rough haircloth worked against his legs and torso, sending the blood surging. At the same time, a piece of porous sandstone in the practiced hands of another servant stripped away the loosened calluses and scales from his boot-roughened feet. A third man massaged still more perfumed oil, hinting of aloe and orange, into his back and along his sides and shoulders. His body had become an invigorated, pliant reed.

They motioned for him to sit up and, as he watched, one of the men produced a mirror and razor. Next he opened a bottle of fragrant liquid and began to apply it to Hawksworth's beard and chest. And then also to his legs and crotch.

"What's the purpose of that razor?"

"We have orders to shave you, Sahib, in our manner." The turbaned man who had greeted him that morning bowed slightly as he signaled the barber to begin. "You are to be shaved completely, as is our custom."

"Trim my beard if you like. But no more. Damn you if you'll shave me like some catamite." Hawksworth started to rise from his stool, but the barber was already over him, the blade flying across his face with a menacing deftness.

"It has been ordered, Sahib." The turbaned man bowed again, and without pausing for a reply produced a short, curved metal device and began to probe Hawksworth's ears, his face intent in concentration as he carefully extracted an enormous ball of gray mud and encrusted sea salt. He scraped the other ear with the same deft twist. Then he flipped the same instrument and began to trim Hawksworth's ragged fingernails.

Hawksworth turned to the mirror to discover that his beard had already disappeared, leaving him clean-faced.

At least I'll be in fashion back home, he thought, if I ever get back. Beards are passing from style.

But what's he doing now? By heaven, no . . .

The razor swept cleanly across Hawksworth's chest, leaving a swath of soft skin in its wake. It came down again, barely missing a nipple as he moved to rise.

"You *must* be still, Sahib. You will harm yourself."

"I told you I'll not have it." Hawksworth pushed the razor away.

"But it is our custom." The man seemed to plead. "Khan Sahib ordered that you be groomed as an honored guest."

"Well, damn your customs. Enough."

There was a moment of silence. Then the turbaned man bowed, his face despondent.

"As the Sahib desires."

He signaled the barber to rub a light coat of saffron-scented oil on Hawksworth's face and then to begin trimming Hawksworth's hair with the pair of silver scissors he had brought. The barber quickly snipped away the growth of the voyage, leaving the hair moderately cropped, in the Moghul fashion.

Hawksworth examined the mirror again.

Damn if I wouldn't make a proper Cheapside dandy. Right in style. And I hate being in style.

Then the turbaned man produced a heavy lead comb and began to work it repeatedly through Hawksworth's hair. Hawksworth watched the mirror in confusion.

What's he doing? It's already been combed. And it's so short there's no point anyway.

Then he noticed the slight traces of gray around the sides beginning to darken, taking on the color of the lead.

"Please open your mouth." The turbaned man stood above him holding a dark piece of wood, frayed at the end and crooked. "And I will scrape your teeth with *nim* root."

"But that's insane. Teeth are cleaned with a piece of cloth and a tooth-pick. Or rubbed with a bit of sugar and salt ash . . ."

The man was scrubbing away at Hawksworth's mouth—tongue, gums, teeth—using a dentifrice that tasted like burnt almond shells. Next he offered a mint-flavored mouth rinse to remove the debris.

The turbaned man then inspected Hawksworth critically from several sides, finally venturing to speak.

"If I may suggest, a bit of collyrium, castor oil darkened with lamp-black, would render your eyes much more striking." Without waiting for confirmation, he applied a few quick strokes to Hawksworth's eyelids, much as an artist might touch up a canvas.

Then one of the eunuchs stepped forward and supplied a silver tray to the turbaned servants. On it were folded garments: a tight-fitting pair of blue trousers, a patterned shirt, and a knee-length coat of thin, peach-colored muslin. They dressed Hawksworth quickly, and then secured a patterned sash about his waist. Waiting on the floor were leather slippers, low-quar-tered with a curved toe and a bent-down back.

"What have you done with my doublet and breeches? And my boots?"

"They are being cleaned today, Sahib. You may have them again when you wish. But you may prefer to wear our garments while our guest." The turbaned man bowed again, then he moved away and held a long mirror for Hawksworth to examine himself.

"Have we pleased you, Sahib?"

Hawksworth scarcely recognized himself. He had been transformed from a rank but honest seaman into a Moghul noble—youthful, smooth-skinned, smelling of spice. The soreness was banished from his limbs, and even his wound had all but disappeared. His hair was clean and completely dark, and his skin glowed. And his new clothes were more elaborate than anything he had ever worn.

"Now if you will please follow us to the garden. Khan Sahib has suggested you begin your day with some *tari* wine."

Hawksworth followed the men through the shuttered doorway into the open courtyard. The morning sun now illuminated the tops of a large grove of palm trees that circled an open cistern. He quickly surveyed the buildings, hoping to gain his bearings.

So I've been quartered in one of the side buildings, off the main palace. But there are many, many rooms. Who's living here?

A group of servants stood waiting at the base of one of the palms. When they saw Hawksworth, they mobilized to action. One young man among them, wearing a white wrap around his lower torso, immediately secured his belt and began to shinny up the leaning palm. When he reached the top he locked his legs around the trunk and carefully detached an earthen pot that hung beneath an incision in the bark of the tree. Balancing the pot in one hand, he stretched and nimbly pulled off a number of leaves from the tree and then lowered himself carrying his load. The moment his feet touched ground he raced toward the veranda and delivered the pot and leaves to a waiting eunuch.

Hawksworth watched as the eunuchs first inspected the items and then ordered them prepared. The leaves were washed thoroughly with water from the cistern and then folded into natural cups. The liquor from the pot was strained through muslin into a crystal decanter and the earthen receptacle discarded. Then one of the turbaned servants poured a large portion of the liquor from the decanter into a palm-leaf cup and offered it to Hawksworth.

"It's *tari* wine, Sahib. One of the pleasures of early morning in India." His matter-of-fact manner could not entirely hide his pride. "Palm wine makes itself overnight. It does not last out the day. When the sun shines the trees only give off vinegar."

Hawksworth gingerly sipped the newly fermented palm sap and was pleasantly surprised by its light flavor, totally unlike ale, or even Canary wine. After the third cup, the world around began to acquire a light sparkle of its own, and he realized the sap was more potent than it seemed.

"Not a bad way to start the day. What do you call it?"

"It comes from the *tari* palm, and some *topiwallahs* call it 'Toddy.'"

"Toddy, it's called? It's more than passable grog."

"Thank you, Sahib. Drink too much and you will spend the day with your head in a buzz." The servant giggled. "So now perhaps you should eat."

He consulted briefly with the eunuchs, who nodded and signaled toward the veranda. Moments later a tray appeared, piled high with honey-covered breads and glass dishes of sweet curds. Some hard cheese also had found its way onto the tray, and Hawksworth wondered if this was to placate his European taste. He sipped more of the Toddy and munched the bread and curds.

Then he saw the women.

There were five. They seemed clustered in a group as they entered the courtyard, but then he realized it was an aristocratic lady surrounded by four maids. They did not know he was there, for none covered her face. As he watched them they seemed preoccupied in an increasingly animated exchange. Then the aristocratic woman stepped determinedly ahead, turned, and curtly gave instructions whose seriousness was clear, even if her words were foreign. Her voice was not strident, but its authority was unmistakable.

The other women paused, then slowly, one by one, they seemed to acknowledge her orders and they bowed. The lady whirled and continued on her way, while the four other women turned toward the direction they had come. Then, as though the resolution of the argument had suddenly made them aware of their surroundings, they all seemed to see Hawksworth at once. All five women froze.

Hawksworth smiled and tried to remember the bow he had seen performed to him so often. But he could not remove his eyes from the first woman, who was more striking than any he had ever before seen. Her skin was fair, with a warm hint of olive, and her high cheekbones stood in stunning relief as they glanced away the golden light of dawn. Her nose was thin and sculptured, while her lips would have been full, had they not been drawn tight in response to some unspecified inner determination. Yet her eyes seemed untouched by what had just transpired. They were clear and receptive, even warm, and Hawksworth asked himself at that moment if this bespoke innocence, or guile.

In dress and adornment she scarcely differed from her maids. All had long black hair, brushed to gleaming and protected from the morning air with a transparent gossamer scarf edged in gold embroidery. At first glance there seemed little to distinguish among the tight strands of pearls each wore at the neck, or the jeweled bands on their wrists and upper arms. Each wore a tight silk halter for a blouse, and to Hawksworth's assessing eyes the maids all seemed to have abundant breasts swelling their halters to overflowing, some—perhaps all—with breasts more generous than the lady herself. Then he noted in amazement that the women actually wore a form of tapered silk trouser, a tight-legged pajama similar to that worn by aristocratic men.

Unlike the male style, however, each woman's body was enveloped by a long transparent skirt, suspended from a band that circled her torso just beneath her breasts. And whereas men all wore a long scarf tied about the waist of their cloaks and hanging down the front, the women all had a long pleated panel tucked directly into the front waistband of their trousers and reaching almost to the ground. He could not help noticing that it clung sensuously to their thighs as they walked, while its gold-embroidered hem tinkled against the gold bracelets each woman wore at her ankles. Their shoes were red Turkish leather, with gold decorations sewn across the top and a pointed toe that curved upward.

The only difference between the lady and her maids seemed to be in the rich fabric of her lightly clinging trousers. Then, too, there was slightly more gold thread in her long transparent skirt, and among the pearls at her neck nestled an unmistakable blue sapphire as large as a walnut.

But her primary distinction was not merely the classic lines of her face or the perfect curve of her waist and thighs, but rather something in her bearing, in her assured but unmannered carriage. Her real beauty lay in her breeding.

All five women stared at Hawksworth in momentary surprise and shock. Then each maid automatically seized her transparent scarf and pulled it across her lower face. The woman also moved instinctively to do the same, but then she seemed to consciously stop herself and with an obvious attempt at restraint she walked on, barefaced, past the courtyard and into the garden beyond. Alone.

Hawksworth watched her form disappear among the clipped hedges and elaborate marble pavilions of the garden. He noticed a curious sensation in his chest as she passed from view, and he suddenly found himself wanting very much to follow her. When he finally turned and looked back, the other women had already vanished.

Only then did he realize that all the servants had been watching him. The one nearest nodded in the direction of the garden and smiled knowingly.

"Perhaps it will not surprise you, Sahib, to learn that she was once the favorite of the *Moghul* himself. And now she is in Surat. Amazing."

"But why's she here?" Hawksworth glanced back at the garden once more to assure himself she was indeed lost to its recesses.

"She is Shirin, the first wife of Khan Sahib." He moved closer to Hawksworth, so that his lowered voice would not reach the eunuchs. "She was removed from the *Moghul*'s *zenana* and married to Khan Sahib last year by Queen Janahara, just before Her Majesty had him appointed the governor of Surat. Some believe she appointed him here to remove Shirin from Agra, because she feared her." The servant's voice became a whisper. "We all know she has refused His Excellency the legal rights of a husband."

The silence of the court was cut by the unmistakable voice of Mukarrab Khan, sounding in anger as he gave some command from within the palace. There followed a chorus of women's wails.

Hawksworth turned to the servant, but the man read his inquiring glance.

"He has ordered the women whipped for disobeying his order to accompany Shirin at all times, even when she walks in the garden."

Then the door opened again, and Mukarrab Khan strode into the morning sunshine.

"Captain Hawksworth, salaam. I trust Allah gave you rest."

"I slept so well I find difficulty remembering all we said last night."

Hawksworth watched him carefully. Will he honor his threat to deliver us to the Viceroy, for a trial at Goa?

"It was an amusing evening. Hardly a time for weighty diplomatic exchange. And did you enjoy my little present?"

Hawksworth pondered his question for a moment, and the drugged dream of the night before suddenly became real.

"You mean the woman? She was very . . . unusual, very different from the women of England."

"Yes, I daresay. She was one of my final gifts from . . . Agra. I often have her entertain my guests. If you like, you may keep her while you stay with me. I already hear she fancies you. The servingwomen call her Kali, after a goddess from their infidel pantheon. I think that one's their deity of destruction."

"Why did they give her that name?"

"Perhaps she'll tell you herself sometime." Mukarrab Khan gestured for a servant to bring his cloak. "I hope you'll forgive me, but I regret I must abandon you for a time. Among my least pleasant duties is a monthly journey to Cambay, our northern port in this province. It always requires almost a week, but I have no choice. Their Shahbandar would rob the *Moghul's* treasury itself if he were not watched. But I think you'll enjoy yourself in my absence."

"I would enjoy it more if I could be with my men."

"And forgo the endless intrigues my Kali undoubtedly plans for you?" He monitored Hawksworth's unsettled expression. "Or perhaps it's a boy you'd prefer. Very well, if you wish you may even have . . ."

"I'm more interested in the safety of our merchants and seamen. And our cargo. I haven't seen the men since yesterday, at the customs house."

"They're all quite well. I've lodged them with a port official who speaks Portuguese, which your Chief Merchant also seems to understand. I'm told, by the way, he's a thoroughly unpleasant specimen."

"When can I see them?"

"Why any time you choose. You have only to speak to one of the eunuchs. But why trouble yourself today? Spend it here and rest. Perhaps enjoy the grounds and the garden. Tomorrow is time enough to reenter the wearisome halls of commerce."

Hawksworth decided that the time had come to raise the critical question. "And what about the Portugals? And their false charges?"

"I think that tiresome matter can be resolved with time. I've sent notice to the court in Agra, officially, that you wish to travel there. When the reply is received, matters can be settled. In the meantime, I must insist you stay here in the palace. It's a matter of your position. And frankly, your safety. The Portuguese do not always employ upright means to achieve their ends." He tightened his traveling cloak. "Don't worry yourself unduly. Just try to make the most of my humble hospitality. The palace grounds are at your disposal. Perhaps you'll find something in all this to engage your curiosity." Mukarrab Khan brushed away a fly from his cloak. "There's the garden. And if you're bored by that, then you might wish to examine the Persian observatory constructed by my predecessor. You're a seaman and, I presume, a navigator. Perhaps *you* can fathom how it all works. I've never been able to make anything out of it. Ask the servants to show you. Or just have some *tari* wine on the veranda and enjoy the view."

He bowed with official decorum and was gone, his entourage of guards in tow.

Hawksworth turned to see the servants waiting politely. The turbaned man, whose high forehead and noble visage were even more striking now in the direct sunshine, was dictating in a low voice to the others, discreetly translating Mukarrab Khan's orders into Hindi, the language that seemed common to all the servants.

"The palace and its grounds are at your disposal, Sahib." The servant with the large white turban stood waiting. "Our pleasure is to serve you."

"I'd like to be alone for a while. To think about . . . to enjoy the beauty of the garden."

"Of course, Sahib. Perhaps I could have the honor of being your guide."

"I think I'd prefer to see it alone."

The servant's dismay was transparent, but he merely bowed and immediately seemed to dissolve into the marble porticoes of the veranda, as did all the others.

Hawksworth watched in amazement. They really *do* follow orders. Now if I can start to figure out this place. I don't need guides. All I need are my eyes. And luck.

The garden spread out before him. Unlike the closely clipped geometry of the courtyard he had seen the night before, this was less formal and more natural, with a long waterway receding into the horizon. The pond was flanked by parallel arbors along each side, shading wide, paved walkways. He noticed there were no flowers, the main focus in an English garden, only gravel walks and the marble-tiled watercourse. The sense was one of sublime control.

Several dark-skinned gardeners in loincloths were wading knee-deep in the shallow reservoir, adjusting the flow from bubbling fountains that spewed from its surface at geometrically regular spacings, while others were intently pruning—in what seemed a superfluous, almost compulsive act—the already immaculate hedges.

As Hawksworth walked past, self-consciously trying to absorb a sense of place, the gardeners appraised him mutely with quick, flicking sweeps of their eyes. But none made any move to acknowledge his presence.

The sun burned through the almost limitless sky, whose blue was polished to a ceramic glaze, and the air was clean and perfumed with nectar. The garden lay about him like a mosaic of naturalism perfected. Through the conspicuous hand of man, nature had been coerced, or charmed, to exquisite refinement.

The gravel pathway ended abruptly as he reached the pond's far shore, terminated by a row of marble flagstones. Beyond lay geometrical arbors of fruit-laden trees—mangoes, apples, pears, lemons, and even oranges. Hawksworth tightened his new robe about his waist and entered one of the orchard's many pathways, marveling.

I've found the Garden of Eden.

The rows of trees spread out in perfect regularity, squared as carefully as the columns of the palace verandas and organized by species of fruit. As he explored the man-made forest, he began to find its regularity satisfying and curiously calming. Then in the distance, over the treetops, a high stone wall came into view, and from beyond could be heard the splashes of men laboring in the moat. He realized he had reached the farthest extent of the palace grounds.

As he neared the wall, the orchard gave way to an abandoned clearing in whose center stood a moss-covered marble stairway projecting upward into space, leading nowhere. The original polish on its steps was now buried in layers of dust and overgrowth.

Was there once a villa here? But where's the . . . ?

Then he saw the rest. Curving upward on either side of the stairway was a moss-covered band of marble over two feet wide and almost twenty feet in length, concave, etched, and numbered.

It's some sort of sundial. But it's enormous.

He turned and realized he was standing next to yet another stone instrument, a round plaque in red and white marble, like the dial of a water clock, on which Persian symbols for the zodiac had been inscribed. And beyond that was the remains of a circular building, perforated with dozens of doorways, with a tall pillar in the middle. Next to it was a shallow marble well, half a hemisphere sunk into the ground, with precise gradations etched all across the bottom.

Hawksworth walked in among the marble instruments, his astonishment growing. They were all etched to a precision he had never before seen in stone.

This observatory is incredible. The sundial is obvious, even if the purpose of the stairway over its center isn't. But what's the round vertical plaque? Or that round building there, and the curious marble well? Could those be some sort of Persian astrolabe, like navigators use to estimate latitude by fixing the elevation of the sun or stars?

What are they all for? Some to fix stars? Others to predict eclipses? But there has to be more. These are for observation. Which means there have to be charts. Or computations? Or something.

It's said the Persians once mastered a level of mathematics and astronomy far beyond anything known in Europe. Is this some forgotten outpost of that time? Just waiting to be rediscovered?

He turned and examined the instruments again, finding himself wondering for an instant if they could somehow be hoisted aboard the *Discovery* and returned to England.

And if the observatory's still here, perhaps the charts are here somewhere too.

His excitement mounted as he searched the rest of the clearing. Then he saw what he wanted.

It has to be there.

Abutting the stone wall was a small hut of rough-hewn stone, with slatted windows and a weathered wooden door that was wedged ajar, its base permanently encrusted in the dried mud of the rainy season. The wall behind was so weathered that the metal spikes along its top had actually rusted away.

This whole place must have been deserted for years. What a waste.

As he approached the weathered stone hut, he tried to dampen his own hopes.

How can there be anything left? Who knows how long it's been abandoned? And even if there are calculations—or maybe even books!—they're most likely written in Persian. Or Arabic.

He took hold of the rotting door, which left a layer of decaying wood on his hand, and wrenched it open wider, kicking a path for its base through the crusted mud. Then he slipped sideways through the opening.

A stifled, startled cry cut the dense air of the hut, and an oil lamp glowing in the black was smothered in a single movement. Then came a woman's voice.

"You're not allowed here. Servants are forbidden beyond the orchard." She had begun in Persian, then repeated herself in Hindi.

"Who are you?" Hawksworth, startled by the unknown languages, began in English and then switched to Turkish. "I thought . . ."

"The English *feringhi*." The voice suddenly found control, and its Turki was flawless. "You were in the courtyard this morning." She advanced slowly toward the shaft of light from the doorway. "What are you doing here? Khan Sahib could have you killed if the eunuchs discover you."

He watched as her face emerged from the shadows. Then his heart skipped.

It was Shirin.

"The govern . . . Khan Sahib told me about this observatory. He said I . . ."

"Stars do not shine in the day, nor the sun in this room. What are you doing in here?"

"I thought there might be charts, or a library." Hawksworth heard his own voice echo against the raw stone walls of the room. He studied her face in the half light, realizing with a shock that she was even more striking now than in the sunshine of the garden.

"Did he also tell you to plunder all you find in the palace grounds?"

"He said I might find the observatory curious, as a navigator. He was right. But there must be some charts. I thought this room might . . ."

"There are some old papers here. Perhaps he thought this place would keep you occupied. Or test you one more time."

"What do you mean?"

She answered with a hard laugh, then circled Hawksworth and examined him in the glancing morning light. Her dark hair was backlighted now from the sun streaming through the doorway, her gauze head scarf glistening like spun gold.

"Yes, you're a *feringhi*. Just like all the rest." Her eyes flashed. "How many more like you are there in Europe? Enough, I would guess, to amuse our debauched governor forever."

"I didn't double the Cape for his amusement. Or yours." What's the matter? Everybody talks in riddles. "Does this room have a library?"

"Yes, but the writings are in Persian. Which you don't understand."

"How do you know what I understand?"

She looked at him with open astonishment. "Do you suppose there's anyone in the palace who doesn't already know all about you?"

"And what do you know about me?"

Silence held the room for a moment. Then she spoke.

"I know you're a *feringhi*. Like the Portuguese. Here for gold. And . . . the rest." She turned and walked back into the darkness. There was a spark of light and the lamp glowed again. "As for this room, there's nothing here you would understand. And when you return to the palace, and to His Excellency's *affion* and his *nautch* girls, remember what happens to a man who is discovered with another's wife. I will forget I saw you here. You should forget also, if you wish to see the sun tomorrow."

Hawksworth found himself watching her spellbound, almost not hearing her words. He stood motionless for a moment, then walked directly toward her, trying not to feel self-conscious in his new Moghul clothes. "I want to talk with you. To find out what's going on. I'll begin with this place. It's an observatory, or was. What harm can there be in looking around this room?"

She stared at him without moving. "You certainly have a *feringhi's* manner. If you won't leave, then I'll ask *you* some questions. What do *you* say is your reason for coming to India? It's rumored you're here for the English king."

"What else have you heard?"

"Other things as well." She moved closer and her perfume enveloped him. Her eyes were intense, almost overwhelming the jewel at her throat. "But I'd like to hear them from you. There's much dismay about you, about the battle, about the letter."

Hawksworth studied her wistfully. "You know about the letter?"

"Of course. Everyone knows." She sighed at his naïveté. "The contents of your chest were examined very carefully last night . . . but no one dared touch the seal on the letter, for fear of the *Moghul*. Is it true the English king may send an armada to attack Goa?"

"And if it were?"

"It could make a great deal of difference. To many people here."

"Who?"

"People who matter."

"The only one who should matter is the *Moghul*."

She laughed again. "He's the very last one who matters. I see you comprehend very little." She paused and examined him closely. "But you're an interesting man. We all listened to you play the English sitar last night. And today the first place you chose to come was here. You're the first *feringhi* ever to seek out this place, which was once famous throughout India. Did you truly come here this morning just to learn?"

"I haven't learned very much so far. At least in this room." He looked about them, noticing for the first time a small table on which there was a book and fresh writings. "You've not told what *you're* doing here. Or why you can come here when the servants are forbidden."

"Servants once tried to steal some of the marble steps for a house. But the reason I come here is not really your concern, Captain Hawksworth. . . ." She caught his startled look and laughed. "Of course I know your name. I also know you should learn not to drink *bhang* with Kali. She's more than your equal."

Hawksworth stifled his embarrassment and tried to ignore the barb. "There surely must be charts here. What harm if I merely look around?"

Shirin stiffened. "Not now. Not today. You have to leave."

"But *are* there calculations, or charts?"

"More than likely. But I told you they're in Persian."

"Then maybe you could translate."

"I could. But not today. I've told you, you have to leave. Really you must." She pushed the door open wider and stood waiting.

"I'll be back." He paused in the doorway and turned. "Will you be here tomorrow?"

"Possibly."

"Then I'll be back for sure."

She looked at him and shook her head resignedly. "You truly don't realize how dangerous it is for you to come here."

"Are you afraid?"

"I'm always afraid. You should be too." She studied him in the sunshine, examining his eyes, and for a moment her face softened slightly. "But if you do come, will you bring your English sitar? I'd like very much to hear it once more."

"And what will you do for me in return?"

She laughed. "I'll try to excavate some musty Persian books here that might tell you something about the observatory. But remember. No one must ever know. Now, please." She urged him out, then reached and pulled the door tightly closed.

Hawksworth suddenly realized the heat had grown intense, and now the sun cut a sharp line down the face of the red marble dial, telling that mid-morning approached. He examined the dial quickly and then turned to look again at the stone hut.

With the door closed, the ramshackle hut again looked completely deserted.

What in Christ's name can she be doing? No matter, she's astonishing. And there's something in the way she handles herself. Little wonder she was the favorite concubine, or whatever they call it, of the *Moghul*. And it's easy to see why his queen married her off to Mukarrab Khan and sent them both here to get her out of the way. A clever way to banish . . .

Hawksworth froze.

That's the word the pilot Karim used! From the Quran. "As for women from whom you fear rebellion, *banish* them to . . . beds apart."

Could this be the woman he meant? But what rebellion? Whatever's going on, nobody's talking. All I see are armed guards. And fear. This palace is like a jewel-set dagger—exquisite, and deadly.

He stared again at the moss-covered marble instruments.

But I'll be back. If she'll be here, absolutely nothing could stop me.

CHAPTER NINE

The two *chitahs* tensed at the same instant and pulled taut the chains on their jewel-studded collars. They were tawny, dark-spotted Indian hunting leopards, and they rode in carpeted litters, one on each side of the elephant's back. Each wore a brocade saddlecloth signifying its rank, and now both began to flick the black-and-white striped tips of their tails in anticipation.

Prince Jadar caught their motion and reined in his dun stallion; the

bright morning sunshine glanced off his freshly oiled olive skin and high-
lighted the crevices of his lean angular face and his tightly trimmed short
beard. He wore a forest-green hunting turban, secured with a heavy strand of
pearls, and a dark green jacket emblazoned with his own royal crest. His
fifty-man Rajput guard had drawn alongside, and their horses tossed their
heads and pawed impatiently, rattling the arrows in the brocade quivers by
each man's saddle.

Then Jadar spotted the *nilgai*, large bovine Indian deer, grazing in a
herd upwind near the base of a low-lying hill. With a flick of his hand he
signaled the keepers who rode alongside the *chitahs* to begin removing the
leopards' saddlecloths. He watched as first the male and then the female
shook themselves and stretched their paws in readiness.

"Fifty rupees the male will make the first kill." Jadar spoke quietly to
Vasant Rao, the moustachioed young Rajput captain who rode alongside.
The commander of the prince's personal guard, he was the only man in
India Jadar trusted fully.

"Then give me two hundred on the female, Highness."

"A hundred. And half the hides for your regiment's shield maker." Jadar
turned toward the waiting keepers. "Release the female. Then count to a
hundred and release the male."

In moments the *chitahs* were bulleting toward the unsuspecting deer,
darting from bush to bush, occasionally kicking up dust with their forefeet
and hind legs to create camouflage. Then, as they approached the final clearing, they suddenly parted—the female to the north, the male to the south.
Seconds later, as though on some private signal, the female sprang. She
seemed to cover the remaining twenty yards in less than a second, and before
the *nilgai* realized she was there, she had already pawed down a bleating
straggler.

The striped ears of the other *nilgai* shot erect at the sound, and the
herd panicked, sweeping blindly away from her—and directly toward the
cover where the male crouched. He waited coolly, and then, as the deer
darted by, pounced. What followed was a fearsome devastation, as he
brought down one after another of the confused prey with his powerful
claws.

"The female killed first, Highness. I assume our bet was in gold coins,
not silver." Vasant Rao laughed lightly and turned to study the brooding
man at his side. Can it be true what many suspect about the prince? he
again found himself wondering. That he choses his strategy for a campaign
from the final hunt of his *chitahs*?

But what strategy is left for us? The Deccanis have already reclaimed
the city of Ahmadnagar, deep in their territory, and once again made it their
rebel capital. They drove the Moghul garrison north to the fort at Burhanpur, and now they threaten that city as well, the most important station in

the vital route between Agra and Surat. We haven't the men and horse to turn them back. Not this time.

This was Prince Jadar's second campaign in the Deccan, India's revolt-torn central plains, which lay far south of Agra and east of the port of Surat, and the second time he had led his army to regain cities lost to Malik Ambar, the Abyssinian adventurer and military genius who periodically rose to lead the Deccan against Moghul rule. The Deccan had never been secure, even under the *Moghul*'s father, Akman, but under Arangbar it had become a burial ground of reputation. One of the *Moghul*'s finest generals, whose dispatches from Ahmadnagar only the previous year had boasted that the Deccan was finally subdued, now cowered in the fortress at Burhanpur. Arangbar had no choice but to send Jadar again.

"Did you see how they planned their attack?" Jadar fingered the edges of his short beard, then pointed. "She drove them toward his trap. By attacking the weak, she frightened the strong, who flew to their doom."

"We're not facing *nilgai*, Highness." Vasant Rao shifted in his saddle to face the prince and shielded his eyes against the sun. "And our position is much worse than on the last campaign. This time we have only eighteen thousand men, all encamped here at Ujjain, all weary to their bones from our siege at the Kangra, north in the Punjab, and then the long march down country. While Malik Ambar waits rested and secure in Ahmadnagar, his own capital, a two months' march south."

"We'll bring Ambar to terms just as before, three years ago. By fear."

Jadar watched as the keepers began measuring the rations of meat to reward the *chitahs*. And he reflected over the secret envoy received early that morning from the commander of the fortress at Mandu, the northern outpost of the Deccan.

"Your Highness is respectfully advised the situation is worse, much worse, than told in the reports sent by Ghulam Adl." They were alone in Jadar's tent and the envoy was on his knees, prostrate, terrified at his obligation to bring ill tidings to the son of the *Moghul*. Ghulam Adl was the general in charge of the Deccan, who had abandoned Ahmadnagar to Malik Ambar and retreated north to Burhanpur. His official reports still maintained an air of bravado, claiming a few reinforcements were all that was required to drive the rebels to final extinction.

"We have asked Ghulam Adl for troops to help defend Mandu, but he cannot leave Burhanpur," the envoy continued. "The Deccanis have surrounded the city, but they do not trouble themselves with a siege. They know he cannot move. So they have sent eight thousand light cavalry, Maratha irregulars, north across the Narbada River to plunder outlying districts. They are approaching Mandu, and will be at the fortress within the week."

"Why doesn't Ghulam Adl call up troops from among the *mansabdars*. They've all been granted their annual allowance for maintenance of cavalry."

Mansabdars were nobles of the Moghul empire who had been given rank by the *Moghul* and were allowed to collect revenue from a specified number of estates and villages, allotted lands called *jagirs*, as a reward for service and loyalty. They collected taxes for the Imperial treasury in Agra, which allowed them a portion to maintain cavalry and equipage at the ready. Assignment of a *jagir* always carried the responsibility of maintaining a specified number of troops and cavalry, which they were obliged to muster when requested by the *Moghul*.

"The *mansabdars* have no men to muster, may it please Your Highness." The envoy's face was buried in the carpet, showing to Jadar only the dust-covered back of his turban. "Conditions have been severe over the past year. Crops have been bad, and many *mansabdars* could not collect taxes because of the Deccani raids. Many have not paid their cavalry for over a year. The *mansabdars* still feed the horses that have been branded and placed in their care. But they have not fed the men who must ride. Most of those have returned to their villages. There can be no army without coin to lure them back. The *mansabdars* are fearful of Malik Ambar now, and many have secretly agreed with him not to muster even the troops they still have."

"How many Deccani troops are encamped around Burhanpur?"

"Our spies report as many as eighty thousand, Highness. Ghulam Adl dares not leave the fort in the center of the city. He has no more than five thousand men still remaining loyal, and his supplies are short."

Jadar had ordered immediate solitary confinement for the envoy, lest the news reach the camp. Now, watching his *chitahs* feed, he calculated his next move.

I have to requisition silver coin from the treasury at Agra, and hope a supply caravan can still get through. In the meantime I'll muster the remaining cavalry from the *mansabdars*, on the threat their *jagirs* will be confiscated if they fail to deliver. It won't raise many men, but it will slow defections.

But if we're to recall the men still loyal, we must have silver. To raise the thirty thousand men we need, men who've not been paid for a year, will require at least five million rupees, fifty *lakhs*. I must have it by the time we reach Burhanpur. If we can hold that city, we can raise the army from there.

"Malik Ambar sued for peace three years ago because his alliance came apart." Vasant Rao spoke again, watching Jadar carefully, knowing that the prince was deeply troubled, had imprisoned a courier that very morning—for which there could only be one reason—then released pigeons that flew north.

"And his alliance will come apart again. If we sow enough fear." Jadar seemed annoyed at the delay as the waiting *chitahs* were reharnessed and the last carcasses of blue *nilgai* were loaded onto the ox-drawn wagons for return to the camp. "You still haven't learned to think like a *chitah*."

Jadar signaled the hunt was finished and wheeled his horse back toward the camp. Vasant Rao rode a few paces behind, asking himself how long that regal head would remain on those royal shoulders.

You're threatened now on every side. You cannot be as oblivious as you seem.

He thought back over Prince Jadar's career. Of the *Moghul's* four sons, Prince Jadar was the obvious one to succeed. Jadar's elder brother Khusrav had been blinded by the *Moghul* years before for attempting a palace revolt. Jadar's brother Parwaz, also older than the prince, was a notorious drunkard and unacceptably dissolute, even by the lax standards of the *Moghul's* court. And Jadar's younger brother, Allaudin, was the handsome but witless son of a concubine, who well deserved his secret nickname, *Nashudani*, "the good-for-nothing." Since there was no law in India that the oldest must automatically succeed, power devolved to the fittest. Only Jadar, son of a royal Rajput mother, could lead an army, or rule India. Among the *Moghul's* four sons, he was the obvious, deserving heir.

But ability alone was never enough to ensure success in the mire of palace intrigue. One must also have a powerful friend.

For years Prince Jadar had the most powerful friend of all.

The grooming of Jadar for office had begun over five years earlier, when he was taken under the protection of Queen Janahara. She had made herself the guardian of Jadar's interests at court; and two years ago she had induced the *Moghul* to elevate Jadar's *mansab*, his honorary rank, to twelve thousand *zat*. In income and prestige he had soared far beyond his brothers.

As is always the case, Jadar was expected to repay his obligation. On the day he ascended to the throne and assumed power from the ailing, opium-sotted Arangbar, he was expected to share that power with Queen Janahara.

But their unofficial alliance had begun to go wrong. Very wrong. And what had gone wrong was the most obvious problem of all. Jadar had lived half his life in army camps, fighting the *Moghul's* wars because he was the only son who could fight them, and he no longer saw any reason to relinquish his battle-earned inheritance to the queen.

What will the queen do? Vasant Rao asked himself again. I know she has turned on the prince. I know she tried to marry her Persian daughter to Jadar's blinded brother Khusrav, but Jadar discovered this and demanded Khusrav be sent out of Agra, to be kept in confinement by a raja loyal to the prince. But the queen is still in Agra, and sooner or later she will produce another successor, a creature she can dominate. Her task will be easy if Jadar fails in this campaign.

"I have reports Maratha irregulars may be at the fort at Mandu within a week." Jadar broke the silence between them as they rode. The noisy Rajput horsemen rode discreetly well behind, cursing, laughing, wagering. The flawless blue sky seemed to cloud as Jadar spoke. "Tell me what you would do?"

"Strike camp and march south. We have no choice."

"Sometimes you Rajputs show less wit than your monkey god, Hanu-manji." Jadar laughed good-naturedly. "You learned nothing from the hunt today. Don't you see that would merely scatter them? They'll never dare meet us if we march in force. They'll only stage small raids. Harass our baggage train. No, we must do just the opposite." Jadar reined in his horse, turned to Vasant Rao, and lowered his voice. "Think like a *chitah* for once, not like an impulsive Rajput. We'll send a small cavalry force only—five hundred horse, you will help me pick them—who will disperse, ride separately, never show their numbers. Like a *chitah* stalks. No supply contingent. No elephants. No wagons. And, after the Marathas have set their siege at Mandu, our cavalry will quietly group and attack their flank. As they fall back, which they always do when facing a disciplined unit, the cavalry in the fort will ride out in force, forming the second arm of a pincer. And that will be the last we see of Malik Ambar's famous Maratha irregulars. They'll return to pillaging baggage trains and helpless villages."

"And after that?"

"We'll march directly on Burhanpur. We should reach it in less than a month."

"The Marathas will begin to harass our supply trains as soon as we cross the Narbada River. If they don't attack us *while* we cross."

"After Mandu, that's the one thing they will *not* do. Remember the *chitahs*. The Marathas will never know where our Mandu cavalry may be waiting in ambush."

"And when we reach Burhanpur?"

"We'll make our camp there, and muster cavalry from all the *mansabdars*." Jadar passed over how he intended to do this. "That will be the end of Ambar's many alliances. We'll have the men we need to march in force on the south, on to Ahmadnagar, within the week. And Malik Ambar will sue for peace and return the territory he's seized, just like before."

Vasant Rao nodded in silent acknowledgment, asking himself what the prince was withholding. The strategy was far too straightforward for Jadar.

The camp was coming into view now. A vast movable city, it was easily several miles in circuit. Even from afar, however, Jadar's massive central tent dominated. It was bright red and stationed in the center of the *gulal bar*, a restricted central zone almost two hundred yards on the side that formed the focal point of the camp. Behind Jadar's tent, separated by a figured satin partition, were the red chintz tents of the women, where his first wife, Mumtaz, and her attendants stayed. Directly in front of Jadar's tent was a canopied platform with four massive corner pillars, called the *sarachah*, where Jadar held private briefings.

The entire *gulal bar* was sealed from common view by a high cloth wall. Near the entrance to Jadar's enclosure was the camp artillery, including the cannon, and the tents of the lead horses and war elephants. Its entry was guarded by mounted horsemen, and next to these were the tents for Jadar's leopards. Around the perimeter were the striped tents of the nobles and officers, whose respective colors flew above for easy identification. And spreading out from each officer's tent were the tents of his men, their wives, and their bazaar. The camp itself was laid out with such consistent precision that a soldier might easily find his tent in total darkness, regardless of where the army might be.

As Jadar dismounted at the entry to the *gulal bar* and strode toward his tent, his mind sorted through the moves that lay ahead. He had notified the *Moghul* of the envoy's secret report and asked for five million rupees in silver coin. It was the price for the Deccan. Surely he could not refuse. Arangbar's own administrators, who were supposed to monitor the *mansabdars*, were to blame.

There were also other, new and disquieting, complexities. Word had come through Surat only the day before that the Portuguese were secretly planning to arm Malik Ambar. Why? It was common enough knowledge they feared and hated Jadar, because he distrusted all Christians and said so. And they certainly were aware that if he should someday unite the rebel-infested province of Gujarat, where their ports of Daimon and Diu were situated, he would undoubtedly try to regain these ports for India. But they would not dare to openly, or even secretly, support rebels within the Moghul empire unless they were sure there would be no reprisals from Agra. Which meant they had powerful accomplices in court. Accomplices who would venture to endanger the empire itself to ruin Jadar.

Whose interests in Agra were served if the Deccan remained in turmoil? If Jadar were kept occupied and harried in the south?

The question virtually answered itself.

If this were not perplexing enough, news had arrived two days before telling of an incredible incident. Two merchant frigates of another European nation, calling themselves English, had appeared off the bar of Surat. And humiliated four Portuguese warships. Jadar had released pigeons for Surat immediately, ordering that the English be protected until he could determine their intentions.

The dispatch received the following morning, yesterday, reported that his orders had been timely. A Portuguese ambush of the English as they came up the Tapti River had been averted, by Rajputs using arrows stolen from the governor's own guard. And this morning there had been another message from Surat, with news that the governor had sent the *Moghul* a dispatch claiming credit for the action—this only *after* he discovered the English captain had gifts for Arangbar!

But who knew the intentions of the captain of this English fleet? Or the content of a letter he had brought for the *Moghul*? Reports said only that he was "quartered" in the governor's palace. Where he could no longer be protected.

His eunuchs bowed and relayed an urgent message from Mumtaz. His wife begged to receive His Highness the moment he returned.

Without entering his own tent, Jadar proceeded through the circle of guards protecting the women's quarters. Mumtaz was waiting, surrounded by two of her women and the now-constant midwife. She was almost to term with Jadar's third child. The first two had been daughters. His first thought when he saw her was that this birth *must* be male. Merciful Allah, make this a son.

Mumtaz's gleaming black hair had been tightly braided, and she wore a shawl and trousers of gold-threaded silk. She had a pronounced fondness for gold and silk: few other luxuries were to be found in the army camps that had been her home for most of their marriage. Mumtaz's features were delicate, with high Persian cheeks, and she was well over thirty—the age at which most Muslim women ceased to interest their mates. But she had found ways to remain the center of Jadar's life, if not dominate it.

The flash of her eyes told Jadar she was in an extreme temper.

"Pigeons arrived just after you left. The report from Agra is astonishing."

"What 'report' do you mean? Do you and your women receive my dispatches now?"

"Which are rarely worth the bother. No, I receive my own. From Father." Mumtaz was the daughter of Nadir Sharif, prime minister of the Moghul empire and brother of Queen Janahara. "I had the sense to leave him pigeons for here at Ujjain. And also for Burhanpur . . . which may prove to be vital for you, assuming that city is not overrun by Deccanis by the time you reach it."

"What message did Nadir Sharif ever send that wasn't dictated by our noble queen?"

"You're a fool not to trust him. But you'd do well to begin. And soon." Mumtaz's eyes snapped momentary fire, matching the hard red jewel on her forehead, and she eased herself slowly onto a well-traveled velvet bolster to lighten the weight of the child. "I think you'll discover your many friends may be difficult to find if we ever return to the capital."

"Come to the point. I want to see the *chitahs* into their tent. They killed well today." Jadar was always amused by Mumtaz's temper. He had long ago despaired of receiving proper respect from her. She defied him exactly the way Janahara defied the *Moghul*. And he delighted in it. Perhaps all Persian wives were incorrigible. Perhaps it was a racial trait.

"Very well. You should be pleased to know that His Majesty has already forgotten you exist. He has agreed to the queen's outrageous scheme. An affront to sense, but it will be the end of you nonetheless."

"Agreed to what?"

"The very marriage I warned you about, but you wouldn't listen. You were too clever. Yes, you were brilliant. You sent the wrong brother away from Agra. You sent Khusrav, the competent one. You should have sent Allaudin."

"I don't believe it."

"I do. And I told you it would happen. The queen has foisted her scrawny offspring, the simpering Princess Layla, onto Allaudin. But it's the perfect match. The *Moghul*'s youngest son, the notorious 'good-for-nothing,' betrothed to that fumbling little sparrow. Both weak and useless."

"What could Allaudin possibly do? Even Arangbar realizes he's incompetent."

"But Arangbar will soon be dead. So what he knows won't matter. It's perfect for the queen. She'll rule them both. In the meantime, she'll make sure you're nowhere near Agra. Your next appointment will probably be the Punjab, or perhaps the Himalayas. Where you can chase yak with your leopards." Mumtaz could scarcely contain her anger and frustration. "The time will come, and soon, when the *Moghul* will chance his twenty glasses of wine and his twelve grains of opium one night too many. And the next day, while you're somewhere sporting with your *chitahs*, she'll summon her lackey general Inayat Latif and his Bengal *mansabdars* to Agra. And declare Allaudin the next *Moghul*."

Jadar was stunned. Allaudin was incapable of anything, except bowing to the queen's orders like a hand puppet. Once *Moghul*, he certainly could not rule. She would rule for him. Or probably eliminate him entirely after a few months.

So Janahara had finally made her move. To challenge Prince Jadar, the son who had earned the throne, for his rightful place. The battle had been joined.

"So what do you propose to do? She waited just long enough to trap you in the Deccan." Mumtaz's fury was turning to despair. "If you go back now, you'll be accused of abandoning Burhanpur. If you march on south, you'll be unable to return for months. And by that time Allaudin will be married. Father said she has convinced the *Moghul* to give him a personal *mansab* rank of eight thousand *zat* and a horse rank of four thousand *suwar*. Allaudin, who scarcely knows a bow from a wine bowl, will now have his own cavalry."

Jadar was looking at her, but he no longer heard.

This changes everything. There'll be no silver. The queen will see to that.

And no silver means no troops can be recalled from the Deccan *mansab-dars*.

Which means we lose the Deccan. But she'd gladly give the Deccan to destroy me.

Jadar looked at Mumtaz and smiled. "Yes, I must do something. But right now I'll see my *chitahs* fed." And he turned and strode briskly back toward his tent.

A dense mantle of evening smoke enveloped the camp as the three generals passed through the entry of the *gulal bar*. They advanced to the front of the *sarachah* platform and halted to wait for Jadar. Each had brought a silver cup, as Jadar had instructed.

All three were seasoned military leaders. Abdullah Khan, a young Moghul warrior, had been promoted to a rank of three thousand *suwar* after the successful siege at the northern fortress of Kangra. Under the prince he had risen from the rank of foot soldier to cavalry, and now he commanded his own division. The next was Abul Hasan, a cool-headed Afghan strategist with rank of five thousand *suwar*, who had led Prince Jadar to his first victory in the Deccan three years before. Finally there was Raja Vikramajit, a bearded Rajput of royal blood, who led the Hindus. He scorned matchlocks and fought only with his sword, and he was the bravest man in battle that Jadar had ever known.

Moments later Prince Jadar emerged through the smoke, carrying his heavy sword and accompanied by Vasant Rao. A servant trailed after them bearing a crystal decanter of wine and two silver goblets on a tray.

The prince assumed his seat in the center of the platform and ordered the servant to place the decanter on a small table by his side. Then he motioned away the servant and all the surrounding guards.

"I propose we all take a glass of wine to clear our thoughts. It's Persian, and I had it cooled in the saltpeter tent especially for this evening."

Jadar personally poured wine for each of the men, then filled the two goblets on the tray for Vasant Rao and for himself.

"I hereby propose a toast to Ahmadnagar, which Malik Ambar now calls his own capital. And to its recapture within a hundred days."

The men raised their goblets and drank in silence. Skepticism filled their eyes.

Jadar looked at them and smiled. "You do not agree? Then let me tell you more. The situation is very bad. How bad even you do not yet know. But battles are more than a matter of numbers. They are a test of the will to win. That's why I called you here tonight." Jadar paused. "But first, is the wine to your liking?"

The men nodded silent assent.

"Good. Drink deeply, for none of us will drink again until we drink in Ahmadnagar. Now I will take your cups."

Jadar reached for each man's cup individually and placed them in a row alongside the tray, together with his own and that of Vasant Rao. Then he laid his own cup on its side on the tray and slowly drew his heavy sword from its scabbard. With a fierce swing he sliced the cup in half. Then the next cup, and the next, until all were destroyed. The men watched him spellbound.

"Assemble your ranks in the bazaar at midnight. In full battle dress. I will address them. And at dawn, we march."

Jadar rose and as quickly as he had come disappeared into the darkness.

Battle gear—helmets, bucklers, pikes, swords, muskets—glistened in the torchlight as Jadar rode a fully armored war elephant slowly down the center of the main bazaar. The bristling infantry, arrayed in rows on either side, watched him expectantly. A midnight muster was unheard of. But rumors had already swept the camp telling of the pending marriage of the queen's daughter to Allaudin. All knew Jadar had been betrayed. And with him, all of them as well.

Then they noticed carts following him, with barrels of wine from Jadar's tent. When the prince reached the center of the bazaar, he raised his arms for silence.

For a moment all that could be heard was the neigh of horses from the stables, and the cries of infants in the far reaches of the camp.

He began in Urdu, a hybrid camp tongue of Persian and Hindi, his voice ringing toward Abul Hasan's Muslim troops.

"Tonight we are many." Jadar paused deliberately. "But in battle the many are nothing. In battle there is only the one. Each of you is that one." Again a pause. Then he shouted in a voice that carried to the far hills. "Is there a Believer among us tonight who would fight to the death for our victory?"

A roar of assent sounded from the men.

"Will you swear it? On the Holy Quran?"

This time the roar shook the tent poles of the bazaar.

"Is there one who would not?"

Silence.

Suddenly Jadar turned to the troops of Moghul lineage and switched his language to exquisite Persian.

"Some here tonight swear to embrace death itself for our victory. But I know not the will of all. Is there among you a man who would give his life for us?"

Again a roar of assent.

"What man will swear it?"

The roar seemed to envelop the camp.

Without pausing, Jadar turned to the Rajput contingent, addressing them easily in their native Rajasthani.

"Does any among you know how to fight?"

Cheers.

"Does any know how to die?"

More cheers. And then the Rajputs began banging their swords on their bucklers. Jadar bellowed above the sudden din.

"I know Hindus cannot take an oath. But if you could, would it be to fight to the death for our victory?"

Bedlam seized the camp. And the chant "Jadar-o-Akbar," Jadar is Great, swept through the ranks. Jadar let the chant continue for a time, and as he listened, he saw that Mumtaz and her women had appeared at the gateway of the *gulal bar*, as he had instructed them. All activity had ceased in the camp, and even in the far background the women had gathered in the shadows of the tents, listening intently. Then Jadar motioned for silence and continued.

"Tonight we each will make a pledge. I to you. You to me. First my pledge to you."

Jadar commanded his elephant to kneel, and he dismounted and walked directly to the waiting wagons containing his wine barrels. He was handed a silver-handled battle axe, and with a powerful overhand swing he shattered the first barrel. Then he signaled his waiting guard, and in moments every barrel had been axed. The center of the bazaar ran red, and the air was filled with the wine's sweet Persian perfume.

Then he motioned toward the entry of the *gulal bar* and his women emerged, followed by an elephant whose *howdah*, the livery on its back, was filled with silver utensils. When the procession reached the clearing where Jadar stood, the elephant's *mahout* commanded it to kneel.

Without a word Jadar walked directly to the *howdah*. As though meeting an enemy in ambush, he suddenly drew his long sword and swung it through the livery, leaving a wide gash in its embroidered side. A glittering array of silver and gold plate, goblets, jewelry poured onto the ground. With a single motion he sheathed the sword and again took the axe.

While the assembled camp watched spellbound, he quickly, methodically, smashed each of the silver and gold objects into small shards. Then he broke the silver handle of the axe and again mounted the elephant.

"My pledge to you." His voice pierced the stunned silence of the camp as he repeated each sentence in three languages. "My pledge to you is not to touch wine, not to lie with woman, not to look on silver or gold until we have taken Ahmadnagar."

The camp seemed to come apart with the cheer that followed, and again came the chant "Jadar-o-Akbar," "Jadar-o-Akbar." The sound was as one voice, and now even the distant hills echoed back the sound. Again Jadar stopped them.

"Your pledge to me must be the same. And together we will take Ahmadnagar in a hundred days. By the head of the Prophet I swear it to you."

Again the chant. And again Jadar stopped them.

"Tonight I offer to fight for you. You must be ready to fight for me. And each must hold the other to his pledge."

More cheers.

"I have spilled my wine. I will stay apart from my women. I have smashed my gold and silver. I will give it to you. Each tent will have a shard. But my eyes must never see it again."

The roar of approval was deafening.

"That is my pledge. You must also give me yours. Leave your women in their tents and lie beside me under the stars. Empty your wine flasks into the Narbada River as we cross. As your oath to fight to the death. And all your silver, that of your vessels, that on your saddles, that on your women, must be brought here tonight. Mark it with your seal, and leave it under guard in my own wagons, away from all eyes, until the day we reach Ahmadnagar. Then we will drink wine, we will have women, we will wear our finest in victory."

Jadar paused dramatically. "Tonight we are many. Tomorrow we are one. We march at sunrise!"

The cheers began again, and immediately the pile of silver started to grow. Muslim nobles began bringing silver-trimmed saddles, plates, even jewelry. But the most silver came from the Hindu infantry, as their women were stripped of the silver bracelets and massive silver anklets that had been their dowries.

Jadar sat unmoving on his elephant as the men began to come forward with items of silver. Soon there was a line stretching into the dark of the tents. He watched the pile growing, and his calculations began.

Will it be enough? The weight must be enough or the Shahbandar, motherless thief that he is, will never agree. But I think we will have it.

He thought back over the plan. It had required almost the entire afternoon to refine. But when he had convinced himself that it would succeed, he had posted the pigeons to Surat.

Where, he had asked himself, can I find fifty *lakhs* of silver, five million rupees, within a month, and have them at Burhanpur when we arrive? I'll not squeeze a copper *pice*, penny, from Agra.

If not Agra, where?

And slowly in his mind a form had taken shape. He had examined it, almost touched it, puzzled over it. And then he knew what it was.

The mint at Surat. Where foreign coin is melted and recast as rupees.

Fifty *lakhs* of silver rupees would scarcely be missed. Especially if the Shah-bandar would allow his minters to work a normal day. The backlog of foreign coin he holds unmelted, creating an artificial shortage of silver, would easily cover fifty *lakhs* of rupees. I need only borrow what I need, and with it buy back into service the cavalry I need to reclaim the Deccan.

The Shahbandar.

But will he do it?

He will. If I can show him collateral.

I don't have enough collateral. Not in my own funds. Not even in the local treasuries.

But there must be enough silver in eighteen thousand tents to assemble five million rupees.

I will hold it, and give *him* a note of obligation using it as collateral. If we reach Ahmadnagar, I will squeeze the five million rupees many times over from every traitorous *mansabdar* I do not hang. I will confiscate their *jagir* estates and let them buy them back. I can easily confiscate enough to return the Shahbandar his loan, and then my men will have back their silver.

If we do not reach Ahmadnagar, it will be because we are dead. So what will it matter? We will make an oath to reach the city or die.

Only one problem remains.

How to move the coin from Surat to Burhanpur. Secretly. No one must know where it came from or that it's being transferred. But a train with fifty *lakhs* of rupees must be heavily guarded. And the guards will betray its value.

Unless there can be some other reason for a heavily guarded train from Surat to Burhanpur. A reason that would not automatically evoke suspicion. Possibly a person of importance. Someone whom all India knows cannot be touched. Someone important to the *Moghul*.

And then the perfect answer came. The most obvious answer of all. Who will soon be traveling from Surat to Burhanpur, en route to Agra, under safe conduct of the *Moghul?*

The Englishman.

The infidel *feringhi* need never know. That with him will be the silver that will save Prince Jadar.

CHAPTER TEN

Brian Hawksworth stepped lightly off the prow of the barge as it eased into the riverbank and worked his way through the knee-deep tidal mud onto the sandy shore. Even here, across the harbor, the water still stank of the sewers of Surat. Then he turned and surveyed the sprawling city, back across the broad estuary, astonished that they could have crossed the harbor so easily on nothing more substantial than a wide raft of boards lashed with rope, what the Indians called a bark.

Ahead, waiting on the shore, was a line of loaded bullock carts—conveyances with two wooden wheels higher than a man's head, a flat bed some six feet wide, and a heavy bamboo pole for a tongue—each yoked to two tall, hump-backed gray cattle with conspicuous ribs. The carts stretched down the muddy road that emerged from the tangle of coastal scrub and were piled to overflowing with rolls of English wool cloth. The turbaned drivers now shouted Hindi obscenities as they walked alongside and lashed the sullen cattle into place for unloading. As Hawksworth watched, the porters who had ridden with him splashed their way toward the shore and began driving stakes to secure the mooring lines of the bark. Wool would be ferried across the harbor and cotton brought back with each trip.

Then Hawksworth caught sight of George Elkington's ragged hat bobbing in the midday sunshine as the Chief Merchant and his aide, Humphrey Spencer, climbed down from their two-wheeled Indian coach, drawn by two white oxen, which had been loaned by Mukarrab Khan. Farther down the line of carts was a detail of English seamen, led by red-haired Mackintosh, and all carrying muskets, who had walked the fifteen-mile, two-day trek to guard the cargo.

The trading season was well underway, and over the past three weeks a motley assemblage of cargo vessels from the length of the Indian Ocean had appeared downriver at the bar to commence unlading. Foreign traders normally transported goods inland to Surat on the barks that plied the Tapti between the port and the shallow bar at the river mouth. But these vessels had arrived at the bar with the blessings of Portugal, for they all had acquired a Portuguese license and paid duty on their cargo at some Portuguese-controlled tax point.

After evaluating the risk of exposing his English frigates at the bar—where maneuverability was limited and the possibility of Portuguese surprise great—Brian Hawksworth had elected to unlade directly onshore from their protected anchorage north of the river mouth, the cove called Swalley, then haul the goods overland to the banks of the Tapti opposite Surat. There would be no risk of Portuguese interference inland and, once across from the port, the goods could be easily barged to the *maidan*.

He turned again toward the river and examined the town of Surat from his new vantage. It was easy to see now why this location had been chosen for the port, for here the river curved and widened, creating a natural, protected harbor. The most conspicuous landmarks visible from across the harbor were three stone villas along the riverfront, all owned by the Shahbandar, and the square stone fort that stood on the downriver side of the harbor, its heavy ordnance trained perpetually on the water. The fort was surrounded by a moat on three sides and on the fourth by the river. Entry could only be gained through a gate on the riverside, or a drawbridge that connected its entrance to the open *maidan*, the square where traders congregated.

The square had swarmed with merchants and brokers as they passed through, and he had watched as two brokers stood together near its center—one from Ahmedabad, up-country, and the other from Surat—arguing loudly over the price and quality of a pile of indigo. The porters explained that the Surat broker was accusing the other of mixing sand with the indigo to increase its weight, then disguising his deception by also adding enough oil that the indigo would still float on water, the test used to establish purity of the dried extract of the indigo leaf. As the argument grew more vigorous, Hawksworth noticed the men join hands beneath a piece of cloth, where they began negotiating the actual price by means of their fingers, a figure undoubtedly little related to the movement of their tongues.

Now that the high trading season of September–January had begun, Surat's narrow streets were one loud bazaar, swollen to almost two hundred thousand grasping traders, bargaining seamen, hawking merchants. A dozen languages stirred the air as a motley mélange of up-country Indian traders, Arabs, Jains, Parsis, Persians, Jews, Egyptians, Portuguese, and returning Muslim pilgrims—every nationality known to the Indian Ocean—swaggered through the garbage-sodden mud paths called streets.

Hawksworth gazed back at the city and reflected over the curious events of the past three weeks. The English had, inexplicably, been received first with open hostility, and then with suspiciously cordial deference—first by the governor, and afterward by the Shahbandar. Something is very wrong, he told himself. A contest of wills is underway between the Shahbandar, Mirza Nuruddin, and the governor, Mukarrab Khan. And so far, Mukarrab Khan seems to be winning. Or is he?

Six days before, the governor had suddenly reversed his policy of noninterference in port affairs and authorized a license for the English to sell their cargo in Surat and buy Indian goods, something the Shahbandar had found one excuse after another to delay. However, Mukarrab Khan had delivered this license directly to the English, rather than forwarding it to the Shahbandar through normal channels, leaving Brian Hawksworth the unpleasant responsibility of presenting this document to the Shahbandar in person. But the meeting turned out to be nothing like Hawksworth had expected.

"Once more you astound me, Captain." The close, torchlit chamber of the customs house office had fallen expectantly silent as the Shahbandar drew slowly on his *hookah* and squinted with his opaque, glassy eyes at the black seal of Mukarrab Khan affixed to the top of the page. Hawksworth had waited for a glimmer of anger at this insulting breach of port protocol— which surely was Mukarrab Khan's reason for insisting the license be delivered by the English Captain-General. But the Shahbandar's eyes never lost their noncommittal squint. Instead he had turned to Hawksworth with a cordial smile. "Your refusal to negotiate seems to have worked remarkable dispatch with His Excellency's officials. I can't recall ever seeing them act this quickly."

Hawksworth had been amazed. How could Mirza Nuruddin possibly know the terms he had demanded of the governor: produce a license for trade within ten days or the two English frigates would weigh anchor and sail; and accept English sovereigns at bullion value rather than the prevailing discount rate of 4½ percent required to circumvent "minting time," the weeks "required" by the Shahbandar's minters to melt down foreign coin and remint it as Indian rupees.

No one could have been more surprised than Brian Hawksworth when Mukarrab Khan had immediately conceded the English terms and approved the license—valid for sixty days—to land goods, and to buy and sell. Why had the governor agreed so readily, overriding the Shahbandar's dawdling clerks?

"Naturally you'll need an officer here to schedule the river barks." The Shahbandar's voice was even, but Hawksworth thought he sensed an air of tension suddenly grip the room. "Normally barks are reserved weeks in advance now during the high season, but we can always accommodate friends of Mukarrab Khan."

It was then that Hawksworth had told the Shahbandar he would not be bringing cargo up the river, that instead it would be transported overland from their protected anchorage using bullock carts arranged for by Mukarrab Khan.

"The cove you call Swalley is several leagues up the coast, Captain. Foreign cargo has never before been unladed there, nor has it ever been brought overland as you propose." He had seemed genuinely disturbed. "I suggest it's both irregular and unworkable."

"I think you understand why we have to unlade from the cove. The decision is made." Hawksworth tried to keep his voice as firm as that of Mirza Nuruddin. "We'll unload the bullock carts just across the river from the port here, and we'll only need a bark to ferry goods across the harbor."

"As you wish. I'll arrange to have one at your disposal." The Shahbandar drew pensively on the *hookah*, ejecting coils of smoke into the already dense air of the chamber, and examined Hawksworth. Then he continued. "I understand your frigates are some five hundred tons each. Full unlading will require at least three weeks, perhaps four. Is that a reasonable estimate?"

"We'll arrange the scheduling. Why do you ask?"

"Merely for information, Captain." Again the Shahbandar flashed his empty smile. Then he bowed as lightly as protocol would admit and called for a tray of rolled betel leaves, signifying the meeting was ended. As Hawksworth took one, he marveled that he had so quickly acquired a taste for their strange alkaline sweetness. Then he looked again at Mirza Nuruddin's impassive eyes.

Damn him. Does he know what the Portugals are planning? And was he hoping we'd be caught unlading in the shallows at the river mouth? He knows I've just spoiled their plans.

As he had passed back through the customs shed headed toward the *maidan* and sunshine, Hawksworth could feel the hostile stares. And he knew the reason.

The new English visitors had already made an unforgettable impression on the town of Surat. The merchants George Elkington and Humphrey Spencer had been given accommodations by a Portuguese-speaking Muslim, whom Elkington had immediately outraged by demanding they be served pork. The other men had been temporarily lodged in a vacant house owned by an indigo broker. After the hard-drinking English seamen had disrupted orderly proceedings in three separate brothels, and been banned in turn by each, the Shahbandar had ordered five *nautch* girls sent to them at the house. But with fewer women than men, a fight inevitably had ensued, with thorough demolition of the plaster walls and shutters.

Worst of all, bosun's mate John Garway had gone on a drunken spree in the streets and, in a flourish of exuberance, severed the tail of a bullock calf—an animal sacred to the Hindus—with his seaman's knife. A riot in the Hindu quarter had erupted soon after, forcing Mukarrab Khan to remove the English seamen outside the town walls, in tents erected by the "tank," the city reservoir.

Yes, Hawksworth sighed, it'll be a long time before India forgets her first taste of the English.

The barge bobbed lightly as two Indian porters, knee-deep in the mud, hoisted the first roll of woolen cloth onto the planking. This begins the final leg of the India voyage, Hawksworth thought to himself. And this has been the easiest part of all.

Almost *too* easy.

Pox on it, believe in your luck for a change. The voyage will post a fortune in pepper. Lancaster was knighted for little more than bringing home his vessels. He reached Java, but he found no trade. He'd have sailed home a pauper if he hadn't ambushed a rich Portuguese galleon in the harbor at Sumatra.

How many weeks to a knighthood? Three? Four? No, we'll make it in less. We'll man every watch. Woolens aland, cotton out. I'll have the frigates laded, stores on board—we can buy cattle and sheep from villages up the coast—and all repairs completed in two weeks. I'll have both frigates in open seas inside a fortnight, where not a Portugal bottom afloat can touch us.

And if permission for the trip to Agra comes, I'll be out of Surat too.

If I live that long.

He reached into his belt and drew out a long Portuguese stiletto. An elaborate cross was etched into the blade, and the handle was silver, with a ram's head at the butt. The ram's eyes were two small rubies. He had been carrying it for two days, and he reflected again on what had happened, still puzzling.

He had returned to the observatory the next morning after he had met Shirin, and this time he brought his lute. But she did not come. That morning, or the morning after, or the morning after. Finally he swallowed his disappointment and concluded he would not see her again. Then it was he had gone to work cleaning away the moss and accumulated mud from the stone instruments. Parts of some seemed to be missing, and he had searched the hut for these without success. All he had found was a hand-held astrolabe, an instrument used to take the altitude of the sun. But he also found tables, piles of handwritten tables, that seemed to hold the key to the use of the instruments. His hopes had soared. It seemed possible, just possible, that buried somewhere in the hut was the key to the greatest mystery of all time —how to determine longitude at sea.

Hawksworth had often pondered the difficulties of navigation in the deep ocean, where only the sun and stars were guides. They were the primary determent to England's new ambition to explore the globe, for English navigators were still far less experienced than those of the Spanish and Portuguese.

The problem seemed overwhelming. Since the great earth was curved, no line on its surface was straight, and once at sea there was absolutely no way to determine *exactly* where you were, which way you were going, or how fast.

The least uncertain measurement was probably latitude, a ship's location north or south of the equator. In the northern hemisphere the height of the polestar was a reasonably accurate determinant of latitude, although it was a full three degrees distant from the northernmost point in the sky. Another measure of latitude was the height of the sun at midday, corrected for the specific day of the year. The problem lay in how to measure either of these elevations accurately.

A hundred years before, the Portuguese had come across an ingenious Arab device for telling the elevation of the sun. It consisted of a board with a knotted length of string run through the middle. If a mariner held the board vertically and sighted the horizon at one end and some object in the sky at the other, the length of the string between the board and his eye could be used to calculate the elevation of the object. In a short time a version appeared in Europe—with a second board replacing the string—called the cross-staff.

However, since locating both the horizon and a star was almost impossible at any time except dawn or dusk, this device worked best for sighting the sun—save that it required staring into the disc of the sun to find its exact center. Also, the cross-staff could not be used when the sun was high in the sky, which was the case in equatorial waters. Another version of the cross-staff was the astrolabe, a round brass dial etched with degree markings and provided with a movable sight that permitted taking the elevation of the sun by its shadow. But even with the astrolabe there was the problem of catching the sun precisely at midday. And on a rolling ship the error in reading it could easily be four degrees.

For longitude, a ship's location east or west on the globe, there were no fixed references at all; but as a mariner traveled east or west, the sun would come up somewhat earlier or later each day, and precisely how much earlier or later could be used to compute how far he had gone. Therefore, calculating longitude depended solely on keeping time extremely accurately—something completely impossible. The best timekeeping device available was the hourglass or "sandglass," invented somewhere in the western Mediterranean in the eleventh or twelfth century. Sandglass makers never achieved real accuracy or consistency, and careful mariners always used several at once, hoping to average out variations. But on a long voyage seamen soon totally lost track of absolute time.

Since they were unable to determine a ship's location from the skies, mariners also tried to compute it from a vessel's speed and direction. Speed was estimated by throwing a log with a knotted rope attached overboard and timing the rate at which the knots in the rope played out—using a sandglass. Margins of error in computing speed were usually substantial. Direction, too, was never known completely accurately. A compass pointed to magnetic north, not true north, and the difference between these seemed to vary unaccountably at different locations on the globe. Some thought it had to do with the lodestone used to magnetize the needle, and others, like the Grand Pilot of the king of Spain, maintained seamen were merely lying to cover their own errors.

For it all, however, longitude was the most vital unknown. Many attempts had been made to find a way to fix longitude, but nothing ever worked. Seamen found the only real solution to the problem was "latitude sailing," a time-consuming and expensive procedure whereby a captain would sail north or south to the approximate latitude of his destination and then sail due east or west, rather than trying to sail on the diagonal. King Philip III of Spain had offered a fortune to the first man who discovered how to tell longitude at sea.

Hawksworth spent days poring through the piles of tables, many of which were strewn about the floor of the room and damaged from mildew and rot. Next he carefully copied the symbols off the walls of the circular building and matched these with those on several of the charts. Were these the names of the major stars, or constellations of the zodiac, or . . . what? The number was twenty-eight.

And then it came to him: they were the daily stations of the moon.

As he continued to sift through the documents, he realized that the scholar who wrote them had predicted eclipses of the moon for many years in advance. Then he found a book, obviously old, with charts that seemed to provide geometric corrections for the distortion caused by the atmosphere when sighting stars near the horizon, something that always had been troublesome for navigators.

He also found other writings. New. Some appeared to be verses, and others, tables of names and numbers. Sums of money were written next to some of the names. But none of it meant anything without the Persian, which he could not read. And Shirin had never returned to the observatory, at least not when he was there.

Until two days ago.

At the observatory that morning the sky had been a perfect ice blue, the garden and orchard still, the air dry and exhilarating. No workmen were splashing in the moat beyond the wall that day. Only the buzz of gnats intruded on the silence. He had brought a bottle of dry Persian wine to make the work go faster, finding he was growing accustomed to its taste. And he had brought his lute, as always, in hope Shirin would come again.

He was in the stone hut, cleaning and sorting pages of manuscript, when she appeared silently in the doorway. He looked up and felt a sudden rush in his chest.

"Have you uncovered all of Jamshid Beg's secrets?" Her voice was lilting, but with a trace of unease. "I've found out that was our famous astronomer's name. He was originally from Samarkand."

"I think I'm beginning to understand some of the tables." Hawksworth kept his tone matter-of-fact. "He should have been a navigator. He could have been a fellow at Trinity House."

"What is that?"

"It's a guild in England. Where navigators are trained."

She laughed. "I think he preferred a world made only of numbers." Her laugh was gone as quickly as it had come, and she moved toward him with a vaguely troubled look. "What have you found?"

"A lot of things. Take a look at this drawing." Hawksworth tried to remain nonchalant as he moved the lamp back to the table from where he had placed it on the floor. "He identified what we call parallax, the slight circular motion of the moon throughout the day caused by the fact it's not sighted from the center of the earth, but from a spot on its surface that moves as the earth rotates. Now if he could measure that accurately enough with these instruments . . ."

Shirin waved her hand and laughed again. "If you understand all this, why not just take the papers back to the palace and work with them there?" She was in the room now, her olive cheeks exquisitely shadowed by the flickering lamp. Her closely braided hair was backlighted perfectly by the partially open door, where flickering shadows played lightly through the brilliant sunshine. "Today I'd rather hear you play your English instrument."

"With pleasure. I've been trying to learn an Indian raga." He kept his voice even and moved himself deftly between Shirin and the doorway, blocking her exit. "But it sounds wrong on the lute. When I get to Agra I'm thinking I'll have a sitar made . . ."

He reached as though for the lute, then swung his hand upward and clapped it over Shirin's mouth. Before she could move he shoved her against the wall beside the door and stretched with his other hand to seize the heavy brass astrolabe that rested on a stand by the table. He caught a look of pure terror in her eyes, and for a moment he thought she might scream. He pressed her harder against the wall to seal her mouth, and as the shaft of light from the doorway dimmed momentarily he stepped forward and swung the brass astrolabe upward.

There was a soft sound of impact, followed by a choked groan and the clatter of metal against the wooden door. He drew back the astrolabe, now with a trace of blood along its sharp edge and the remains of a tooth wedged between its discs. Then he looked out to see a dark-skinned Indian man in a loincloth rolling himself across the top of the garden wall. A faint splash followed, as he dropped into the moat.

When Hawksworth released Shirin and placed the astrolabe back on its stand, he caught the glint of sunshine off a stiletto lying in the doorway. He bent down to retrieve it and suddenly she was next to him, holding his arm and staring at the place where the man had scaled the wall.

"He was a Sudra, a low caste." She looked at the stiletto in Hawksworth's hand, and her voice turned to scorn. "It's Portuguese. Only the Portuguese would hire someone like that, instead of a Rajput." Then she laughed nervously. "If they'd hired a Rajput, someone would be dead now. Hire a Sudra and you get a Sudra's work."

"Who was it?"

"Who knows? The horse bazaar is full of men who would kill for ten rupees." She pointed toward the wall. "Do you see that piece of cloth? There on the old spike. I think it's a piece of his *dhoti*. Would you get it for me?"

After Hawksworth had retrieved the shred of cotton loincloth, brown from a hundred washings in the river, she had taken it from him without a word.

"What will you do with it?"

"Don't." She touched a finger to his lips. "There are things it's best not to ask." Then she tucked the brown scrap into the silken sash at her waist and moved toward the door. "And it would be better if you forgot about today."

Hawksworth watched her for a second, then seized her arm and turned her facing him. "I may not know what's going on yet. But, by Jesus, I'll know before you leave. And you can start by telling me why you come here."

She stared back at him for a moment, meeting his eyes. There was something in them he had never seen there before, almost admiration. Then she caught herself and drew back, dropping into a chair. "Very well. Perhaps you do deserve to know." She slipped the translucent scarf from her hair and tossed it across the table. "Why don't you open the wine you brought? I'll not tell you everything, because you shouldn't want me to, but I'll tell you what's important for you."

Hawksworth remembered how he had slowly poured the wine for her, his hand still trembling.

"Have you ever heard of Samad?" she had begun, taking a small sip.

"I think he's the poet Mukarrab Khan quoted once. He called him a Sufi rascal."

"Is that what he said? Good. That only confirms once again what I think of His Excellency." She laughed with contempt. "Samad is a great poet. He's perhaps the last great Persian writer, in the tradition of Omar Khayyam. He has favored me by allowing me to be one of his disciples."

"So you come here to write poems?"

"When I feel something I want to say."

"But I've also found lists of names here, and numbers."

"I told you I can't tell you everything." Shirin's look darkened momentarily as she drank again lightly from the cup, then settled it on the table. He found himself watching her face, drawn to her by something he could not fully understand. "But I can tell you this. There's someone in India who will one day rid us of the infidel Portuguese. Do you know of Prince Jadar?"

"He's the son of the *Moghul*. I'm guessing he'll probably succeed one day."

"He should. If he's not betrayed. Things are very unsettled in Agra. He has many enemies there." She paused. "He has enemies here."

"I'm not sure I understand."

"Then you should. Because what happens in Agra will affect everyone. Even you."

"But what does Agra politics have to do with me? The knife was Portuguese."

"To understand what's happening, you should first know about Akman, the one we remember now as the *Great Moghul*. He was the father of

Arangbar, the *Moghul* now. I was only a small girl when Akman died, but I still remember my sadness, my feeling the universe would collapse. We worshiped him almost. It's not talked about now, but the truth is Akman didn't really want Arangbar to succeed him, nobody did. But he had no choice. In fact, when Akman died, Arangbar's eldest son started a rebellion to deny him the throne, but that son's troops betrayed him, and after they surrendered Arangbar blinded him in punishment. Khusrav, his own son. Although Prince Jadar was still only a young boy then, we all thought after that he would be *Moghul* himself one day. But that was before the Persians came to power in Agra."

"But aren't you Persian yourself?"

"I was born in India, but yes, I have the great fortune to be of Persian blood. There are many Persians in India. You know, Persians still intimidate the Moghuls. Ours is a magnificent culture, an ancient culture, and Persians never let the Moghuls forget it." Shirin had dabbed at her brow and rose to peer out the door of the observatory building, as though by instinct. "Did you know that the first Moghul came to India less than a hundred years ago, actually after the Portuguese? He was named Babur, a distant descendant of the Mongol warrior Genghis Khan, and he was from Central Asia. Babur was the grandfather of Akman. They say he had wanted to invade Persia but that the ruling dynasty, the Safavis, was too strong. So he invaded India instead, and the Moghuls have been trying to make it into Persia ever since. That's why Persians can always find work in India. They teach their language at court, and give lessons in fashion, and in painting and garden design. Samad came here from Persia, and now he's the national poet."

"What do these Persians have to do with whatever's happening in Agra? Are you, or your family, somehow involved too?"

"My father was Shayhk Mirak." She hesitated a moment, as though expecting a response. Then she continued evenly, "Of course, you'd not know of him. He was a court painter. He came to India when Akman was *Moghul* and took a position under the Persian Mir Sayyid Ali, who directed the painting studio Akman founded. You know, I've always found it amusing that Akman had to use Persian artists to create the Moghul school of Indian painting. Anyway, my father was very skilled at Moghul portraits, which everybody now says were invented by Akman. And when Akman died, Arangbar named my father to head the school. It lasted until *she* was brought to Agra."

"Who?"

"The queen, the one called Janahara."

"But why was your father sent away?"

"Because *I* was sent away."

Hawksworth thought he sensed a kind of nervous intensity quivering behind Shirin's voice. It's *your* story, he told himself, that I'd *really* like to hear. But he said nothing, and the silence swelled. Finally she spoke again.

"To understand the trouble now, you must understand about the queen. Her story is almost amazing, and already legends are growing around her. It's said she was born the day her father, Zainul Beg, left Persia as an adventurer bound for India. He ordered her abandoned in the sun to die, but after the caravan traveled on his wife lamented for the baby so much he decided to return for her. Although the sun was intense, they found her still alive. It's said a cobra was shading her with his hood." Shirin turned to Hawksworth, her dark eyes seeming to snap. "Can you believe such a story?"

"No. It sounds like a fable."

"Neither can I. But half the people in India do. Her father finally reached Lahore, the city in India where Akman was staying, and managed to enter his service. Like any Persian he did very well, and before long Akman gave him a *mansab* rank of three hundred *zat*. His wife and daughter were allowed to come and go among the palace women. Then, when she was seventeen, this little Persian girl of the cobra began her plan. She repeatedly threw herself across the path of the *Moghul's* son Arangbar, whom she rightly guessed would be next in line for the throne. He was no match for her, and now people say she won his heart before he knew it himself. My own belief is she cast a spell on him."

"And he married her?"

"Of course not. Akman was no fool. He knew she was a schemer, and when he saw what she was doing he immediately had her married to a Persian general named Sher Afgan, whom he then appointed governor of Bengal, a province in the distant east of India. Akman died a few years after that, still thinking he had saved Arangbar from her, but he hadn't counted on the spell."

"So how did she get back to Agra, and become queen?"

"That part I know very well." Shirin laughed bitterly. "I was there. You see, Arangbar never forgot his Persian cobra girl, even after he became *Moghul* himself. And he found a way to get her back. One day he announced he was receiving reports of unrest in Bengal, where Sher Afgan was still governor, and he summoned the governor to Agra to explain. When no answer came, he sent troops. Nobody knows what happened, but the story was given out that Sher Afgan drew a sword on Arangbar's men. Perhaps he did. They say he was impulsive. But the Imperial troops cut him down. Then Arangbar ordered Sher Afgan's Persian wife and her little daughter, Layla, back to Agra and put them under the protection of his mother, the dowager queen. Then, just as we'd all predicted, he married her. At first he was going to put her in the *zenana*, the harem, but she refused. She demanded to be made his queen, an equal. And that's what he did. Except now she's actually more. She's the real ruler of India."

"And you were in the harem, the *zenana*, then?" Hawksworth decided to gamble on the story he had heard.

Shirin stared at him, trying to hide what seemed to be surprise. "You know." For a moment he thought she might reach out and touch his hand, but then she drew back into herself. "Yes, I was still in the *zenana* then, but not for long. The first thing Janahara did was find out which women Arangbar favored, and she then had us all married off to governors of provinces far from Agra. You know a Muslim man is allowed four wives, so there's always room for one more. Mukarrab Khan got me."

"She seems very clever."

"You haven't heard even half her story yet. Next she arranged to have her brother, Nadir Sharif, appointed prime minister, and her father, Zainul Beg, made chief adviser to Arangbar. So now she and her family control the *Moghul* and everyone around him." Shirin paused. "Not quite everyone. Yet. Not Prince Jadar."

"But he'll be the next *Moghul*. When that happens, what becomes of her?"

"He *should* be the next *Moghul*. And if he is, her power will be gone. That's why she wants to destroy him now."

"But how can she, if he's the rightful heir?" Hawksworth found himself suddenly dismayed by the specter of Agra in turmoil.

"No one knows. But she'll think of a way. And then she'll find someone she can control to be the next *Moghul*."

"But why do you care so much who succeeds Arangbar?"

"One reason I care is because of Samad." Her eyes suddenly saddened.

"Now I *really* don't understand. He's a poet. Why should it matter to him?"

"Because the queen would like to see him dead. He has too much influence. You must understand that the queen and her family are Shi'ites, a Persian sect of Islam. They believe all men should bow to some dogmatic mullah, whom they call an imam. But this was never in the teachings given to the Prophet."

A curse on all religions, Hawksworth had thought. Am I caught in the middle of some Muslim holy war?

"But why do these Persians, or their imams, want to be rid of Samad?"

"Because he's a Sufi, a mystic, who teaches that we all should find God within our own selves. Without the mullahs. That's why the Persian Shi'ites despise him and want him dead."

"Then he's supporting Prince Jadar?"

"Samad does not concern himself with politics. But it's the duty of the others of us, those who understand what is happening, to help Prince Jadar. Because we know he will stop the Persians and their Shi'ites who are now spreading their poison of hate in India. And he'll also rid India of the Portuguese. I'm sure of it." She paused for a moment. "You know, it's always seemed ironic that the Persians and the Portuguese should actually work together. But in a way each needs the other. The Portuguese have made the Persians, particularly the queen and her brother, Nadir Sharif, very rich, and in return they're allowed to send their Jesuits to preach. So both the Persians and the Portuguese want to prevent Prince Jadar from becoming the next *Moghul,* since they know he'd like nothing better than to rid India of them both."

"But what does this have to do with me? I just want a trading *firman* from Arangbar. He's still alive and healthy, and he should know the Portugals can't stop English trading ships from coming here. Why shouldn't he give us a *firman?*"

"Can't you see? The English can never be allowed to trade here. It would be the beginning of the end for the Portuguese. It would show all the world they no longer can control India's ports. But what I'm really trying to make you see is that it's not only the Portuguese who want to stop you. It's also the people who support them. So no one can aid you openly. The Persians are already too powerful. Still, there are those here who would protect you."

"Who do you mean?"

"How could I possibly tell you?" She held him with her eyes. "I scarcely know you. But you should listen to your intuition. Samad says we all have an inner voice that tells us what is true."

This time she did reach and touch his hand, and her touch was strangely warm in the chill of the room. "I can't tell you any more, really. So now will you play for me? Something tender, perhaps. A song you would play for the woman you left behind you in England."

"I didn't have all that much to leave behind." He picked up the lute. "But I'll be happy to play for you."

"You have no one?"

"There was a woman in London. But she married while I was . . . gone."

"She wouldn't wait while you were away?" Shirin sipped again from her cup and her eyes darkened. "That must have been very sad for you."

"It could be she didn't think I was worth waiting for." He hesitated. "I've had some time to think about it since. In a way it was probably my own fault. I think she wanted more than I was ready to give."

She looked at him and smiled. "Perhaps what she wanted was *you.* And you wouldn't give *yourself.* Tell me what she was like."

"What was she like?" He looked away, remembering Maggie's face with a strange mixture of longing and bitterness. "Well, she's like nobody I've seen in India. Red hair, blue eyes . . . and a salty tongue." He laughed. "If she was ever anybody's fourth wife, I'd pity the other three." He felt his laugh fade. "I missed her a lot when I was away before. But now . . ." He tried to shrug.

She looked at him as though she understood it all. "Then if you won't play for her any more, will you play just for me? One of your English ragas?"

"What if I played a suite by Dowland, one of our English composers? It's one of my favorites." He found himself smiling again, the lute comfortable and reassuring in his grasp. "I hope you won't think it sounds too out of place."

"We're both out of place here now." She returned his smile wistfully and glanced at the papers on the desk. "You *and* me."

Hawksworth saw George Elkington approaching and dropped the dagger quickly into his boot.

" 'Twill take a lifetime the rate these heathens dawdle." Elkington wiped a sweaty arm across his brow. Deep bags sagged under his bloodshot eyes. "An' we'll be months movin' the lead and ironwork with these damn'd rickety carts. Not to mention the silver bullion for buyin' commodity. We'll have to get a barge."

"How many more trips do you need to bring in the wool?"

"Can't say. But 'tis clear we'll need more of these damn'd carts, for what little they're worth." As Elkington turned to spit, he spotted a porter who had let a roll of woolen cloth dip into the river, and his neck veins pulsed. "Hey, you heathen bastard, mind the water!" He stumbled after the terrified man trailing a stream of oaths.

Hawksworth leaned against the wooden spokes of a bullock cart and quickly passed the stiletto from his boot back to his belt. As he watched, the bark tipped, beginning to list dangerously, and then he heard Elkington command the porters to stop the loading and prepare to get underway. Only five of the twenty-five bullock carts had been emptied, and the sun was already approaching midafternoon. As Hawksworth had watched the men at work, some corner of his mind had become dimly aware of a curious anomaly. Whereas the Shahbandar's porters were working at full speed, the drivers of the bullock carts seemed actually to be hindering the unloading— moving the carts around in a confused way that always kept the work disorganized. And a number of answers began, just began, to fall into place.

"Captain-General Hawksworth, do you expect to be joinin' us?" George Elkington stalked up and began to scrape his muddy boots on the spokes of the bullock cart.

"Elkington, I want you to dismiss these drivers." Hawksworth ignored his sarcastic tone. "I want the Shahbandar to supply all our men from now on."

"What the bloody hell for?" Elkington tightened his hat and hitched up his belt.

"Something's wrong. Did you have any accidents coming in from Swalley?"

"Accidents? Nay, not a bleedin' one. Unless you'd call the axle of a cart breakin' the first day and blockin' a narrow turn in the road, with mud on both sides so we couldn't pass and had to unload the whole bleedin' lot and look half the mornin' for another cart to hire. An' then the drivers had a fight over who was responsible, and who'd pay for what, and we couldn't start till after midday. And yesterday one of their damn'd bullocks died, right in the road. Which is scarce wonder, considerin' how worn out they are. Nay, we had no accidents. The whole bleedin' trip was an accident."

"Then let's get rid of them all. Men, carts, bullocks, the lot. And hire new. Let the Shahbandar hire them for us. We pay in silver, and give him his commission, and I'm sure he'll provide us what we need."

"Think he can do any better?" Elkington's skeptical eyes squinted against the sun. "These damn'd heathens all appear similar."

"I think he'll make a difference. They all seem terrified of him. We have to try." Hawksworth started for the barge.

"You don't have much time left." Shirin had said. "Try to understand what's happening."

The porters were loosening the lines on the pegs. The bark was ready to get underway.

"Don't assume you know who'll aid you," she had said. "Help may come in a way that surprises you. It can't be known who's helping you."

He waded through the mud and pulled himself onto the bark. Then he turned and rolled over onto a bale of cloth. The sky was flawless and empty.

"Just trust what feels right," she had said, and for no reason at all she had reached out and touched his lute. "Learn to trust your senses. Most of all"—she had taken his hand and held it longer than she should have— "learn to open yourself."

They were underway.

The Shahbandar watched from the *maidan* as the bark of English woolens moved in short spurts toward the steps below him. Oars sparkled in the sunshine, and the faint chant of the rowers bounced, garbled, across the waves. Behind him two short, surly-eyed men held the large umbrella that shaded his face and rotund belly. A circle of guards with poles pushed away traders who shouted begs and bribes for a moment of his time in their tent, to inspect their goods please and render them salable commodity with his *chapp* and an invoice stating their worth, preferably undervalued. The 2½ percent duty was prescribed by the *Moghul*. The assessed value was not.

Mirza Nuruddin ignored them. He was calculating time, not rupees.

His latest report was that four weeks more were needed for the Viceroy to outfit the galleons and fireships. But the single-masted *frigatta* bringing the news from Goa was two weeks in travel. Which means the galleons will be here within three, perhaps two weeks, he told himself. A Portuguese armada of twelve warships. The Englishman's luck has run out. They'll be caught unlading and burned.

He fingered the shred of dirty cloth tucked in his waist. It had been sent by Shirin, wrapped with a gift of *aga* of the rose. Her cryptic note had told him all he had needed to know. When his spies reported no one recently injured among the servants of the Portuguese Jesuits, the search had begun in the horse bazaar. They had found the man the next day. The truth had come quickly when Mirza Nuruddin's name was mentioned.

And nothing had been learned. The man had been given the knife by Hindi-speaking servants. Their master's name was never divulged. But they knew well the routine of the Englishman, and the location of the observatory.

And now I must tamper with your destiny, English captain. We are all —you, I, the prince—captives of a world we no longer can fully control.

He asked himself again why he had made the choice, finally. To take the risks Jadar had asked, when the odds against the prince were growing daily. It was stupid to support him now, and Mirza Nuruddin had always held absolute contempt for stupidity, particularly when it meant supporting a hopeless cause.

If the queen crushes him, as she very likely will, I've jeopardized my position, my holdings, probably my life.

The prince does not understand how difficult my task is. The infidel Englishman is almost too clever.

I had planned it perfectly. I had shown them the opportunity for great profit, then denied it to them. They were preparing to leave, but surely they would have returned, with a fleet. Then Mukarrab Khan approved their trade, after waiting until he was certain the Portuguese preparations were almost complete. So now they remain, awaiting their own destruction, never to leave again. And when these frigates are destroyed, will any English ever return?

The Englishman will surely be dead, or sent to Goa. There'll be no trip to Agra. And Arangbar will never know why.

But the silver coin will soon be ready. And the prince's cipher today said Vasant Rao himself will arrive in ten days to escort the Englishman and the silver as far as Burhanpur. Time is running out.

There's only one solution left. Will it work?

The barge eased into the shallows and the porters slid into the water, each already carrying a roll of cloth.

"I expected this difficulty, Captain Hawksworth. But your path is of your own making. You yourself chose to unlade at that distance from the port." They were in Mirza Nuruddin's chamber, and the Shahbandar faced Hawksworth and Elkington with his rheumy, fogbound eyes. The chamber had been emptied, as Hawksworth had demanded. "I propose you consider the following. Unlade the woolens from your smaller frigate immediately, and let me oversee their transport here." He drew nonchalantly on the *hookah*. "My fee would be a small commission above the cost of hiring the carts. One percent if they are delivered here within two weeks. Two percent if they are delivered within one week. Do you accept?"

Hawksworth decided not to translate the terms for Elkington.

"We accept." It seems fair, he told himself. This is no time to bargain.

"You show yourself reasonable. Now, the lead and ironwork you have cargoed is another matter. Bullock carts are totally unsuitable for those weights in this sandy coastal delta. The weights involved require they be transported by river bark. And that means unlading at the river mouth."

Hawksworth shook his head. "We'll dump the cargo first. We can't take the risk now."

"Captain, there is risk and there is risk. What is life itself if not risk? Without risk what man can call himself alive?" Mirza Nuruddin thought of his own risk at this moment, how his offer of help to the English would immediately be misconstrued by the entire port. Until the plan had played through to its ending. Then the thought of the ending buoyed him and he continued, his voice full of solicitude. "I can suggest a strategy for unlading your ironwork at the river mouth in reasonable safety, after your frigates have been lightened of their wool. With an experienced pilot, you can sail along the shoreline, south to the bar, and anchor under cover of dark. Barks can be waiting to unlade you. If the lead and ironwork are ready for unlading, perhaps it can be completed in one night. You can unlade the smaller frigate first, return it to the cove you call Swalley, and then unlade the other vessel. That way only one frigate is exposed at a time."

As Hawksworth and Elkington listened, Mirza Nuruddin outlined the details of his offer. He would hire whatever men were needed. He normally did this for foreign traders, and took a percentage from them—as well as from the meager salary of the men he hired. And he already had a pilot in mind, a man who knew every shoal and sandbar on the coastline.

As Hawksworth listened his senses suddenly told him to beware. Hadn't Shirin told him to trust his intuition? And this scheme was too pat. This time his guts told him to dump the lead in the bay and write off the loss. But Elkington would never agree. *He* would want to believe they could unlade and sell the lead. *His* responsibility was profit on the cargo, not the risk of a vessel.

So he would take this final risk. Perhaps Mirza Nuruddin was right. Risk exhilarated.

He smiled inwardly and thought again of Shirin. And of what she had said about trusting his instincts.

Then, ignoring them, he agreed to Mirza Nuruddin's plan.

And the Shahbandar produced a document already prepared for their signature.

CHAPTER ELEVEN

"Now we will begin. As my guest, you have first throw of the dice." Mirza Nuruddin fingered the gold and ivory inlay of the wooden dice cup as he passed it to Hawksworth. Then he drew a heavy gurgle of smoke from his *hookah*, savoring the way it raced his heart for that brief instant before its marvelous calm washed over his nerves. He needed the calm. He knew that any plan, even one as carefully conceived as the one tonight, could fail through the blundering of incompetents. Or betrayal. But tonight, he told himself, tonight you will win the game.

The marble-paved inner court of the Shahbandar's sprawling brick estate house was crowded almost to overflowing: with wealthy Hindu moneylenders, whose mercenary hearts were as black as their robes were white; Muslim port officials in silks and jewels, private riches gleaned at public expense; the turbaned captains of Arab cargo ships anchored at the bar, hard men in varicolored robes who sat sweltering, smoking, and drinking steaming coffee; and a sprinkling of Portuguese in starched doublets, the captains and officers of the three Portuguese trading *frigatta* now anchored at the bar downriver.

Servants wearing only white loincloths circulated decanters of wine and boxes of rolled betel leaves as an antidote to the stifling air that lingered even now, almost at midnight, from a broiling day. The torchbearers of Mirza Nuruddin's household stood on the balconies continuously dousing a mixture of coconut oil and rose attar onto their huge flambeaux. Behind latticework screens the *nautch* girls waited in boredom, braiding their hair, smoothing their skintight trousers, inspecting themselves in the ring-mirror on their right thumb, and chewing betel. The dancing would not begin until well after midnight.

As Hawksworth took the dice cup, the sweating crowd fell expectantly silent, and for the first time he noticed the gentle splash of the river below them, through the trees.

He stared for a moment at the lined board lying on the carpet between them, then he wished himself luck and tossed the three dice along its side. They were ivory and rectangular, their four long sides numbered one, two, five, and six with inlaid teakwood dots. He had thrown a one and two sixes.

"A propitious start. You English embrace fortune as Brahmin his birthright." The Shahbandar turned and smiled toward the Portuguese captains loitering behind him, who watched mutely, scarcely masking their displeasure at being thrown together with the heretic English captain. But an invitation from the Shahbandar was not something a prudent trader declined. "The night will be long, however. This is only your beginning."

Hawksworth passed the cup to the Shahbandar and stared at the board, trying to understand the rules of *chaupar*, the favorite game of India from the *Moghul's zenana* to the lowliest loitering scribe. The board was divided into four quadrants and a central square, using two sets of parallel lines, which formed a large cross in its middle. Each quadrant was divided into three rows, marked with spaces for moving pieces. Two or four could play, and each player had four pieces of colored teak that were placed initially at the back of two of the three spaced rows. After each dice throw, pieces were moved forward one or more spaces in a row until reaching its end, then up the next row, until they reached the square in the center. A piece reaching the center was called *rasida*, arrived.

Hawksworth remembered that a double six allowed him to move two of his pieces, those standing together, a full twelve spaces ahead. As he moved the pieces forward, groans and oaths in a number of languages sounded through the night air. Betting had been heavy on the Shahbandar, who had challenged both Hawksworth and the senior Portuguese captain to a set of games. Only an adventurous few in the crowd would straddle their wagers and accept the long odds that the English captain would, or could, be so impractical as to defeat the man who must value and apply duty to his goods.

"Did I tell you, Captain Hawksworth, that *chaupar* was favored by the *Great Moghul*, Akman?" The Shahbandar rattled the dice in the cup for a long moment. "There's a story, hundreds of years old, that once a ruler of India sent the game of chess, what we call *chaturanga* in India, to Persia as a challenge to their court. They in return sent *chaupar* to India." He paused dramatically. "It's a lie invented by a Persian."

He led the explosion of laughter and threw the dice. A servant called the numbers and the laughter died as suddenly as it had come.

"The Merciful Prophet's wives were serpent-tongued Bengalis."

He had thrown three ones.

A terrified servant moved the pieces while Mirza Nuruddin took a betel leaf from a tray and munched it sullenly. The crowd's tension was almost palpable.

Hawksworth took the cup and swirled it again. He absently noted that the moon had emerged from the trees and was now directly overhead. The Shahbandar seemed to notice it as well.

Mackintosh watched as the last grains of red marble sand slipped through the two-foot-high hourglass by the binnacle and then he mechanically flipped it over. The moon now cast the shadow of the mainmast yard precisely across the waist of the ship, and the tide had begun to flow in rapidly. The men of the new watch were silently working their way up the shrouds.

"Midnight. The tide's up. There's nae need to wait more." He turned to Captain Kerridge, who stood beside him on the quartdeck of the *Resolve*. George Elkington stood directly behind Kerridge.

"Let's get under sail." Elkington tapped out his pipe on the railing. Then he turned to Kerridge. "Did you remember to douse the stern lantern?"

"I give the orders, Mr. Elkington. And you can save your questions for the pilot." Captain Jonathan Kerridge was a small, weasel-faced man with no chin and large bulging eyes. He signaled the *Resolve*'s quartermaster and the anchor chain began to rattle slowly up the side. Then the mainsail dropped, hung slack for a moment, and bellied against the wind, sending a groan through the mast. They were underway. The only light on board was a small, shielded lantern by the binnacle, for reading the large boxed compass.

The needle showed their course to be almost due south, toward the bar at the mouth of the Tapti. On their right was the empty bay and on their left the glimmer of occasional fires from the shoreline. The whipstaff had been taken by the Indian pilot, a wrinkled nut-brown man the Shahbandar had introduced as Ahmet. He spoke a smattering of Portuguese and had succeeded in explaining that he could reliably cover the eight-mile stretch south from Swalley to the unloading bar at the Tapti river mouth in one turn of the hourglass, if Allah willed. With high tide, he had also managed to explain, there were only two sandbars they would have to avoid.

And there would be no hostiles abroad this night. Even the Portuguese trading frigates were safely at anchor off the river mouth, for this evening their captains had been honored by an invitation to attend the gathering at Mirza Nuruddin's estate.

"Your beginning has been impressive, Captain Hawksworth. But now you must still maintain your advantage." Mirza Nuruddin watched as Hawksworth threw a double five and a two, advancing two of his four pieces into the central square. The crowd groaned, coins began to change hands.

"You have gained *rasida* for two pieces. I'll save time and concede this game. But we have six more to play. *Chaupar* is a bit like life. It favors those with endurance."

As the board was cleared for the next game, Mirza Nuruddin rose and strode to the end of the court. The wind was coming up now, as it always did on this monthly night of full moon and tide, sweeping up the river bringing the fresh salt air of the sea. And the currents would be shifting along the coast, as sandbars one by one were submerged by the incoming tide. He barked an inconsequential order to a hovering servant and then made his way back to the board, his guests parting automatically before him. The drinking crowd had already begun to turn boisterous, impatient for the appearance of the women. As always, the *nautch* girls would remain for additional entertainment after their dance, in private quarters available in the rambling new palace.

"This game I will throw first." The Shahbandar seated himself, and watched as Hawksworth drew on a tankard of brandy, especially provided for the Europeans present. Then Mirza Nuruddin made a deft twist of the cup and the ivories dropped on the carpet in a neat row of three sixes. A servant barked the numbers and the crowd pressed forward as one to watch.

"Fifteen fathom and falling." The bosun leaned back from the railing and shouted toward the quarterdeck. In disbelief he quickly drew the line in over the gunwale at the waist of the *Resolve* and fed it out again.

"Now she reads thirteen fathom."

Kerridge glanced at the hourglass. The sand was half gone, and the compass reading still gave their course as due south. Ahead the sea was blind dark but on the left the fires of shore still flickered, now perhaps even brighter than he had remembered them. Then he realized a cloud had drifted momentarily over the moon, and he told himself this was why. The pilot held the whipstaff on a steady course.

"I'd reef the foresail a notch, Cap'n, and ease her two points to starboard. I'll lay a hundred sovereigns the current's chang'd on us." Mackintosh ventured to break protocol and speak, his concern growing.

I do na like the feel of this, he told himself. We're driftin' too fast. I can feel it.

"Eight fathoms, sir." The bosun's voice again cut the dark.

"Jesus, Cap'n," Mackintosh erupted. "Take her about. The pox-rotted current's . . ."

"She'll ride in three fathom. I've sailed the *James*, six hundred ton, in less. Let her run." He turned to Elkington. "Ask the Moor how much longer to the river mouth."

George Elkington turned and shot a stream of questions rapidly at the pilot, whose eyes glazed in his partial comprehension. He shook his head in a way that seemed to mean both yes and no simultaneously and then pointed into the dark and shrugged, emitting fragments of Portuguese.

"*Em frente*, Sahib. *Diretamente em frente.*"

Then he gestured toward the waist of the ship and seemed to be asking the depth reading.

As though in answer, the bosun's voice came again, trembling.

"Five fathom, Cap'n, and still dropping."

"*Cinco.*" Elkington translated, but his concerned tone was a question. What does it mean?

The pilot shouted an alarm in Gujarati and threw his fragile weight against the whipstaff. The *Resolve* pitched and shuddered, groaning like some mourning animal at tether, but it no longer seemed to respond to the rudder.

Kerridge glared at the pilot in dismay.

"Tell the blathering heathen steady as she goes. She'll take . . ."

The deck tipped crazily sideways, and a low grind seemed to pass up through its timbers. Then the whipstaff kicked to port, strained against its rope, and with a snap from somewhere below, drifted free. The *Resolve* careened dangerously into the wind, while a wave caught the waist of the ship and swept the bosun and his sounding line into the dark.

"Whorin' Mary, Mother of God, we've lost the rudder." Mackintosh lunged down the companionway toward the main deck, drawing a heavy knife from his belt. As the frightened seamen clung to the tilting deck and braced themselves against the shrouds, he began slashing the lines securing the main sail.

Another wave seemed to catch the *Resolve* somewhere beneath her stern quarter gallery and lifted her again. She poised in midair for a long moment, then groaned farther into the sand. As the frigate tipped, Mackintosh felt a rumble from the deck below and at that instant he knew with perfect certainty the *Resolve* was doomed to go down. A cannon had snapped its securing lines and jumped its blocks. He grabbed a shroud and braced himself.

Then it came, the muffled sound of splintering as the cannon bore directly through the hull, well below the waterline of the heeling frigate.

"Takin' water in the hold." A frightened shout trailed out through the scuttles.

The seamen on decks still clung to the shrouds, wedging themselves against the gunwales.

"Man the pumps in the well, you fatherless pimps." Mackintosh shouted at the paralyzed seamen, knowing it was already too late, and then he began to sever the moorings of the longboat lashed to the mainmast.

Elkington was clinging to the lateen mast, winding a safety line about his waist and bellowing unintelligible instructions into the dark for hoisting the chests of silver bullion from the hold.

No one on the quarterdeck had noticed when its railing splintered, sending Captain Kerridge and the Indian pilot into the dark sea.

"The strumpet luck seems to have switched her men tonight, Captain Hawksworth, like a *nautch* girl when her *karwa*'s rupees are spent." Mirza Nuruddin signaled for his *hookah* to be relighted. He had just thrown another row of three sixes, and was now near to taking the seventh game, giving him six to Hawksworth's one. All betting on Hawksworth had stopped after the fourth game. "But the infinite will of God is always mysterious, mercifully granting us what we need more often than what we want."

Hawksworth had studied the last throw carefully, through the haze of brandy, and he suddenly realized Mirza Nuruddin had been cheating.

By Jesus, the dice are weighted. He sets them up somehow in the cup, then slides them quickly across the carpet. Damn me if he's not a thief. But why bother to cheat me? I only laid five sovereigns on the game.

He pushed aside the confusion and reflected again on the astounding genius who sat before him now, cheating at dice.

His plan was masterful. Host a gathering for the captains at the bar the night we will unload. Even the Portuguese. No one in command of a ship will be at the river mouth, no one who could possibly interfere. And his porters are waiting there now, with barks he reserved especially for us. All our wool's already been unladed and brought overland to Surat. Then we transferred the ironwork and lead on the *Discovery* to the *Resolve*. So all the lead and ironwork in cargo will be unladed by moonlight tonight and on its way upriver by morning, before the Portugals here even sleep off their liquor.

And the *Resolve* will be underway again by dawn, back to Swalley with no one to challenge her. Not even the Portuguese trading *frigatta*, with their laughable eight-pound stern chasers. The *Discovery* is almost laded with cotton. Another couple of days should finish her. And then the *Resolve*. Another two weeks at most, and they'll be underway.

The East India Company, the Worshipful damned East India Company, will earn a fortune on this voyage. And a certain captain named Brian Hawksworth will be toasted the length of Cheapside as the man who did what Lancaster couldn't. The man who sent the East India Company's frigates home with a cargo of the cheapest pepper in history. The Butterbox Hollanders will be buying pepper from the East India Company next year and cursing Captain Brian Hawksworth.

Or will it be Sir Brian Hawksworth?

He tried the name on his tongue as he swirled the dice for one last throw. This time he tried to duplicate the Shahbandar's technique.

Easy swirls and then just let them slide onto the carpet as you make some distracting remark.

"Perhaps it's Allah's will that a man make his own luck. Is that written somewhere?" The dice slid onto the carpet and Hawksworth reached for his brandy.

Three sixes.

Mirza Nuruddin studied the three ivories indifferently as he drew on his *hookah*. But traces of a smile showed at the corner of his lips and his foggy eyes sparkled for an instant.

"You see, Captain Hawksworth, you never know the hand of fortune till you play to the end." He motioned to a servant. "Refresh the English captain's glass. I think he's starting to learn our game."

The longboat scraped crazily across the deck and into the surf. Then another wave washed over the deck, chilling the half-naked seamen who struggled to secure the longboat's line. Two chests of silver bullion, newly hoisted from the hold, were now wedged against the mainmast. Elkington clung to their handles, shouting between waves for the seamen to lower them into the longboat.

Mackintosh ignored him.

"Hoist the line to the poop. We'll board her from the stern gallery. Take the longboat under and drop a ladder. You and you, Garway and Davies, bring the line about, to the gallery rail."

The current tugged at the longboat, but its line held secure and the seamen passed the end up the companionway and toward the stern gallery, where the rope ladder was being played out.

"The longboat'll not take all the men *and* the silver. Blessed Jesus, there's ten thousand pound sterling in these chests." Elkington gasped as another wave washed over him, sending his hat into the surf. He seized a running seaman by the neck and yanked him toward the chests. "Take one end, you whoreson bastard, and help hoist it through the companionway to the poop."

But the man twisted free and disappeared toward the stern. With an oath, Elkington began dragging the chest across the deck and down the companionway. By the time he reached the gallery, the ladder had already been dropped into the longboat.

And five seamen were waiting with half-pikes.

"I'll send you to hell if you try loadin' that chest." Bosun's mate John Garway held his pike in Elkington's face. "We'll all not make it as 'tis."

Then Thomas Davies, acting on the thought in every man's mind, thrust his pike through the lock hinge on the chest and wrenched it off with a single powerful twist. "Who needs the money more, say I, the bleedin' Worshipful Company, or a man who knows how to spend it?"

In moments a dozen hands had ripped away the lid of the chest, and seamen began shoveling coins into their pockets. Elkington was pushed sprawling into the companionway. Other seamen ran to begin rifling the second chest. Silver spilled from their pockets as the men poured down the swaying ladder into the longboat. As Elkington fought his way back toward the stern, he took a long last look at the half-empty chests, then began stuffing the pockets of his own doublet.

Mackintosh emerged from the Great Cabin holding the ship's log. As he waited for the last seaman to board the longboat, he too lightened the *Resolve* of a pocketful of silver.

With all men on board the longboat's gunwales rode a scant three inches above waterline. Bailing began after the first wave washed over her. Then they hoisted sail and began to row for the dark shore.

"Tonight you may have been luckier than you suppose, Captain Hawksworth." The Shahbandar's fingers deftly counted the five sovereigns through the leather pouch Hawksworth had handed him. Around them the final side bets were being placed against the Portuguese captain who would play Mirza Nuruddin next.

"It's hard to see how."

"For the price of a mere five sovereigns, Captain, you've learned a truth some men fail to master in a lifetime." Mirza Nuruddin motioned away the Portuguese captain, his doublet stained with wine, who waited to take his place at the board. "I really must call the dancers now, lest some of my old friends lose regard for our hospitality. I hope you'll find them entertaining, Captain Hawksworth. If you've never seen the *nautch*, you've yet to call yourself a man."

Hawksworth pulled himself up and thought about the river and slowly worked his way through the crowd to the edge of the marble court. The damp, chill air purged the torch smoke from his lungs and began to sweep away the haze of brandy from his brain. He stared into the dark and asked the winds if they knew of the *Resolve*.

Could it all have been a trap? What if he'd told the Portugals, and they had warships waiting?

Without warning, the slow, almost reverent strains of a *sarangi*, the Indian violin, stirred from the corner of the courtyard, and the crowd shifted expectantly. Hawksworth turned to notice that a carpeted platform had been erected directly in the center of the court, and as he watched, a group of women, perhaps twenty, slowly began to mount steps along its side. The torches had grown dim, but he could still see enough to tell they all wore the veil of purdah and long skirts over their trousers. As they moved chastely toward the center of the platform he thought they looked remarkably like village women going to a well, save they wore rows of tiny bells around their ankles and heavy bangles on their wrists.

The air was rent by a burst of drumming, and the courtyard suddenly flared as servants threw oil on the smoldering torches around the balcony. At that instant, in a gesture of high drama, the women ripped away their turquoise veils and flung them skyward. The crowd erupted in a roar.

Hawksworth stared at the women in astonishment.

Their skirts, the skintight trousers beneath, and their short halters—were all gossamer, completely transparent.

The dance was underway. Hips jerked spasmodically, in perfect time with the drummer's accelerating, hypnotic rhythms—arching now to the side, now suggestively forward. Hawksworth found himself exploring the dancers' masklike faces, all heavily painted and expressionless. Then he watched their hands, which moved in sculptural arcs through a kind of sign language certain Indians in the crowd seemed to know. Other hand messages were understood by all, as the women stroked themselves intimately, in what seemed almost a parody of sensuality. As the rhythm continued to intensify, they began to rip away their garments one by one, beginning with their parted waist wraps. Next their halters were thrown to the crowd, though their breasts had long since found release from whatever minimal containment they might have known at the beginning of the dance. Their earth-brown skin now glistened bare in the perfumed torchlight.

The dance seemed to Hawksworth to go on and on, incredibly building to ever more frantic levels of intensity. The drunken crowd swayed with the women, its excitement and expectation swelling. Then at last the women's trousers also were ripped away, leaving them adorned with only bangles and reflecting jewels. Yet the dance continued still, as they writhed onto their knees at the edge of the platform. Then slowly, as though by some unseen hand, the platform lowered to the level of the courtyard and they glided into the drunken crowd, thrusting breasts, thighs, against the ecstatic onlookers. The cheers had grown deafening.

Hawksworth finally turned away and walked slowly down the embankment to the river. There, in the first hint of dawn, bathers had begun to assemble for Hindu prayers and a ritual morning bath. Among them were young village girls, swathed head to foot in bright-colored wraps, who descended one by one into the chilled water and began to modestly change garments while they bathed, chastely coiling a fresh cloth around themselves even as the other was removed.

They had never seemed more beautiful.

Hawksworth was standing on the steps of the *maidan* when the sail of the English longboat showed at the turn of the river. News of the shipwreck had reached Surat by village runner an hour after sunup, and barks had already been sent to try to recover the remaining silver before the ship broke apart. The frigate was reportedly no more than a thousand yards off the coast, and all the men, even Kerridge, the bosun, and the pilot, had been safely carried ashore by the current.

Hawksworth watched the longboat's sail being lowered in preparation for landing and tried to think over his next step, how to minimize the delay and loss.

We can't risk staying on past another day or two, not with only one vessel. If we're caught at anchor in the cove, there's nothing one ship can do. The Portugals can send in fireships and there'll be no way to sink them with crossfire. The *Discovery* has to sail immediately. We've enough cotton laded now to fill the hold with pepper in Java.

Damn Kerridge. Why was he steering so close to shore? Didn't he realize there'd be a current?

Or was it the pilot?

Were we steered into this disaster on the orders of our new friend Mirza Nuruddin? Has he been playing false with us all along, only claiming to help us stay clear of the Portugals? By the looks of the traders on the *maidan* this morning I can tell they all think we were played for fools.

He tried to remember all the Shahbandar had said the night before, particularly the remarks he had not understood, but now the evening seemed swallowed in a fog of brandy.

But the game, he finally realized, had been more than a game.

"The voyage will be lucky to break even now." George Elkington slid from the back of the sweating porter and collapsed heavily on the stone steps. "The *Resolve* was old, but 'twill take forty thousand pound to replace her."

"What do you plan to do?" Hawksworth eyed Kerridge as he mounted the steps, his doublet unrecognizable under the smeared mud, and decided to ignore him.

"Not a damn'd thing we can do now, save lade the last of the cotton and some indigo on the *Discovery* and weigh anchor. And day after tomorrow's not too soon, by my thinkin'." Elkington examined Hawksworth and silently cursed him. He still had not swallowed his disbelief when Hawksworth had announced, only three days before, that he planned to leave the ships and travel to Agra with a letter from King James.

"The Shahbandar has asked to meet with you." Hawksworth motioned to Elkington as the last seaman climbed over the side of the longboat and onto the back of a waiting porter. "We may as well go in."

A crowd of the curious swarmed about them as they made their way across the *maidan* and through the customs house. Mirza Nuruddin was waiting on his bolster.

"Captain, my sincere condolences to you and to Mr. Elkington. Please be sure that worthless pilot will never work out of this port again. I cannot believe he was at fault, but he'll be dealt with nonetheless." Which is partially true, Mirza Nuruddin told himself, since my cousin Muhammad Haidar, *nakuda* of the *Rahimi*, will take him on the pilgrim ship for the next Aden run, and allow him to work there until his reputation is repaired. "You were fortunate, at least, that the largest part of her cargo had already been unladed."

Elkington listened to Hawksworth's translation, his face growing ever more florid. "'Twas the damned pilot's knavery. Tell him I'd see him hanged if this was England."

Mirza Nuruddin listened, then sighed. "Perhaps the pilot was at fault, perhaps not. I don't quite know whose story to believe. But you should know that in India only the *Moghul* can impose the death penalty. This matter of the pilot is past saving, however. It's best we move on. So tell me, what do you propose to do now?"

"Settle our accounts, weigh anchor, and be gone." Elkington bristled. "But you've not heard the last o' the East India Company, I'll warrant you. We'll be back with a fleet soon enough, and next time we'll do our own hirin' of a pilot."

"As you wish. I'll have our accountants total your invoices." Mirza Nuruddin's face did not change as he heard the translation, but his spirit exulted.

It worked! They'll be well at sea within the week, days before the Portuguese warships arrive. Not even that genius of intrigue Mukarrab Khan will know I planned it all. And by saving these greedy English from certain disaster, I've lured to our seas the only Europeans with the spirit to drive out the Portuguese forever, after a century of humiliation.

India's historic tradition of free trade, the Shahbandar had often thought, had also brought her undoing. Openhanded to all who came to buy and sell, India had thrived since the beginning of time. Until the Portuguese came.

In those forgotten days huge single-masted arks, vast as eight hundred tons, freely plied the length of the Arabian Sea. From Mecca's Jidda they came, groaning with the gold, silver, copper, wool, and brocades of Italy, Greece, Damascus, or with the pearls, horses, silks of Persia and Afghanistan. They put in at India's northern port of Cambay, where they laded India's prized cotton, or sailed farther south, to India's port of Calicut, where they bargained for the hard black pepper of India's Malabar Coast, for ginger and cinnamon from Ceylon. India's own merchants sailed eastward, to the Moluccas, where they bought silks and porcelains from Chinese traders, or cloves, nutmeg, and mace from the islanders. India's ports linked China on the east with Europe on the west, and touched all that moved between. The

Arabian Sea was free as the air, and the richest traders who sailed it prayed to Allah, the One True God.

Then, a hundred years ago, the Portuguese came. They seized strategic ocean outlooks from the mouth of the Persian Gulf to the coast of China. On these they built strongholds, forts to control not the lands of Asia, but its seas. And if no man could remember the centuries of freedom, today all knew well the simple device that held the Arabian Sea in bondage. It was a small slip of paper, on which was the signature of a Portuguese governor or the captain of a Portuguese fort. Today no vessel, not even the smallest bark, dared venture the Arabian Sea without a Portuguese *cartaz*. This hated license must name the captain of a vessel and verify its tonnage, its cargo, its crew, its destination, and its armament. Vessels could trade only at ports controlled or approved by the Portuguese, where they must pay a duty of 8 percent on all cargo in and out. Indian and Arab vessels no longer could carry spices, pepper, copper, or iron—the richest cargo and now the monopoly of Portuguese shippers.

An Indian vessel caught at sea without a *cartaz*, or steering south when its stated destination was north, was confiscated; its captain and crew were executed immediately, if they were lucky, or sent to the galleys if they were not. Fleets of armed galleons cruised the coastlines in patrol. If a vessel gave cause for suspicion, Portuguese soldiers boarded her in full battle dress, with naked swords and battle cries of "Santiago." And while their commander inspected the ship's *cartaz*, Portuguese soldiers relieved passengers of any jewelry salable in the streets of Goa. *Cartaz* enforcement was strict, and—since a percentage of all seized cargo went to captains and crews of patrol galleons —enthusiastic. The seas off India were theirs by right, the Portuguese liked to explain, because they were the first ever to have the ingenuity to make claim to them.

The revenues the *cartaz* brought Portugal were immense—not because it was expensive to obtain, it cost only a few rupees, but because it funneled every ounce of commodity traded in the Arabian Sea through a Portuguese tax port.

And it is the Portuguese taxes, Mirza Nuruddin told himself, not just their galleons, that the English will one day drive from our ports. And on that day, our merchant ships will again lade the best cargo, sail the richest routes, return with the boldest profits.

"There seems nothing further then, Mr. Elkington, I can do for you." The Shahbandar smiled and bowed his small, ceremonial salaam. "Save wish you a fair wind and Allah's blessing."

So it's over, Hawksworth thought as they turned to leave, the last time I'll ever see you, and thank you very much, you unscrupulous deceiving son of a whore.

"Captain Hawksworth, perhaps you and I can share a further word. You are not, as I understand, planning to depart India. At least not immediately. I'd like you always to know my modest offices remain at your behest."

Elkington paused, as did Hawksworth, but one of the Shahbandar's officials took the merchant's arm and urged him firmly toward the door of the chamber. Too firmly, Hawksworth thought.

"I think you've done about all for us you can." Hawksworth made no attempt to strain the irony from his voice.

"Be that as it may, I've heard rumors that your trip to Agra may be approved. Should that happen, you must know you cannot travel alone, Captain. No man in India is that foolhardy. The roads here are no more safe than those, so I hear, in Europe. All travelers inland need a guide, and an armed escort."

"Are you proposing to help me secure a guide? Equal in competence, may I presume, to the pilot you hired for the *Resolve?*"

"Captain Hawksworth, please. God's will is mysterious." He sighed. "No man can thwart mischance if it is his destiny. Hear me out. I have just learned there's currently a man in Surat who knows the road to Burhanpur like his own sword handle. In fact, he only just arrived from the east, and I understand he expects to return when his affairs here, apparently brief, are resolved. By a fortuitous coincidence he happens to have an armed escort of guards with him. I suggest it might be wise to attempt to engage him while you still have a chance."

"And who is this man?"

"A Rajput captain with the army. A soldier of no small reputation, I can assure you. His name is Vasant Rao."

Mukarrab Khan reread the order carefully, scrutinized the black ink seal at the top of the page to assure himself it was indeed the *Moghul's*, and then placed it aside. So at last it had come. The prospect of English presents was too great a temptation for the acquisitive Arangbar, ever anxious for new baubles. The Englishman would be going to Agra. No one at court could have prevented it.

But that road—east through bandit-infested Chopda to now-threatened Burhanpur, then north, the long road through Mandu, Ujjain, and Gwalior to Agra—was a journey of two hard months. The *Moghul's* seal meant less than nothing to highwaymen, or to servants and drivers whose loyalties were always for sale. It's a long road, Englishman, and mishaps on that road are common as summer mildew.

He smiled to himself and took up the other silver-trimmed bamboo tube. It had arrived by the same runner. The date on the outside was one week old.

It always amazed Mukarrab Khan that India's runners, the Mewras, were actually swifter than post horses. This message had traveled the three hundred *kos* south from Agra to Burhanpur and then the remaining hundred and fifty *kos* west to Surat—a combined distance of almost seven hundred English miles—in only seven days.

Runners were stationed at posts spaced five *kos* apart along the great road that Akman had built to link Agra to the seaport of Surat. They wore an identifying plume at their head and two bells at their belt, and they gained energy by eating *postibangh,* a mixture of opium and hemp extract. Akman even conceived of lining the sides of the road with white stones so his Mewras could run in darkest midnight without lanterns. There were now some four thousand runners stationed along India's five main arteries.

The only things swifter, Mukarrab Khan had often told himself, are lightning . . . and a blue, white-throated Rath pigeon. A distance requiring a full day for a runner could be covered by a pigeon in one *pahar,* three hours, given good weather. Arangbar kept pigeons all over India, even in Surat—but then so did everyone else at court. Recently, it seemed, everyone was training pigeons.

Next to the date was the seal of Nadir Sharif, prime minister and brother of the queen. Mukarrab Khan knew Nadir Sharif well. A dispatch from Nadir Sharif, though it always reflected the wishes of the *Moghul* or the queen, could be relied upon to be reasonable. If the *Moghul* in fury condemned a man over some trivial transgression, Nadir Sharif always forgot to deliver the sentence until the next day, having found that Arangbar often tended to reverse sentences of death when musing in his evening wine cups. This order will be reasonable, Mukarrab Khan told himself, but it will have to be obeyed, eventually.

As always, Mukarrab Khan tried to guess the message before unsealing the two-inch-long silver cap attached to the end of the tube. Probably taxes, late delivery. Or perhaps there's been a discrepancy between the open report filed from my chamber by the *wakianavis,* the public reporters, and the private report, which I supposedly do not see, sent directly to the *Moghul* by the *harkaras,* the confidential reporters. And if that's the complaint, it will disprove my suspicion that no one in the Imperial chancery ever actually reads the reports. I deliberately inserted a difference of one-half *lakh* of rupees as reported logged at the mint last month, just to see if they would catch it.

Mukarrab Khan unrolled the dispatch. And his heart stopped.

Clasping the paper he wandered distractedly out of the now-empty audience hall and down the stairs toward the courtyard. When he reached the veranda he only half-noted the heavy clouds threatening in the west, toward the sea, and the moist air promising one last spatter of the monsoon. Servants were removing the tapestried canopy that shaded his cushioned bench, and when they saw him they discreetly melted out of sight, leaving one side of the cloth still dangling from the poles. He dropped heavily onto the bench and reread the order carefully, his disbelief growing.

On the recommendation of Queen Janahara, Mukarrab Khan had just been appointed India's first ambassador to Portuguese Goa. He would leave in two weeks.

CHAPTER TWELVE

The moon was high, bathing the sleeping veranda in a wash of glistening silver, and the air was deliciously moist, heavy with perfume from the garden below. From somewhere among the distant rooftops came the thread of a man's voice, entoning a high-pitched melody, trilling out wordless syllables like some intense poetry of sound.

Hawksworth leaned back against one of the carved juniper-wood posts supporting the canopy above his sleeping couch and explored Kali's body with his gaze, as a mariner might search a map for unknown islands and inlets. She lounged opposite him, resting against an oblong velvet bolster, examining him with half-shut eyes while she drew contentedly on a *hookah* fired with black tobacco and a concentrated *bhang* the Arabs called *hashish*.

Her hair hung loose, in gleaming black strands reaching almost to her waist, and her head was circled by a thin tiara of gold and pearls, supporting the large green emerald that always hung suspended in the center of her forehead—even when she made love. The gold she wore—long bracelets at her wrists and upper arms, swinging earrings, even tiny bells at her ankles— seemed to excite her in a way Hawksworth could never understand. Her eyes and eyebrows were kohl-darkened and her lips carefully painted a deep red, matching the color of her fingernails and toenails. And as always she had dyed her palms and the soles of her feet red with henna. Four different strands of pearls hung in perfect array beneath her transparent blouse, glistening white against her delicate, amber-tinted skin. He noticed, too, that her nipples had been rouged, and told himself this was the only thing about her that recalled the women in London.

"Tonight your thoughts were far away, my love. Do you weary of me so soon?" She laid aside the *rome-chauri*, the rubber ring impregnated with powdered hair that she often asked him to wear for her, then took a vial of rose attar from beside the couch and dabbed herself absently along the arms. "Tell me the truth. Are you now beginning to recoil from women, like so many bragging and posturing men I've known, and to long for a boy who fears to seek his own pleasure? Or a subservient *feringhi* woman whose parts are dry from lack of desire?"

Hawksworth studied her for a moment without replying. In truth he did not know what to say. Your nightly visits to this couch have been the most astonishing experience of my life. To imagine I once thought being with the same woman night after night would eventually grow monotonous. But you always come here as someone different, always with something new. You play on my senses like an instrument—with touch, with scent, with tongue. Until they seem to merge with my mind. Or is it the reverse? But you're right when you say the mind must surrender itself first. When that's done, when the mind is given up to the body, then you somehow forget your own self and think only of the other. And eventually there grows a union of plea-sure, a bond that's intense, overwhelming.

But tonight he could not repress his vagrant mind. His feeling of failure churned too deep. It had stolen his spirit.

Day after tomorrow the *Discovery* weighs anchor, he told himself, with half the cargo we'd planned and twice the men she needs, while the *Resolve* slowly breaks apart on a sandbar. I've failed the Company . . . and myself. And there's nothing that can be done. Kali, dear Kali. The woman I really want to be with tonight is Shirin. Why can't I drive her from my mind? Half the time when you're in my arms, I pretend you're her. Do you sense that too?

"I'm sorry. I'm not myself tonight." You're right as always, he marveled, the mind and the body are one. As he paused, the singer's voice cut the stillness between them. "How did you know?"

"It's my duty as your courtesan to feel your moods. And to try to lift the weight of the world from your heart."

"You do it very well. It's just that sometimes there's too much to lift." He studied her, wondering what she was *really* thinking, then leaned back and looked at the stars. "Tell me, what do you do when the world weighs on *you*?"

"That's never your worry, my love. I'm here to think of you, not you of me."

"Tell me anyway. Say it's a *feringhi*'s curiosity."

"What do *I* do?" She smiled wistfully and drew again on the *hookah*, sending a tiny gurgle into the quiet. "I escape with *bhang*. And I remember when I was in Agra, in the *zenana*."

She lay aside the mouthpiece of the *hookah* and began to roll betel leaves for them both, carefully measuring in a portion of nutmeg, her favor-ite aphrodisiac.

"Tell me how you came to be here, away from Agra."

"Is it really me you wish to hear about?" She looked at him squarely, her voice quiet. "Or is it Shirin?"

"You," Hawksworth lied, and absently stroked the edge of her foot, where the henna line began. Then he looked into her dark eyes and he knew she knew.

"Will we make love again if I tell you?"

"Possibly."

"I know how to make you keep your promise." She took his toe in her mouth and brushed it playfully with her tongue before biting it, ever so lightly. "So I will tell you anything you want to know."

He scarcely knew where to start.

"What was it about the harem, the *zenana*, that you liked so much?"

She sighed. "We had everything there. Wine and sweet *bhang*. And we bribed the eunuchs to bring us opium and nutmeg and tobacco. We could wear tight trousers, which none of the women here in Surat dare for fear the mullahs will condemn them." As she spoke, her eyes grew distant. "We wore jewels the way women in Surat wear scarves. And silks from China the way they wear their dreary cotton here. There was always music, dance, pigeon-flying. And we had all the perfumes—musk, scented oil, attar of rose—we could want. The *Moghul* had melons brought by runner from Kabul, pome-granates and pears from Samarkand, apples from Kashmir, pineapples from Goa." She remembered herself and reached to place a rolled betel leaf in his mouth. "About the only thing we weren't supposed to have was cucum-bers . . ." She giggled and took a betel leaf for herself. "I think His Majesty was afraid he might suffer in comparison. But we bribed the eunuchs and got them anyway. And we also pleasured each other."

Hawksworth studied her, not quite sure whether to believe it all. "I've heard the harems of the Turks in the Levant are said to be like some sort of prison. Was it like that?"

"Not at all." She smiled easily. A bit too easily, he thought. "We used to take trips to the countryside, or even go with His Majesty when he went to Kashmir in the hot summer. In a way we were freer than the poor third wife of some stingy merchant."

"But weren't you always under guard?"

"Of course. You know the word 'harem' is actually Arabic for 'forbidden sanctuary.' Here we call it by the Persian name *zenana*, but it's still the same. It's really a city of women. All cities must have guards. But we each re-ceived a salary and were like government officials, with our own servants. We each had our own apartment, immense and decorated with paintings and bubbling fountains at the door. Except there were no doors, since we were always supposed to be open to receive His Majesty."

"Wasn't there anything about it you *didn't* like?" He examined her skeptically. "It seems to me I could list a few drawbacks."

"A few things. I didn't like the intrigues. All the women scheming how to lure His Majesty to their apartment, and giving him aphrodisiacs to try to prolong his time there. The beautiful ones were constantly afraid of being poisoned, or spied on by the older women and the female slaves. And some of the women were always trying to bribe eunuchs to bring in young men disguised as servingwomen." She took the stem of a flower and began to weave it between his toes. "But there are always intrigues anywhere. It's the price we pay for life."

"You've never told me how you came to be in the *zenana* in the first place. Were you bought, the way women are in the Levant?"

Kali burst into laughter. "*Feringhis* can be such simpletons sometimes. What wonderful legends must be told in this place called Europe." Then she sobered. "I was there because my mother was very clever. The *zenana* is powerful, and she did everything she could to get me there. She knew if His Majesty liked me, there could be a good post for my father. She planned it for years. And when I finally reached fifteen she took me to the annual *mina bazaar* that Arangbar always holds on the Persian New Year, just like his father Akman did."

"What's that?"

"It's a mock 'bazaar' held on the grounds of the palace, and only women can go. Anyone who wants to be seen by His Majesty sets up a stall, made of silk and gauze, and pretends to sell handiwork, things like lace and perfume. But no woman can get in who isn't beautiful."

"Was that where the *Moghul* first saw you?"

"Of course. Arangbar came to visit all the stalls, riding around on a litter that some Tartar women from the *zenana* carried, surrounded by his eunuchs. He would pretend to bargain for the handiwork, calling the women pretty thieves, but he was really inspecting them, and the daughters they'd brought. I was there with my mother, and I wore a thin silk blouse because my breasts were lovely." She paused and looked at him hopefully, brushing a red-tipped finger across one nipple. "Don't you think they still are? A little?"

"Everything about you is beautiful." It was all too true. As he looked at her, he told himself he much preferred her now to how she must have looked at fifteen.

"Well, I suppose Arangbar must have thought so too, because the next day he sent a broker to pay my mother to let me come to the *zenana*."

Hawksworth paused, then forced nonchalance into his voice. "Did Shirin, or her mother, do the same?"

"Of course not." Kali seemed appalled at the absurdity of the idea. "She's Persian. Her father was already some kind of official. He was far too dignified to allow his women to go to the *mina bazaar*. The *Moghul* must have seen her somewhere else. But if he wanted her, her father could not refuse."

"What eventually happened to you . . . and to her?"

"She became his favorite." Kali took out her betel leaf and tossed it aside. "That's always very dangerous. She was in great trouble after the queen came to Agra."

"I've heard something about that." He found himself wanting to hear a lot more about it, but he held back. "And what happened to you after *you* entered the *zenana?*"

"His Majesty only came to me once, as was his duty." She laughed but there was no mirth in her voice. "Remember I was only fifteen then. I knew nothing about lovemaking, though I tried very hard to please him. But by that time he was already entranced with Shirin. He began to call for her almost every afternoon."

"So what did you do after that?"

"I began to make love to the other women there. I suppose it sounds strange to you, but I found I actually enjoyed other women's bodies very much."

"Weren't you ever lonely?"

"A little. But I'm lonely here sometimes too." She paused and looked away. "A courtesan is always lonely. No man will ever truly love her. He'll listen to her sing to him and joke with him, but his heart will never be hers, regardless of all the sweet promises he'll think to make her."

Hawksworth watched her quickly mask the sadness in her eyes as she reached for the *hookah*. At that moment he wanted more than anything in the world to tell her it wasn't always true, but he knew she would hate the lie. Instead he took out his own betel leaf and cleared his throat awkwardly.

"You've never told me how you came to be called Kali. Mukarrab Khan said that's not your real name."

She looked at him and her eyes became ice. "He's a truly vicious man. What did he say?"

"That you would tell me." He paused, bewildered. "Don't you want to?"

She wiped her eyes with a quick motion. "Why not? You may as well know. Before someone else tells you. But please try to understand I was very lonely. You can't know how lonely it becomes in the *zenana*. How you long for a man to touch you, just once. You can't imagine. After a while you become . . . sort of mad. It becomes your obsession. Can you understand? Even a little?"

"I've seen men at sea for months at a time. I could tell you a few stories about that that might shock you."

She laughed. "Nothing, absolutely nothing, shocks me any more. But now I'll shock you. There was this beautiful eunuch who guarded the *zenana* at night. He was Abyssinian, very tall and striking, and he was named Abnus because he was the color of ebony. He was truly exquisite."

"A eunuch?" Hawksworth stared at her, disbelieving. "I always thought . . ."

She stopped him. "I probably know what you always thought. But eunuchs are not all the same. The Bengali eunuchs like Mukarrab Khan has were sold by their parents when they were very young, and they've had everything cut away with a razor. Muslim merchants buy boys in Bengal and take them to Egypt, where Coptic monks specialize in the operation. That's the type called *sandali*. They even have to pass water through a straw. But the operation is so dangerous few of the boys live, so they're very expensive. Abnus had been sent to His Majesty as a gift from some Arab merchant, who was so stingy he simply crushed the testicles of one of his grown slaves instead of buying a Bengali boy. No one realized Abnus could still do almost everything any man can do. It was our secret."

"So you made love to a eunuch?" Hawksworth found himself incredulous.

Kali smiled and nodded. "Then one day our Kashmiri ward servant entered my apartment unannounced. She had suspected us. I didn't know until that moment she was a spy for the palace." She stopped and a small shiver seemed to pass through her. "We were both condemned to death. I didn't care. I didn't want to live anyway. He was killed the next day, left on a pike to die in the sun."

Kali paused and her lips quivered slightly. Then she continued. "I was buried up to the neck in the courtyard. To watch him die. Then, in late afternoon some Imperial guards came and uncovered me. And they took me back into the palace. I was delirious. They took me into this room, and there she was."

"Who?"

"Queen Janahara. She offered me a chance to live. I didn't know what I was doing, where I was, anything. Before I thought I'd already agreed." At last a tear came. "And I've never told anyone. I'm so ashamed." She wiped her eyes and stiffened. "But I've never done what I told her I would do. Not once."

"What was that?"

Kali looked at him and laughed. "To come here with Mukarrab Khan. And spy on Shirin. So now and then I just send some silly nonsense to Her Majesty. I know what Shirin is doing . . . and I admire her for it."

Hawksworth tried to keep his voice even. "What exactly is it she's doing?"

Kali stopped abruptly and stared at him. "That's the one thing I can't tell you. But I *will* tell you that I'm now also supposed to be spying on you too, for Khan Sahib." She laughed again. "But you never say anything for me to report."

Hawksworth found himself stunned. Before he could speak, she continued.

"But you asked about my name. It's probably the real reason I despise Janahara so much. Before, I was named Mira. My father was Hakim Ali, and he came to India from Arabia back when Akman was *Moghul*. But the queen said I could never use those names again. She said that because I'd caused Abnus' death, she was renaming me Kali, the name the Hindus have for their bloodthirsty goddess of death and destruction. She said it would remind me always of what I'd done. I hate the name."

"Then I'll call you Mira."

She took his hand and brushed it against her cheek. "It doesn't matter now. Besides, I'll probably never see you again after tonight. Tomorrow you'll be getting ready to leave for Agra. Khan Sahib told me I'm not to come to you any more after this. I think he's very upset about something that happened with your ships."

"I'm very upset about it too." Hawksworth studied her. "What exactly did he say?"

"No, I've told you enough already. Too much." She pinched his toe. "Now. You *will* keep your promise, my love. And then after tonight you can forget me."

Hawksworth was watching her, entranced. "I'll never forget you."

She tried to smile. "Oh yes you will. I know men better than that. But I'll always remember you. When a man and a woman share their bodies with each other, a bond is made between them. It's never entirely forgotten, at least by me. So tonight, our last night, I want you to let me give you something of mine to keep."

She reached under the couch and withdrew a box, teakwood and trimmed in gold. She placed it on the velvet tapestry between them.

"I've never shown this to a *feringhi* before, but I want you to have it. To make you remember me, at least for a while."

"I've never had a present from an Indian woman before." Hawksworth carefully opened the box's gold latch. Inside was a book, bound in leather and gilded, with exquisite calligraphy on its cover.

"It's called the *Ananga-Ranga,* the Pleasures of Women. It was written over a hundred years ago by a Brahmin poet who called himself Kalyana Mal. He wrote it in Sanskrit for his patron, the Viceroy of Gujarat, the same province where you are now."

"But why are you giving it to me?" Hawksworth looked into her eyes. "I'll remember you without a book. I promise."

"And I'll remember you. You've given me much pleasure. But there are those in India who believe the union of man and woman should be more than pleasure. The Hindus believe this union is an expression of all the sacred forces of life. You know I'm not a Hindu. I'm a Muslim courtesan. So for me lovemaking is only to give you pleasure. But I want you to know there's still more, beyond what we've had together, beyond my skills and knowledge. According to the Hindu teachings, the union of male and female is a way to reach the divine nature. That's why I want you to have this book.

It describes the many different orders of women, and tells how to share pleasure with each. It tells of many things beyond what I know."

She took the leatherbound copy of the *Ananga-Ranga* and opened it to the first page. The calligraphy was bold and sensuous.

"In this book Kalyana Mal explains that there are four orders of women. The three highest orders he calls the Lotus Woman, the Art Woman, and the Conch Woman. The rest he dismisses as Elephant Women."

Hawksworth took the book and examined its pages for a time. There were many paintings, small colored miniatures of couples pleasuring one another in postures that seemed astounding. Finally he mounted his courage.

"Which 'order' of woman are you?"

"I think I must be the third order, the Conch Woman. The book says that the Conch Woman delights in clothes, flowers, red ornaments. That she is given to fits of amorous passion, which make her head and mind confused, and at the moment of exquisite pleasure, she thrusts her nails into the man's flesh. Have you ever noticed me do that?"

Hawksworth felt the scratches along his chest and smiled. Only in India, he thought, could you make love so many ways, all kneeling before a woman rather than lying with her. So she scratches you on the chest.

"So far it sounds a bit like you."

"And it says the Conch Woman's love cleft, what the Hindus call her yoni, is always moist with *kama salila*, the woman's love seed. And its taste is salt. Does that also remind you of me?"

Hawksworth was startled with wry delight when he realized he actually knew the answer. Something he'd never had the slightest desire to know about a woman in England.

In England. Where baths were limited to the face, neck, hands, and feet—and those only once every few weeks. Where women wore unwashed petticoats and stays until they literally fell off. Where a member of the peerage was recently quoted as complaining "the nobler parts are never in this island washed by the women; they are left to be lathered by the men."

But Kali was scrubbed and perfumed each day like a flower. And she had taught him the pleasure in the taste of all her body.

"I guess that makes you a Conch Woman. But what are the others supposed to be like?"

"Let me tell you what it says." She reached and took back the book. "The next one, the Art Woman, has a voice like a peacock, and she delights in singing and poetry. Her carnal desire may be less strong than the Conch Woman, at least until she's properly aroused, but then her *kama salila* is hot, with a perfume like honey. And it's abundant, producing a sound with the act of union. She is sensuous, but for her lovemaking is always a kind of art."

"Who would be an Art Woman?"

She looked at him and smiled wryly. "I think Shirin, the one who fascinates you so much, may well be an Art Woman. But I don't know her body well."

But I will, Hawksworth told himself. I'll know all of her. Somehow. I swear it.

"And what about the Lotus Woman?"

"According to Kalyana Mal she's actually the highest order of woman. She's a spiritual being, who loves to converse with teachers and Hindu priests. She's always very beautiful, never dark, and her breasts are full and high. Her yoni is like an opening lotus bud and her *kama salila* is perfumed like a lily newly burst."

"And who would be a Lotus Woman?"

"The only one I've ever known for sure is in Agra now. She's a classical dancer, a Hindu temple dancer. Her name is Kamala."

"I saw a few dancers recently. At the Shahbandar's estate house. In my *feringhi* opinion they weren't of a very high order."

"Those were *nautch* girls, common whores. They degrade and debase the classical dance of India for the purpose of enticing customers. Kamala is nothing like them. She's a great artist. For her the dance, and lovemaking, are a kind of worship of the Hindu gods. I don't entirely understand it, but I could sense her power the one time I saw her dance. When I saw her I began to believe what people say, that she embodies the female principle, the divine female principle that defines India for the Hindu people. Believe me when I tell you she's very different from anyone here in Surat. She knows things that no one else knows. People say they're explained in a very old book she has."

"How can there possibly be any more to know?" Hawksworth thought of the hundreds of pleasure tricks Kali had taught him, delights unknown in Europe. "What's left to put in this other book?"

"Her book is one I've never actually seen. I've only heard about it. It's a sacred text of the Hindus', an ancient *sutra*, in which the union of man and woman are shown to be a way of finding your own divine natures, the God within you both. I'm told it's called the *Kama Sutra*, the Scripture of Love and Pleasure."

Hawksworth found himself beginning to be overwhelmed. "Maybe we'd better start with this book. What exactly does it say?"

"The *Ananga-Ranga* explains that each order of woman must be aroused, must be awakened to her pleasure, in a different way. At different times of day, with different caresses, different kinds of kisses and scratches and bites, different words, different embraces during union. It says if you learn to know women well, you will understand how to give and receive the greatest enjoyment with each."

"Is it really so complicated?"

"Now you're starting to sound like some Muslim men I know, who lock their women away and make love to boys, claiming women are insatiable. With desires ten times stronger than those of a man. But they're actually afraid of a woman, so they believe she's to be enjoyed quickly and as little as possible. They care nothing for her own pleasure. But a woman must be aroused to enjoy union to its fullest. That's why this book is so important. I happen to think you are one who cares about a woman's pleasure."

Hawksworth stroked her smooth leg mischievously, then took the book and gently laid it aside. "Tell me what it says about a Conch Woman. What have I been doing that's right and wrong?"

"The book says that the Conch Woman prefers union with a man in the third *pahar* of the night."

"When is that?"

"Time is counted in India by *pahar*. The day and the night are each divided into four *pahars*. The first *pahar* of the night would be between six and nine in the evening by *feringhi* time. The third *pahar* would be your hours between midnight and three in the morning. Is that not the very time I come to your couch?"

"That's convenient."

"It also says that on certain days of the moon, which it tells, the Conch Woman particularly enjoys having her body pressed with the nails of the man. Some days roughly, some days gently. And on certain days the embrace must be forceful, on certain days gentle. There are many special ways to touch and embrace a Conch Woman, and they are explained here. Also there are certain ways of kissing her, of biting her, of scratching her. For example, you may kiss her upper lip, or her lower lip, or you may kiss her with your tongue only."

"And how am I supposed to be able to kiss you with my tongue only?" Hawksworth cast a skeptical glance at the book.

"It's very easy." She smiled at him slyly. "Perhaps it's easier if I show you."

She took his lower lip gently with the tips of her fingers, passed her tongue over it slowly and languorously, and then suddenly nipped it playfully. He started in surprise.

"There. You see there are many ways to please a woman, to kiss her, to bite her, to scratch her. When you have become a true lover of women, my strong *feringhi*, you will know them all."

Hawksworth shifted uncomfortably. "What next?"

"The book also tells of the bodies of women. Foolish men often do not know these things, my love, but I think you are beginning to learn. It tells that in the upper cleft of the yoni there's a small organ it likens to a plan-tain-shoot sprouting from the ground. This is the seat of pleasure in a woman, and when it is excited, her *kama salila* flows in profusion."

"And then?"

"When the woman is ready, you may both enjoy the act of union to its fullest. And there are many, many ways this may be done. The book tells of thirty-two. It is the great wisdom of Kalyana Mal that a woman must have variety in her love couch. If she does not find this with one man, she will seek others. It is the same with men, I think."

Hawksworth nodded noncommittally, not wishing to appear overly enthusiastic.

"Finally, he tells the importance of a woman reaching her moment of enjoyment. If she does not, she will be unsatisfied and may seek pleasure elsewhere. In India, a woman is taught to signify this moment by the *sitkrita*, the drawing in of breath between the closed teeth. There are many different ways a woman may do this, but you will know, my love."

"Enough of the book." He took it and replaced it in the box. "Somehow I think I've already had a lot of its lessons."

"That was merely my duty to you. To be a new woman for you each night. And I think you've learned well." She took the box and settled it beside the couch. Then she laughed lightly. "But you still have a few things to learn. Tonight, for our last time together, I will show you the most erotic embrace I know." She examined him with her half-closed eyes, and drew one last burst of smoke from the *hookah*. Then she carefully positioned the large velvet bolster in the center of the couch. "Are you capable of it?"

"Try me."

"Very well. But I must be deeply aroused to enjoy this fully. Come and let me show you all the places you must bite."

The sun was directly overhead when Vasant Rao reined his iron-gray stallion to a halt at the Abidjan Gate. Behind him, beyond the grove of mango and tamarind trees, lay the stone reservoir of Surat. It was almost a mile in circumference, and he had chosen its far bank as campground for his Rajput guard. Accommodations in Surat were nonexistent during the season, and although he could have cleared a guest house with a single name, Prince Jadar, he had chosen to remain inconspicuous.

Through the dark bamboo slats of the gate he could now see the Englishman riding toward him, holding his Arabian mare at an easy pace. Vasant Rao studied the gait carefully. He had learned he could always judge the character of a man by observing that man's handling of a mount. He casually stroked his moustache and judged Brian Hawksworth.

The Englishman is unpracticed, yet there's an unmistakable sense of command about him. Not unlike the control the prince holds over a horse. He handles the mare almost without her knowing it, forcing discipline onto her natural gait. Perhaps our treacherous friend Mirza Nuruddin was right. Perhaps the Englishman will suit our requirements.

Vasant Rao remembered that Jadar had been insistent on the point.

"The English captain must be a man of character and nerve, or he must never reach Burhanpur. You need only be seen providing his guard as you depart Surat. If he's weak, like a Christian, he will not serve our needs."

The times ahead will be difficult enough, Vasant Rao told himself, without having to worry about the Englishman. The prince has been trapped in the south, and now there's news Inayat Latif and his troops are being recalled to Agra from Bengal. The queen will soon have at her right hand the most able general in the *Moghul's* army.

Vasant Rao turned his eyes from the Englishman to look again at his own Rajput guard, and his pride in them restored his spirit. Only Rajputs would have the courage to one day face the numerically superior troops of Inayat Latif.

The origin of the warrior clans who called themselves Rajputs, "sons of kings," was lost in legend. They had appeared mysteriously in western India over half a millennium before the arrival of the Moghuls, and they had royalty, and honor, in their blood. They had always demanded to be known as Kshatriya, the ancient Hindu warrior caste.

The men, and women, of the warrior Kshatriya clans lived and died by the sword, and maintained a timeless tradition of personal honor. Theirs was a profession of arms, and they lived by rules of conduct unvaried since India's epic age. A member of the warrior caste must never turn his back in battle, must never strike with concealed weapons. No warrior could strike a foe who was fleeing, who asked for mercy, whose own sword was broken, who slept, who had lost his armor, who was merely an onlooker, who was facing another foe. Surrender was unthinkable. A Rajput defeated in battle need not return home, since his wife would turn him out in dishonor for not having given his life. But if a Rajput perished with a sword in his hand, the highest honor, his wife would proudly follow him in death, joining his body on the funeral pyre. And many times, in centuries past, Rajput women themselves had taken up swords to defend the honor of their clan.

When they had no external foes, the Rajput clans warred among themselves, since they knew no other life. For convenience, each clan decreed its immediate neighboring clans its enemies, and an elaborate code was devised to justify war over even the smallest slight. Their martial skills were never allowed to gather rust, even if the cost was perpetual slaughter of each other.

Though they were divided among themselves, the Rajput clans had for centuries defended their lands from the Muslim invaders of India. Only with the coming of the great Moghul genius Akman was there a Muslim ruler with the wisdom to understand the Rajputs could be more valuable as allies than as foes. He abandoned attempts to subdue them, instead making them partners in his empire. He married Rajput princesses; and he used Rajput fighting prowess to extend Moghul control south and west in India.

The men with Vasant Rao were the elite of the dominant Chauhan clan, and all claimed descent from royal blood. They held strong loyalties, powerful beliefs, and absolutely no fear of what lay beyond death. They also were men from the northwest mountains of India, who had never before seen Surat, never before seen the sea, never before seen a *feringhi*.

But Vasant Rao had seen *feringhi*, when he had stood by the side of Prince Jadar in Agra, when Jesuit fathers had been called to dispute with Muslim mullahs before Arangbar. He had seen their tight, assured faces, and heard their narrow, intolerant views. Could this *feringhi* be any different?

Already he had witnessed the Englishman's nerve, and it had reminded him, curiously, of Jadar. The Englishman had refused to come to their camp, claiming this demeaned his office of ambassador. And Vasant Rao, representative of Prince Jadar, had refused to meet the Englishman inside Surat. Finally it was agreed that they would meet at the wall of the city, at the Abidjan Gate.

"*Nimaste*, Ambassador Hawksworth. His Highness, Prince Jadar, conveys his most respectful greetings to you and to the English king." Vasant Rao's Turki had been excellent since his boyhood, and he tried to remember the phrases Mirza Nuruddin had coached. Then he watched through the bamboo poles of the gate as Hawksworth performed a lordly salaam from horseback.

The gate opened.

"I am pleased to offer my good offices to you and your king," Vasant Rao continued, "in the name of His Highness, the prince. It is his pleasure, and my honor, to provide you escort for your journey east to Burhanpur. From there His Highness will arrange a further escort for the trip north to Agra."

"His Majesty, King James, is honored by His Highness' concern." Hawksworth examined the waiting Rajputs, his apprehension mounting. Their eyes were expressionless beneath their leather helmets, but their horses pawed impatiently. He found himself wondering if Mirza Nuruddin had contrived to provide more "help," and yet another surprise. "But my route is not yet decided. Although I'm grateful for His Highness' offer, I'm not certain traveling east on the Burhanpur road is best. His Excellency, Mukarrab Khan, has offered to provide an escort if I take the Udaipur road, north past Cambay and then east."

Vasant Rao examined Hawksworth, choosing his words carefully. "We have orders to remain here for three days, Captain, and then to return to Burhanpur. It would be considered appropriate by the prince, who has full authority to administer this province, if we rode escort for you."

Hawksworth shifted in the saddle.

This isn't an offer. It's an ultimatum.

"Is His Highness aware I have with me a large sea chest? It will require a cart, which I plan to hire. Perhaps the delay this will impose would inconvenience you and your men, since you surely prefer to ride swiftly."

"On the contrary, Captain. We will have with us a small convoy of supplies, lead for molding shot. We will travel at a pace that best suits us all. Your chest presents no difficulty."

But there will be many difficulties, he told himself. And he thought again about Mirza Nuruddin and the terms he had demanded. Twenty percent interest on the loan, and only a hundred and eighty days to repay both the new silver coin and the interest.

But why, Vasant Rao asked himself again, did the Shahbandar agree to the plan at all? Is this Mirza Nuruddin's final wager? That Jadar will win?

"Will three days be sufficient for your preparations, Captain Hawksworth?"

"It will. If I decide to use the Burhanpur road." Hawksworth wondered how long he could taunt the Rajput.

"Perhaps I should tell you something about travel in India, Ambassador. There are, as you say, two possible routes between Surat and Agra. Both present certain risks. The northern route, through Udaipur and Rajputana, is at first appearance faster, since the roads are drier and the rivers there have already subsided from the monsoon. But it is not a part if India where travelers are always welcomed by the local Rajput clans. You may well find yourself in the middle of a local war, or the reluctant guest of a petty raja who judges you worth a ransom.

"On the other hand, if you travel east, through Burhanpur, you may find that some rivers are still heavy from the monsoon, at least for another month. But the clans there are loyal to Prince Jadar, and only near Chopda, halfway to Burhanpur, will you encounter any local brigands. Theirs, however, is an honorable profession, and they are always willing to accept bribes in return for safe passage. We ordinarily do not kill them, though we easily could, since petty robbery—they view it as a toll—is their livelihood and their tradition. They are weak and they make weak demands. Such is not true of the rajas in Rajputana. The choice is yours, but if you value your goods, and your life, you will join us as we make our way east to Burhanpur."

Hawksworth studied the bearded Rajput guards as Vasant Rao spoke.

I'm either a captive of the prince or of Mukarrab Khan, regardless of what I do. Which one wants me dead more?

"My frigate sails tomorrow. I can leave the following day."

"Good, it's agreed then. Our convoy will leave in three days. It will be my pleasure to travel with you, Captain Hawksworth. Your reputation has already reached His Highness. We will meet you here at the beginning of the second *pahar*. I believe that's your hour of nine in the morning." He smiled with a warmth that was almost genuine. "You should consider yourself fortunate. Few *feringhi* have ever traveled inland. You will find the interior far different from Surat. Until then."

He bowed lightly and snapped a command to the waiting horsemen. In moments they were lost among the trees.

"This evening must be a time of farewell for us both, Captain Hawksworth. You know, the Hindus believe life and death are an endless cycle that dooms them to repeat their miserable existence over and over again. I myself prefer to think that this one life is itself cyclical, ever renewing. What was new, exciting, yesterday is today tedious and tiresome. So tomorrow brings us both rebirth. For you it is Agra, for me Goa. But I expect to see Surat again, as no doubt do you. Who knows when our paths will cross once more?" Mukarrab Khan watched as a eunuch shoved wide the door leading onto the torchlit garden. "You have been a most gracious visitor, tolerating with exemplary forbearance my unworthy hospitality. Tonight perhaps you will endure one last evening of my company, even if I have little else left to offer."

The courtyard was a confused jumble of packing cases and household goods. Servants were everywhere, wrapping and crating rolled carpets, bolsters, furniture, vases, and women's clothing. Elephants stood near the back of the courtyard, *howdahs* on their backs, waiting to be loaded. Goods would be transferred to barks for the trip downriver to the bar, where they would be loaded aboard a waiting Portuguese frigate.

"My dining hall has been dismantled, its carpet rolled. We have no choice but to dine this evening in the open air, like soldiers on the march."

Hawksworth was no longer hearing Mukarrab Khan. He was staring past him, through the smoke, not quite believing what he saw. But it was all too real. Standing in the corner of the courtyard were two Europeans in black cassocks. Portuguese Jesuits.

Mukarrab Khan noticed Hawksworth's diplomatic smile suddenly freeze on his face, and turned to follow his gaze.

"Ah, I must introduce you. You do understand the Portuguese language, Captain?"

"Enough."

"I should have thought so. I personally find it abominable and refuse to study it. But both the fathers here have studied Persian in Goa, and I think one of them knows a bit of Turki, from his time in Agra."

"What are they doing here?" Hawksworth tried to maintain his composure.

"They returned to Surat just today from Goa, where they've been these past few weeks. I understand they're en route to the Jesuit mission in Lahore, a city in the Punjab, well to the north of Agra. They specifically asked to meet you." He laughed. "They're carrying no cannon, Captain, and I assumed you had no objection."

"You assumed wrong. I have nothing to say to a Jesuit."

"You'll meet Jesuits enough in Agra, Captain, at the *Moghul*'s court. Consider this evening a foretaste." Mukarrab Khan tried to smile politely, but there was a strained look in his eyes and he fingered his jeweled ring uncomfortably. "You would favor me by speaking to them."

The two Europeans were now moving toward them, working their way through the swarm of servants and crates in the courtyard. The ruby-studded crucifixes they wore against their black cassocks seemed to shoot red sparks into the evening air. Mukarrab Khan urged Hawksworth forward apprehensively.

"May I have the pleasure to present Ambassador Brian Hawksworth, who represents His Majesty, King James of England, and is also, I believe, an official of England's East India Company.

"And to you, Ambassador, I have the honor to introduce Father Alvarez Sarmento, Superior for the Society of Jesus' mission in Lahore, and Father Francisco da Silva."

Hawksworth nodded lightly and examined them. Although Sarmento was aged, his face remained strong and purposeful, with hard cheeks and eyes that might burn through marble. The younger priest could not have been more different. His ruddy neck bulged from the tight collar of his cassock, and his eyes shifted uncomfortably behind his puffed cheeks. Hawksworth wondered absently how long his bloat—too much capon and port wine—would last if Mackintosh had him on the third watch for a month.

"You are a celebrated man, Captain Hawksworth." Father Sarmento spoke in flawless Turki, but his voice was like ice. "There is much talk of you in Goa. The new Viceroy himself requested that we meet you, and convey a message."

"His last message was to order an unlawful attack on my merchantmen. I think he still remembers my reply. Is he now offering to abide by the treaty your Spanish king signed with King James?"

"That treaty has no force in Asia, Captain. His Excellency has asked us to inform you that your mission to Agra will not succeed. Our fathers have already informed the *Moghul* that England is a lawless nation living outside the grace of the Church. Perhaps you are unaware of the esteem he now holds for our Agra mission. We have a church there now, and through it we have led many carnal-minded Moors to God. We have refuted the Islamic mullahs in His Majesty's very presence, and shown him the falsity of their Prophet and his laws. Indeed, it is only because of the esteem we have earned that he now sends an ambassador to the Portuguese Viceroy."

Before Hawksworth could respond, Father Sarmento suddenly reached out and touched his arm imploringly. "Captain, let me speak now not for

the Viceroy, but for the Holy Church." Hawksworth realized with a shock
that he was speaking English. "Do you understand the importance of God's
work in this sea of damned souls? For decades we have toiled in this vine-
yard, teaching the Grace of God and His Holy Church, and now at last our
prayers are near to answer. When Arangbar became *Moghul*, our Third Mission had already been here for ten long, fruitless years. We strove to teach
the Grace of God to his father, Akman, but his damnation was he could
never accept a single True Church. He would harken to a heathen fakir as
readily as to a disciple of God. At first Arangbar seemed like him, save his
failing was not ecumenicity. It was indifference, and suspicion. Now, after
years of ignomy, we have secured his trust. And with that trust will soon
come his soul." Sarmento paused to cross himself. "When at last a Christian
holds the throne of India, there will be rejoicing at the Throne of Heaven.
You may choose to live outside the Mystery of the Most Holy Sacrament,
my son, but surely you would not wish to undo God's great work. I implore
you not to go before the *Moghul* now, not to sow unrest in his believing
mind with stories of the quarrels and hatreds of Europe. England was once
in the bosom of the Holy Church, until your heretic King Henry; and England had returned again, before your last, heretic queen led you once more
to damnation. Know the Church always stands with open heart to receive
you, or any apostate Lutheran, who wishes to repent and save his immortal
soul."

"I see now why Jesuits are made diplomats. Is your concern the loss of
the *Moghul's* soul, or the loss of his trade revenues in Goa?" Hawksworth
deliberately answered in Turki. "Tell your pope to stop trying to meddle in
England's politics, and tell your Viceroy to honor our treaty and there'll be
no 'quarrels' between us here."

"Will you believe my word, sworn before God, that I have told His Excellency that very thing? That this new war could destroy our years of work
and prayer." Sarmento still spoke in English. "But he is a man with a personal vendetta toward the English. It is our great tragedy. The Viceroy of
Goa, His Excellency, Miguel Vaijantes, is a man nourished by hatred. May
God forgive him."

Hawksworth stood speechless as Father Sarmento crossed himself.

"What did you say his name was?"

"Miguel Vaijantes. He was in Goa as a young captain, and now he has
returned as Viceroy. We must endure him for three more years. The Anti-
christ himself could not have made our cup more bitter, could not have
given us a greater test of our Christian love. Do you understand now why I
beg you in God's name to halt this war between us?"

Hawksworth felt suddenly numb. He stumbled past the aged priest and
blindly stared into the torchlit courtyard, trying to remember precisely what
Roger Symmes had said that day so many years ago in the offices of the

Levant Company. One of the few things he had never forgotten from Symmes's monologue of hallucinations and dreams was the name Miguel Vaijantes.

Hawksworth slowly turned to face Father Sarmento and switched to English.

"I will promise you this, Father. If I reach Agra, I will never speak of popery unless asked. It honestly doesn't interest me. I'm here on a mission, not a crusade. And in return I would ask one favor of you. I would like you to send a message to Miguel Vaijantes. Tell him that twenty years ago in Goa he once ordered the death of an English captain named Hawksworth on the *strappado*. Tell him . . ."

The crash of shattering glass from the hallway of the palace severed the air between them. Then the heavy bronze door swung wide and Shirin emerged, grasping the broken base of a Chinese vase. Her eyes blazed and her disheveled hair streamed out behind her. Hawksworth thought he saw a stain on one cheek where a tear had trailed, but now that trail was dry. She strode directly to Mukarrab Khan and dashed the remainder of the vase at his feet, where it shattered to powder on the marble tiles of the veranda.

"That is my gift to the queen. You may send it with a message in your next dispatch. Tell her that I too am Persian, that I too know the name of my father's father, of his father's father, of his father's father, for ten generations. But unlike her, I was born in India. And it is in India that I will stay. She can banish me to the remotest village of the Punjab, but she will never send me to Goa. To live among unwashed Portuguese. Never. She does not have the power. And if you were a man, you would divorce me. Here. Tonight. For all to see. And I will return to my father, or go where I wish. Or you may kill me, as you have already tried to do. But you must decide."

Mukarrab Khan's face was lost in shock. The courtyard stood lifeless, caught in a silence more powerful than any Hawksworth had ever known. He looked in confusion at Father Sarmento, and the old Jesuit quietly whispered a translation of the Persian, his own eyes wide in disbelief. Never before had he seen a Muslim woman defy her husband publicly. The humiliation was unthinkable. Mukarrab Khan had no power to order her death. He had no choice but to divorce her as she demanded. But everyone knew why she was his wife. What would a divorce mean?

"You will proceed to Goa as my wife, or you will spend the rest of your days, and what little remains of your fading beauty, as a *nautch* girl at the port. Your price will be one copper *pice*. I will order it in the morning."

"His Majesty will know of it within a week. I have friends enough in Agra."

"As do I. And mine have the power to act."

"Then divorce me."

Mukarrab Khan paused painfully, then glanced down and absently whisked a fleck of lint from his brocade sleeve. "Which form do you wish?"

An audible gasp passed through the servants, and not one breathed as they waited for the answer. There were three forms of divorce for Muslims. The first, called a revocable divorce, was performed when a man said "I have divorced you" only once. He had three months to reconsider and reconcile before it became final. The second form, called irrevocable, required the phrase be repeated twice, after which she could only become his wife again through a second marriage ceremony. The third, absolute, required three repetitions of the phrase and became effective the day her next reproductive cycle ended. There could be no remarriage unless she had, in the interim, been married to another.

"Absolute."

"Do you 'insist'?"

"I do."

"Then by law you must return the entire marriage settlement."

"You took it from me and squandered it long ago on *affion* and pretty boys. What is left to return?"

"Then it is done."

Hawksworth watched in disbelief as Mukarrab Khan repeated three times the Arabic phrase from the Quran that cast her out. The two Jesuits also stood silently, their faces horrified.

Shirin listened impassively as his voice echoed across the stunned courtyard. Then without a word she ripped the strands of pearls from her neck and threw them at his feet. Before Mukarrab Khan could speak again, she had turned and disappeared through the doorway of the palace.

"In the eyes of God, Excellency, you will always be man and wife." Father Sarmento broke the silence. "What He has joined, man cannot rend."

A look of great weariness seemed to flood Mukarrab Khan's face as he groped to find the facade of calm that protected him. Then, with an almost visible act of will, it came again.

"Perhaps you understand now, Father, why the Prophet's laws grant us more than one wife. Allah allows for certain . . . mistakes." He forced a smile, then whirled on a wide-eyed eunuch. "Will the packing be finished by morning?"

"As ordered, Khan Sahib." The eunuch snapped to formality.

"Then see dinner is served my guests, or put my kitchen *wallahs* to the lash." He turned back to Hawksworth. "I'm told you met her once, Ambassador. I trust she was more pleasant then."

"Merely by accident, Excellency. While I was at the . . . in the garden."

"She does very little by accident. You should mark her well."

"Your counsel is always welcome, Excellency." Hawksworth felt his pulse surge. "What will she do now?"

"I think she will have all her wishes granted." He turned wearily toward the marble columns of the veranda. "You will forgive me if I must leave you now for a while. You understand I have further dispatches to prepare."

He turned and was gone. After a moment's pause, the despairing Jesuits trailed after.

And suddenly the courtyard seemed empty.

The waves curled gently against the shore, breaking iridescent over the staves of a half-buried keg. Before him the sea spread wide and empty. Only a single sail broke the horizon. His mare pawed impatiently, but Hawksworth could not bring himself to turn her back toward the road. Not yet. Only when the sail's white had blended with the sea did he rein her around and, with one last glance at the empty blue, give her the spur.

He rode briskly past the nodding palms along the shore, then turned inland toward Surat, through villages of thatch-roofed houses on low stilts. Women watched from the wide porches, sewing, nursing infants. After a time he no longer saw them, no longer urged the mare. His thoughts were filled with images from the tumultuous evening past.

He had paced the vacant rooms of the palace till the early hours of morning, his mind in turmoil. Sleep was never a possibility. When the courtyard at last grew still, he had slipped back into the garden, wanting its openness, the feel of its order. In the moonlight it lay deserted, and as he strolled alongside the bubbling fountain, he felt himself even more lost in this alien place, this alien land. The pilot Karim had been right. India had already unsettled him more than he thought he could bear.

In time he found himself wandering once more through the orchard, amid the wistful calls of night birds. The trees formed a roof of leafy shadows, cold and joyless as the moon above. Even then, all he could see was Shirin, poised defiant in the stark torchlight, taunting the queen. She had offered herself up to almost certain death, for reasons he scarcely comprehended.

Before he fully realized where he was, he looked up and saw the observatory. A tiny blinking owl perched atop the staircase, studying him critically as he approached. Around him the marble instruments glistened like silver, while ahead stood the stone hut, forlorn now, more ramshackle than he had ever remembered, more abandoned. He reflected sadly that it probably would soon be forgotten entirely. Who would ever come here again?

The door of the hut was sealed tightly and for a time he stood simply looking at it, trying to recall all that had passed inside. Finally he reached with a determined hand and pulled it wide.

Shirin stared up from the table in shock, grabbing the lamp as though to extinguish it. Then she recognized him in the flickering light.

"Why . . . why are you here?"

Before he could answer, she moved in front of the table, masking it from his view. "You should not have come. If you're seen . . ."

As his own surprise passed, he felt himself suddenly wanting to take her in his arms. "What does it matter now? You're divorced." The words filled him with momentary exhilaration, till he remembered the rest. "You're also in danger, whether I'm seen or not."

"That's my concern."

"What are you planning to do?"

"Leave. But I still have friends."

He reached out and took the lamp from her, to feel the touch of her hand. It was soft and warm. "Will I ever see you again?"

"Who knows what will happen now?" The wildness in her eyes was beginning to gentle. She moved back from the table and dropped into a chair. He realized it was the same chair she had sat in when telling him about the queen. On the table before her were piles of papers, tied into small, neat bundles. She examined him for a few moments in silence, then reached to brush the hair back from her eyes. "Did you come here just to see me?"

"Not really . . ." He stopped, then laughed. "I think maybe I did. I think I somehow knew you would be here, without realizing I knew. I've been thinking about you all night."

"Why?" Her voice quickened just enough for him to notice.

"I'm not sure. I do know I'm very worried about what may happen to you."

"No one else seems to be. No one will talk to me now, not even the servants. Suddenly I don't exist." Her eyes softened. "Thank you. Thank you for coming. It means you're not afraid. I'm glad."

"Why do you care whether I came or not?" He asked almost before realizing what he was saying.

She hesitated, and unconsciously ran her glance down his frame. "To see you one more time." He thought he saw something enter her eyes, rising up unbidden. "Don't you realize you've become very special for me?"

"Tell me." He studied her eyes in the lamplight, watching them soften even more.

"You're not like anyone I've ever known. You're part of something that's very strange to me. I sometimes find myself dreaming of you. You're . . . you're very powerful. Something about you." She caught herself, then laughed. "But maybe it's not really you I dream about at all. Maybe it's what you are."

"What do you mean?"

"You're a man, from the West. There's a strength about you I can't fully understand." He watched her holding herself in check.

"Go on."

"Maybe it's partly the way you touch and master the things around you." She looked at him directly. "Let me try to explain what I mean. For most people in India, the world that matters most is the world within. We explore the seas inside our own mind. And so we wait, we wait for the world outside to be brought to us. But for you the inner world seems secondary." She laughed again, and now her voice was controlled and even. "Perhaps I'm not explaining it well. Let me try again. Do you remember the first thing you did on your very first morning in the palace?"

"I walked out here, to the observatory."

"But why did you?"

"Because I'm a seaman, and I thought . . ."

"No, that's only partly the reason." She smiled. "I think you came to see it because it belongs to the world of things. Like a good European, you felt you must first and always be the master of things. Of ships, of guns, even of the stars. Maybe that's why I find you so strong." She paused, then reached out and touched his hand. The gesture had been impulsive, and when she realized what she'd done, she moved to pull it back, then stopped herself.

He looked at her in the lamplight, then gently placed his other hand over hers and held it firm. "Then let me tell *you* something. I find you just as hard to understand. I find myself drawn to something about you, and it troubles me."

"Why should it trouble you?"

"Because I don't know who you are. What you are. Even what you're doing, or why. You've risked everything for principles that are completely outside me." He looked into her eyes, trying to find words. "And regardless of what you say, I think you somehow know everything there is to know about me. I don't even have to tell you."

"Things pass between a man and woman that go beyond words. Not everything has to be said." She shifted her gaze away. "You've had great sadness in your life. And I think it's killed some part of you. You no longer allow yourself to trust or to love."

"I've had some bad experiences with trust."

"But don't let it die." Her eyes met his. "It's the thing most worthwhile."

He looked at her a long moment, feeling the tenderness beneath her strength, and he knew he wanted her more than anything. Before he thought, he had slipped his arm around her waist and drawn her up to him. He later remembered his amazement at her softness, her warmth as he pulled her body against his own. Before she could speak, he had kissed her, bringing her mouth full to his lips. He had thought for an instant she would resist, and he meant to draw her closer. Only then did he realize it was she who had come to him, pressing her body against his. They clung together in the lamplight, neither wanting the moment to end. At last, with an act of will, she pulled herself away.

"No." Her breath was coming almost faster than his own. "It's impossible."

"Nothing's impossible." He suddenly knew, with an absolute certainty, that he had to make her his own. "Come with me to Agra. Together . . ."

"Don't say it." She stopped his lips with her finger. "Not yet." She glanced at the papers on the table, then reached for his hand, bringing it to her moist cheek. "Not yet."

"You're leaving. So am I. We'll leave together."

"I can't." She was slipping from him. He felt it. "I'll think of you when you're in Agra. And when we're ready, we'll find each other, I promise it."

Before he knew, she had turned and gathered the bundles. When she reached for the lamp, suddenly her hand stopped.

"Let's leave it." She looked toward him. "Still burning." Then she reached out and brushed his lips with her fingertips one last time. He watched in dismay as she passed on through the doorway. In moments she was lost among the shadows of the orchard.

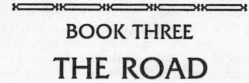

BOOK THREE
THE ROAD

CHAPTER THIRTEEN

East along the Tapti River valley the land was a verdant paradise, a patchwork of mango and pipal groves and freshly turned dark earth. By mid-October the fields of cotton, corn, and sugarcane were in harvest; and in the lowlands paired buffalo strained to turn the crusted mud to readiness for broadcast sowing the grain crops of autumn: millet, wheat, and barley. The monsoon-washed roads had again grown passable, and now they were a continual procession, as mile-long caravans of corn-laden bullock carts inched ponderously west toward the shipping port of Surat.

The distance from Surat to Burhanpur was one hundred and fifty *kos*, and in dry weather it could be traversed in just over a fortnight. Vasant Rao had hired fifty carts to transport the sealed bundles—which he said were lead—to Burhanpur, swelling his entourage of forty Rajput horsemen by fifty low-caste drivers and bullock teams. He had also hired five additional carts to carry provisions.

Brian Hawksworth had contracted for his own cart and driver, negotiating a price of twenty rupees for cartage of his belongings all the way from Surat to Agra. He was amused to reflect that the chest containing King James's gifts for the *Moghul* of India traveled lashed to the bed of a ramshackle, wooden-wheeled cart originally intended for hay.

The caravan had been scheduled to depart early on a Saturday morning, but the drivers had suddenly refused to budge until the following day. Hawksworth had confronted his driver, Nayka, a dark-skinned low-caste man with the spindly limbs of the underfed, and demanded to know why. Nayka had twisted his head deferentially, riveting his eyes on the ground, and explained in halting Turki.

"Today is Saturday, Captain Sahib. Saturdays and Tuesdays are sacred to the goddess Devi, the Divine Mother. Journeys begun on those days always meet disaster. Bandits, tigers, washed-out roads. A Mussalman once made my cousin bring a cart of indigo to Surat from a village down the river on a Tuesday, and a bridge broke under his load. Both of his bullocks were drowned."

It was midafternoon on Sunday when the caravan finally pulled out from the water tank at Surat's Abidjan Gate. By nightfall they had traveled three *kos*, reaching the outskirts of the village of Cossaria. The next day they made twelve *kos* east-northeast to reach the town of Karod, a strategic fort on the Tapti, dominated by a hilltop castle that garrisoned two hundred Rajput soldiers. The next three days their camp stages had been the towns of Viara, Corka, and the large garrison city of Narayanpur.

On the insistence of Mirza Nuruddin, Hawksworth had carried only a minimal amount of money with him. Instead he had adopted the practice of Indian merchants, leaving a chest of silver in Surat and receiving a letter of credit, which could be debited for cash at major stops along the road to Agra. Moneylenders received negotiable notes against the silver deposit, which would be paid in Surat at 7 percent surcharge, thereby allowing travelers along the bandit-infested roads to carry cheques instead of cash.

Hawksworth found himself annoyed that Vasant Rao never allowed the caravan to stop inside the towns, where traditional Indian guest houses—a stone floor and a roof—were available free for travelers. Instead they camped each evening on the outskirts, while a few Rajputs rode in to the town bazaar to buy fresh vegetables, bricks of cow dung for cooking, and betel leaves for the drivers.

The evening they reached Narayanpur, the governor of the garrison, Partab Shah, had paid a surprise visit to their camp, bringing his own troup of *nautch* women. While the women entertained the Rajputs with an evening of dance and low-priced sex, Partab Shah whispered warnings to Hawksworth that the road farther east was no longer safe now that civil rule in the Deccan was teetering. The governor had offered to provide additional troops to escort the English ambassador and his gifts for the *Moghul* safely through the district. To the governor's—and Hawksworth's—dismay, Vasant Rao had politely declined.

It had been well after midnight when the governor and his aides rose to return to Narayanpur. Vasant Rao had insisted that the women be sent with him. Then he convened the Rajputs and drivers and announced that they would assemble the caravan two hours before sunup the following morning, an hour earlier than usual. They would try to reach and ford the Tapti before nightfall, then veer northeast for Burhanpur. Hawksworth thought he detected a trace of worry in Vasant Rao's voice for the first time.

They were well underway by sunup the next day, and as he fought off sleep in the rising heat, Hawksworth reflected on what he had seen along the road. It was clear the larger towns were collection depots for the Surat region, centers where grain, cotton, indigo, and hemp were assembled for delivery to the port. As their caravan rumbled through town after town, Hawksworth began to find them merely a provincial version of Surat, equally frenetic and self-absorbed. Their bazaars bustled with haggling brokers and an air of commerce triumphant. After a time he began to find them more wearisome than exotic.

But between these towns lived the other India, one of villages unchanged for centuries. To a Londoner and seaman they were another world, and Hawksworth understood almost nothing of what he saw. Several times he had started to ask Vasant Rao some question about a village, but the time never seemed right. The Rajput was constantly occupied with the progress of the caravan and never spoke unless he was giving an order. The long silence of the road had gathered between them until it was almost an invisible wall.

For no apparent reason this changed suddenly on the afternoon after Narayanpur, as the caravan rumbled into the small village of Nimgul and began working its way along the single road through the town. Vasant Rao drew his mount alongside Hawksworth's and pointed to a white plaster building up ahead that dominated the center of the village.

"I grew to manhood in a village such as this, Captain, in a house much like that one there."

Hawksworth examined the well-kept house, and then the village around it. Spreading away on all sides were tumbledown thatch-roofed homes of sticks and clay, many raised on foot-high stilts to keep them above the seasonal mud. Gaunt, naked children swarmed about the few remaining trees, their voices piping shrilly at play, while elderly men lounged on the porches smoking *hookahs*. Most of the able-bodied men seemed to be in the fields, leaving their women—unsmiling laborers in drab body-length wraps, a large marriage ring dangling from one nostril—to toil in the midday sun combing seeds from large stacks of cotton, shelling piles of small-eared corn, and boiling a dense brown liquid in wide iron pans.

Vasant Rao drew up his horse in front of the pans and spoke rapidly with one of the sad-eyed women. There was a tinkle of her heavy silver bracelets as she bowed to him, then turned to ask a turbaned overseer to offer them two clay cups of the liquid. Vasant Rao threw the man a small coin, a copper *pice*, and passed one of the cups to Hawksworth. It was viscous and sweeter than anything he had ever tasted. Vasant Rao savored a mouthful, then discarded the cup into the road.

"They're boiling cane juice to make *gur*, those brown blocks of sugar you see in the bazaars, for the Brahmin landholders to sell. She's a Camar, a low caste, and she works from sunup to dusk for a day's supply of *chapattis*, fried wheat cakes, for her household. Wages haven't risen in the villages since I was a boy."

"Why did she ask the overseer to bring you the cup?"

"Because I'm a Rajput." Vasant Rao seemed startled by the question.

"I would pollute my caste if I took a cup from the hand of a Camar. If a Rajput or a Brahmin eats food that's been handled by a member of the low castes, he may be obligated to undergo ritual purification. If you are born to a high caste, Captain, you must honor its obligations."

Hawksworth studied him, wondering why he had finally decided to talk.

Security had been unaccountably tight for a shipment of lead. Vasant Rao had insisted that all carts be kept within the perimeter of the camp, inside the circle of guards. No one, neither drivers nor guards, had been allowed to touch the contents of the carts: sealed packages individually wrapped and lashed in bricks.

"Did you grow up around here?" Hawksworth tried to widen the opening.

"No, of course not." He laughed sharply. "Only a *feringhi* would ask that. I was born in the foothills of the Himalayas, hundreds of *kos* north of Agra. In a Rajput village. The villages in the Surat district are ruled by Brahmins."

"Are Rajput villages like this?"

"All villages are more or less the same, Captain. How could it be otherwise? They're all Hindu. This is the real India, my friend. Muslims and Moghuls, and now Christians, come and go. This stays the same. These villages will endure long after the marble cities of the Moghuls are dust. That's why I feel peace here. Knowing this cannot be destroyed, no matter who rules in Agra."

Hawksworth looked about the village. It seemed to be ruled by cattle. They roamed freely, arrogantly, secure in the centuries-old instinct that they were sacred and inviolable. Naked children had begun to swarm after the carts, and a few young women paused to cast discreet glances at the handsome Rajput horsemen. But the main work pressed monotonously forward. It was a place untouched by the world beyond its horizons.

"You said this was a Brahmin village. Are all the men here priests?"

"Of course not." Vasant Rao grunted a laugh and gestured toward the fields beyond. "Who would do the work? There must be the other castes, or the Brahmins would starve. Brahmins and Rajputs are forbidden by the laws of caste from working the land. I meant this village is ruled by Brahmins, although I'd guess no more than one family in ten is high caste. The brick and plaster homes there in the center of the village probably belong to Brahmins. The villages of India, Captain Hawksworth, are not ruled by the Moghuls. They're ruled by the high castes. Here, the Brahmins, in other villages, the Rajputs. These, together with somes merchants called Banias, make up the high-caste Hindus, the wearers of the sacred thread of the twice born, the real owners and rulers of India. All the other castes exist to serve them."

"I thought there were only four castes."

Hawksworth remembered that Mukarrab Khan had once described the caste system of the Hindus with obvious Muslim disgust. There are four castes, he had explained, each striving to exploit those below. The greatest exploiters called themselves Brahmin, probably Aryan invaders who had arrived thousands of years past and now proclaimed themselves "preservers of tradition." That tradition, which they invented, was mainly subjugation of all the others. Next came the Kshatriya, the warrior caste, which had been claimed by Rajput tribes who also had invaded India, probably well after the Brahmins. The third caste, also "high," was called Vaisya, and was supposed to be made up of society's producers of foods and goods. Now it was the caste claimed by rich, grasping Hindu merchants. Below all these were the Sudra, who were in effect the servants and laborers for the powerful "high" castes. But even the Sudra had someone to exploit, for beneath them were the Untouchables, those unfortunates in whose veins probably ran the blood of the original inhabitants of India. The Untouchables had no caste. The part that annoyed Mukarrab Khan the most was that high-caste Hindus regarded all Muslims as part of the mass of Untouchables.

"The four main castes are those prescribed in the order of the *varna*, the ancient Aryan scriptures. But the world of the village has little to do with the *varna*. Today there are many castes," Vasant Rao continued, reflecting to himself how he loathed most Brahmins, who took every opportunity to claim caste superiority over Rajputs. "For example, the Brahmins here probably have two subcastes—one for the priests, who think up ceremonies as an excuse to collect money, and the other for the landowners, most of whom are also moneylenders. "There"—he pointed—"that man is a Brahmin."

Hawksworth saw a shirtless man standing by one of the white plaster homes. He wore a dingy loincloth beneath his enormous belly, and as Hawksworth examined him he noticed a strand of thread that circled around his neck and under his left arm.

"Why is he wearing a cord around his shoulder?"

"That's the sacred thread of the high castes. I wear one myself." Vasant Rao opened his shirt to reveal a strand of three colored threads, woven together. "It's consecrated and given to boys around age ten at a very important ceremony. Before the thread ceremony a boy has no caste. An orthodox Brahmin won't even eat with his son until after the boy's thread ceremony."

Hawksworth examined the thread. It was the first time he'd noticed it.

"What about the men who don't wear a thread?"

"They're the middle castes, the ones who do the work in a village. Carpenters, potters, weavers, barbers. They serve the high castes and each other. The barber shaves the potter; the potter makes his vessels. The Brahmins here probably won't sell them any land, so they'll always be poor. That's why the middle castes live in houses of mud and thatch instead of brick. And below them are the unclean castes. Sweepers, servants, shoemakers."

And below *them* are the non-Hindus, Hawksworth thought. Me.

"What the hell's the reason for all this? It's worse than the class system in England. I'll drink with any man, high or low. I have. And I usually prefer to drink with the low."

"That may explain why most *feringhis* seem so confused and unhappy. Caste is the most important thing in life." Vasant Rao glanced over his shoulder at the receding village. "It's the reason India's civilization has lasted for thousands of years. I pity your misfortune, Captain Hawksworth, not to have been born a Hindu. Perhaps you were once, and will be again in some future life. I think you'll someday be reborn a Kshatriya, a member of the warrior caste. Then you'll know who you are, what you must do. Unlike the Moghuls and the other Muslims, who have no caste and never know their purpose in life, a Rajput always knows."

As they rode on through the countryside Hawksworth tried to understand the purpose of castes. Its absurdity annoyed him.

Mukarrab Khan was right for once. It's just a class system, devised by the highborn to keep the others in submission. But why do they all seem to believe in it? Why don't the so-called lower castes just tell the others to go to hell?

As they neared the next village, he decided to try to guess who was in which caste. But the central road in the village was deserted. Instead all the villagers, men and women, were clustered around a tall, brightly painted pole that had been erected near one of the dingy thatch homes. Vasant Rao's face brightened when he saw the pole.

"There must be a wedding here today. Have you ever seen one?"

"No. Not in India."

"This is a powerful moment, Captain, when you feel the force of *prahna*, the life spirit."

Vasant Rao pointed toward a pavilion that had been erected next to the marriage pole. From horseback Hawksworth could just make out the bride and groom, both dressed in red wraps trimmed in silver. The groom wore a high turban, on top of which were ceremonial decorations, and the bride was so encrusted with precious metals she might have been a life-size ornament: her hands, wrists, feet, ankles, and her head were all adorned with elaborately worked silver rings, bracelets, medallions. Her necklace was a string of large gold coins.

"Where'd she get all the silver and gold?"

"Her father is probably a big landowner. Those ornaments are her savings and part of her dowry. Look, all the women wear thick bracelets of silver on their ankles. There's much gold and silver in India, Captain."

As Hawksworth watched, a Brahmin priest, his forehead streaked with white clay, finished lighting a fire in a central brazier and then began to recite.

"The priest is reciting from the Vedas, Sanskrit scriptures thousands of years old," Vasant Rao continued as they watched. "This is a ritual going back to the dawn of time."

The couple began repeating the priest's verses, their faces intent and solemn.

"They're taking the marriage vows now. There are seven. The most important is the wife's vow of complete obedience to her husband. See the silver knife he carries? That's to symbolize his dominion over her. But really, she will belong to his entire family when she finally comes to live at his house."

"What do you mean by 'finally'?"

"These things take time. To begin with, a marriage proposal must come from the family of the girl. As she approaches womanhood, her father will hire a marriage broker, probably the village barber, to go to surrounding villages to look for a suitable match. I remember when I was young and they used to come to my village." Vasant Rao's face assumed a faraway expression. "I didn't want to marry and I dreaded seeing them, but unfortunately I was a good catch. My subcaste is high, and I had many sisters, which meant more women to share the work in our house. Then one day my father ordered the priest to cast my horoscope and I knew I was lost. A broker had brought an inquiry from a girl who had a compatible horoscope. Soon after, the engagement ceremony was held in our house. The girl was not there, of course; I didn't see her until three years later. When we finally had the ceremony you see here."

The bride and groom were standing together now, and they began to circle the fire while the women standing nearby sang a monotonous, repetitive song. Hawksworth counted seven turns of the fire. Then they seated themselves and the priest placed a red dot on the forehead of man and wife.

"They'll feast tonight, and then the groom will return to his village." Vasant Rao spurred his mount to catch up with the caravan. "Later she and her family will go there for more ceremonies. After that the groom may not see her again for several years, until the day her father decides she's ready for the *gauna*, the consummation of the marriage. I didn't see my bride again for two years."

"What happened then?"

"She came to my village for a few days and stayed in the women's quarters—the men and women sleep apart in these villages—and I had to go there and try to find her cot. After that she went back home and it was several months later before I saw her again. Then she came back, for a longer time. Finally she moved to my village, but by then I was nineteen and soon after I left on a campaign. She stayed with my younger brother while I was gone, and when I returned, she was with child. Who can say whether it was mine or his? But none of it matters, for she died in childbirth." He spurred his horse past the line of carts. "Let's try to make the river before sundown."

Hawksworth couldn't believe what he had heard, and he whipped his mount to catch up.

"Your brother kept your wife while you were away?"

"Of course. I don't know how it is *here*, but in the part of India where I was born, brothers normally share each other's wives. I used to go to my older brother's house when he was gone and visit his wife. She expected it and would have been upset if I hadn't come to her." Vasant Rao was puzzled by Hawksworth's surprise. "Don't brothers share one another's wives in England?"

"Well, not . . . usually. I mean . . . no. Hell no. It's damned close to incest. The truth is a husband would have grounds to call out a man he caught with his wife. And especially a brother."

" 'Call him out,' Captain? What does that mean?"

"A duel. With swords. Or maybe pistols."

Vasant Rao was incredulous.

"But what if a man goes away on a campaign? His wife will grow frustrated. Hindus believe a woman has seven times the sexual energy of a man. She would start meeting other men in the village if a man didn't have a brother to keep her satisfied. In the village were I grew up, if a man and woman met together by chance in the forest, and they had the same caste, we all assumed they would make the most of the opportunity. So it's better for the honor of the family if your brothers care for your wife. It's an important duty for brothers. And besides, as long as a woman attends to her own husband's needs, what does it matter if his brother enjoys her also?"

Hawksworth found himself astonished.

"How does . . . I mean, what about this brother's own wife? What does she think about all this?"

"If her husband wants to visit his brothers' wives, what should she care? It's normal. She'll also find ways to meet her husband's brothers for the same purpose. Women married to brothers often try to send each other away on errands, in order to enjoy the other's husband. So wives have no reason to complain. In fact, if a woman returns to her own village for a visit, she will probably seek out some of the men she knew when she was young and enjoy them, since her husband is not around and no one in her own village would tell him. Hindus in the villages don't lock away their women the way the Muslims do, Captain Hawksworth. And because they're free to enjoy whoever they wish, they aren't frustrated and unhappy the way Muslim women are. Surely your England is an advanced country where women have the same freedom."

Hawksworth puzzled for a minute before trying to answer. The truth is there's a big difference between what's said and what's done. With chastity praised from the pulpits and whores the length of London. And highborn

ladies thronging the playhouses, ready to cuckold their husbands with any
cavalier who'll give them a look. How can I explain it?

"I guess you'd say upper-class women have the most freedom to take
lovers. Usually young gallants or soldiers. And no one is surprised if her husband makes full use of his serving wench."

"Are these soldiers and servingwomen from a lower caste?"

"Well, we don't exactly have . . ." Hawksworth paused for a moment.
"Actually I guess you could say they're a lower 'caste,' in a way."

Vasant reined in his mount and inspected Hawksworth for a moment in
disgust.

"Please excuse me if I say yours must be a very immoral country, Captain. Such a thing would never happen in India. No Rajput would touch the
body of a low caste. It would be pollution."

"You don't care what your women do? All that matters is who they do
it with?" Hawksworth suddenly realized he found it all too absurd to believe.
It sounds like another tale of the Indies. Concocted to entertain credulous
seamen. "All right, then, what about your own wife? Did she have other
men besides your brothers?"

"How would I know?" Vasant Rao waved his hand, dismissing the question as insignificant. "I suppose it's possible. But after she died I decided I'd
had enough of wives and women. I took a vow of chastity. There's the legend
of a god named Hanumanji, who took on the flesh of a monkey and who
gained insuperable strength by retaining his semen. It made him invulnerable." Vasant Rao smiled. "So far it's worked for me as well. But to protect the charm, I eat no meat and drink a glass of opium each day."

The Rajput suddenly spurred his mount toward the head of the caravan. The sun had disappeared behind a heavy bank of storm clouds in the
west, and the road had already begun to darken. The river was probably still
another hour away, perhaps two hours.

Hawksworth studied Vasant Rao's tall, commanding form, sitting erect
and easy in the saddle.

Sweet Jesus, he thinks he's invulnerable because he avoids women and
drinks opium. Rajputs are even madder than the damned Turks. And he
thinks the high castes rule by the will of God. I wonder what the low castes
think?

Hawksworth puzzled through the Rajput's words and half-dozed in the
saddle until he realized they were finally approaching the river. Ahead, past
groves of mango trees, lay a sandy expanse leading down toward the water's
edge. As they approached, Vasant Rao sent some of his horsemen to scout
along the riverbank in both directions to find a shallow spot for crossing.
The caravan followed the stream for half a *kos*, then halted on a sandy plain
that sloped gradually down toward the wide stream. The water rippled

slightly all the way across, signifying there were no lurking depths to swallow a cart.

The sun was dying, washing a veneer of gold over the high dark clouds threatening in the east. The smell of rain hinted in the evening air. Vasant Rao peered across the water's darkening surface for a time, while the drivers waited patiently for orders to begin crossing, then he turned to the waiting Rajputs.

"The light is too far gone." He stroked the mane of his gray stallion and again studied the clouds building where the sun had been. "It's safer to camp here and cross in the morning."

He signaled the head driver and pointed the Rajputs toward a sandy expanse close to the water's edge. In moments the drivers were urging their teams toward the spot, circling them in preparation for the night.

"The carts will go on the riverside, and we'll camp here." He specified areas for the Rajputs and the drivers, and then he turned to Hawksworth and pointed out a large mango tree. "Your tent can go there."

Hawksworth had been required by the Rajputs to keep a separate area for his campfire and cooking. Vasant Rao had explained the reasons the first evening of the journey.

"Food is merely an external part of the body, Captain, so naturally it must be kept from pollution. Food is transformed into blood, and the blood eventually turns to flesh, the flesh to fat, and the fat to marrow. The marrow turns to semen, the life-force. Since you have no caste, a Rajput would become polluted if he allowed you to touch his food, or even the pots in which he cooked."

Hawksworth's driver, being a low caste, had no objection to cooking and eating with the English ambassador. Their diet on the trip had been simple. The Rajputs lived mainly on game they killed as they rode, though some occasionally ate fish. A few seemed to subsist on rice, wheat cakes, and boiled lentils. That night, as an experiment, Hawksworth ordered his driver, Nayka, to prepare a dinner of whatever he himself was having. Then he reclined against his saddle, poured himself a tankard of brandy, and watched the preparations.

Nayka struck up a fire of twigs, to ignite the chips of dried cow dung used for the real cooking, and then he began to heat a curved pan containing ghee, butter that had been boiled and strained to prevent rancidity. Although the Rajputs cooked in vegetable oil, Nayka had insisted from the first that a personage as important as the English feringhi should eat only clarified butter. The smoldering chips of dung took a long time to heat, but finally the ghee seemed ready. Nayka had ground spices as he waited, and he began to throw them into the hot fat to sputter. Then he chopped vegetables and dropped them in to fry. In a separate pot he was already boiling lentils, together with a yellow spice he called turmeric. As the meal neared readiness, he began to fry *chappatis*, thin patties of unleavened wheat flour mixed with water and *ghee*. Then Hawksworth watched in shock as Nayka discreetly dropped a coal of burning cow dung into the pot of cooking lentils.

"What the *hell* was that?"

"Flavoring, Captain Sahib." Nayka's Turkish had been learned through procuring women for Turkish seamen, and it was heavily accented and abrupt. "It's the secret of the flavor of our lentils."

"Is that 'high-caste' practice?"

"I think it is the same for all." Nayka examined him for a moment, twisting his head deferentially. "Does the Sahib know about caste?"

"I know it's a damnable practice."

"The Sahib says what the Sahib says, but caste is a very good thing."

"How do you figure that?"

"Because I will be reborn a Brahmin. I went to a soothsayer who told me. My next life will be marvelous."

"But what about this life?"

"My present birth was due to a very grave mistake. The soothsayer explained it. He said that in my last life I was a Rajput. Once I ordered my cook to prepare a gift for some Brahmins, to bake bread for them, and inside the bread I had put gold. It was an act of great merit. But the faithless cook betrayed me. He stole the gold and put stones in its place. The Brahmins were very insulted, but no one ever told me why. Because I had insulted Brahmins, I was reborn as I am. But my next life will be different. I will be rich and have many women. Like a Brahmin or a Rajput." Nayka's eyes gleamed in anticipation.

"The improvement in money I can understand." Hawksworth examined Nayka's ragged *dhoti*. "But what does it matter when it comes to women? There seem to be plenty of randy women to go around, in all castes."

"That's true if you are a Rajput or a Brahmin. Then no woman of any caste can refuse you. But if you are a low caste, and you are caught with a high-caste woman, you'll probably be beaten to death by the Rajputs. They would say you were polluting her caste."

"Wait a minute. I thought Rajputs would have nothing to do with a low-caste woman." Hawksworth remembered Vasant Rao's stern denial.

"Who told you that?" Nayka smiled at Hawksworth's naïveté. "I would guess a Rajput. They always deny it to strangers, so you won't form unfavorable ideas about the high castes. Let me tell you that it is a lie, Captain Sahib. They take our women all the time, and there is nothing we can say. But a low-caste man with a high-caste woman is another matter."

"But what about their 'ritual pollution'? They're not supposed to touch the low castes."

"It's very simple. A Rajput can take one of our women if he chooses, and then just take a bath afterward and he is clean again."

"But can't a high-caste woman do the same, if she's been with a low-caste man?"

"No, Captain Sahib. Because they say her pollution is *internal*. She has the polluting emissions of the low-caste man within her. So there is no way she can be purified. It's the way the high castes control their women. But if you're a man, you can have any woman you please, and there's nothing anyone can say." Again Nayka's eyes brightened. "It will be wonderful the day I am reborn. Caste is a wonderful thing."

Hawksworth studied the half-starved, almost toothless man who stood before him barefoot, grinning happily.

Well, enjoy your dreams, you poor miserable son-of-a-bitch. I'll not be the one to tell you this life is all you get.

He took a slug of brandy and returned to his dung-flavored lentils. Taken with some of the charcoal-flavored bread they were actually better than he'd expected.

Vasant Rao had already summoned the Rajputs and made assignments for the evening guard duty. Guards were to be doubled. Hawksworth remained astounded by the Rajput concept of security. A large kettledrum was set up at the head of the camp and continually beaten from dusk to dawn. A detail of Rajputs would march around the perimeter of the camp throughout the night, and on the quarter hour a shout of "*khabardar*," meaning "take heed," would circle the camp. The first night Hawksworth had found it impossible to sleep for the noise, but the second night and thereafter his weariness overtook him.

He poured himself another brandy and watched as Nayka scrubbed out the cooking pans with ashes and sand. Then the driver rolled a betel leaf for Hawksworth and another for himself and set to work erecting the tent, which was nothing more than four poles with a canopy. After this he unloaded Hawksworth's cot, a foot-high wooden frame strung with hemp. None of the Rajputs used cots; they preferred a thin pallet on the ground.

Nayka seemed to work more slowly as he started unrolling the bedding onto the hemp strings of the cot, and he began to glance nervously at the sky. Suddenly he stopped and slipped quietly to where the other drivers were encamped, seated on their haunches around a fire, passing the mouthpiece of a *hookah*. A long discussion followed, with much pointing at the sky. Then Nayka returned and approached Hawksworth, twisting his head in the deferential bow all Indians seemed to use to superiors. He stood for a moment in hesitation, and then summoned the courage to speak.

"It is not well tonight, Sahib. We have traveled this road many times." He pointed east into the dark, where new lightning played across the hovering bank of clouds. "There has been rain near Chopda, farther east where the river forks. In two *pahars* time, six of your hours, the river will begin to rise here."

"How much will it rise?"

"Only the gods can tell. But the river will spread beyond its banks and reach this camp. I have seen it. And it will remain impassable for three days."

"How can you be sure?"

"I have seen it before, Sahib. The drivers all know and they are becoming afraid. We know the treachery of this river very well. But the other bank is near high ground. If we crossed tonight we would be safe." Again he shifted his head deferentially. "Will you please tell the raja?"

To the drivers, Vasant Rao could only be a raja, a hereditary prince. All important Rajputs were automatically called rajas.

"Tell him yourself."

"We would rather you tell him, Captain Sahib. He is a high caste. It would not be right for us to tell a raja what to do."

Hawksworth watched for a moment as the Rajput guards began taking their place around the perimeter of the camp, and then he looked sadly at his waiting cot.

Damn. Crossing in the dark could be a needless risk. Why didn't the drivers say something while we still had light? God curse them and their castes.

Then with a shrug of resignation he rose and made his way to Vasant Rao's tent.

The Rajput leader had already removed his helmet, but after listening to Hawksworth he reluctantly strapped it back on and called for his second in command. Together they examined the clouds and then walked down to the river.

In the dark no one could tell if it had begun to rise. Vasant Rao ordered three Rajputs to ride across carrying torches, to test the depth and mark out a path. The river was wide, but it still was no more than a foot or two deep. When the third Rajput finally reached the far shore, over a hundred yards away, Vasant Rao issued orders to assemble the convoy.

The drivers moved quickly to harness their bullocks, which had been tethered to stakes near bundles of hay. The weary cattle tossed their heads and sniffed suspiciously at the moist air as they were whipped into harness. Meanwhile the Rajput guards began saddling their horses.

Hawksworth saddled his own mare and watched as his cot and tent were rolled and strapped into the cart alongside his chest. He stared again into the darkness that enveloped the river. Nothing could be seen except the three torches on the distant shore. Suddenly he seemed to hear a warning bell in the back of his mind.

We're too exposed. Half the guard will be in the river while we cross. And there'll be no way to group the carts if we need to.

He paused a moment, then retrieved his sword from the cart and buckled it on. Next he checked the prime on the two matchlock pocket pistols he carried, one in each boot.

Five mounted Rajputs holding torches led as the convoy started across the sandy alluvium toward the river. Hawksworth's cart was the first to move, and as he drew his mare alongside, Nayka threw him a grateful smile through the flickering light of the torch strapped against one of the cart's poles.

"You've saved us all, Captain Sahib. When the river grows angry, nothing can appease her."

The bullocks nosed warily at the water, but Nayka gave them the lash and they waded in without protest. The bed was gravel, smoothed by the long action of the stream, and the water was still shallow, allowing the large wheels of the carts to roll easily. Hawksworth pulled his mount close to the cart and let its enormous wheel splash coolness against his horse's flank.

The current grew swifter as they reached the center of the stream, but the bullocks plodded along evenly, almost as though they were on dry ground. Then the current eased again, and Hawksworth noticed that the Rajputs riding ahead had already reined in their mounts, signifying they had gained the far shore. Their five torches merged with the three of the Rajputs already waiting, and together they lined the water's edge.

Hawksworth twisted in the saddle and looked back at the line of carts. They traveled abreast in pairs, a torchman riding between, and the caravan had become an eerie procession of waving lights and shadows against the dark water. The last carts were in the river now, and Vasant Rao was riding rapidly toward him, carrying a torch.

Looks like I was wrong again, Hawksworth thought, and he turned to rein his horse as it stumbled against a submerged rock.

The torches along the shore were gone.

He stared in disbelief for a moment, and then he saw them sputtering in the water's edge. Lightning flashed in the east, revealing the silhouettes of the Rajputs' mounts, stumbling along the shore, their saddles empty. He whirled to check the caravan behind him, and at that moment an arrow ricocheted off the pole of the cart and ripped cleanly through the side of his jerkin. He suddenly realized the torch lashed to the side of the cart illuminated him brilliantly, and he drew his sword and swung at its base, slicing it in half. As it fell, sputtering, he saw a second arrow catch Nayka squarely in the throat and he watched the driver spin and slump wordlessly into the water.

Godforsaken luckless Hindu. Now you can be reborn a Brahmin. Only sooner than you thought.

A shout of alarm erupted from behind, and he looked to see the remaining Rajputs charging in formation, bows already drawn. The water churned around him as they dashed by, advancing on the shore. The Rajputs' horn bows hissed in rapid succession as they sent volleys of bamboo arrows into the darkness. But the returning rain of arrows was dense and deadly. He saw the Rajput nearest him suddenly pivot backward in the saddle, an arrow lodged in his groin, below his leather chest guard. Hawksworth watched incredulously as the man clung to his saddle horn for a long last moment, pulling himself erect and releasing a final arrow before tumbling into the water.

Again lightning flared across the sky, and in the sudden illumination Hawksworth could see shapes along the shore, an army of mounted horsemen, well over a hundred. They were drawn in tight formation, calmly firing into the approaching Rajputs. The lightning flashed once more, a broad sheet of fire across the sky, and at that moment Hawksworth saw Vasant Rao gain the shore, where he was instantly surrounded by a menacing wall of shields and pikes.

Then more of the Rajputs gained the shore, and he could hear their chant of "Ram Ram," their famous battle cry. The horsemen were moving on the caravan now, and when the lightning blazed again Hawksworth realized he had been surrounded.

The dark figure in the lead seized Hawksworth's right arm from behind and began to grapple for his sword. As he struggled to draw it away, the butt end of a pike came down hard on his forearm. A shot of pain pierced through to his mind, clearing away the last haze of the brandy.

"You bastard." Hawksworth realized he was shouting in English. "Get ready to die."

He twisted forward and with his free hand stretched for the pistol in his boot. Slowly his grip closed about the cool horn of the handle, and with a single motion he drew it upward, still grasping the sword.

As he raised himself erect he caught the outline of a dark object swinging above him in the air. Then the lightning flashed again, glinting off the three large silver knobs. They were being swung by the man who held his sword arm.

My God, it's a *gurz*, the three-headed club some of the Rajputs carry on their saddle. It's a killer.

He heard it arc above him, singing through the dark. Unlike the Rajputs, he had no leather helmet, no padded armor. There was no time to avoid the blow, but he had the pistol now, and he shoved it into the man's gut and squeezed.

There was a sudden blinding flash of light. It started at his hand, but then it seemed to explode inside his skull. The world had grown white, like the marble walls of Mukarrab Khan's music room, and for a moment he thought he heard again the echo of drumbeats. The cycle swelled sensuously, then suddenly reached its culmination, when all pent-up emotion dissolved. In the silence that followed, there was only the face of Mukarrab Khan, surrounded by his eunuchs, his smile slowly fading into black.

CHAPTER FOURTEEN

The light of a single flame tip burned through the haze of his vision, and then he heard words around him, in a terse language as ancient as time. He tried to move, and an aching soreness shot through his shoulders and into his groin. His head seemed afire.

I must be dead. Why is there still pain?

He forced his swollen eyelids wider, and a room slowly began to take form. It was a cell, with heavy bamboo slats over the windows and an ancient wooden latch on the door. The floor was earth and the walls gray mud with occasional inscriptions in red. Next to him was a silhouette, the outline of a man squatting before an oil lamp and slowly repeating a sharp, toneless verse. He puzzled at the words as he studied the figure.

It's the language of the priest at the wedding. It must be Sanskrit. But who . . . ?

He pulled himself upward on an elbow and turned toward the figure, which seemed to flicker in the undulating shadows. Then he recognized the profile of Vasant Rao. The verses stopped abruptly and the Rajput turned to examine him.

"So you're not dead? That could be a mistake you'll regret." Vasant Rao's face sagged and his once-haughty moustache was an unkempt tangle. He stared at Hawksworth a moment more, then turned back to the lamp. The Sanskrit verses resumed.

"Where the hell are we?"

Vasant Rao paused, and then slowly revolved toward Hawksworth.

"In the fortress village of Bhandu, ten *kos* northwest of the town of Chopda. It's the mountain stronghold of the Chandella dynasty of Rajputs."

"And who the hell are they?"

"They claim direct descent from the ancient solar race of Rajputs described in the *Puranas*. Who knows, but that's what they believe. What we all *do* know is they've defended these hills for all of time."

"Did they take the caravan?"

A bolt of humiliation and pain swept through Vasant Rao's eyes for a moment and then his reserve returned. "Yes, it was taken."

"So your mighty 'solar race' is really a breed of God-cursed common bandits."

"Bandits, they are. They always have been. Common, no. They're professionals, honorable men of high caste."

"High-caste thieves. Like some of the merchants I've met." Hawksworth paused and tried to find his tongue. His mouth was like cotton. "How long've we been here?"

"This is the morning of our second day. We arrived yesterday, after traveling all night."

"I feel like I've been keelhauled for a week." Hawksworth gingerly touched his forehead and there was a pulse of pain.

Vasant Rao listened with a puzzled expression. "You were tied over your horse. Some of the clan wanted to kill you and leave you there, but then they decided that would give you too much honor."

"What the hell are you talking about? I remember I gave them a fight."

"You used a pistol. You killed a man, the head of this dynasty, with a pistol."

The words seemed to cut through the shadows of the room. The pain returned and ached through Hawksworth's body.

More deaths. The two men who died on the *Discovery*. I saw Nayka die with an arrow in his throat. And how many of the Rajput guards died? Why am I always in the middle of fighting and death?

"The bastards killed my driver."

"The driver was nothing. A low caste." He shrugged it away. "You are an important *feringhi*. You would not have been harmed. You should never have drawn a pistol. And then you allowed yourself to be captured. It was an act beneath honor. The women spat on you and your horse when you were brought through the streets. I have no doubt they'll kill us both now."

"Who's left alive?"

"No one. My men died like Rajputs." A trace of pride flashed through his eyes before they dimmed again with sadness. "When they knew they could not win, that they had failed the prince, they vowed to die fighting. And all did."

"But you're still alive."

The words seemed almost like a knife in the Rajput's heart.

"They would not kill me. Or let me die honorably." He paused and stared at Hawksworth. "There was a reason, but it doesn't concern you."

"So all the men died? But why did they kill the drivers?"

"The drivers weren't killed." Vasant Rao looked surprised. "I never said that."

I keep forgetting, Hawksworth told himself, that only high castes count as men in this God-forgotten land.

"This whole damned country is mad." The absurdity overwhelmed him. "Low castes, your own people, handled like slaves, and high castes who kill each other in the name of honor. A pox on Rajputs and their fornicating honor."

"Honor is very important. Without honor what is left? We may as well be without caste. The warrior caste lives by a code set down in the Laws of Manu many thousands of years ago." He saw Hawksworth's impatience and smiled sadly. "Do you understand what's meant by *dharma?*"

"It sounds like another damned Hindu invention. Another excuse to take life."

"*Dharma* is something, Captain Hawksworth, without which life no longer matters. No Christian, or Muslim, has ever been able to understand *dharma*, since it is the order that defines our castes—and those born outside India are doomed to live forever without a caste. *Dharma* defines who we are and what we must do if we are to maintain our caste. Warfare is the *dharma* of the Kshatriya, the warrior caste."

"And I say a pox on caste. What's so honorable about Rajputs slaughtering each other?"

"Warriors are bound by their *dharma* to join in battle against other warriors. A warrior who fails in his duty sins against the *dharma* of his caste." Vasant Rao paused. "But why am I bothering to tell you this? I sound like Krishna, lecturing Arjuna on his duty as a warrior."

"Who's Krishna? Another Rajput?"

"He's a god, Captain Hawksworth, sacred to all Rajputs. He teaches us that a warrior must always honor his *dharma*."

Vasant Rao's eyes seemed to burn through the shadows of the cell. From outside Hawksworth heard the distant chantings of some village ceremony.

"If you'll listen, *feringhi* captain, I'll tell you something about a warrior's *dharma*. There's a legend, many thousands of years old, of a great battle joined between two branches of a powerful dynasty in ancient India. Two kings were brothers, and they shared a kingdom, but their sons could not live in peace. One branch wished to destroy the other. Eventually a battle was joined, a battle to the death. As they waited on the field for the sound of the conch shell, to summon the forces, the leader of those sons who had been wronged suddenly declared that he could not bring himself to kill his own kinsmen. But the god Krishna, who was charioteer for this son, reminded him he must follow his *dharma*. That there is no greater good for a warrior than to join battle for what is right. It's wrong only if he is attached to the fruits of battle, if he does it for gain. It's told in the Bhagavad-Gita, a Sanskrit scripture sacred to all warriors. I was reciting a verse from Chapter Twelve when you woke."

"What did this god Krishna say?"

"He declared that all who live must die, and all who die will be reborn. The spirit within us all, the *atman*, cannot be destroyed. It travels through us on its journey from birth to rebirth. But it's not correct to say merely that it exists. It *is* existence. It is the only reality. It is present in everything because it *is* everything. Therefore there's no need to mourn for death. There is no death. The body is merely an appearance, by which the *atman* reveals itself. The body is only its guardian. But a warrior who turns away from the duty of his caste sins against his honor and his *dharma*. Krishna warned that this loss of honor could one day lead to the mixture of castes, and then the *dharma* of the universe, its necessary order, would be destroyed. It's not wrong for a Rajput to kill a worthy foe, Captain Hawksworth, it's his duty. Just as it's also his duty to die a worthy death."

"Why all this killing in the name of 'honor' and 'duty'?"

"Non-Hindus always want to know 'why.' To 'understand.' You always seem to believe that words somehow contain all truth. But *dharma* simply *is*. It is the air we breathe, the changeless order around us. We're part of it. Does the earth ask why the monsoons come? Does the seed ask why the sun shines each day? No. It's *dharma*. The *dharma* of the seed is to bear fruit. The *dharma* of the warrior caste is to do battle. Only *feringhi*, who live outside our *dharma*, ask 'why.' Truth is not something you 'understand.' It's something you're part of. It's something you feel with your being. And when you try to catch it with words, it's gone. Can the eagle tell you how he flies, Captain Hawksworth, or 'why'? If he could, he would no longer be an eagle. This is the great wisdom of India. We've learned it's wasted on *feringhi*, Captain, as I fear it's now wasted on you."

The talk left Hawksworth feeling strangely insecure, his mind wrestling with ideas that defied rationality.

"I know there are things you understand with your gut, not with your head."

"Then there may be hope for you, Captain Hawksworth. Now we will see if you can die like a Rajput. If you can, perhaps you will be reborn one of us."

"Then I might even learn to be a bandit."

"All Rajputs are not the same, Captain. There are many tribes, descended from different dynasties. Each has its own tradition and genealogy. I'm from the north. From the races descended from the moon. This tribe claims descent from the solar dynasty, which also began in the north. I think their genealogy goes back to the god Indra, who they claim brought them into being with the aid of the sun."

Vasant Rao turned and continued reciting in Sanskrit. His face again became a mask.

Hawksworth rubbed his head in confusion and suddenly felt a hard lump where the club had dropped. The fear began to well up in his stomach as he remembered the stony-faced riders who had surrounded him in the river. But he pushed aside thoughts of death.

Dharma be damned. What did he mean, they're members of a clan descended from the "solar dynasty"? They're killers, looking for an excuse to plunder.

I'm not planning to die like a Rajput just yet. Or be reborn as one. Life is too sweet just as it is. I'm beginning to feel alive here, for the first time ever. Shirin is free. I've got a feeling I'll be seeing her again. Whatever happens, I don't care to die in this piss hole, with empty talk about honor. Think.

He remembered the river again, and quickly felt in his boot. The other pistol was still there.

We'll find a way to get out. Somehow. We may just lose a few days' time, that's all. We made good time so far. Six days. We left on Sunday, and we've been here two days. So today is probably Monday.

He suddenly froze.

"Where are the carts?"

"At the south end of the village. Where they have the *chans*, the cattle sheds. The drivers are there too."

"Is my chest there?"

"No. It's right there. Behind you." Vasant Rao pointed into the dark. "I told them it belonged to the *Moghul*, and they brought it here. I guess the *Moghul* still counts for something here. Maybe they're superstitious about him."

Hawksworth pulled himself up and reached behind him. The chest was there. He fingered the cool metal of the lock and his mind began to clear even more. Quickly he began to search his jerkin for the key. Its pockets were empty.

Of course. If I was tied over a horse it . . .

Then he remembered. For safety he had transferred it to the pocket of his breeches the second day out. He felt down his leg, fighting the ache in his arm.

Miraculously the key was still there.

He tried to hold his excitement as he twisted it into the lock on the chest. Once, twice, and it clicked.

He quickly checked the contents. Lute on top. Letter, still wrapped. Clothes. Then he felt deeper and touched the metal. Slowly he drew it out, holding his breath. It was still intact.

The light from the lamp glanced off the burnished brass of the Persian astrolabe from the observatory. It had been Mukarrab Khan's parting gift.

He carried it to the slatted window and carefully twisted each slat until the sun began to stream through.

Thank God it's late in the year, when the sun's already lower at midday.

He took a quick reading of the sun's elevation. It had not yet reached its zenith. He made a mental note of the reading and began to wait. Five

minutes passed—they seemed hours—and he checked the elevation again.
The sun was still climbing, but he knew it would soon reach its highest
point.

Vasant Rao continued to chant verses from the Bhagavad-Gita in terse,
toneless Sanskrit.

He probably thinks I'm praying too, Hawksworth smiled to himself.

The reading increased, then stayed the same, then began to decrease.
The sun had passed its zenith, and he had the exact reading of its elevation.

He mentally recorded the reading, then began to rummage in the bottom of the chest for the seaman's book he always carried with him.

We left Surat on October twenty-fourth. So October twenty-fifth was
Karod, the twenty-sixth was Viara, the twenty-seventh was Corka, the twenty-
eighth was Narayanpur, the twenty-ninth was the river. Today has to be
October thirty-first.

The book was there, its pages still musty from the moist air at sea. He
reached the page he wanted and ran his finger down a column of figures
until he reached the one he had read off the astrolabe.

From the reading the latitude here is 21 degrees and 20 minutes north.

Then he began to search the chest for a sheaf of papers and finally his
fingers closed around them, buried beneath his spare jerkin. He squinted in
the half light as he went through the pages, the handwriting hurried from
hasty work in the observatory. Finally he found what he wanted. He had
copied it directly from the old Samarkand astronomer's calculations. The nu-
merals were as bold as the day he had written them. The latitude was there,
and the date.

With a tight smile that pained his aching face he carefully wrapped the
astrolabe and returned it to the bottom of the chest, together with the
books. He snapped the lock in place just as the door of the cell swung open.

He looked up to see the face of the man who had swung the club.

Good Jesus, I thought he was dead. And he looks even younger . . .

Then Hawksworth realized it had to be his son. But the heavy brow, the
dark beard, the narrow eyes, were all the same, almost as though his father's
blood had flowed directly into his veins. He wore no helmet or breastplate
now, only a simple robe, entirely white.

The man spoke curtly to Vasant Rao in a language Hawksworth did not
understand.

"He has ordered us to come with him. It's time for the ceremony. He
says you must watch how the man you killed is honored."

Vasant Rao rose easily and pinched out the oil lamp. In the darkened
silence Hawksworth heard the lowing of cattle, as well as the distant drone
of a chant. Outside the guards were waiting. He noted they carried sheathed
swords. And they too were dressed in white.

In the midday sunshine he quickly tried to survey the terrain. Jagged

rock outcrops seemed to ring the village, with a gorge providing an easily
protected entrance.

He was right. It's a fortress. And probably impregnable.

The road was wide, with rows of mud-brick homes on either side, and
ahead was an open square, where a crowd had gathered. Facing the square,
at the far end, was an immense house of baked brick, the largest in the fortress village, with a wide front and a high porch.

As they approached the square, Hawksworth realized a deep pit had
been newly excavated directly in the center. Mourners clustered nearby,
silently waiting, while a group of women—five in all—held hands and moved
slowly around the pit entoning a dirge.

As they reached the side of the opening he saw the Rajput's body, lying
face up on a fragrant bier of sandalwood and neem branches. His head and
beard had been shaved and his body bound in a silk winding sheet. He was
surrounded by garlands of flowers. The wood in the pit smelled of *ghee* and
rose-scented coconut oil. Nearby, Brahmin priests recited in Sanskrit.

"His body will be cremated with the full honor of a Rajput warrior."
Vasant Rao stood alongside. "It's clear the Brahmins have been paid
enough."

Hawksworth looked around at the square and the nearby houses, their
shutters all sealed in mourning. Chanting priests in ceremonial robes had
stationed themselves near the large house, and an Arabian mare, all white
and bedecked with flowers, was tied at the entrance. Suddenly the tones of
mournful, discordant music sounded around him.

As Hawksworth watched, the heavy wooden doors of the great house
opened slowly and a woman stepped into the midday sunshine. Even from
their distance he could see that she was resplendent—in an immaculate
white wrap that sparkled with gold ornaments—and her movements regal as
she descended the steps and was helped onto the horse. As she rode slowly in
the direction of the pit, she was supported on each side by Brahmin priests,
long-haired men with stripes of white clay painted down their forehead.

"She is his wife." Vasant Rao had also turned to watch. "Now you'll see
a woman of the warrior caste follow her *dharma*."

As the woman rode slowly by, Hawksworth sensed she was only barely
conscious of her surroundings, as though she had been drugged. She circled
the pit three times, then stopped near where Hawksworth and Vasant Rao
were standing. As the priests helped her down from the mare, one urged her
to drink again from a cup of dense liquid he carried. Her silk robe was fragrant with scented oil, and Hawksworth saw that decorations of saffron and
sandalwood paste had been applied to her arms and forehead.

It's a curious form of mourning. She's dressed and perfumed as though
for a banquet, not a funeral. And what's she drinking? From the way she
moves I'd guess it's some opium concoction.

She paused at the edge of the pit and seemed to glare for an instant at the five women who moved around her. Then she drank again from the cup, and calmly began removing her jewels, handing them to the priests, until her only ornament was a necklace of dark seeds. Next the Brahmins sprinkled her head with water from a pot and, as a bell began to toll, started helping her into the pit. Hawksworth watched in disbelief as she knelt next to her husband's body and lovingly cradled his head against her lap. Her eyes were lifeless but serene.

The realization of what was happening struck Hawksworth like a blow in the chest. But how could it be true? It was unthinkable.

Then the man who had brought them, the son, held out his hand and one of the Brahmins bowed and handed him a burning torch. It flared brilliant against the dark pile of earth at the front of the pit.

God Almighty! No! Hawksworth instinctively started to reach for his pistol.

A deafening chorus of wails burst from the waiting women as the young man flung the torch directly by the head of the bier. Next the priests threw more lighted torches alongside the corpse, followed by more oil. The flames licked tentatively around the edges of the wood, then burst across the top of the pyre. The fire swirled around the woman, and in an instant her oil-soaked robes flared, enveloping her body and igniting her hair. Hawksworth saw her open her mouth and say something, words he did not understand, and then the pain overcame her and she screamed and tried frantically to move toward the edge of the pit. As she reached the edge she saw the hovering priests, waiting with long poles to push her away, and she stumbled backward. Her last screams were drowned by the chorus of wailing women as she collapsed across the body of her husband, a human torch.

Hawksworth stepped back in horror and whirled on Vasant Rao, who stood watching impassively.

"This is murder! Is this more of your Rajput 'tradition'?"

"It is what we call *sati*, when a brave woman joins her husband in death. Did you hear what she said? She pronounced the words 'five, two' as the life-spirit left her. At the moment of death we sometimes have the gift of prophecy. She was saying this is the fifth time she has burned herself with the same husband, and that only two times more are required to release her from the cycle of birth and death, to render her a perfect being."

"I can't believe she burned herself willingly."

"Of course she did. Rajput women are noble. It was the way she honored her husband, and her caste. It was her *dharma*."

Hawksworth stared again at the pit. Priests were throwing more oil on the raging flames, which already had enveloped the two bodies and now licked around the edges, almost at Hawksworth's feet. The five women seemed crazed with grief, as they held hands and moved along the edge in a delirious dance. The heat had become intense, and Hawksworth instinctively stepped back as tongues of fire licked over the edge of the pit. The mourning women appeared heedless of their own danger as they continued to circle, their light cloth robes now only inches from the flame. The air was filled with the smell of death and burning flesh.

They must be mad with grief. They'll catch their clothes . . .

At that instant the hem of one of the women's robes ignited. She examined the whipping flame with a wild, empty gaze, almost as though not seeing it. Then she turned on the other women, terror and confusion in her eyes.

Hawksworth was already peeling off his jerkin. He'd seen enough fires on the gun deck to know the man whose clothes caught always panicked.

If I can reach her in time I can smother the robe before she's burned and maimed. Her legs . . .

Before he could move, the woman suddenly turned and poised herself at the edge of the roaring pit. She emitted one long intense wail, then threw herself directly into the fire. At that moment the robes of a second woman caught, and she too turned and plunged head-first into the flames.

Merciful God! What are they doing!

The three remaining women paused for a moment. Then they clasped hands and, as though on a private signal, plunged over the edge into the inferno, their hair and robes igniting like dry tinder in a furnace. The women all clung together as the flames enveloped them.

Hawksworth tried to look again into the pit, but turned away in revulsion.

"What in hell is happening?"

Vasant Rao's eyes were flooded with disbelief.

"They must have been his concubines. Or his other wives. Only his first wife was allowed to have the place of honor beside his body. I've . . ." The Rajput struggled for composure. "I've never seen so many women die in a *sati*. It's . . ." He seemed unable to find words. "It's almost too much."

"How did such a murderous custom begin?" Hawksworth's eyes were seared now from the smoke and the smell of burning flesh. "It's unworthy of humanity."

"We believe aristocratic Rajput women have always wished to do it. To honor their brave warriors. The *Moghul* has tried to stop it, however. He claims it began only a few centuries ago, when a Rajput raja suspected the women in his palace were trying to poison him and his ministers. Some believe the raja decreed the custom as protection for his own life, and then others followed. But I don't think that's true. I believe women in India have always done it, from ancient times. But what does it matter when it began. Now all rani, the wives of rajas, follow their husbands in death, and consider it a great honor. Today it seems his other women also insisted on joining her. I think it was against her wishes. She did not want to share her moment of glory. *Sati* is a noble custom, Captain Hawksworth, part of that Rajput strength of character wanting in other races."

A hand seized Hawksworth's arm roughly and jerked him back through the crowd, a sea of eyes burning with contempt. Amid the drifting smoke he caught a glimpse of the bullock carts of the caravan, lined along the far end of the road leading into the fortress. The drivers were nowhere to be seen, but near the carts were cattle sheds for the bullocks.

If they can send innocent women to their death, life means nothing here. They'll kill us for sure.

He turned to Vasant Rao, whose face showed no trace of fear. The Rajput seemed oblivious to the smell of death as smoke from the fire engulfed the palms that lined the village roads. They were approaching the porch of the great house where the head of the dynasty had lived.

Two guards shoved Hawksworth roughly to his knees. He looked up to see, standing on the porch of the house, the young man who had tossed the torch into the pit. He began speaking to them, in the tones of an announcement.

"He's the son of the man you killed. He has claimed leadership of the dynasty, and calls himself Raj Singh." Vasant Rao translated rapidly, as the man continued speaking. "He says that tomorrow there will be an eclipse of the sun here. It is predicted in the Panjika, the Hindu manual of astrology. His father, the leader of this dynasty of the sun, has died, and tomorrow the sun will die also for a time. The Brahmins have said it is fitting that you die with it. For high castes in India the death of the sun is an evil time, a time when the two great powers of the sky are in conflict. On the day of an eclipse no fires are lit in our homes. Food is discarded and all open earthenware pots are smashed. No one who wears the sacred thread of the twice-born can be out of doors during an eclipse. The Brahmin astrologers have judged it is the proper time for you to pay for your cowardly act. You will be left on a pike to die in the center of the square."

Hawksworth drew himself up, his eyes still smarting from the smoke, and tried to fix the man's eyes. Then he spoke, in a voice he hoped would carry to all the waiting crowd.

"Tell him his Brahmin astrologers know not the truth, neither past nor future." Hawksworth forced himself to still the tremble in his voice. "There will be no eclipse tomorrow. His Brahmins, who cannot foretell the great events in the heavens, should have no right to work their will on earth."

"Have you gone mad?" Vasant Rao turned and glared at him as he spat the words in disgust. "Why not try to die with dignity."

"Tell him."

Vasant Rao stared at Hawksworth in dumb amazement. "Do you think we're all fools. The eclipse is foretold in the Panjika. It is the sacred book of the Brahmins. It's used to pick auspicious days for ceremonies, for weddings, for planting crops. Eclipses are predicted many years ahead in the Panjika. They have been forecast in India for centuries. Don't Europeans know an eclipse is a meeting of the sun and moon? Nothing can change that."

"Tell him what I said. Exactly."

Vasant Rao hesitated for a few moments and then reluctantly translated. The Rajput chieftain's face did not change and his reply was curt.

Vasant Rao turned to Hawksworth. "He says you are a fool as well as an Untouchable."

"Tell him that if I am to die with the sun, he must kill me now. I spit on his Brahmins and their Panjika. I say the eclipse will be this very day. In less than three hours."

"In one *pahar?*"

"Yes."

"No god, and certainly no man, can control such things. Why tell him this invention?" Vasant Rao's voice rose with his anger. "When this thing does not happen, you will die in even greater dishonor."

"Tell him."

Vasant Rao again translated, his voice hesitant. Raj Singh examined Hawksworth skeptically. Then he turned and spoke to one of the tall Rajputs standing nearby, who walked to the end of the porch and summoned several Brahmin priests. After a conference marked by much angry shouting and gesturing, one of the Brahmins turned and left. Moments later he reappeared carrying a book.

"They have consulted the Panjika again." Vasant Rao pointed toward the book as one of the Brahmins directed a stream of language at Raj Singh. "He says there is no mistaking the date of the eclipse, and the time. It is in the lunar month of *Asvina*, which is your September-October. Here in the Deccan the month begins and ends with the full moon. The *tithi* or lunar day of the eclipse begins tomorrow."

As Hawksworth listened, he felt his heart begin to race.

The calculations at the observatory had a lot to say about your Panjika's lunar calendar. And they showed how unwieldy it is compared to the solar calendar the Arabs and Europeans use. A cycle of the moon doesn't divide evenly into the days in a year. So your astrologers have to keep adding and subtracting days and months to keep years the same length. It's almost impossible to relate a lunar calendar accurately to a solar year. Jamshid Beg, the astronomer from Samarkand, loved to check out the predictions in the Hindu Panjika.

If I deciphered his calculations right, this is one eclipse the Panjika called wrong. The astrologer must have miscopied his calculations. Or maybe he just bungled one of the main rules of lunar bookkeeping. Solar days begin at sunrise, but lunar days are different. The moon can rise at any time of day. According to the system, the lunar day current at sunrise is supposed to be the day that's counted. But if the moon rises just after sunrise, and sets before sunrise the next day, then that whole lunar "day" has to be dropped from the count.

Today was one of those days. It should have been dropped from the lunar calendar, but it wasn't. So the prediction in the Panjika is a day off.

According to Jamshid Beg's calculations, at least. God help me if he was wrong.

"Tell him his Panjika is false. If I'm to be killed the day of the eclipse, he must kill me now, today."

Raj Singh listened with increasing disquiet as Vasant Rao translated. He glanced nervously at the Brahmins and then replied in a low voice.

Vasant Rao turned to Hawksworth. "He asks what proof you have of your forecast?"

Hawksworth looked around. What proof could there be of an impending eclipse?

"My word is my word."

Another exchange followed.

"He is most doubtful you are wiser than the Panjika." Vasant Rao paused for a moment, then continued. "I am doubtful as well. He says that if you have invented a lie you are very foolish. And we will all soon know."

"Tell him he can believe as he chooses. The eclipse will be today."

Again there was an exchange. Then Vasant Rao turned to Hawksworth, a mystified expression on his face.

"He says if what you say is true, then you are an avatar, the incarnation of a god. If the eclipse is today, as you say, then the village must begin to prepare immediately. People must all move indoors. Once more, is what you say true?"

"It's true." Hawksworth strained to keep his voice confident, and his eyes on the Rajput chieftain as he spoke. "It doesn't matter whether he believes or not."

Raj Singh consulted again with the Brahmin priests, who had now gathered around. They shifted nervously, and several spat to emphasize their skepticism. Then the Rajput leader returned and spoke again to Vasant Rao.

"He says that he will take the precaution of ordering the high castes indoors. If what you say comes to pass, then you have saved the village from a great harm."

Hawksworth started to speak but Vasant Rao silenced him with a gesture.

"He also says that if what you say is a lie, he will not wait until tomorrow to kill you. You will be buried alive at sunset today, up to the throat.

Then you will be stoned to death by the women and children of the village.
It is the death of criminal Untouchables."

As the smoke from the funeral pyre continued to drift through the village, the high-caste men and women entered their homes and sealed their
doors. Women took their babies in their laps and began their prayers. Only
low castes and children too young to wear the sacred thread remained outside. Even Vasant Rao was allowed to return to the room where they had
been held prisoner. Hawksworth suddenly found himself without guards, and
he wandered back to the square to look once more at the pit where the
funeral pyre had been. All that remained of the bodies were charred
skeletons.

An hour ago there was life. Now there's death. The difference is the
will to live.

And luck. The turn of chance.

Was Jamshid Beg right? If not, God help me . . .

He knelt down beside the pit. To look at death and to wait.

CHAPTER FIFTEEN

Prince Jadar passed the signal to the waiting guards as he strode briskly
down the stone-floored hallway and they nodded imperceptibly in acknowledgment. There was no sound in the torchlit corridor save the pad of his
leather-soled riding slippers.

It was the beginning of the third *pahar*, midday, and he had come
directly from the hunt when the runner brought word that Mumtaz had entered labor. It would have been unseemly to have gone to her side, so he had
spoken briefly with the *dai*, midwife. He had overruled the Hindu woman's
suggestion that Mumtaz be made to give birth squatting by a bed, so that a
broom could be pressed against her abdomen as the midwife rubbed her
back. It was, he knew, the barbarous practice of unbelievers, and he cursed
himself for taking on the woman in the first place. It had been a symbolic
gesture for the Hindu troops, to quell concern that all the important details
attending the birth would be Muslim. Jadar had insisted that Mumtaz be
moved to a velvet mat on the floor of her room and carefully positioned with
her head north and her feet south. In case she should die in childbirth—and
he fervently prayed she would not—this was the position in which she would
be buried, her face directed toward Mecca. He had ordered all cannon of the
fort primed with powder, to be fired in the traditional Muslim salute if a
male child was the issue.

Preparations also were underway for the naming ceremony. He had
prayed for many days that this time a son would be named. There were two

daughters already, and yet another would merely mean one more intriguing woman to be locked away forever, for he knew he could never allow a daughter to marry. The complications of yet another aspiring family in the palace circle were inconceivable. The scheming Persian Shi'ites, like the queen and her family, who had descended on Agra would like nothing better than another opportunity to use marriage to dilute the influence of Sunni Muslims at court.

Allah, this time it *has* to be a son. Hasn't everything possible been done? And if Akman was right, that a change of residence during the term ensures a male heir, then I'll have a son twelve times over from this birthing. She's been in a dozen cities. And camps. I even tested the augury of the Hindus and had a household snake killed and tossed in the air by one of their Brahmin unbelievers, to see how it would land. And it landed on its back, which they say augurs a boy. Also, the milk squeezed from her breasts three days ago was thin, which the Hindus believe foretells a son.

Still, the omens have been mixed. The eclipse. Why did it come a day earlier than the Hindu astrologers had predicted? Now I realize it was exactly seven days before the birth. No one can recall when they failed to compute an eclipse correctly.

What did it mean? That my line will die out? Or that a son will be born here who will one day overshadow me?

Who can know the future? What Allah wills must be.

And, he told himself, the meeting set for the third *pahar* must still take place, regardless of the birth. Unless he did what he had planned, the birth would be meaningless. All the years of planning now could be forfeited in this single campaign.

If I fail now, what will happen to the legacy of Akman, his great work to unify India? Will India return to warring fiefdoms, neighbor pitted against neighbor, or fall to the Shi'ites? The very air around me hints of treachery.

With that thought he momentarily inspected the placement of his personal crest on the thick wooden door of the fortress reception hall, and pushed it wide. A phalanx of guards trailed behind him into the room, which he had claimed as his command post for the duration of his stay in Burhanpur. The immense central carpet had been freshly garlanded around the edges with flowers.

The fortress, the only secure post remaining in the city, had been commandeered by Jadar and his hand-picked guard. His officers had taken accommodations in the town, and the troops had erected an enormous tent complex along the road leading into the city from the north. Their women now swarmed over the bazaar, accumulating stores for the march south. Bullock carts of fresh produce glutted the roads leading into the city, for word had reached the surrounding villages that Burhanpur was host to the retinue of the prince and his soldiers from the north—buyers accustomed to high northern prices. The villagers also knew from long experience that a wise man would strip his fields and gardens and orchards now and sell, before an army on the march simply took what it wanted.

Rumors had already reached the city that the army of Malik Ambar, Abyssinian leader of the Deccanis, was marching north toward Burhanpur with eighty thousand infantry and horsemen. An advance contingent was already encamped no more than ten *kos* south of the city.

Jadar inspected the reception room until he was certain it was secure, with every doorway under command of his men. Then he signaled the leader of the Rajput guard, who relayed a message to a courier waiting outside. Finally he settled himself against an immense velvet bolster, relishing this moment of quiet to clear his mind.

The Deccan, the central plains of India. Will they ever be ours? How many more campaigns must there be?

He recalled with chagrin all the humiliations dealt Arangbar by the Deccanis.

When Arangbar took the throne at Akman's death, he had announced he would continue his father's policy of military control of the Deccan. A general named Ghulam Adl had requested, and received, confirmation of his existing post of Khan Khanan, "Khan of Khans," the supreme commander of the Moghul armies in the south. To subdue the Deccan once and for all, Arangbar had sent an additional twelve thousand cavalry south and had given Ghulam Adl a million rupees to refurbish his army. But in spite of these forces, the Abyssinian Malik Ambar soon had set up a rebel capital at Ahmadnagar and declared himself prime minister.

In disgust Arangbar had taken the command from Ghulam Adl and given it to his own son, the second oldest, Parwaz. This dissolute prince marched south with great pomp. Once there he set up an extravagant military headquarters, a royal court in miniature, and spent several years drinking and bragging of his inevitable victory. Ghulam Adl had watched this with growing resentment, and finally he succumbed to bribes by Malik Ambar and retreated with his own army.

In anger Arangbar then appointed two other generals to march on the Deccan, one from the north and one from the west, hoping to trap Malik Ambar in a pincer. But the Abyssinian deftly kept them apart, and badly defeated each in turn. Eventually both were driven back to the north, with heavy losses.

This time, on the advice of Queen Janahara, Arangbar transferred his son Parwaz out of the Deccan, to Allahbad, and in his place sent Prince Jadar. The younger prince had marched on the Deccan with forty thousand additional troops to supplement the existing forces.

When Jadar and his massive army reached Burhanpur, Malik Ambar

wisely proposed a truce and negotiations. He returned the fort at Ahmadnagar to the *Moghul* and withdrew his troops. Arangbar was jubilant and rewarded Jadar with sixteen *lakhs* of rupees and a prize diamond. Triumphant,
Jadar had returned to Agra and begun to think of becoming the next
Moghul. That had been three long years ago.

But Malik Ambar had the cunning of a jackal, and his "surrender" had
been merely a ruse to remove the Moghul troops again to the north. This
year he had waited for the monsoon, when conventional armies could not
move rapidly, and again risen in rebellion, easily driving Ghulam Adl's army
north from Ahmadnagar, reclaiming the city, and laying siege to its Moghul
garrison. The despairing Arangbar again appealed to Jadar to lead troops
south to relieve the permanent forces of Ghulam Adl. After demanding and
receiving a substantial increase in *mansab* rank and personal cavalry, Jadar
had agreed.

The wide wooden door of the reception hall opened and Ghulam Adl
strode regally into the room, wearing a gold-braided turban with a feather
and a great sword at his belt. His beard was longer than Jadar had remembered, and now it had been reddened with henna—perhaps, Jadar thought,
to hide the gray. But his deep-set eyes were still haughty and self-assured, and
his swagger seemed to belie reports he had barely escaped with his life from
the besieged fortress at Ahmadnagar only five weeks before.

Ghulam Adl's gaze quickly swept the room, but his eyes betrayed no notice of the exceptional size of Jadar's guard. With an immense show of dignity he nodded a perfunctory bow, hands clasped at the sparkling jewel of
his turban.

"Salaam, Highness. May Allah lay His hand on both our swords and
temper them once more with fire." He seated himself easily, as he might
with an equal, and when no servant came forward, he poured himself a glass
of wine from the decanter that waited on the carpet beside his bolster. Is
there anything, he wondered, I despise more than these presumptuous young
princes from Agra? "I rejoice your journey was swift. You've arrived in time
to witness my army savage the Abyssinian unbeliever and his rabble."

"How many troops are left?" Jadar seemed not to hear the boast.

"Waiting are fifty thousand men, Highness, and twenty thousand horse,
ready to tender their lives at my command." Ghulam Adl delicately shielded
his beard as he drank off the glass of wine and—when again no servant appeared—poured himself another.

Jadar remained expressionless.

"My reports give you only five thousand men left, most *chelas*." *Chelas*,
from the Hindi slang for "slave," was a reference to the mercenary troops,
taken in childhood and raised in the camp, that commanders maintained
as a kernel of their forces. Unlike soldiers from the villages, they were loyal

even in misfortune, because they literally had no place to return to. "What troops do you have from the *mansabdars*, who've been granted stipends from their *jagir* estate revenue to maintain men and horse?"

"Those were the ones I mean, Highness." Ghulam Adl's hand trembled slightly as he again lifted the wineglass. "The *mansabdars* have assured me we have only to sound the call, and their men will muster. In due time."

"Then pay is not in arrears for their men and cavalry."

"Highness, it's well known pay must always be in arrears. How else are men's loyalties to be guaranteed? A commander foolish enough to pay his troops on time will lose them at the slightest setback, since they have no reason to remain with him in adversity." Ghulam Adl eased his wineglass on the carpet and bent forward. "I concede some of the *mansabdars* may have allowed matters of pay to slip longer than is wise. But they assure me that when the time is right their men will muster nonetheless."

"Then why not call the muster? In another twenty days Ambar's troops will be encamped at our doorstep. He could well control all lands south of the Narbada River."

And that, Ghulam Adl smiled to himself, is precisely the plan.

He thought of the arrangement that had been worked out. Jadar was to be kept in Burhanpur for another three weeks, delayed by any means possible. By then Malik Ambar would have the city surrounded, all access cut off. The Imperial troops would be isolated and demoralized. No troops would be forthcoming from the *mansabdars*. Only promises of troops. Cut off from Agra and provisions, Jadar would have no choice but to sign a treaty. The paper had already been prepared. Malik Ambar would rule the Deccan from his new capital at Ahmadnagar, and Ghulam Adl would be appointed governor of all provinces north from Ahmadnagar to the Narbada River. With their combined troops holding the borders, no Moghul army could ever again challenge the Deccan. Ghulam Adl knew the *mansabdars* would support him, because he had offered to cut their taxes in half. He had neglected to specify for how long.

"I respectfully submit the time for muster is premature, Highness. Crops are not yet in. The revenues of the *mansabdars'* *jagir* estates will suffer if men are called now." Ghulam Adl shifted uncomfortably.

"They'll have no revenues at all if they don't muster immediately. I'll confiscate the *jagir* of any *mansabdar* who has not mustered his men and cavalry within seven days." Jadar watched Ghulam Adl's throat muscles tense, and he asked himself if a *jagir* granted by the *Moghul* could be legally confiscated. Probably not. But the threat would serve to reveal loyalties, and reveal them quickly.

"But there's no possible way to pay the men now, Highness." Ghulam Adl easily retained his poise. Hold firm and this aspiring young upstart will waver and then agree. Give him numbers. First make it sound hopeless, then show him a way he can still win. "There's not enough silver in all the Deccan. Let me give you some idea of the problem. Assume it would require a year's back pay to muster the troops, not unreasonable since most of the *mansabdars* are at least two years behind now. The usual yearly allowance for cavalry here is three hundred rupees for a Muslim and two hundred and forty for a Hindu. You will certainly need to raise a minimum of thirty thousand men from the *mansabdars*. Assuming some loyal troops might possibly muster on notes of promise, you'd still need almost fifty *lakhs* of rupees. An impossible sum. It's clear the *mansabdars* won't have the revenues to pay their men until the fall crops are harvested."

"Then I'll confiscate their *jagirs* now and pay the troops myself. And deduct the sum from their next revenues."

"That's impossible. The money is nowhere to be found." Ghulam Adl realized with relief that Jadar was bluffing; the prince could not possibly raise the money needed. He shifted closer and smiled warmly. "But listen carefully. If we wait but two months, everything will be changed. Then it'll be simple to squeeze the revenue from the *mansabdars*, and we can pay the men ourselves if we need. Until then we can easily contain the Abyssinian and his rabble. Perhaps we could raise a few men and horse from the *mansabdars* now, but frankly I advise against it. Why trouble them yet? With the troops we have we can keep Malik Ambar diverted for weeks, months even. Then when the time is right we sound the call, march south with our combined forces, and drive him into the southern jungles forever."

But that call will raise no men, Ghulam Adl told himself, not a single wagon driver. It has been agreed. "We'll wait a few weeks until Ambar has his supply lines extended. Then we'll begin to harass him. In no time he'll begin to fall back to Ahmadnagar to wait for winter. And by that time we'll have our full strength. We'll march in force and crush him. I'll lead the men personally. You need never leave Burhanpur, Highness." He took another sip of wine. "Though I daresay its pleasures must seem rustic for one accustomed to the more luxurious diversions of Agra."

Jadar examined the commander and a slight, knowing smile played across his lips. "Let me propose a slight alternative." He began evenly. "I will lead the army this time, and *you* will remain here at the fortress. I called you here today to notify you that as of this moment you are relieved of your command and confined to the fort." Jadar watched Ghulam Adl stiffen and his sly grin freeze on his face. "I will assemble the army myself and march south in ten days."

"This is a weak jest, Highness." Ghulam Adl tried to laugh. "No one knows the Deccan the way I and my commanders know it. The terrain is treacherous."

"Your knowledge of the terrain admittedly is excellent. You and your commanders have retreated the length of the Deccan year after year. This time I will use my own generals. Abdullah Khan will command the advance guard, with three thousand horse from our own troops. Abul Hasan will take the left flank, and Raja Vikramajit the right. I will personally command the center." Jadar fixed Ghulam Adl squarely. "You will be confined to the fort, where you'll send no ciphers to Ambar. Your remaining troops will be divided and put under our command. You will order it in writing today and I will send the dispatches."

"For your sake I trust this is a jest, Highness. You dare not carry it out." Ghulam Adl slammed his glass onto the carpet, spilling his wine. The Rajputs around Jadar stiffened but made no move. "I have the full support of the *Moghul* himself. Your current position in Agra is already talked about here in the south. Do you think we're so far away we hear nothing? Your return this time, *if* you are allowed to return, will be nothing like the grand celebrations three years ago. If I were you, I'd be marching back now. Leave the Deccan to those who know it."

"You're right about Agra on one point. It *is* far away. And this campaign is mine, not the *Moghul's*."

"You'll never raise the troops, young prince. Only I can induce the *mansabdars* to muster."

"I'll muster the men. With full pay."

"You'll muster nothing, Highness. You'll be Ambar's prisoner inside a month. I can swear it. If you are still alive." Ghulam Adl bowed low and his hand shot for his sword. By the time it touched the handle the Rajputs were there. He was circled by drawn blades. Jadar watched impassively for a moment, and then signaled the guards to escort Ghulam Adl from the audience room.

"I'll see you dead." He shouted over his shoulder as the men dragged him toward the door. "Within the month."

Jadar watched Ghulam Adl's turban disappear through the torchlit opening and down the corridor. His sword remained on the carpet, where it had been removed by the Rajput guards. Jadar stared at it for a moment, admiring the silver trim along the handle, and it reminded him of the silver shipment. And the Englishman.

Vasant Rao blundered badly with the English captain. He should have found a way to disarm him in advance. Always disarm a *feringhi*. Their instincts are too erratic. The whole scenario fell apart after he killed the headman of the dynasty. My Rajput games almost became a war.

But what happened in the village? Did the *feringhi* work sorcery? Why was the caravan released so suddenly? The horsemen I had massed in the valley, in case of an emergency, panicked after the eclipse began. They became just so many terrified Hindus. Then suddenly the caravan assembled and left, with Rajputs from the village riding guard, escorting them all the way back to the river.

And even now Vasant Rao refuses to talk about what really happened. It seems his honor is too besmirched. He refuses even to eat with the other men.

Allah the Merciful. Rajputs and their cursed honor.

But I've learned what I need to know about the English *feringhi*. His nerve is astonishing. How could he dare refuse to attend my morning *durbar* audience in the reception room? Should I accept his claim that he's an ambassador and therefore I should come to him. Should I simply have him brought before me?

No. I have a better idea. But tomorrow. After the child is born and I've sent runners to the *mansabdars* . . .

A member of Mumtaz's guard burst through the doorway, then remembered himself and salaamed deeply to the prince. Guards around Jadar already had their swords half drawn.

"Forgive a fool, Highness." He fell to his knees, just in case. "I'm ordered to report that your son is born. The *dai* says he's perfectly formed and has the lungs of a cavalry commander."

Cheers swept the room, and the air blossomed with flying turbans. Jadar motioned the terrified man closer and he nervously knelt again, this time directly before Jadar.

"The *dai* respectfully asks if it would please Your Highness to witness the cord-cutting ceremony. She suggests a gold knife, instead of the usual silver."

Jadar barely heard the words, but he did recall that tradition allowed the midwife to keep the knife.

"She can have her knife of gold, and you are granted a thousand gold *mohurs*. But the cord will be cut with a string." This ceremony must be a signal to all India, Jadar told himself, and he tried to recall exactly the tradition started by Akman for newborn Moghul princes. The birth cord of all Akman's three sons was cut with a silken string, then placed in a velvet bag with writings from the Quran, and kept under the new child's pillow for forty days.

The guard salaamed once more, his face in the carpet, and then scurried toward the door, praising Allah. As Jadar rose and made his way toward the corridor, a chant of "Jadar-o-Akbar," "Jadar is Great," rose from the cheering Rajputs. Every man knew that with an heir, the prince was at last ready to claim his birthright. And they would fight beside him for it.

Mumtaz lay against a bolster, a fresh scarf tied around her head and a roller bound about her abdomen, taking a draft of strong, garlic-scented asafetida gum as Jadar came into the room. He immediately knew she was well, for this anti-cold precaution was taken only after the placenta was expelled and the mother's well-being assured. Next to her side was a box of betel leaves, rolled especially with myrrh to purge the taste of the asafetida.

"My congratulations, Highness." The *dai* salaamed awkwardly from the bedside. "May it please you to know the child is blind of an eye."

Jadar stared at her dumbfounded, then remembered she was a local Hindu midwife, from Gujarat province, where the birth of a boy is never spoken of, lest the gods grow jealous of the parents' good fortune and loose the Evil Eye. Instead, boys were announced by declaring the child blind in one eye. No precautions against divine jealousy were thought necessary for a girl child, a financial liability no plausible god would covet.

The *dai* returned to washing Mumtaz's breasts, stroking them carefully with wet blades of grass. Jadar knew this local ritual was believed to ensure fortune for the child and he did not interrupt. He merely returned Mumtaz's weak smile and strode to the silver basin resting by the bedside, where another midwife was washing his new son in a murky mixture of gram flour and water.

The frightened woman dried off the child, brushed his head with perfumed oil, and placed him on a thin pillow of quilted calico for Jadar to see. He was red and wrinkled and his dark eyes were startled. But he was a prince.

Jadar touched the infant's warm hand as he examined him for imperfections. There were none.

Someday, my first son, you may rule India as *Moghul*. If we both live that long.

"Is he well?" Mumtaz spoke at last, her normally shrill voice now scarcely above a whisper. "Are you pleased?"

"He'll do for now." Jadar smiled as he examined her tired face. She had never seemed as beautiful as she did at this moment. He knew there was no way he could ever show his great love for her, but he knew she understood. And returned it. "Do these unbelievers know enough to follow Muslim tradition?"

"Yes. A mullah has been summoned to sound the *azan*, the call to prayer, in his ear."

"But a male child must first be announced with artillery. So he'll never be afraid to fight." Jadar wasn't sure how much belief he put in all these Muslim traditions, but the troops expected it and every ceremony for *this* prince had to be observed. Lest superstitions begin that he was somehow ill-fated. Superstitions are impossible to bury. "This one is a prince. He will be greeted with cannon. Then I'll immediately have his horoscope cast—for the Hindu troops—and schedule his naming ceremony—for the Believers."

"What will you name him?"

"His first name will be Nushirvan. You can pick the others."

"Nushirvan was a haughty Persian king. And it's an ugly name."

"It's the name I've chosen." Jadar smiled wickedly, still mulling over what name he would eventually pick.

Mumtaz did not argue. She had already selected the name Salaman, the handsome young man Persian legends said was once created by a wise magician. Salaman was an ideal lover. Whatever name Jadar chose, Salaman would be his second name. And the one she would call him all the coming years in the *zenana*, when he would creep into her bed after Jadar had departed for his own quarters.

And we'll see what name he answers to seven years hence, on his circumcision day.

The *dai* was busy spooning a mixture of honey, *ghee*, and opium into the child's mouth. Then a drop of milk was pressed from Mumtaz's breast and rubbed on the breast of the wet nurse. Jadar watched the ritual with approval. Now for the most important tradition, the one begun by Akman.

"Is the wrap ready?"

Akman had believed that the first clothes a Moghul prince wore should be fashioned from an old garment of a Muslim holy man, and he had requested a garment from the revered Sayyid Ali Shjirazi for his first son. The custom had become fixed for the royal family.

"It's here. The woman in Surat heard a child was due and had this sent to me in Agra before we left." She pointed to a folded loincloth, which had been washed to a perfect white. "It was once worn by that Sufi you adore, Samad."

"Good. I'm glad it's from Samad. But what woman in Surat do you mean?"

"You know who she is." Mumtaz looked around the crowded room, and switched from Turki to Persian. "She sent the weekly reports of Mukarrab Khan's affairs, and handled all the payments to those who collected information in Surat."

Jadar nodded almost imperceptibly. "That one. Of course I remember her. Her reports were always more reliable than the Shahbandar's. I find I can never trust any number that thief gives me. I always have to ask myself what he would *wish* it to be, and then adjust. But what happened to her? I learned a month ago that Mukarrab Khan was being sent to Goa. I think a certain woman of power in Agra finally realized I was learning everything that went on at the port before she was, and thought Mukarrab Khan had betrayed her."

"The Surat woman didn't go to Goa with Mukarrab Khan. She made him divorce her. It was a scandal." Mumtaz smiled mysteriously. "You should come to the women's quarters more often, and learn the news."

"But what happened to her?"

"There's a rumor in Surat that the Shahbandar, Mirza Nuruddin, is hiding her in the women's quarters of his estate house. But actually she left for

Agra the next day, by the northern road. I'm very worried what may happen
to her there."

"How do you know all this? It sounds like bazaar gossip."

"It's all true enough. She sent a pigeon, to the fortress here. The message was waiting when we arrived."

"It's good she's out of Surat. With Mukarrab Khan gone, she's no
longer any help there. But I've always wanted to thank her somehow. She's
one of the best. And our only woman. I don't think anyone ever guessed
what she really did."

"I will thank her for you. Her message was a request. Something only I
could arrange. A favor for a favor."

"And what was that?"

"Just something between women, my love. Nothing to do with armies
and wars." Mumtaz shifted on the bolster and took a perfumed *pan*. "Allah,
I'm tired."

Jadar studied her face again, marveling as always how it seemed to attest
to her spirit.

"Then rest. I hope the cannon won't disturb you."

"It should have been another girl. Then there'd be no cannon."

"And no heir." Jadar turned to leave and Mumtaz eased herself back on
the bolster. Then she lifted herself again and called Jadar.

"Who is escorting the English *feringhi* to Agra?"

"Unfortunately it's Vasant Rao. And just when I need him. But he
demanded to do it personally."

"I'm glad." Mumtaz smiled weakly. "Have him see one of my servants
before they leave."

"Why should I bother him with that?"

"To humor me." She paused. "Is this *feringhi* handsome?"

"Why do you ask?"

"A woman's curiosity."

"I haven't seen him yet. I do suspect he's quick. Perhaps too quick. But
I'll find out more tomorrow. And then I'll decide what I have to do." Jadar
paused at the doorway, while the *dai* pulled aside the curtains that had been
newly hung. "Sleep. And watch over my new prince. He's our first victory in
the Deccan. I pray to Allah he's not our last."

He turned and was gone. Minutes later the cannon salutes began.

Hawksworth began to count the stone stairs after the third twisting turn
of the descending corridor, and his eyes searched through the smoke and
flickering torchlight for some order in the arched doorways that opened out
on each level as they went farther and farther down. An object struck him
across the face and his hand plunged for his sword, before he remembered he

had left it in his quarters, on Jadar's command. Then he heard the high-pitched shriek of a bat and saw it flutter into the shadows. The torchbearers were ten Rajputs of Jadar's personal guard, armed with the usual swords and half-pikes. None spoke as their footsteps clattered through the musty subterranean air.

Hawksworth felt the dankness against the beads of sweat forming on his skin. As the old memory of a dark prison welled up, he suddenly realized he was terrified.

Why did I agree to meet him here? This is not "the lower level of the fortress." This is a dungeon. But he can't detain me, not with a safe conduct pass from the *Moghul*.

Still, he might try. If he wants to keep me out of Agra while he's away on campaign. And he may. I already smell this campaign is doomed.

It was the evening of Hawksworth's third day in the Burhanpur fortress. When the convoy arrived at the village of Bahadurpur, three *kos* west of Burhanpur, they had been met by Jadar's personal guards and escorted through the city and into the walled compound of the fortress. He had been given spacious, carpeted quarters, always guarded, and had seen no one, not even Vasant Rao. Communications with Jadar had been by courier, and finally they had agreed on a neutral meeting place. Jadar had suggested a location in the palace where they would have privacy, yet be outside his official quarters. Since they would meet as officials of state, Jadar had insisted on no weapons.

No visible weapons, Hawksworth told himself, glad he wore boots.

The corridor narrowed slightly, then ended abruptly at a heavy wooden door. Iron braces were patterned over the face of the door and in its center was a small window, secured with heavy bars. Armed Rajputs stood on either side and as Hawksworth's party approached they snapped about, hands at their swords. Then the leader of Hawksworth's guards spoke through the smoke-filled air, his voice echoing off the stone walls.

"Krishna plays his flute."

A voice came from the sentries at the door.

"And longing *gopis* burn."

Again Hawksworth's guard.

"With a maid's desire."

Immediately the sentries slid back the ancient iron bolt that spanned the face of the door. Then came the rasping scrape of another bolt on the inside being released. When he heard the sound, Hawksworth felt a surge of fear and stared around wildly at the faces of the guards. They all stood menacingly, with a regal bearing and expressionless faces. Each man had his hand loosely on his sword.

The door creaked slowly inward, and Hawksworth realized it was almost a foot thick and probably weighed tons. The guards motioned him forward and stood stiffly waiting for him to move. He calculated his chances one more time, and with a shrug, walked through.

The room was enormous, with a high vaulted stone ceiling and a back wall lost in its smoky recesses. Rows of oil lamps trailed down the walls on either side of the door. The walls themselves were heavy gray blocks of cut stone, carefully smoothed until they fit seamlessly together without mortar. He asked himself how air reached the room, then he traced the lamp smoke upward and noticed it disappeared through ornate carvings that decorated the high roof of the chamber.

A heavy slam echoed off the walls and he turned to see the door had been sealed. As his eyes adjusted to the lamplight he searched the chamber. All he could see were long, neat rows of bundles, lining the length of the stone floor. With a shock he realized they were the bundles from the caravan. Otherwise the room seemed empty.

At that moment he caught a flicker of movement, a tall figure at the far end of the chamber, passing shadowlike among the bundles, an apparition. Then a voice sounded through the dense air.

"At last we meet." The stone walls threw back an eerie echo. "Is the place to your liking?"

"I prefer sunlight." Hawksworth felt the cool of the room envelop his skin. "Where I can see who I'm talking to."

"You are speaking to Prince Shapur Firdawsi Jadar, third son of the *Moghul*. It's customary to salaam, Captain-General Hawksworth."

"I speak for His Majesty, King James the First of England. The sons of kings normally bow before him."

"When I meet him, perhaps I will bow." Jadar emerged from among the bundles. He had an elegant short beard and seemed much younger, somehow, than Hawksworth had expected. "I'm surprised to see you alive, Captain. How is it you still live while so many of my Rajputs died?"

"I live by my wits, not by my caste."

Jadar roared with genuine delight.

"Spoken like a Moghul." Then he sobered. "You'd be wise never to say that to a Rajput, however. I often wonder how an army of Moghul troops would fare against a division of Hindu unbelievers. I pray to Allah I never find out." Jadar suddenly slipped a dagger from his waist and held it loosely, fingering the blade. "*Feringhi* Christians would be another matter entirely, however. Did you come unarmed, Captain, as we agreed?"

"I did." Hawksworth stared at the knife in dismay.

"Come, Captain, please don't ask me to believe you'd be such a fool." Jadar slipped the dagger into his other hand with a quick twist and tossed it atop one of the bundles. "But this meeting must be held in trust. I ask that you leave your weapon beside mine."

Hawksworth hesitated, then slowly reached into his boot and withdrew a small stiletto, the Portuguese knife left at the observatory. As he dropped it beside Jadar's weapon, he noticed the prince's knife was missing half its handle.

Jadar smiled. "You know, Captain, if I killed you here, now, there would be no witness to the deed, save your Christian God."

"Do you plan to try?"

"I do not 'try' to do anything, Captain." Jadar opened his hand to reveal that a dagger remained. It was the other side of his original knife, which had been two blades fitted to appear as one. "What I do, Captain, is merely a matter of what I *decide* to do. Right now I have serious misgivings about your intentions in India."

Jadar's blade glinted in the lamplight as he moved toward Hawksworth.

"Is this your greeting for any who refuse to salaam?"

Hawksworth took a step backward toward the door, feinted toward his boot, and rose with a cocked pistol leveled directly at Jadar. "What game is this?"

The prince exploded with laughter, and before Hawksworth caught the quick motion of his arm, the knife thudded deeply into the wooden door behind him.

"Well done, Captain. Very well done." Jadar beamed in appreciation. "You are, as I suspected, truly without the smallest shred of Rajput honor. Put away your pistol. I think we can talk. And by the way, there are twenty matchlocks trained on you right now." He waved toward the vaulted ceiling of the crypt, where dark musket barrels were visible through slits in the carved decoration. He barked a command in Urdu and the barrels slowly withdrew.

"Why don't we talk about releasing me and my chest to travel on to Agra." Hawksworth lowered the pistol, but kept it still cocked, in his hand.

"Agra, you say? Captain, there are already Europeans in Agra." Jadar leaned against one of the bundles. "Portuguese. They've been there many years. How many more Christians can India endure? You infidel Europeans are beginning to annoy me more than I can tell you."

"What do you mean?" Hawksworth tried to read Jadar's eyes, remembering Shirin's story of the Persians and Portuguese both hating the prince.

"Tell me about your English ships, Captain." Jadar seemed not to hear Hawksworth's question. "Tell me how you defeated the Portuguese so easily."

"English frigates are better designed than the Portugals' galleons. And English seamen are better gunners and sailors."

"Words, Captain. Easy words. Perhaps the Portuguese allowed themselves to be defeated. This one time. Waiting for a bigger prize. How can you know?"

"Is that what the Portugals say happened?"

"I asked you."

"A well-manned English frigate is the match of any two galleons."

"Then how many of your 'frigates' would it take to blockade the port at Goa?"

Hawksworth saw a small flicker in Jadar's eyes as the prince waited for the answer. "I think a dozen could do it. If we caught their fleet in the harbor, before they could put out to sea."

"Christians typically exaggerate their strength. How many would it really take? Five times what you've said? Ten times?"

"I said it depends on seamanship. And surprise."

"Christians always seem to have answers. Particularly when there is no answer." Jadar turned and pointed to the stacks of bundles. "By the way, do you know what the caravan carried, Captain?"

"I doubt very much it was lead. So it's probably silver." Hawksworth marveled at the way Jadar seemed to lead the conversation, always getting what he wanted before what he wanted had become obvious. And then quickly moving on.

"Your 'probably' is exactly right. And do you know *why* it carried silver?"

"You have a long supply line. You needed to buy supplies and arms."

"I see you don't think like a Moghul after all." Jadar moved closer, studying Hawksworth's eyes. "Why bother to buy what I could easily take? No, my Christian captain, or ambassador, or spy, I needed men. What is it about human character that allows men to be bought like so many *nautch* girls?"

"Not every man is born to wealth." Hawksworth glared directly at Jadar, beginning to find the conversation growing sinister.

"And few men are without a price, Captain. I think I could even find yours if I looked enough for it." Jadar paused reflectively for a moment, then continued. "Tell me, should I be pleased with your presence here?"

"You have no reason not to be. My only mission here is to open trade between our kings."

"You know your 'mission' has brought about many deaths since you landed in India. The most recent were the deaths of forty of my best men."

"I didn't order the attack on the caravan. Those men's lives are on the head of whoever did." Hawksworth stopped, and as he looked at Jadar something clicked in his mind. Something about the attack that had bothered him ever since.

"Your caravan was attacked by bandits, Captain. Who could order them to do anything? But the men I provided as escort gave their lives protecting you."

"Those men were murdered. They never had a chance."

Hawksworth's mind was racing. Suddenly the pieces of the puzzle began to fall together. Everything fit. Vasant Rao had been too nervous. He must have known the attack was coming, but not when. It was all a game. Some deadly serious war game. And none of the other men knew.

"But I think I have an idea who *did* order the attack." Hawksworth continued, glaring at Jadar. "And you do too."

"Your Rajput guards were growing careless, Captain. They made a foolish mistake. What commander can afford men who make mistakes? Even if they are Rajputs. All men grow complacent if they are never tested."

"It was vicious."

"It was discipline. Security has improved considerably here since that incident." Jadar continued evenly, ignoring the look on Hawksworth's face. "The only real difficulties that night were caused by you. It was very imprudent of you to kill one of the bandits with a pistol. They were instructed merely to disarm you. You were completely safe. But after your rash killing it became much more difficult for me to try to rescue you. And after the eclipse, it actually became impossible." Jadar wanted to ask Hawksworth what had really happened, but he suppressed the impulse. "Still, after your first mistake, you appear to have handled yourself reasonably well. That's why we're having this talk."

"In a dungeon? Surrounded by muskets?"

"In a room surrounded by silver. More, I suspect, than you have ever known. How many sailing ships, your 'frigates,' could be bought with this much silver?"

"I don't know exactly. I do know English frigates are not for sale."

"Come, Captain. Would you have me believe your king never has allies who share a common cause? That he never aids those who war against his enemies?"

"Allies have been known to become enemies. If they grow too ambitious. Just who would your frigates, assuming you had them and the trained seamen to man them, be used against? The Portugals? Or against the English eventually?"

"Sometimes, unfortunately, an ally becomes a tyrant, forcing you to act in your own interest. I know it all too well." Jadar was silent for a moment, then he smiled smoothly. "But tell me about your plans when you reach Agra. You'll have no frigates there. What do you hope to gain?"

"Open trade. That and nothing more. England wants no war with the Portugals."

"Truly? I believe they may think otherwise. Time will tell. There may be changes in Agra soon. The Christian Portuguese may find their time has run out. If that happens, what will you do?"

"I'll wait and see."

"There may be no time to 'wait,' English Captain Hawksworth. The times may require you to choose. If the Portuguese decide to act in the interest of one party here, will England act in the interest of the other? I want to know."

"The king of England acts in his own interest."

"But your king will not be here. You will be here."

"Then *I* will act in his interest." Hawksworth fixed Jadar squarely. "And the king of England is not interested in who rules India. Only in free trade between us."

"But the one who rules India will have the power to permit or deny that trade. You know, there's an Indian folk tale of a Brahmin who once discovered a tiger in a well. He gave aid to the tiger, helped him escape from the well, and years later when the Brahmin was starving the tiger brought him a necklace of gold and jewels won from a rich man in a battle to the death. Do you understand?"

"I understand. But I still serve my king first."

Jadar listened silently, but his eyes were intent.

"And that king is English. For now." Jadar filled the last words with a tone of presumption that left Hawksworth uncomfortable. "But enough. Let's talk of other matters. I assume you are aware the Portuguese will probably try to have you assassinated when you reach Agra. Already there are many rumors about you there. Perhaps you should remember your own personal interests too. As well as your king's. One day, I think, we will meet again. *If* you are still alive."

"And if you are still alive."

Jadar smiled lightly. "We're both difficult to kill. So we both must think of the future. Now I have a last question for you."

Jadar retrieved his knife from atop the bundles and deftly ripped open the side of one. Rolls of new silver coin glistened in the light. "What do you see in this package, Ambassador Hawksworth?"

"A king's ransom in silver."

"I'm surprised at you, Captain. For a seaman you have remarkably bad eyesight. What you see here, what came with you from Surat, is lead, Captain. Ingots of lead."

"That forty men died to protect."

"Those men died protecting you, Captain. Don't you remember? Your safety is very important to me. So important that it may be necessary to keep you under guard here in the fortress until this campaign is over. Look again at the bundle and tell me once more what you see."

"You can't hold me here. I have a safe conduct pass from the *Moghul* himself."

"Do you? Good. In that case there shouldn't be any difficulty. I'll only need to examine it to make sure it's not a forgery. There should be an opportunity sometime after I return from this campaign."

Hawksworth examined Jadar and realized the threat was not empty.

"There's no reason for me to stay. You have your lead."

Jadar smiled an empty grin, but with a trace of bizarre warmth. "At last we're beginning to understand each other. Neither of us has a Rajput's honor." He tossed Hawksworth the Portuguese stiletto. "An interesting knife. Did you know it took me almost two weeks to find out for sure who really hired the assassin? And for all that trouble it was exactly who you'd expect."

Hawksworth examined him in amazement, and decided to gamble another guess.

"I suppose I haven't thanked you yet for saving us from the Portugals' ambush on the river, the day we made landfall."

Jadar waved his hand in dismissal. "Mere curiosity, nothing more. If I had allowed them to kill you, we could never have had this interesting talk. But you still have many troubles ahead."

"We both do."

"But I know who my enemies are, Captain. That's the difference."

The door had begun to swing slowly inward.

"Yes, these are interesting times, Captain. You may find it difficult to stay alive, but somehow I think you'll manage for a while longer."

Hawksworth watched nervously as the Rajput guards filed into the room and stationed themselves by the door.

"I plan to march south in ten days. You would be wise to leave tomorrow for the north, while the roads are still secure. Vasant Rao has asked to accompany you, and I'm afraid I have no choice but to humor him. I need him here, but he is a man of temperament. I will provide guards for you as far north as the Narbada River. After that he will hire his own horsemen. I'll give him a letter for a raja in Mandu, who can supply whatever he needs." Jadar studied Hawksworth one last time, his eyes calculating. "We both have difficult times ahead, but I think we'll meet again. Time may change a few things for both of us."

As Hawksworth passed through the open doorway, he looked back to see the prince leaning easily against a stack of bundles, flipping a large silver coin. And suddenly he wanted to leave the fortress of Burhanpur more than he had ever wanted anything in his life.

The next morning Vasant Rao and forty horsemen were waiting with Hawksworth's cart. By midday they had left Burhanpur far behind, and were well on the way north. The journey north through Mandu, Ujjain, and Gwalior to Agra normally took six weeks, but when roads were dry it was an easy trip.

Two days later five prominent *mansabdars* in the northern Deccan died painfully in separate ambushes by bandits. Their *jagirs* were confiscated immediately by Prince Jadar. Ten days from that time he moved south with eighty thousand men and thirty thousand horse.

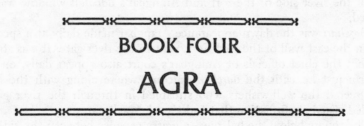

BOOK FOUR

AGRA

CHAPTER SIXTEEN

Nadir Sharif leaned uneasily against the rooftop railing of his sprawling riverside palace, above the second-floor *zenana*, and absently watched his Kabuli pigeons wing past the curve of the Jamuna River, headed toward the Red Fort. They swept over the heavy battlements at the river gate and then veered precisely upward, along the sheer eastern wall of the fort, until they reached the gold minaret atop the Jasmine Tower, the private quarters of Queen Janahara. They circled her tower once, then coalesced into a plumed spear driving directly upward toward the dawn-tinged cloud bank that hovered over Agra from the east.

Imported Kabuli pigeons, with their flawless white eyes and blue-tipped wings, were Nadir Sharif's secret joy. Unlike the inferior local breeds of the other devoted pigeon-fliers along the west bank of the Jamuna, Agra's palace-lined showplace, his Kabulis did not flit aimlessly from rooftop to rooftop on their daily morning flight. After he opened the shutters on their rooftop grill-work cage, they would trace a single circle of his palace, next wing past the Red Fort in a salute to the queen, then simply disappear into the infinite for fully half a day, returning as regally as they had first taken wing.

Nadir Sharif was the prime minister of the Moghul empire, the brother of Queen Janahara, and the father of Prince Jadar's favorite wife, Mumtaz. Even in the first light of dawn there was no mistaking he was Persian and proud. The early sun glanced off his finely woven gauze cape and quickened a warm glow in the gold thread laced through his yellow cloak and his pastel morning turban. His quick eyes, plump face, and graying moustache testified to his almost sixty years of life, thirty spent at the Moghul court as close adviser to Arangbar and, before that, to Arangbar's father, the great empire-builder Akman. In power and authority he was exceeded only by the *Moghul* himself.

Nadir Sharif's palace was deliberately situated next to the Red Fort, just around the broad curve of the Jamuna. The Red Fort, home of the *Moghul*, was a vast, rambling fortress whose river side towered over a hundred feet above the western curve of the Jamuna. From Nadir Sharif's rooftop the view of the river side of the fort and Arangbar's *darshan* window was unobstructed.

Darshan was the dawn appearance Arangbar made daily at a special balcony in the east wall of the Red Fort, next to the river gate. It was strict custom that the chief officials of Arangbar's court also appear daily, on a high platform just beneath the *darshan* balcony, where along with the *Moghul* they greeted the well-wishers who streamed in through the river gate and provided visual confirmation that India's rule was intact.

The square below the balcony—a grassy expanse between the side of the fort and the river wall, where Arangbar held noontime elephant fights and, on Tuesdays, executions by specially trained elephants—had already filled almost to capacity. Agra's most prominent noblemen were there, as prudence required, and today there also were clusters of important visitors. Several Rajput chieftains from the northwest, astride prancing Arabian horses, passed regally through the river gate and assumed prominent positions. Then a path was cleared for a large embassy of Safavid Persian diplomats, each of whose palanquins was borne by four slaves in gleaming velvet liveries; next several desert Uzbek khans in leather headdress rode into the square; and finally three Portuguese Jesuits in black cassocks trooped through the river gate and moved imperiously to the front of the crowd.

Nadir Sharif watched as his pigeons were swallowed by the morning haze and then settled himself onto a canopied couch to observe *darshan*. The eunuchs of the *zenana* had whispered that this morning would be different, that there would be a precedent-shattering occurrence. For once a *zenana* rumor seemed all too plausible, and late the previous evening he had sent a dispatch through a *qazi*, a high judge, pleading illness and excusing himself from *darshan*. And now he had stationed himself to watch. How would the court officials react? Had they too heard the rumors? And what of those who had gathered below to salute Arangbar with the traditional *teslim?*

Most importantly, what of Nadir Sharif? This day could well be a turning point in the course of India's history . . . and in the three decades of his preeminence at court. If the rumors were true.

Nadir Sharif was easily the most accomplished courtier in India, a skill that had earned him the most splendid palace in Agra after the *Moghul* himself. His position brought with it not merely a palace, but also the *mansab* rank and *jagir* wealth required to maintain it. Only enormous wealth could sustain the hungry host of slaves, eunuchs, concubines, musicians, dancers, and wives who thronged his Agra palace.

Success for Nadir Sharif had always seemed so effortless, so inevitable, he often marveled that so few others had ever grasped the elementary secret. His simple formula for longevity, in a court where favorites daily rose and fell, was first to establish with certainty which side of a difference would inevitably triumph, and then to unveil his own supporting views.

He had made a lifelong habit of seeing everything. And saying almost nothing. He understood well that thoughts unsaid often served better than those voiced too hastily. Whereas the way of others might be flawed by a penchant for the *zenana*, or jewels, or those intoxicants the Prophet had so futilely prohibited, Nadir Sharif's sole worldly obsession was power—from which nothing, absolutely nothing, had ever turned his head. For a decade he had ruled the *Moghul*'s empire in all but name, forwarding to Arangbar only those petitions he favored, holding in advisement any he opposed, counseling the *Moghul* at every turn—but always through other, unsuspecting voices if the advice was anything save disguised flattery.

His meticulous attention to affairs at court did not exclude foreign trade. For years his voice had been raised against any who counseled Arangbar in directions adverse to Portuguese interests. This attention did not pass unnoticed in Goa, and when a kingly jewel was sent to Arangbar, another of only slightly inferior dimensions always found its way into the hands of Nadir Sharif.

The first rays of sun struck the hard ocher sandstone of the Red Fort's east wall and suddenly it glowed like an inflamed ruby, throwing its warmth across the face of the Jamuna River. Moments later the heightening sun illuminated the rooftops of Agra, a sea of red tile and thatch that spread out in a wide arc west of the fort.

Agra, the capital of Moghul India, was one of the great cities of the East. It was home to over half a million, more than lived in any capital of Europe, and some said a man on horseback could scarcely circle it in a day. Yet most of the city was far from grand. It was a jumble of two-story brick and tile merchant houses, clay-faced homes of Hindu tradesmen, and a spreading sea of mud and thatch one-room hovels that sheltered the rest.

But along the river on either side of the Red Fort had been created a different world. There glistened the mansions of Moghul grandees like Nadir Sharif, magical and remote, behind whose walls lay spacious gardens cooled by marble fountains and gilded rooms filled with carpets from Persia, porcelains from China, imported crystal from Venice. Their *zenanas* thronging with exquisite, dark-eyed women, and their tapestried halls with hosts of slaves and eunuchs.

Nadir Sharif inhaled the clean air of morning and surveyed the palaces on either side along the riverbank. They were all sumptuous, but none more than his own. A vainer man might have swelled with pride at such a moment, but Nadir Sharif knew from years of court experience that vanity always led, inevitably, to excess, and finally to debt and ruin. To keep one's place, he often told himself, one must know it. He also knew that to hold one's ground, one must know when to shift.

His reverie was abruptly dispelled by the noise of shuffling feet, and then a hesitant voice.

"A man is at the outer gate, Sharif Sahib, asking to see you."

Nadir Sharif turned to see the eunuch's spotless white turban bowing toward him. He flared inwardly that his orders for absolute privacy had been ignored, and then, as always, he waited a few seconds for composure before speaking.

"I'm too ill to receive. Have you already forgotten my orders?"

"Forgive me, Sharif Sahib." The eunuch bowed even lower and raised his clasped palms in involuntary supplication. "He has demanded an audience. He claimed he had arrived last night from the Deccan. He was with the prince . . ."

Nadir Sharif's body tensed perceptibly. "What name did he give?"

"A Rajput name, Sharif Sahib. He said he was requested by Her Highness, the princess, to report to you immediately on arriving."

Nadir Sharif's heart skipped a beat. Does this mean the English *feringhi* has arrived? Allah! On this of all days.

"Tell him I am at home." The voice was coolly matter-of-fact.

The eunuch bowed again and disappeared without a word. As Nadir Sharif watched his skirt vanish past the doorway tapestry, he tried to clear his mind and decide quickly what now must be done. Involuntarily he turned once more to monitor the *darshan* balcony. Still nothing. Then he smiled fleetingly, realizing that the fate of the Englishman would depend very much on what happened at *darshan* this very morning.

The visitor appeared, in freshly brushed red turban and jeweled earrings, and wordlessly strode past the eunuch at the doorway, pushing the partially opened tapestry aside as though a foe in battle. There was about the man the haughty carriage and contemptuous eyes always encountered among Rajputs in high places, and Nadir Sharif recognized him immediately. The prime minister also knew this particular Rajput had never trusted him, and never would.

"*Nimaste*, Sharif Sahib." Vasant Rao's salaam was correct but cold. "It's always a pleasure to see you."

"When did you arrive?"

"Last evening."

"Have you arranged lodgings for the English *feringhi*? Even before informing me you were here?"

"He has no lodging yet, Sharif Sahib, only rooms at a guest house. The *feringhi* insisted no one be informed of his arrival. He did not say why." Vasant Rao returned Nadir Sharif's expressionless stare. "The prince's orders were to honor the *feringhi*'s requests whenever possible."

Nadir Sharif's face betrayed none of his anger as he turned again toward the *darshan* balcony. A flock of vagrant pigeons darted overhead, following the line of palaces along the river.

"How is the child?"

"He is well formed, Sharif Sahib. Your daughter, Her Highness, was also well when I left Burhanpur. She gave me this dispatch for you."

Nadir Sharif accepted the bamboo tube and, controlling his expression, tossed it aside as though it were of no more consequence than a gardener's report brought by a eunuch. "I've received no pigeons from her for four weeks. Only official dispatches from Ghulam Adl's secretary in Burhanpur, which tell nothing. Why isn't he in the field with Jadar? What is happening?"

"I'm not with the army now, Sharif Sahib." Vasant Rao casually stroked his moustache. "Perhaps the prince has ordered secrecy to protect his movements toward the south."

Nadir Sharif started to reply, but immediately thought better of it. Instead he traced his finger along the railing of the balcony in silence and seemed to listen to the distant pigeons as he rotated the answer in his mind, knowing it was a lie and quickly evaluating the possible reasons why.

In the north, dispatching pigeons in the field might be a risk, but never in the south, where the infidel Deccanis always know the deployment of our army better than its own commanders. No. There's something planned that Jadar does not want me to know. Which can only mean His impulsive Highness, Prince Jadar has undertaken something foolish. I know him too well.

After a moment Nadir Sharif broke the silence, without turning his face from the *darshan* balcony.

"Tell my about the *feringhi*."

"Do you mean what he says? Or what I think about him?"

"Both."

"He claims to be an ambassador for the English king, but his only credentials are a letter he brings, said to request a trading *firman* from His Majesty."

"What are the intentions of this *feringhi* king? Trade, or eventual meddling?"

"No one has seen the letter, Sharif Sahib, but the Englishman says his king merely asks to trade yearly at Surat."

"Which means the English must again contest with the Portuguese. Until one of them eventually abandons our ports. They cannot both trade. The Portuguese Viceroy would never allow it."

"What you say seems true. It's said the Christians in Europe are having a holy war. I don't understand the cause, but the English and the Portuguese seem to be historic enemies because of it. However, the Englishman claims their disputes in Europe are now over, and that the Portuguese attack on his ships was in violation of a treaty of peace recently signed. Whether this is actually true no one knows. The English ships are gone now, but if they come again, who can say what will happen."

"Will they come again?" Nadir Sharif's eyes told nothing of his thoughts, but his voice sharpened. "Soon?"

"The Englishman has not said. Perhaps next year. Perhaps before that." Vasant Rao caught the inflection in Nadir Sharif's voice, and it triggered a chain of improbable possibilities.

"Goa will never allow them open access to Surat. There must be war on our seas if the English return." Nadir Sharif paused for a moment and then continued. "Who do you think will triumph?"

"Ask those who claim the gift of prophecy, Sharif Sahib. I'm only a soldier."

"That's why I asked you."

"I can only say that if other English are like this man, then they are a determined race. He seems to seek the new because it is there, yet perhaps not knowing what he will do with it once it is his."

"What do you mean?"

"The Englishman, Hawksworth. He claims to be here for his king and his king only. But I sense this is only partly true. He is a man of complex desires."

"Then why *is* he here?"

"I think he is here also for himself. He wants something."

"Perhaps it's to make war on the Portuguese?"

"He will not shrink from it. But I think his own coming to India is to find something. He is searching, for what I cannot say. He is a man of curious parts. He spoke once of spending time in prison. And he is devoted to playing a small stringed instrument. He understands the tongue of the Moghuls, and he questions all he sees. He is beginning to know India, because he has made it his purpose to know India. If he stays, he could become very troubling for the Portuguese."

"And that will bring no good to affairs here?" Nadir Sharif paused. "Will it?"

"I do not follow matters of state, Sharif Sahib."

Nadir Sharif let the silence swell, then in a voice brittle as ice he spoke. "Why did the prince meet with him?"

Vasant Rao tried without success to mask his surprise. Lord Krishna, they know everything in Agra.

"There was a meeting." Vasant Rao hesitated, then decided to maintain discretion. "But neither spoke of it afterwards."

Nadir Sharif studied him, pondering if it were true. Then he turned to glance at the *darshan* balcony as he spoke.

"The *Moghul* has demanded that the English *feringhi* be brought to *durbar* immediately after he arrives."

"Does that mean today?" Vasant Rao shifted with surprise.

"His Majesty will hear soon enough he has arrived. There is no choice."

"Then the *feringhi* must be told to prepare, Sharif Sahib. He has a chest containing gifts, and the letter."

"I know what he has. Tell him he must bring the gifts to *durbar*. For his sake I hope they're not trifles. His Majesty is most anxious to see them."

And the queen is even more anxious to see the letter, Nadir Sharif told himself. Then he smiled as he realized he would see it first.

It will be an interesting afternoon.

A fanfare of drums sounded faintly from the ramparts of the Red Fort, and for a moment the morning sun seemed to glow even brighter against the gleaming panels of the Jasmine Tower. Nadir Sharif turned toward the *darshan* balcony. From the shadow of its embroidered satin awning a figure had suddenly emerged. It was just possible to make out the man's glistening robe and his elaborate, patterned turban. Then the heavy jewels of his earrings momentarily caught the morning sunshine and sent streams of light flashing outward. All the waiting crowd bowed low, each man touching the back of his right hand to the ground and then bringing the palm to his forehead as he drew erect. It was the formal *teslim* given the *Moghul*, signifying each man's readiness to give himself as an offering.

Nadir Sharif scrutinized the scene carefully and drew an almost audible sigh of relief. Then he turned to Vasant Rao.

"Have you ever seen the *Moghul* at morning *darshan?*" He continued on distractedly, neglecting to pause for an answer. "You know, it's actually a custom begun by Akman, who worshiped the sun as one of the gods. But Arangbar appears in order to maintain his own authority. If he missed *darshan* for a day, rumors would begin he was dead. Three days and there would be anarchy."

Suddenly the cheers from the courtyard died abruptly. In the silence that followed, a single pigeon's cry could be heard from overhead. Nadir Sharif whirled to see a second figure now standing on the balcony beside Arangbar.

It was a dark-haired woman. He could not tell if she wore a veil, but her tiara of jewels glistened in the early sun. The color drained from Nadir Sharif's face as he watched.

So the rumor was true. For the first time in history, she has appeared beside him at *darshan*, to be worshiped equally.

Vasant Rao found himself staring in astonishment.

Queen Janahara. This is truly the beginning of the end for the prince. He will never see Agra again. Unless he's at the head of an army, or in chains.

"What does it mean?" Vasant Rao could think of nothing else to say.

"Times and fashions change. Perhaps it's a whim of His Majesty." Nadir Sharif did not turn his gaze from the balcony. He did not want Vasant Rao to see his eyes.

"Escort the *feringhi* to *durbar* today. He's not safe here alone."

"As you wish, Sharif Sahib." Vasant Rao paused and studied the back of Nadir Sharif's turban. "Do you have a message for the prince when I return?"

"Official channels will serve for any message I have to give the prince." The prime minister whirled with uncharacteristic abruptness. "That will be all. You would be wise to be out of Agra when the sun rises tomorrow."

As Vasant Rao made his way past the waiting eunuchs, Nadir Sharif turned once more to examine the *darshan* balcony. He watched in growing dismay as the courtiers on the platform began salaams to Queen Janahara, who now stood boldly at the forefront of the canopied marble portico.

Then he recalled the dispatch from Mumtaz.

A line of mounted Imperial guards cleared a pathway through the narrow street, now a midday throng of bullock carts, dark-skinned porters, ambling cattle, and black-veiled women balancing heavy brass pots atop their heads. Along both sides of the street tan awnings shielded lines of quick-eyed, bearded merchants, who squatted on their porches beckoning all to inspect their unprecedented bargains in cloth, reeds, betel leaves. Vendors sizzled flat bread in charcoal-fired round pans and dropped balls of brown dough into dark pots of smoking oil, seasoning the dusty air with piquant spice. Above the clatter of their horses' hooves came a cacophony of street Hindi, squeaking cart wheels, children's discordant piping.

Between the open shops were ornate doorways, framed in delicate plasterwork scallops, leading upward to overhead balconies supported by red sandstone brackets. Behind the latticework screens that fronted these balconies—some carved rosewood, some filigreed marble—Hawksworth could see clusters of idle women chewing betel and fanning themselves as they leaned forward to inspect the procession below.

Hawksworth studied the helmeted guards around him, whose ornate shields bore and *Moghul*'s personal seal, and reflected on his introduction to Agra. His caravan from the south had arrived at the city's outskirts the evening before, after the sun's light had died away, and as he requested, Vasant Rao had found a traditional guest house for them. It was near the center of town, inconspicuous, and its primary amenities were a rainproof thatch roof and a stone floor. Tomorrow, the Rajput had told him, he must find a house befitting an ambassador.

The guards accompanying them into Agra had not even dismounted, had turned back immediately for the south, and only Vasant Rao stayed to share the evening meal. They had dined quickly on fried bread and lentils and afterward the Rajput had retrieved his saddle from the stable and, pillowing it under his helmet, immediately fallen asleep, curved sword in hand. Hawksworth had lain awake listening to the night sounds of Agra, wondering what his next move should be. Sleep finally overtook him just before dawn broke.

He awoke to discover Vasant Rao already gone. But the Rajput had mysteriously returned in time to share a breakfast of more fried bread and spiced curds. After eating, Vasant Rao had announced that Arangbar expected him in *durbar* that afternoon. The rest of the morning had been spent hastily procuring bearers for his chest of gifts and cleaning the mildewed doublet and hose he had been instructed by the Company to wear. Just after noon, a contingent of the *Moghul*'s personal guard had arrived unexpectedly with orders to escort them through the center of Agra, directly to the *Moghul*'s private entrance to the Red Fort.

Their horses emerged abruptly from the narrow, jostling street and Hawksworth realized they had entered a wide, sunlit plaza opening outward from the fort's south gate. The close, acrid smells of the town were immediately scourged by the searing midday heat. Hawksworth reined in his horse and stared at the fort, incredulous at its immensity.

They were facing two concentric walls of polished red sandstone, the outer easily forty feet high and the inner at least seventy. Both were obviously thick, with battlements loopholed for musketry and crowned by rampart-ways. A wide wooden drawbridge leading to the entrance spanned a thirty-foot, water-filled moat that followed the outer wall in both directions as far as the eye could see.

It had to be the largest, most powerfully built fortress Hawksworth had ever seen. No story he had heard, no imagined grandeur, had prepared him for this first view. The sight was at once awesome and chilling.

No wonder the *Moghul* frightens all of India. It's impregnable. The outer blocks of the walls seem to be linked by massive iron rings and the round towers spaced along them have slots designed for heavy ordnance. With two thick walls, which probably also have a moat between, it would be impossible to storm. And cannon would be almost useless.

Vasant Rao monitored Hawksworth's reaction, and his dark eyes betrayed his pride. "Do you understand now why the *Moghul* is held in such regard? No king in the world could have a palace as grand as this. Did you know that the distance around the walls is over one *kos*. What would that be? Around two of your English miles?"

Hawksworth nodded assent as their guards led them directly across the wide drawbridge and through a passageway. The outer edge of the drawbridge was connected by heavy chains to rollers at the top of the entryway. The two rollers worked in a stone channel cut upward into the steep walls of the passage and were held in place by iron bars inserted into the channel. The bridge would lift automatically by simple removal of the iron bars. Around them now was a small, heavily defended barbican and ahead, between the outer and inner wall, was a gateway set in a towering portal almost eighty feet high that was faced with gleaming blue enamel tiles.

"How many gates like this are there?"

"The Red Fort actually has four gates, one on the river and one on each of the other sides. This is the southern gate, which the *Moghul* recently renamed the Amar Singh Gate"—Vasant Rao lowered his voice—"after a defiant Rajput who he murdered. I have never seen it before, but it is even more beautiful than the public Delhi Gate, on the north, which is inlaid marble. The Red Fort is truly astonishing. Tell me, Captain, is there anything in your England to compare?"

"Nothing." Hawksworth searched for his voice. "Why is it so large?"

"This is the place where India is governed. And the *Moghul* does not live alone. He has to house over a thousand women, an army to protect him and his treasury, and more servants than man can count." The Rajput seemed momentarily puzzled by the question. Then he continued with a sly smile. "The fort was built by the *Moghul*'s father, the great Akman. People say it required over eight years to complete. He also built another complete city in the desert a few *kos* west of here, but later he abandoned it and moved back to Agra. Surely your English king governs from a palace."

"His Majesty, King James, has a palace at Hampton Court." Hawksworth paused. "But England is governed by laws made in Parliament, which has its own place to meet."

"It sounds like you have a very weak king, Captain Hawksworth, if he cannot rule." Vasant Rao glanced nervously at the guards. "You would do well not to tell that to Arangbar. In India there is only one law, the word of the *Moghul*."

As they entered the portico of the Amar Singh Gate, Hawksworth glanced behind him, relieved to see that their porters still followed, one at each side of his sea chest. Vasant Rao had cautioned him not to deliver all the gifts at once, since Arangbar would expect a new gift each time they met. King James's letter he carried personally, carefully secreted inside his doublet.

Inside the archway of the gate were sets of thick wooden doors, opened back against the sides. These inner doors bristled with long iron spikes, and as Hawksworth puzzled over them, Vasant Rao caught his questioning look.

"Those spikes embedded in the doors are to prevent war elephants from battering them in with their foreheads. It's common in a fortress." He smiled. "But then I keep forgetting your England probably has no elephants."

Ahead, at the terminus of the archway, the path was blocked by a heavy chain and armed sentries. The guards reined in their horses and began to dismount, while their leader passed brusque orders to Vasant Rao.

"We ride no farther," Vasant Rao translated as he swung from the saddle. "He says no one except the *Moghul* himself, his sons, or his women is allowed to ride through the Amar Singh Gate. It's strictly enforced."

Hawksworth paused one last time, feeling about him the weight of the thick walls and the ornate tower rising above them, a great blue jewel in the afternoon sun. For a moment he had the curious sensation of entering a giant tomb. He took a deep breath and slowly dismounted, feeling suddenly conspicuous in his formal silk hose and ruffled doublet.

Vasant Rao passed the reins of his horse to a waiting servant and drew alongside, his eyes intent. "Does it seem strange to you that the *Moghul* would name one of the four gates to the Red Fort after a Rajput?" He stroked the curl of his moustache, and lowered his voice. "It's a story you should hear. It's not meant as an honor."

"What do you mean?"

"It's intended to be a warning to all Rajputs of what happens when he is defied. There was, several years ago, a Rajput adventurer named Amar Singh. He sought to rise to position in Arangbar's court—he eventually did rise to the rank of a thousand horse—and along the way he asked and received the help of an old courtier who had influence. Only later did the Rajput find out that this man expected his youngest daughter in payment." Vasant Rao smiled wryly. "They say she was incredibly beautiful. Well, Amar Singh was a true Rajput, and he was outraged. Naturally he refused. So the courtier who had helped him decided to have revenge, and he went to Arangbar and told him about a certain beautiful Rajput girl who would make an excellent addition to the *zenana*. The *Moghul* immediately sent some of his personal guards to Amar Singh's house to take the girl. When Amar Singh realized why the guards had come, he called for the girl and stabbed her to death before their eyes. Then he took horse and rode to the Red Fort, even riding through this gate. He rode into the audience hall and demanded that Arangbar appear and explain. Such things, Captain, are simply not done in Agra. The moment he dismounted he was cut to pieces by a dozen of Arangbar's guards. Then the *Moghul* decided to name this gate after him, to remind all Rajputs of his fate. But he need not have bothered. No Rajput will ever forget."

Leaving the servants with their horses, they proceeded on foot up a wide, inclined path that led through an enclosed square. Around the sides of the square were porticoes and galleries, where horsemen with swords and pikes waited.

"Those men are on their *chauki*, their seventh-day watch." Vasant Rao pointed to the porticoes. "Every soldier in Agra must stand watch once every seven days. Either here or in the large square inside, where we're going. It's the *Moghul's* law."

They passed through another large gate and suddenly a half dozen turbaned guards, in leather armor and wearing long curved swords, drew alongside, as though expecting them. Now with a double escort they began the ascent of a long walkway, perhaps twenty paces wide, situated between two high brick walls. Hawksworth's leather shoes padded against the square paving stones, which had been striated to permit easy footing for the *Moghul's* horses and elephants. As they reached the end, they emerged into another large court, comprising the southeast corner of the fort.

Ahead was yet a fourth gate. As they passed through, Hawksworth realized it was protected by more mounted horsemen in the recessed lower porticoes, and archers in elevated galleries. They walked past the wide wooden doors and into a vast milling square. It was several hundred feet on the side and ringed with arcades where still more mounted horsemen waited. A wide roadway divided the square.

"This is the quadrangle. I only saw it once before, but then I entered from the public side." Vasant Rao indicated an identical gate, directly opposite. "Over there."

The guards directed them toward a large multicolored silk canopy fanning out from the tall buildings on their right. The area beneath the canopy was cordoned off from the square by a red velvet railing, and porters with cudgels stood around the perimeter. Vasant Rao seemed increasingly nervous as their escorts led them forward, past the guards at the entry to the canopy. Hawksworth noticed that the air beneath the canopy was heavy with incense —ambergris and aloe—burning in gold and silver censers hanging from poles.

"The arcade ahead is the *Diwan-i-Am*, the Hall of Public Audience, where the *Moghul* holds his daily *durbar*." Vasant Rao pointed toward the steps that led upward to a large open pavilion at the far end of the canopy. It was several stories high and over a hundred feet on each side. The roof was borne by marble arches supported by rows of white columns. "No man with rank under five hundred horse is allowed to enter inside the railing. I think that's why we have a special escort."

Above the crowd, at the far end of the hall, was a raised platform of white marble, standing about three feet from the floor and covered by its own tapestried canopy. The platform was surrounded by a silver railing, and several turbaned men holding rolls of documents were now struggling to gain a position at the rail. All around them the crowd buzzed with anticipation.

Behind and above the platform, in a marble gallery set in the wall, rested an immense throne carved from black marble. At its four corners were life-sized silver statues of rearing lions, each spangled with jewels, which supported in their silver paws a canopy of pure gold. The walls on either side of the throne were latticework marble screens, through which the *zenana* women could watch.

"I've never seen the throne this close before. It's famous." Vasant Rao paused. "And there are some in Agra who would sell their brother to have it."

The Imperial guards suddenly saluted, fists against their leather shields, turned and marched down the steps of the *Diwan-i-Am* and back into the square. Vasant Rao watched them disappear into the crowd and then he shook the left sleeve of his riding cloak and a naked *katar*, the deadly "tiger knife" all Rajputs carried, dropped into his hand. Its handle was a gold-plated grip between two prongs, designed to be held in the fist and thrust directly forward. Without a word he slipped it into a sheath secured in the sash of his belt.

Hawksworth pretended not to notice and instead turned to examine the crowd. Next to them an assembly of Persian diplomats, wearing heavy robes and jewel-encrusted turbans, eyed Hawksworth's plain doublet and hose with open contempt. The air was thick with sweat and incense and the sparkle of gold and jewels.

Uniformed servants sounded a drum roll on two large brass kettles at the back of the throne and the velvet curtains behind the throne parted. Two guards with gold-handled swords entered briskly and stood at attention, one on either side of the parted curtains.

Hawksworth felt his pulse surge as the next figure entered through the curtains.

He was of middle height, with a small moustache and glistening diamond earrings. He wore a tight patterned turban, a blue robe secured by a gold brocade sash, jeweled rings on both hands, and a massive string of pearls. A golden-handled sword and dagger were at his waist, and two feline cubs frisked by his side. Hawksworth studied them in confusion, and after a moment realized they must be baby lions, an animal famous in English folklore but never actually seen firsthand by anyone in England.

At that instant a din of kettledrums erupted from galleries at the sides of the square. Almost as one those waiting called out a salaam, bent forward, and touched the back of their right hand to the ground and then to their forehead as they drew erect. The *durbar* of the *Moghul* had begun.

"You did not perform the *teslim*." Vasant Rao turned to Hawksworth with dismay in his voice. "He may have taken note of it. That was unwise, my friend."

"An ambassador for a king doesn't prostrate himself."

"You're new to India. That may be taken as an excuse. The other ambassadors here know better."

As they watched, three other men slowly emerged from behind the throne and took their places on the marble platform, standing beside the *Moghul*. They all wore jeweled turbans and each had a sash of gold cloth about the waist. Hawksworth turned to Vasant Rao in time to see a look of hatred flash through his eyes.

"Who are they?"

"The two younger men are his sons. I saw them once before in Agra. It's traditional that his sons join him at the *durbar* when they are here. The younger one is Allaudin. He will be married next month to Queen Janahara's daughter. The other one is his drunken brother Parwaz. The older man is Zainul Beg, the *Moghul's wazir*, his chief counsel. He's the father of Nadir Sharif, the prime minister, and he's also the father of Queen Janahara."

Hawksworth watched as yet another man emerged through the curtain, walked casually past the throne, and was helped onto the marble platform directly in front. He turned to the silver rail, where a dozen petitions were immediately thrust up to him.

Vasant Rao nudged Hawksworth and pointed. "And that's Nadir Sharif, the prime minister. Remember him well. No one reaches the *Moghul* without his consent."

The prime minister paused to study the faces below, and then reached out for a petition. He unrolled it, scanned it quickly, and turned to Arangbar, passing it upward with a comment only those by the throne could hear. The business of the day was underway.

Arangbar listened with obvious boredom as one petition after another was set before him. He held counsel with his sons and with the *wazir*, and frequently he would turn to the marble screen off the right side of the throne and discuss a petition with someone waiting behind it.

Below the platform several ambassadors shuffled, trying to mask their impatience. Hawksworth suddenly realized that the jeweled-encrusted boxes they held, many of beaten gold, contained presents for the *Moghul*. He looked at his own leatherbound wooden chest, shabby by comparison, and his heart began to sink.

After a short while, the *Moghul* seemed to lose patience with the petitions and, ignoring the waiting nobles, abruptly signaled for a review of the day's elephant troops. Moments later, a line of war elephants entered through the public gate and began to march single-file across the back of the square. Their tusks were wreathed with gold bands and they wore coverings of embroidered cloth which were strung with tinkling bells and tassels of Tibetan yak hair. As each reached a spot directly in front of the *Diwan-i-Am* it stopped, kneeled, and trumpeted to Arangbar.

When the last elephant had passed, drums were sounded again and a group of eight men came into the square leading a snarling beast by heavy chains attached to its iron collar. It was tawny, with a heavy mane and powerful paws, and it roared out its displeasure as it writhed and clawed at the chains.

Hawksworth took one look and realized it was a fully grown male lion.

"That seems to be His Majesty's new toy." Vasant Rao pointed nervously. "He collects lions as pets. That one must have just been captured."

Arangbar studied the lion with obvious delight. Then he bent down and stroked one of the cubs by his side, lifting it to better view the new prize. The assembly watched spellbound for a moment, then burst into cheers.

As Hawksworth watched, Arangbar set down the lion cub and spoke with his *wazir*. Zainul Beg stared into the crowd and then pointed. Moments later the black cassock of a Jesuit appeared at the railing. With a start Hawksworth recognized Father Alvarez Sarmento, last seen in the courtyard of Mukarrab Khan's palace in Surat. The Jesuit listened to the *wazir's* instructions and then turned to the crowd. His announcement was in English.

"His Majesty orders the ambassador from England to come forward."

Vasant Rao touched Hawksworth's arm and reached out to clasp his hand.

"This is your moment, my friend. By the time *durbar* is through I will be far from here."

"Why are you leaving?" Hawksworth turned and looked into his eyes, suddenly realizing that Vasant Rao was the closest thing he had to a friend in India.

"It's impossible for me to stay longer." Vasant Rao paused, and Hawksworth sensed his warmth was genuine. Suddenly the Rajput reached into the sash at his belt and drew out his sheathed *katar*. "You saved my life once, in the village, and I've never found the words to thank you. Perhaps this can say it for me. Take it as a token of friendship from a Rajput. It was given to me by my father, and it has tasted blood more times than I can count. You're a brave and honest man, and I think we'll meet again."

Before Hawksworth could speak, Vasant Rao embraced him warmly and melted into the crowd.

A pathway was clearing through the glaring nobles, and Hawksworth quickly slipped the *katar* into his doublet as he leaned over to secure the chest. When he reached the silver railing, Sarmento was waiting.

"Let me welcome you to Agra, Captain." The Jesuit spoke quietly in English, his face a hard mask. "I pray God gave you a pleasant journey."

"I thought you were bound for Lahore."

"In time, Captain, in time. But we have an Agra mission as well. Our flock here grows. It must be tended. And do you remember what we agreed that night in Surat?"

"Translate for the Inglish ambassador." Arangbar's voice interrupted, speaking in Persian. "I would know his name."

"He asks your name." Sarmento spoke quietly to Hawksworth in English. "You must bow when you give it."

"I am Captain-General Brian Hawksworth, ambassador of His Majesty, King James the First of England." Hawksworth replied in Turkish, trying to remember the speech he had been told to deliver. A look of delighted surprise flashed through Arangbar's eyes. Hawksworth bowed and then continued. "His Majesty, King James, has asked me to convey his friendship to His Most Noble Majesty, Arangbar, *Moghul* of India, together with certain unworthy tokens of his regard." Hawksworth tried to think quickly of a way to explain the unimpressive gifts King James had sent. "Those trifles he sends are not intended as gifts deserving of Your Majesty, for that would be a bounty no single man could deliver. Instead he has asked me to bring certain common products of our country, not as gifts, for they are too unworthy, but as samples of English workmanship that Your Majesty may examine personally the goods he offers your merchants in trade. These are the first of many, more-worthy gifts he is now assembling for Your Majesty, to be sent on future voyages to your land."

"You speak the tongue of the Moghuls, Ambassador. Already your king does me honor. I welcome you in his name." Arangbar leaned forward to watch as Hawksworth opened the clasp on the chest.

The first items were samples of English woolens, lace, and brocade, crafted into doublets. Hawksworth laid these aside and took out a silver-trimmed brace of pistols, a gold-handled sword, an hourglass in carved ivory, and finally a gold whistle studded with small diamonds. The *Moghul* peered down from his marble throne impassively, and then called for them to be brought to him.

While he examined each gift briefly, assessing it with a quick glance and calling for the next, Hawksworth reached into the corner of the box and withdrew the next present, a three-cornered English hat topped with a feather. When Arangbar saw the hat his eyes brightened.

"At last I can look like a *topiwallah*." He pushed aside the other gifts and called for the hat. He turned it in his hand for a moment, then removed his jeweled turban and clapped it on his head with delight.

"The *feringhi* hat is a puzzling invention, Ambassador Khawksworth." Arangbar stumbled over the pronunciation of the name as he signaled for a mirror. "What purpose it serves I have never understood. You, I observe, do not wear one yourself."

"Hats are not to my taste, may it please Your Majesty." Hawksworth bowed again and then continued. "His Majesty, King James of England, also has asked me to deliver a portrait of himself to Your Majesty, together with letter expressing his desire for friendship between your land and his." Hawksworth produced a small framed watercolor from the wooden chest. It was a miniature on vellum, scarcely more than an inch square, by Isaac Oliver, a celebrated artist from the school of Nicholas Hilliard, who had been fashionable under Queen Elizabeth. While Arangbar examined the painting, scrutinizing the workmanship as might a connoisseur, Hawksworth reached into his doublet and withdrew the letter. It was passed to Nadir Sharif, who presented it to Arangbar.

The *Moghul* reluctantly handed the portrait to Allaudin, then inspected the leather binding of the letter. Finally he broke the red wax seal and began to study the writing, a quizzical expression spreading over his face.

"The seal and script are worthy of a king. But it is in a language of Europe."

"There are two copies, Your Majesty. One in English, the language of my king, and one in Spanish, a language something like the Portugals speak."

"Then we will have Father Sarmento translate."

Sarmento moved to the silver railing and took the leatherbound letter with a distasteful expression. He examined it for a moment and then began to read it silently, the color slowly draining from his face.

"What message does your king send, Ambassador?"

"His admiration for Your Majesty, whose reputation has reached even Europe. And his offer of full and open trade between your nation and his."

"The letter is basely penned, Your Majesty." Sarmento's face was red with dismay as he turned to Arangbar. "Its style is unworthy of a great prince."

Arangbar examined the Jesuit with a troubled gaze and shifted on his throne.

"May it please Your Majesty, this man is the enemy of England." Hawksworth pointed at Sarmento. "How can my king's letter be ill-penned, when he entreats Your Majesty's friendship?"

Arangbar paused a moment and then he smiled broadly. "A reasonable reply. The Inglish, I see, are a blunt-spoken race." He glanced at Sarmento. "And we have already seen their seamanship."

"Your words honor my king, Your Majesty." Hawksworth found himself bowing again and wondering how to respond.

"We would hear more of England. Is it large?"

"Not nearly as large as India, Your Majesty. It is an island, but the queen of all the islands of the West."

"It is a rocky, barren speck in the great seas of Europe, Your Majesty," Sarmento interjected himself, straining to hold his composure. "A breeder of drunken fishermen and pirates. Its king is a heretic, a sovereign of lawless privateers and an enemy of the Holy Church."

"It is a noble land, Your Majesty, ruled by a free king, not by a Spanish tyrant or an Italian pope, like the land of the Portugals. Our cannon are the best in the world, our ships the swiftest, our men the bravest. No flag but our own has ever flown above our soil. Our ships have sailed all the seas of the world, from the East to the West. My king's seamen have explored the seas north of England, searching for a northeast passage to the Indies, and the Americas, searching for a northwest passage. Off your own shores we have met the galleons of Portugal, as Your Majesty must know, and in the West Indies we have challenged and overcome the carracks of Papist Spain. There brave English captains named Hawkins and Drake stood off Spaniards ten times their number. The very name of England strikes fear in the heart of a Portugal or a Spaniard."

Arangbar toyed with the jeweled whistle as he listened. "Your England interests us, Ambassador Khawksworth." He paused for a moment and reviewed the small, dispiriting assemblage of gifts. "We would know when your king's next voyage will be."

"Very soon, may it please Your Majesty." Hawksworth squirmed, and noticed Nadir Sharif suddenly edge closer to listen.

"But your king must send out voyages regularly? We have heard of the English traders in our southern seas. Do you not know when the next voyage will be, or what gifts your king is preparing? Surely he will send them this year?"

"May it please Your Majesty"—Hawksworth fumbled with the railing, trying to gain time—"I . . ."

Prince Parwaz suddenly plucked at Arangbar's arm and pointed into the crowd. A tall bearded man with a vast turban and two ornate swords at his side had moved next to the silver railing, near Hawksworth, holding a petition in his hand.

"He is the man I spoke of yesterday." Parwaz spoke in Turki, and his words seemed slurred. Hawksworth realized he was tipsy. "I told him to bring his petition today personally. He's a commander with the rank of a thousand horse. His stipend is eight thousand rupees a month. He claims he has served honorably, most recently in the siege of Qandahar, but that he must resign his *mansab* and dismiss his men and horse unless his stipend is increased."

Arangbar examined the man for a moment, then addressed him in Turki.

"What is your name and rank?"

"I am Amanat Mubarik, Your Majesty. I maintain a thousand horse, the finest Arabian blood in India." The man stood straight and spoke with a loud, clear voice.

"Is not your stipend the amount prescribed any man who maintains that number?"

"It is, Your Highness. But I am not any man. I am a Pathan, and my father was Fath Shah. No enemy of Your Majesty has ever seen the back of my shield. His Highness, Prince Parwaz, saw me defend the royal encampment five years ago when he moved south of the Narbada. With my cavalry I held position when all others called for retreat. I challenge any man here today to do me battle in your presence. With any weapon. On horseback or on foot. Then you may decide if I am as other men."

The *Moghul* examined him carefully for a long moment.

"If you are not like other men, then I will let you prove it." Arangbar pointed beyond the marble porticoes. "Will you fight with the lion?"

The Pathan commander turned and stared blankly into the sunlit square, where the captured lion was snarling and pawing at its chains.

"A lion is a wild beast, Your Majesty. What trial is it for a man to contest with a lion?"

"I think it would be the best trial of all." Arangbar's eyes began to glow.

"A beast has no understanding, Majesty." He shifted nervously as he realized Arangbar was not jesting. "It's not a fit thing for a man to fight."

"You *will* joust with him." The fancy seemed to flood Arangbar with pleasure, and he turned abruptly to one of the guards. "Give him a glove and a truncheon. That should suffice for a man who claims bravery above all others."

Hawksworth watched in disbelief as the dazed commander was led from the *Diwan-i-Am* and into the quadrangle. A murmur of amazement passed through the crowd.

The square cleared quickly as the lion was brought forward by its keepers. Still incredulous, the Pathan slowly pulled the heavy glove onto his left hand, then he took the truncheon, no more than a foot and a half long, in his right. Guards took his swords and turban and in moments he and the lion were faced off in the afternoon sunshine.

Hawksworth forced himself to watch as the commander began to spar with the lion, a young male with powerful claws. He managed to cudgel the lion several times, with the effect that it became more enraged than harmed. Then with a roar it sprang, pulling free of its keepers, and they went down together, rolling in the dust of the square.

The Pathan continued to bravely cudgel the lion, even while its claws ripped across his face and arms. Hawksworth watched the lion's hard tail whip for balance as it pawed again and again at the truncheon. Suddenly the man pulled free of its grasp and, with a wide arcing swing, brought the truncheon directly across the crown of the lion's head. Its rear haunches clawed upward spastically and then it pitched unconscious into the bloody dust, its body still twitching.

A cheer rose from the crowd of onlookers as the Pathan slowly drew himself erect. Hawksworth realized that the right side of his face had been completely ripped away by the lion's sharp claws. He made a few halting steps toward the *Diwan-i-Am*, wheeled dizzily, and collapsed in a pool of blood. He was dead by the time the guards reached him.

Arangbar had watched in spellbound delight. He clapped his hands and turned to Parwaz, whose glazed eyes seemed not to have fully comprehended the spectacle.

"Astounding. I never knew a man could kill a lion with a mere club. He was braver than he knew. If he has sons, I will allow them to keep half his estate." Arangbar turned to the guard captain standing by the curtained entrance. "Tomorrow select ten of your best men and we will bring more lions. What better test of bravery?"

The uniformed men standing at attention around the perimeter of the *Diwan-i-Am* all blanched but their eyes remained fixed straight ahead. Then Arangbar suddenly remembered Hawksworth.

"Does England have men as brave as ours, Ambassador?"

Hawksworth felt a cold sweat in his palms.

"No man in England would dare challenge one of Your Majesty's lions."

Arangbar laughed loudly. Before he could respond, the *wazir* was whispering in his ear. He glanced at the marble screen directly behind his throne and nodded. Then he turned to Hawksworth.

"We are called away, Ambassador. I'm told I must take my afternoon rest. This is the time of day I retire to the *zenana* for one *pahar*." He winked and gestured toward the marble screen. "Her Majesty rules our time. But I want to speak more with you today about this island of England. And about your king's schedule for trade. You will attend me in the *Diwan-i-Khas* this evening."

"As Your Majesty pleases."

As Arangbar rose his eye caught the painting. He picked it up and scrutinized it, then turned to Hawksworth.

"Is this a fair example of Inglish painting?"

"It came from the school of a celebrated artist, Your Majesty. His Majesty, King James, sat to have it painted especially for you." Hawksworth sensed that Arangbar had taken more interest in the painting than in any of the other gifts, except perhaps the hat. "The painters of England are the finest in the world."

The *Moghul* stirred slightly and then summoned a small, wiry man with heavy brows from the first row of courtiers. He briskly moved to the front and salaamed to Arangbar. The *Moghul* passed the painting to him and together they studied it, conversing quietly in Persian. Then Arangbar turned to Hawksworth.

"We have a school of artists here in the palace, Ambassador Khawks-worth. This man, who directs the school, says this portrait's background is too dark, the eyes lifeless. And it is neither three-quarter nor full face, as is our proven convention. Consequently it gives no sense of your king's depth of character." Arangbar smiled. "He also says the portraits he and his men execute are far more difficult. They catch the soul of the man, not merely his physical likeness."

"May it please Your Majesty, I cannot accept what he says."

Arangbar translated to the artist, who replied quickly in Persian, casting a quick, contemptuous glance at Hawksworth.

"He declares he could easily duplicate this simple portrait of your king, in a likeness so exact you could not tell his copy from the original."

"Such a thing is not possible, Your Majesty. No man in the world could execute this exact painting, save the man who first put it on paper."

Arangbar again translated for his painter, who replied animatedly.

"My Chief Painter says he and his workshop could easily produce four copies of this, any one of which would pass for the original."

"May it please Your Majesty, I say it is impossible. European painting is a centuries' old tradition, requiring years of apprenticeship and study."

The men around Hawksworth had begun to shift uncomfortably. The *Moghul* was never contradicted. Yet he seemed to relish the dispute.

"Then we'll set a wager. What will you wager me, Ambassador, that I can make this one painting of your king into five?"

"I know not what to lay with so great a prince, nor does it befit me to name a sum to Your Majesty." Hawksworth shifted uneasily, unsure of the protocol of betting with kings.

"Then if you'll not wager with me, wager with my painter."

"Begging Your Majesty's pardon, your painter is no more suited to wager with an ambassador than I am to wager with Your Majesty."

"Then wager with my prime minister." He turned to Nadir Sharif. "What will you lay?"

"Five thousand gold *mohurs*, Majesty."

Hawksworth swallowed hard, realizing the amount was almost ten thousand pounds English sterling, more money than he had ever seen.

"Money is not an honorable bet among those who speak for great princes, Your Majesty." Hawksworth glanced about wildly, then an idea came. "But perhaps I could wager your prime minister a horse, a fine Arabian stallion."

"Done." Arangbar beamed. "I'll have the paintings tonight."

The painter stared at Arangbar in dismay.

"It's not possible, Majesty. There's not time."

"You'll find a way. Or you'll owe Nadir Sharif a horse."

Arangbar passed the painting back to the painter and whirled with a flourish to leave. Around Hawksworth the nobles all bowed to the ground.

Hawksworth turned quickly to scan the back of the crowd, but Vasant Rao had disappeared. Then guards surrounded him and before he knew what was happening he was swept past Sarmento, whose eyes still glowed with hatred, toward a marble doorway at the corner of the *Diwan-i-Am*.

CHAPTER SEVENTEEN

"Ambassador Hawksworth, His Majesty has asked me to ensure you are wanting in nothing while you wait." Nadir Sharif was standing on the wide marble balcony when Hawksworth emerged from the stairs that led upward from the *Diwan-i-Am* to the interior courtyard of the palace. He salaamed with practiced dignity even as his darting eyes assessed Hawksworth in a quick sweep. "As prime minister for His Majesty it is my duty, indeed my pleasure, to attend your comfort and acquaint you with our protocol."

"I thank you on behalf of His Majesty, King James." Hawksworth awkwardly tried to salaam in return, careful not to bend as low as the prime minister.

"Perhaps I can begin by acquainting you with the palace." He gestured toward the open courtyard, where workmen thronged installing marble fountains, and the rest of the encircling second-story balcony. "The stalls below us are where the wives of merchants sometimes come to offer finery to the women of the *zenana*. Now they are being readied for His Majesty's birthday celebration. And there, across the way"—he pointed to a massive silk canopy covering a pavilion opposite the square, on the riverside of the palace—"is the *Diwan-i-Khas*, where His Majesty holds his evening gatherings. To the left are His Majesty's baths and on the right, projecting out over the river, is the Jasmine Tower of Queen Janahara. Now please follow me. His Majesty has honored you by inviting you to wait for him in the *Diwan-i-Khas*. The only other *feringhis* ever to see it are the Jesuits he sometimes invites here to debate with the mullahs."

Around them the marble porticoes had been carved in relief, a profusion of flowers and vines, creating a monochromatic garden in stone. The floors were patterned marble and the walls decorated with hanging tapestries. As they entered the *Diwan-i-Khas* Hawksworth noticed its floor was covered with a vast Persian carpet, over which had been scattered bolsters and pillows for lounging. On the side nearest the interior square was a foot-high platform in white marble and on the opposite side, facing a gallery overlooking the arena below and the Jamuna River beyond, was a similar platform in black marble. Both were padded with rich carpets.

"His Majesty uses the white throne in evenings, and the black in the afternoons, when he sometimes comes here to watch elephant fights in the square below. The doorway there leads to Her Majesty's apartments."

"Where is His Majesty now?"

"He has retired to the *zenana* for one *pahar*, three hours, where he dines on roasted meats, some wine, and passes the time agreeably. Each afternoon Her Majesty selects a woman for him." Nadir Sharif smiled. "Naturally it's never the same one. Her Majesty is always first in his heart, but she never allows his wanton affections to wander. Afterward he comes here for his evening gathering." Nadir Sharif walked to the gallery and looked down on the river. Far below, on the opposite bank, a caravan of heavily loaded camels passed silently. "By the way, His Majesty has asked me to inquire if you have a lodging yet, Ambassador."

"I have references for brokers, and tomorrow I'll begin to look."

"And personal servants?"

"I'd hoped they'd be provided with the house."

"His Majesty may wish to arrange lodgings for you." Nadir Sharif turned back toward Hawksworth and paused for a moment before continuing. "In Agra ambassadors must acquire their lodgings and servants with care. There is, regrettably, a certain amount of intrigue in our city. Trustworthy and efficient servants are not always the easiest thing to find. Perhaps I should raise the matter of your lodging and servants with His Majesty."

"There's no reason to trouble His Majesty. I'll contact the brokers tomorrow." Hawksworth's tone was level but firm, suspecting that any servants picked for him would be spies. And if they turned out to be "trustworthy and efficient" rather than lazy and begrudging, there would be no doubt.

"The matter rests with His Majesty." Nadir Sharif watched as a eunuch entered bearing a tray with glasses of *sharbat*. A *sarangi* player followed him and settled in the corner, striking up a mournful-sounding tune on an instrument that looked like a bloated violin and sounded, to Hawksworth, like a distressed cat.

"Have you engaged an agent yet, Ambassador?" Nadir Sharif directed the tray toward Hawksworth.

"What do you mean?"

"If your king wishes to trade large quantities of commodity, he will certainly require an agent here in Agra. To ensure that documents and approvals are handled efficiently." Nadir Sharif sighed. "Officials here naturally prefer to work with someone who understands their . . . requirements. An agent will be essential, if your king expects to trade heavily." Nadir Sharif paused. "I presume that *is* his intention, assuming His Majesty approves the *firman*?"

Hawksworth examined Nadir Sharif for a moment, assuming *he* was offering to be the agent for King James. Or was he merely hoping to elicit trade information to pass on to the Portuguese.

"I'll engage an agent when the time seems proper. For now I have no *firman*." Then a light suddenly dawned somewhere in Hawksworth's brain. "But I suppose I'll need an 'agent' for that as well?"

"It could prove useful. His Majesty can be distressingly absentminded."

"And what would be this agent's fee?"

"It depends on the difficulty involved." Nadir Sharif's face remained impassive.

"I would say it also depends on whether he's successful."

"So it would. But he would need more information on English trading intentions than you have divulged so far."

"That will come in time, when I know more about the 'agent.'"

"Naturally." Nadir Sharif cleared his throat. "But enough of affairs. Permit me to toast your arrival. When your request for a safe-conduct pass arrived from Surat, we all wondered if a *feringhi* new to India could successfully travel our bandit-infested roads, even with the *Moghul's* pass." He took a delicate sip of the beverage. "I trust your journey was without mishap."

"For the most part."

"A diplomatic answer. But you seem to have survived all parts well enough. Did you take the Burhanpur road?"

"I did."

"Ah, then perhaps you passed Prince Jadar. I understand he was there recently." Nadir Sharif smiled disarmingly. "I always welcome news of him. You may know he's married to my first daughter, Mumtaz. I hear she just presented him with his first son."

"He was in Burhanpur when I arrived. But I was only there for three days."

"Not a very interesting city, I'm told. But they say the Deccan itself is quite beautiful in harvest. I envy you your trip. I, alas, rarely can escape Agra, except when His Majesty goes to Kashmir in the heat of summer." Nadir Sharif signaled the eunuch to refill Hawksworth's cup. The *sarangi* player had been joined by a drummer, who took up a slow, even rhythm. "Did I understand you to say you met the prince while you were there?"

Hawksworth hesitated and studied Nadir Sharif, not remembering he had mentioned meeting Jadar. "Actually I did see him briefly once. He was in the fortress, where I stayed."

"Ah yes, the fortress. That was wise of you, considering the situation now. I'm pleased he invited you to join him."

"As it happened, I traveled from Surat with men from his guard. Their destination was the fortress."

"His guards? Then you were most fortunate indeed." Nadir Sharif seemed to listen absently to the melody for a moment. "I'm always a bit stupid about military campaigns. What would men from his guards be doing in Surat?"

Hawksworth heard an inner alarm suddenly sound. "I think they were there to accompany a convoy."

"A convoy? From Surat? Odd. But then I rarely understand these things. What was it bringing?" Nadir Sharif chuckled congenially. "Barrels of Persian wine for the prince, I would venture to guess?"

"I understand it was lead for shot."

Nadir Sharif gave Hawksworth a quick, troubled glance. "I see. Yes, lead would require a guard. But Prince Jadar's Rajputs virtually scorn to use muskets, so I assume it was rather a small number of carts."

Hawksworth straightened his doublet, shifting the location of Vasant Rao's *katar*. "I don't recall the precise number."

"Naturally. I'm confused by numbers myself. Probably something like twenty, I suppose. Certainly, I would presume, no more than fifty?"

"I didn't count the exact number."

"Too many to count? I see." Nadir Sharif seemed to be only half attentive to the conversation, as he swung his head from side to side in appreciation of the accelerating tempo of the drummer. "Doubtless it was some of the very lead I'm told you brought for trade."

"It wasn't English."

"Ah, then I suppose it was Portuguese. I assume you must have noticed."

"Not actually." Hawksworth paused. "It wasn't really my concern."

"Yes, quite so." Nadir Sharif walked again to the gallery and stood silent, still swinging his head absently to the time of the music. The pieces of the puzzle had already dropped into place.

So *that's* how Jadar did it. And only one man in Surat could have provided the prince the silver he needed, that contemptible son of a moneylender Mirza Nuruddin. He's uncontrollable. But even if the prince survives the Deccan, what can he do? The Imperial army . . .

Allah, it's obvious! There's only one way he can ever march north with enough men to meet Janahara's army. By the Merciful Prophet, he's mad!

Nadir Sharif coughed lightly and turned back toward the room. "Ambassador Hawksworth, would you care for some wine? You need not be squeamish, His Majesty has always admired men who drink. I would join you, but regrettably I cannot. While His Majesty retires, the rest of us must labor on."

"A glass would be welcome."

"A glass, Ambassador? Did you say 'a glass'?" Nadir Sharif laughed. "You'll need more than a glass if you drink with His Majesty. I'll send the servants." He bowed again at the doorway of the vestibule. "I'll rejoin you when I can. In the meantime, summon the eunuchs if you require anything."

He turned and was gone. In what seemed only moments, two turbaned servants appeared, smiling as they placed a large chalice of wine on the carpet next to Hawksworth's bolster.

"It's all too incredible." Queen Janahara slumped onto a velvet divan and distractedly took a rolled betel leaf from the silver tray offered by a hovering eunuch. Behind her a female *zenana* slave fanned a plume of peacock feathers against the afternoon heat. As she spoke she brushed back her gold-threaded scarf, revealing gleaming dark hair—the few gray strands had been perfectly dyed—pulled back tightly against her head and secured with a golden band. Her only jewels were in a necklace, diamonds with a massive blue sapphire that complemented her dark eyes. She was nearing fifty, but still possessed of a beauty that had, with the years, evolved to magnificent dignity. Her face was statuesque and her Persian was both elegant and mellifluous. "He's still marching south. I think he actually enjoys living in the field, surrounded by mud and Rajputs. How much longer can he continue?"

"Be assured this time the prince will bring his own undoing." Nadir Sharif accepted a betel leaf from the tray, a gesture, and absently rolled it between his thumb and finger. He wondered nervously why she had summoned him to the Jasmine Tower the minute he left the English *feringhi*. He normally enjoyed meeting her there, amid the marble screens, where they could recline on the carpeted terrace and admire the broad Jamuna. As her brother and prime minister, it was not unseemly for him to visit her in her quarters. "The campaign in the Deccan will change everything, Your Majesty. It cannot end as did the last one, with Malik Ambar surrendering out of fright. The Abyssinian surely suspects by now that Jadar is isolated."

Queen Janahara was no longer listening. Her thoughts were seething over the two surprises of the day. The first was Nadir Sharif's absence from her historic appearance at the *darshan* balcony. She had already been informed of his absence by four separate eunuchs. All assumed it was deliberate.

Nadir Sharif. My own brother. Can he be wavering? Or merely bargaining?

Why? Has something happened with Jadar? The march south should have been the end of him. The mansabdars *and their troops south of the Narbada were in shambles. But somehow Jadar has managed to recall enough cavalry to continue his campaign. What is he planning?*

That question called to mind the second problem of the day.

The Englishman.

She knew, as Arangbar did not, that the Englishman had already met with Jadar. Why had Jadar contrived such a meeting? The prince must know that both she and Nadir Sharif had full support of the Viceroy of Goa. Did he also know that the Viceroy had even offered secretly to help arm the Deccanis against him, an arrangement she was now negotiating?

What of the English *feringhi*, his letter, his meeting with Jadar? She had studied him carefully through her screen when he appeared at the afternoon *durbar* and she had ordered a Persian translation of his letter prepared immediately. And what she read was disturbing. The English king had, it was true, asked merely for a trading *firman*. But who knew what sea power waited behind the English appearance at Surat?

She knew Jadar despised Christians, but he would not scruple to use them one against the other. Where would it lead, if Jadar could enlist English sea power in the struggle that loomed ahead, and somehow neutralize the influence of the Portuguese? Maddeningly, the *Moghul* seemed amused by the Englishman, by his rude manner.

"Why did His Majesty invite the *feringhi* to the *Diwan-i-Khas* tonight?"

"My esteemed sister, you were at today's *durbar*. You know His Majesty's whims far better than I. Perhaps he was fascinated by finding a *feringhi* who speaks his barbarous Turki. For His Majesty the new *feringhi* cannot be anything more than merely a new toy, like a new dog or horse. He will amuse himself with the *feringhi*, dangle promises before him, and wait to see if more gifts are forthcoming. You know he is the same with all ambassadors."

"This one I think is different. Did you see him refuse to *teslim?* I think His Majesty is already awed by him. I fear for India if the English ever gain influence here. Do you really believe the English king wants nothing more than trade?" Janahara found herself searching for the key to Nadir Sharif's thoughts. "What do you suppose would happen if these English defy the Portuguese, and one day decide to blockade Surat? To allow trade only to those who have supported them at court." She paused as she studied him. "Could there be some here already who are fearful enough to pretend friendship to the Englishman?"

"Who could know these things?" Nadir Sharif walked to the white marble railing and gazed along the side of the fort, where the Jamuna lapped gently against the thick red walls. He remembered his pigeons, and then he remembered the morning *darshan* and Janahara's unprecedented appearance.

The Englishman is hardly a problem, my dear sister. He is already tamed. *You* are the problem now. You and your newfound power. But if you fear this harmless *feringhi*, more than you fear me, then I have at last found a way to manage you as well. At long last.

"Tonight I will drink with the English *feringhi*, and then we may learn something useful. A man lounging with a wine cup in his hands says things he would never utter standing at *durbar*. I think His Majesty may also be wondering about the intentions of his king."

Janahara chewed silently on the betel leaf and eyed him, knowing he had met that morning with the Rajput who brought the English *feringhi* to Agra and wondering why. Whatever the reason, she told herself, Nadir Sharif would never be so foolish as to side with Jadar. Not so long as the prince was isolated and weak. Nadir Sharif did not gamble.

"The *feringhi* must be watched closely. Find a way. We need to know what he is doing, what he is thinking. Do you understand?"

"To hear is to obey." Nadir Sharif bowed lightly.

"And you will be at *darshan* tomorrow morning. Even if you were not there today."

"Naturally had I but known, Majesty . . ."

"Father made you prime minister. You can be just as easily removed."

"Your Majesty." Nadir Sharif bowed, and with an unseen flick sent the rolled betel leaf spinning past the railing, toward the dark waters of the Jamuna below.

Hawksworth sipped from the new cup of wine, his third, and watched the musicians begin to retune. Around him the members of Arangbar's inner circle were assembling in the *Diwan-i-Khas*. This must be evening dress in Agra, he marveled: silk turbans studded with rubies and sapphires, diamond earrings, swords trimmed in gold and silver, pearl necklaces, cloaks of rich brocade, velvet slippers. The faces around him all betrayed the indolent eyes and pasty cheeks of men long indulged in rich food, hard spirits, sensuality.

It was, he now realized, the fairyland that Symmes had described that freezing day so long ago in the offices of the Levant Company. What man not a Papist monk could resist the wordly seductions of the *Moghul's* court?

Then he remembered the brave Pathan who had been torn apart by a lion that very afternoon, while all Arangbar's nobles watched unprotesting.

On the signal of a eunuch standing by the doorway the drummer suddenly pounded out a loud, rhythmic fanfare, and then the sitarist took up a martial motif. The brocade drapery hanging inside a marble archway at the back of the room was drawn aside by a guard and a moment later Arangbar swept into the room. The courtiers all bowed in the *teslim*, rising with their hands on their forehead.

Arangbar had changed to evening dress. He wore a dark velvet turban encrusted with jewels, tight-fitting patterned trousers beneath a transparent muslin skirt, and a gold brocade cinch at his waist. He clapped his hands in delight when he saw Hawksworth holding a wine cup.

"The ambassador has already tasted our Persian wine. How do you find it, Ambassador . . . Khaw . . . ?" He stumbled over the name. "Wait. The first thing we must do is rename you. Henceforth we will call you 'Inglish.' Now, have we pronounced that properly?"

"Perfectly, Your Majesty. And, so please Your Majesty, the wine is excellent, though perhaps not as sweet as the wines of Europe."

"Every *feringhi* says the same, Inglish. But we will civilize you. And also teach you something about painting." He seized a glass of wine from a waiting eunuch and then shouted to Nadir Sharif, who had entered moments before from the back. "Where are my five paintings?"

"I'm told they will be ready before Your Majesty retires. The painters are still hard at work, so please Your Majesty."

"It does not please me, but then I have no wager." He roared with amusement. "Your stables will be reduced by a prize stallion come morning if the paintings are not ready soon. Look to it."

As Nadir Sharif bowed in acknowledgment, Arangbar whirled to Hawksworth.

"Tell me something about your king, Inglish? How many wives does he have? We have hundreds."

"He has but one, Your Majesty, and I believe she is mostly for show. King James prefers the company of young men."

"Very like most Christians I've met. And you, Inglish. Have you any wives?" Arangbar had already finished his first glass of wine and taken a second.

"I have none, Your Majesty."

"But you, I suspect, are not a Jesuit, or a eunuch."

"No, Your Majesty."

"Then we shall find you a wife, Inglish." He took a ball of opium and washed it down with wine. "No, we will find you two. Yes, you shall be well wived."

"May it please Your Majesty, I have no means to care for a wife. I am here for only a season." Hawksworth shifted uncomfortably.

"You will only leave Agra, Inglish, when it is our pleasure. But if you will not have a wife, you must at least have a house."

"I am arranging it now, Your Majesty."

Arangbar looked at Hawksworth sharply, then continued as though he had not heard.

"Now tell us more about your king. We would know what he's like."

Hawksworth bowed as he tried to collect his thoughts. The wine was already toying with his brain. Although most of what he knew about King James was hearsay, he knew he did not care for England's new king overly much. No English subject did. And idle seamen had reason to dislike him the most of all. He was not the sovereign Elizabeth had been.

"He's of middle stature, Your Majesty, not overly fat though he seems so since he always wears quilted, stiletto-proof doublets."

Arangbar seemed surprised. "Is he not safe? Has he no guards?"

"He's a prudent man, Your Majesty, as befits a sovereign." And, Hawksworth thought, also a coward, if you believe the talk in London. What all men know for fact, though, is that he's a weakling, whose legs are so spindly he has to be helped to walk, leaning on other men's shoulders while he fiddles spastically with his codpiece.

"Does your king wear many jewels, Ambassador Inglish?"

"Of course, Your Majesty." Hawksworth drank calmly from his wine cup, hoping the lie would pass unnoticed.

What would the *Moghul* think if he knew the truth, Hawksworth asked himself? That King James of England only changes his clothes when they are rags, and his fashion never. He was once, they say, given a Spanish-style hat, and he cast it away, swearing he loved neither them nor their fashions. Another time he was given shoes with brocade roses on them, and he railed at the giver, asking if he was to be made a ruff-footed dove.

"Is your king generous of nature, Ambassador? We are loved by our people because we give of our bounty on every holy day. Baskets of silver rupees are flung down the streets of Agra."

"King James is giving also, Your Majesty." With the moneys of others. He'd part willingly with a hundred pounds not in his own keeping before he'd release ten shillings from his private purse. And it's said he'd rather spend a hundred thousand pounds on embassies abroad, buying peace with bribes, than ten thousand on an army that would enforce peace with honor. "He is a man among men, Your Majesty, admired and loved by all his subjects."

"As are we, Ambassador." Arangbar took another ball of opium and washed it down with a third glass of wine. "Tell me, does your king drink spirits?"

"It is said he drinks often, Your Majesty, though many declare it is more out of custom than delight. He drinks strong liquors—Frontiniack, Canary, High Canary wine, Tent wine, Scottish ale—but never, it's said, more than a few spoonfuls."

"Then he could never drink with the *Moghul* of India, Ambassador. We have twenty cups of wine a night. And twelve grains of opium." Arangbar paused as he accepted yet another glass. His voice had begun to slur slightly. "But perhaps your king can trade with me. When will the ships from your king's next voyage arrive? And how many of your king's frigates will we see yearly if we grant him the trading *firman* he requests?"

Hawksworth noticed out of the corner of his eye that Nadir Sharif had now moved directly beside him. The prime minister held a glass of wine from which he sipped delicately. Around him the other courtiers were already drinking heavily, to the obvious approval of Arangbar.

He'll not finish a single glass of wine, if my guess is right. Nadir Sharif'll find a way to stay stone sober while the rest of the room sinks into its cups. And they'll all be too drunk to notice.

"King James will one day send an armada of frigates, Your Majesty." Keep Arangbar's mind off the next voyage. He just may try to hold you here until it comes, or refuse to grant a *firman* until he sees the next batch of presents. "His Majesty, King James, is always eager to trade the seas where his ships are welcome."

"Even if other nations of Europe would quarrel with his rights to those seas?"

"England has no quarrels in Europe, Your Majesty. If you refer to the engagement off Surat, you should know that was caused by a misunderstanding of the treaties that now exist in Europe. England is at peace with all her neighbors."

A skeptical silence seemed to envelop the room. Arangbar took another cup of wine and drank it off. Then he turned to Hawksworth.

"The matter, Ambassador Inglish, does not seem to us to be that simple. But we will examine it more later. Nights are made for beauty, days for affairs of state." Arangbar's voice had begun to slur even more noticeably. "You may have heard there will be a wedding here soon. My youngest prince is betrothed to the daughter of my queen. The wedding will be held one month after my own birthday celebration, and it will be an event to remember. Tonight I begin the always-pleasant task of selecting the women who will dance. Do you know anything of Indian dance?"

"Very little, Your Majesty. I have only seen it once. In Surat. At a gathering one evening at the palace of the Shahbandar."

Arangbar roared and seized another glass of wine. "I can well imagine the kind of entertainment the Shahbandar of Surat provides for his guests. No, Ambassador, I mean the real dance of India. The dance of great artists? Perhaps you have classical dance in England?"

"No, Your Majesty. We have nothing similar. At least similar to the dance I saw."

"Then a pleasant surprise awaits you." Arangbar examined Hawksworth's cup and motioned for a servant to refill it. "Drink up, Inglish. The evening is only beginning."

Arangbar clapped drunkenly and the guests began to settle themselves around the bolsters that had been strewn about the carpet. An ornate silk pillow was provided for each man to rest against, and a number of large *hookahs*, each with several mouthpieces, were lighted and stationed about the room. The servants also distributed garlands of yellow flowers, and as

Nadir Sharif took his place next to Hawksworth, he wrapped one of the garlands about his left wrist. With the other hand he set down his wineglass, still full, and signaled a servant to replenish Hawksworth's. Arangbar was reclining now on the throne, against his own bolster, and the oil lamps around the side of the room were lowered, leaving illumination only on the musicians and on a bare spot in the center of the carpet. The air was rich with the aroma of roses as servants passed shaking rosewater on the guests from long-necked silver decanters.

The musicians were completing their tuning, and Hawksworth noticed that now there were two drummers, a sitar player, and a new musician holding a *sarangi*. In the background another man sat methodically strumming a simple upright instrument, shaped like the sitar save it provided nothing more than a low-pitched droning, against which the other instruments had been tuned. Next a man entered, wearing a simple white shirt, and settled himself on the carpet in front of the musicians. As silence gripped the room, Arangbar signaled to the seated man with his wineglass and the man began to sing a low, soulful melody that seemed to consist of only a few syllables. "Ga, Ma, Pa." The voice soared upward. "Da, Ni, Sa." After a few moments Hawksworth guessed he must be singing the names of the notes in the Indian scale. They were virtually identical to the Western scale, except certain notes seemed to be a few microtones higher or lower, depending whether approached from ascent or descent.

The singer's voice soared slowly upward in pitch and volume, growing more intense as it quavered around certain of the high notes, while the *sarangi* player listened attentively and bowed the exact notes he sang, always seeming to guess which note he would find next. The song was melodic, and gradually what had at first seemed almost a dirge grew to be a poignant line of beauty.

Suddenly the singer's voice cut the air with a fast-tempo phrase, which was brief and immediately repeated, the second time to the accompaniment of the drum, as both players picked up the notes. On the third repetition of the phrase, the curtains on Arangbar's right were swept aside and a young woman seemed to fairly burst across the room, her every skipping step announced by a band of tiny bells bound around her ankles and across the tops of her bare feet.

As she spun into the light, she whirled a fast pirouette that sent her long braided pigtail—so long the end was attached to her waist—whistling in an arc behind her. Her flowered silk tunic flew outward from her spinning body, revealing all of her tight-fitting white trousers. She wore a crown of jewels, straight pendant earrings of emerald, and an inch-long string of diamonds dangled from the center of her nose.

She paused for an instant, whirled toward Arangbar, and performed a salaam with her right hand, fingers slightly bent, thumb across her palm as she raised her hand to her forehead. The movement was possessed of so much grace it seemed a perfect dance figure.

"May I take the liberty of interpreting for you, Ambassador?" Nadir Sharif ignored the *hookah* mouthpiece that another, slightly tipsy, guest was urging on him and slid closer to Hawksworth. "Kathak is an art, like painting or pigeon-flying, best appreciated when you know the rules." He pointed toward the dancer. "Her name is Sangeeta, and she has just performed the invocation. For the Hindus it is a salute to their elephant-headed god Ganesh. For Muslims, it is a salaam."

Next she turned slowly toward the guests and struck a pose, one foot crossed behind the other, arms bent as though holding a drawn bow. As the *sarangi* played a slow, tuneful melody, she seemed to control the rhythm of the drums by quietly stroking together again and again the thumb and forefinger of each hand. The explosive tension in her body seemed focused entirely in this single, virtually imperceptible motion, almost as a glass marshals the power of the sun to a tiny point. Then her eyes began to dart from side to side, and first one eyebrow and then the other lifted seductively. Gradually the rhythm was taken up by her head, as it began to glide from side to side in a subtle, elegant expression that seemed an extension of the music.

She had possessed the room almost as a spirit of pure dance, chaste, powerful, disciplined, and there was nothing of the overt suggestiveness of the *nautch* dancers of the Shahbandar's courtyard. She wore a low-cut, tight vest of brocade over a long-sleeved silk shirt, and of her body only her hands, feet, and face were visible. It was these, Hawksworth realized, not her body, that were the elements of Kathak dance.

"Now she'll begin the second section of the dance. It's the introduction and corresponds to the opening of a raga. It sets the atmosphere and makes you long for more. I know of no *feringhi* who has ever seen Kathak, but perhaps you can understand. Do you feel it?"

Hawksworth sipped his wine slowly and tried to clear his head. In truth he felt very little, save the intensity that seemed to be held in check.

"It appears to be rather subtle. Very little seems to be happening." Hawksworth drank again and found himself longing for a lively hornpipe.

"A great deal will happen, Ambassador, and very soon. In India you must learn patience."

Almost at that moment the drummers erupted with a dense rhythmic cycle and the *sarangi* took up a single repetitive phrase. Sangeeta looked directly at Hawksworth and called out a complex series of rhythmic syllables, in a melodic if slightly strident voice, all the while duplicating the exact pattern of sounds by slapping the henna-reddened soles of her feet against the

carpet. Then she glided across the carpet in a series of syncopated foot movements, saluting each of the guests in turn and calling out strings of syllables,
after which she would dance a sequence that replicated the rhythm exactly,
her feet a precise percussion instrument.

"The syllables she recites are called *bols*, Ambassador, which are the
names of the many different strokes on the tabla drums. Drummers sometimes call out a sequence before they play it. She does the same, except she
uses her feet almost as a drummer uses his hands."

As Hawksworth watched, Sangeeta called strings of syllables that were
increasingly longer and more complex. He could not understand the *bols*, or
perceive the rhythms as she danced them, but the drunken men around him
were smiling and swinging their heads from side to side in what he took to
be appreciative approval. Suddenly Arangbar shouted something to her and
pointed toward the first drummer. The drummer beamed, nodded, and as
Sangeeta watched, called out a dense series of *bols*. Then she proceeded to
dance the sequence with her feet. The room exploded with cries of appreciation when she finished the sequence, and Hawksworth assumed she had
managed to capture the instructions the musician had called. Then Arangbar
pointed to the other drummer and he also called out a string of *bols*, which
again Sangeeta repeated. Finally the singer called a rhythm sequence, the
most complex yet, and both dancer and drummer repeated them precisely together.

As the tempo became wilder, Sangeeta began a series of lightning spins,
still pounding the carpet with her reddened soles, and in time she seemed to
transform into a whirling top, her pigtail loose now and singing through the
air like a deadly whip. She had become a blur, and for a brief moment she
appeared to have two heads. Hawksworth watched in wonder and sipped
from his wine cup.

"Now she'll begin the last part, Ambassador, the most demanding of
all."

The rhythm became almost a frenzy now. Then as suddenly as they had
begun the whirls ended. Sangeeta struck a statuesque pose, arms extended in
rigid curves, and began a display of intensely rhythmic footwork. Her body
seemed frozen in space as nothing moved save her feet. The bells on her ankles became a continuous chime, increasing in tempo with the drum and the
sarangi until the rhythmic phrase itself was nothing more than a dense blur
of notes. Suddenly the drummer and instrumentalist fell silent, conceding
the room to Sangeeta's whirring bells. She seemed, at the last, to be treading
on pure air, her feet almost invisible. When the intensity of her rhythm became almost unbearable, the drummers and *sarangi* player reentered, urging
the excitement to a crescendo. A final phrase was introduced, repeated with
greater intensity, and then a third and final time, ending with a powerful
crash on the large drum that seemed to explode the tension in the room. Sev-

eral of the musicians cried out involuntarily, almost orgasmically, in exulta-
tion. In the spellbound silence that followed, the nobles around Hawksworth
burst into cheers.

Sangeeta seemed near collapse as she bowed to Arangbar. The *Moghul*
smiled broadly, withdrew a velvet purse of coins from his cloak, and threw it
at her feet. Moments later several others in the room followed suit. With a
second bow she scooped the purses from the carpet and vanished through
the curtains. The cheers followed her long after she was gone.

"What do you think, Ambassador? You know half the men here would
give a thousand gold *mohurs* to have her tonight." Nadir Sharif beamed mischievously. "The other half two thousand."

"Come forward." Arangbar motioned to the singer sitting on the carpet.
He was, Hawksworth now realized, an aging, portly man with short white hair
and a painful limp. As he approached Arangbar's dais, he began removing
the tiny cymbals attached to the fingers of one hand that he had used to
keep time for the dancer.

"He's her *guru*, her teacher." Nadir Sharif pointed to the man as he
bowed obsequiously before the *Moghul*. "If His Majesty decides to select
Sangeeta to dance at the wedding, his fortune will be made. Frankly I
thought she was good, though there is still a trifle too much flair in her style,
too many tricks. But then she's young, and perhaps it's too soon to expect
genuine maturity. Still, I noticed His Majesty was taken with her. She could
well find herself in the *zenana* soon."

Arangbar flipped another purse of coins to the man, and then spoke to
him curtly in Persian.

"His Majesty has expressed his admiration, and says he may call him
again after he has seen the other dancers." Nadir Sharif winked. "Choosing
the dancers is a weighty responsibility. Naturally His Majesty will want to
carefully review all the women."

The lamps brightened again and servants bustled about the carpet
filling glasses and exchanging the burned-out tobacco *chillum*, clay bowls at
the top of each *hookah*. When they had finished, Arangbar took another
glass of wine and signaled for the lamps to be lowered once more. A new
group of musicians began filing into the room, carrying instruments Hawksworth had never before seen. First came the drummer, who carried not the
two short tabla drums but rather a single long instrument, designed to be
played at both ends simultaneously. A singer entered next, already wearing
small gold cymbals on each hand. Finally a third man entered, carrying
nothing but a piece of inch-thick bamboo, less than two feet in length and
perforated with a line of holes.

Arangbar looked quizzically at Nadir Sharif.

As though reading the question, the prime minister rose and spoke in
Turki. "This one's name is Kamala, Your Majesty. She is originally from the

south, but now she is famous among the Hindus in Agra. Although I have never seen her dance, I assumed Your Majesty would want to humor the Hindus by auditioning her."

"We are a sovereign of all our subjects. I have never seen this Hindu dance. Nor these instruments of the south. What are they called?"

"The drum is called a *mirdanga*, Majesty. They use it in the south with a type of sitar they call the veena. The other instrument is a bamboo flute."

Arangbar shifted impatiently. "Tell them this should be brief."

Nadir Sharif spoke quickly to the musicians in a language few in the room seemed to understand. They nodded and immediately the flautist began a haunting lyric line that bathed the room in a soft, echoing melody. Hawksworth was startled that so simple an instrument could produce such rich, warm tones.

The curtains parted and a tall, elaborately jeweled woman swept across the carpet. She took command of the space around her, possessed it, almost as though it were part of her being. Her long silk *sari* had been gathered about each leg so that it seemed like trousers, and her every step was announced by dense bracelets of bells at her ankles. Most striking, however, was her carriage. Hawksworth had never before seen such dignity of motion.

As he stared at her, he realized she was wearing an immense, diamond-encrusted nose ring and long pendant earrings, also of diamonds. Not even the *Moghul* wore stones to equal hers. Her face was heavily painted, but still he suspected she might no longer be in the first bloom of youth. Her self-assurance was too secure. She knew exactly who she was.

She turned her back to Arangbar as she reverently gave an invocation, both hands together and raised above her head, to some absent god. The only sound was the slow, measured cadence of the drum. Suddenly it seemed as though her body had captured some perfect moment of balance, a feeling of timelessness within time.

Hawksworth glanced toward Arangbar, whose irritation was obvious.

How can she be so imprudent as to ignore him? Aren't Hindus afraid of him? What was her name? Kamala?

His eyes shot back to the woman.

Kamala.

Can she be the woman Kali spoke of that last night in Surat? The Lotus Woman? Nadir Sharif said she was famous.

"Just who are you?" Arangbar's voice cut through the carpeted room, toward the woman's back. He was speaking Turki, and he was outraged.

Kamala whirled on him. "One who dances for Shiva, in his aspect as Nataraj, the god of the dance. For him and for him alone."

"What do you call this dance for your infidel god?"

"Bharata Natyam. The dance of the temple. The sacred tradition as old as India itself. The god Shiva set the world in motion by the rhythms of his dance. My dance is a prayer to Shiva." Kamala's eyes snapped with hatred. "I dance for no one else."

"You were summoned here to dance for *me*." Arangbar pulled himself drunkenly erect. Around the room the nobles began to shift uneasily, their bleary eyes filling with alarm.

"Then I will not dance. You have the world in your hands. But you cannot possess the dance of Shiva. Our dance is prescribed in the Natya Shastra of the ancient sage Bharata. Over a thousand years ago he declared that dance is not merely for pleasure; dance is the blending of all art, religion, philosophy. It gives mankind wisdom, discipline, endurance. Through dance we are allowed to know the totality of all that is. My dance is not for your sport."

Arangbar's anger increased, but now it was leavened with puzzlement.

"If you will not dance your Shiva dance, then dance Kathak."

"The dance Muslims call Kathak is the perversion of yet another of our sacred traditions. Perhaps there are some Hindu dancers who will, for Muslim gold, debase the ancient Kathak dance of India, will make it a display of empty technique for the amusement of India's oppressors. Muslims and"—she turned and glared at Hawksworth—"now *feringhi*. But I will not do it. The Kathak you want to see is no longer true Kathak. It has been made empty, without meaning. I will never debase our true Kathak dance for you, as others have done, any more than I will dedicate a performance of Bharata Natyam to a mortal man."

The guards near the entrance of the *Diwan-i-Khas* had all tensed, their hands dropping uneasily to their swords.

"I have heard enough. A man who dared speak to me as you have would be sent to the elephants. You, I think, deserve more. Since you speak to your god through dance, you do not need a tongue."

Arangbar turned to summon the waiting guards when, at the rear of the *Diwan-i-Khas*, the figure of the Chief Painter emerged, his assistants trailing behind. They carried a long, thin board.

Nadir Sharif spotted them and immediately leaped to his feet, almost as though he had been expecting their entrance.

"Your Majesty." He quickly moved between Arangbar and Kamala, who stood motionless. "The paintings have arrived. I'm ready for my horse. Let the English ambassador see them now."

Arangbar looked up in confusion, his eyes half closed from the opium. Then he saw the painters and remembered.

"Bring them in." Suddenly his alertness seemed to return. "I want to see five Inglish kings."

The paintings were brought to the foot of Arangbar's dais, and he inspected them drunkenly, but with obvious satisfaction.

"Ambassador Inglish. Have a look." Arangbar called toward the hushed

shadows of the seated guests. A path immediately cleared among the
bolsters, as *hookahs* were pushed aside, wineglasses seized.

Hawksworth walked unsteadily forward, his mind still stunned by the
imminent death sentence waiting for the woman. As he passed her, he
sensed her powerful presence and inhaled her musky perfume. There was no
hint of fear in her eyes as she stood waiting, statuesque and defiant.

By the time he reached the throne, eunuchs were waiting with candles,
one on each side of the board, bathing it in flickering light. On it was a line
of five English miniatures of King James, each approximately an inch square.

Good Jesus, they're identical. Am I so drunk I can't tell a painting of
King James?

He looked up shakily at Arangbar, whose smile was a gloat.

"Well, Ambassador Inglish. What say you? Are the painters of my
school equal to any your king has?"

"One moment, Majesty. Until my eyes adjust." Hawksworth grasped
one edge of the board to steady himself. Behind him there were murmurs of
delight and he caught the word *"feringhi."*

As he walked along the board, studying each painting in turn, he suddenly noticed that the reflection of the candlelight was different for one.

The paint is still wet on the new portraits. That's the difference. Or is it?
Are my eyes playing tricks? Damn me for letting Nadir Sharif fill my wineglass every chance he had.

"Come, Ambassador Inglish. We do not have all night." Arangbar's
voice was brimming with triumph.

Hawksworth studied the paintings more closely. Yes, there's a slight
difference. The colors on the one painting are slightly different. Duller.

They didn't use varnish. And there are fewer shadows. Theirs are more
two-dimensional.

"I'm astounded, Your Majesty. But I believe this is the one by Isaac
Oliver." Hawksworth pointed to the painting second from the right end.

"Let me see them again." Arangbar's voice was a husky slur. "I will tell
if you have guessed correctly."

The board was handed up. Arangbar glanced at the paintings for only
an instant. "You have guessed right, Ambassador Inglish. And I realize how
you did it. The light from the candles."

"The portraits are identical, Your Majesty. I confess it."

"So we have won our point. And you won the wager, Inglish. Still, you
won only because of my haste. Tomorrow you would not have known. Do
you admit it?"

"I do, Your Majesty." Hawksworth bowed slightly.

"So, you did not really win the wager after all. We lost it. But I am a
man of honor. We will release Nadir Sharif from his pledge. I am the one
who must pay. What would you have? Perhaps a diamond?"

"The wager was only for a horse, Your Majesty." Hawksworth was stunned.

"No. That was the wager of Nadir Sharif. You have won a wager from a king. Yours must be the payment of a king. If not a jewel, then what would you have?"

Before Hawksworth could reply, Nadir Sharif stepped forward and bent toward Arangbar.

"If I may be allowed to suggest, Your Majesty, the *feringhi* needs a woman. Give him this dancer. Let him amuse himself with her until you can find a suitable wife for him."

Arangbar looked toward Hawksworth with glazed eyes. It was obvious he had already forgotten about Kamala.

"The Kathak dancer who was here? She was excellent. Yes, that would be perfect."

"Your Majesty of course means the woman standing here now." Nadir Sharif directed Arangbar's groggy gaze toward Kamala, who stood mutely, eyes flashing.

"There she is. Of course. What do you say to her, Inglish?"

Hawksworth was astounded by Nadir Sharif's quickness of wit. He's saved the woman. He's a genius. Of course I'll take her. Good Jesus, there's been enough bloodshed today.

"The woman would be the gift of a great prince, Your Majesty."

"So there's manhood about you after all, Inglish. I had begun to think you were like your king." Arangbar laughed in delight. "So it's a woman you would have, Ambassador? Merciful Allah, I have too many now. Perhaps you would like two. I recall there's an Armenian Christian somewhere in the *zenana*. Perhaps several. They're said to be as lusty as the Portuguese harlots in Goa." He choked for a moment on laughter. "Let me summon the eunuchs."

"This one will do for now, Your Majesty." Think how to phrase this. "Merely to serve me."

"Yes, she will 'serve' you, Ambassador. Or we will have her head. If she would amuse you, she's yours."

Kamala's look met Hawksworth's. It was strangely without emotion.

Then Arangbar suddenly remembered Kamala's defiance and turned to study her again with half-closed eyes.

"But not this one. It must be the other one you want. This one will be hanged tonight, in a room far beneath the *zenana*. After she has answered for her words. Tomorrow her carcass will pollute the Jamuna. A man in her place would already be dead."

"May it please Your Majesty, it would satisfy me even more to have this one." Hawksworth paused. "Perhaps it's what the English call honor. We both know I did not win our wager fairly. Only by taking something of no value, like this woman, could I maintain my honor, and my king's."

"You are persuasive, Inglish, and I am drunk. But not too drunk to suspect you've taken a fancy to this infidel. But if you prefer her to the other, then so be it. We offered you whatever you wished. She's yours. But never let her be seen on the streets of Agra again. We will have her cut down."

"As please Your Majesty."

"It's done." Arangbar turned to Nadir Sharif. "Is it true you've found a house for the Inglish?"

"I have, Your Majesty."

"Then send her there." He turned to Hawksworth. "Allah protect you from these infidel Hindus, Inglish. They have none of your Inglish honor."

"I humbly thank Your Majesty." Jesus Christ, I've just been imprisoned in a house staffed by Nadir Sharif's hand-picked spies.

"Enough. We've been told to retire early tonight. Her Majesty thinks we drink to excess." He laughed a slurred chortle. "But we will see you tomorrow, Inglish. To talk more. We have much to discuss. We want to hear what gifts your king is preparing for us. We would very much like a large mastiff from Europe. We hear they hunt game like a *chitah*."

Arangbar drew himself up shakily and two eunuchs immediately were at his side, helping him from the white marble throne. None of the guests moved until he had passed through the curtains. Immediately the eunuchs began moving about the room, extinguishing the lamps. By the time the guests assembled to leave, the room was virtually dark. Kamala and the musicians had been escorted from the room by Arangbar's guards. Suddenly Hawksworth felt Nadir Sharif's hand on his arm.

"That was a noble thing you did, Ambassador. We all owe you a debt of thanks. I have rarely seen His Majesty so out of temper. The repercussions could have been distressing for many of us."

"It was your idea."

"Merely a quick fancy, an act of desperation. But without your cooperation it would have been impossible. I do thank you."

"There's nothing to thank me for." Hawksworth drew his arm away. "Where's this house you've found for me?"

Nadir Sharif sighed. "Finding a secure lodging these days is more difficult than you might first imagine, Ambassador. But you were in luck. I remembered there's a small lodge in my palace grounds that is unoccupied. I did not reckon on quarters for two, but of course the woman will be living with your servants. The house should serve until something more fitting can be found."

"My thanks." Damn you. "When do I move there?"

"Your effects have already been moved, on His Majesty's authority. You can come tonight. My men will show you there. Your dinner is probably waiting."

At that moment the last lamp was extinguished. Along with the other guests they groped their way out of the *Diwan-i-Khas* in total darkness.

CHAPTER EIGHTEEN

"Many years ago I was a *devadasi*." Kamala sat, pillowless, on the carpet, watching as Hawksworth ate. Her musicians, the flautist and the drummer, knelt silently behind her. Nadir Sharif's servants stood by, nervously attentive, pretending to ignore everyone but Hawksworth. The white plaster walls of the lamplit room fairly flashed with Kamala's diamonds. "Do you know what that is?"

Hawksworth shook his head, his mouth gorged with roast lamb. The room was filled with its aroma. It was his first lamb since Burhanpur, and he was ravenous.

"Does that mean yes?" Kamala's Turki was surprisingly good.

Hawksworth suddenly remembered the curious Indian convention of swinging the head from side to side to signify concurrence. He had meant to say no, which in Indian body language was an almost unreproduceable twist of the neck. He swallowed the lamb and reached for another shank.

"No. I meant no. Is that a kind of dancer?"

"It means 'a servant of the gods.' In south India there's a special caste of women who serve in the great stone temples, who are married to the god of the temple. When we are very young we have a marriage ceremony, like any wedding. Except we are a bride of the temple. And then we serve its god with music and with our dance."

Hawksworth examined her quizzically. "You mean you were like a nun?"

"What is that?"

"They're something like Papist priests. Women who give themselves to God, or at least to the pope's Church." Hawksworth paused awkwardly. "And claim to be married to Christ, so they never lie with a man."

Kamala looked at him with surprise.

"Not even the high-caste men who come to the temple? But how, then, do they serve this Christian God? By dance only?"

"Nuns aren't known to do much dancing. They mainly . . . well, I don't really know what they do, except claim to be virgins."

"Virgins!" Kamala exploded in laughter. "This Christian God must be a eunuch. We *devadasis* serve the temple with our bodies, not with empty words."

"Then what exactly did you do?" Hawksworth looked up and examined her.

"I was at the famous Shiva temple of Brihadishwari in Tanjore, the great fountainhead of Bharata Natyam dance in India. There we danced for the god of the temple, and we danced too at the courts of the Dravidian kings of the south." She hesitated, then continued. "*Devadasis* there also honor the temple god by lying with men of high caste who come to worship, and by wearing the jewels they give us. It's all part of our sacred tradition."

She laughed as she watched the disbelief flood Hawksworth's face. "I gather we must be quite different from your Christian 'nuns.' But you know *devadasis* are honored in the south. Many are granted lands by the men they know, and though they can never marry, *devadasis* sometimes become attached to a man and bear his children. But our children always take our name and are dedicated to the temple. Our daughters become *devadasis* also, and our sons temple musicians. Our dance *gurus* are part of a hereditary guild, and they are esteemed above all men. They are the ones who preserve and pass down the sacred Bharata Natyam dance. You may not believe me when I tell you we are highly revered by the kings who reign in the south, lands where the Moghuls fear to tread. They know we are special among women. We are cultivated artists, and among the few Hindu women in India who teach our daughters to read and write."

"I'll believe you." Hawksworth studied her, not quite sure it was true. "But if you're dedicated to a temple in the south, why are you here in Agra?"

Kamala's dark eyes grew lifeless, and then she turned away. "I'm no longer a true *devadasi*. In truth, I have not danced at my temple for many years. The first time the *Moghul's* army invaded the south, a Rajput officer who had deserted came to our temple to hide. He fell in love with me and forced me to come with him when he returned to Agra, telling me I must dance for him only." Her voice hardened. "But I never danced for him, not once. And three years later he was killed in a campaign in Bengal. Since that time I have had to live by my own hand. For many years now I've lived by teaching dance to the *tavaifs* in Agra."

"Who?"

"*Tavaifs*. Muslim dancing girls. Courtesans who live in beautiful houses here and entertain men. There are many in Agra and in the city of Lucknow to the east." Kamala's tone grew vague. "And I teach them other things as well."

"But why did you insult the *Moghul* tonight? Do you really believe all the things you said?"

"What I said was not a 'belief.' I don't understand what you mean by that. Things either are or they are not. What does it matter whether we 'believe' them? But what I did was foolish, I agree. Impulsive. I so despise the

Moghuls. You know, I told the *Moghul's* prime minister this afternoon I would never dance for Arangbar, that nothing could make me, but he forced me to come anyway."

Hawksworth's eyes narrowed, and he dropped the shank of lamb he was holding. "What did you say! Nadir Sharif knew all along you would refuse to dance for Arangbar?"

"Of course he knew. And I knew Arangbar would order me killed. That's why I wore all my diamonds. I thought if I was to die, it must be my *dharma.*" She paused. "And you know, it's strange but I felt nothing. Except perhaps pity for my pretty little courtesans. Some of them are only girls, and I wondered who would teach them after I was gone."

Hawksworth was no longer listening. He was trying to remember the exact sequence of what had happened in the *Diwan-i-Khas.*

He arranged it, the bastard. Even the paintings. Nadir Sharif played with me like a puppet. Just so he could send her here. He knew I'd try to save her. But why would he do it, and in such a way I was never supposed to know? Is this so-called dancer supposed to be another of his spies?

"You said you worshiped a god named Shiva. I thought Hindus worshiped Krishna."

Kamala looked at him with surprise. "You know of Krishna? Yes, he is the god worshiped by the Rajputs of the north. But he is a young god. Lord Shiva is the ancient god of south India. He presides over the generation of life. His lingam symbolizes the male half of the force that created the universe."

"And I suppose you're about to tell me *that's* the part of him you worship." Hawksworth kept a straight face.

"He is revered in many aspects, including Nataraj, the God of the Dance. But yes, his lingam is worshiped. Have you seen the round stone pillars wreathed in garlands of flowers?"

"As a matter of fact . . ." Hawksworth paused, then looked at her sharply. "There was something of that sort in the porters' lodge of the customs house at Surat, where my men and I were kept the morning we arrived."

"Those pillars symbolize Shiva's lingam. Let me tell you about it. Once, back in the time of the gods, Lord Shiva was burdened with unhappiness. He was bereaved of his consort and weary with his being. And he wandered into a forest, where there were sages and their wives. But the sages scorned Lord Shiva, because he was haggard, and they forsook him in his time of sadness. So he had to make his way through the forest begging alms. However, the women of these sages felt love for him, and they left the beds of their men and followed him. When the sages saw their wives leaving to follow Shiva, they set a curse on him. Their curse was that his lingam would fall to the ground. Then one day Shiva did shed his lingam. And he was gone. Only his lingam remained, emerging upright from the earth. It had become stone, and it was of infinite length. All the other gods came to worship it, and told mankind to do likewise. They said that if it was worshiped, Shiva's consort, the goddess Parvati, would come to receive the lingam in her yoni, and the earth would be made fertile. And even now we worship the stone lingam, set erect with a stone yoni as its base. We honor them with flowers and fire and incense. Shiva and Parvati are a symbol of the creation of life." She looked at him, puzzling. "Don't Christians have such a symbol?"

"Not quite like that one." Hawksworth suppressed a grin. "I guess the main symbol for Christians is the cross."

"What do you mean?"

"Christians believe the Son of the Christian God came down to earth and sacrificed Himself on a cross. So the cross became a symbol for that act."

"Yes, I've seen that symbol. Jesuits wear them, covered with jewels. But I never knew its meaning." Kamala paused, seeming to ponder the idea. "Somehow though it seems very static. Surely there are other symbols the Christians have, symbols more dynamic and powerful."

"I suppose Christians think it's pretty powerful."

"But don't Christians have any symbols like our bronze statues of the Dancing Shiva? Lord Shiva, in his aspect as Nataraj, the God of the Dance, embodies everything in the world."

"That's what you said to Arangbar." Hawksworth examined her and tried to clear his mind of the wine. "But I don't understand why you think symbols are so important, whatever their meaning."

"Symbols are a visible sign of things we know but can't actually see, like an idea." Kamala's voice was soft and warm.

"All right. But it's hard to imagine how one symbol could contain everything, no matter what it is."

"But the Dancing Shiva does, my handsome *feringhi*. Perhaps you have not seen it. It came out of the great civilization of the south. Let me explain it for you, and then perhaps you will understand why dance is the deepest form of worship." Kamala rose, bells tinkling, and assumed a dance posture, arms outstretched, one foot raised across the other. Nadir Sharif's Muslim servants paused to stare in amazement. "The bronze statues of Dancing Shiva have four arms, so you will have to imagine the other two. One leg is crossed over the other and raised, as you see now. And the figure stands inside a great circle of bronze." She made a momentary sweep around her body with her hands. "On this circle are flame tips everywhere pointing outward. The circle signifies the world as we know it, the world of time and of things, and the flame tips are the limitless energy of the universe. Lord Shiva dances within this great circle, because he is everywhere. In fact, the universe itself was created through his dance. And our world here is merely his *lila,* his sport."

"You mean he created both good and bad? Christians believe there's evil only because woman tempted man into sin somewhere along the way."

"Sin? What do you mean by that?" Kamala stared at him blankly for a moment. "Whatever it is, Shiva created it. His dance created everything in nature."

"What does he look like, besides having four arms?"

"First, he has long hair, which represents the hair of the *yogi,* the contemplative one, and this long hair streams out from his head, to the very ends of the universe, since he has all knowledge. And each of his four arms has a different meaning. In this one, the upper right arm, he holds a small drum, signifying sound, music and words, the first thing that appeared in the universe. And in his left hand he holds a burning fire, his symbol of destruction. He creates and he also destroys. His lower right hand is held up in a sign." She held up her hand, palm out as though in a blessing. "This is a *mudra,* part of the hand language we use in the dance, and it means 'fear not'; it is his benediction of peace. The fourth hand points down toward his feet. One foot is crushing a repugnant, powerful dwarf, who represents man's willfulness, and the other is held up against the forces of the earth, signifying man's spiritual freedom." Kamala paused and looked at Hawksworth hopefully. "Do you understand? Do you see how the Dancing Shiva symbolizes everything—space, time, creation, destruction? And also hope."

Hawksworth scratched his head in silent confoundment. Kamala watched him, then sighed and resumed her seat on the floor.

"Then just try to feel what I am saying. Words really cannot express these ideas as well as dance. When we dance we invoke the energy, and the life force, that moves through the world, outside its great cycles of time."

Hawksworth picked up his wineglass and drew on it. "To tell the truth, I find your Hindu symbols a trifle abstract."

"But they're not, really. They merely embody truths already within us. Like the life force. We do not have to think about it. It's simply there. And we can reach out and experience this force when woman and man join together in union. That is our *lila, our* play. That's why we worship Lord Shiva with dance, and with *kama.*"

As Hawksworth watched, sipping his wine and scarcely understanding her words, he realized he had begun to desire this bizarre woman intensely.

"You haven't told me what *kama* is."

"That's because I'm not sure you can understand." She scrutinized him professionally. "How old are you?"

"I'm closer to forty than thirty."

"Time, I think, has treated you harshly. Or is it the spirits you drink?"

"What's wrong with a bit of grog now and then?"

"I think you should not drink so much. I drink nothing. Look at me."
She pushed back the hair from both sides of her forehead. Her face was
flawless. "You know most Muslims despise their women after thirty, usually
before, but many young officers still ask to visit me. Can you guess how old I
am?"

"A woman only asks that if she thinks she looks younger than she is."

"I'm over fifty." She examined him directly, invitingly. "How much
over you must only speculate."

"I don't want to. I'm still trying to figure out what exactly happened tonight." He studied her. "But whatever it was, I'm not sure I care anymore."

Hawksworth shoved aside his plates of lamb and rice pilaf and watched
as the servants began hastily clearing the carpet.

In the quiet that followed he reached behind him to his chest, opened
the latch, and took out his lute. Kamala watched with curiosity.

"What instrument is that?"

"Someone in Surat once called it an English sitar."

Kamala laughed. "It's far too plain for that. But it does have a simple
beauty. Will you play it for me?"

"For you, and for me." Hawksworth strummed a chord. The white plaster walls echoed back the wave of notes, a choir of thin voices. "It brings
back my sea legs when I'm ashore."

"Now I do not understand you. But I will listen."

He began a short, plaintive galliard. Suddenly his heart was in London,
with honest English faces, clear English air. And he felt an overwhelming
ache of separation. He played through to the end, then wistfully laid the
lute aside. After a moment Kamala reached for his wineglass and held it for
him, waiting.

"The music of your English sitar is simple, young Ambassador. Like the
instrument itself. But I think it moves you. Perhaps I felt something of your
loneliness in the notes." She paused and studied him quietly. "But you yourself are not simple. Nothing about you comes easily. I sense you are filled
with something you cannot express." She looked at him a moment longer,
and then her voice came again, soft as the wine. "Why did you say what you
did to Arangbar tonight? I was nothing to you. You violated my *dharma*.
Perhaps it is true, as many tell me, that I have mastered the arts of *kama*
more fully than any woman in Agra, but still there is less and less pleasure in
my life. What will you do now? Perhaps you think I belong to you, like
some courtesan you have bought. But you are wrong. I belong to no man."

"You're here because someone wanted you here." Hawksworth glanced
around them. The room was empty now save for Kamala's two musicians. "I
don't know why, but I do know you're the first person I've met in a long

time who was not afraid of Arangbar. The last one was a woman in Surat."
Hawksworth paused suddenly. "I'm starting to wonder if you know her."

"I don't know anyone in Surat." She swept him with her eyes. "But what does some woman in Surat have to do with me?"

"Perhaps someone thought I should meet you."

"Who? Someone in Surat? But why?"

"Perhaps she thought I needed . . . I don't know exactly."

"Then tell me what you mean by 'need'? That's an odd phrase, a *feringhi* expression. Perhaps you mean our meeting is part of your *dharma?*"

"You mean like it's a Rajput's *dharma* to be a warrior and kill?"

"*Dharma* can be many things. It's what each of us must do, our purpose."

"That's something I've heard before."

"But do you know what your *dharma* is?"

"I'm still trying to find it. Maybe it's to be here . . ."

"And then what?"

"I'm . . . I guess I'm still working out the rest."

"Well, for Hindus there's a second aim in life besides our honoring our *dharma*. We call it *artha*. That aim is to have things. Knowledge, wealth, friends. Is that part of why you're here?" Kamala smiled scornfully. "Some merchants seem to believe *artha* is their primary aim."

"It can't be for me. I somehow always manage to lose whatever I have."

"Hindus also believe there's a third aim in life, my handsome *feringhi*. And that's *kama*. It's to take pleasure in the senses."

"I think I like the sound of that better than the other two."

"Do not speak of it lightly. For Hindus it is just as essential as the other two aims. *Kama* is taught by Lord Shiva and his consort Parvati. It means love, pleasure, the primal force of desire." She stared at Hawksworth for a long moment, and then at the lute standing in the corner. "Music is part of *kama*. It's one way we experience beauty and pleasure. That's the *kama* of the heart. But there's also *kama* of the body, and I do not think you yet know it. Your music betrays you. You are a man of sensuality." Kamala looked at him regretfully. "But not of the sensuous. Do you even understand the difference?"

"How do you know what I am?"

"Remember I was once a *devadasi*. It's my *dharma* to know the hearts of men. Who they are and what gives them pleasure." She fell silent for a moment, then continued. "The sensualist is one who only knows his own feelings; the one who is sensuous knows also how to give."

Hawksworth shifted uncomfortably, uncertain how to reply.

"Do you, Ambassador *Feringhi*, touch a woman with the same feeling you touch the strings of your English sitar?"

"I don't see any connection."

"The arts of *kama* are not unlike the mastery of your sitar. You can spend a lifetime learning to sound its notes, but you do not create music unless your hand is in touch with your heart, with *prahna*, the breath of life. It's the same with *kama*." She paused discreetly. "Have you ever known it with a woman in India."

"Well . . . I knew a courtesan in Surat who . . ."

Kamala's eyes hardened, but her voice remained dulcet. "Is this the woman you spoke of?"

"No, this was a different woman. Her name was Kali and she was thrown out of Arangbar's *zenana*."

"Ah, she was probably badly trained. But still. Did you feel the force of *kama* with this Surat courtesan?"

Hawksworth shifted again, uneasily. "That's not the type of thing we normally talk about in England."

"Don't be foolish. You judge the skill of a musician. Why not of a courtesan?" She turned and said something Hawksworth did not understand. Both musicians immediately rose and moved a screen across the corner of the room where they were sitting. Then, from behind the screen came the first notes of a simple, poignant melody, the soft tones of the bamboo swelling slowly to envelop the room in their gentleness. "I have asked him to play the *alap*, the opening section, of a south Indian raga for you. To help you understand. His music has the life breath of *prahna*. He speaks to Lord Shiva with his music. *Kama* too must come from the heart. If we are worthy, we evoke the life-giving power within us." Her eyes snapped back to Hawksworth. "But tell me more about this Surat courtesan."

"Perhaps I'm not entirely qualified to judge. She certainly knew more tricks than most women in England."

"That's not surprising. It's well known *feringhi* women know nothing of pleasure." Kamala paused and studied Hawksworth carefully with her dark eyes. "But I've never known a *feringhi* who could move my senses with music. You did that just now, even though I don't understand how. I cannot dance for you; that is for Shiva. But I want to touch you." She shifted on the carpet until she was at Hawksworth's feet. With a gentle motion she removed a boot and quickly ran a finger across one toe. Nerves throughout his body tingled unexpectedly.

"What did you do just then?"

"The secret of *kama* is touch. To touch and be touched by one we desire always gives pleasure. Do you understand what I mean?"

"Is that *kama*?"

"A very small part."

"You know, the courtesan in Surat actually told me about you. She said you had a book . . . an ancient text."

Kamala laughed and began to remove the other boot. "And *I've* always heard that *feringhi* think everything can be put in books. You probably mean the *Kama Sutra*. Whoever told you about it has probably never seen it. Of course I have it, and I can tell you it is one of the great frauds of India. It was compiled by a musty scholar named Vatsyayana, who obviously knew nothing about giving pleasure, and simply copied things here and there from much older books. It's amusing, perhaps, but it's also pedantic and ignorant. It's certainly not sensuous, and the reason is he knew nothing about desire. He probably had none. He only knew how to make lists of things, like ways of biting and scratching during love play, but he had no idea *why* these are exciting."

She stroked the other foot very lightly along the arch with her long red fingernail, and again a bolt of sensation shot through him.

"I'm beginning to see your point."

"I don't think you understand anything yet. Did you know the pleasure, the power, the beauty possible in your music on the very first day you touched a string of this instrument?"

"I knew there was something in music that moved me, but I wasn't sure what it was."

"And now, many years later, you know." She shifted next to him and began unfastening the bells on her ankles. They chimed gently as she carefully laid them aside. Then she opened a small silver box she had brought and placed a red dot in the middle of her forehead, just below the pendant jewel.

"I sense the first stirrings of *kama* inside me now. The awakening of desire. And because I feel it, I know you must feel it too." She loosened his doublet and pushed him gently against the bolster. The notes of the flute wound through the dark air around them. Kamala listened a moment in silence, then slowly rose off the bolster.

She stood before him, holding his gaze with her eyes, and pulled away the heavy, jeweled belt at the waist of her dance *sari*. She dropped it at his feet, never averting her eyes. Then she made a half turn and twisted her hip gracefully into a voluptuous bulge. The silk clung even tighter to the statuesque curve of her legs as she crossed her feet with an almost ceremonial deliberation. Wordlessly she slowly drew the silk end of the *sari* from across her shoulder and let it drop before her, revealing the curve of a perfectly spherical breast. Seen from behind her body was fixed in a perfect double curve, a sensuous "S" whose top was the full line of her half-revealed breast and whose bottom was the rounded edge of her hip.

In those few simple motions she had transmuted her body, as though through some deep cultural memory, into an ancient fertility totem, a prayer for the bounty of the human loins. It was, Hawksworth suddenly realized, a pose identical to that of a statue he'd seen in a mossy temple in Mandu, on the way north from Burhanpur. It was the essence of the female principle, sharing with the earth itself the power of life. That stone goddess had automatically stirred his desire, as it had the desire of man thousands of years before, as it was meant to do. Now it stood before him.

Before he could move, she turned again and swept up the pleats of silk that comprised the front of her *sari*. She whipped the loose ends of silk about her head once, twice, and magically it seemed to evaporate from her body. All that remained was a small drape of silk about her waist, held in place by a thin band of jade.

Her body was like ivory, perfect from the band at her neck to the small rings on her toes, and her breasts billowed full and geometrically round, a long necklace of pearls nestled between them. As Hawksworth stared at her dumbfounded, the drummer commenced a finely metered rhythm timed exactly with his heartbeat.

She moved to Hawksworth's side and slid her left hand beneath his open doublet. "The very first note of a raga can contain everything if it is sounded with *prahna*. And the first touch between a man and a woman can become the OM, the syllable that carries the totality of creation."

Her hand glided over his body with the gentleness of a feather, and in moments his ambassador's ensemble slipped away like some superfluous ancient skin. He looked at her again, still overwhelmed by her physical perfection, and reached to touch the curve of her breast.

Her hand stopped his in midair.

"Shiva, in his dance, had four hands. But he did not use them for touch. Do you want to feel the touch of my breasts? Then feel them with your body."

She guided him over, across the round bolster, then rose above him.

"Your body is hard and firm, like the stone lingam of Shiva. But your skin still has a hidden softness, like a covering of raw silk."

He felt the hard touch of her nipple as it began to trace the crease of his back. It moved slowly, tantalizingly, trailing just at the skin. Now the musk of her perfume had begun to hover about his head, fogging his mind even more. But the sensation of her touch, and the knowledge it was the breast he wanted exquisitely to hold, attuned his starved senses to everything around him, even the quiet rhythm of her breath.

Suddenly, without warning, she slid the tip of her long red fingernail sharply down the same crease in his back, where his nerves strained for sensation. He felt a delicious burst of pain, and whirled to meet her smiling eyes.

"What . . . ?"

"Do you see now how your sense of touch can be awakened? Now you may touch my breasts, but only with the nails of your fingers. Here."

She drew him to his feet and twined one leg about his body, her heel in the small of his back, enveloping him with her warmth as though it were a cloak. Then she embraced him with her thighs and took his hands in her own, forcing a pattern of scratches on each of her breasts with his nails. Each was different, and each time she pressed his hand, she named the shape of the mark. Her breathing grew increasingly rapid from the pain, and soon both her breasts were decorated with a garland of hard red lines.

At last Hawksworth tried to speak, but she seized his lower lip between her teeth while her nails quickly imprinted a pattern of identical scratches across his own chest. He found the pain oddly exhilarating. It seemed to flow between their bodies, attuning them deeply one to the other. Instinctively he moved to take her, but she twined herself even tighter about him, unattainable. Then, when he thought he could endure it no longer, she lowered herself easily against the bolster.

He scarcely noticed as the pace of the drum intensified.

"Remember, you cannot touch with your hands. Anything else is allowed."

The wine had saturated his mind, but now he found the pleasure of desiring of her body overwhelming. He moved across her lightly with the tip of his tongue, first tasting her lips, then her dark nipples, then the ivory-smooth arch beneath her arms. There her skin was soft as a child's and so sensitive he caused her to shudder involuntarily. He teased her slowly, languorously, until she erupted with cries of pleasure. Then he moved his tongue slowly down her body, trailing the circle of the navel lightly to find the few light wisps of down she had failed to banish. These he teased lightly with his breath until he sensed she could endure it no longer. Then he traced his sex along the inside of her thighs, upward to the fringe of her silk wrap, until at last they were both lost in desire.

With a quick motion she rose and drew astride his body, still scarcely touching him. The silk at her waist came away in her hands and without a sound she twined it into a moist rope. Kneeling above him now she drew it slowly across the tips of her own nipples, then across his. Then she pulled the binding of jewels from her hair and with a toss of her head spread the dark strands across his chest. As he watched, she seized the ends of her hair and began to draw them slowly, expertly, against the sensitive underside of the phallus that stood beneath her. Her breath came in short bursts as she drew close enough to tease her own sex as well.

He knew he had lost when he felt his last attempts at restraint dissolve. Then her breath told him she had lost as well. With their eyes joined, each exquisitely aware of the other's imminent resolution, she quickly slipped her left hand beneath her and caught the uppermost tip of the phallus with her nails, holding it taut, the pain intensifying his pleasure.

She had directed the pulse at the point of her own ecstasy, guiding the warm seed exactly as she wanted, against her own hard bud. As it struck her, she gave the *sitkrita* cry of release and with a hard shudder fell across him, loin against loin, exquisitely replete.

As the drummer pounded the final *sum* of the raga, Hawksworth realized she used his resolution to bring her own. Without their bodies touching.

The room lay silent about them, as though enfolded in their content. Only their hard breath remained.

"I never knew lovemaking could be so intense." He startled himself by his own admission.

"Because I loved you with more than just with my body." She smiled at him carefully and reached out to touch the marks on his chest. "But that was merely the first stage of *kama*. Are you ready now for the second?"

CHAPTER NINETEEN

Nadir Sharif studied the pigeon as it glided onto the red sandstone ledge and rustled its feathers in exhausted satisfaction. It cocked its white-spotted head for a moment as it examined the prime minister, then waddled contentedly toward the water cup waiting just inside the carved stone pigeon house.

He immediately recognized it as one of the birds he kept stationed in Gwalior, his last pigeon stage en route to Agra from the south. The cylinder bound to its leg, however, was not one of his own. Imprinted on its silver cap was the seal of the new Portuguese Viceroy of Goa, Miguel Vaijantes.

Nadir Sharif waited patiently for the pigeon to drink. He knew well the rewards of patience. He had waited patiently, studying the *feringhi*, for a full week. And he had learned almost all he needed to know.

The Englishman had been invited to *durbar* every day since his arrival. Arangbar was diverted by his stories and bemused by his rustic gifts. (The only gift that had *not* entertained Arangbar was the book of maps he had wheedled out of the Englishman, which upon inspection showed India as something far less than the greatest continent on the globe. But Arangbar found the map's rendering of India's coastline to be sufficiently naïve to cast the accuracy of the entire book into question.) This was the first *feringhi* Arangbar had ever met who could speak Turkish and understand his native Turki, and the *Moghul* rejoiced in being able to snub the Jesuits and dispense with their services as translators.

But most of all, Arangbar loved to challenge the Englishman to drinking bouts, as night after night they matched cups in the *Diwan-i-Khas* until near midnight. As Arangbar and the Englishman drew closer, the Jesuits had grown distraught to near madness. The hard-drinking Englishman bragged

of the East India Company and its bold plans for trade, of the old Levant
Company and its disputes with Spain over Mediterranean routes, of English
privateering in the West Indies. Of everything . . . except when the next
voyage would come.

Nadir Sharif had listened closely to their expansive talk all those nights,
and he had finally deciphered to his own satisfaction the answer to the question uppermost in Arangbar's mind.

The Englishman is bluffing. England has no fleet. At least no fleet that
can ever hope to threaten Portuguese control of the Indian Ocean. There'll
be no more voyages, and no more presents, for at least a year. The Englishman is living a fool's dream.

When his European presents are gone, and he's spent what's left of his
money buying jewels and gifts for the *Moghul*, he'll be dropped from court.
Arangbar plays him like a puppet, always hinting the *firman* will be ready tomorrow. But there'll be no *firman* unless Arangbar can be convinced the English king is powerful enough to protect Indian shipping from Portuguese reprisals at sea. And this the English clearly cannot do. At least not now, not
without a fleet. The Englishman is living on borrowed time.

And I'm beginning to think he suspects it himself. He drinks more than
a man in his place should. He's always able to stay in control, but just
barely. If Arangbar were not always drunk himself, he would have noticed it
also.

Nadir Sharif glanced at the silver cylinder and smiled to himself. So His
Excellency, Miguel Vaijantes, is worried. Undoubtedly he's demanding I
contain the Englishman, isolate him from Arangbar.

It will hardly be necessary. The Englishman is destined to be forgotten
soon. How much longer can he hold the *Moghul's* attention? A month? Two
months? I know his supply of trifles for Arangbar is already half depleted.

But why burden the Viceroy with this insight? Bargain with him. Let
him pay enough and I will guarantee with my life that the sun will rise tomorrow morning. The end of the Englishman is no less sure.

Nadir Sharif stroked the pigeon lovingly as he began to unwind the silk
binding holding the cylinder, and it reminded him again of the Deccan.

Still no pigeons from Mumtaz. How curious that her one dispatch in
the last month, the one brought by the Rajput, was merely to request that
small accommodation for the Englishman. Who knows why she asked it?
Perhaps it was a joke of the prince's.

Nadir Sharif congratulated himself on how easy it had been. The
Englishman had never known.

And it was obvious the woman Kamala *had* changed him, smoothed
him. Was the prince grooming him for something? If so, why send the
request through Mumtaz? Whatever the reason, it had been a pleasure to

grant this one favor for the daughter he doted on. He also realized it might well be the last favor he could ever do for her.

It was clear now that Prince Jadar would be banished from Agra forever. The events of the next four weeks were inexorable.

Today Arangbar's birthday celebrations begin. Next week Allaudin will be guest of honor at a *shikar*, a royal hunt. Two weeks after that, the wedding formalities begin, and the following week is the wedding itself. Four weeks and Jadar will be finished. Even if he returned to Agra today, he could not forestall the inevitable.

Nadir Sharif took the pigeon on his wrist and offered it a few grains of soaked *dal* from his own hand as he gently slipped off the silver cylinder. When the bird was pecking contentedly he eased it onto the ledge, twisted away the silver cap of the cylinder, and settled against the rooftop divan to translate the cipher.

The morning wind from the Jamuna grew suddenly chill against his skin. Then, as the message slowly emerged, the wind from the Jamuna became ice.

Nadir Sharif translated the cipher again, to be sure. But there could be no mistaking what it said. Or what it meant. He would have declared its contents an absurd hoax, perhaps even a hoax inspired by the Englishman, had not the message been intercepted by the Portuguese, by capture of one of Jadar's own pigeons.

The cipher did not say so, but doubtless a copy had also been sent to Arangbar. Even had it not, the *Moghul* still would hear the news within the day. His own intelligence network was the best in India, after that of the queen.

He closed the door of the pigeon house, picked up a small silver bell beside the divan, and rang lightly. Almost before he had replaced the bell, a eunuch was waiting.

"Your pleasure, Sharif Sahib."

"The Englishman. Where is he now?"

"In the garden, Sharif Sahib. He's always there at this time of day, with the Hindu woman."

"What's he doing there?"

"Who can say, Sharif Sahib? All we know is he goes into the garden every day around noon—I think the Hindu woman may be teaching him to play the sitar there—before going to *durbar* in the Red Fort. But he will be leaving soon now, as you must, to be present for His Majesty's birthday weighings."

"The English *feringhi* was invited?" Nadir Sharif was momentarily startled.

"He received an invitation, Sharif Sahib."

"Bring him to the reception room. I will see him now, before he leaves."

The eunuch snapped around and was gone. Nadir Sharif paused to translate the cipher one last time before ringing for his turban.

"Ambassador Hawksworth, please forgive my preoccupation these past few days." Nadir Sharif was bowing, it seemed, unusually low. "We're not always privileged to entertain our guests as we might wish. Preparations for today's birthday ceremonies have kept me rushing about the palace. But please, be seated."

Hawksworth's gaze swept the room. It was cavernous, hung with thick tapestries on every wall, and lightly perfumed with rose incense. Before he could reply a bowing servant was proffering a chalice of Persian wine. As Nadir Sharif watched a glass being poured, his voice continued, silken.

"Have you found anything here to pass the time? They tell me you've developed an interest in the sitar. A marvelous instrument really. And in my garden. Tell me, what do you think of it?"

"I can't decide." Hawksworth felt his caution rising automatically, as it did any time he found himself alone with Nadir Sharif. "It reminds me of some of the Tudor gardens connected with English castles, but still it's different. I like the precise geometry of the walkways and hedges, and the running water. It's a soothing place to sit and practice."

"So you find the Persian garden soothing? It *is* Persian, you know. The whole idea of a symmetrical garden comes from Persia. Not from this barbarous wasteland." Nadir Sharif motioned him to a bolster, and paused until he was seated. "Yes, it's soothing. I agree with you. But of course, that's one of the purposes of a garden." Nadir Sharif eased himself against a bolster and accepted a glass of *sharbat*. "It pleases me that you enjoy my garden. You see, Ambassador, to a man in the desert an oasis, a spot of water and green, is like a paradise. So we sometimes believe we are creating a bit of Allah's Paradise when we create a garden. You know, the Holy Quran itself tells us that Paradise will be something like a garden."

"But whose idea was it to build Persian gardens here?"

"When the first Moghul conqueror arrived in India, almost a century ago, he declared the land here around Agra to be particularly barren and depressing. So he immediately built a Persian garden. But we must all do our share, so today there are many gardens, all over India. The garden, you see, is our tribute to nature."

"But why so geometrical? Your garden uses water, stones, and plants to create designs that seem almost like the marble floors of your palace."

"Mathematics, Ambassador, principles of law. Islam is the rule of law. Why do you think we have so many mathematicians? I deliberately designed this garden with calculated geometric divisions. It provides me great satisfaction to impose order on the willfulness of nature."

"But why are the stone pathways all elevated above the level of the garden? In English gardens they're at ground level and lined with shrubs."

"But surely that's obvious as well. Our gardens are really concealed waterways, with water constantly flowing from one end to the other. We must put the walkways above the water." Nadir Sharif waved his hand. "But all of that is merely mechanics. The garden is where we find peace. It's where we wait to greet the spring, whose arrival we celebrate at the Persian New Year."

Nadir Sharif strolled to a window and looked out on the garden. "Spring in India seems to come up from the south. It's said that buds appear each day a few *kos* farther north, like a tender army on the march. But we Persians believe that spring must have a haven if she is to stay. And that's another reason we build gardens."

"I don't understand."

"There's a famous poem in Persian, by the poet Farrukhi, about gardens and spring. He once wrote of a place where spring always arrived feeling lowly and despised, because there was no land for her save desert, a place of rocks and thistles. But then a rich man—actually the patron of Farrukhi, whom he was writing to flatter—built a garden for her and the next year spring came forth from the south and found a home there." Nadir Sharif smiled. "In fact the poem begins by comparing spring's original arrivals to that of a bankrupt *feringhi*'s, who appeared with no carpet, no livelihood. But after spring discovered the garden, she brought from the south turquoise for the willows, rubies for the rose."

Nadir Sharif smiled. "What do you think of Farrukhi's poem, Ambassador?"

"What do you mean?"

"Curiosity. I was wondering what are the chances that spring will come again from the south this year? Did the 'bankrupt *feringhi*' merely come to see if the garden was ready? Was the first arrival of spring false, with the real arrival yet to come?"

Hawksworth studied Nadir Sharif's face. "I don't understand what you're trying to say. But I would like to know if you've spoken to His Majesty about the *firman*."

"Please believe I mention it daily. I think now he'll soon agree to terms."

"Then there's nothing yet?" Hawksworth set down the glass of wine. "I assumed that was why you wanted to speak to me. But you just wanted to talk about Persian gardens and Persian poets."

"Ambassador, I'm not a man for idle talk. Surely we know each other better than that." Nadir Sharif turned and banished the servants and eunuchs with a wave of his hand.

"Tell me. I know you met Prince Jadar once. Give me your honest opinion. Do you think he's a clever man?"

Hawksworth nodded noncommittally.

"I can assure you, Ambassador, that he's very clever indeed. Even his staunchest detractors would agree on that. And he's also resourceful. Not many here are aware he has a full intelligence network of his own. He does not, of course, have access to the dispatches of the official court reporters in the provinces, the *wakianavis*, or the dispatches of His Majesty's confidential reporters, the *harkaras*." Nadir Sharif paused. "At least we do not think he has access to their reports. But in a way he doesn't really need them. You see, he has his own system of reporters, which we know he began creating over two years ago. Spies whose identity is carefully guarded. We do not know any of their names, but we do know he calls them his *swanih-nigars*, and they prepare detailed information on anything in the provinces he asks them to. His network is extensive and, I understand, quite effective."

Hawksworth suddenly found himself remembering Shirin, the papers in the observatory, and wondering . . .

"Naturally he has agents along the southern coast. But at times they can be a bit too careless about the information they gather. For example, a cipher intended for the prince—sent by one of Jadar's secret *swanih-nigars* stationed in Cochin, on the far southern end of the Malabar Coast—was just intercepted by a Portuguese shipping agent at the port of Mangalore, down the coast south of Goa. The message was of great interest to the Portuguese, and they saw fit to forward it to me. What do you suppose the message contained?"

Hawksworth pulled himself alert.

"I have no idea."

"Tell me, Ambassador. The East India Company does trade on Java, am I correct?"

"Six years ago the Company established a factory . . . a trading station . . . at Bantam, the main port on the island."

"Was there a voyage to Bantam this year?"

"The *Discovery* was bound for Bantam this year, with cargo from Surat."

"Ambassador, the time for games is over. Your charade has made things very difficult for those of us who would try to help you." Nadir Sharif studied Hawksworth deliberately, almost sadly. "It would have been helpful if you had told me everything sooner. It's embarrassing that I must receive my information through captured intelligence, when I'm authorized to serve as your agent. I'm sure it will not surprise you that the Portuguese Viceroy, His Excellency, Miguel Vaijantes, is most disturbed at the news. There will be consequences."

"What are you talking about?"

"The cipher for Jadar. You could have told me sooner of your king's plans. It would have made all the difference." Nadir Sharif stared coldly at Hawksworth. "There's no longer any need to pretend you don't know. The fleet was sighted off the Malabar Coast, by coastal fishing barks, only three days ago. Four armed frigates, showing English colors, with a course north by northwest, which means they will stand to sea and avoid the Portuguese patrols along the coast. It was only by the slightest chance that they were seen. And then another accident that the cipher intended for Jadar was intercepted. Otherwise no one would have known. It was very resourceful of your East India Company, Ambassador, to have a second fleet sail up our west coast from the English factory at Java. Unless the Portuguese had intercepted and decoded Jadar's cipher, they would have been taken completely by surprise. Now they estimate the English fleet is scheduled to reach Surat within the month. Unless they are met and engaged . . . which they most assuredly will be."

The perfumed air of midmorning still seemed to hover above the inner courtyard of Arangbar's palace as Hawksworth approached its towering wooden gates. The astonishing news of the English fleet had sent his spirits soaring, and he had donned his finest doublet and hose for the occasion. As scimitared eunuchs scrutinized his gilded invitation and bowed obsequiously for him to pass, he suddenly felt he was walking through the portals of a Persian dreamland.

For the past two months servants and slaves had toiled through the crisp autumn nights transforming the courtyard of the Red Fort's inner palace from an open-air marble arcade into a vast, magnificent reception room for Arangbar's five-day lunar birthday fete. The surrounding galleries had been softened with rich carpets, their walls cloaked in new tapestries; and in the central square a flowering garden, freshened by interlocking marble fountains, had appeared out of nothing. In this new garden time had ceased to flow, night and day knew not their passage one into the other, for the sky itself was now a vast canopy of imperial red velvet, embroidered in gold and held aloft by silver-sheathed poles forty feet high and the size of ship's masts. The horizons of this velvet sky were secured to protruding stone eyelets along the second-story galleries by multicolored cotton cords the thickness of cable.

The centerpiece of the upcoming celebration was an enormous balance, the scale on which Arangbar's yearly weight would be taken. By that weight his physicians would foretell the future estate of his body, and if his weight had increased since the previous year, there was universal rejoicing. But, greater or less, his weight always seemed to augur well for India. His physicians inevitably found it reason to forecast another hundred years of his benevolent rule.

Nor was the balance itself suggestive of anything less than a portentous occasion. The measure of a king demanded kingly measures. Its weighing pans were two cushioned platforms, gilded and inlaid with jewels, suspended from each end of a central beam by heavy gold chains interwoven with silken cords. The beam itself, and its supports, were carved from rosewood, inlaid with jewels, and plated with gold leaf.

This event of universal joy was never witnessed by more than a few of Arangbar's closest circle. The first tier of court officials were permitted to watch, family members, favored officers with rank above five thousand horse, and a minuscule list of select foreign ambassadors.

Hawksworth tried to look formal and attentive, but his mind was still reeling from the news. All the way to the Red Fort he had tried to sort out the implications.

That crafty bastard Spencer. He well deserves to be Director of the East India Company. It's perfect. He timed it perfectly.

Why did he decide to send a second voyage? Did they accidentally rendezvous with the *Discovery* at Bantam? Or was it no accident? Could Elkington have ordered them north? Or maybe it's some sort of scheme with the Hollanders? Who could the Captain-General be?

Spencer, you deceiving whoremaster. You double-crossed Elkington, never told him about the letter from King James, and now you, or somebody, has double-crossed me.

Or saved the mission.

There's sure to be a bounty of gifts for Arangbar. If they can make it around Goa, and avoid the Portugals . . .

"Ambassador, this way." Nadir Sharif was standing near the balance, motioning him to the front.

"Ambassador, His Majesty is overjoyed at the news of the English fleet. He has asked that I seat you here, next to me, so I may translate the Persian for you and allow you to prepare a full report to your king." The prime minister had changed to formal dress, with a tapestried turban and cloak, under which were skin-tight, pastel-striped pants. He wore a necklace of enormous pearls and in the sash at his waist was a gold-handled *katar* set with emeralds. He was barefoot. "This is an ancient yearly custom of all the *Great Moghuls.*"

Hawksworth quickly unbuckled his shoes and tossed them by the edge of the vast carpet, near the arcade.

"Seat yourself here next to me and I will explain everything to you. His Majesty thinks the news of your trading fleet is extremely auspicious, coming as it did on the first day of his birthday celebration. He wants to return the

honor by allowing you to join him in the royal circle at the wedding of
Prince Allaudin and Princess Layla."

"That's very gracious of His Majesty. And when do you think he's planning to sign the *firman* approving English trade?"

"Your *firman* should be little more than a formality now, Ambassador.
He has already accepted in principle the terms you requested, but you must
realize he is quite preoccupied. I think you will have what you want in a few
more weeks. His Majesty has assumed a natural fondness for you, but I still
foresee various encumbrances from our friends in Goa. Much depends on
the fleet, and what happens if the Portuguese intercept it."

Nadir Sharif moved closer and lowered his voice. "You know, Ambassador, the appearance of your fleet brings nearer the time we should work
more closely together. Someday soon perhaps we can discuss the price of
English wool. I have five *jagirs* in northern Gujarat that produce superb indigo. They are convenient to the port of Cambay, just a few *kos* north of
Surat. And, as it happens, I have a private understanding with the Shahbandar of Cambay. It may be possible to make arrangements that would help
us both avoid some of the normal customs duties. I suggest we explore it."

Hawksworth looked at him and smiled. I'll trade with you the day after
hell turns to ice, you unscrupulous son of a whore.

Kettledrums sounded at the back of the square and Hawksworth turned
to see Arangbar making his entry, followed by Allaudin and a gray-bearded
wazir. The men around Hawksworth bounded to their feet as one, performed the *teslim*, and then settled again on the carpets. On Nadir Sharif's
whispered urgings, Hawksworth also rose and bowed, without the *teslim* . . .
causing Nadir Sharif's eyes to flash momentary disapproval as they both resumed their seats.

The *Moghul* was outfitted in the most magnificent attire Hawksworth
had ever seen. He seemed to be clothed in a fabric of jewels: diamonds,
rubies, pearls were woven into his cloak, and his sword handle appeared to
consist entirely of emeralds. His fingers were covered with jeweled rings and
chains from which dangled walnut-sized rubies. His chest was covered with
sparkling necklaces, and even his turban was bejeweled.

The crowd watched with anticipation as Arangbar strode directly to the
nearest platform of the balance and tested its cushions with a sparkling
hand. He waited with a broad smile while it was lowered to the carpet, then
without a word seated himself onto the cushions, in the hunched squat all
Indians preferred. Allaudin and the *wazir* stood on either side and steadied
him as officials from the mint, all wearing bright red turbans, approached
bearing dark brown bags.

Bag after bag was piled onto the opposite platform, until Arangbar's
side slowly began to levitate off the carpet. When a perfect balance had
been achieved, his side was tipped gently back down by Allaudin and the

wazir, while the officials began to remove and count the bags on the opposite platform. When the bags were counted, the weighing commenced again, this time with bags of purple silk.

"The first weighing is in silver rupees," Nadir Sharif whispered through the reverential silence. "Afterwards they are taken back to the mint and distributed to the poor by His Majesty. Today is one of great rejoicing in Agra."

"How much does he weigh?"

"His usual weight is about nine thousand silver rupees."

"That's over a thousand pounds in English sterling."

"Is that a large amount in your king's coinage, Ambassador?"

"It's a substantial sum of money."

"Over the following year, during the evenings, His Majesty will call the poor of Agra to come before him and he will give them the money with his own hand."

"How far will nine thousand rupees go to feed all the poor of Agra?"

"I don't understand your question, Ambassador?"

"Nothing. I . . . I was just wondering if perhaps King James should do the same."

"It is an old Moghul tradition here." Nadir Sharif turned back to the scales, where Arangbar was calling for the next weighing. "But watch. Now he will be weighed against gold *mohurs.*"

The pile of bags was mounting, and again Arangbar's platform slowly began to rise into the air.

"There are twelve weighings in all. You will see. After the gold coins, he is weighed against gold cloth that has been given to him on his birthday by the women of the *zenana.* Then bags of jewels that were contributed by the governors of India's provinces, carpets and brocades from Agra nobles, and so forth. He is also weighed against silk, linen, spices, and even *ghee* and grains, which are distributed later to the Hindu merchant caste."

Arangbar continued to smile serenely as the weighing proceeded. During the weighing of silk, he spotted Hawksworth and winked, raising a hand to flash a diamond the size of a bullet. Hawksworth noted wryly that he had not seen any of the wealth actually being distributed, that it was all in fact returned directly to the palace.

When all the weighings were completed, Arangbar drew himself erect and regally moved to a raised platform that had been constructed at the back of the arcade. He then signaled for the massive balance to be removed and in moments it had disappeared into the recesses of the palace.

The crowd had begun to shuffle expectantly. As Hawksworth watched, he suddenly realized why.

Large covered baskets were being brought before Arangbar, and when their lids were removed, Hawksworth caught the glisten of silver. Arangbar took the first basket and stood to his full height on the dais. Then with a swing he flung the contents over the top of the crowd. The air seemed to rain silver and the assembled nobles began scrambling over the carpet retrieving the silver objects. Nadir Sharif picked up one and handed it to Hawksworth.

It was a silver nutmeg, life-sized and topped with a tiny gold flower. Hawksworth rolled it over . . . and it deflated to a thin piece of foil.

Arangbar flung another basket and the turmoil intensified. Only Hawksworth stood firm, as even Nadir Sharif could not resist scooping up several of the foil replicas of nuts, fruits, and spices that scattered on the carpet around them. The dignified assemblage had been reduced to bedlam. Then the beaming Arangbar spotted Hawksworth and called out.

"Ambassador Inglish. Is there nothing you would have?"

"May it please Your Majesty, an ambassador of the English king does not scramble for toys."

"Then come forward and you'll not have to."

When Hawksworth reached the dais he bowed lightly, and as he drew himself up, Arangbar seized the front of his doublet and dumped a basket of gold foil flowers down the front of his shirt.

Before he could move, the nobles were there, pulling open his doublet and scooping up the worked foil. In moments his doublet was plucked clean. He looked about in disbelief, and saw that Arangbar was already tossing more baskets to the turbaned crowd.

When the silver and gold were gone, Arangbar spoke quickly to the eunuchs, and trays appeared with chalices of hard spirits. The assembled nobles all toasted the *Moghul's* health and he joined in as the drinking began. Musicians appeared, followed by food on plates of silver worked in gold. Finally *hookahs* were set about the carpet, together with more drinks, and a singer arrived to perform an afternoon raga.

"This is an auspicious day for us both, Inglish." Arangbar beamed down from his throne as he motioned Hawksworth forward. "The news just reached me. Was this meant to be a surprise?"

"The English fleet is my king's birthday gift to Your Majesty."

"Nothing could gratify me more." Arangbar drank from a large cup of wine. "We think it might be time we considered sending an ambassador of our own to the court of your Inglish king. We just sent our first ambassador to Goa."

"King James would be most honored, Your Majesty."

"Tell me, Ambassador Inglish. When will these ships reach the port at Surat?"

"It depends on whether the Portugals want to honor the treaty between Spain and England and allow our fleet to pass unchallenged. Sailing up from the islands will mean tacking against the wind, but the fleet could possibly make landfall within a month." Hawksworth paused. "Your Majesty must realize this adds urgency to the matter of the trading *firman*."

"Within the week or so, Inglish. Within a week or so."

Hawksworth caught a slight elevation of Nadir Sharif's eyebrows.

"How long now do you intend to be staying with us, Inglish?" Arangbar popped a ball of opium into his mouth . . . a bit too early in the day, Hawksworth thought.

"Until you've signed the *firman* for trade, Your Majesty. I'll return it to King James by the next shipping west."

"We would prefer that you stayed with us awhile longer, Inglish."

"No one regrets more than I that it's not possible, Your Majesty. But my king awaits Your Majesty's pleasure regarding the terms of the *firman*."

"We have conceived a new idea, Inglish. We will send the *firman* to your king by our own ambassador. Then you can remain here with us until your king sends another ambassador to replace you." Arangbar laughed. "But he must be a man who drinks as well as you, or we may send him back."

Hawksworth felt his stomach tighten. "Who can say when another ambassador will be sent, Your Majesty? Should Your Majesty approve the *firman*, my duties here will be resolved."

"But you must remain here to ensure we keep our word, Inglish." Arangbar winked broadly. "Else our heart could grow fickle."

"I am honored, Your Majesty." Hawksworth shifted. "But my first duty is to my king."

"We have been thinking perhaps you should have other duties . . ." Arangbar's voice trailed off as he sipped on his wine and studied Hawksworth. Then he looked up and his glance fell on the Portuguese Jesuits lingering at the back of the courtyard. As he examined them, he recalled the many long evenings when he had allowed the Jesuit Pinheiro and his superior, Father Sarmento, to debate with him the merits of Christianity. And again he found himself marveling how refreshingly different the Englishman was.

Out of curiosity he had once inquired of the Jesuits how exactly a king such as himself could become a Christian, and the very first thing they had said was he must select only one of all his wives and dismiss the rest.

He had tried to point out to them the absurdity of allowing a man only one wife, without even the option to rid oneself of her once she grew tiresome. And what, he had asked, was this king to do if his single remaining wife suddenly became blind one day? Was he to keep her still? Of course, they had replied, blindness in no way interferes with the act of marriage. And what if she becomes a leper? Patience, they had counseled, aided by God's grace, which renders all things easy. Such patience, he had pointed out, might be customary for a Jesuit, who had abstained from women all his life, but what about one who had not? And they had replied that Christians also were sometimes known to sin, but that the Grace of Christ provided the remedy of penitence, even for those who transgressed against the law of chastity. He had listened with mounting astonishment as they next proceeded to describe how Jesuits scourged themselves to still the fires of the flesh.

At this last, he had realized that Christian doctrines were incomprehensible and unworthy of further inquiry. From that time forward he had never bothered to take the Jesuits seriously.

But this Englishman is different, he told himself. A real man, who'll drink a cup of wine or eye a pretty woman with plenty of unchaste thoughts on his sleeve.

"From this day forth you'll be serving us, Inglish, as well as your king. We have decided to make you a khan."

Hawksworth stared at him uncomprehending. A murmur swept the crowd, but quickly died away to stunned silence.

"A khan, Your Majesty?"

"Khan is a title given to high-ranking officers in our service. It carries with it great honor. And a salary. No feringhi has ever before been made a khan by us. You will be the first." He laughed broadly. "So now you must stay in India and drink with us. You are in our hire."

"I'm flattered by Your Majesty's generosity." Hawksworth found himself stunned—by the honor and also by the disquieting implications for his planned return to England. "What are the duties of a khan?"

"First, Inglish, we must have a ceremony, to invest you properly." Arangbar seemed to ignore the looks of disbelief on the faces around him. "You will be given a personal honorary rank, called zat, of four hundred. And a horse rank, called suwar, of fifty."

"Does it mean I have to maintain that many cavalry?" Hawksworth blanched, realizing his money was already growing short.

"If you do, you will be the first khan in India who ever did. No, Inglish, you will be provided salary for that number, but you need not maintain more than twenty or thirty. We will personally select them for you after the wedding."

Arangbar turned and motioned to Nadir Sharif. The prime minister came forward and one of the eunuchs handed him a small box, of teakwood worked in gold. He motioned for Hawksworth to kneel directly in front of Arangbar. The nobles around them still could not disguise their astonished looks.

Nadir Sharif moved directly above where Hawksworth was kneeling and opened the box. "His Majesty, by this symbol, initiates you into discipleship. It is bestowed only on the very few." He took out a small gold medal, attached to a chain, and slipped the chain over Hawksworth's head. Hawksworth noted that the medal had the likeness of Arangbar imprinted on both sides. "Now you must prostrate yourself before His Majesty."

"May it please His Majesty, the ambassador of a king must show his gratitude after the custom of his own country," Hawksworth replied to Nadir Sharif, then bowed lightly to Arangbar. "I humbly thank Your Majesty in the name of King James."

Nadir Sharif's face darkened. "You must *teslim* to His Majesty."

"No, not the Inglish." Arangbar waved Nadir Sharif aside. "He must follow his own custom. Now, give him the pearl."

Nadir Sharif took a large pearl from the box and stood before Hawksworth.

"This you must wear in your left ear, where your gold earring is now."

Hawksworth examined the pearl. It was immense, and perfect.

"Again I thank Your Majesty." Hawksworth looked up to see Arangbar beaming. "How shall I wear it?"

"My jeweler will fit it for you, Inglish."

A wry, portly man stepped forward and quickly removed the small gold earring from Hawksworth's ear. Just as deftly, he attached the pearl where it had been.

"And now, Inglish, I will bestow on you the highest favor of my court." He turned and signaled another eunuch to come forward. The eunuch carried a cloak woven with gold. "This cloak I have myself worn, then kept aside to bestow on a worthy disciple. It is for you."

Arangbar took the cloak himself and laid it over Hawksworth's shoulders.

"I thank Your Majesty. The honor is more than I could ever merit."

"That may well be true, Inglish." Arangbar roared. "But it's yours. You speak my tongue and you drink almost as well. Few men here today can equal you. And you have the wits of ten Portuguese. I think you deserve to be one of my khans." Arangbar signaled for him to rise. "Your salary will begin with the next lunar month. After that you will be known in this court as the Inglish Khan. Day after tomorrow you will ride with us in *shikar*, the royal hunt. You may soon decide you like India better than England. Have you ever seen a tiger?"

"Never, Your Majesty."

"You will soon enough. Day after tomorrow. So you had best do your drinking now, for tigers require a clear head." Arangbar laughed again and clapped and the tension in the courtyard seemed to evaporate. The singer immediately began a second raga.

As Hawksworth fingered the earring, the medal, and the cloak, he found himself remembering Huyghen's burning eyes that day in the London alehouse. "You'll forget who you are," the old seaman had said. Could this be what he meant?

But maybe it's not so bad after all, he told himself. It's like a dream come true. And when the fleet makes landfall . . .

"Of course I've heard. It was my idea. Although His Majesty naturally assumes he thought of it all by himself. Making the *feringhi* a khan will confuse the Portuguese. And it will take everyone's mind off the *firman* for a while." Queen Janahara had received Nadir Sharif immediately after Arangbar retired to the *zenana* for his afternoon dalliance. The balcony of the Jasmine Tower was empty, the servants all ordered back to the *zenana*. I'm more interested in the English fleet. Do you know what has happened?"

"What do you mean, Majesty?" Nadir Sharif noted that he had not been invited to sit.

"There was another message today, a private message from His Excellency, Miguel Vaijantes." Janahara raised a silver, hourglass-shaped cuspidor to her lips and delicately discharged red betel juice. "Can you guess what he was dared to do?"

"What do you mean?"

"Miguel Vaijantes is a man without courage. The understanding was very clear."

"The understanding, Your Majesty?"

"We have kept our side of the agreement. There has been no *firman* for the English *feringhi*. But now His Excellency has declared that he must off-load the arms. He has begun assembling an armada to sail north and intercept the English."

"The arms, Your Majesty?" Nadir Sharif moved closer. "Miguel Vaijantes was shipping arms?"

"Surely you knew. My dear brother, has anything ever escaped your rapacious eyes." She smiled, then spat again. "For Ahmadnagar. Small arms and cannon."

"You were arming Malik Ambar? Against Jadar?" Nadir Sharif could not strain the surprise from his voice.

"We were not arming him. The Portuguese were. Miguel Vaijantes was to have armed a Maratha division on the western coast, off-loading at a Portuguese port called Bom Bahia, on the coast west of Ahmadnagar. He had his own reasons, but now it seems he has lost his nerve. I had no idea how alarmed these Portuguese were by the English."

Nadir Sharif's mind was reeling. Say something, anything.

"If I may inject a word on His Excellency's behalf, Majesty, you must understand that matters between the Portuguese and the English are extremely delicate at the moment." Nadir Sharif's voice grew more statesmanlike as he spoke. He scarcely heard of his own words as his mind plowed through the consequences of it all. And the treachery. "The English could conceivably interrupt the entire trade of the Portuguese. All the prince could ever possibly do would be to tighten restrictions on our ports at Surat and Cambay. The Viceroy's decision is clearly strategic, nothing more. I'm sure the regard he holds for Your Majesty remains undiminished."

"That is a touching consolation." Janahara's voice was frigid, and she seemed suddenly much older.

Footsteps sounded through the marble corridor and Allaudin appeared at the doorway. He had changed to a foppish green turban, set off by an effeminate necklace of rubies. His elaborate *katar* was secured by a sash of gold-threaded brocade, and an emerald was set at the top of each slipper. He wore heavy perfume.

"Your Majesty." He salaamed to Queen Janahara and then stood attentively, somewhat sheepishly, until she gestured for him to sit.

"You're late."

"I was detained in my quarters, Majesty."

Janahara seemed completely preoccupied, unable even to look at the prince. "The question now is what to do about the Englishman."

"What do you mean?" Allaudin did not trouble to mask his sneer. "It's perfectly clear. His Majesty adores the *feringhi*. He'll surely sign the *firman* for English trade. Then there'll be a war on the seas. It's really most exciting."

"The *firman* is not yet signed." Janahara moved to the balcony and studied the river below. Her walk was purposeful, yet still the perfection of elegance. "Nor do I think it ever will be. His Majesty will not have the time. The wedding will be moved forward. Before His Highness, Prince Jadar, has the leisure to trouble us more."

Janahara turned and examined the two men, one her brother and one her future son-in-law, finding herself astonished by their credulity. Somehow, she told herself, the hand of Jadar lies behind all this. The coincidence was just too great. First, he had succeeded in raising troops from the southern *mansabdars*. And now the Deccanis could not be armed. Could he possibly still forge a peace in the Deccan. Still, after the wedding he would be isolated. Then what he did would no longer matter. But if the *firman* were signed, there would no longer be leverage with the Portuguese.

Janahara looked directly at Nadir Sharif. "If His Majesty signs the *firman* before the wedding, you will be held responsible."

"I understand, Majesty." Nadir Sharif shifted. "When will the wedding be?"

"I think it would be auspicious to hold it the week following the birthday celebration. Which means the preparations must begin now."

"Hold the wedding immediately after the hunt? There's scarcely time."

"There will be time. For that and more." Janahara turned to Allaudin. "And you would do well to start spending more time with a sword and bow, and less with your pretty slave girls. I will know before long if you are a match for Jadar. I pray to Allah I don't already suspect the answer."

CHAPTER TWENTY

"There, on that hill, Inglish, is where I was born." Arangbar pointed to the high sandstone walls of a distant hilltop fortress, outlined against the midday sky. "It's called Fatehpur Sekri. It was a great city during the time of my father Akman, but now it's abandoned. It's romantic, but it's also forbidding. I've only been back once in my life, and that was enough."

Hawksworth's elephant was half a length behind those of Arangbar and Allaudin, even with that of Nadir Sharif. It was the second morning of their ride, and they were nearing the locale of the royal hunt. It seemed to him that half of Agra had traveled along. The queen and her retinue were behind them, as were many of Arangbar's favorite women, his guard, his eunuchs, the entire palace staff. The location of the hunt was a two-day ride from Agra.

"What's there now?"

"It's abandoned, Inglish. Except for a few Sufi Muslims. They were there before, and I guess they'll be there forever."

"What do you mean 'they were there before'? Before what?"

"Ah, Inglish. We had a very romantic birth. You seem to know nothing of it. You see, my father, the Great Akman, had tried for many years to have a son before I was born. Many hundreds of women, Inglish, but not one could give him a son. Once twin boys were born to a Rajput princess he had wived, but both died a few days later. Gradually he became obsessed with fears of death, of dying without a lineage, and he began calling holy men to the *Diwan-i-Khas* every evening to question them about mortality. Once a Hindu holy man came who told Akman the greatest duty of a king is to leave a male heir, who can carry his lineage forward. The Great Akman was plunged into even greater sadness by this, and he resolved to renounce everything until he could have a son.

"He walked all the way from Agra to that mountain, Inglish." Arangbar pointed toward the fortress. "He came to see a holy Sufi living there, among the rocks and wild beasts. It was a momentous meeting. Akman fell at the feet of the holy man, and the Sufi held out his arms in welcome to the *Great Moghul* of India. In later years many of Akman's artists painted the scene. Akman told him that he had come to find the peace of Allah. To find his own destiny. As a seeker after truth. The Sufi offered this great warrior berries to eat, and gave him his own simple hut for an abode. Akman stayed for many days, meditating with the Sufi, and finally, when he made ready to leave, the Sufi told him he would have three sons.

"And now," Arangbar grinned, "we reach the interesting part. When next a wife announced she was with child, Akman moved her out here, to stay in the same abode as the holy man. And, as the Sufi predicted, a male child was born."

"And the child was . . ."

"You are riding beside him, Inglish. That is the story of my birth. Akman was so elated that he decided to build an entire city here, and move the capital from Agra. He built the city, but it was an obvious act of excess. He never found time to live there, and soon it was abandoned. So now the mountain is like it was before my birth, home to wild birds and a few mad Sufis. The only difference is they have a magnificent abandoned city to live in, instead of straw huts." He laughed again. "Perhaps I owe my very life to a Sufi. Incidentally, descendants of that holy man still live there."

"Are they all Sufis?"

"Who knows, Inglish? I think holy men from all over India can be found there from time to time. It's become a kind of retreat."

"I'd like permission to visit it sometime, Majesty."

"Of course, Inglish. You'll find it's magnificent."

Hawksworth squinted against the sun and studied the distant red walls of the city-fortress. Something about its remote purity beckoned him. After the hunt, he told himself, when there's time. Right after the hunt.

Arangbar fell silent, and Hawksworth leaned back in his *howdah* as it rocked gently along. Elephants made better mounts than he had first suspected. He thought again of the previous morning, and his first reaction when told he would be riding an elephant for the next two days. He had arrived at the Red Fort, to be greeted by Nadir Sharif, who directed him to the royal elephants being readied in the courtyard of the *Diwan-i-Am*.

"His Majesty has selected one of his favorites for you. Her name is Kumada." Nadir Sharif had pointed toward a large female elephant, her body dyed black and festooned with golden bells, yak-tail tassels, gold tusk rings.

"What does the name mean?"

"The infidel Hindus believe the eight points of the earth are each guarded by a heavenly being in the shape of an elephant. Your English fleet is coming to us out of our ocean from the southwest, and Kumada is the name Hindus give to the elephant who guards that point of the Hindu compass. His Majesty believes this elephant will be auspicious for you."

"I'm most grateful to His Majesty." Hawksworth surveyed the assembled crowd in astonishment. Around him nobles wearing jeweled turbans and silk trousers were selecting elephants. He had worn seaboots and a leather jerkin.

Nadir Sharif signaled toward the *mahout* perched atop the neck of Kumada, and the man tapped her flapping ear with a short barbed rod and gave her directions in Hindi as he guided her toward Hawksworth. She lumbered forward to where Hawksworth stood, and then her mountainous flesh seemed to roll like a wave as she kneeled, front legs out, back legs bent at the knee, ready to be mounted. Two keepers were there, opening the gate of the gold-trimmed *howdah* and then kneeling, ready to hoist the *feringhi* aboard.

"Have you ever ridden an elephant before, Ambassador?" Nadir Sharif monitored Hawksworth's apprehensive expression with delight.

"Never. I've never actually been this close to one before." Hawksworth eyed the elephant warily, mistrusting her seeming docility. Elizabethans circulated fabulous tales about this mountainous beast, that it could pull down great trees with the power of its trunk, that it had two hearts—one it used when calm, the other when incensed—and that in Ethiopia there were dragons who killed elephants merely to drink their blood, said to be ice cold at all times.

"You will find an elephant has more wit than most men. His Majesty keeps a thousand in his stables here in the Red Fort. The Great Akman used to trap them in the wild, using a female in heat, but then he learned to induce tame ones to couple. Your elephant, I believe, is second-ranked. She's a fine-tempered animal."

Kumada examined Hawksworth with her sad, dark eyes, and waved her fanlike ears skeptically.

"I'm not entirely sure she's taken to me."

"Here, Ambassador." Nadir Sharif slipped a paper-wrapped stick of sugarcane into Hawksworth's hand and nodded his head toward the elephant.

Hawksworth gingerly approached her and began unwrapping the paper. No sooner was the cane in view than Kumada nipped it deftly from his hand with a flourish of her trunk. She popped the cane into her mouth and flapped her ears with obvious pleasure as she cracked it with her immense teeth. For a second Hawksworth thought he caught a flash of appreciation in her eyes. He paused a moment, then walked close enough to stroke the heavy skin at her neck.

"She'll not forget you now, Ambassador." Nadir Sharif was feeding his own elephant. "It's said these animals have a memory longer than a man's."

Hawksworth vaulted into the *howdah* and the entire world suddenly seemed to shudder as her *mahout* signaled Kumada to rise. He seized the railing surrounding him and gasped as she rumbled to her feet.

"You'll soon ride like a Rajput, Ambassador."

The elephant rocked into motion. It was worse than heavy weather at sea.

"I think it may take practice."

"Women from the *zenana* ride elephants all the way to Kashmir in the summer. I'm sure you'll manage a two-day hunt." Nadir Sharif swung easily into his *howdah*. Around them other elephants were kneeling for nobles to mount.

"Where will the hunt be?"

"This time we're going west, out toward the old city of Fatehpur Sekri. But His Majesty has hunting preserves all over. In the neighborhood of Agra and near the small town of Delhi north of here, along the course of the Jamuna and reaching into the mountains, there is much uncultivated land. There are many places with grasses over six feet high and copse wood. This land is guarded with great care by the army, and no person, high or low, is allowed to hunt there except for partridge, quail, and hare—which are caught with nets. So the game—*nilgai*, deer, antelope, *chitah*, tiger, even some lions—is plentiful. Some of His Majesty's hunting preserves may extend as far as ten *kos* in every direction—I believe that's around twenty of your miles."

"You said preparations for the hunt had been underway for days?"

"Of course. When His Majesty announces a *shikar*, a royal hunt, the grand master of the hunt in that particular location has to begin extensive preparations. The hunts now are usually a *qamargha*, which was invented by Akman."

"What's that?"

"First, sentries are posted on all the roads leading into the preserve to keep villagers out, and then the entire preserve is surrounded by beaters, we call them *qarawals*, who begin to close the circle and drive in the game. For this week's hunt he used thirty thousand *qarawals*. The grand master of the hunt informs His Majesty when the game has been brought together. The next day the court and officers from the army leave early, to be at the appointed place to greet His Majesty when he arrives. His Majesty usually hunts alone at first, if there are no tigers, and everyone else must wait at a distance of about one *kos*. Only some members of the Imperial army are allowed to accompany him, for protection. After His Majesty wearies of the kill, then others of his choosing are allowed to enter the circle. Finally the circle is opened and anyone who wishes is allowed to kill the last of the game. But if tigers are to be hunted, it's customary that only His Majesty and the royal family enter the circle. It's always been the tradition of Moghul rulers that only they and their kinsmen are allowed to hunt tigers. But this hunt will be different. This time His Majesty will merely watch."

"Who'll do the killing then?"

"That may surprise you, Ambassador. Let me merely say that it is no man. You will see."

Hawksworth was still wondering what he meant. But the time was not far away when he would know. They were nearing the area that Nadir Sharif had said was designated for the hunt.

"Inglish," Arangbar shouted back over his shoulder. "Does your king hunt?"

"Rarely, Your Majesty. But he has no elephants."

"Perhaps we should send him some. But then I assume he has no tigers either. Should we also send him some tigers to run free in Ingland so he can hunt them?"

"I'll remember to ask His Majesty."

"But first you must see our tigers for yourself, Inglish. Today you and Nadir Sharif will join us as we go into the *qur*, the hunting round. Have your elephants fitted with leather armor."

Nadir Sharif started with surprise. "I thank Your Majesty for the honor."

Allaudin stirred in his *howdah*, and Hawksworth caught the disdain in his eyes. "Majesty, why are you inviting the *feringhi* into the *qur*?"

"Her Majesty suggested it. And it amuses me." Arangbar seemed to dismiss Allaudin's question. "He will not have a weapon. All he'll do is watch."

As servants rushed forward to begin fitting the leather armor, Hawksworth saw the queen's elephant approach. This was the closest he had ever been to her, and still he could not see her. Her *howdah* was completely enclosed with curtains, which now flapped lightly in the midday breeze.

"Her Majesty, Queen Janahara, will be going into the hunting circle." Nadir Sharif's voice was discreet as he spoke to Hawksworth. "She rarely joins in *shikar*, but she is an excellent shot. This is a rare honor for you, Ambassador."

Hawksworth studied the closed *howdah* and wondered why the "honor" seemed to leave him with such an uneasy feeling.

The waiting nobles formed a line with their elephants as the Imperial entourage moved past. Armed guards followed on horseback at a distance. Leather padding had been fitted over the face and shanks of Hawksworth's and Nadir Sharif's elephants, and they joined the end of the procession.

Hawksworth held firmly to the side of the *howdah* as his elephant rocked along, with only occasional instructions from her *mahout*. Now they followed a winding road, which was surrounded on either side by tall, brown grass. He warily studied every sway of the grass, imagining tigers waiting to spring.

"Why don't we have guns?" He turned to Nadir Sharif, who rode alongside, rocking placidly in his swaying *howdah*.

"There's no need, Ambassador. I told you the tiger will not be killed with guns today. Of course, His Majesty and Prince Allaudin have guns, but they're merely for protection, in case there's some minor difficulty."

"Minor difficulty? What are *we* supposed to do if there's a 'minor difficulty'?"

"The army will be there, men with half-pikes." He smiled easily. "You're in no danger."

Ahead the woods seemed to open up, and the grass was shorter, perhaps only as high as a man's waist. Deer darted wildly from side to side, contained by high nets that had been erected around the sides of the clearing. As they approached, Hawksworth saw a long line of several hundred water buffalo waiting, heavy bovine animals with thick curved horns dipping back against their hands, each fitted with a leather saddle and reined by a rider on its back. The reins, which passed through the buffalo's nostrils, were held in one hand by a mounted soldier, whose other hand grasped a naked broadsword.

"Those men may well be the bravest soldiers in the army." Nadir Sharif pointed to the riders, who were all saluting Arangbar's arrival. "Theirs is a task I do not envy."

"What do they do?"

"You will see for yourself, Ambassador, in just a few moments."

From beyond the other side of the clearing, as though on an agreed signal, came the sound of beaters. As the Imperial elephants drew near the gray line of buffalo, their riders began to urge them ahead. The buffalo snorted, knowing what waited in the grass, and then they lumbered forward, tossing their heads in disquiet. The line of buffalo was curved in the shape of a half-moon, and Arangbar urged his elephant directly behind them. The grass ahead swarmed with frightened game, as deer and antelope dashed against the nets and were thrown back, and from the woods beyond, the clatter and shouts of the beaters increased.

Suddenly from out of the grass a tawny head appeared, with gold and black stripes and heavy whiskers. The animal dashed for the side of the enclosure, sprang for freedom, and was thrown back by the heavy net. Hawksworth watched it speechless, unprepared for the size and ferocity of an Indian tiger. It was enormous, with powerful haunches and a long striped tail. The tiger flipped to its feet and turned to face the line of buffalo with an angry growl.

Arangbar clapped his hands with delight and shouted in Urdu to the line of riders, all—Hawksworth now realized—Rajputs. The buffalo snorted and tried to turn back, but their riders whipped them forward. The tiger assumed a crouching stalk along the gray, horned wall, eyeing a large dark buffalo with a bearded rider. Then it sprang.

The buffalo's head went down, and when it came up a heavy curved horn had pierced the tiger's neck. There was a snort and a savage toss of the head that flung the wounded tiger upward. As it whirled in the air, Hawksworth saw a deep gash across its throat. The Rajput riders nearby slipped to

the ground and formed a wall of swords between Arangbar and the tiger as
the line of buffalo closed in, bellowing for the kill. In what seemed only moments the tiger was horned and pawed to a lifeless pulp.

"Superb!" Arangbar shouted something to the enclosed *howdah* that
Hawksworth did not understand. "A hundred gold *mohurs* to every man on
the line."

The Rajputs remounted their buffalo, retrieving the reins from the
bloody grass, and the line again moved forward.

"This is a variation on His Majesty's usual tiger hunt," Nadir Sharif
shouted through the dust, above the din of bellowing buffalo and trumpeting elephants. "Often he shoots, but today His Majesty elected merely to
watch. Actually, animal fights have long been a favorite pastime in India."

At that moment a pair of tigers emerged from the grass and stared at
the approaching line of buffalo. They did not seem frightened, as had the
first, and they watched the line coolly, as though selecting a strategy. Then
they dropped into a crouching stalk, moving directly toward the center of
the line.

Hawksworth noticed Arangbar suddenly order his *mahout* to hold back
his elephant. The other Imperial elephants had also paused to wait. Then
Arangbar turned and ordered the servant who rode behind him to pass forward a long-barreled, large-caliber sporting piece. Allaudin, whose fright was
transparent, also signaled for a gun.

Hawksworth's *mahout* pulled his elephant directly behind Arangbar's, as
though for protection.

The tigers seemed in no hurry to engage the buffalo. They scrutinized
the approaching line and waited for their moment. Then, when the buffalo
were no more than ten feet away, both sprang simultaneously.

The female was speared on the horn of a buffalo, but she flipped in
midair and sank her teeth into the leather shielding on its neck. As its Rajput rider slipped to the ground, the male of the pair dashed past his mate
and sprang for him. The Rajput swung his broadsword, catching the tiger in
the flank, but it swatted him aside with a powerful sweep of its paw and he
crumpled, his neck shattered. Other Rajputs rushed the male tiger with their
swords, as their buffalo closed in to kill the female, but it eluded their
thrusts as it circled Arangbar's elephant. Soldiers with half-pikes had already
rushed to form a barricade between Arangbar's elephant and the tiger, but
the *Moghul* seemed unperturbed. While the panting male tiger stalked
Arangbar, the female tiger was forgotten.

As Hawksworth watched spellbound, his pulse pounding, he caught a
yellow flicker out of the corner of his eye and turned to see the female tiger
slip past the ring of buffalo and dash toward the rear of Arangbar's elephant.
It was on the opposite side from the armed soldiers, where the *Moghul*'s elephant was undefended.

Hawksworth opened his mouth to shout just as the female tiger sprang for Arangbar, but at that moment a shot rang out from the enclosed *howdah* of Queen Janahara and the female tiger crumpled in midair, curving into a lifeless ball as it smashed against the side of the *Moghul's* mount.

The jolt caused Arangbar's shot at the male tiger to go wide, merely grazing its foreleg. A dozen half-pikes pierced its side as it stumbled forward, and it whirled to slap at the Rajputs. Allaudin also fired his tiger gun, but his shot missed entirely, almost hitting one of the men trying to hold the tiger back. It whirled in a bloody circle for a moment, and then stopped.

It was staring at Hawksworth.

He heard his *mahout* shout in terror as the tiger sprang for the head of their elephant. A wrap of yellow fur seemed to twist itself around the elephant's forehead as the tiger dug its claws into the protective leather padding. As Kumada tossed her head in panic, the *mahout* screamed again and plunged for safety, rolling through a clump of brown grass and scrambling toward the soldiers.

The tiger caught Hawksworth's eyes with a hypnotic gaze as it began pulling itself over the forehead of the terrified elephant, directly toward his *howdah*. Kumada had begun to whirl in a circle and shake her head, futilely trying to dislodge the wounded fury slashing at her leather armor. The tiger slipped momentarily, then caught its claws more firmly and began to climb again.

Almost without thinking, Hawksworth reached forward and grabbed the *ankus*, the short pike and claw used for guiding an elephant, that the *mahout* had left lodged in a leather fold behind the elephant's head. He wrenched it free and began to tease the tiger back.

Kumada was running now, wildly it seemed, toward a large pipal tree at the edge of the clearing. But the tiger had pulled itself atop her head and, as Hawksworth jabbed its whiskered face with the *ankus*, he heard a deep growl and saw a flash of yellow and claw as a sharp pain cut through his shoulder.

He knew he was falling, dizzily, hands grasping against smooth leather as he slipped past the neck of the elephant, past its flapping ear, against a thundering foot that slammed the dust next to his face.

Kumada had suddenly stopped dead still, throwing him sprawling against the base of the pipal tree. He looked up to see the tiger suspended above him, glaring down, clawing at the face of the elephant and bellowing with pain.

Then he heard the snap of the tiger's spine, as Kumada slammed it again and again against the massive trunk of the tree. Only when the tiger was motionless did she let it drop, carefully tossing its body away from Hawksworth as it tumbled lifeless onto the grass.

Hawksworth looked up through the dust to see Arangbar pulling his elephant alongside.

"That was most auspicious, Inglish. It's an ominous and evil portent for the state if a tiger I have shot escapes the hunt. If that beast had succeeded in going free, we would have had to send the entire army into the country-side to find and kill it. Your Kumada saved me the trouble. The gods of the southwest have been auspicious for our reign today. I think you brought us luck."

"I thank Your Majesty." Hawksworth found himself gasping for breath.

"No, it is you we must thank. You were quick-witted enough to keep the tiger where Kumada could crush it." Arangbar called for his own ele-phant to kneel, and he walked briskly to Kumada, who was still quivering from fright. He stroked her face beneath the eye and she gentled perceptibly. It was obvious she loved Arangbar. "She's magnificent. Only once before have I ever seen an elephant do that. I hereby promote her immediately to First Rank, even though a female." He turned to Nadir Sharif. "Have it recorded."

As Hawksworth tried to rise, he felt a bolt of pain through the shoulder where the tiger had slapped him. He looked to see his leather jerkin shred-ded. Arangbar seemed to notice it too and he turned and motioned to Nadir Sharif, who signaled to another man, who called yet another. Moments later a physician was bending over Hawksworth. He probed the skin for a painful moment and then slammed a knee against Hawksworth's side, giving the pained arm a quick twist.

Hawksworth heard himself cry out from the pain and for a moment he thought he might lose consciousness. But then his mind began to clear and he realized he could move the arm again. The pain was already starting to abate.

"I suggest the shoulder be treated with compresses for a few days, Maj-esty." Nadir Sharif had dismounted from his elephant and was there, atten-tive as always.

"Then he must be sent back to Agra."

"Of course, Majesty." Nadir Sharif stepped closer to Arangbar. "But perhaps it would be equally wise to let the *feringhi* rest somewhere near here. Perhaps at the old city." He turned and pointed toward the west. "There at Fatehpur. I think there may still be a few Sufi hermits there who could attend the shoulder until *shikar* is over. Then he could return with us."

Arangbar turned and shaded his eyes as he stared at the horizon. Above the treeline could be seen the gate of the fortress at Fatehpur Sekri.

"But my shoulder is fine now." Hawksworth tried to move into the cir-cle of conversation. "There's no need . . ."

"Very reasonable." Arangbar seemed to ignore Hawksworth as he turned back to Nadir Sharif. "You can escort the Inglish to the fortress. Call up a palanquin for him. Leave your elephant here and take a horse."

As the physician bound Hawksworth's arm in readiness, a palanquin was brought from among the women's elephants. "A contingent of Rajputs can go with him." Arangbar shouted instructions to the captain of his guard and watched the men fall into formation. Then he remounted his elephant and signaled for the buffalo to resume their sweep of the tall grass.

As the party started forward, Hawksworth saw Nadir Sharif shout orders to one of the servants attending him. And as four Rajputs lifted Hawksworth's palanquin off the ground, a servant rushed forward to shove a flask inside.

It was brandy. Hawksworth turned to see Nadir Sharif grinning, a gleam in his eye.

She watched the palanquin ease up the weathered, winding path leading to the fortress gate. The procession had moved slowly through the gate at the northeast corner of the city's walls and now the Rajputs were clustered around the palanquin and the lone rider. The night was still, awash in a wild desert fragrance, and the moon was curing slowly from white to a rarefied gold. Her vantage, in a corner turret of the wall, was shadowless and perfect. She examined the rider and smiled when she recognized the face.

Nadir Sharif. You have kept your part of the bargain. All of it.

As she studied him through the half light, she wondered why they were coming a day earlier than planned. Then the palanquin stopped and the other figure emerged. She hesitated before looking, at last forcing herself, willing her eyes to see.

After a long moment she turned to the tall man standing next to her. His beard was white, as were his robes. His eyes saw what she saw, but he did not smile. He turned to her and nodded wordlessly. Then he tightened his white robe and moved easily down the stone staircase toward the courtyard below.

Hawksworth had sensed the autumn light begin to fall rapidly as they approached the gates of the fortress-city. Already there was a pale moon, promising fullness. In size and grandeur the portals of the gate reminded Hawksworth of the Red Fort in Agra, only the walls themselves were considerably less formidable. The palace itself sat atop a wooded hill, and already the stones of the abandoned roadway leading up the hill were becoming overgrown. There was a small village at the bottom of the hill, where smoke from evening cooking fires had begun to rise, but from the fortress itself there was no smoke, no hint of life or habitation.

He alighted from the palanquin at the bottom of a steep stairway leading to the palace gate and together with Nadir Sharif passed slowly up the abandoned steps. The Rajputs trailed behind them as they reached the top and passed under the shadow of a tulip-curved arch that framed the gateway.

The dark surrounded them like an envelope, and the Rajput guards pushed forward, toward the black outline of two massive wooden doors at the back of the recess. They pushed open the doors, and before them lay a vast open courtyard, empty in the moonlight.

"Is this place completely abandoned? I still don't understand why I'm here."

Nadir Sharif smiled. "On the contrary, Ambassador. It's far from abandoned. But it appears so, does it not?"

Then Hawksworth saw a figure approaching them, gliding noiselessly across the red sandstone pavement of the court. The figure carried an oil lamp, which illuminated a bearded face framed in a white shawl.

"You are welcome in the name of Allah." The figure bowed a greeting. "What brings armed men to our door? It is too late now to pray. We long ago sounded the last *azan*."

"His Majesty has sent a *feringhi* here, to be cared for by you for two days." Nadir Sharif stepped forward. "He was injured today during *shikar*."

"Our hands are always open." The figure turned and moved across the plaza toward a building that looked, in the new moonlight, to be a mosque. When they reached the entrance, the man turned and spoke to the Rajputs in a language Hawksworth did not understand.

"He says this is the house of God," Nadir Sharif translated. "He has commanded the Rajputs to leave their shoes and their weapons here if they wish to follow. I think they will refuse. Perhaps it would be best if we all left you now. You'll be well cared for. Day after tomorrow I'll send a horse for you."

"What's going on? You mean I'm going to be here alone?" Hawksworth suddenly realized he was being abandoned, at an abandoned city. He whirled on Nadir Sharif. "You suggested this. You brought me here. What the hell is this for? I could have returned to Agra, or even stayed with the hunt."

"You're a perceptive man, Ambassador." Nadir Sharif smiled and looked up at the moon. "But as far as I know, you're here entirely by coincidence. I cannot be responsible for anything that happens to you, or anyone you see. This is merely the hand of chance. Please try to understand."

"What do you mean?"

"I will see you in two days, Ambassador. Enjoy your rest."

Nadir Sharif bowed, and in moments he and the Rajputs had melted into the moonlight.

Hawksworth watched them leave with a mounting sense of disquiet. Then he turned and peered past the hooded figure, who stood waiting. The mosque looked empty, a cavern of flickering shadows against intricate plaster calligraphy. He unbuckled the sheath of his sword and passed it to the man as he kicked away his loose slippers. The man took the sword without a word, examined it for a moment as though evaluating its workmanship, then turned to lead the way.

They moved silently across the polished stone floor, past enormous columns that disappeared into the darkness of the vaulted space above them. Hawksworth relished the coolness of the stones against his bare feet, then ducked barely in time to avoid a hanging lamp, extinguished now, its polished metalwork almost invisible against the gloom.

Ahead a lamp flickered through the dark. They passed beneath it, then stopped at a closed door at the rear of the mosque. The man spoke a word Hawksworth did not understand and the door was swung open from the inside, revealing an illuminated passageway.

Four men were waiting. As Hawksworth and his guide passed through, the door closed behind them and the men silently drew around.

The passageway was long, freshly plastered, and floored in marble mosaic. It was cool, as though immune from the heat of the day, and scented faintly with rose incense that had been blended with the oil in the hanging lamps.

At the end of the corridor was another stairway, again of white marble, and as they moved up its steps the man who had greeted Hawksworth extinguished his lamp with a brass cup he carried.

Beyond the stair was another corridor, then another door that opened as they approached. Hawksworth realized they were in an upper story of a large building directly behind the mosque. They passed through the door and emerged into a room facing a balcony that overlooked the abandoned square below.

In the center of the room was a raised dais, covered with a thick Persian carpet. The man who had been Hawksworth's guide moved to the dais, mounted it, and seated himself. With a flourish he dropped his white hood and the wrap that had been around him. Hawksworth realized with a shock that his long white hair streamed to his waist. He was naked save for a loincloth. He gestured for Hawksworth to sit, indicating a bolster.

"Welcome, English." He waited until the surprise had registered in Hawksworth's face. "We've been expecting you, but not quite so soon."

"Who are you?"

"I was once a Persian." He smiled. "But I've almost forgotten my country's manners. First I should offer you some refreshment, and only then turn to affairs. Normally I would offer *sharbat*, but I understand you prefer wine?"

Hawksworth stared at him speechless. No pious Muslim would drink wine. That much he knew.

"Don't look so surprised. We Persian poets often drink wine . . . for divine inspiration." He laughed broadly. "At least that's our excuse. Perhaps Allah will forgive us.

> "A *garden of flowers, a cup of wine,*
> *Mark the repose of a joyous mind.*"

He signaled one of the men, and a chalice of wine appeared, seemingly from nowhere. "I once learned a Latin expression, 'in vino veritas.' As a Christian you must know it. 'In wine there is truth.' Have some wine and we will search for truth together."

"Let's start with some truth from you. How do you know so much about me? And you still haven't told me who you are."

"Who am I? You know, that's the most important question you can ask any man. Let us say I am one who has forsworn everything the world would have . . . and thereby found the one thing most others have lost." He smiled easily. "Can you guess what that is?"

"Tell me."

"My own freedom. To make verse, to drink wine, to love. I have nothing now that can be taken away, so I live without fear. I am a Muslim reviled by the mullahs, a poet denounced by the Moghul's court versifiers, a teacher rejected by those who no longer care to learn. I live here because there is no other place I can be. Perhaps I soon will be gone, but right here, right now, I am free. Because I bear nothing but love for those who would harm me." He stared out over the balcony for a moment in silence. "Show me the man who lives in fear of death, and I will show you one already dead in his soul. Show me the man who knows hate, and I will show you one who can never truly know love." He paused again and once more the room grew heavy with silence. "Love, English, love is the sweetness of desert honey. It is life itself. But you, I think, have yet to know its taste. Because you are a slave to your own striving. But until you give all else over, as I have done, you can never truly know love."

"How do you think you know so much about me? I know nothing about you. Or about why I'm here."

"But I think you've heard of me."

Hawksworth stared at him for a moment, and suddenly everything came together. He could have shouted his realization.

"You're Samad. The Sufi . . ." He stopped, his heart racing. "Where is . . . ?"

"Yes, I'm a poet, and I'm called a Sufi because there is nothing else to call me."

"You're not really a Sufi?"

"Who knows what a Sufi is, my English friend? Not even a Sufi knows. Sufis do not teach beliefs. They merely ask that you know who you are."

"I thought they're supposed to be mystics, like some of the Spanish Catholics."

"Mystics yearn to merge with God. To find that part within us all that is God. Sufis teach methods for clearing away the clutter that obscures our knowledge of who we are. So perhaps we're mystics. But we're not beloved by the mullahs."

"Why not? Sufis are Muslims."

"Because Sufis ignore them. The mullahs say we must guide our lives by the Laws of the Prophet, but Sufis know God can only be reached through love. A pure life counts for nothing if the heart is impure. Prayers five times a day are empty words if there is no love." Samad paused again, and then spoke slowly and quietly. "I am trying to decide if there is love about you, English."

"You seem to think you know a lot about me. There's only one person who wanted me to meet you. And she was in Surat. Where is she now? Is she here?"

"She's no longer in Surat. Be sure of that. But at this moment you are here with me. Why always seek after what you do not have? You see, I do know much about you. You're a pilgrim." He waved his hand absently. "But then we all are pilgrims. All searching for something. We call it different names—fulfillment, knowledge, beauty, God. But you still have not found what you seek, is that not true?" Samad watched Hawksworth in silence as he drank from his own wineglass. "Yes, it is given many names, but it is in fact only one thing. We are all searching, my English, for our own self. But the self is not easy to find, so we travel afar, hoping it lies elsewhere. Searching inward is a much more difficult journey."

Hawksworth started to speak, but Samad silenced him with a wave of the hand. "Know that you will find the thing you most want only when you cease to search. Only then can you listen to the quiet of the heart, only then can you find true content." Samad drank again from his wine. "This last week you have found, so you think, your fortune. You have received worldly honors from the *Moghul*, you have news of imminent success for your English king. But these things will only bring you despair in the end."

"I don't understand what you mean."

Samad laughed and finished off his glass. "Then let me tell you a story about myself, English. I was born a Persian Jew, a merchant at my birth by historic family vocation. But my people have ignored the greatest Prophet of all, the Prophet Mohammed. His voice invites all, and I heard that voice. I became Muslim, but still I was a merchant. A Persian merchant. And, perhaps not unlike you, I traveled to India in search of . . . not the greater Prophet, but the baser profit. And here, my English, I found the other thing I searched for. I found love. Pure love, consuming love. The kind of love few men are privileged to know. The love of a boy whose beauty and purity could only have come from God. But this love was mistaken by the world, was called impure, and he was hidden from me. So the only one left for me to love was God. Thus I cast away my garments, my worldliness, and gave myself to Him. And once more I was misunderstood."

Samad paused and called for another glass of wine. Then he turned back to Hawksworth. "So I have told the world my story in verse. And now there are many who understand. Not the mullahs, but the people. I have given them words that could only come from a pure heart, words of joy that all men can share." Samad stopped and smiled. "You know we Persians are born poets. It's said we changed Sufism from mystic speculation to mystic art. All I know is the great poets of Persia found in Sufism a vehicle for their art that gave back to Islam almost more than it took. But then a poet's vocation must always be to give. I have given the people of India my heart, and they have loved me in return. Yet such love engenders envy in the minds of men who know it not. The Shi'ite mullahs would have condemned me for heresy long ago were it not for one man, a man who has understood and protected me. The only man in India who is not afraid of the Persian Shi'ites at court. And now he too is gone. With him went my life."

"And who was that?"

"Can you not guess? You have already met him." Samad smiled. "Prince Jadar."

Hawksworth suddenly felt as though the world had closed about him.

"Why did you contrive to get me here tonight?"

"Because I wished to see you. And I can no longer walk abroad. It has been forbidden on pain of death. But death is something I am almost ready to welcome. One day soon I will walk the streets of Agra once more, for the last time."

Hawksworth wondered if the claim was bravado, or truth.

"But why did you want to see me?" Hawksworth studied Samad closely. Suddenly he decided to ask the question directly. "To ask me to help Jadar? You can tell him for me that I want no part of his politics. I'm here to get a trade agreement, a *firman*. That's my mission, why I was sent."

Samad settled his wineglass on the carpet with a sigh of resignation. "You've heard nothing I have said. I am telling you it would be best for you to forget about your 'mission.' Your destiny is no longer in your hands. But if you will open your heart, you will find it has riches to compensate you manyfold. Still, they can be yours only if you can know love. But now, I fear, the only love you know is self-love, ambition. You have not yet understood it is empty as a mirror.

> *"The world is but a waking dream,*
> *The eye of heart sees clear,*
> *The garden of this tempting world,*
> *Is wrought of sand and tear."*

Hawksworth shifted and stared about the room. It was darker now but several men had entered. Few of them seemed to understand Samad's Turki.

"So what do I do now?"

"Stay with us for a while. Learn to know yourself." Samad rose and stepped off the dais. "Perhaps then you will at last find what you want."

He motioned for Hawksworth to walk with him to the balcony. Across the courtyard a single lamp burned in the turret of one of the buildings. "Tonight must be remembered as a dream, my English. And like a dream, it is to be recalled on waking as mere light and shadow." He turned and led Hawksworth to the door. The men stood aside for them. "And now I bid you farewell. Others will attend you."

Hawksworth walked into the marble corridor.

Standing in the half light, her face warm in the glow of a lamp, was Shirin.

CHAPTER TWENTY-ONE

The night sky above the courtyard was afire, an overturned jewel box strewn about an ivory moon. They passed through a gateway of carved columns and ornate brackets, into a smaller plaza. The mosque was left behind: around them now were empty pavilions, several stories high, decorated with whimsical carvings, railings, cornices. Now they were alone in the abandoned palace, surrounded by silence and moonlight. Only then did she speak, her voice opening through the stillness.

"I promised to think of you, and I have, more than you can know. Tonight I want to share this with you. The private palace of the Great Akman. The most beautiful place in all India." She paused and pointed to a wide marble pond in the middle of the plaza. In its center was a platform, surrounded by a railing and joined to the banks by delicate bridges. "They say when Akman's court musician, the revered Tansen, sat there and sang a raga for the rainy season, the clouds themselves would come to listen, and bless the earth with their tears. Once all this was covered by one magnificent canopy. Tonight we have only the stars."

"How did you arrange this?" He still was lost in astonishment.

"Don't ask me to tell you now. Can we just share this moment?"

She took his arm and motioned ahead. There, glistening in the moonlight, were the open arcades of a palace pavilion. "I've prepared something especially for us." She guided him through a wide open archway and into a large arcade, illuminated by a single oil lamp atop a stone table. In front of them, on the walls, were brilliantly colored renderings of elephants, horses, birds. She picked up the lamp and led him past the paintings and into the next room, a vast red chamber whose floor was a fragrant standing pool of water. In the flickering light he could see a marble stairway leading to a red sandstone platform projecting out over the water, supported by square stone columns topped by ornate brackets.

"This is where Akman spent the hot summer nights. Up there, on the platform, above a cooling pool of rosewater. From there he would summon his women to come to him from the *zenana*."

Hawksworth dipped his fingers into the water and brought it to his lips. It was like perfume. He turned to her and she smiled.

"Yes, the Sufis still keep rosewater here, in memory of Akman." She urged him forward, up the stairs. "Come and together we'll try to imagine how it must have felt to be the *Great Moghul* of India."

As they emerged onto the platform, the vaulted ceilings above them glowed a ruby red from the lamp. Under their feet was a thick carpet, strewn with small velvet bolsters. At the farthest edge was a large sleeping couch, fashioned from red marble, its dark velvet canopy held aloft by four finely worked stone columns. The covering of the couch was a patterned blue velvet, bordered in gold lace.

"Just for tonight I've made this room like it was when Akman slept here, with his chosen from the *zenana*." She slipped the gauze wrap from her shoulders. He looked at her dark hair, secured with a transparent scarf and a strand of pearls, and realized it contrasted perfectly with the green emerald brooch that swung gently against her forehead. She wore a necklace of pearl strands and about each upper arm was a band ringed with pearl drops. Her eyes and eyebrows were painted dark with kohl and her lips were a brilliant red.

Without a word she took a garland of yellow flowers from the bed and gently slipped it over his head. Next to the couch was a round rosewood table holding several small brass vials of perfume and incense. "Tonight this room is like a bridal chamber. For us."

A second garland of flowers lay on the bed next to the one she had taken. Without thinking, he reached and took it and slipped it around her neck. Then he drew his fingertips slowly down her arm, sending a small shiver through them both. Seeing her in the lamplight, he realized again how he had ached for her.

"A wedding? For us?"

"Not a wedding. Can we just call it a new beginning? The end of one journey and the beginning of another."

Hawksworth heard a sudden rustling behind him and then a sound. He turned and searched the gloom, where two eyes peered out of the darkness, reflecting the lamplight. He was reaching for his pistol when she stopped his arm.

"That's one of the little green parrots who live here. They've never been harmed, and they've never been caged. So they're unafraid." She turned and called to it. "If they're caught and imprisoned, their spirit dies and their beauty starts to fade."

The bird ruffled its wings again and flew to the top of the bolster beside

Shirin. Hawksworth watched her for a moment, still incredulous, then settled himself on the carpet next to a chalice of wine that sat waiting. She
reached and touched his arm. "I never asked you what your lovers call you.
You're so important, nobody in India knows your first name, just your titles."

"My only other name is Brian." He found her touch had already begun
to stir him.

"Brian. Will you tell me everything about you, what you like and what
you don't?" She began to pour the wine for them. "Did I ever tell you what
I like most about you?"

"In Surat you said you liked the fact I was a European. Who always
had to be master of worldly things."

"Well, I've thought about you a lot since then." Her expression grew
pensive. "I've decided it's not so simple. There's a directness about you, and
an openness, an honesty, that's very appealing."

"That's European. We're not very good at intrigue. What we're thinking always shows on our face."

She laughed. "And I think I know what you're thinking right now. But
let me finish. I feel I must tell you this. There's something else about you
that may also be European, but I think it's just your special quality. You're
always ready to watch and learn from what you see. Looking for new things
and new ideas. Is that also European?"

"I think it probably is."

"It's rare here. Most Indians think everything they have and everything
they do is absolutely perfect, exactly the way it is. They might take something foreign and use it, or copy it, but they always have to appear disdainful
of anything not Indian."

"You're right. I'm always being told everything here is better." He
reached for her. "Sometimes it's even true."

"Won't you let me tell you the rest?" She took his hand and held it. "I
also think you have more concern for those around you than most Indians
do. You respect the dignity of others, regardless of their station, something
you'll seldom see here, particularly among the high castes. And there's a
kindness about you too. I feel it when you're with me." She laughed again.
"You know, it's a tragic thing about Muslim men. They claim to honor
women; they write poems to their beauty; but I don't think they could ever
truly *love* a woman. They believe she's a willful thing whom it's their duty
to contain."

She paused, then continued. "But you're so very different. It's hard to
comprehend you sometimes. You love your European music, but now I
think you're starting to understand and love the music of India. I even heard
you're learning the sitar. You're sensitive to all beauty, almost the way
Samad is. It makes me feel very comfortable with you. But you're also a lot

like Prince Jadar. You're not afraid of risks. You guide your own destiny. Instead of just accepting whatever happens, the way most Indians do." She smiled and traced her fingers down his chest. "That part makes you very exciting."

She hesitated again. "And do you know what I like least about you? It's the *feringhi* clothes you wear."

He burst into laughter. "Tell me why."

"They're so . . . undignified. When I first saw you, that night you came to Mukarrab Khan's palace, I couldn't believe you could be anyone of importance. Then the next morning, at the observatory, you looked like a nobleman. Tonight, you're dressed like a *feringhi* again."

"I like boots and a leather jerkin. When I'm wearing a fancy doublet and hose, then I feel I have to be false, false as the clothes. And when I dress like a Moghul, I always wonder if people think I'm trying to be something I'm not."

"All right." She smiled resignedly. "But perhaps sometime tonight you'll at least take off your leather jerkin. I would enjoy seeing you."

He looked at her in wonderment. "I still don't understand you at all. You once said you thought I was powerful. But you seem to be pretty powerful yourself. Nobody I know could force Mukarrab Khan or Nadir Sharif to do anything. Yet you made the governor divorce you, and then you made the prime minister deceive half of Agra to arrange this. You're so many different things."

"Don't forget. Sometimes I'm also a woman."

She rose and began to slowly draw out the long cinch holding the waist of her wrap. Her halter seemed to trouble her as she tried to loosen it. She laughed at her own awkwardness, and then it too came away. She was left with only her jewels and the long scarf over her hair, which she did not remove. Then she turned to him.

"Do you still remember our last night in Surat?"

"Do you?" He looked at her in the dim lamplight. The line of her body was flawless, with gently rounded breasts, perfect thighs, legs lithe yet strong.

"I remember what I felt when I kissed you."

He laughed and moved to take her in his arms. "But I thought *I* was the one who kissed you."

"Maybe we should try it once more and decide." With a mischievous look she caught his arms and wrapped herself around him. As he touched her lips, she turned abruptly and the world suddenly seemed to twist crazily around them, sending his head spinning. In shock he opened his mouth to speak and it was flooded with the essence of rose.

The pool beneath the platform had broken their fall. He came up gasping and found her lips.

She tasted of another world. Sweet, fragrant. He enclosed her slowly in his arms, clasping her lean body gently at first; then feeling more and more of her warmth he pressed her to him, both of them still gasping. They seemed to float, weightless, serene in the darkness. Awkwardly he began pulling away his wet jerkin.

"You're just as I imagined." Her hands traveled across his chest, lightly caressing his skin, while the lamp flickered against the paintings on the walls above them. "There's a strength about you, a roughness." She nuzzled his chest with her face. "Tonight will you let me be your poet?"

"Tonight you can be anything you want."

"I want to sing of you—a man I adore—of the desire I feel for you. After we know each other fully, the great longing will be gone. The most intense moment we can ever share will be past. The ache of wanting."

"What you just said reminds me of something John Donne once wrote."

"Who is he?"

"One of our English poets and songwriters. But he had a slightly different idea." He hesitated, then smiled. "To tell the truth, I think I may like his better."

She lifted herself up in the water, rose petals patterned across her body. "Then tell me what he said."

"It's the only poem of his I can still remember, but only the first verse. For some reason I'll never forget it. I sometimes think of it when I think of you. Let me say it in English first and then try to translate.

"I wonder, by my troth, what thou and I
Did, till we lov'd? Were we not wean'd till then?
But suck'd on country pleasures, childishly?
Or snorted we in the Seven Sleepers' den?
'Twas so; but this, all pleasures fancies be;
If ever any beauty I did see,
Which I desir'd, and got, 'twas but a dream of thee."

She listened to the hard English rhythm and then to his translation, awkward and halting. Then she was silent for a moment, floating her hand across the surface of the pond.

"You know, I also wonder now what I did before I met you. Before I held you."

She slipped her hands about his neck, and as she did he drew her up out of the water and cradled her against him. Then he lifted her, her body still strewn with rose petals, and carried her slowly up the marble stairs to the couch of Akman. He felt her cling to him like no woman ever had, and as he placed her on the bed, she took his face in her hands and kissed him for a long moment. Then he heard her whisper.

"Tonight we will know just each other. And there will be nothing else."

And they gave each to each until there was nothing more to give because each *was* the other. Together, complete.

He was on the quarterdeck, the whipstaff aching against his hand, the mainsail furled as storm winds lashed the waist of the ship with wave after powerful wave. The ship was the *Queen's Hope*, his vessel when he sailed for the Levant Company, and the rocks that towered off his starboard bow were Gibraltar. He shouted into the dark for the quartermaster to reef the tops'ls, and he leaned on the whipstaff to bring her about, but neither responded. He had no crew. He was being swept, helpless, toward the empty darkness that lay ahead. Another wave caught him across the face, and somewhere in the dark came a screech, as though the sea had given up some dying Leviathan beast. His seaboots were losing their hold on the quarterdeck, and now the whipstaff had grown sharp talons that cut into his hand. Then a woman's voice, a distant siren calling him. Again the screech and then yet another wave cut across his face.

The water tasted of roses.

He jerked violently awake. On his hand a green parrot was perched, preening itself and ruffling its feathers. And from the pool below Shirin was flinging handfuls of water up over the side of the platform, laughing as she tried to splash his face.

She was floating, naked, below him, her hair streaming out across the surface of the water, tangled among the drifting rose petals. He looked about and saw his own wet clothes, mingled among her silks and jewels. For a moment he felt again the terror of the dream, the rudderless ship impelled by something beyond control, and then he caught the edge of the platform and slipped over the side.

The water was cool against his skin and involuntarily he caught his breath. Then he reached out and wrapped her in his arms, pulling her against him. She turned her face to his, twined her hair around his head, and crushed his lips with her own. Just as suddenly, she threw back her head and laughed with joy. He found himself laughing with her.

"Why don't we both just stay? I don't have to be back in Agra until the wedding. We could have a week." He studied the perfect lines of her face, the dark eyes at once defiant and anxious, and wished he could hold her forever. The Worshipful East India Company be damned.

"But we both have things we must do." She revolved in the flowered water and drew her face above his. She kissed him again, languorously. Then she drew herself out of the water and twisted a wrap around her, covering her breasts. "Both you and I."

"And what's this thing you have to do?"

Her eyes shadowed. "One thing I must try to do is convince Samad he cannot stay here any longer. He has to go south, where Prince Jadar can protect him. But he refuses to listen. And time is growing short now. I truly fear for what may happen to him after the wedding. The Persian Shi'ite mullahs will certainly be powerful enough then to demand he be tried and executed on charges of heresy. For violating some obscure precept of Islamic law. It will be the end for him." She paused. "And for anyone who has helped him."

"Then if he won't leave, at least you should." He lifted himself out of the water and settled beside her on the marble paving. "Why don't you come back to England with me? When the fleet from Bantam makes landfall at Surat, Arangbar will surely have the courage to sign the *firman,* and then my mission will be finished. It should only be a matter of weeks, regardless of what the Portugals try to do."

She studied the water of the pool with sadness in her eyes and said nothing for a moment as she kicked the surface lightly.

"Neither of us is master of what will happen. Things are going to soon be out of control. For both of us. Things are going to happen that you will not understand."

Hawksworth squinted through the half light. "What's going to happen?"

"Who can know? But I would not be surprised to see the prince betrayed totally, in one final act that will eventually destroy him. He is too isolated. Too weak. And when that happens we're all doomed. Even you, though I don't think you'll believe that now."

"Why should I? I'm not betting on Prince Jadar. I agree with you. I don't think he has a chance. I'm betting on a *firman* from Arangbar, and soon."

"You'll never get a *firman* from the *Moghul.* And Arangbar will be gone in half a year. The queen has already started appearing at morning *darshan* and directing his decisions at afternoon *durbar.* As soon as she has Allaudin under her control, Arangbar will be finished. Mark it. He'll die from too much opium, or from some mysterious poison or accident. He will cease to exist, to matter."

"I don't believe it. He seems pretty well in control."

"If that's what you think, then you are very deceived. He can't live much longer. Everyone knows it. Perhaps even he knows it in his heart. Soon he will give up even the appearance of rule. Then the queen will take full command of the Imperial army, and Prince Jadar will be hunted down like a wild boar."

He studied her, not sure he could reasonably contradict her, and felt his stomach knot. "What will happen to you, if the queen takes over?"

"I don't know. But I do know I love you. I truly do. How sad it makes me that I can't tell you everything." Her eyes darkened and she took his hand. "Please understand I did not know the prince would use you the way he has. But it is for good. Try to believe that."

"What do you mean?"

She hesitated and looked away. "Let me ask you this. What do *you* think the prince will do after the wedding?"

"I don't know, but I think he'd be very wise to keep clear of Agra. Nobody at court will even talk about him now, at least not openly. Still, I think he might be able to stay alive if he's careful. If he survives the campaign in the Deccan, maybe he can bargain something out of the queen. But I agree with you about one thing. She can finish him any time she wants. I understand she already has *de facto* control of the Imperial army, in Arangbar's name of course. What can Jadar do? He's outnumbered beyond any reasonable odds. Maybe she'll make him a governor in the south if he doesn't challenge her."

"Do you really believe he'd accept that? Can't you see that's impossible? You've met Prince Jadar. Do you think he'll just give up? That's the one thing he'll never do. He has a son now. The people will support him." She pulled herself next to him. "I feel so isolated and hopeless just thinking about it all. I'm so glad Nadir Sharif brought you here."

He slipped his arm around her. "So am I. Will you tell me now how you managed to make him do it?"

"I still have friends left in Agra." She smiled. "And Nadir Sharif still has a few indiscretions he'd like kept buried. Sometimes he can be persuaded . . ."

"Did he know Samad was here?"

"If he didn't before, he does now. But he won't say anything. Anyway, it hardly matters any more. The queen probably already knows Samad's here." She sighed. "The worst is still waiting. For him. And for both of us."

He caught a handful of water and splashed it against her thigh. "Then let's not talk about it. Until tomorrow."

The worry in her eyes seemed to dissolve and she laughed. "Do you realize how much you've changed since I first met you? You were as stiff as a Portuguese Jesuit then, before Kali and Kamala got their painted fingernails into you. Kali, the lover of the flesh, and Kamala, the lover of the spirit." She glared momentarily. "Now I must take care, lest you start comparing me with them. Never forget. I'm different. I believe love should be both."

He pulled her away and looked at her face. "I'm amazed by how different you are. I still have no idea what you're really like. What you really think."

"About what?"

"Anything. Everything." He shrugged. "About this even."

"You mean being here with you? Making love with you?"

"That's a perfect place to start."

She smiled and eased back in the water, silently toying for a moment with the rose petals drifting around her. "I think making love with someone is how we share our deepest feelings. Things we can't express any other way. It's how I tell you my love for you." She paused. "The way music or poetry reveal the soul of the one who creates them."

"Are you saying you think lovemaking is like creating music?" He examined her, puzzling.

"They both express what we feel inside."

He lifted up a handful of water and watched it trickle back into the pool. "I've never thought of it quite like that before."

"Why not? It's true. Before you can create music, you have to teach both your body *and* your heart. It's the same with making love."

"What do you mean?"

She reached and touched his thigh. "When we're very young, lovemaking is mostly just desire. We may think it's more, but it isn't really. Then gradually we learn more of its ways, how to give and receive. But even then we still don't fully understand its deeper significance. We're like a novice who has learned the techniques of the sitar, the way to strike and pull a string to make one note blend into another, but who still doesn't comprehend the spiritual depth of a raga. Its power to move our heart. We still don't understand that its meaning and feeling can only come from within. And love, like a raga, is an expression of reverence and of wonder. Wonder at what we are and can be. So even after all the techniques are mastered, we still must learn to experience this wonder, this sense of our spirit becoming one with the other. Otherwise it's somehow still empty. Like perfect music that has no feeling, no life."

He was silent for a moment, trying to comprehend what she was saying. "If you look at it like that, I suppose you could be right."

"With music, we first have to learn its language, then learn to open our spirit. Lovemaking is just the same."

She nestled her head against his chest, sending her warmth through him. As he held her, he noticed lying alongside the pool the garland of flowers she had worn the night before. He reached and took it and slipped it over her head. Then he kissed her gently, finding he was indeed filled with wonder at the feeling he had for her.

He held her silently for a time, looking at the paintings on the walls of the palace around them. Then he noticed a large straw basket at the entryway.

"What is that?" He pointed.

She rose and looked. "I think it's something Samad had left for us."

She lifted herself out of the water and, holding her wrap against her, brought the basket. It was filled with fruits and melons.

"They're not from Samarkand or Kabul, like you've probably grown accustomed to at the palace in Agra. But I think you'll like them anyway." She squinted across the square, in the direction of the mosque. "I love Samad dearly. He did all of this for me. But he refuses to listen to anything I say." She handed him an apple, then reached and took some grapes. "You know, I think he secretly wants to die a martyr. Like a lover eager to die for his or her beloved. He wants to die for his wild freedom, for what he thinks is beautiful. Perhaps to be remembered as one who never bowed to anyone. I wish I had his strength."

"Where's he now?"

"You won't see him any more. But he's still here. He'll have food sent to us. He loves me like a daughter, and he's happy when I am. And he knows now you make me happy. But you mustn't see him here again, even know that he's here. It would be too dangerous for you. Perhaps someday, if we're all still alive."

He took her face in his hands and held it up to him. "You have as much strength as anyone, including Samad. And I want to get you away from here before your strength makes you do something foolish. I love you more than my own life."

"And I love you. Like I've never loved anyone."

"Not even the *Great Moghul*? When you were in his *zenana?*"

She laughed. "You know that was very different. I was scarcely more than a girl then. I didn't know anything."

"You learned a few things somewhere." He remembered the night past, still astonished. The way she had . . .

"In the *zenana* you learn everything about lovemaking. But nothing about love." She rose and took his hand. Together they walked to the open portico of the palace. Around them the red pavilions were empty in the early sunshine. The morning was still, save for the cries of the green parrots who scurried across eaves and peered down impassively from weathered red railings and banisters. His gaze followed the wide arches, then turned to her dark shining hair. He reached out and stroked it.

"Tell me more about you. How did you learn Turki?"

"In the *zenana*. We had to learn it, even though Arangbar speaks perfect Persian." She turned to him. "And how did you learn to understand it?"

"In a Turkish prison." He laughed. "It seems about the same to me. I had to learn it too."

"Will you tell me about it? Why were you in prison?"

"Like you, I had no choice. The Turks took a ship I was commanding, in the Mediterranean."

"Tell me what happened."

He stopped and looked at her. "All right. We'll trade. You tell me all about you and I'll tell you everything about me. We'll leave out nothing. Agreed?"

She reached and kissed him. "Will you begin first?"

CHAPTER TWENTY-TWO

The imminent wedding of Prince Allaudin and Princess Layla was a momentous event in the history of the Moghul empire. It represented the final merging of two dynasties. One, that of the *Moghul* Akman and his first son Arangbar, was in direct descent from the Mongols of the steppes who had conquered India by the sword less than a century before, melding under one rule a disorganized array of Muslim and Hindu states. The other dynasty, that of Queen Janahara, her Persian father Zainul Beg, her brother Nadir Sharif, and now her daughter Layla, represented a very different kind of conqueror. At court they were called, always in whispers, the "Persian junta."

Whereas no combination of forces indigenous to India—even the recalcitrant Rajput warrior chieftains of the northwest—had ever succeeded in wresting power from the invading Moghuls, this extraordinary Persian family had, in one generation, come to rule India virtually as equals with the dynasty of Akman, assuming the power that the decadent Arangbar had let slowly slip away. With the marriage of Queen Janahara's daughter to the weakling son of Arangbar, a son she was carefully promoting to the role of heir-apparent, the last element in the Persian strategy would be in place. When Arangbar died, or was dethroned, the powerful line of Akman, who had unified India by a blend of force and diplomatic marriages, would be supplanted by what was, in effect, a palace coup. The "Persian junta" would have positioned itself to assume effective control of India: Prince Allaudin, for so long as he was allowed to maintain even the appearance of rule, would be nothing more than a titular sovereign. Queen Janahara, together with her father and her brother, would be the real ruler of India.

The queen could, of course, have contented herself for a time longer merely to direct Arangbar from beside the throne, but that could never be entirely satisfactory. Arangbar still wielded power when he so chose, and that power could be enormous.

India had no independent judiciary, no parliament, no constitution. There was, instead and only, the word of the *Moghul*. Criminals were brought before him to be tried and sentenced. Offices of state were filled, or vacated, on his personal whim. The army marched at his word. And he owned, in effect, a large part of Indian soil, since large estates went not to heirs but returned to the *Moghul* when their current "owner" died. He granted lands and salaries as reward for loyalty and service. And he alone granted titles. Seldom in history had a land so vast, and a people so diverse, been held so absolutely under the unquestioned rule of a single hand. Queen Janahara now looked confidently forward to the day that hand would be hers.

The power Arangbar now possessed was thought by many to have brought his own undoing. Originally an introspective if sometimes whimsical sovereign—whose early memoirs were filled with scientific observations on India's fauna and flora, and statesman-like ruminations on the philosophy of governing—he had become slowly dissolute to the point of incapacity. A man who had forsworn both alcohol and drugs until well into his third decade of life, he was now hopelessly addicted to both. In consequence his judgment and instincts had grown ever more unreliable. And since all appointments of salary and place depended on his word alone, no career or fortune was truly secure. It was into this vacuum of sound leadership that the "Persian junta" of Janahara's family had moved.

The Persian junta was supported by all those at court who feared Arangbar's growing caprice, by other influential Persians, by the powerful mullahs of the Shi'ite sect of Islam, by Hindus who still harbored historic grievances against Moghul rule . . . and by the Portuguese. The "Persian junta" was not loved. But it did not need to be loved; it enjoyed an even more compelling ingredient for success: it was feared. Even those who might have preferred the succession of Prince Jadar wisely held silent. The tides of history were there for all to see.

Even Brian Hawksworth saw them.

The private palace of Zainul Beg, father of Janahara and Nadir Sharif and grandfather of Princess Layla, was more modest than that of Nadir Sharif, and its architecture more Persian, almost consciously reminiscent of the land of his birth. It lay on the banks of the Jamuna River, farther down from the palace of Nadir Sharif, and this evening it was brilliantly illuminated by bonfires along the riverside. Even the river itself was lighted. A dozen barks filled with lamps had been towed upriver from the Red Fort, and now their camphor-oil flames cast a dazzling white sheen over the pink turrets of the palace. On the opposite bank of the Jamuna, men were lighting candles and floating them in hollow clay pots across the surface of the water, where they drifted gently downstream toward the Red Fort, creating a line of illumination that would eventually stretch for miles.

Although Hawksworth's money was starting to grow short, he had used a large portion of what was left to purchase a new pair of striped Indian trousers, an expensive brocade turban, and ornate velvet slippers. He alighted from his palanquin at the palace gate looking like a Moghul grandee, to be greeted almost immediately by Zainul Beg's eunuchs and ushered into the main hall. As he entered, the eunuchs directed him toward a large silver fish stationed by the door. It was ornamented with green lapis lazuli scales and fitted with seven spouts shooting thin streams of rosewater outward into a large basin. Hawksworth was by now accustomed to this Moghul ritual, and he quickly removed his new slippers and splashed his feet in the basin to the minimal extent acceptable. Then he turned and made his way through the line of nobles reverently awaiting the arrival of Arangbar. He had become such a familiar sight at royal gatherings that his presence excited no unusual notice.

The marble walls of the hall were hung with new Persian tapestries and the floors covered with silk carpets embroidered with silver and gold. At the corners were immense vases of solid gold studded with precious stones that sparkled in the lamplight. Incense burners wrought from silver hung from the walls. Servants circulated among the crowd bearing trays of rolled betel leaves, glasses of lemony *sharbat*, and cups of green milky *bhang*. In deference to the ceremonial significance of this holy Muslim occasion, there would be no wine until after the Shi'ite mullahs had left. Hawksworth decided to take a glass of *sharbat* and wait for the wine.

He strolled through the buzzing crowd of bejeweled men and anonymous, veiled women and reflected on the bizarre ceremonies of a Moghul marriage.

His first taste had come only the previous evening, when he had been invited to the Red Fort to witness and take part in the *henna bandi* ceremony. The square just below the *Diwan-i-Khas*, where Arangbar's birthday weighing was held only two weeks before, had been cleared and made ready for the henna ceremony. Hawksworth had arrived and been granted a place near Nadir Sharif and Arangbar. The crowd was already being entertained by music and dancing women. Allaudin was there, slightly nervous in anticipation of his upcoming ordeal.

Then the procession arrived: women of the *zenana* rode into the courtyard on palanquins, in a flower-bedecked line bearing henna—a red paste extracted from the plant of the same name—and gifts sent from Layla to Allaudin. The bride was not present; she had not yet been seen by Allaudin or any of his family, including Arangbar. The women of the *zenana*, all veiled, spread before the *Moghul* the gifts that, on this night, the bride was expected to present to the bridegroom. The eunuchs bore trays which had been covered with basketwork raised in domes, over which were thrown draperies of gold cloth and brocade in a rainbow of colors. They were brought before Allaudin and Arangbar and uncovered one by one. The first tray was of beaten silver and it held a new suit for the bridegroom, a tailored cloak and trousers woven with strands of gold. Others bore gold and silver vessels containing cosmetics and toiletries—collyrium, kohl, musky perfumes —and plates of sweets, betel leaves tied with strings of gold, and a confectionary of dried fruits and preserves. The eunuchs also brought in sprays of flowers containing disguised fireworks wheels, which were ignited as they entered to create a startling, fiery garden of color.

Next the women led Allaudin to rooms behind the *Diwan-i-Khas*, where he was dressed in the new clothes provided for him by the bride. Bamboo slats were placed across the doorway to enable the *zenana* women to watch the ceremony. While he was gone, an opening was prepared in the screen separating the *zenana* from the courtyard and a low stool was placed just outside. The screen was specially constructed to allow the hands and feet of the one sitting on the stool to be reached from behind it.

When Allaudin returned, he assumed his place again beside Arangbar, shifting occasionally in mild discomfort from the stiff new clothes. It was obvious to Hawksworth that he wished to appear bored by the ceremonies, but his eyes betrayed his apprehension.

Then a eunuch approached and announced to the male assembly—Arangbar, Allaudin, Nadir Sharif, Zainul Beg, and a retinue of other men with vague ties to royal blood who were waiting at the center of the courtyard—that "the bridegroom is wanted."

"Go quickly." Arangbar pushed Allaudin toward the stool waiting in front of the screen covering the entrance to the *zenana*. "It's always a man's fate to be made the fool by his women."

Allaudin marched across the courtyard with as much dignity as his stiff new clothes allowed, and seated himself with a flourish on the stool. The air was rich with incense and music from the upper balconies. As Hawksworth and the other male guests watched, women from behind the screen ordered Allaudin to insert his hands and feet through the new holes. He was then teased and fed small lumps of sugar candy while the women behind the screen began to tie dark red cloths, soaked in a paste of moist leaves of henna, onto his hands and feet.

"This ceremony is very important, Inglish." Arangbar had beamed with satisfaction as he watched. "Henna is a charm to promote their union. The women anoint the bride with it also, in private. It will make him virile and her fertile."

As the women continued to dye Allaudin's hands and feet with the paste, musicians and singers began to entertain him. Some of the songs, all extemporary, lauded him as a prince among men, while others rhapsodized over the beauty of the bride. Listening to their songs, Hawksworth had to remind himself that none of the singers had actually seen the bride, whose beauty they now extolled as that of one woman in thousands. Then the singers sang of the impending happiness of the pair, as inevitable, they declared, as that Paradise awaiting Believers after life on earth is past.

After the women had finished their task, Allaudin turned to face the assembled men wearing a vaguely sheepish expression. Hawksworth had caught himself laughing out loud at the preposterous figure Allaudin struck, standing before them with hands and feet dripping red with henna.

Then he noticed a group of veiled women filing out from behind the screen and approaching. They carried a silver chalice filled with red henna paste. The women stopped in front of Arangbar, bowed with the *teslim*, and began to anoint his fingers with henna. Then they tied each reddened finger with a small, gold-embroidered handkerchief. He smiled widely and signaled a eunuch to bring him a ball of opium. Next the women proceeded to Zainul Beg and reddened his fingers also, then Nadir Sharif, then all the other family members. Finally they stopped in front of Hawksworth.

A robust woman from the *zenana* seized his fingers and began to daub them with henna paste. It was thick and smelled of saffron. He watched helplessly as his fingers disappeared into the red, after which they too were swathed in the small kerchiefs of silk and gold.

"It will make you virile too, Inglish. This is a great omen for your good fortune," Arangbar observed wryly, delighted by the confused look on Hawksworth's face.

The women disappeared back into the *zenana* and the music began again, now with more dancers. Hawksworth recognized among them the young woman Sangeeta, who had danced Kathak for Arangbar that first night in the *Diwan-i-Khas*. She was resplendent, and her face announced her pride in being selected for the first night of the wedding celebrations.

After she had finished her dance, the veiled women again emerged from the *zenana*, carrying a large silver vessel, and saluted Allaudin. He was brought to the center of the square, where they began to remove the red bindings on his hands and feet. His hands, then his feet, were bathed in rosewater. After they were dried, he was taken back to the *Diwan-i-Khas* and attired in yet another of the new suits of clothes given to him by the bride. He returned to the general cheers of the assembled guests, whose hands had also been washed while he was gone.

As the formal ceremonies drew to a close, Arangbar produced heavy brocade waist sashes for all the male guests. Hawksworth was last, and when he received his from Arangbar's hand, he bowed in thanks and examined it quizzically.

"It is a *kamar-band*, Inglish, for you to wear tomorrow night at the wedding." Arangbar took Hawksworth's red-stained fingers and examined them for a moment. "If you can get the rest of the henna off your fingers by then."

He roared with delight and signaled the musicians to start again. Allaudin was escorted from the square by a number of young men in foppish cloaks—Hawksworth assumed they were his friends—and then, as midnight approached, servants appeared with the evening's meal.

While the men drank and dined, Sangeeta entertained them with more Kathak dance. When she was near exhaustion, other dancers were brought out, and the music and dance continued undiminished through the short hours remaining before dawn. Only when the eastern sky began to lighten did Arangbar rise and bid the guests farewell. The courtyard cleared in moments.

As the crowd dispersed, Hawksworth watched the *Moghul* down another ball of opium and call for Sangeeta to accompany him into the palace. She was escorted by the eunuchs, her smile brighter than the rising sun.

Hawksworth was momentarily startled as a fanfare of trumpets announced to the guests in Zainul Beg's hall that Arangbar was approaching. The center of the hall cleared, leaving a pathway from the entrance to a low platform at the opposite end, on which were two large cushions fashioned from gold cloth. On some unseen command musicians in an adjacent room began to play, and then the doors of the hall opened wide.

Women from Arangbar's *zenana* entered first, sweeping past the guests in a glitter of silks and jewels unlike anything Hawksworth had ever seen. The women displayed heavy gold necklaces and multiple strands of pearls. Their arms were scarcely visible beneath their wide gold bracelets. For this evening, all wore a headdress of silver cloth and a veil.

More trumpets sounded as Arangbar himself entered, Queen Janahara striding imperiously behind him. Hawksworth examined her hard features with curiosity for a moment before the significance of the scene registered. She was not wearing a veil.

He looked about him and realized that the other guests had noticed as well.

Nadir Sharif trailed behind the royal couple, and after him came a few select officials of the court, including the *qazi* who would perform the ceremony and officially record the marriage.

As Arangbar and Janahara seated themselves on the cushioned platform, the guests all performed the *teslim*. Arangbar motioned for the crowd to be seated, and Hawksworth was already halfway to the carpet before he noticed that no one else had moved. Only after Arangbar had demanded three times that the guests seat themselves did those around Hawksworth accede to his request.

More trays of rolled betel leaves and *sharbat* were circulated, and the guests settled to listen to a lively raga performed on sitar and tabla drums by musicians who were seated on a small dais at the opposite end of the hall. The time was approaching eight o'clock when the musicians brought the music to a rousing finish.

Hawksworth found himself beginning to wonder where the bride and groom were. They were nowhere to be seen.

No sooner had the last notes of the raga melted into the tapestried walls than there came a knocking at the closed doors of the hall. There were sounds of a raucous, but not rancorous, argument. Everyone around Hawksworth fell silent to listen. There were more words, and he managed to grasp that the family of the bride was demanding a payment for entry, apparently a mock ritual. Finally there was the jingle of coins dropping into a cup. The money seemed to settle the dispute, for the doors of the hall suddenly burst open, to the sounds of a trumpet fanfare.

Hawksworth looked through the doorway to see a horse and rider, surrounded by a milling crowd.

In the lamplight he could see the horse was covered with a fine brocade tapestry, into which fresh flowers had been woven. Its legs, tail, and mane had been dyed red with henna, and all its body outside the tapestry was covered with glistening spangles. The rider's cloak and turban were heavy with gold thread, and his face was hidden behind a thick veil of silver cloth attached to the top of his turban and hanging to his waist. On either side of the horse two young men stood, each carrying a large paper umbrella, which they held over the rider's head. Behind them clustered singers, dancers, musicians, and a mob of tipsy young men in extravagant finery.

The crowd cheered the veiled rider and he saluted them. From the chatter of the guests, Hawksworth gathered that the horse had led a procession through the streets of Agra for the past two hours in preparation for this grand entrance.

The rider, whom Hawksworth assumed to be Prince Allaudin, was helped onto the back of one of the young men. He was carried to the dais where Arangbar and Janahara sat and gently lowered to the ground. The silver veil was removed and he performed the *teslim*, the fatigue in his face beginning to show.

Arangbar beckoned him to rise, and two eunuchs who had been part of the *Moghul*'s train stepped forward and placed two large silver boxes beside him on the dais. Arangbar opened the first and drew out a string of large pearls. He admired them for a moment, showed them to Janahara, then looped them around Allaudin's neck. Next he opened the other box and drew out a crown of silver trimmed in gold. He rose to his feet and held it aloft.

"Two months past I presented a *sachaq*, a marriage present, of two *lakhs* of silver rupees to honor the bride. And tonight I bestow on my son the same *sehra*, the same bridegroom's crown, that was placed on my head the night I wed Her Majesty, Queen Janahara."

Allaudin slipped off his turban and knelt before Arangbar. After the crown was fitted, he stood erect to acknowledge the cheers of the crowd.

Without further ceremony, Arangbar turned and spoke to Zainul Beg.

The old *wazir* beckoned two eunuchs forward and passed an order. There were shouts, and torches were lighted in the upper balcony of the hall. Then, as Hawksworth watched in amazement, the tapestries at the far end of the hall were drawn away, opening the pavilion to the riverfront.

Arangbar and Janahara revolved on their cushions to face the water, which was now a sea of floating candles and lamps. The guests surged forward toward the opening, and as Hawksworth passed near the royal dais, Arangbar's voice cut through the din.

"Inglish, come and join us. There will be no henna on your fingers tonight." He gestured toward the carpet near his feet. "Sit here. I would have your opinion of this."

"Thank you, Your Majesty." Hawksworth sensed that Arangbar was already partly drunk. "What will happen now?"

"Just more tradition, Inglish, but the part I always enjoy most." He pointed toward the river, where servants were carrying torches in the direction of three decorated wheels, each several feet across, mounted atop what appeared to be small-gauge cannon. "Tell me if your king has anything to equal this."

As he spoke the servants touched the torches to the center of each wheel. Lines of burning sulfur traced their spokes, then ignited the squibs attached around their perimeter. At that instant, other servants stepped forward and thrust a burning taper to the touchhole of each cannon. The cannon spewed flame, lofting the wheels upward over the river. They suddenly began to rotate, creating a whirling circle of colored flame tips in the night sky. Just as they reached the top of their trajectory, they began to explode one by one, showering sparks and fire across the face of the Jamuna.

The turbaned crowd scarcely had time to exclaim its delight before a blue flame suddenly appeared from behind where the wheels had been, illuminating the palace walls in a shimmering, ghostly light. As it grew, Hawksworth realized it was an artificial tree whose branches were saturated with black powder and brimstone. Next more flames spewed from the tops of five towers that had been erected near the riverfront. There were sharp reports, as though a musket had been fired, and dense streaks of red billowed into the sky. All around powder pots began to explode, hurtling lightning, dazzling white with camphor, and writhing serpents of flame into the smoky night air.

"Well, Inglish, what do you think?" Arangbar turned to Hawksworth with a delighted smile. "Have you ever seen anything to compare?"

"We have fireworks in England too, Your Majesty, particularly on the eve of St. John's Day, when we have barges of fireworks on the Thames. And sometimes they're used in plays and pageants. And at the wedding of His Majesty's daughter, four of King James's gunners gave a show with a fiery castle, a dragon, a damsel, and St. George. But English fireworks generally make more noise than these." Hawksworth paused, wondering how much to tell. "And some countries in Europe use fireworks in battle, Majesty. Helmets that throw fire, swords and lances with fiery points, and bucklers that give out flames when struck.

Arangbar gave him a puzzled glance. "But what good are those, Inglish? In battle the most important use of flame is the fire lance. What use are sparking swords? Watch and you will see what I mean."

Arangbar pointed to a line of Rajput marksmen, carrying horn bows and heavy spears, who had assembled at one side of the clearing. While they fell into a formation perpendicular to the river, servants were placing clay pots on small stands at the opposite side, perhaps seventy yards away. The Rajputs watched impassively as the arrows in their bows were lighted, and then on the shout of their commander they lifted their bows and fired in unison.

Ten streaks of flame shot across the riverfront, and the crowd fell expectantly silent. All the arrows seemed to reach their target at precisely the same instant. Each had been aimed at a separate pot, and as they impacted, the silence was rent by what sounded like a single explosion. The pots, Hawksworth realized, had been primed with powder, ready to detonate.

The smoke was still drifting across the grounds when torch carriers with large flambeaux moved to the center, illuminating scaffolding that had been hastily erected. More clay pots, painted white, hung suspended from the scaffolds on long ropes. The servants set the pots swinging and then fell back, while the Rajputs ignited the tips of their spears.

Again flame streaked across the clearing and again there was a simultaneous explosion as the spears caught the swinging pots.

Arangbar joined the cheers, then turned and slapped Hawksworth on the shoulder. "That, Inglish, is how you use fire in battle. You must put it where you want it. No soldier of India would be daunted by trick swords and bucklers."

"My king agrees with you, Majesty. He leaves such toys to the Germans."

The display continued for almost an hour, as one exotic device after another was carried next to the riverfront. The water became littered with burning paper and the air so dense with smoke that Queen Janahara finally started to cough. Arangbar immediately ordered an end to the fireworks, and as the crowd filed back into the hall, the tapestries were lowered to again conceal the smoky view of the river.

Now the music began, and the dancing, as musicians and women moved to the center of the hall. Servants circulated with more betel leaves and *sharbat*, and Arangbar took his first ball of opium.

Hawksworth glanced guardedly at the queen. Her manner was imperious, regal, everything a sovereign should be. Everything Allaudin was not. And, he thought, probably a lot Arangbar himself is not.

She'll soon have India by the *cojones*, not a doubt on it. And then it's farewell Jadar. And probably farewell Arangbar too. Will I get a signed *firman* for trade before it's too late?

As midnight neared, the music and dance were suddenly interrupted by trumpets and a drum roll and shouts of "the bride comes." The curtains covering a large doorway leading into the palace were drawn open, and a closed palanquin was brought in by four eunuchs. It was accompanied by veiled women singing something Hawksworth did not understand. The palanquin was carried to the center of the room, where a low platform covered with gold brocade had been positioned, and then the eunuchs lowered it to the marble floor. The curtains were drawn aside and a veiled woman emerged, her small body almost smothered in a dress that seemed made of multiple layers of beaten gold. She was helped to the middle of the platform, still wearing a veil that covered her entire face. Chants of "Hail to the bride" arose on all sides.

Then Allaudin was escorted forward, taking his place on the platform beside her. He stole a quick, distasteful glance at the veiled figure beside him, then an official smile illuminated his face and he sat patiently as the *qazi* was summoned in front of them. The official was bearded, stern-faced, and transparently arrogant. He stood before the veiled bride and motioned around him for silence.

"Is it by your own consent that this marriage take place with Prince Allaudin, son of His Royal Majesty?"

From beneath the layers of the veil came a muffled, almost hesitant, "It is by my consent."

The *qazi* seemed satisfied and began reading a passage from the Quran, informing her that marriage depends on three circumstances: the assent of the bride and groom, the evidence of two witnesses, and the marriage settlement. He then turned to Allaudin and asked him to name the sum he brought.

Allaudin mumbled a figure that Hawksworth did not catch, but then the *qazi* repeated it for the guests. Hawksworth caught his breath when he realized the amount named was fifty *lakhs* of rupees. Then Allaudin said something else, which the *qazi* did not repeat.

Later Hawksworth learned that Allaudin had added he was giving only ten *lakhs* of rupees then, and the balance at some indefinite future time.

The *qazi* blessed the royal pair, praying that they would be blissful in this world and in eternity, and then wrote something quickly in a book he carried. Finally the eunuchs appeared again and assisted the bride into the palanquin. The marriage ceremony seemed to be over.

A glass of wine was placed in Hawksworth's hand, and he looked up to see Arangbar beaming with satisfaction.

"Now we drink, Inglish. Come, sit closer and help me toast the bridegroom."

"It was truly a royal wedding, Your Majesty."

"But it's not over, Inglish." Arangbar roared with laughter. "The hardest part is yet to come. Does my son have the strength to complete the work he's offered to undertake? No one can leave until we're sure."

Hawksworth had begun his third glass of wine when Princess Layla reappeared, wearing a lighter dress, though still resplendent. Behind her eunuchs carried several palanquins piled high with vessels and trays of silver. Following them were servants bearing bundles on their heads.

"Those are the wares she brings to the marriage, Inglish, and her servants. I think she will make him a good wife."

The royal pair moved together, Layla still veiled, and then Queen Janahara stepped down from the dais and took a large mirror handed her by a turbaned eunuch. She walked to the couple and stopped directly in front of them. As they stood facing her, she held the mirror before Allaudin and reached to lift Layla's veil, giving him his first glimpse of his bride.

Hawksworth studied her with curiosity. She was plain. And she looked very frightened.

"It's auspicious, Inglish, if his first sight of his bride is in a mirror. I have not seen her before either." Arangbar examined her for a moment, then turned to Nadir Sharif. "What do you think? Should I buy him another one for his *bed?*"

"She's a goddess of beauty, Majesty. Inspiration for a poet."

"Is that what you think?" Arangbar sipped pensively from his cup. "Well, perhaps it's true. We'll discover soon enough if she inspires her groom."

The guests watched as Allaudin and Layla were helped into a large palanquin. In moments their procession was winding out of the palace, followed by Layla's household silver, to a great fanfare of drums and trumpets and the shouts of servants.

"Peace on the Prophet!"

"There is no nobility but the nobility of Mohammed!"

"Allah be with Him, the noblest, the purest, the highest!"

Hawksworth settled back against his bolster and realized groggily that it was already past two o'clock in the morning.

When the wedding procession had disappeared from view, the jubilant servants immediately turned to preparations for the banquet.

"Sometimes life can be sweet, Inglish." Arangbar leaned back against a bolster and pinched Janahara's hand. "I think he should have more wives. You know there's a saying in India: 'A man should have four wives: A Persian to have someone to talk to; a Khurasani to keep his house; a big-breasted Hindu from the South to nurse his children; and a Bengali to whip, as a warning to the other three.' So far he has only the Persian."

Hawksworth noticed that Janahara did not join in the general laughter. Then Arangbar took another drink and turned to Hawksworth.

"But you know I don't entirely agree with that wisdom, Inglish. The Holy Prophet, on whom be peace, wisely realized a man needs more than one wife. He also demanded of us that we give each of them equal attention, never to turn away from any one of them. What man can do that, even with Allah's help? It is never possible. So we all do the best we can. It is the will of Allah." Arangbar paused to swallow a ball of *affion* as he watched the trays of lamb being placed before them. "Tell me, Inglish, have you found a wife for yourself yet?"

"Not as yet, Your Majesty." He paused. "There are so many to choose."

"Then take more than one, Inglish." Arangbar washed down the opium.

"It's not allowed for a Christian, Majesty."

"Then become a Muslim." Arangbar smiled and took another sip from his glass. "Are you circumcised, Inglish?"

"Majesty?"

"Never mind." Arangbar laughed out loud. "Neither am I. How are the mullahs to know? My father, Akman, actually wanted to start his own religion, combining the wisdom of India, Persia, and the West. He thought circumcision was an absurd practice. You know, there was once a *feringhi* here, I believe he was Portuguese, who decided to become a Muslim, a True Believer. Apparently he had found a Muslim woman he wanted to marry, and her father declared she could never marry a Christian. So he had himself circumcised." Arangbar paused dramatically. "And immediately bled to death. But doubtless he was healed by the time he reached Paradise. Perhaps he made up there for what he missed here." Arangbar chuckled and took a sip of wine. Hawksworth noticed that Queen Janahara was trying with great difficulty to retain her pleased expression. "Do you believe there is a Paradise after death, Inglish?"

"What man can say, Majesty? No one has returned from death to tell what he found. I think life is best lived in the present."

"I've always believed the same, Inglish. And I've lived as few men on Allah's earth have lived." Arangbar settled himself against his bolster and reached for another glass. He was starting to grow visibly tipsy. "I now enjoy all Allah could possibly grant to a living man. There is nothing on earth I cannot have. And yet, do you know, I still have many griefs. Show me the man whose heart is free of grief." He took a piece of lamb from a dish and washed it down. "So I find my greatest happiness with wine. Like a low-caste camel driver. Why must I still endure sorrow, Inglish?"

"We all are mortal, Majesty."

"That we are, Inglish. But I will soon see this Paradise, if it exists. I will find out the truth soon enough. And when I'm finally wise, who will then come after me? Now my sons practically war among themselves. Someday, Inglish, I fear they may decide to war against me as well. And what of those I see around me? Do they think I am blind to their deceit?" Arangbar leaned farther back on the bolster. Nadir Sharif sat listening, rolling a ball of lamb between his fingers. "Sometimes I think you may be the only honest man left in India, Inglish. You are the only one who has ever dared refuse to *teslim*. It is only with the greatest forbearance that I do not order you hanged."

"I thank Your Majesty." Hawksworth took a decanter and poured more wine into Arangbar's glass before replenishing his own.

"No, Inglish, instead you should thank your Christian God. If He listens to you. But sometimes I wonder. I've heard you called a heretic more than once."

"And I have names for the Jesuits, Your Majesty. Would you care to hear them?"

"No, Inglish. Frankly, I have names for them too. But tell me, what am I to do to find peace?" Arangbar lowered his voice, but only slightly. "I see around me an army of sycophants, *nautch* women dressed as men. Whom dare I trust? You know, my own people were once warriors, Mongols of the steppes. They knew that the only ties that last are blood. And that's why this wedding cheers me. It is blood to blood." Arangbar turned and again touched Janahara's hand. Her face was expressionless as she accepted the gesture. "The only person in India I dare trust completely is my own queen. She is the only one who cannot, will not deceive me. Never. I feel it is true, as I feel nothing else in life. Nothing else."

Janahara's face remained a mask as Arangbar drank again. Nadir Sharif was watching wordlessly, his face beginning to turn noticeably grim. Hawksworth realized he had not been mentioned.

"I have loved her since I was a youth, Inglish," Arangbar continued, his voice growing maudlin. "And she has never betrayed my trust. That's the reason I would do anything she asked me. Anything, anytime. I always know it is right."

Hawksworth found himself marveling as he glanced at Janahara's calculating eyes.

I'd not trust her with two pence. He must be God's own fool.

Arangbar sat silent for a moment, savoring his own pronouncement, then he turned to Janahara and spoke to her in a dull slur.

"Ask something of me. Let me prove to the Inglish that I can never deny you."

Janahara turned as though she had not been listening. Hawksworth knew she had been straining for every word.

"What could I ask, Majesty? You have given me all I could ever want. Tonight you even gave me a husband for my daughter. Now I can die with the peace of Allah."

"But I must give you something." He settled his wine cup shakily on the carpet, jostling red splashes across the Persian design. "You must name it."

"But there is nothing I could ask that I do not already have."

"Sometimes you vex me with your good nature. The Inglish will now suspect the *Moghul* of India is a vain braggart." He fumbled with his turban, trying to detach the large blue sapphire attached to the front. "I will give you a jewel, even though you have not asked it."

"I beg Your Majesty." She reached to stay his hand. "There is nothing more I could ever want."

"But I must give you something."

She smiled in defeat. "If you must bestow a present, why not give something to the bride and groom? This is their wedding, not mine."

"Then at least you must name it. It will be my gift to you through them." He turned to Hawksworth. "Whatever else you do, Inglish, never marry a Persian. They forever study to try your patience."

Hawksworth noticed Nadir Sharif's eyes harden as he listened. He slowly gripped the side of his bolster and absently pulled away a piece of gold fringe.

"Then give them a small token, to show your confidence in Allaudin."

"I asked you to name it."

"Very well. Perhaps you could grant him the royal *jagirs* in Dholpur, those closest to Agra."

Arangbar's sleepy eyes widened slightly.

"Those *jagirs* always go to the prince nearest the throne. I granted them only last year to Prince Jadar, as part of his price to undertake the campaign in the Deccan."

"But Prince Allaudin can administer them more easily. He's here. And you can compensate Jadar with others. Perhaps some in the north, near the fortress of Qandahar? You'll have to send him there after the campaign in the Deccan." Janahara's voice was silken now.

Hawksworth turned to see Nadir Sharif's face growing ashen.

She's trying to drive Jadar into oblivion. Rob him of his best estates, then send him to defend a piece of mountain rock. Surely Arangbar will refuse. Jadar will never agree. She must know that. Nadir Sharif certainly knows it.

"What would Prince Jadar say to such a trade?" Arangbar sipped from his wineglass and shifted slightly, his eyes again barely in focus.

"Why should he object? He's never here. And surely he'll be ready to obey Your Majesty and return to defend Qandahar after he completes his campaign in the south. The threat from the Persian Safavis in the north is already growing."

"I doubt very much he will agree so easily to march north again. Not yet. Though I pray to Allah that he would."

"Then this will give him all the more reason."

"He may not see it as a reason. He may see it as a betrayal. You know he's temperamental."

Hawksworth suddenly found himself wondering if the trade had been planned with Allaudin. It was obvious Nadir Sharif had been taken completely by surprise.

"Then I suppose it's best dropped." Janahara turned her face away. "You can just forget I ever asked."

Arangbar looked crushed. He sipped thoughtfully on his wine for a moment.

"Perhaps if I consulted Prince Jadar first." He paused to study his empty wine cup. "The *jagirs* were granted . . ."

"Perhaps Your Majesty thinks Prince Allaudin should have no estates at all? Perhaps you think he is not yet fit?"

"He's fit, by Allah. He's my son." Arangbar impulsively seized another ball of opium and began to chew on it thoughtfully. "I'll find a way to compensate Jadar. Surely he'll be reasonable. After all, there must be a wedding gift."

"Then you'll agree to grant it?" Janahara's tone was quiet and inquiring.

"Majesty." Nadir Sharif's voice seemed strangely unguarded. "Prince Jadar . . ."

Arangbar seemed not to hear him. "I grant it. In the morning I'll summon the *qazi*, and let this be recorded as my gift to my youngest son and his new bride." Arangbar's tenseness seemed to dissolve as he leaned back on the bolster and took another ball of opium. "But only on the condition that he perform his duty tonight. Let him plow the field he has before he's granted more."

Arangbar turned to Hawksworth. "Do you know what else will happen, Inglish, if he fails in his duty the first night?"

"No, Majesty."

"Some of her women will send him a distaff, which they use with their spinning wheels. With a message that since he cannot do a man's work, it is fitting he should do a woman's. But I think he'll succeed." Arangbar turned to Janahara with a wink. "He's been practicing for months with the *nautch* girls in the palace."

The queen did not smile as she took a rolled betel leaf from a tray.

A messenger appeared at the foot of the dais and performed the *teslim*. His voice was quivering. "The sheet has not yet come out, may it please Your Majesty."

Arangbar laughed. "Then perhaps the furrow is too narrow to receive his plow. Have a mullah bless some water and send it in to him. And tell him I'm waiting to see if he's yet a man."

"A Shi'ite mullah, Your Majesty, or a Sunni?"

"From this night forward, he will have Shi'ite mullahs perform all the duties for his household," Janahara interrupted.

The messenger performed the *teslim* to the queen and backed from the room. Arangbar sat silent, drinking.

"What does it matter?" He finally turned to her. "Let him have whatever he pleases."

"That is easy for you to say. But it does not please Allah. Tonight should be taken as an omen."

"Tonight is an omen of nothing. Tonight my son is charged to make a woman out of a Persian girl of fifteen, who knows nothing of her duties in bed. But he'll succeed. Give him time."

"I think tonight is an omen. Allah is not pleased when you allow open heresies to flourish."

Arangbar was watching a dancer who had approached the dais to begin a suggestive *nautch* dance for him. It seemed to Hawksworth that they were already well acquainted, for she smiled at him knowingly, avoiding the queen's glance.

"I care nothing for heresies." Arangbar turned back to Janahara. "I only care for the honor of my reign."

"But a faith divided does you no honor."

"Then unite it if you care so much. I have other duties." Arangbar turned again to watch the dancer. She had a large ring in one side of her nose, and her eyes seemed to snap as she slapped her bare feet against the carpeted floor. "I never knew she was so good." He turned to Nadir Sharif. "Send her a small ruby and find out for me tomorrow what her salary is. Whatever it is, I think she should have more."

"As you wish, Majesty." Nadir Sharif bowed lightly and turned again to watch the dancer.

Hawksworth studied the prime minister's face. It was grim, leaden.

It's everything Shirin said would happen. Prince Jadar has been stripped of his lands, and the queen has been granted license to start an inquisition.

You'd better get the *firman* signed, before the country starts coming apart.

The doors of the hall burst open, and a crowd of women entered. They carried a silver plate, on which was a folded silk sheet. They moved quickly before the queen and performed the *teslim*. Then one held out the plate.

The queen took the sheet and inspected it. Hawksworth watched her, puzzling, then remembered that in Muslim society a bloodstained wedding sheet is considered evidence, vital to the honor of both the families, of the bride's virginity and the groom's virility. With a triumphant smile, Janahara nodded and turned to exhibit the sheet to Arangbar.

There were light pink traces across the white silk.

"He's a man after all." Arangbar passed the sheet to Zainul Beg, who beamed and passed it to Nadir Sharif. The prime minister smiled with approval.

"He has earned his *jagirs*." Arangbar turned to Janahara. "Let it be recorded. And now we feast."

More silver dishes of baked lamb appeared from inside the palace, brought by eunuchs who inspected them carefully before handing them to servingwomen. The music and dancing were exultant now and lasted until the light of dawn showed. The drunken guests waited reverently until Arangbar, who had gone to sleep, was carried from the hall on a palanquin. Then they began to disperse.

Hawksworth reached Nadir Sharif's side as the prime minister was moving out through the large, tapestry-adorned doorway.

"What really happened tonight?"

"What do you mean, Ambassador?"

"The transfer of *jagirs*. What will Jadar do?"

"Ambassador, that's a matter for the rulers of India to decide. It's not your affair." Nadir Sharif did not look around. "Instead let me ask *you* a question. When will your English fleet make landfall? They are overdue, but there have been no further sightings. I'm beginning to wonder if there really is a fleet."

"Perhaps the weather's been against them." Hawksworth tried to steady himself on his feet. "After all, it *was* sighted by Jadar's men."

"Was it? Or did you and Prince Jadar deceive us all? If there's no fleet, Ambassador, you're in very serious trouble. There will be no *firman*. His Majesty is hardly a fool."

"He promised to sign the *firman* long before the sighting."

"You do not know him as I do. You have another week, perhaps two, and then . . . Let me merely say you cannot drink the fleet into existence. We are both going to have difficulty explaining this deception to His Majesty. You met with the prince. I'm beginning to wonder now if you both planned this. If you did, it was most unwise."

"Then wait two weeks and see." Hawksworth felt his palms grow moist. "Two weeks is not so long a time."

"It is a very long time, Ambassador. Much is happening. You have made many of the wrong friends. Good evening, Ambassador. I must speak to Her Majesty." Nadir Sharif turned and was swallowed by the crowd.

As Hawksworth moved into the street, he saw that the front of the palace was already bathed in morning light. And Agra was beginning to come to life. He strolled for a time along the side of the Jamuna, where burned-out candles still floated, and studied the outline of the Red Fort against the morning sky.

What if there really is no fleet? What if it really *was* a trick by Jadar, for some reason of his own? To destroy my mission? Has he cozened us all?

Midmorning was approaching when he finally reached his lodge at the rear of Nadir Sharif's estate. As he passed through the curtained doorway, he saw Kamala waiting, her eyes dark. She was wearing none of her jewels.

"Have you heard?" She took his turban and knelt to remove his *kamarband*.

"Heard what?"

"Do you know the Sufi Samad? And the Persian woman who was with him?"

Hawksworth examined her, wondering who else knew of his stay in Fatehpur Sekri.

"Why do you ask?"

"If you do know them, it is no longer wise to admit it."

"Why?" Hawksworth felt his gut tighten. Suddenly Kamala's touch no longer stirred him.

"The news is already spreading in Agra." She began removing his cloak, pausing to smooth her hand across his chest. "They were arrested last night, while the wedding was underway. In the bazaar this morning they said he is sure to be condemned to death for heresy, and she for aiding him. People think they will both be executed within the week."

CHAPTER TWENTY-THREE

Father Manoel Pinheiro's clean-shaven face was grim and his lips set tightly against the brisk air as he pushed a path through the crowded alley, headed toward the riverside palace of Nadir Sharif. Around him large black cauldrons of frying bread filled the dawn with the aroma of oil and spice. He had slipped from the mission house at first light and, clasping his peaked black hat tightly over his forehead, he had tried to melt inconspicuously among the rattling bullock carts and noisy street vendors. Now he paused for breath and watched as a large white cow licked the few grains of rice from the begging bowl of a dozing leper. The image seemed to capture all the despair of India, and he suddenly felt himself overwhelmed by the enormity of the Church's burden. Before he could move on, a crowd of chanting Hindus jostled him against a wall as they poured into a small, garishly decorated temple brimming with polycolored heathen idols. On either side Hindu fakirs sat listlessly, long white hair streaming down over their streaked faces, their limpid eyes devoid of God's understanding. He shook his head sadly as he made the sign of the cross over them, and found his heart near bursting.

On every hand, he told himself, the fields are ripe unto harvest, the flocks wanting a keeper. For every soul in this forgotten land we bring to God and the Church, a hundred, nay a thousand, are born into eternal darkness, damned forever. Our task is overwhelming, even with God's help.

He thought of the Holy Church, the Society of Jesus, and their long years of disappointment in India. But now, at last, it seemed their hopes and prayers might be nearing fulfillment. After all the years of humiliation and ignominy, there seemed a chance, a genuine chance, that Arangbar, the *Great Moghul* himself, would at last consent to be baptized into the Holy Church. After him, all of India would surely soon follow.

Father Pinheiro crossed himself again, and prayed silently that God would make him a worthy instrument of His will.

The burden of India was by now a Jesuit legend. It had been taken up when the first mission came to the court of Akman over three decades before. And even now the pagan fields of India remained, in many ways, the greatest challenge of the Society of Jesus and the Holy Church.

India had, it was true, been held in the grip of Portuguese sea power for many years before the first mission arrived in Agra. But Portuguese arms and trade had not served the work of the Church. They had served the greed of Portuguese merchants and the coffers of Portuguese royalty. The lost souls of India were denied the Grace of the Holy Church.

Then, in 1540, a priest named Ignatius Loyola, once a nobleman and a soldier, founded the Society of Jesus, whose dual purpose was to defend the Holy Church against the Protestant Reformation and begin preaching the True Faith to the pagan lands of Asia and the Americas. In 1542 the Society of Jesus reached Portuguese Goa, on the very shores of India, in the person of Francis Xavier, a close friend of Ignatius Loyola's from student days at the University of Paris.

With Goa as base of operations, the society had immediately pushed farther eastward, reaching Japan and Macao a few short years later. Paradoxically, it was India itself that had initially eluded their influence. Finally, in 1573, the Great Akman journeyed south and encountered the members of the Society of Jesus for the first time. He was awed by their learning and moral integrity, and soon thereafter he posted an envoy to Goa requesting that a Jesuit mission be sent to his court. Three Jesuit fathers traveled to Fatehpur Sekri.

The Jesuits' hopes soared when they were immediately invited to debate the orthodox Islamic mullahs at Akman's court. The leader of the mission, a soft-spoken Italian father with encyclopedic learning, knew the Quran well in translation and easily refuted the mullahs' absolutist arguments—to the obvious delight of Akman. It was only after several months at Fatehpur Sekri that the three learned fathers began to suspect that Akman's real purpose in inviting them was to have on hand skilled debaters for entertainment.

Akman may have had scant patience with Islam, but it had grown obvious he had no desire to become a Christian either. He was an intellectual who amused himself by questioning the ideas and teachings of all faiths; with the inevitable result that he always found something in each to affront his own reason. He was, in fact, beginning to form the notion that he himself was as great a leader as any of the spiritual teachers he had heard about, and accordingly should simply declare himself an object of worship. After a decade the three Jesuits finally conceded their first mission was a failure and abjectly returned to Goa.

Almost a decade later, in 1590, Akman again requested that Jesuit fathers be sent to his court. Once more a mission was sent, and once more its members eventually concluded Akman had no real intention of encouraging Christianity in India. The second mission was also abandoned.

There remained some, however, in Goa and in Rome, who believed the *Great Moghul* Akman still could be converted. Furthermore, as the Protestant countries began to venture into the Indies, the political usefulness of having Portuguese priests near the ruler of India became increasingly obvious. Thus, in 1595, a third mission was sent to Akman's court. Father Pinheiro remembered well their instructions upon departing Goa. They would convert Akman if they could; but equally important now, they would ensure that Portuguese trading interests were protected.

The Jesuit fathers drew close to Akman, became valued advisers, and found themselves being consulted on questions ranging from whether Jesus was the Son of God or merely a Prophet, to the advisability of smoking tobacco. Still, the only lasting achievement of the mission was to extract from Akman a *firman* granting Jesuits the right to free exercise of the Catholic religion. They wanted his soul, and through it the soul of India, but the most they ever attained was his protection. He died a royal skeptic, but a sovereign whose religious tolerance shocked the dogmatic sixteenth-century world.

Father Pinheiro paused to study the outline of the Red Fort against the morning sky and listened to the *azan* call to Islamic prayer sounding from a nearby mosque. He smiled to think that the schism between the rule of Arangbar and the rule of Islam might soon be complete. Like Akman, Arangbar had never bothered to hide his distaste for the mullahs who flooded his court. He collected Italian paintings of the Virgin for his palace, even scandalizing the mullahs by hanging one in the *Diwan-i-Am*, and whenever one of the Jesuit fathers journeyed to Goa, there was always a request for more Christian art. True the *Moghul's* understanding of blasphemy was erratic, as evidenced by a recent evening in the *Diwan-i-Khas* when, drunk and roaring with laughter, Arangbar had set a wager with the Jesuits on how

long he could stand with his arms outstretched as a cross. But then he had
built a church for the mission, and also provided them a house, which he
now visited ever more frequently to secretly indulge his passion for forbidden
pork.

A scant two months before, Arangbar had taken an action that sent the
mission's hopes soaring. He had summoned the Jesuit fathers to baptize two
of his young nephews, ordering the boys to become Christians. The mullahs
had been outraged, immediately spreading the pernicious rumor he had done
so merely to better remove them from the line of succession. In Goa, however, the mission was roundly congratulated on nearing its goal. If Arangbar
became a Christian, many in his court and perhaps eventually all of India
would someday follow.

This had all been before the arrival of the English heretic, Hawksworth.
At the very moment when Arangbar's mind seemed within their grasp, there
had now emerged the specter that all their work might be undone. Arangbar
had treated the Englishman as though he were qualified to speak on theological matters and had even questioned him about the most Holy Sacrament,
when the Church's doctrine regarding this Mystery had already been fully
expounded to him by Father Sarmento himself. Arangbar had listened with
seeming interest while the Englishman proceeded to tell him much that was
contrary to the Truth and to Church teaching. When asked point blank, the
Englishman had even denied that His Holiness, the pope, should be acknowledged head of the Universal Church, going on to characterize His Holiness' political concerns in almost scatological terms. Father Sarmento, normally the most forbearing of priests, was nearing despair.

Most disturbing of all, Arangbar had only last week asked the Englishman by what means the Portuguese fortress at the northern port of Diu
could be recaptured by India. The Englishman had confided that he
believed a blockade by a dozen English frigates, supported by an Indian land
army of no more than twenty thousand, could force the Portuguese garrison
to capitulate from hunger!

Clearly Arangbar was growing eccentric. The English heretic had
beguiled him and was near to becoming a serious detriment to Portuguese
interests. To make matters worse, there was the latest dispatch from Goa,
which had arrived only the previous evening. Father Pinheiro had studied it
well into the night, and finally concluded that the time had come to stop
the Englishman. He also concluded it was time to make this unmistakably
clear to Nadir Sharif. As the situation continued to deteriorate, only the
influence of Nadir Sharif could still neutralize the Englishman.

Father Pinheiro moved on through the jostling street, occasionally swab-
bing his brow. And as he looked about him, he began to dream of the day
there would be a Christian India. It would be the society's greatest triumph.
What would it be like? What would Arangbar do to silence the heretical

mullahs? Would the time come when India, like Europe, would require an Inquisition to purify the sovereignty of the Church?

One thing was certain. With a Catholic monarch in India, there would be no further English trade, no Dutch trade, no Protestant trade. The declining fortunes of Portuguese commerce at Goa, the Protestant challenge to Portuguese supremacy in the Indies, would both be permanently reversed in a single stroke.

The thought heartened him as he looked up to see the sandstone turrets of Nadir Sharif's palace gleaming in the morning sun.

"Father, it is always a pleasure to see you." Nadir Sharif bowed lightly and indicated a bolster. He did not order refreshments from the servants. "No matter what the hour."

"I realize the time is early. I wanted to find you at home. And to come here when there were the fewest possible eyes on the street." Pinheiro paused and then decided to sit. He was perspiring heavily from the walk, even though the real heat of the day lay hours ahead.

Nadir Sharif flinched at the Jesuit's school-book Persian and examined him with ill-concealed disdain, knowing word of his visit surely had already found the ears of the queen.

"Then I should ask the occasion for this unexpected pleasure." Nadir Sharif seated himself and discreetly examined the Jesuit's soiled black habit.

"The English trading fleet, Excellency. The news is most disturbing. I received a pigeon last evening from His Excellency, Miguel Vaijantes. The armada he dispatched along the coast to sweep for the English fleet returned three days ago, finding nothing. The English may have eluded us. He has now ordered the armada to sail north from Goa, into the bay, but by now the English fleet could be nearing Surat, or perhaps they have veered north to the port of Cambay. His Excellency fears that they may possibly escape our patrols entirely and make landfall. He has asked me to inform you privately that the *firman* for English trade must be delayed at all costs, until the English fleet can be sighted and engaged."

"I have made every effort. The Viceroy knows that." Nadir Sharif casually adjusted the jewel on his turban. "It has been stopped so far."

"But if the fleet lands? And if the heretic English king has sent new gifts for His Majesty?" Pinheiro tried to maintain his dignity as he nervously wiped his face with the black fold of a sleeve.

"If the English do make landfall, and dispatch more gifts for His Majesty, I fear no power in Agra can stop him from signing the *firman*." Nadir Sharif's face assumed an expression of conciliatory resignation. "The English will undoubtedly make the trading *firman* a condition of further presents."

"You know that is unacceptable, Excellency." Pinheiro's eyes narrowed. "The mission cannot allow it. You know that as well as I."

"Forgive me, but I've always understood your mission here was not to concern itself with trade."

"The Holy Church is not engaged in trade, Excellency. But our position here is dependent, as you are well aware, on the fortunes of Goa. The two are entwined, as are all secular and spiritual aspects of life. Whatever disturbs one must inevitably affect the other. It cannot be otherwise."

"Obviously." Nadir Sharif stroked the tip of his moustache a moment in thought. "So what would you have me do? The English *feringhi* cannot be harmed. He drinks every evening with His Majesty."

"There are other ways to negate the heretic's influence. Perhaps the Englishman's . . . situation with His Majesty can be rendered less intimate. Perhaps he could be removed from favor. If only for a time."

"So you have come to ask me to work miracles for you, when you do nothing for yourself." Nadir Sharif rose and strolled to a latticework window. He studied the garden for a moment, then spoke without turning. "Have you advised His Majesty in explicit terms of the Viceroy's displeasure with the English intrusion into our . . . into Portuguese waters?"

"It has been made known. Many times."

"But have you suggested the consequences?" Nadir Sharif turned and gazed past Pinheiro, his eyes playing on the scalloped marble arch of the entryway.

"The consequences are obvious. The warships at Goa are capable of terminating all trade in the Indian Ocean if His Excellency so pleases."

"Then you should merely engage the English." Nadir Sharif consciously deleted the irony from his voice.

"That is an entirely separate matter. The English frigates are of a new design, very swift. They may possibly have eluded us for a time." Pinheiro's voice hardened. "But do not doubt our galleons are swifter than any of the trading vessels of His Majesty's fleet. India's own Red Sea trade continues only at the Viceroy's discretion."

"That is true enough. But are you prepared to demonstrate your . . . displeasure." Nadir Sharif revolved back to the window. "I do not think His Majesty actually believes the Viceroy would ever take hostile action."

"What are you suggesting?" Pinheiro's voice betrayed momentary disbelief.

"Nothing that you have not already brought to His Majesty's attention. But possibly he does not believe you have the conviction, or the strength, to carry it through. The English *feringhi* constantly brags to him of English superiority at sea, hinting that his king will soon drive Portugal from the Indian Ocean. I've heard it so often myself I confess I'm near to believing him too."

"I can assure you that the protection, and control, of India's ports will always remain in Portuguese hands."

"Then you would still have me believe you have the power to impound Indian shipping, even a vessel owned by His Majesty, thereby exposing the English as helpless to prevent it?" Nadir Sharif seemed absorbed in the garden, his hands clasped easily behind him in perfect repose.

"Of course." Pinheiro stood dazed at the implications of Nadir Sharif's words. He paused for a moment, digesting them. "Do I understand you to be suggesting the Viceroy take hostile action against one of His Majesty's own trading ships?"

"You have contested the Englishman with words, and he seems to be winning." Nadir Sharif turned and examined Pinheiro. "Your Viceroy is undoubtedly aware that Her Majesty, Queen Janahara, is equally disturbed by the Englishman. She too is concerned with the possible effects on her . . . trading arrangements if the English gain undue influence."

"Would she be willing to speak to His Majesty?"

"Again you talk merely of words. What have they gained you?"

"Father Sarmento would never consent to an overt action. He would be too fearful of the possible consequences to the mission."

"Bold measures are for bold men. I think His Excellency, Miguel Vaijantes, understands boldness. And His Majesty understands boldness better than anyone." Nadir Sharif paused. "It may be of interest to His Excellency to know that His Majesty currently has a vessel en route from the Red Sea, with cargo owned by the mother of His Majesty, the dowager Maryam Zamani. It is due to make landfall within the week, if it has managed to hold its schedule. The vessel's safety is, quite naturally, of utmost concern to His Majesty . . ."

"I think I understand." Father Pinheiro again swabbed the moisture from his brow. "But Father Sarmento . . ."

"What possible concern could Father Sarmento have with decisions made by His Excellency, Miguel Vaijantes? He is the Viceroy." Nadir Sharif nodded toward a pudgy eunuch hovering at the doorway, who immediately entered with a tray of betel leaves, signaling that the meeting was adjourned.

"His Excellency will undoubtedly be most appreciative of your thoughts." Pinheiro paused. "Still, wouldn't it be prudent to advise Her Majesty, lest she mistake our Viceroy's intentions?"

"I will attend to it." Nadir Sharif smiled warmly. "You must be aware, however, that if His Majesty chooses to respond irresponsibly, I will know nothing about any action that may be taken. The Viceroy must weather his own seas."

"Naturally." Pinheiro bowed. "You have always been a friend. I thank you, and bless you in God's name."

"Your thanks are sufficient." Nadir Sharif smiled again and watched as the Jesuit was led through the scalloped doorway by the waiting eunuch.

Only when he turned back to the window did he realize his palms were drenched with perspiration.

Arangbar moved groggily through the arched corridor carrying a fresh silver cup of wine and quietly humming the motif of his favorite Hindustani raga. His afternoon nap in the *zenana* had been fitful, unusually so, and when he finally admitted to himself why, he had dismissed the two young women who waited to pleasure him, retrieved his jeweled turban, and waved aside the attending eunuchs. He had announced he wanted to stroll among the fruit trees in the courtyard of the Anguri Bagh, which lay down the marble steps from the Khas Mahal, the breezy upper pavilion of the *zenana*. But when he reached the trees, he had turned and slipped through his private doorway leading to the women's apartments in the lower level of the fort.

The *zenana* was quiet, even the eunuchs were dozing, and no one noticed when he passed along the shadowed afternoon corridor toward the circular staircase leading to the lower apartments. As he began to descend the curved stone steps, he felt his legs momentarily grow unsteady, and he paused to rest against the hard polished wall, tightening his light brocade cloak against the cooler air and taking a short sip of wine for warmth. Then he continued on, carefully feeling for each step in the dim light of the overhead oil lamps.

He emerged on the next level and stopped to catch his breath on the balcony that opened out over the Jamuna. This was the level where he had built private apartments for his favorite women, and behind him was the large room, with a painted cupola ceiling high above a large rose-shaped marble fountain, which he had granted to one of his Hindu wives. (Now he could no longer recall precisely who she was; she had reached thirty some time past and he had not summoned her to his couch in many years.) Since she was a devout Hindu, he had ordered it decorated with brilliantly colored scenes from the Ramayana. The room itself was cooled by a high waterfall in the rear that murmured down an inclined and striated marble slab. Stairways on either side of the room curved around to an overhead balcony, directly above where he now stood, which was the post where eunuchs waited when the women came to cool themselves by the fountain.

The balcony where he now stood jutted out from the fort, supported by thick sandstone columns, and from his position he could look along the side of the fort and see the Jasmine Tower of Queen Janahara. When he realized he also could be seen, he instinctively stepped back into the cool corridor.

The women were inside their apartments, asleep, and the corridor empty as he began to descend the circular stairs leading to the next level below, the quarters for eunuchs and female servants. As he rounded the last curve of the stair and emerged into the light, three eunuchs stared up in shock from their game of cards. It vaguely registered that they probably were gambling, which he had strictly prohibited in the *zenana*, but he decided to ignore it this afternoon.

The circular pasteboard cards of the eunuchs' scattered across the stone floor as they hurried to *teslim*. He paused to drink again from the cup and absently studied the painted faces on the cards dropped by the eunuch nearest him. It was not a bad hand. Lying on the marble were four high cards from the *bishbar*, powerful, suits—the lord of horses, the king of elephants, the king of infantry, and the throned *wazir* of the fort—and three from the *kambar*, weaker, suits—the king of snakes, the king of divinities, and the throned queen. He stared for a moment at the king of elephants, the suit he always preferred to play, and wondered at the happenstance that the king had fallen beneath the queen, whose face covered his golden crown. He shrugged it away as coincidence and turned toward the stairs leading to the next lower level.

Two more levels remained.

The air was increasingly musty now, noticeably smoky from the lamps, and he hurried on, reaching the next landing without stopping. The windows on this level had shrunk to only a few hand spans, and now they were secured with heavy stone latticework. The eunuchs were arguing at the other end of the corridor and failed even to notice him. He told himself to try to remember this, and drank again as he paused to listen to the metrical splash of the Jamuna lapping against the outer wall. Then he stepped quietly down the last flight of stairs.

The final level. As he emerged into the corridor, two guarding eunuchs who had been dozing leaped to their feet and drew swords before recognizing him. Both fell on their face in *teslim*, their turbans tumbling across the stone floor.

Arangbar said nothing, merely pointed toward a doorway at the end of the corridor. The startled eunuchs strained against their fat as they lifted torches from the walls and then turned officiously to lead the way. As they walked, Arangbar paused to stare through an arched doorway leading into a large domed room off the side of the hall. A dozen eunuchs were inside, some holding torches while others laced a white cotton rope through a wooden pulley attached to the lower side of a heavy wooden beam that spanned the room, approximately ten feet above the floor.

The two eunuchs with Arangbar also stopped, wondering if His Majesty had come to supervise the hanging that afternoon of the two *zenana* women who had been discovered in a flagrant sexual act in the Shish Mahal, the mirrored *zenana* baths.

Arangbar studied the hanging room for a moment with glazed eyes, not remembering that he had sentenced the women that same morning, and then waved the guards on along the corridor, past the doors that secured dark cells. These were the cells used to confine women who had broken *zenana* regulations.

At the end of the corridor was a door wider than the others, and behind it was a special cell, with a window overlooking the Jamuna. He walked directly to the door and drank again from his cup as he ordered it opened. The guards were there at once, keys jangling. The door was massive and thick, and it creaked heavily on its hinges as they pushed it slowly inward.

From the gloom came the unmistakable fragrance of musk and sandalwood. He inhaled it for a moment and it seemed to penetrate his memory, calling up long forgotten pleasures. Grasping the door for support, he moved past the bowing guards and into the cell. There, standing by the small barred window, her face caught in a shaft of afternoon sun, was Shirin.

Her eyes were carefully darkened with kohl and her mouth red and fresh. She wore a gossamer scarf decorated with gold thread, and a thin skirt that betrayed the curve of her thighs against the outline of her flowered trousers. The musty air of the room was immersed in her perfume, as though by her very being she would defy the walls of her prison. She looked just as he had remembered.

She turned and stared at him for a moment, seeming not to believe what she saw. Then her eyes hardened.

"Shall I *teslim* before my sentence?"

Arangbar said nothing as he examined her wordlessly, sipping slowly from his almost-empty cup. Now more than ever he realized why she had once been his favorite. She could bring him to ecstasy, and then recite Persian poetry to him for hours. She had been exquisite.

"You're as beautiful as ever. Too beautiful. What do you expect me to do with you?"

"I expect that I will die, Your Majesty. That, I think, is the usual sentence for the women who disobey you."

"You could have stayed in Surat, where you were sent. Or gone on to Goa with the husband I gave you. But instead you returned here. Why?" Arangbar eased himself onto the stone bench beside the door.

"I don't think you would understand, Majesty."

"Did you come because of the Inglish *feringhi*? I learned yesterday that you conspired to meet with him. It displeased me very much."

"He was not responsible, Majesty. I met with him because I chose to. But I came to Agra to be with Samad again." Her voice began to tremble slightly. "Samad is guilty of nothing, except defiance of the Shi'ite mullahs. You know that as well as I. If you want to hear me beg for him, I will."

Arangbar seemed not to notice the tear that stained the kohl beneath one eye. "It was a death sentence for you to disobey me and come back. Perhaps you actually want to die."

"Is there nothing you would die for, Majesty?"

Arangbar stared for a moment at the window, its hexagonal grillwork throwing a pattern across his glazed eyes. He seemed to be searching for words. "Yes, perhaps I might die for India. Perhaps someday soon I will. But I would never die for the glory of Islam." His gaze came back to Shirin. "And certainly not for some half-naked Sufi mullah."

"Samad is not a mullah." By force of will she held any trace of shrillness from her voice. "He is a Persian poet. One of the greatest ever. You know that. He defies the Shi'ites because he will not bow to their dogma."

"The Shi'ites want his head." Arangbar examined his empty cup and tossed it to the floor, listening as the silver rang hard against the stone. "It seems a small price for tranquillity."

"Whose tranquillity? Theirs?" The tears were gone now, her eyes again defiant.

"Mine. Every day I'm flooded with petitions about this or that heresy. It wearies and consumes me. Samad ignored the laws of Islam, and he has followers."

"*You* ignore the laws of Islam."

Arangbar laughed. "It's true. Between us, I despise the mullahs. You know I once told them I had decided to become a Christian, because I enjoyed eating pork and the Prophet denied it to all men. The next day they brought the Quran and declared although it was true pork was denied to *men*, the Prophet said nothing specifically about what a *king* could eat. So there was no need for me to become a Christian." He paused and sobered. "But Samad is not a king. He is a well-known Sufi. The mullahs claim that if he's dead, the inspiration for heresy will die with him. They say his death will serve as an example. I hear this everywhere, even from Her Majesty."

"Her Majesty?" Shirin searched for his eyes as she spoke, but they were shrouded in shadow. "Does she make laws for you now?"

"She disrupts my tranquillity with all her talk about Islam and Shi'ites. Perhaps it's age. She never used to talk about the Shi'ites. But now she wants to bring the Islam of Persia to India. She forbade Sunni mullahs even to attend the wedding. But if it pleases her, what does it matter? I despise them all."

"But why Samad? Why sentence him to death?"

"Frankly I don't really care about this poet, either way. But he has not tried to help himself. When I allowed him to confront the mullahs who accused him, he refused to recite the Kalima, 'There is no God but Allah.'"

"What did he say?"

"Perhaps just to spite them, he would only recite the first phrase, 'There is no God,' the negation. He refused to recite the rest, the affirmation. He said he was still searching for truth. That when he finally saw God he would recite the remainder; that to affirm His existence without proof would be giving false evidence. I thought the mullahs would strangle him on the spot."

Arangbar laughed to himself as he watched her turn again to the window. "You have to admit that qualifies as blasphemy, by any measure. So if the mullahs want him so badly, why not let them have him?"

"But Samad is a mystic, a pantheist." Shirin returned her eyes to Arangbar. "For him God is everywhere, not just where the mullahs choose to put Him. Do you remember those quatrains in his *Rubaiyat* that say,

> "*Here in the garden the sunshine glows,*
> *A Presence moves in all that grows.*
> *He is the lover, the belov'd too.*
> *He is the bramble and the rose.*
> *We know Him when our hearts are moved;*
> *He, our lover and our loved.*
> *Open your eyes with joy and see*
> *The hundred ways His love is proved.*"

"I've seen his poetry. It sings of the love of some God, although his God sounds a bit too benign to be Allah. But I also know his *Rubaiyat* will not save him. It may make him immortal someday, but he'll be long since dead by then."

Arangbar rose unsteadily and moved beside her, staring out onto the glinting surface of the Jamuna. For a moment he watched a fleet of barges pass, piled high with dark bundles of indigo. "I believe I myself will die someday soon. I can almost feel my strength ebbing. But I hope I'll be remembered as my father Akman is, a ruler who tolerated all faiths. I've protected Hindus from the bigoted followers of Mohammed's religion, who would convert them forcibly to Islam, and I've allowed all religions to build places of worship. Did you know I've even built a church for the Portuguese Jesuits, who have to buy most of their converts with bribes? I even gave them a stipend, since they would starve otherwise. They tell me they're astonished I allow so much religious freedom here, since it's unheard of in Europe. But I can do all this only if I remain the nominal defender of Islam. Islam holds the power in India, and as India's ruler I must acknowledge that. I can defy the mullahs myself now and then. But I can't permit your Sufi mystic to do it too. There's a limit."

"You can do anything. If you wish. The orthodox mullahs have always hated mystics. The Shi'ite mullahs are men who live on hate. You see it burning in their eyes. They even hate their own women, can't you see? They keep them prisoner, claiming that's the way they honor and respect them. The mullahs even resent that Samad allows me to come into his presence without a veil."

"They say he's a poison in Islam."

"Yes, his example is poison. His poetry is filled with love. The mullahs cannot bear it, since their own lives are filled with hate. God help India if it ever becomes an 'Islamic' state. There'll be mobs in the streets murdering Hindus in the name of 'God.' Is that the tranquillity you want?"

"I want to die in peace. Just like your poet. And I want to be remembered, for the good I've done for India." Arangbar paused, seeming to search on the stone ledge for his cup. "I think Samad will be remembered too. Tomorrow I'll make him famous. Let him live on through his words. He knows, and I know, that he must die. We understand each other perfectly. I can't disappoint him now."

Arangbar suddenly recalled the high-ranking Rajput raja who had asked for an early audience in the *Diwan-i-Khas*, and he turned and moved unsteadily toward the door. When he reached it, he revolved and looked back sadly at Shirin.

"I found myself dreaming about you this afternoon. I don't know why. So I decided to come and see you, alone. I didn't come to talk about Samad. It's you I'm uncertain about. Her Majesty wants you hanged. But I cannot yet find the courage to sentence you." Arangbar continued on wearily toward the door. "Where will it all end?" He paused and, as though remembering something, turned again. "Jadar is plotting something against me, I sense it. But I don't know what he can do. Recently I've heard rumors you're part of it. Have you turned against me?"

"If you kill Samad, I will defy you with every power I have."

"Then perhaps I *should* execute you." He stared at her, trying to focus. "But you have no powers left. Unless you're plotting something with the Inglish. If you are, then I will kill you both." He turned to leave, tightening his cloak against the chill. The guards saw him emerge and hurried from the far end of the corridor. Arangbar watched them for a moment, then turned and looked one last time at Shirin. "Samad will die tomorrow. You will have to wait."

Brian Hawksworth's lean frame towered above the crowd, conspicuous in jerkin and seaboots. He had heard the rumor and he had come to the plaza to watch, mingling among the turbaned assembly of nobles, shopkeepers, mullahs, and assorted street touts. His presence was immediately noted by all, especially the crippled beggars in dirty brown *dhotis*, who dragged themselves through the crowd, their leprosy-withered hands upturned, calling for a *pice* in the name of Allah. They knew from experience that, however ragged a *feringhi* might appear, he was always more likely to be moved by their plight than a wealthy Indian merchant.

The plaza was a confined area between the steep eastern side of the Red Fort and the outer wall of the fortress. Beyond the fortress wall lay the wide Jamuna River, while high above, and with a commanding view of the plaza, sat Arangbar, watching from the black throne at the outer edge of the *Di-*

wan-i-Khas. Next to him sat Queen Janahara and Allaudin. The day was Tuesday and the sun was approaching midday. As Hawksworth pushed his way to the front of the crowd, the last elephant fight of the morning had just begun.

Two First-ranked bull elephants were locked head to head in the dusty square. Their blunted tusks were wreathed with brass rings, and the back of each was covered with a brocaded canvas on which sat two riders. Perched on each animal's neck and directing it was its *mahout,* and on its rump sat its Second-ranked keeper, whose assignment was to urge the animal to greater frenzy.

The dusty air was alive with a festive clanging from large bells attached to each elephant's harness. Hawksworth noticed that a long chain, called the *lor langar,* was secured to the left foreleg of each elephant and circled over its back, where it was attached to a heavy log held by the second rider. Both elephants also had other keepers who ran alongside holding long poles, at the end of which was crossed a foot-long piece of paper-covered bamboo. Nearby another keeper stood holding a smoldering taper.

Hawksworth watched in awe as the elephants backed away and lunged together again and again, tusk resounding against tusk, often rearing on their hind legs as each strained for advantage.

"Do you have a favorite, *feringhi* Sahib?" A brown-skinned man with a slightly soiled turban was tugging at Hawksworth's sleeve. "There is still time to wager."

"No thanks." Hawksworth moved to brush him aside.

"But it is our habit in India to wager on the elephants, Sahib. Perhaps the Sahib does not yet know Indian customs?" He pushed closer, directly in Hawksworth's face. His few remaining teeth were stained red with betel. "I myself am a poor judge of elephants. I can never guess which will win. Still I love to wager. May Allah forgive me."

"I'm not here to bet."

"Just this once, Sahib. For my weakness." He turned and pointed through the dust. "Although the dark elephant is smaller and already growing tired, I will even offer to bet on him to give you, a guest in India, a chance to win. So when you return to your *feringhistan* someday, you will say there is one honest man in India. I will wager you ten rupees the dark one will be declared the winner." The man backed away for an instant and discreetly assessed Hawksworth's worn jerkin with a quick glance. "If ten rupees are too much, I will wager you five."

Hawksworth studied the two elephants again. The dark one *was* slightly smaller, and *did* seem to be growing tired. The other elephant, larger and brown, had a *mahout* less skilled but he also clearly was gaining the advantage.

"All right. I'll take the brown." Hawksworth reached for his purse, feeling slightly relieved that it was still there. "And I'll lay twenty rupees."

"As pleases the Sahib." The man smiled broadly. "The Sahib must be a very rich man in his *feringhistan*."

Even as he spoke, the large brown elephant wheeled and slammed its black adversary in the side with its tusks, barely missing the leg of the *mahout*. The black elephant staggered backward, against the side of the fort. It was now clearly on the defensive, as the larger elephant began slamming it repeatedly in the side.

Hawksworth found himself caught up in the taste of imminent victory.

"*Charkhi! Charkhi!*" A cry began to rise from the crowd. The man holding the burning taper looked up toward Arangbar, who signaled lightly with his hand. Then the men holding the long poles tipped them toward the taper, and the two ends of papered bamboo were quickly ignited.

The bamboo sticks started to whirl like pinwheels, popping and throwing sparks from the gunpowder packed inside. The keepers turned and thrust the poles under the face of the brown elephant, sending him rearing backward in fright.

Although the black elephant now lay crushed against the wall, the brown was too distracted by the sudden noise to press his advantage. Instead he wheeled away from the exploding bamboo and began to charge wildly toward the edge of the crowd. Retreating bodies pummeled about Hawksworth, and there were frightened calls of "*lor langar*." As the elephant neared the crowd, its second rider, with a look of infinite regret, threw down the log chained to its forefoot. The chain whipped against its leg, and in moments it was tangled and stumbling.

By then the smaller black elephant had recovered its feet and came galloping in chase. In moments he was there, slamming his larger adversary with his tusks. The brown elephant stumbled awkwardly, tangled in the chain, and then collapsed into the dust. With a victory yell the *mahout* of the black elephant pulled a cord releasing a canvas cloth over its eyes. The heaving animal immediately began to gentle, and its jubilant keepers ran forward to lead it away.

"Your elephant lost, Sahib. My regrettings. May I have the twenty rupees?"

"But it was fixed!" Hawksworth held tightly to his purse. "The brown was clearly winning before he was frightened by the damned fireworks."

"Did I neglect to tell the Sahib that the black elephant is a *khasa*, from His Majesty's private stable? His Majesty does not like to see his elephants lose."

"You conniving bastard."

"His Majesty makes the rules, Sahib. It is permitted to use the *charkhi*

fireworks once during a contest, if His Majesty judges that the elephants need
to be disciplined. May Allah grant you better luck next week." The man
stood waiting, hand outstretched.

"You're a damned thief."

"That is a harsh judgment, Sahib. I am merely a poor man who must
live. If you wait, you will see what happens to criminals here."

With a sigh of resignation Hawksworth began to count out the twenty
silver rupees, trying to look as sporting as he could muster. He found himself
in grudging admiration of the swindler's style. Then he suddenly realized
what the man had said.

The rumors must have been right.

"You mean there'll be an execution?"

"This is the day. His Majesty always has executions on Tuesday, after
the elephant fights."

Hawksworth looked up to see another bull elephant being ridden into the
plaza. He had sharpened tusks, each decorated with a single heavy brass ring,
and was guided by a single rider, a fierce-looking, unshaven *mahout*. The elephant was festooned with bells, but there were no chains about any of its
legs.

At the other end of the square a balding man, with a short black beard
and a ragged green cloak, was being dragged forward by Imperial guards.
Hawksworth noticed that his arms had been bound behind him, by a heavy
cord circled just above the elbows. His eyes brimmed with fear.

The guards shoved him struggling toward the middle of the plaza. When
they reached the central clearing, the officer of the guard knocked him to his
knees with the butt end of a lance. The stunned prisoner turned to watch in
terror as the elephant lumbered toward him, flapping its ears in anticipation.

"He was sentenced yesterday, Sahib."

"What did he do? Steal some nobleman's sheep? In England that's a
hanging offense."

"Oh no, Sahib, Islamic law does not give the death penalty for theft, unless a thief is notorious. And even then he must be caught in the act. If it is
proved you have stolen something worth more than a certain amount, then
the sentence is to have your right hand cut off. But for that to happen there
must either be two witnesses or the thief must himself confess. Islamic law is
not cruel; it is just."

"What's this man accused of then?"

"He was tried and found guilty under Islamic law of *qatlul-'amd*, a willful murder. His name is Kaliyan, and he is a Hindu and the son of Bijai Ganga
Ram. He is accused of having kept a common Muslim woman as his concubine, and when the woman's father discovered this and went to reclaim
her to restore his family's honor, this man murdered him and buried him

behind his house. He confessed the act yesterday morning before His Majesty."

The elephant moved with calm deliberation toward the kneeling prisoner, guided by the *mahout*, until it towered directly over the quivering man. Suddenly it whipped its trunk about the man's torso and lifted him squirming into the air, holding him firmly against its banded tusks. It swung the screaming man back and forth in delight for a long moment, seeming to relish the torment, then dashed him violently to the ground.

The prisoner hit on his back, gasping, and weakly tried to roll to his feet. Before he could gain his footing, the elephant was there again, seizing him once more with its leathery trunk and again slamming him to the ground.

"The elephant will torment him for a time, Sahib. Before the moment of death." The small brown man's eyes shone in anticipation.

Again the prisoner was lifted and again dashed to the ground. Now he no longer attempted to struggle; he merely lay moaning in a broken voice.

Then the *mahout* shouted something to the elephant and the animal suddenly reared above the man, crushing down on him with both front feet. There was a final, rending scream and then silence, as blood sprayed over the dust. The elephant reared again, and again mashed the lifeless body. Then again. Finally the animal placed one foot on the man's lower torso and seized his crushed chest with its trunk, wrenching upward and rending the body in two. Maddened by the smell of blood, he whipped the torn half upward and slammed it once more against the hard earth. Finally the *mahout* tapped the blood-spattered elephant with his *ankus* and began guiding it toward the back of the square. The crowd, which had held a spellbound silence, erupted into cheers.

"That's the most brutal death I've ever seen." Hawksworth found his voice only after the initial shock had passed.

"It's why so few men dare to commit murder, Sahib. But His Majesty is very just. All criminals are given a full Islamic trial before they are executed."

Hawksworth looked up to see yet another man being led into the plaza. The cheers of the crowd died abruptly. He wore only a loincloth, which was pure white, and his hands were bound not behind him but in front, secured through a large wooden clamp that had been locked together like European stocks. Hawksworth took one look and felt his own groin tighten.

"All praise to Allah the Merciful. And to the Holy Prophet, on whom be peace," one of the white-bearded mullahs shouted through the silence. He wore a gray turban, a dingy collarless shirt that reached to his knees, and over that a long black vest. He carried a staff and was barefoot. Other mullahs clustered around him immediately joined his call.

"Murder! Murder!" Another voice began to chant, from a young man

standing near Hawksworth. Then other young men with him took up the cry
and began to surge forward. They were fresh-faced, with clean white shirts
and trousers, and they awkwardly began to brandish short swords.

Imperial guards immediately threw a line across the crowd and held the
young men back with short pikes. While the crowd watched, the prisoner
continued to walk alone and unescorted toward the center of the square.

Hawksworth studied the face again, the deep sad eyes above a flowing
white beard, and there was no doubt. He turned to the man standing beside
him.

"Do you know who that is?"

"Of course, Sahib. He's the heretic poet Samad. Did you hear that he denied the existence of Allah in an Islamic court? He has been sentenced to
death."

"Who are those men with the swords?"

"They're his disciples. I think they came today to try to save him."

Hawksworth turned to see the elephant again being urged forward.

"What about . . . what about the Persian woman I heard was arrested
with him?"

"I do not think she has been executed yet, Sahib. They say she will be
hanged, secretly, in the fort. Women are not executed by elephant."

"When . . ." Hawksworth struggled to contain his voice. "When do they
say she'll be hanged?"

"Perhaps in a week or two. Perhaps she is already dead." He moved forward to watch. "What do poor Believers know of justice inside the fort? But
the heretic Samad will die for all to see, so there will be no rumors that he
still lives. Already there are stories in Agra that he had escaped to Persia."

Samad had reached the center of the square. As the elephant approached,
he turned to the crowd of young men, raising his bound hands toward them
in a gesture of recognition.

"Do not grieve for this weak clay." His voice was sonorous, hypnotic, and
the crowd fell curiously quiet. "Grieve for yourselves, you who must travel
on a short while, sorrowing still."

The crowd erupted again, the mullahs and many others urging his death,
the young followers decrying it. Again he lifted his hands, and his voice
seemed to bring silence around it.

"I say to you do not grieve. You will all soon know far greater sorrow.
Soon death will lay his dark hand across the city of Agra, upon Muslim and
Hindu alike, upon woman and child. Many will perish without cause. Therefore grieve not for me. Grieve for yourselves, when death will descend upon
your doorsteps, there to take the innocent. Sorrow for your own."

The crowd had listened in hushed silence. Then a bearded mullah
shouted "Death to the heretic" and others took up the cry.

Samad watched the elephant quietly as it continued to lumber forward. When it reached him, he bowed to it with an ironic smile. The *mahout* looked upward toward the black throne of the *Diwan-i-Khas*, where Arangbar and Janahara sat waiting. Arangbar turned to the queen, with what seemed a question, and she replied without moving her stare from the court below. Arangbar paused a moment, then signaled the *mahout* to proceed. The bearded *mahout* saluted the *Moghul*, then urged the elephant forward with his sharp *ankus*.

The elephant flapped its bloodstained ears in confusion but did not move.

The *mahout* goaded it again and shouted something in its ear, but it merely waved its trunk and trumpeted.

"Merciful Allah. The elephant does not smell his crime." The small man caught Hawksworth's questioning look. "The Great Akman believed elephants would not kill an innocent man, that they can always smell a man's guilt. But I have never before seen one refuse to kill a prisoner. I think Samad must be a wizard, who has entranced the animal."

"Innocent," a young man from the group of disciples yelled out above the silence.

The *mahout* goaded the elephant once more, but still it stood unmoving.

"Innocent." More cries went up from Samad's young followers, and again they pressed forward, swords in hand. In moments the plaza became a battleground, blood staining the earth as the Imperial guards began turning their pikes against the line of disciples. Then others in the crowd, mullahs leading them, broke through and joined the battle against the young men. Sword rang against sword and calls to Allah rent the air.

Samad stood quietly watching as the battle edged toward him. Then suddenly a group of bearded mullahs broke from the crowd and surged toward him, swords drawn. Hawksworth instinctively reached for his own weapon, but the man beside him caught his arm. He looked down to see a small, rust-handled *katar* pointed against his chest.

"This is the will of Allah. An infidel must not interfere."

The mullahs had formed a ring around Samad. He stood silently, waiting, as the leader stepped forward and thrust a long sword into the bare skin of his lower stomach. He jerked but did not fall, standing tall as another swung a sharp blade across his open neck. His head dropped to one side and he slumped forward, as two more men thrust swords into his belly. In seconds he disappeared beneath a crowd of black cloaks.

From a low latticework window down the east side of the Red Fort, past the Jasmine Tower and many levels below the Khas Mahal, it was just possible to see the center of the plaza. A woman stood by the window watching as the crowd turned on the young men and, one by one, cut them down.

Then she saw a bloodstained body being hoisted above a black-cloaked assembly and carried triumphantly toward the river gate.

There had been tears as Shirin watched. But as she turned away, toward the darkness of the cell, her eyes were hard and dry.

CHAPTER TWENTY-FOUR

Hawksworth waited anxiously by the rear entryway of the *Diwan-i-Khas* and watched the three Jesuits file silently through the tapestried archway beside him. Father Alvarez Sarmento, imperious in his freshly laundered black habit, moved directly to the silver railing that circled the throne. The old priest's eyes seemed to fairly glow in triumph. Behind him trailed Father Pinheiro and the pudgy father Francisco da Silva, their attempts at poise marred by shifting, anxious glances of disquiet. Hawksworth studied all three and puzzled even more what could be afoot.

Over a week had passed since the death of Samad, and since that day he had no longer been invited to Arangbar's evenings in the *Diwan-i-Khas*. Even his requests for an audience had been ignored. Before the poet's death, it had been possible for him to believe that the absurdity of Samad and Shirin's arrest would eventually resolve itself, that the nightmare would fade into reality and bring their release. But the killing of Samad had blotted out that illusion. When he saw Arangbar, presiding high above the square, signal the Sufi's death, he had realized finally the nightmare was all too real. Since that time he had spent the sleepless nights alone, distraught, counting the passage of each hour as he awaited news Shirin was also dead. In his mind he had conceived a dozen stratagems to try to save her, a dozen arguments, threats, bargains for her release, but nothing could be done if he was denied even an audience with the *Moghul*.

That they should have tasted so much, only to lose it all. He found himself aware, for the first time ever, how much he could want, could need, a woman like Shirin beside him. With her, life itself seemed renewed. She was like no other he had ever known: strong, beautiful, self-willed. He had found himself admiring the last most of all, even though he still found it startling. But the love he had known with her in his arms now only made the despair deeper. Nothing was left. Now there was only abiding sorrow, loss beyond healing. She had given him something he had never known, something he realized—for the first time ever—he no longer wanted to live without. He would have taken her place a hundred times over, but even that seemed impossible.

Then, that morning, hope had appeared, almost a miracle. A sudden, urgent message had been delivered, instructing him to appear once more in the *Diwan-i-Khas*. It almost certainly meant Arangbar had received word of the

English fleet. If Shirin were still alive, and there had been no news of her death, it must mean that the *Moghul* was uncertain about her guilt: he was not a man who normally waited to act. And if she was alive, all things again became possible . . .

He had asked himself again and again over the past week why he had suddenly been forgotten by Arangbar. He finally concluded it was the distracting turmoil that had gripped Agra and the court since Samad's death.

The Sufi's last words had been repeated throughout the city, and already there were rumors of impending calamity: the bazaars were alive with talk of a Persian Safavid invasion from the northwest, a rebellion among the Imperial guards, an impending holocaust that would burn all Agra to ash, a universal plague. The streets had an apocalyptic air, with omens foreseen in every temple.

Another reason for Arangbar's preoccupation could be the rumors from the south. Word was sweeping Agra that Prince Jadar and his army had been savaged by the Deccani forces and were now retreating northward, with Malik Ambar in pursuit. If this story were true, then the Abyssinian's defeat of Jadar must have been overwhelming, since rebels did not normally pursue Moghul forces. But this story was still merely rumor. There had been no actual reports of any engagements in the south.

Jadar's possible defeat, so the talk in Agra went, had gone very heavily with Arangbar, and accounted for his increasing dependence on opium and wine. Those who had seen him reported the *Moghul* was growing noticeably weaker. And as his strength waned, so too did his authority. Ever since the night of the wedding, Queen Janahara had been moving to assume more and more of the prerogatives of power. Arangbar already seemed to be becoming a figurehead. The only sanctuary she had not yet invaded was the *Diwan-i-Khas*.

Those evening gatherings Arangbar still ruled like a god, and the unusual note he had sent to Hawksworth was worded almost more like an order than an invitation. It confirmed vividly the reports that Arangbar was growing more erratic by the day.

Around Hawksworth sat the usual assembly of Arangbar's closest advisers, men whose perpetually smiling faces he had come to know well over the past weeks. Prominent among them as always was Nadir Sharif, who now seemed to be avoiding Hawksworth's glance. Also in attendance was a special contingent of Rajput guards, in Imperial turbans and tunics. Hawksworth could never remember having seen these particular guards in the *Diwan-i-Khas* before.

When the last official had arrived, the Rajput guards moved across the doorway and the kettledrum was sounded. Moments later the tapestry behind the throne was pushed aside by two eunuchs and Arangbar emerged into the light. He stumbled momentarily on the edge of a carpet, then recovered his balance and took his seat on the white marble throne. His dull eyes glistened against the lamplight as the men in the room dropped to *teslim*. For the first time he seemed more annoyed than amused when Hawksworth failed to bow to the carpet. He glared at him for a long moment and then spoke to Nadir Sharif, who stood waiting by his side. The prime minister turned to the room.

"Ambassador Hawksworth, His Majesty commands you to come forward."

It was abrupt language rarely heard in the *Diwan-i-Khas*, and the room immediately fell silent. Hawksworth rose and tightened his belt, feeling his apprehension rising. As he neared the throne, he found himself seeing not Arangbar's expressionless gaze, but the face of Shirin as she waited for help.

"Inglish, stand there." He pointed to the side of the throne opposite the Jesuits. "Tell me, any fresh news of your king's fleet?"

Hawksworth felt his heart explode, realizing there was no arrival—and no possibility of using King James's presents to bargain for Shirin. "I expect it any day, Your Majesty. Possibly the winds have been against them."

"The winds." Arangbar turned to Father Sarmento, his voice sarcastic. "Do you think the winds have been against them, Padre?"

"Undoubtedly, Majesty." Sarmento could not suppress a malicious smile. "The winds of truth. They have been arrested in a gale of deception."

"I object, Your Majesty, to this Papist's innuendos." Hawksworth felt himself suddenly bristle. "An Englishman does not accept insults from a Portugal."

"You will listen quietly to what you are about to hear, Inglish, or you will be removed by my guards." Arangbar again turned to Father Sarmento. "Padre, repeat to the Inglish conspirator what you told me this afternoon."

"May it please Your Majesty, not only is the English a heretic before God and the Holy Church, he is also a liar." Sarmento paused with the dramatic timing of a practiced orator. "*There is no English fleet.*"

Hawksworth stared at the Jesuit in speechless dismay. His entire being seemed to crash down about him as Sarmento continued.

"Because of the foresight of His Excellency, Miguel Vaijantes, Viceroy of Goa, we have now uncovered the truth, Your Majesty. After his patrols encountered no English merchantmen, either north or south, he began to grow suspicious. He ordered his personal guards to find and detain the man who claimed to have intercepted Jadar's cipher reporting the fleet. The traitor was found, not surprisingly, in a Goan brothel, where he had been for many days, spending more money than such a man could normally earn in a lifetime. He was brought to the palace and interrogated on the *strappado*." Sarmento turned triumphantly to Hawksworth. "Where he readily admitted being paid to bring a false report."

"And who do you believe paid him?"

"On that His Excellency is still uncertain, Your Majesty. He was paid by agents in the south."

"But who does the Viceroy *believe* paid the money?"

"The coins were assayed and traced to the mint at Surat, Your Majesty. They were part of a special minting that took place just before the English, Hawksworth, left the city. The assay also revealed they were a debased alloy, slightly lower in silver content than is normal, although not enough to be readily detectable. Similar coins have begun to be used throughout the Deccan. Reportedly they were given out recently by Prince Jadar as back pay to the troops of certain *mansabdars*."

"Who were the coins minted for?"

"The Shahbandar at Surat, Mirza Nuruddin, claims to have misplaced the records for this particular minting. However, he maintains the lower silver content was probably due to a minter's oversight. The former governor of Surat, Mukarrab Khan, is returning to the city to investigate. The minting run appears to have been approximately fifty *lakhs* of rupees. But the actual silver content was only forty-nine *lakhs* of rupees." He paused for breath. "The Shahbandar says he has no idea what could have happened to the other *lakh*'s worth of silver bullion authorized to be used in the minting."

"That's not so difficult to explain, knowing Mirza Nuruddin." Arangbar seemed to be talking to himself. Then he glanced again at Sarmento. "Of course, the discrepancy would probably never have been detected if the coins given to the traitor had not been melted down and assayed. The question remains who ordered him paid?" Arangbar turned to Hawksworth, who stood with his mind churning, refusing to accept the consequences of what he was hearing. It meant the end of everything. "Perhaps the Inglish ambassador can help explain it."

"I have no idea why there was a false report, Majesty. I believed it too."

"Did you, Inglish?" Arangbar glared down drunkenly from his throne. "Or did you plot this with Prince Jadar when you met with him in Burhanpur? Did you and he conspire together to deceive me, exchanging bribes in the pocket of the prince with some of this debased silver coin for his help in a ruse you thought would produce a *firman* when brought to my ears?"

"I gave nothing to the prince, Majesty. And I asked nothing from him. That is the truth."

"The truth from you is not always easy to obtain, Inglish. Your deceptions have distressed me very much. And, curiously enough, Her Majesty even more. There is no fleet, Inglish. Instead there are lies, by you and, I'm beginning to suspect now, by my own son. I no longer have any idea what he is doing in the south. But I fear his arrogance has brought ruin to his army. I am recalling him to Agra, immediately, for an inquiry, and I am hereby ordering you to leave India."

Hawksworth noticed Nadir Sharif shoot a troubled glance toward the Jesuits.

"May it please Your Majesty, neither I nor my king have had anything to do with the reports of the fleet, whether true or false. There will be other voyages and soon. My king has promised it, and he is a sovereign who honors his word."

"Your Inglish king posts a conspirator and a traitor to my court. He will never have a *firman* from my hand, no matter how many voyages he may send."

"If there is indeed no fleet now, then I agree Your Majesty has been deceived. But I have been also. We have both been used by those around us, for purposes unknown. But my king would not knowingly play false with Your Majesty. Nor would I. Those who would deceive you, whoever they may be, sit much closer to Your Majesty's throne."

"It is not your place, Inglish, to tell me mine is a court of liars. Your forgeries in India are ended. You will be gone from Agra within the week, or I will not answer for your life. After that you no longer may use the title of ambassador. You will be treated as the conspirator you are. And as of this moment you are stripped of your title of khan." He motioned to the Rajput guards. "Take him away."

Hawksworth turned to see Father Sarmento beaming.

"Alas it seems we soon must part, Ambassador. May God in His mercy grant you a pleasant and speedy journey. Should you wish to travel through Goa, I can give you a letter to His Excellency, Miguel Vaijantes, requesting safe passage on a westbound galleon."

"Damn your Viceroy." As Hawksworth turned back toward Arangbar, he felt rough hands close about his arms. Before he could speak, he was being guided through the rear doorway and into the long gallery leading to the public square.

"Majesty." Nadir Sharif watched the curtains close behind Hawksworth, then rose and moved closer to the throne. "May it please you, the Englishman unfortunately remains my guest. At least for a few more days. As his host I feel a trifling obligation to see he finds his way home safely. I ask leave to excuse myself for a few moments to ensure he finds a palanquin."

"As you wish." Arangbar was watching a eunuch bring in a box of opium.

When Nadir Sharif moved toward the doorway, Father Pinheiro rose unobtrusively and slipped out behind him. As the Jesuit moved into the hallway, he appeared not to hurry, but his brisk walk brought him alongside the prime minister midway down the corridor.

"Have you told Her Majesty, as we agreed?"

"Told her what?" Nadir Sharif did not break his pace or remove his eyes from Hawksworth, still being led by the guards several yards ahead.

"About the ship that would be seized."

Nadir Sharif stopped as though hit by an arrow. "But surely you'll not take the vessel now! Didn't you see that the Englishman has been ordered out of Agra? He's finished. There'll certainly be no trading *firman* for him now, or ever."

"But the warships were dispatched from Surat day before yesterday, just before the pigeons arrived from Goa with the word of the hoax. His Excellency, Miguel Vaijantes', message revoking their order to sail arrived a day too late. They were already at sea. The Indian ship may have already been seized."

Nadir Sharif inspected him with astonishment. "Your Viceroy must be mad. To take the vessel now? There's no purpose in it. His Majesty will be most annoyed."

"But you were the one who suggested it!" The Jesuit's voice rose, quivering in dismay. "You said that bold measures were for bold men. Those were your words. His Excellency agreed it would be a decisive stroke of firmness."

"And what does Father Sarmento think of this folly?"

"Father Sarmento does not yet know. I thought it best not to inform him." Pinheiro's eyes were despairing. "What did Her Majesty, Queen Janahara, say about the plan?"

"What do you mean?"

"We agreed you would tell her."

"I've not forgotten our agreement. I've been watching carefully for the right moment."

"She does not even know!" Pinheiro seized his arm and stared at him incredulously. "But I told His Excellency you would . . ."

"I planned to tell her any day. The time was approaching. But now, given what has happened . . ." Then he smiled and touched the Jesuit's arm lightly. "But I think she can still bring reason to His Majesty. It can all be readily explained as a misunderstanding."

"But you must tell her immediately." Pinheiro's shock was growing. "If she hears of it before you've explained, she'll think . . ."

"Of course. But there's no reason yet for concern." Nadir Sharif smiled again. "I assure you it all can be handled very routinely. But please tell His Excellency, Miguel Vaijantes, not to do anything else this ill-advised for at least a week. I can only excuse so much at one time."

As Nadir Sharif turned to continue down the corridor, Pinheiro reached out and seized his arm again. "You must also do one other thing. You must make sure the Englishman is removed from Agra immediately. We both know His Majesty may well forget by tomorrow that he has ordered him gone."

"This time I doubt very much His Majesty will forget. It will only be a matter of days, in any case." Nadir Sharif turned and smiled. "And remember what I told you, that as far as His Majesty is concerned, I know nothing about your Viceroy's impetuous act. But I do advise you to inform Father Sarmento, before he hears it in open *durbar*."

"He'll be furious. He'll probably order me back to Goa."

"I doubt it. I'm sure he knows your value here." Nadir Sharif turned without another word and hurried on down the corridor.

Ahead of him Hawksworth was being led by the guards through the marble archways. As they reached the end, facing the doorway leading to the courtyard stairs, he turned one last time and stared back, seeing Nadir Sharif for the first time.

"What do you want now? My money or my life? Or both?"

"I merely came to see you safely home, Ambassador." Nadir Sharif waved the guards back toward the *Diwan-i-Khas*, and they bowed with relief as they turned to retreat. "And to offer my condolences."

"And no doubt to cozen me as well. I intend to find out who played me false. Even if it's Jadar. Somebody has hell to pay."

"That would be most unwise, Ambassador. I'm afraid we were *all* a bit too credulous. I readily confess even I had begun to believe your story."

"It wasn't 'my story'! I knew nothing about . . ."

"But you never denied it, Ambassador. Surely you knew the truth all along. The truth is always wisest. That's my cardinal rule in life."

"But it *could* have been true. It was entirely possible. Why didn't you explain that to Arangbar? You're still supposed to be my agent."

"That would be rather difficult for His Majesty to believe, given what really happened. But I do suppose it's possible." Nadir Sharif patted Hawksworth's shoulder. "I'll see if there's anything I can do. But in the meantime, I suggest you begin preparations to leave. His Majesty was unusually disturbed tonight."

"He's disturbed over a lot of things, most of which have little to do with me."

"If you mean the matter of the prince, I assure you it's alarming to us all. No one is certain what has happened in the south. In fact, you were one of the last men to see Prince Jadar. He seems almost to have disappeared. All sorts of rumors are working their way to the court. Where it will end no one can any longer even guess." Nadir Sharif followed Hawksworth out into the open square of the *Diwan-i-Am*. "Incidentally, Ambassador, did you yourself know anything about the fifty *lakhs* of silver coin spoken of tonight?"

Hawksworth examined him a moment. "Maybe the Shahbandar stole it all."

"That's hardly an answer, Ambassador. It wasn't, by any chance, traveling with you from Surat to Burhanpur? You know, His Majesty has demanded a full investigation. I think he may just summon Mirza Nuruddin to Agra for an explanation."

"Then let him ask Mirza Nuruddin what happened. I'm sure he'll get the truth." Hawksworth turned toward the large gate at the far end of the square.

"Very well, Ambassador." Nadir Sharif smiled warmly. "By the way, I understand Mirza Nuruddin has suggested you may have smuggled it out of Surat yourself, leaving a worthless letter of credit, in order to swindle your merchants."

"The bastard."

"The truth will surely come out, Ambassador, as you say. So I wish you good night and a restful sleep." Nadir Sharif turned and in moments had melted into the darkness.

Hawksworth slowly worked his way down the cobblestone roadway, past the guards at the Amar Singh Gate, and into the Agra night. He turned left and headed toward the banks of the Jamuna, hoping the smells and sounds of water would soothe his mind. When he reached the riverbank, he found himself looking back at the massive walls of the Red Fort, wondering again where Shirin was being kept, wanting to be with her. To hold her one last time. But the high stone walls stood dark and mute as his own despair.

"You are home, Sahib." The servants were waiting, beaming and immaculate in fresh muslin *dhotis*, as Hawksworth pushed open the doors of his compound. It was nearing midnight. "Your house is honored tonight with a special evening."

"What are you planning? My farewell?"

The servants examined him uncomprehending as he pushed past the portiere of the doorway.

The room was heavy with sandalwood incense. In the lamplight he recognized Kamala's musicians: the gray-haired flautist in a long *lungi* wrap and bare to the waist, the drummer smiling widely in a plain white shirt and brown *dhoti*. Although he had not seen them for days, they paused only briefly to acknowledge him. The drummer was absorbed in tuning his instrument, using a small hammer to tap blocks of wood wedged beneath the leather thongs securing the drumhead. As he adjusted the tension on the thongs, he periodically tested the drum's pitch against a note from the flute.

Kamala was nowhere to be seen. Hawksworth stared about the room quizzically, then turned to the musicians. They responded with a puzzled shrug and motioned toward a rear door.

"She summoned them here tonight, Sahib. She did not tell them why.

No one has seen her all day. It is very worrying." The servant shuffled uneasily. "Has the Sahib heard the stories in the bazaar?"

"What stories?"

From behind the curtains came the sudden tinkling of tiny bells. The musicians smiled in recognition.

As the servants edged toward the curtained doorway to look, Hawksworth extracted a half-empty bottle of brandy from his chest and threw himself down against a bolster.

What's this all about? Why can't I be alone for once? Tonight of all nights she does this.

He puzzled a moment over Kamala, her erratic and powerful moods, then his thoughts returned gloomily to the *Diwan-i-Khas* and to Shirin. He could not give up hope. Never. He never gave up hope.

There was another tinkling of bells and the curtain at the doorway was swept aside. Standing there, jewels afire in the lamplight, was Kamala.

He noticed the two musicians stare at her for an instant, then exchange quick, disturbed glances.

She was, it seemed, more striking than he had ever seen her. Her eyes were seductively lined with kohl and her lips were an inviting red, matching the large dot on her forehead. In one side of her nose she wore a small ring studded with diamonds. Her hair was swept back and secured with rows of rubies and her throat and arms were circled with bands of gold imbedded with small green emeralds. She wore a silken wrap folded in pleats about each leg in a way that enhanced the full curve of her hips. Her waist was circled by a belt of beaten gold, and her palms and the soles of her feet had been reddened with henna. As she came toward him, the bands of tiny bells at her ankles punctuated the sensuous sway of her breasts beneath her silk halter.

"You've returned early. I'm glad." As she moved into the light, he thought he caught a glimpse of some profound melancholy in her eyes. He also noted her voice was strangely frail.

"Is there supposed to be a ceremony tonight I didn't know about?" As Hawksworth studied her, he took another long swallow of brandy, its heat burning away at his anguish.

"This is a special evening. I have decided to dance Bharata Natyam one last time, for Lord Shiva."

"What do you mean, one last time?"

She seemed to stare past him for a moment, then she slowly turned. "I'm truly glad you've come. To be here tonight. I would have waited for you, but there was no time. And I wondered if you would really understand. Perhaps I was wrong. Bharata Natyam is never only for the dancer. So it is good you are here. Perhaps it was meant to be. Perhaps you can understand something of what I feel tonight."

"I haven't understood much that's happened tonight so far." Hawksworth settled his brandy bottle awkwardly onto the carpet and forced himself to bring her into focus.

"You do not seem yourself, my *feringhi* Sahib." She studied him for a moment. "Did you hear sad news of your Persian woman?"

"Nothing. But I'm afraid I've just lost my best chance to save her."

"I don't understand."

"It's not your trouble." He examined her wistfully. "It seems I'll be leaving Agra sooner than I thought. So dance if you want, and then I'll wish you well."

"Your trouble is *always* my trouble." She frowned as she studied him. "But you are leaving? So soon?" She seemed not to wait for an answer as she went on. "Never mind, I've never understood the affairs of ambassadors and kings. But our parting must not be sad. Let my dance to Shiva be my farewell to you."

She turned and signaled to the flautist, who began a low-pitched, poignant melody. "Have you ever seen the Bharata Natyam?"

"Never." Hawksworth sipped more brandy from the bottle and found himself wishing he could send them all away and play a suite on his lute, the one he had played for Shirin that day at the observatory.

"Then it may be difficult for you to comprehend at first. With my body and my song I will tell Lord Shiva of my longing for him. Do you think you can understand it?"

"I'll try." Hawksworth looked up at her and again sensed some great sadness in her eyes.

She examined him silently for a moment. "But I want you to understand. Not the words I sing, they're in ancient Sanskrit, but if you watch my hands, they will also speak. I will sing to Lord Shiva, but I give life to his song with my eyes, my hands, my body. I will re-create the poem with my dance. My eyes will speak the desire of my heart. The language of my hands will tell my longing for Lord Shiva. My feet will show the rhythms by which he brings order to the world. If you will try to feel what I feel, perhaps Lord Shiva will touch you and lighten your burden."

"And this is called Bharata Natyam? What does that mean?" Hawksworth slipped off his mud-smeared boots and wearily tossed them next to the carpet.

"The ancient temple dance of India is Bharata Natyam: *bhava* means mood, *raga* means song, *tala* means rhythm. All these are brought together in the dance. Natyam means the merging of dance and story. The true Bharata Natyam has seven movements: some are called pure dance and these are only rhythms, but some also tell a story. If I were to dance them all, as I would in the temple, I would have to dance all night." She tried wanly to smile. "But not now. Tonight I am not so strong. Tonight I will dance only the Varnam, the most important movement. In it I will tell the story of how the goddess Parvati, Shiva's beloved consort, longs for her lord. If I dance well I will become Parvati, and through the story of her love for Shiva, I will tell my own."

"So it's really just a love song?"

"It is Parvati's song of longing for her lord. The words are very simple.

> *"Great with love for you this night,*
> *Am I, oh Lord.*
> *Do not avert yourself from me.*
> *Do not tease me, do not scorn me,*
> *Oh great, oh beautiful God*
> *Of the Brihadishwari temple.*
> *Great God who gives release*
> *From the sorrows of the world . . ."*

Kamala paused to tighten the straps securing the bells around her ankles. "The song goes on to say that she cannot bear even to hear the voice of the nightingale now that she is separated from her Lord Shiva. She cannot endure the dark night now that he has taken himself from her."

"It's a very touching love song." Hawksworth found himself thinking again of Shirin, and of the dark nights they had both endured.

"It is really much more. You see, Lord Shiva is her beloved, but he is also her god. So her song also praises the beauty of the great Shiva in all his many aspects: as her own consort, as one who has the Third Eye of Knowledge, as the great God of the Dance, Nataraj. Through my dance I will show all the many aspects of Shiva—as creator, as destroyer, as lord of the cosmic rhythms of life."

Hawksworth watched in groggy fascination as she rose and, clasping her hands above her head, bowed toward a small bronze statue of the Dancing Shiva she had placed on a corner table. Then, as the drummer took up a steady cadence and the flute began a searching, high-pitched lament, she struck a statuesque pose of her own, feet crossed, arms above her head. Gradually her eyes began to dart seductively from side to side, growing in power until it seemed her entire body might explode. Abruptly she assumed a second pose, reminiscent of the statue. As the drummer's rhythms slowly increased, she began to follow them with her body, next with her feet, slapping heel, then ball, fiercely against the carpet. The drummer began to call out his *bols*, the strokes he was sounding on the drum, and as he did she matched his rhythms with the rows of tiny bells around her ankles.

Hawksworth found himself being drawn into her dance. Her rhythms were not flamboyant like those of the Kathak style, but rather seemed to duplicate some deep natural cadence, as she returned again and again to the pose of the Dancing Shiva. It was pure dance, and he slowly began to feel the power of her controlled sensuality.

Without warning she began a brief song to Shiva in a high-pitched, repetitive refrain. As she sang, her hands formed the signs for woman, for beauty, for desire, for dozens of other words and ideas Hawksworth could not decipher. Yet her expressive eyes exquisitely translated many of the hand signs, while her body left no mistaking the intensity of their emotion.

When the song and its mime reached some climactic plateau, she suddenly resumed the pure dance, with the drummer once more reciting the *bols* as he sounded them. Again she matched his rhythms perfectly.

After a time she began another verse of the song. By her mime Hawksworth concluded she was describing some aspect of Lord Shiva. When the song concluded, the drummer called out more *bols* and again she danced only his rhythms. Then she began yet another verse of the song, followed by still more rhythmic dance. The aspects of Shiva that she created all seemed different. Some wise, some fierce, some clearly of a beauty surpassing words.

As Hawksworth watched, he began to sense some alien power growing around him, enveloping him and his despair, just as she had said. Kamala seemed to be gradually merging with an energy far beyond herself, almost as though she had invoked some primal rhythm of life into existence. And as he watched the growing intensity of her dance he began to experience a deep, almost primitive sense of fear, a stark knowledge of life and death beyond words.

He found himself fighting to resist the force of some malevolent evil settling about the room, beginning to possess it and all it contained. He felt its power begin to draw out his own life, hungry and insistent, terrifying. And still she danced on, now only rhythms, her body dipping and whirling, her arms everywhere at once, her smile frozen in an ecstatic trance.

Forcing himself at last to turn away, he looked toward the musicians. They seemed entranced by her as well, captured by the delirium of her dance. He finally caught the eye of the drummer and weakly signaled him to stop. But the man stared as though not comprehending, spellbound. Her dance had now grown to a frenzy, surpassing human limits.

Summoning his last strength, he tried to pull himself up off the bolster, but he discovered his legs were no longer his own. The room had become a whirling pattern of color and sound, beyond all control.

Uncertainly he turned and began to feel about the carpet for his boots. His grip closed about a sheath of soft leather and he probed inside. There, strapped and still loaded, was his remaining pocket pistol. Shakily he took it in his hand, checked the prime, and began trying to aim at the long drum resting between the musicians. Now the drum seemed to drift back and forth in his vision, while the players smiled at him with glazed eyes.

He heard a hiss and felt his hand fly upward, as though unconnected to his body. Then the world around erupted in smoke and flying splinters of wood.

The shot had been timed perfectly with the end of a rhythm cycle, as the drum exploded into fragments on the *sum*.

The smoky room was suddenly gripped in silence. The musicians stared wildly for a moment, then threw themselves face down on the carpet, pleading in unknown words needing no translation. Hawksworth looked in confusion at the smoking pistol in his hand, not recognizing it. Then he threw it onto the carpet and turned toward Kamala.

She was gazing at him with open, vacant eyes, as though awakened suddenly from a powerful dream. Her breath was coming in short bursts, and her skin seemed afire. She stood motionless for a moment, then tried to move toward him, holding out her arms. After two hesitant steps, she crumpled to the carpet.

When he bolted upward to reach for her, the servants were there, holding him back.

"You must not touch her, Sahib."

"But she's . . ."

"No, Sahib." They gripped his arms tighter. "Can't you see? She has the sickness."

"What are you talking about?"

"It began late today, in the bazaar. Perhaps they do not know of it yet in the fort. At first no one realized what it was. But tonight, while she was dancing, one of the slaves from Sharif Sahib's kitchen came to tell us. Two of the eunuchs and five of his servants have become very sick." He paused to look at Kamala. "I think she must have known. That is why she wanted to dance tonight."

"Knew what? What did she know?"

"The plague, Sahib. The slave who came said that the plague has struck all over Agra. It has never happened in India before." The servant paused. "It is the will of Allah. The prophet Samad foretold it. Now it has come."

Hawksworth turned again to Kamala. She was still watching him with empty, expressionless eyes, as though her life had just poured out of her. He looked down at her for a moment, then reached for a pillow and carefully slipped it beneath her head. Her lips moved as she tried to form words, but at first no sound came. Then, as though again finding some strength beyond herself, her voice came in a whisper.

"Did you see?"

"What . . . ?"

"Did you see him? The Great God Shiva. He came tonight. And danced beside me. Did you see his beauty?" She paused to breathe, then her voice rose again, full and warm. "He was as I knew he would be. Beautiful beyond telling. He danced in a ring of fire, with his hair streaming out in burning strands. He came as Shiva the Destroyer. But his dance was so beautiful. So very, very beautiful."

CHAPTER TWENTY-FIVE

From the *Tuzuk-i-Arangbari*, the court chronicles of His Imperial Majesty:

On the day of *Mubarak-shamba*, the twenty-eighth of the month of Dai, there came first reports of the pestilence in the city of Agra. On this day over five hundred people were stricken.

The first signs are headache and fever and much bleeding at the nose. After this the *dana* of the plague, buboes, form under the armpits, or in the groin, or below the throat. The infected ones turn in color from yellow inclining to black. They vomit and endure much high fever and pain. And then they die.

If one in a household contracts the pestilence and dies, others in the same house inevitably follow after, traveling the same road of annihilation. Those in whom the buboes appeared, if they call another person for water to drink or wash, will also infect the latter with the *sirayat*, the infection. It has come to pass that, through excessive apprehension, none will minister unto those infected.

It has become known from men of great age and from old histories that this disease has never before shown itself in this land of Hindustan. Many physicians and learned men have been questioned as to its cause. Some say it has come because there has been drought for two years in succession; others say it is owing to the corruption of the air. Some attribute it to other causes.

The infection is now spreading to all towns and villages in the region of Agra save one, the noble city of the Great Akman, Fatehpur.

Wisdom is of Allah, and all men must submit.

Written this last day of the Muharram in the Hijri year after the Prophet of 1028 A.H., by Mu'tamad Khan, Second *Wazir* to His Imperial Majesty, Arangbar.

Brian Hawksworth walked slowly up worn stone steps leading from the riverside funeral ghats. The pathway was narrow, crowded, and lined with carved statues of Hindu gods: a roly-poly god with human form and the head of an elephant, a god with a lion's body and a grotesquely grinning human face, an austere deity with a pointed head and a trident in his hand. All were ancient, weathered, ill-kept. Tame monkeys, small, brown, malicious, chased among them screeching.

The smoke from the ghats behind him still seared in his lungs. Only when he reached the top of the steps could he force himself to look back. Scavenger birds wheeled in the sky above and small barks with single oarsmen plied the muddy face of the Jamuna. Along the banks were toiling washermen, Untouchables, who wore nothing save a brown loincloth and a kerchief over their heads. They stood in a long row, knee-deep at the water's edge, mechanically slapping folded lengths of cloth against stacks of flat stones. They seemed unconcerned by the nearness of the funeral ghats, stone platforms at the river's edge that were built out above the steps leading down into the water. As he silently surveyed the crowd around him, from somewhere on the street above a voice chanted a funeral litany: *Ram Nam Sach Hai*, the Name of Ram Is Truth Itself.

It had taken four days for Kamala to die. The morning after she had danced, she had begun to show unmistakable symptoms of the plague. She had called for Brahmin priests and, seating herself on a wooden plank in their presence, had removed her *todus*, the ear pendants that were the mark of her *devadasi* caste, and placed them together with twelve gold coins on the plank before her. It was her deconsecration. Then with a look of infinite peace, she had announced she was ready to die.

Next she informed the priests that since she had no sons in Agra, no family at all, she wanted Brian Hawksworth to officiate at her funeral. He had not understood what she wanted until the servants whispered it to him. The Brahmins had been scandalized and at first had refused to agree, insisting he had no caste and consequently was a despicable Untouchable. Finally, after more payments, they had reluctantly consented. Then she had turned to him and explained what she had done.

When he tried to argue, she had appealed to him in the name of Shiva.

"I only ask you do this one last thing for me," she had said, going on to insist his responsibilities would not be difficult. "There are Hindu servants in the palace. Though they are low caste, they know enough Turki to guide you."

After the Brahmins had departed, she called the servants and, as Hawksworth watched, ordered them to remove all her jewels from the rosewood box where she kept them. Then she asked him to accompany them as they took the jewels through the Hindu section of Agra, to a temple of the goddess Mari, who presides over epidemics. They were to donate all her jewels to the goddess. Smiling at Hawksworth's astonishment, she had explained that Hindus believe a person's reincarnation is directly influenced by the amount of alms given in his or her previous life. This last act of charity might even bring her back as a Brahmin.

Two days later she lapsed into a delirium of fever. As death drew near, the Hindu servants again summoned the priests to visit the palace. The plague was spreading now, and with it fear, and at first none had been willing to comply. Only after it was agreed that they would be paid three times the usual price for the ceremonies did the Brahmins come. They had laid Kamala's fevered body on a bed of kusa grass in the open air, sprinkled her head with water brought from the sacred Ganges River, and smeared her brow with Ganges clay. She had seemed only vaguely conscious of what they were doing.

When at last she died, her body was immediately washed, perfumed, and bedecked with flowers. Then she was wrapped in linen, lifted onto a bamboo bier, and carried toward the river ghats by the Hindu servants, winding through the streets with her body held above their heads, intoning a funeral dirge. Hawksworth had led the procession, carrying a firepot with sacred fire provided by Nadir Sharif's Hindu servants.

The riverside was already crowded with mourners, for there had been many deaths, and the air was acrid from the smoke of cremation pyres. On the steps above the ghats was a row of thatch umbrellas, and sitting on a reed mat beneath each was a Brahmin priest. All were shirtless, potbellied, and wore three stripes of white clay down their forehead in honor of Vishnu's trident. The servants approached one of the priests and began to bargain with him. After a time the man rose and signified agreement. The servants whispered to Hawksworth that he was there to provide funeral rites for hire, adding with some satisfaction that Brahmins who served at the ghats were despised as mercenaries by the rest of their caste.

After the bargain had been struck, the priest retired beneath his umbrella to watch while they purchased logs from vendors and began construction of a pyre. When finished, it was small, no more than three feet high, and irregular; but no one seemed to care. Satisfied, they proceeded to douse it with oil.

Then the Brahmin priest was summoned from his umbrella and he rose and came down the steps, bowing to a stone Shiva lingam as he passed. After he had performed a short ceremony, chanting from the Vedas, the winding sheet was cut away and Kamala's body was lifted atop the stack of wood.

A mortal sadness had swept through Hawksworth as he stood holding the torch, listening to the Brahmin chant and studying the flow of the river. He thought again of Kamala, of the times he had secretly admired her erotic bearing, the times she had sat patiently explaining how best to draw the long sensuous notes from his new sitar, the times he had held her in his arms. And he thought again of their last evening, when she had danced with the power of a god.

When at last he moved toward the bier, the servants had touched his arm and pointed him toward her feet, explaining that only if the deceased were a man could the pyre be lighted at the head.

The oil-soaked logs had kindled quickly, sending out the sweet smoke of neem. Soon the pyre was nothing but yellow tongues of fire, and for a moment he thought he glimpsed her once more, in among the flames, dancing as the goddess Parvati, the beloved consort of Shiva.

When he turned to walk away, the servants had caught his sleeve and indicated he must remain. As her "son" it was his duty to ensure that the heat burst her skull, releasing her soul. Otherwise he would have to do it himself.

He waited, the smoke drifting over him, astonished that a religion capable of the beauty of her dance could treat death with such barbarity. At last, to his infinite relief, the servants indicated they could leave. They gathered up the pot of sacred fire and took his arm to lead him away. It was then he had pulled away, wanting to be alone with her one last time. Finally, no longer able to check his tears, he had turned and started blindly up the steps, alone.

Now he stared numbly back, as though awakened from a nightmare. Almost without thinking, he searched the pocket of his jerkin until his fingers closed around a flask of brandy. He drew deeply on it twice before turning to make his way on through the streets of Agra.

"You took an astonishing risk merely to honor the whims of your Hindu dancer, Ambassador." Nadir Sharif had summoned Hawksworth to his reception room at sunset. "Few men here would have done it."

"I've lived through plagues twice before. In 1592 over ten thousand in London died of the plague, and in 1603, in the summer after King James's coronation, over thirty thousand died, one person out of every five. If I were going to die, I would have by now." Hawksworth listened to his own bravado and wondered if it sounded as hollow as it was. He remembered his own haunting fear during the height of the last plague, when rowdy, swearing Bearers, rogues some declared more ill-bred than hangmen, plied the city with rented barrows, their cries of "Cast out your dead" ringing through the deserted streets. They charged sixpence a corpse, and for their fee they carted the bodies to open pits at the city's edge for unconsecrated, anonymous burial, the cutpurse and the alderman piled side by side. As he remembered London again, suddenly the Hindu rites seemed considerably less barbaric.

"You're a brave man, nonetheless, or a foolish one." Nadir Sharif gestured him toward a bolster. "Tell me, have your English physicians determined the cause of the infection?"

"There are many theories. The Puritans say it's God's vengeance; and astrologers point out that there was a conjunction of the planets Jupiter and

Saturn when the last plague struck. But our physicians seem to have two main theories. Some hold it's caused by an excess of corrupt humors in the body, whereas others claim it's spread by poisonous air, which has taken up vapors contrary to nature."

Nadir Sharif sat pensive and silent for a moment, as though pondering the explanations. Then he turned to Hawksworth.

"What you seem to have told me is that your physicians have absolutely no idea what causes the plague. So they have very ingeniously invented names for the main points of their ignorance." He smiled. "Indian physicians have been known to do the same. Tell me then, what do *you* think causes it?"

"I don't know either. It seems to worsen in years after crops have been bad, when there are hungry dogs and rats scavenging in the streets. During the last plague all the dogs in London were killed or sent out of the city, but it didn't seem to help."

"And what about the rats?"

"There've always been men in England who make a living as rat-catchers, but with the dogs gone during the plague, the rats naturally started to multiply."

Nadir smiled thoughtfully. "You know, the Hindus have a book, the Bhagavata Parana, that warns men to quit their house if they see a sickly rat near it. Indians have long assumed vermin bring disease. Have you considered the possibility that the source of the plague might be the rats, rather than the dogs? Perhaps by removing the dogs, you eliminated the best deterrent to the bearer of the plague, the rats?"

"No one has thought of that."

"Well, the European plague has finally reached India, whatever its cause." Nadir Sharif looked away gloomily. "Almost a hundred people died in Agra this past week. Our physicians are still searching for a cure. What remedies do you use in England? I think His Majesty would be most interested to know."

"I suppose the measures are more general than specific. Englishmen try to ward it off by purging the pestilent air around them. They burn rosemary and juniper and bay leaves in their homes. During the last plague the price of rosemary went up from twelve pence an armful to six shillings a handful. But the only people helped seemed to be herb wives and gardeners. One physician claimed the plague could be avoided by wearing a bag of arsenic next to the skin. There's also a belief that if you bury half a dozen peeled onions near your home, they'll gather all the infection in the neighborhood. And some people fumigate the contagious vapors from their rooms by dropping a red-hot brick into a basin of vinegar."

"Do these curious nostrums work?" Nadir Sharif tried to mask his skepticism.

"I suppose it's possible. Who can say for sure? But the plague always diminishes after a time, usually with the onset of winter."

"Doesn't your king do anything?"

"He usually leaves London if an infection starts to spread. In 1603, the year of his coronation, he first went to Richmond, then to Southampton, then to Wilton. He traveled all summer and only returned in the autumn."

"Is that all he did? Travel?"

"There were Plague Orders in all the infected towns. And any house where someone was infected had to have a red cross painted on the door and a Plague Bill attached. No one inside could leave. Anyone caught outside was whipped and set in the stocks."

"And did these measures help?"

"Englishmen resent being told they can't leave home. So people would tear the Plague Bills off their doors and go about their business. Some towns hired warders at sixpence a day to watch the houses and make sure no one left. But when so many are infected, it's impossible to watch everyone. So there were also orders forbidding assemblies. King James banned the holding of fairs within fifty miles of London. And all gatherings in London were prohibited by a city order—playhouses, gaming houses, cockpits, bear-baiting, bowling, football. Even ballad singers were told to stay off the streets."

"His Majesty may find that interesting." Nadir Sharif turned and signaled for *sharbat* from the servants. "Perhaps he should issue laws forbidding assembly before he leaves Agra."

"Is he leaving?" Hawksworth felt his heart stop.

"Day after tomorrow." Nadir Sharif watched as the tray of *sharbat* cups arrived and immediately directed it toward Hawksworth.

"I have to see him one last time before he leaves. Before I leave."

"I really think that's impossible now. He's canceled the daily *durbar*. No one can see him. Even I have difficulty meeting with him." Nadir Sharif accepted a cup from the tray and examined Hawksworth sorrowfully as he sipped it. "In any case, I fear a meeting would do you little good, Ambassador. He's busy arranging the departure for all the court, including the *zenana*. There are thousands of people to move, and on very short notice. In fact, I've been trying to see Her Majesty for several days, but she has received no one." He smiled evenly. "Not even her own brother."

"Where's His Majesty planning to go?"

"Not so very far, actually. Ordinarily he probably would travel north, toward Kashmir. But since winter is approaching, he's decided to go west, to Fatehpur Sekri. The area around the old palace has remained free of the infection."

"But I *have* to see him." Hawksworth hesitated. "Do you know what's happened to Shirin?"

"Nothing, so far as I hear. I believe she's still being held in the fort."

Nadir Sharif studied Hawksworth. "But I would advise you in the strongest possible terms to avoid meddling in the business of that Persian adventuress and her departed Sufi heretic."

"What I do is my affair." Hawksworth set down his cup harder than necessary. "I insist on seeing His Majesty. I want you to arrange it."

"But a formal meeting is really quite impossible, Ambassador. Haven't I made that clear?" Nadir Sharif paused to collect his poise. "But perhaps if you appeared when his entourage is departing Agra, you might be able to speak with him. I have to insist, however, that a meeting now would be pointless and possibly even dangerous, considering His Majesty's disposition at the moment."

"I'll see him before he leaves, somehow. I'll find a way."

"Then I wish you well, Ambassador." Nadir Sharif put down his *sharbat* glass. "Incidentally, there's a large caravan leaving for Surat day after tomorrow. Should I make arrangements for you to join it?"

"I'm not going anywhere until I see the *Moghul*."

"You're a headstrong man, Ambassador. Please believe I wish you well. Notwithstanding His Majesty's current views, I've always regarded you highly." He signaled for a tray of betel leaves and rose, flashing one of his official smiles. "Who knows? Perhaps your luck is due for a change."

Queen Janahara read the dispatch twice, the lines of her mouth growing tighter each time, before passing it back to Arangbar. He studied it again, holding it with a trembling hand, seeming not to fully comprehend its meaning, then extended it to Nadir Sharif. The courtyard off Arangbar's private library was deadly silent, all servants and eunuchs banished. The tapestries shading the inner compartment had been drawn back, permitting the hard light of morning to illuminate the flowered murals on the library's red sandstone walls. Arangbar sipped wine from a gilded cup and studied Nadir Sharif's face while the prime minister read, as though hoping somehow to decipher the document's significance from his expression.

"He has plainly refused, Majesty." Nadir Sharif's voice was strangely calm. "When did this arrive?"

"This morning. It's his reply to the pigeon I sent to Burhanpur the day after the wedding, ordering him to return the command in the south to Ghulam Adl and march to the northwest, to relieve the fortress at Qandahar." Arangbar's eyes were bloodshot and grim. "At least we know now where he is."

"We know nothing." Janahara reached for the document and scrutinized it. "This dispatch was sent four days ago. He could be as far north as Mandu by now, or well on his way to Agra."

"I doubt very much he will march anywhere." Nadir Sharif cut her off without seeming to do so. "Until he receives a response to the terms he has demanded."

"Repeat them to me." Arangbar was having difficulty focusing on the wine cup and he shifted his gaze into the courtyard.

"They are very explicit, Majesty." Nadir Sharif rolled the document and replaced it in the bamboo sleeve. "Jadar has refused to march to defend Qandahar unless his horse rank is raised to thirty thousand, and unless the *jagirs* in Dholpur, those that were granted to Prince Allaudin, are returned. What will you do?"

"There can be no bargaining with an Imperial order," Queen Janahara interjected. "How many times will you be intimidated? Remember he refused to undertake this campaign—which, I should add, he has apparently bungled—until his *suwar* rank was elevated, and his elder brother Khusrav was sent out of Agra. When will his demands end?" Her voice rose. "Even now we do not know what has happened. All we know for sure is that two months ago he marched south from Burhanpur. And four days ago he was there again. Was he driven back when he tried to recapture Ahmadnagar from Malik Ambar? Does the Deccan still belong to the Abyssinian? Prince Jadar has much to answer."

"But the dispatch *was* sent from Burhanpur. At least he hasn't abandoned the city entirely, as some of the rumors said," Nadir Sharif continued evenly. "And I don't believe he has abandoned the south, either. He would not permit it to remain in rebel hands. Whatever else he is, he's a soldier first."

"For all we know he is now isolated at the fortress in Burhanpur." Janahara studied the empty courtyard. "*If* he has not already lost the city."

"So what do you propose be done?" Arangbar's voice was slurred as he sipped from his cup.

"There's only one choice remaining, if you ever hope to control Jadar." She spoke directly to Arangbar. "Order Inayat Latif to mobilize the Imperial army and march south, now. We have to know what's happening there. Inayat Latif is a far abler general than Jadar. He, at least, can ensure the Deccan is secure. Then we can handle the matter of Jadar's demands."

"But that could also give the appearance the Imperial army is marching against Jadar." Nadir Sharif shifted uncomfortably. "He will see it as an ultimatum. Do you really think he will respond to threats? You must know him better than that."

"I know him all too well." Janahara's voice was hard.

"Your Majesty"—Nadir Sharif turned directly to the queen—"perhaps if he is given more time, he will come to better . . . appreciate his position. I suggest the first thing we do is request a clarification of the military situation throughout the Deccan. Then we can send the Imperial army, as reinforcements, if it still seems advisable."

"I'm growing weary of constantly trying to outguess Jadar." Arangbar examined his cup and noted gloomily that it was dry. "First the plague, and now the preparations for the move. I'm exhausted. When do we leave?"

"I'm told the last of the elephants will be ready within one *pahar*, Majesty." Nadir Sharif studied the queen casually, wondering how far she would push her influence with Arangbar. "I agree with you it would be wisest to wait."

"If you insist on doing nothing, at least the Imperial army should be mobilized and made ready." Janahara's dulcet voice was betrayed by the quick flash in her eyes. "Then Jadar will understand we are prepared to act quickly if he remains defiant."

"How many men and horse does Inayat Latif have under his command now?" Arangbar searched the darkened recesses behind them for a servant to summon with more wine.

"There are over a hundred thousand men here, Majesty, and probably fifty thousand cavalry. Over three times the force Jadar took with him to the south." Nadir Sharif paused. "They could always move out within, say, two to three weeks."

"I insist the forces here at least be mobilized, and moved to Fatehpur with the court . . . lest the army itself become contaminated by the plague." Janahara hesitated for a moment and then continued evenly. "I'm prepared to order it in your name today. It would protect the army from infection; you would have them with you if you needed them; and it would also put Jadar on notice."

"Then prepare the orders for my seal, if it pleases you." Arangbar sighed and reached for his turban. "You're usually right."

"You know I'm right." She smiled warmly. "And, regardless, no harm will be done."

"Then it's settled." Arangbar tried unsuccessfully to rise, and Nadir Sharif stepped forward, assisting him to his feet. "I have to hold *durbar* one last time today, quickly before we leave. The Persian Safavid ambassador notified the *wazir* he has gifts and a petition that must be brought to me before the court leaves Agra." He grinned. "The Safavis are so worried I will form an alliance with the northwestern Uzbeks that their Emperor Shah Abbas sends gifts every month."

"You've decided to hold *durbar* today, after all?" Nadir Sharif's eyes quickened. "If so, there's a Portuguese official from Surat who also wishes to present some gifts from the Viceroy and speak with you on a matter he said was delicate."

"What 'delicate' matter does His Excellency have?" Janahara stopped sharply on her way toward the corridor and turned back. "I've heard nothing about it."

"I suppose we'll all discover that in *durbar*, Majesty." Nadir Sharif bowed and was gone.

Brian Hawksworth waited in the crowded square of the *Diwan-i-Am*, holding a large package and hoping the rumored appearance of Arangbar was true. For the past four days the *Moghul* had not held *durbar*, had remained in complete isolation. But only an hour before, talk had circulated in the square that Arangbar would hold a brief reception before departing, probably in a tent pavilion that had been erected in the center of the square. As though to verify the speculation, slaves had unrolled several thick carpets beneath the tent, installed a dais, and were now positioning his throne onto the platform.

Hawksworth stared about the square and felt his palms sweat.

Is this the last time I ever see the *Moghul* of India? And Shirin never again? Is this how it ends?

He had spent the last several days in a private hell, thinking of Shirin and waiting for the first fever, the first nodules that would signal the plague. So far there had been no signs of the disease. And he had heard that the consensus in the bazaar was the infection would subside within the month. Clearly it would be nothing like London in 1603.

Palace rumors said that Shirin was still alive. All executions had ceased after the appearance of the plague. And stories were that the *Moghul* was rarely seen sober. Perhaps, Hawksworth told himself, Arangbar has stayed so drunk he has forgotten her.

He had finally conceived one last plan to try to save her. Then he had packed his chest, settled his accounts, and dismissed his servants. If nothing came of the meeting today . . . if there was a meeting . . . he would have to leave in any case.

He moved closer to the royal pavilion, pushing his way through the melee of shirtless servants. The elephants for the *zenana* had been moved into the square and were now being readied. There were, by Hawksworth's rough count, approximately a hundred elephants to carry Arangbar's women. The *howdahs* for the main wives were fashioned from gold, with gratings of gold wire around the sides to provide a view and an umbrella canopy of silver cloth for shade. A special elephant was waiting for Queen Janahara and Princess Layla, decorated with a canvas of gold brocade and bearing a jewel-studded *howdah*.

As Hawksworth watched, another elephant, shining with black paint and the largest he had ever seen, lumbered regally into the square, ridden by a *mahout* with a gold-braided turban. Its covering was even more lavish than that of the queen's mount, and its *howdah* was emblazoned with the Imperial standard of Arangbar, a long-tailed lion crouching menacingly in front of a golden sun face. Beneath the verandas rows of saddled horses waited for the lesser members of the court, each with a slave stationed alongside bearing an umbrella of gold cloth, and in front of the horses were rows of crimson-colored palanquins, their pearl-embroidered velvet gleaming in the light, ready for high officials.

The roadway leading from the square of the *Diwan-i-Am* had been lined with a guard of three hundred male war elephants, each with a cannon turret on its back. Behind those, three hundred female elephants stood idling in the sunshine, their backs covered with gold cloth marked with the *Moghul's* insignia, waiting to be loaded with household goods from the *zenana*. Just beyond the gate a host of watermen were poised with waterskins slung from their backs, ready to run before the *Moghul's* procession sprinkling the roadway to banish dust. Near them a small party of men stood holding the harness of a camel bearing a roll of white cloth, used to cover and banish from sight any dead animals that might lie along the route of the *Moghul's* party.

The courtyard erupted with a sudden blare of trumpets and kettledrums, and Hawksworth turned to see Arangbar being carried in on an open palanquin, supported by uniformed eunuchs. A slave walked along one side, holding a satin umbrella over his head for shade, while on the other, two chubby eunuchs walked fanning him with sprays of peacock feathers attached to long poles.

As the palanquin neared the tent, Hawksworth pushed through the crowd to gain a better view. Arangbar was dressed for a ceremonial occasion, wearing a velvet turban with a plume of white herne feathers almost two feet in length. A walnut-sized ruby dangled from one side of the turban, and on the other side was a massive diamond, paired with a heart-shaped emerald. Around his turban was a sash wreathed with a chain of pearls. Rings bearing flashing jewels decorated every finger, and his cloak was gold brocade, decorated with jeweled armlets.

As he descended from the palanquin, at the entry of the pavilion, the nobles near him yelled "*Padshah Salamat,*" Long Live the Emperor, and performed the *teslim*. As he moved toward his throne two more eunuchs were waiting. One stepped forward and presented an enormous pink carp on a silver tray, while the other held out a dish of starchy white liquid. Arangbar dipped his finger in the liquid, touched it to the fish, then rubbed his own forehead—a Moghul ceremony presaging good omens for a march.

Next, another eunuch stepped forward, bowed, and presented him with a sword. He stared at it for a moment as though confused, then shakily ran his finger along the diamonds set in the scabbard and the braided gold belt. As the eunuch urged it toward him, he nodded and allowed it to be buckled at his waist. Another eunuch then presented him with a golden quiver containing thin bamboo arrows and a gleaming lacquer bow.

As he mounted the dais, two eunuchs moved to his side, each waving a gold-handled tail of white yak hair intended to drive away flies. Another fanfare of trumpets and drums cut the air as the eunuchs helped him onto the throne.

Only when Arangbar was seated did Hawksworth notice that Nadir Sharif and Zainul Beg were already waiting at the foot of the dais. He also noted Queen Janahara was not present. And then he realized why. The servants had neglected to erect her screen, the one she normally sat behind to dictate his decisions. Since the appearance of Arangbar's solitary rule still had to be maintained, she could not be seen publicly issuing orders, at least not yet.

Hawksworth smiled to himself, wondering whose head would roll for the oversight. Then, as he watched Nadir Sharif begin explaining petitions to Arangbar, he thought he sensed a gleam of triumph in the prime minister's eye. Could it be the failure to install a screen was deliberate?

The Persian Safavid ambassador approached with the obligatory gift, this time an ornamental case containing a ruby on a gold chain, and then handed up a paper. Arangbar listened to Nadir Sharif explain the document, then appeared to ponder it a moment. Finally he waved his arms lightly and agreed to something Hawksworth did not catch. The ambassador bowed his appreciation, revolved with enormous dignity, and retreated into the sunshine.

Arangbar was already beginning to grow restless, clearly anxious to dismiss everyone and begin loading the *zenana* women onto their elephants. He turned and spoke to Nadir Sharif, who replied quickly and motioned toward a Portuguese emissary in a starched doublet who stood waiting, together with Father Sarmento. It was the first time Hawksworth had noticed them, and he felt his gut knot in hatred as he shoved his own way forward toward the pavilion.

Arangbar listened with a glazed expression, nodding occasionally, as the Portuguese emissary delivered an elaborate speech, translated by Sarmento, and began laying out the contents of a chest he carried. With theatrical flair he drew out several large silver candlesticks, a brace of gold-handled knives with jewel-embossed sheaths, a dozen wine cups of Venetian crystal. Then he produced a leather packet with a red wax seal. He spoke a few more words and passed it to Nadir Sharif.

The prime minister examined it, broke the seal to extract the parchment, then gestured for Sarmento to come forward to translate. The Jesuit suddenly looked very old and very uneasy as he adjusted his peaked black hat and took the paper.

Hawksworth shoved closer, and for the first time Arangbar seemed to notice him. The *Moghul's* eyes darkened and he started to say something in Hawksworth's direction, but Sarmento had already begun the translation into Turki.

"His Excellency, Miguel Vaijantes, sends this message of his high regard and everlasting friendship for His Most High Majesty, the *Great Moghul* of India. He bows before you and hopes you will honor him by accepting these few small tokens of his admiration."

Sarmento shifted and cleared his throat. Arangbar's eyes had fluttered partially closed and his head seemed to nod sleepily at the conventional flattery.

"His Excellency asks Your Majesty's indulgence of a grievous misdeed last week by a captain of one of our patrol vessels. He assures Your Majesty that the captain will be stripped of all rank and returned in chains to Goa within the month."

Arangbar's eyes had again opened and he shifted slightly on the throne. "What 'misdeed' is referred to?"

Sarmento looked at the emissary, who quickly replied in Portuguese. The Jesuit turned again to Arangbar.

"Your Majesty will doubtless receive a dispatch from Surat within a short time describing an unfortunate incident. His Excellency wants you to understand in advance that it was a mistaken order, undertaken entirely without his knowledge or approval."

Arangbar was fully awake now and staring down at the two Portuguese.

"What order? Did the Viceroy order something he now wishes to disown? What was it?"

"It's the unfortunate matter of the *Fatima*, Your Majesty." Sarmento turned helplessly toward the Portuguese emissary, as though he too were searching for an explanation.

"What about the *Fatima*? She's my largest cargo vessel. She's due in Surat in two days, with goods from Persia." Arangbar's face was sober now. "Her Highness, Maryam Zamani, had eighty *lakhs* of rupees . . ."

"The *Fatima* is safe, Your Majesty. She has only been detained at sea, on a mistaken interpretation of His Excellency's orders." Sarmento seemed to be blurting out the words. "But he wishes to assure you . . ."

"Impossible!" Arangbar's voice was suddenly a roar. "He would not dare! He knows the cargo was under my seal. I have a copy of the *cartaz* sent to Goa."

"It was a grievous mistake, Majesty. His Excellency sends his deepest apologies and offers to . . ."

"It was done on *someone's* order! It had to be his. How can it be a 'mistake'!" Arangbar's face had gone purple. "Why was it ordered in the first place?"

Sarmento stood speechless while the envoy spoke rapidly into his ear. Then he looked back at Arangbar. "Mistakes are always possible, Majesty. His Excellency wishes to assure you the vessel and all cargo will be released within two weeks."

"I demand it be released immediately! And damages equal the value of the cargo brought to me personally." Arangbar's face was livid. "Or he will never again have a *pice* of trade in an Indian port."

Sarmento turned and translated quickly to the emissary. The Portuguese's face dropped over his moustache and he hesitantly spoke something to Sarmento.

"We regret we have no power at this time to authorize a payment for damages, Majesty. But we assure you His Excellency will . . ."

"Then 'His Excellency' will have no more trade in India." Arangbar turned, his face overflowing with rage, and shouted to the guards standing behind him. As they ran to his side he drew his sword and waved it drunkenly at the emissary, whose face had gone white. "Take him away."

As the guards seized the terrified Portuguese by the arms, sending his hat tumbling onto the carpet, he looked imploringly at Nadir Sharif. But the prime minister's face was a mask. Then Arangbar turned on Father Sarmento. "If His Excellency has anything else to say to me, he will say it himself, or he will send someone with the authority to answer me. I do not receive his *peons*."

Sarmento flinched at the insulting Goan slang for dockhand. "Your Majesty, again I assure you . . ."

"*You* will never again assure me of anything. I've listened to your assurances for years, largely on matters about which you have only belief, never proof. You assured me of the power of the Christian God, but never once would you accept the challenge of the Islamic mullahs to cast a Bible and the Quran into a fire together, to show once and for all which held sacred truth. But their test is no longer needed. Your Christian lies are over." Arangbar rose unsteadily from his throne, his brow harrowed by his fury. "I order your stipend terminated and your church in Agra closed. And your mission in Lahore. There will never again be a Christian church in India. Never."

"Your Majesty, there are many Christians in India." Sarmento's voice was pleading. "They must have a priest, to minister the Holy Sacrament."

"Then do it in your lodgings. You no longer have a church." Arangbar settled back on the throne, his anger seeming to overwhelm him. "Never see me again unless you bring news the ship is released, and my demands met. Never."

Sarmento watched in horror as Arangbar dismissed him with a gesture of his arm. The old Jesuit turned and moved trembling into the crowd that had pushed around the sides of the pavilion. As he passed by Hawksworth, he suddenly stopped.

"This was all because of you." His voice quivered. "I learned of this only today from my foolish prodigal, Pinheiro. May God have mercy on you, heretic. You and your accomplices have destroyed all His work in India."

As Hawksworth tried to find an answer he heard a drunken shout.

"Inglish! What are you doing here? Come forward and explain yourself."

He looked up to see Arangbar motioning at him.

"Are you deaf? Come forward." Arangbar glared mischievously. "Why are you still in Agra? We were told we sent you away, almost a week ago. I think I may decide to have you and every other Christian in India hanged."

"May it please Your Majesty, I came to request an audience." Hawksworth moved quickly forward, past the confused guards, carrying the package he had brought.

"And what have *you* stolen of ours, Inglish? Have you come now to tell us it was all a mistake, before I order your hand cut off?"

"Englishmen are not Portugals, Your Majesty. We do not take what is not our own. What have I ever taken that Your Majesty did not freely give?"

"It's true what you say, Inglish. You are not a Portuguese." Arangbar suddenly beamed as a thought flashed through his eyes. "Tell me, Inglish, will your king destroy their fleets for me now?"

"Why would he do so, Your Majesty? You have denied him the right to trade; you have refused to grant the *firman* he requested."

"Not if he will rout the Portuguese infidels from our seas, Inglish. They are a pestilence, a plague, that sickens all it touches." Arangbar waved in the direction of a eunuch, ordering wine for himself. "You deceived me once, Inglish, but you did not rob me. Perhaps we will have you stay here a few days longer."

"I have already made preparations to depart, Your Majesty, on your orders."

"You cannot travel without our permission, Inglish. We still rule India, despite what the Portuguese Viceroy may think." Arangbar paused and drank thirstily from the glass of wine. "So why did you want an audience, Inglish, if you were planning to leave?"

Hawksworth paused, thinking of the decision he had made, wondering again if there was a chance.

"I've come to make a trifling request of Your Majesty." He moved forward and bowed, presenting his parcel, the obligatory gift.

"What's this have you brought us, Inglish?"

"May it please Your Majesty, after settling my accounts in Agra, I have no money remaining to purchase gifts worthy of Your Majesty. I have only this remaining. I offer it to Your Majesty, in hopes you will understand its unworthiness in your eyes is matched only by its unequaled value to me. It is my treasure. I have had it by my side for over twenty years, at sea and on land."

Arangbar accepted the parcel with curiosity and flipped aside the velvet wrap. An English lute sparkled against the sunshine.

"What is this, Inglish?" Arangbar turned it in his hand, examining the polished cedar staves that curved to form its melon-shaped back.

"An instrument of England, Your Majesty, which we hold in the same esteem you grant your Indian sitar."

"This is a curious toy, Inglish. It has so few strings." He examined it a moment longer, then turned to Hawksworth. "Do you yourself play this instrument?"

"I do, Your Majesty."

"Then we will hear it." Arangbar passed the lute back to Hawksworth, while the nobles around them buzzed in astonishment.

Hawksworth cradled it against him. The feel of its body flooded him with sadness as he realized he would never play it again. Memories of London, Tunis, Gibraltar, a dozen cabins and lodgings, flooded over him. He inhaled deeply and began a short suite by Dowland. It was the one he had played for Shirin that afternoon so long ago in the observatory in Surat.

The clear notes flooded the canopied pavilion with their rich full voice, then drifted outward into the square, settling silence in their path. The suite was melancholy, a lament of lost love and beauty, and Hawksworth found his own eyes misting as he played. When he reached the end, the last crisp note died into a void that seemed to be his own heart. He held the lute a moment longer, then turned to pass it back to Arangbar.

The *Moghul's* eyes seemed to be misting as well.

"I have never heard anything quite like it, Inglish. It has a sadness we never hear in a raga. Why have you never played for us before?"

"Your Majesty has musicians of your own."

"But no instrument like this, Inglish. Will you have your king send us one?"

"But I have given you mine, Majesty."

Arangbar examined the lute once more, then looked at Hawksworth and smiled. "But if I keep this instrument now, Inglish, I will most probably forget by tomorrow where I have put it." He winked at Hawksworth and handed back the lute. "Have your king send us one, Inglish, and a teacher to instruct our musicians."

Hawksworth could not believe what he was hearing. "I humbly thank Your Majesty. I . . ."

"Now what was it you came to ask of us, Inglish?" Arangbar continued to study the lute as he sipped from his wine. "Ask it quickly."

"Merely a trifling indulgence of Your Majesty."

"Then tell us what it is, Inglish." Arangbar turned and searched the square with his eyes, as though monitoring the state of preparations.

Hawksworth cleared his throat and tried to still his pulse. "Your Majesty's release of the Persian woman Shirin, who is guilty of no crime against Your Majesty."

Arangbar's smile faded as he turned back to Hawksworth.

"We have not yet decided her fate, Inglish. She does not concern you."

"May it please Your Majesty, she concerns me very much. I come to ask Your Majesty's permission to make her my wife, and to take her back to England with me, if Your Majesty will release her. She will be gone from India soon, and will trouble Your Majesty no further."

"But we just told you you are not returning, Inglish. Not until we permit it." He grinned. "You must stay and play this instrument for us more."

"Then I beg that her life be spared until the time I *am* allowed to leave."

Arangbar studied Hawksworth and a grudging smile played on his lips. "You are an excellent judge of women, Inglish. Perhaps too much so. I suspected it the first time I saw you."

"She wishes no ill toward Your Majesty. There is no purpose in taking her life."

"How do you know what she wishes for us, Inglish? I think we know better than you." Arangbar paused to sip again from his wine cup. "But we will spare her for now, *if* your king will agree to send warships to drive the infidel Portuguese from our shores. And if you will agree to play more for me."

"Will Your Majesty order her release?"

"I will move her to my *zenana* for now, Inglish. Until matters are settled. I will order her brought with us to Fatehpur. That is my part of the bargain. What will you do about yours?"

"I will inform my king of Your Majesty's wishes."

"And he will comply, if he wants to trade in India." Arangbar turned to Nadir Sharif. "Order a horse for the Inglish. He will ride with us today. And have the woman Shirin sent to the *zenana*."

Nadir Sharif bowed and edged next to Arangbar, adopting a confidential tone.

"If I may be allowed, Your Majesty, you are aware the woman Shirin would not be entirely welcome in the *zenana* by Her Majesty, Queen Janahara."

"Her Majesty is not the *Moghul* of India." Arangbar seemed suddenly exhilarated by the absence of the queen. "I have ordered it."

"To hear is to obey." Nadir Sharif bowed low, casting a worried glance toward Hawksworth. "But perhaps it would be equally pleasing to Your Majesty . . . and to Her Majesty as well . . . to allow the woman to travel to Fatehpur under the cognizance of the English ambassador."

Arangbar glanced toward the palace, and his exhilaration seemed to dissolve as suddenly as it had come. "Until Fatehpur, then. After that we will decide where she will be kept until the Inglish satisfies his part of the bargain." Arangbar turned to Hawksworth. "Agreed, Inglish?"

"I bow to Your Majesty's will."

"*Durbar* is concluded." Arangbar rose by himself and moved to the edge of the tent pavilion. As the trumpets and drums again sounded, the fanning eunuchs scurried to stay beside him. He stepped into the sunshine, stared about the square for a moment, then turned to Nadir Sharif.

"Order everyone cleared and the women brought. I am suddenly growing weary of Agra."

Nadir Sharif bowed again and spoke quickly to the captain of the guard. As the order was circulated, he quietly moved next to Hawksworth.

"So it seems your luck changed after all, Ambassador. For now. But I fear it may not last. As a friend I suggest you make the most of it."

CHAPTER TWENTY-SIX

The dark sky had begun to show pale in the east, heralding the first traces of day. Hawksworth stood in the shadows of his tent, at the edge of the vast Imperial camp, and pulled his frayed leather jerkin tighter against the cold. He watched as the elephants filed past, bulky silhouettes against the dawn. They were being led from the temporary stables on the hill behind him toward the valley below, where cauldrons of water were being stoked for their morning bath. Heating the water for the elephant baths had become routine during the reign of Akman, who had noticed his elephants shivering from their baths on chilly mornings and decreed their bath water warmed henceforth.

As he watched the line of giant animals winding their way through the camp, waving their trunks in the morning air, he realized they were not docile female *zenana* elephants, but male war elephants, first and second rank.

First-ranked war elephants, called "full blood," were selected from young males who had demonstrated the endurance and even temper essential in battle; those granted Second Rank, called "tiger-seizing," were slightly smaller, but with the same temperament and strength. Each elephant had five keepers and was placed under the training of a special military superintendent—whose responsibility was to school the animal in boldness amid artillery fire. The keepers were monitored monthly by Imperial inspectors, who fined them a month's wages if their elephant had noticeably lost weight. Should an elephant lose a tusk through its keepers' inattention to an infection, they were fined one eighth the value of the animal, and if an elephant died in their care, they received a penalty of three months' wages and a year's suspension. But the position of elephant keeper was a coveted place of great responsibility. A well-trained war elephant could be valued at a hundred thousand rupees, a full *lakh*, and experienced commanders had been known to declare one good elephant worth five hundred horses in a battle.

Hawksworth studied the elephants, admiring their disciplined stride and easy footing, and wondered again why the army had stationed its stables so near the Imperial camp. Did Arangbar somehow feel he needed protection?

"They're magnificent, don't you think?" Shirin emerged from her tent to join him, absently running her hand across the back of his jerkin. It had been six days since they had left Agra, and it seemed to Hawksworth she had grown more beautiful each day, more loving each night. The nightmare of the past weeks had already faded to a distant memory. She was fully dressed now, with a transparent scarf pinned to her dark hair by a band of pearls, thick gold bracelets, flowered trousers beneath a translucent skirt, and dark kohl highlighting her eyes and eyebrows. He watched enthralled as she pulled a light cloak over her shoulders. "Especially in the morning. They say Akman used to train his royal elephants to dance to music, and to shoot a bow."

"I don't think I'll ever get used to elephants." Hawksworth admired her a moment longer in the dawn light, then looked back at the immense forms lumbering past, trying to push aside the uneasy feeling their presence gave him. "You'd be very amused to hear what people in London think they're like. Nobody there has ever seen an elephant, but there are lots of fables about them. It's said elephants won't ford a clear stream during the day, because they're afraid of their reflection, so they only cross streams at night."

Shirin laughed out loud and reached to kiss him quickly on the cheek. "I never know whether to believe your stories of England."

"I swear it."

"And the horse-drawn coaches you told me about. Describe one again."

"It has four wheels, instead of two like your carts have, and it really is pulled by horses, usually two but sometimes four. It's enclosed and inside there are seats and cushions . . . almost like a palanquin."

"Does that mean your king's *zenana* women all ride in these strange coaches, instead of on elephants?"

"In the first place, King James has no *zenana*. I don't think he'd know what to do with that many women. And there are absolutely *no* elephants in England. Not even one."

"Can you possibly understand how hard it is for me to imagine a place without elephants and *zenanas*?" She looked at him and smiled. "And no camels either?"

"No camels. But we have lots of stories about camels too. Tell me, is it true that if you're poisoned, you can be put inside a newly slain camel and it will draw out the poison?"

Shirin laughed again and looked up the hill toward the stables, where pack camels were being fed and massaged with sesame oil. The bells on their chest ropes sounded lightly as their keepers began harnessing them, in strings of five. Hawksworth turned to watch as the men began fitting two of the camels to carry a *mihaffa*, a wooden turret suspended between them by heavy wooden poles. All the camels were groaning pitifully and biting at their keepers, their customary response to the prospect of work.

"That sounds like some tale you'd hear in the bazaar. Why should a dead camel draw out poison?" She turned back to Hawksworth. "Sometimes you make the English sound awfully naïve. Tell me what it's really like there."

"It is truly beautiful. The fairest land there is, especially in the late spring and early summer, when it's green and cool." Hawksworth watched the sun emerge from behind a distant hill, beginning to blaze savagely against the parched winter landscape almost the moment it appeared. Thoughts of England suddenly made him long for shade, and he took Shirin's arm, leading her around the side of their rise and back into the morning cool. Ahead of them lay yet another bleak valley, rocky and sere. "I sometimes wonder how you can survive here in summer. It was already autumn when I made landfall and the heat was still unbearable."

"Late spring is even worse than summer. At least in summer there's rain. But we're accustomed to the heat. We say no *feringhi* ever gets used to it. I don't think anyone from your England could ever really love or understand India."

"Don't give up hope yet. I'm starting to like it." He took her chin in his hand and carefully studied her face with a scrutinizing frown, his eyes playing critically from her eyes to her mouth to her vaguely aquiline Persian nose. "What part do I like best?" He laughed and kissed the tip of her nose. "I think it's the diamond you wear in your left nostril."

"All women wear those!" She bit at him. "So I have to also. But I've never liked it. You'd better think of something else."

He slipped his arm around her and held her next to him, wondering if he should tell her of his bargain with Arangbar—that she had been released only because he had offered to take her from India forever. For a moment the temptation was powerful, but he resisted. Not yet. Don't give her a chance to turn headstrong and refuse.

"You know, I think you'd like England once you saw it. Even with no elephants, and no slaves to fan away the flies. We're not as primitive as you seem to imagine. We have music, and if you'd learn our language, you might discover England has many fine poets."

"Like the one you once recited for me?" She turned to face him. "What was his name?"

"That was John Donne. I hear he's a cleric now, so I doubt he's writing his randy poems and songs any more. But there are others. Like Sir Walter

Raleigh, a staunch adventurer who writes passable verse, and there's also Ben
Jonson, who writes poems, and plays also. In fact, lots of English plays are in
verse."

"What do you mean by plays?"

"English plays. They're like nothing else in the world." He stared
wistfully into the parched valley spread out before them. "Sometimes
I think they're what I miss most about London when I'm away."

"Well, what are they?"

"They're stories that are acted out by players. In playhouses."

She laughed. "Then perhaps you should begin by explaining a play-
house."

"The best one is the Globe, which is just across the Thames from London, in the Bankside edge of Southwark, near the bridge. It was built by
some merchants and by an actor from Stratford-up-on-Avon, who also writes
their plays. It's three stories high and circular, with high balconies. And
there's a covered stage at one side, where the players perform."

"Do the women in these plays dance, like our *devadasis*?"

"Actually the players are all men. Sometimes they take the roles of
women, but I've never seen them dance all that much. There are plays about
famous English kings, and sometimes there are stories of thwarted love, usually set in Italy. Plays are a new thing in England, and there's nothing like
them anywhere else."

Shirin settled against a boulder and watched the shadows cast by the rising sun stretch out across the valley. She sat thoughtfully for a moment and
then she laughed. "What would you say if I told you India had dramas
about kings and thwarted love over a thousand years ago? They were in
Sanskrit, and they were written by men named Bhavabhuti and Bhasa and
Kalidasa, whose lives are legends now. A *pandit*, that's the title Hindus give
their scholars, once told me about a play called *The Clay Cart*. It was about
a poor king who fell in love with a rich courtesan. But there are no plays
here now, unless you count the dance dramas they have in the south.
Sanskrit is a dead language, and Muslims don't really care for plays."

"I'll wager you'd like the plays in London. They're exciting, and sometimes the poetry can be very moving."

"What's it like to go to see one?"

"First, on the day a play is performed they fly a big white banner of silk
from a staff atop the Globe, and you can see it all over London. The admission is only a penny for old plays and two pence for new ones. That's all you
ever have to pay if you're willing to stand in the pit. If you want to pay a little more, you can get a seat in the galleries around the side, up out of the
dust and chips, and for a little extra you can get a cushion for the seat. Or
for sixpence you can enter directly through the stage door and sit in a stall at
the side of the stage. Just before the play begins there's a trumpet fanfare—

like Arangbar has when he enters the *Diwan-i-Am*—and the doorkeepers pass through the galleries to collect the money."

"What do they do with it?"

"They put it into a locked box," Hawksworth grinned, "which wags have taken to calling the box office, because they're so officious about it. But the money's perfectly safe. Plays are in the afternoon, while there's daylight.

"But aren't they performed inside this building?" Shirin seemed to be only half listening.

"The Globe has an open roof except over the stage. But if it gets too dull on winter afternoons, they light the stage with torches of burning pitch or tar."

"Who exactly goes to these playhouses?"

"Everyone. Except maybe the Puritans. Anybody can afford a penny. And the Globe is not that far from the Southwark bear gardens, so a lot of people come after they've been to see bearbaiting. The pit is usually full of rowdy tradesmen, who stand around the stage and turn the air blue with tobacco smoke."

"So high-caste women and women from good families wouldn't go."

"Of course women go." Hawksworth tried unsuccessfully to suppress a smile. "There are gallants in London who'll tell you the Globe is the perfect place to spot a comely wench, or even a woman of fashion looking for some sport while her husband's drunk at a gaming house."

"I don't believe such things happen."

"Well that's the way it is in England." Hawksworth settled against the boulder. "You have to understand women there don't let themselves be locked up and hidden behind veils. So if a cavalier spies a comely woman at the Globe, he'll find a way to praise her dress, or her figure, and then he'll offer to sit next to her, you know, just to make sure some rude fellow doesn't trod on the hem of her petticoats with muddy boots, and no chips fall in her lap. Then after the play begins, he'll buy her a bag of roasted chestnuts, or maybe some oranges from one of the orange-wenches walking through the galleries. And if she carries on with him a bit, he'll offer to squire her home."

"I suppose you've done just that?" She examined him in dismay.

Hawksworth shifted, avoiding her gaze. "I've mainly heard of it."

"Well, I don't enjoy hearing about it. What about the honor of these women's families? They sound reprehensible, with less dignity than *nautch* girls."

"Oh no, they're very different." He turned with a wink and tweaked her ear. "They don't dance."

"That's even worse. At least most *nautch* girls have some training."

"You already think English women are wicked, and you've never even met one. That's not fair. But I think you'd come to love England. If we were in London now, right this minute, we could hire one of those coaches

you don't believe exist . . . a coach with two horses and a coachman cost
scarcely more than ten shillings a day, if prices haven't gone up . . . and ride
out to a country inn. Just outside London the country is as green as Nadir
Sharif's palace garden, with fields and hedgerows that look like a great patchwork coverlet sewed by some sotted alewife." Hawksworth's chest tightened
with homesickness. "If you want to look like an Englishwoman, you could
powder your breasts with white lead, and rouge your nipples, and maybe
paste some beauty stars on your cheeks. I'll dine you on goose and veal and
capon and nappy English ale. And English mutton dripping with more fat
than any lamb you'll taste in Agra."

Shirin studied him silently for a moment. "You love to talk of England,
don't you? But I'd rather you talked about India. I want you to stay. Why
would you ever want to leave?"

"I'm trying to tell you you'd love England if you gave yourself a chance.
I'll have the *firman* soon, and when I return the East India Company
will . . ."

"Arangbar will never sign a *firman* for the English king to trade. Don't
you realize Queen Janahara will never allow it?"

"Right now I'm less worried about the queen than about Jadar. I think
he wants to stop the *firman* too, why I don't know, but he's succeeded so far.
He almost stopped it permanently with his false rumor about the fleet. He
did it deliberately to raise Arangbar's hopes and then disappoint him, with
the blame falling on me. Who knows what he'll think to do next?"

"You're so wrong about him. That had nothing to do with you. Don't
you understand why he had to do that? You never once asked me."

Hawksworth stared at her. "Tell me why."

"To divert the Portuguese fleet. It's so obvious. He somehow discovered
Queen Janahara had paid the Portuguese Viceroy to ship cannons to Malik
Ambar. If the Marathas had gotten cannon, they could have defended Ahmadnagar forever. So he tricked the Portuguese into searching for the English fleet that wasn't there. The Portuguese are a lot more worried about
their trade monopoly than about what happens to Prince Jadar. He knew
they would be."

"I know you support him, but for my money he's still a certified bastard." Hawksworth studied her for a moment, wondering whether to believe
her words. If it were actually true it would all make sense, would fill out a bizarre tapestry of palace deception. But in the end his ruse had done Jadar no
good. "And for all his scheming, he was still defeated in the south. I hear
the rumors too." Hawksworth rose and took Shirin's arm. She started to
reply, then stopped herself. They began to walk slowly back toward his tent.
"So he deceived everyone to no purpose."

As they rounded the curve of the slope and emerged into the sunshine,
Hawksworth noted that some of the war elephants had already been led

back to their stables and were being harnessed. He looked across the valley toward the tents of the Imperial army and thought he sensed a growing urgency in the air, as though men and horse were being quietly mobilized to move out.

"But don't you realize? The prince is not retreating." Shirin finally seized his arm and stopped him. "No one here yet realizes that Malik Ambar has . . ." Her voice trailed off as she looked ahead. A group of Rajput officers was loitering, aimlessly, near the entrance to her tent. "I wish I could tell you now what's happening." Her voice grew quieter. "Just be ready to ride."

Hawksworth stared at her, uncomprehending. "Ride where?" He reached to touch her hand, but she glanced at the Rajputs and quickly pulled it away. "I don't want to ride anywhere. I want to tell you more about England. Don't you think you'd like to see it someday?"

"I don't know. Perhaps." She shifted her gaze away from the Rajputs. For an instant Hawksworth thought he saw her make a quick movement with her hands urging them to leave. Or had she? They casually moved on down the hill, their rhino-hide shields swinging loosely from their shoulder straps. "After . . . after things are settled."

"After what? After Arangbar signs the *firman*?"

"I can't seem to make you understand." She turned to face him squarely. "About Prince Jadar. Even if you got a *firman* it would soon be worthless."

"I understand this much. If he's thinking to challenge Arangbar, and the queen, then he's God's own fool. Haven't you seen the army traveling with us? It's three times the size of Jadar's." He turned and continued to walk. "His Imperial Majesty may be a sot, but he's in no peril from young Prince Jadar."

As they approached the entrance to his tent, she paused for a moment to look at him, her eyes a mixture of longing and apprehension.

"I can't stay now. Not today." She kissed him quickly and before he could speak she was moving rapidly down the hill, in the direction the Rajputs had gone.

Queen Janahara studied Allaudin thoughtfully as he strode toward her tent. His floral turban was set rakishly to one side in the latest style, and his purple gauze cloak was too effeminate for anyone but a eunuch or a dandy. She caught a flash from the jewel-handled *katar* at his waist, too ornamental ever to be used, and suddenly realized that she had never seen him actually hold a knife, or a sword. She had never seen him respond to any crisis. And Princess Layla had hinted he was not quite the husband she had envisioned, whatever that might imply.

Suddenly it all mattered. It had only been a week since Jadar's demands had been refused, and already he had taken the initiative. Now, she sighed, she would have to protect her *nashudani,* her "good-for-nothing" son-in-law. He could never protect himself, not from Jadar.

"Your Majesty." Allaudin salaamed formally as he dipped below the tapestried portiere of her tent, never forgetting that his new mother-in-law was also the queen. "The princess sends her wishes for your health this morning."

"Sit down." Janahara continued to examine him with her brooding dark eyes. "Where is Nadir Sharif?"

"The eunuchs said he would be a few moments late."

"He always tries to irritate me." Her voice trailed off as she watched Allaudin ensconce himself with a wide flourish against a velvet bolster. "Tell me, are you content with your bride?"

"She is very pleasing to me, Majesty."

"Are you satisfying your obligations as a husband?"

"Majesty?" Allaudin looked up at her as though not comprehending the question.

"Your duties are not merely to her. Or to me. They're also to India. Jadar has a male heir now. Such things matter in Agra, or weren't you aware?"

Allaudin giggled. "I visit her tent every night, Majesty."

"But for what purpose? After you're drunk and you've spent yourself with a *nautch* dancer. Don't deny it. I know it's true. Do you forget she has servants? There are no secrets in this camp. I think you'll sooner sire an heir on a slave girl than on my daughter. I will not have it."

"Majesty." Allaudin twisted uncomfortably and glanced up with relief to see Nadir Sharif pushing aside the portiere of the tent. As he entered, Janahara motioned toward the servants and eunuchs waiting in attendance and in moments they had disappeared through the curtained doorways at the rear.

"You're late."

"My sincerest apologies, Majesty. There are endless matters to attend. You know His Majesty still holds morning *darshan* from his tent, and has two *durbar* audiences a day. The difficulties . . ."

"Your 'difficulties' are only beginning." She was extracting a dispatch from a gilded bamboo tube. "Read this."

Nadir Sharif took the document and moved into the light at the entrance. He had always despised the red chintz tents of the Imperial family, whose doorways were forever sealed with Persian hangings that kept in all the smoke and lamp soot. As he studied the dispatch he moved even closer to the light, astonishment growing in his eyes. He read it through twice before turning back to Janahara.

"Has His Majesty seen this yet?"

"Of course not. But he will have to eventually."

"Who is it from?" Allaudin stared up from the bolster, his voice uneasy.

"Your brother." Janahara studied him with eyes verging on contempt. "Jadar has declared he is no longer under the authority of the *Moghul*." She paused to make sure the news had reached Allaudin. "Do you understand what that means? Jadar has rebelled. He's probably marching on Agra right now with his army."

"That's impossible! As long as His Majesty lives . . ."

"Jadar has declared His Majesty is no longer fit to reign. He has offered to assume the 'burden' himself. It's a preposterous affront to legitimate rule."

"Then he must be brought to Agra for trial." Allaudin's voice swelled with determination.

"Obviously." Nadir Sharif moved toward the door of the tent and stared into the sunshine for a long moment. Then he turned to Janahara. "We have no choice now but to send the Imperial army. Your intuition about Jadar last week was all too correct."

"And now you agree? After a week has been lost." Janahara had followed him with her eyes. "Now you concede that the army must move."

"There's nothing else to be done." Nadir Sharif seemed to study the parched landscape of the valley below. "Although containing Jadar may well be more difficult than we first assumed."

"Why should it be difficult?" Allaudin watched Nadir Sharif in bewilderment. "His forces were very small to begin with. And after his defeat by Malik Ambar, how many men and cavalry can he have left?"

"Perhaps you should read the dispatch." Nadir Sharif tossed the scrolled paper into Allaudin's lap. "Jadar never engaged Malik Ambar. Instead he forged an alliance. It would appear his 'retreat' north to Burhanpur was merely a ruse. He never met the Maratha armies in the first place, so he did not lose a single infantryman. Instead he intimidated Malik Ambar and struck a truce with him. There's no knowing how large his army is now, or even where he is. This dispatch came from Mandu, so he's already well on his way north. I think he'll probably lay siege to Agra within two weeks if he's not stopped."

"Merciful Allah." Allaudin's voice was suddenly tremulous. "What do we do?" Then he looked imploringly at Janahara. "I'll lead the army myself if you want."

Janahara seemed not to hear him as she rose and walked toward the door of the tent. Nadir Sharif stepped aside as she shoved back the tapestry and stared out into the valley.

"This morning I ordered Inayat Latif to mobilize and march."

"Without telling His Majesty!" Nadir Sharif stared at her incredulously.

"I ordered it in his name. I suspected something like this might happen, so I had him sign and stamp the order four days ago."

"Was his Majesty entirely sob . . ." Nadir Sharif hesitated. "Was he in full understanding of what he was authorizing?"

"That hardly matters now. But you must place the seal you keep on the order also before it's forwarded to the *wazir* to be officially recorded." She did not shift her gaze from the sunlit valley. "It's on the table behind you."

Nadir Sharif turned and stared down at the gold-inlaid stand. The order was there, a single folded piece of paper inside a gilded leather cover. The string which would secure it had not yet been tied.

"You were wise to have taken this precaution, Majesty." Nadir Sharif glanced back at Janahara, his voice flowing with admiration. "There's no predicting His Majesty's mind these days. Only yesterday I discovered he had completely forgotten . . ."

"Have you stamped it?"

"My seal is not here, Majesty." He paused. "And I was wondering . . . would it be wise to review our strategy briefly with His Majesty, lest he become confused later and forget he authorized the order? Perhaps even countermand it?"

"Your seal will be sufficient. It's in the pocket of your cloak where you always carry it, the pocket on the left."

"Your Majesty's memory is astonishing sometimes." Nadir Sharif quickly extracted the metal case, flipped off the cover, and with a flourish imprinted the black Seal of the Realm on the top of the order, beneath Arangbar's signature and the impression of his royal signet ring. "When will the army be able to move?"

"Tomorrow. Most of the elephants are moving out this morning." Janahara turned back and glanced at the paper with satisfaction. "And tomorrow we will all return to Agra. The plague is subsiding, and I think His Majesty should be in the fort."

"I agree entirely. Has it been ordered?"

"I will order it later today. Jadar cannot move his army *that* rapidly."

"I will begin preparations to go with the army." Allaudin rose and adjusted the jeweled *katar* at his belt.

"You will be returning to the Red Fort, with His Majesty and with me." Janahara did not look at him as she spoke.

"But I want to face Jadar. I insist." He tightened his gauze cloak. "I will demand an audience with His Majesty if you refuse."

Janahara studied him silently for a moment. "I have an even better idea. Since Jadar has refused to lead the army to defend the fortress at Qandahar, how would you like to be appointed in his place?"

Allaudin's eyes brightened. "What rank would I have?"

"I think we can persuade His Majesty to raise your personal rank to twelve thousand *zat* and your horse rank to eight thousand *suwar*, twice what you have now."

"Then I will go." Allaudin tightened his cloak, beaming. "I'll drive the Safavid king's Persian troops back into the desert."

"You are as sensible as you are brave. I will speak to His Majesty tonight."

Allaudin grinned a parting salaam, squared his shoulders, and pushed his way through the portiere and into the sunshine. Nadir Sharif watched without a word until he had disappeared into his own tent.

"Was that entirely wise, Majesty?"

"What else do you propose we do? It will keep him in Agra. I'll see to that. You don't really think I'd allow him to leave? Anyway, it's time his rank was elevated. Now all he needs is a son."

"I'm sure he'll have one in time, Majesty. The Hindu astrologers all say Princess Layla's horoscope is favorable."

"The Hindu astrologers may have to help him do a husband's work if they want to save their reputation."

"Give him time, Majesty." Nadir Sharif smiled. "And he'll have more heirs than the Holy Prophet."

"All the Prophet's children were daughters." She took the paper, inserted it into the gold case, and began tying the string. "There are times you do not entirely amuse me."

"I'm always half distracted by worrying." Nadir Sharif followed her with his eyes. "Even now."

"What in particular worries you at the moment?" Janahara paused as she was slipping the case into her sleeve.

"I'm thinking just now about the Imperial army. The loyalty of some of the men."

"What do you mean? Inayat Latif is entirely beholden to His Majesty. He would gladly give his life for the *Moghul*. I've heard it from his own lips, and I know it's true."

"I've never questioned your commander's loyalty. But now you . . . His Majesty will be ordering the men to march against Jadar. Are you aware that fully a third of the army is under Rajput field commanders, officers from the northwest. Some of the rajas there still bear ill feelings toward His Majesty, because of Inayat Latif's campaign there ten years ago. These Rajputs sometimes have long memories. And who knows what Jadar could be promising them? Remember his treachery with Malik Ambar."

"What are you suggesting? That the Rajput commanders will not fight for His Majesty, the legitimate *Moghul*? That's absurd. No one respects authority more than the Rajput rajas."

"I'm not suggesting it at all. But I do believe the Rajputs here should

be monitored closely nonetheless. Any discontent should be addressed before
it grows . . . unwieldy. Perhaps their commanders should be placed under a
separate authority, someone who could reason with them in His Majesty's
name if there are signs of unrest. Inayat Latif is an able general, but he's no
diplomat."

Janahara studied him closely. "Do you believe there would be unrest?"

"Your Majesty is perhaps not always fully informed as to the activities
of some of the more militant Rajput loyalists. I have ordered them watched
at all times."

"What are you suggesting then? That the Rajputs should be placed
under a separate top command? Some raja whose loyalty is unquestionable?"

"I'm suggesting precisely that. If there were extensive defections, it
would be demoralizing for the rest of the army, at the very least."

"Who do you propose?"

"There are any number of Rajput commanders I would trust. To a
point. But it's always difficult to know where their final loyalties lie." Nadir
Sharif paused, lost in thought. "Perhaps an alternate solution might be to
allow someone of unquestioned loyalty to monitor the Rajput field commanders, someone experienced in handling Rajput concerns, though not necessarily a general. Then the command could remain unified, with orders passing through this other individual, who would ensure compliance."

"Again, is there someone you would recommend?"

"There are several men near His Majesty who could serve. It is, of
course, essential their loyalty to you be beyond question. In a way it's a pity
Prince Allaudin is not . . . older. Blood is always best."

"That leaves only you, or Father, who is far too old."

"My responsibilities here would really make it impossible for me."
Nadir Sharif turned and walked again to the door of the tent, pulling back
the portiere. "Certainly I could not leave His Majesty for an extended campaign."

"But if the campaign were short?"

"Perhaps for a few weeks."

Janahara studied him silently, her thoughts churning. At times even
Nadir Sharif's loyalty seemed problematical. But now there was a perfect
way to test it in advance . . .

"I will advise Inayat Latif you are now in charge of the Rajput commanders."

"Your Majesty." Nadir Sharif bowed lightly. "I'm honored by your
confidence."

"I'm sure it's well placed." She did not smile. "But before I make the
arrangements, there's one other assignment for you. Totally confidential."

"Anything within my power." Nadir Sharif bowed elegantly.

"Tonight I want you to order the Imperial guards stationed in your compound to execute the Englishman and the woman Shirin. On your sole authority."

"Of course." Nadir Sharif's smile did not flicker.

Hawksworth finally returned to his compound near midnight, carrying his empty flask of brandy. He had wandered the length of the chaotic tent city searching for Shirin. Over the past five hours he had combed the wide streets of the bazaar, searched through the half-empty elephant stables, and circled the high chintz border of the Imperial enclosure. The periphery of the camp swarmed with infantrymen and their wives gathering supplies for the march, and already there had been numerous fights in the bazaar, where prices had soared after the announcement the army would march.

As he neared his tent, he looked up at the stars, brilliant even through the lingering evening smoke from the cooking fires, and mused about Jadar. The rebel prince would soon be facing Inayat Latif, just recalled to Agra two months earlier after a brutally successful campaign in Bengal extending the Imperial frontier against local Hindu chieftains. Inayat Latif was a fifty-five-year-old veteran commander who revered the *Moghul* and would do anything in his power to protect him. Although he had made no secret of his dislike of the "Persian junta," he shared their common alarm at the threat of Jadar's rebellion. It was Arangbar he would be fighting to defend, not the queen.

The Imperial army is invincible now, Hawksworth told himself, its cavalry outnumbers Jadar's easily three to one, and its officers are at full strength. There are at least a hundred and fifty thousand men ready to march. How many can Jadar have? Fifty thousand? Perhaps less. Jadar can never meet them. The most he can possibly do is skirmish and retreat.

Perhaps, he thought ruefully, it was all just as well. A decisive defeat for Jadar would resolve the paralysis at court, and the indecision in Shirin's mind. She would realize finally that Jadar had attempted to move too fast.

The mission might still be saved. With the Portuguese resistance neutralized—there were even rumors that Arangbar had ordered Father Sarmento back to Goa—there would be no voices in Agra to poison Arangbar's mind daily against the *firman* for King James. After all, he asked himself, who else could Arangbar turn to? England alone has the naval strength to challenge Portugal, even if it might require years to break their monopoly completely. He would bargain for a *firman* in exchange for a vague promise of King James's help against the Portuguese. It was a bargain England surely could keep. Eventually.

He slipped through the doorway of his tent and groped for the lamp, an open bronze dish of oil with a wick protruding through the spout. It rested where he had left it, on a stand near his sea chest, and he sparked a flint against the wick. Suddenly the striped cotton walls of the tent glowed around him. He removed the sword at his belt and slipped it onto the carpet. Then he removed his leather jerkin and dropped against a bolster, still puzzling about Shirin.

Her status during the past few days had been ambiguous. As a divorced Muslim woman, she was free to move about as she chose. But everyone knew she was on very uncertain terms with the *Moghul*. After they had arrived outside the western wall of the old city of Fatehpur, Arangbar had been too preoccupied to remember his threat to move her into the *zenana*. She had remained free, able to move inconspicuously about the camp, mingling with the other Muslim women. And each night, after the final watch was announced, Hawksworth had been able to slip unnoticed to her tent. Once, late one night, he had suggested they try to return to the old palace of Akman, inside the walls of Fatehpur, but they both finally decided the risk would be too great.

He had hoped the days, and nights, at the camp would bring them closer together. And in a way they had, although Shirin still seemed to retreat at times into a special realm of mourning she had devised for herself. She could never stop remembering Samad and his brutal death.

Something, he told himself, has to change. He had begun to wonder if he should gamble and tell her of the terms the *Moghul* had demanded for her release. Would she then understand she had no choice but to return to England with him?

He rose and rummaged through his sea chest, finding another bottle of brandy, almost his last, and to fight his despondency he poured himself a cup. The liquor burned its way down, like a warm soothing salve, and he turned to begin assembling his few belongings for packing in the morning. He had reprimed and loaded his remaining pistol, and now he laid it on the table beside his chest. Then he drew his sword from its scabbard to check its edge and the polish on the metal. Holding it to the lamp, he spotted a few random flecks of rust, and he found a cloth and burnished them away.

His few clothes were already piled haphazardly in the chest, now virtually empty save for his lute. He found his leather purse at the bottom and counted his remaining money. Five hundred rupees. He counted them twice, beginning to wonder if he might eventually have to walk all the way back to Surat.

He searched the floor for stray items, and came across Vasant Rao's *katar* caught between the folds of the carpet. It seemed years now since the Rajput aide of Jadar had slipped it into his hand in the square of the *Diwan-i-Am*, and he had almost forgotten he had it. With a smile of recollection he gingerly slipped it from its brocade sheath and held it in his hand, puzzling how such a curiously constructed weapon could be so lethal. The grip was diagonal to the blade, so that it could only be used to thrust, like a pike head growing out of your fist. Rajputs were said to kill tigers with only a *katar* and a leather shield, but he wasn't sure he believed the stories. He grasped it and made a few trial thrusts, its ten-inch blade shining in the lamplight like a mirror, then tossed it atop his sea chest. It would make a nice memento of the trip; every fighting man in India seemed to carry one. Who in London would ever believe such a weapon unless they saw it?

Out of the corner of his eye he caught a flutter in the portiere of his tent, and he looked up to see Shirin standing silently in the doorway.

"What . . . ?" He looked up to greet her, unsure whether to betray his relief by taking her immediately in his arms, or to scold and tease her a bit first.

She silenced him with a wave of her hand.

"Are you ready?" Her voice was barely above a whisper.

"Ready for what? Where in Christ's name have you been? I've been . . ."

Again she silenced him as she moved inside.

"Are you ready to ride?" She glanced in dismay at the belongings he had scattered about the tent. "We have to leave now, before dawn."

"Have you gone mad?" He stared at her. "We're returning to Agra day after tomorrow. The *Moghul* has . . ."

"We have to leave now, tonight." She examined him in the lamplight, consternation growing in her eyes. "The prince . . ."

"Jadar is finished." He cut her off. "Don't be a sentimental fool. He brought this on himself. You can't help him. Nobody can now."

They stood, eyes locked together, for a moment that seemed as long as eternity. Hawksworth did not move from his place on the carpet. Gradually her eyes clouded with sorrow, and he thought he saw her begin to turn.

He was on his feet, seizing her arm, pulling her toward him. "I'm not letting you die for Jadar. If he's meant to win, he'll do it without either of . . ."

He sensed a movement in the portiere behind her, and looked up to see the glint of a sword thrust exactly where she had been standing. She caught his bewildered look and revolved in time to see the sword slash through the fringed cloth. An Imperial guard, wearing light chain mail and a red turban, moved through the doorway, weapon in hand.

"You son of a whore!" Hawksworth reached back for the naked sword lying on the carpet behind him and grabbed his leather jerkin. Holding the leather as a shield, he lunged at the attacker.

As Hawksworth's sword thrust reached him, the guard caught the blade with his own and instinctively parried it aside, throwing Hawksworth against a tent pole.

As he tried to regain his footing, he heard Shirin cry out and turned to see a heavy sword cut through the side of the tent behind them, creating a second opening. A hand ripped away the striped chintz and another Imperial guard entered, weapon in hand.

"Jesus! Shirin, get back!" Hawksworth shouted in English and shoved her across his sea chest, sending her tumbling away from the second attacker. As she fell, he saw her grab the pocket pistol lying on the table and turn to face the guard approaching her.

Hawksworth felt a blade rip through the jerkin in his hand and tangle in the leather. He shoved the jerkin and sword aside and cut upward with his own blade, miraculously imbedding it in the exposed neck of the turbaned guard. The man yelled out and dropped his weapon, which slid harmlessly onto the carpet. Then he stumbled and fell forward, holding his neck. Still incredulous, Hawksworth looked up to see two more Imperial guards standing in the doorway behind him, both with drawn swords. As he moved to keep them at bay with his own weapon, he turned and saw the guard who had entered through the side of the tent advancing menacingly toward Shirin. Just as the guard raised his weapon, Hawksworth heard a sharp report, followed by a moan, and watched the man crumple and fall directly in front of her smoking pistol.

As he fell, two more guards appeared at the opening behind him and began pushing their way through.

"Shirin, the lamp!" Again he shouted in English before realizing she could not understand. Without waiting, he grabbed the open oil lamp and flung it against the uniforms of the guards, bathing them in burning oil. Their turbans and hair ignited and they pulled back against the side of the tent, slapping at the flames.

He turned back to the doorway in time to see the other two guards coming toward him. As he attempted to parry them away, he found his feet tangled in the leather jerkin on the carpet and he stumbled backward, losing his balance long enough for one of the attackers to bring his sword around with a heavy sweep and knock his own weapon spinning into the dark recesses of the tent.

As he grabbed a tent pole for balance he suddenly noticed the dark outline of two more men approaching behind the guards at the door. In the shadows he could tell they were shirtless, wearing only dirty loincloths and the gray turbans of servants. They carried no weapons and had been attracted by the uproar.

Looking quickly around the tent, he noticed the burning outline of his oil-soaked powder horn lying on the carpet near his feet. He kicked it toward the approaching guard and as it struck his leg, the cap jarred free, sending hissing powder flaming through the tent. The man stumbled backward in surprise and lowered his sword. Just as he did, Hawksworth saw one of the servants standing at the doorway slip a naked *katar* from his loincloth and seize the guard by the neck. He pulled the attacker around and with a flash of steel gutted him silently with a savage upward thrust. The other Imperial guard at the doorway turned just in time to watch the *katar* drawn by the second servant enter his own throat.

Hawksworth stared in astonishment, realizing he had never before seen the two servants. Even now their faces were largely obscured by the loose ends of their turbans.

He revolved to see the other two guards turning back toward the opening that had been cut through the side of the tent, still slapping at the burning oil on their uniforms. As they reached the opening, they seemed to hesitate momentarily, then stumbled backward. As they sprawled across the carpet in front of him, their throats cut, he saw two more grimy servants standing in the opening, holding bloody *katars*.

The burning oil blazed across the fringe of a carpet and suddenly the interior of the tent was crisscrossed with fire. The four alien servants, all still holding *katars*, seemed to ignore the flames as they advanced on Shirin and Hawksworth without a word.

He watched them for a moment in horror, then reached and groped blindly across the top of his sea chest. It was bare. Then he remembered Shirin's fall and he felt along the carpet behind the chest, next to where she stood.

Just as the first man reached the edge of the chest, Hawksworth's hand closed around the handle of his *katar*.

Jesus, what do they want? Did they kill the Imperial guards so they could have the pleasure of murdering us themselves?

Bracing himself against the side of the chest, he swung the blade upward. He still could not see the attacker's face, masked behind the end of his turban.

The man stepped deftly to the side and caught Hawksworth's wrist in a grip of iron, laughing out loud.

"Never try to kill a Rajput with his own *katar*, Captain Hawksworth. He knows its temperament too well."

Vasant Rao flipped back the ragged end of his turban.

"What the bloody hell . . . !"

"We've been waiting for you by Shirin's tent. It would appear your welcome here has run out." He glanced mockingly at Shirin. "So much for your famous Muslim hospitality."

"You know very well who's responsible." Her eyes snapped back at him.

"I can probably guess." Vasant Rao released Hawksworth's wrist and stared about the burning tent. "Are you ready to ride?"

"What the hell are *you* doing here?"

"This is hardly the spot for long explanations. The fact is I'm here tonight to lead some of our friends back to the camp of His Highness, the prince. And you, if you cared to join us." Vasant Rao signaled the men around him to move out through the doorway. The smoke was already growing dense. "I'm afraid your fire has made our departure that much more difficult. It wasn't a particularly good idea on your part. Now we have to ride quickly."

"What about all this?" Hawksworth looked about the burning tent. "I have to . . ."

"Just roll what you need in a carpet. If you're going with us, you'll have to leave now. Before the entire Imperial army comes to see us off."

"But who'd want to kill us?" Hawksworth still could not move as he stared through the smoke.

"Whoever it was, they'll probably succeed if we wait here talking much longer."

Hawksworth turned on Shirin.

"You knew!"

"I couldn't tell you before. It would have been too dangerous." She quickly grabbed a carpet from the floor, stamping out the burning fringe, then flipped open Hawksworth's chest. She grabbed his lute, a handful of clothes, his boots, his books, and his depleted purse. As he watched in a daze, she rolled them in the carpet and shoved it into his hands. He looked around the burning tent one last time and caught the glint of his sword lying behind a tent pole. He grabbed it, scooped up his pistol and jerkin, and took Shirin by the arm as they pushed through the smoke toward the entrance, stepping over the bodies of the guards as they emerged into the night air.

Ahead, beside Shirin's tent, waited saddled horses and a group of turbaned riders. As they ran toward the horses, Hawksworth recognized several Rajputs from Arangbar's private guard among the horsemen.

"We were ready to ride." Vasant Rao seized the rein of one of the horses and vaulted into the saddle. "You were out walking or we could have left sooner. Shirin demanded we wait. It was well we did. Lord Krishna still seems to be watching over you, Captain."

"Which way are we headed?" Hawksworth helped Shirin into a saddle, watching as she uncertainly grabbed the horn for balance, then, still clasping the bundle, pulled himself onto a pawing Arabian mare.

"West. The rest of the men are already waiting at the end of the valley." Vasant Rao whipped his horse and led the way as they galloped toward the perimeter of the tent city. "This will be a long ride, my friend."

As Hawksworth watched the last of the tents recede into the dark, he saw disappearing with them his final chance for a *firman*. He would never see Arangbar again. Probably he would never see London again.

I've traded it all for a woman. And I still wonder if she's mine.

God help me.

BOOK FIVE
PRINCE JADAR

CHAPTER TWENTY-SEVEN

Hawksworth heard the exultant cheer of the Rajputs riding behind him and snapped awake. It was midmorning of the third day and he had been dozing fitfully in the saddle since dawn, fatigue deep in his bones. Through the trees ahead the camp of Prince Jadar lay spread before them, blanketing half the valley.

"I told you we'd make the camp in three days' ride." Vasant Rao smiled wearily at Hawksworth and spurred his lathered mount forward. "Every man with us is eager to be with the prince."

They had covered, it seemed to Hawksworth, well over a hundred miles since departing the environs of Fatehpur. Between five and six hundred Rajputs rode behind them, all heavily armed with an array of swords, pikes, clubs, saddle-axes. Each man's body armor, a woven network of steel and the quilted garment worn beneath it, was secured behind his saddle, ready to be donned for combat. Hanging at the side of each rider was a round leather shield and a large quiver containing his horn bow and arrows. None carried muskets.

Hawksworth glanced back at Shirin, who rode a few paces behind, and they shared a tired smile. She had ridden the distance like a Rajput, but now her eyes were glazed with weariness. He had suddenly realized, the morning after they all galloped out of the camp at Fatehpur, that he had never before seen a woman in India ride. Where had she learned? He had pondered the question for an hour, riding behind her to watch her easy posture in the saddle, and then he had pulled alongside and asked her point-blank. She said nothing, merely smiled and tossed the loose strands of hair back from her face. He understood her well enough to know this meant she had never ridden before . . . and didn't wish Vasant Rao to know.

"This is the moment I've waited for so long." She reined her mount alongside Hawksworth's, reached out and touched his hand. "You must help the prince now too."

"I'm not so sure I'm eager to die for Prince Jadar."

"You can always go back to Agra. And wait to be murdered by Janahara's guards. The prince has saved your life, and mine, once already. What makes you think he'll bother with you again?"

"To tell the truth, he also saved my life several months ago, the night we made landfall at Surat and were ambushed on the Tapti River by the Portugals."

"I know." She spurred her horse ahead. "I received the pigeon from Prince Jadar ordering it. I passed the message to the Shahbandar, Mirza Nuruddin, who sent his personal Rajputs to protect you."

Hawksworth urged his horse back alongside. "So I was right. You *were* one of Jadar's agents in Surat. What did Nadir Sharif once call them . . . *swanih-nigars?*"

"I gathered information for the prince." She smiled in consent. "I kept his accounts and coded his ciphers at the old observatory. Then you came along and started combing through it. You made my work that much more difficult. I never knew when you'd decide to go out there. Or what you'd find."

"Why didn't you just tell me? What did I care?"

"Too much was at risk. The prince once said never to trust a *topi-wallah.*"

Hawksworth laughed. "But surely Mukarrab Khan knew what you were doing?"

"I think he probably guessed. But what could he do? He was only the governor, not Allah. He finally forbade me to go into the palace grounds alone. When I refused to obey, he thought of sending you to the observatory, just to annoy me." She smoothed the mane of her horse. "So I think he knew I was doing something there. But he was too entangled by his own intrigues for Janahara to really care."

"Mukarrab Khan worked for the queen? How?"

"Two ways. Naturally he gathered intelligence for her, mainly about the Portuguese. But he also collected her Portuguese revenues at the ports of Surat and Cambay."

"*Her* revenues? I thought all duties went to the *Moghul's* Imperial treasury."

Shirin stifled a smile. "That's what Arangbar thinks too. And at Surat it's mostly true. She collects very little. Mirza Nuruddin despises her and always finds devious ways to muddle her accounts, probably keeping some of her money for himself. But the Shahbandar at the port of Cambay, where Mukarrab Khan used to go every two weeks, would accept bribes from the Portuguese to undervalue their goods, and then split the money with Mukarrab Khan and Janahara." She paused to watch a bright-winged bird dart past. "Arangbar could never understand why his revenue from Cambay was

so low. I heard he's thinking about closing the port." She laughed. "If only
he knew it's going mostly to Janahara."

Hawksworth rode silently for a moment, thinking. "You know, Nadir
Sharif once proposed the same arrangement for English goods, if I would
trade with him personally through the port of Cambay. I ignored him. I suspected he planned to find some way to confiscate the goods later on, claiming nonpayment of duty."

"No, on that I think Nadir Sharif would have been very fair. He always
honors his agreements, with friend or foe." She looked ahead, her weary eyes
brightening as they approached the first jumble of tents and roaming live-
stock that formed the edge of the camp. Servants in soiled *dhotis* were leading camels bearing huge baskets of fodder along the makeshift streets between the tents. "But their swindle will be finished when Prince Jadar
becomes *Moghul*. He despises the Portuguese traders and their Christian
priests."

The perimeter of the compound reserved for Jadar and his *zenana* was
clearly visible now, towering above the center of the camp. It was bordered
by a ten-foot-high wall of billowing red chintz, decorated with a white hem
at the top and held up with gilded poles spaced no more than two feet apart.
Spreading out around it were clusters of smaller tents—red and white striped
cloth for noblemen, and one-sided lean-to shelters ranging from brocade to
ragged blankets for their troops.

"The prince asked that we all ride directly to the *gulal bar*, his personal
compound," Vasant Rao shouted back over his shoulder at Hawksworth. "I
think he'll particularly want to see you, Captain."

Cheers erupted as they entered the camp. Tents emptied and infantrymen lined the sides of the wide avenue leading to Jadar's compound,
beating their swords against their leather shields. As Hawksworth studied the
forest of flying standards spreading out on either side, he suddenly realized
that each *mansabdar* nobleman was flying his own insignia above his cluster
of tents.

Ahead, rising upward from the center of Jadar's compound, was a pole
some fifty feet high with a huge vessel of burning oil secured on its tip.
Hawksworth examined the flame with astonishment, then drew his horse
alongside Vasant Rao's.

"Why's there a light in the middle of the camp? It can be seen for
miles?"

"That's called the *akas-diya*, Captain, the Light of Heaven. It's the
Great Camp Light and it's used by everyone to keep their bearings at night.
How else could a man find his tent? There are probably fifty thousand men
here, with their women and servants. In the evenings, after all the cow-dung
fires are lighted for cooking, it's so smoky here you can't see your own tent
till you're practically in it."

"This camp's a town almost the size of London. How do the people live?"

"The camp bazaar travels with us, Captain. But you're right. It *is* a city; merely one that moves." He gestured around them. "The prince of course has his own personal supplies, but everyone else must shift for himself. See those small tents on the street over there, between those two high poles bearing standards. That's one of the bazaars for the *banyas*, Hindu merchants who follow the army and sell grain, oil, *ghee*, rice, *dal*, everything you'd find in any town. They feed the men. The horses are fed by sending servants out to gather fodder. They cut grass and bring it back on camels, or baggage ponies, or even on their own head. On a long campaign many of the men bring their women, to cook and carry water. The women have to bring water from any wells or streams nearby." He laughed. "Incidentally, I should warn you the prices these *banyas* ask are as inflated as the market will bear."

"For once I can't fault the merchants. They may well be out of buyers soon."

Vasant Rao snorted and whipped his horse ahead. They were approaching the entry to Jadar's compound, a wide silk awning with the prince's banners flying from atop its posts. On either side stood rows of ornate red tents with yellow fringe along the eaves. As Hawksworth rode by, he noticed a high open tent on the left holding caged hunting leopards. Next to it stood a massive canopy, surrounded by guards, sheltering light artillery. He squinted against the sun to look inside and caught a glimpse of several dozen small-bore cannon mounted on carriages. He also noticed swivel guns fitted with a harness on their base, obviously intended to be mounted atop elephants or camels. In the center were several stacks of long-barreled Indian muskets wrapped in cloth. The last tent on the left, adjacent to the gate, sheltered several gilded palanquins and a row of immaculate bullock carts for Jadar's *zenana* women.

On the opposite side of the avenue was a row of stables for elephants, camels, and horses. Turbaned grooms were busy brushing the animals and fitting harness. Next to the stables were quarters for the animals' superintendents.

"Does all this belong to Jadar?"

"These are for the prince, his women, and guards. Each nobleman also has his own stables and light artillery. The top command is split three ways: with separate field commanders for the Rajputs, for the Muslims, for the men of Moghul descent." Vasant Rao smiled reflectively. "It's always wisest not to mix. For one thing, each needs its own bazaar; no Rajput would eat food handled by an untouchable Muslim."

Their horses drew into the shade of the awning above the entrance to the *gulal bar*. Vasant Rao and the other Rajputs reined in their mounts and began to dismount.

"This is the *naqqara-khana*, Captain Hawksworth, the entry to His Highness' private compound." Vasant Rao waved toward the red awning. "Come. You'll be welcomed warmly by the prince, I promise you. I know he'd hoped you'd join him."

Hawksworth swung down from his dark mare and stroked her one last time, wiping away the lather around the saddle. Then he turned to help Shirin alight. She leaned over and dropped into his arms, the sweat of exhaustion mingled with her perfume.

Grooms from Jadar's stables were already waiting. As they took the horses, the leader of the Rajput riders shouted staccato orders to them in Urdu, the *lingua franca* of the camp, then turned and dismissed his men, who immediately swaggered into the gathering crowd to embrace old acquaintances.

"His Highness is expecting you." Vasant Rao smiled and bowed lightly to the Rajput commander, who was tan and beardless save for a small moustache, with a white skirt, a small turban of braided gold cloth, and a velvet-sheathed *katar* in a red waist sash. The Rajput nodded, then adjusted his turban and retrieved a tightly wrapped brocade bundle from behind his saddle. As he led the way through the *naqqara-khana*, Vasant Rao turned and motioned for Hawksworth and Shirin to follow.

Jadar's guards directed them along a pathway of carpets leading through the outer barbican. Ahead was another gate, decorated with striped chintz and sealed with a hanging tapestry. As they approached it, the guards swept the tapestry aside and ushered them through.

The second compound was floored entirely with carpets and in its center stood an open, satin canopy held aloft by four gilded poles. The canopy shaded a rich Persian carpet and a throne fashioned from velvet bolsters. Several men with shoulder-high kettledrums and long brass trumpets were waiting nearby.

As Hawksworth watched, two eunuchs emerged through a curtain at the far gate and lifted it high. While a fanfare of drums and trumpets filled the air, Prince Jadar strolled jauntily through the entryway, alone.

He was dressed formally, with an elaborate silk cloak in pastel blue and a jeweled turban that reminded Hawksworth of the one worn by the *Moghul* himself. The brocade sash at his waist held a heavy *katar* with a ruby on each side of the handle. His beard was close-trimmed, accenting his dark eyes. Nothing about him suggested the appearance of a man facing impending defeat.

"*Nimaste*, Mahdu, my old friend." Jadar walked directly to the Rajput commander, grasped the man's turban and pressed it to his own breast. "How long since we sat together and ate your Udaipur *lapsi* from the same dish?"

"The New Year's festival of *diwali* two years past, Highness. In my brother's palace. And I wore the gold cloak you gave me in honor of the treaty between your armies and his, five years before."

"And tonight we will dine together again." He smiled. "If my cooks can find enough cane-juice *gur* in all the bazaars to sweeten your *lapsi*."

"Seeing you again, Highness, sweetens my tongue already." He bowed and produced the brocade bundle. "My brother, the maharana, sends this unworthy token, together with his prayers for your victory."

A eunuch stepped forward and brought it to Jadar. When the prince opened the wrapping, a scabbard holding a jewel-handled sword glistened in the midmorning light.

"He does me honor. A Rajput blade knows its friends and its foes." Jadar smiled as he brushed the sword handle. Next he drew out the blade and tested its edge with his finger. The Rajput watched as Jadar sheathed the sword, then lifted the ruby-studded *katar* from his own belt. "To honor him, I grant his brother my own *katar*. May its blade soon be crimson with the blood of his foes."

The Rajput bowed as he received the knife. Jadar admired his new sword a moment longer, then continued. "How many of our friends rode west with you?"

"Half a thousand, Highness. More would have joined us now, but I thought it unwise. Your Highness will understand why. But those who did come I picked carefully. Twenty officers of superior class, and the rest first and second class.

"The eunuchs watched your banners enter the camp. I've already heard some of the names." The prince's voice rose. "I think you've gutted the Rajput field command in the Imperial army."

"Not entirely, Highness."

"Ah, but I know you did." Jadar smiled and leaned forward, dropping his voice again and switching from Turki to Rajasthani. "The tent poles here can repeat my words." He drew himself erect again and signaled for a tray of *pan* leaves from the eunuchs. "A tent has been prepared for you. Tonight we will dine again from the same dish and you can tell me how many white-necked cranes you bagged on Pichola Lake last winter."

The Rajput clasped his hands together and bowed lightly before taking a *pan* leaf. "Tonight, Highness."

As Mahdu marched regally back through the entryway, Jadar turned and studied Shirin thoughtfully for a moment. Then he motioned her forward and smiled toward Vasant Rao. "And who else did you bring? Yet another old friend?"

Shirin salaamed lightly. "I thank Your Highness for still remembering me."

"I remember you very well. But the last I'd heard, Janahara had ordered you imprisoned. I'm astonished to see you still alive."

"I was released by Arangbar, Highness, after Samad was executed." She tried unsuccessfully to disguise the fatigue in her voice. "I still do not know why."

"Perhaps it was his weakness for beauty." Jadar smiled. "But just now I think you need rest. Mumtaz has asked me to invite you to stay with her in the *zenana*."

"Shirin stays with me." Hawksworth heard his own voice, abruptly rising above his exhaustion.

Jadar turned and studied him for a moment, then laughed out loud. "Suddenly I understand many, many things. Mumtaz was right after all. Why is it women always seem to see these things so clearly?" His gaze swept Hawksworth's tattered jerkin. "Well? How are you, Captain Hawksworth? Still alive, I see, just as I foretold. And still the fashionable English ambassador."

"There is no other. Unfortunately, however, my mission was not a complete success."

"First, India must have a just rule. Then trade can be conducted with an even hand." Jadar leaned back on his bolster. "Tell me, Captain, have you seen enough of Agra and court intrigue to rethink the matter we once discussed?"

"I've probably seen all of Agra I'll ever see." Hawksworth fixed Jadar squarely. "But then I'll have much company."

Jadar sobered and regarded Hawksworth a moment in silence.

"I see time still has not mellowed you. Or taught you very much. Do you understand anything at all of land tactics, Sea Captain Hawksworth?"

"I've never claimed to. But I can count infantry."

Jadar laughed again. "You still amuse me, Captain. I'll never know why. It saddens me there'll be so few occasions for us to pass the time together during the next few days. But at least let me show you around my compound. You'll see the next *Moghul* of India does not campaign entirely like a destitute Arab."

"Why don't we start with your fortifications."

Jadar roared as he lifted nimbly from his bolster throne and walked into the sunshine. Then he paused and turned to Shirin. "Join us if you wish. And by the way, where've you decided to stay?"

Shirin looked at Hawksworth for a moment, and their eyes locked. Then he saw a smile flicker across her face. "I'll stay with the English ambassador, Highness."

"As you wish." Jadar's tone was wistful. "I no longer try to reason with the mind of a woman. But just let me caution you. If you stay among the Muslims here, their women will spit on you unless you put on a veil. They've never heard of Persia."

"Then we'll stay with the Rajputs." Shirin tossed her head and followed along as Jadar led them through a side exit in the interior chintz wall and into the outer perimeter of the compound. The kettledrums thundered Jadar's exit.

"This side is for food, Captain." Jadar gestured toward a row of ornate tents that lined the inside of the chintz walls. "The first is for fruit and melons. No man can campaign without them, particularly if he has a hungry *zenana*. The tent over there is for making *sharbat*, and that one is for keeping betel leaves to make *pan*." Jadar smiled. "Try denying a woman her betel and you'll have nothing but squabbles." He led them on, pointing as he walked. "The large tent there is the kitchen, the one beyond it the bakery, and the one past that for grinding spices."

Hawksworth found himself astonished. Who could lead an army amid such extravagance? The tents were all red satin, with gilded poles around the outside, giving them the appearance of luxurious pavilions. Some, like the one for fruits and melons, were raised on a platform above the ground, while others were two-story, with an interior stair. As he watched the servants scurry from tent to tent bearing silver trays, he found it difficult to remember a war was looming.

"You'll soon discover traveling with women is always burdensome, Captain. For example, on the other side of the *gulal bar* I've had to erect a special tent just for their perfumes, another for their tailors, another to hold their wardrobes. Then there's a tent for mattresses, one for basins, and one for lamps and oil. These women rule my life. The things I really need—workshops, guardhouses, my arsenal—I've had to situate back behind the *zenana*, near where the servingwomen stay." Jadar paused, his eyes gleaming mischievously. "Well, what do you think?"

"I think an army camp should have fewer women and more men."

Jadar laughed and looked pointedly at Shirin. "But what is life without women, Captain?"

"Wives don't travel with an army in Europe."

"Then Europe could learn something from India."

"About fighting or about women?"

"Before you're through you may learn a few things about both." Jadar turned and started back down the row of tents. "War here is very different from wars on the seas, Captain. You should see my men fight before you judge them. But my question now is whether *you* know how to fight well enough to be of any help. Tell me, can you handle a bow?"

"Armies don't use bows in England any more. I've certainly never used one. I think the last time bows were issued for battle was back around the time of the Spanish Armada, almost thirty years ago. Some of the local forces in Devonshire equipped eight hundred men with longbows."

Jadar paused uncertainly. "What do you mean by 'longbow'?"

"It's a bow about five feet in length. The best ones are made of yew, but they're also made from ash and elm."

"You mean your bows are made entirely from wood?" Jadar's voice betrayed his skepticism. "What weight did they pull?"

"I don't know exactly, but they were powerful enough. You can draw a longbow all the way back to your ear. During the time of King Harry it was forbidden to practice with a longbow using a range less than a full furlong. The English longbow drove the crossbow right out of Europe. I've heard it said a longbow can pierce a four-inch-thick oak door."

"But you don't use them now?"

"We prefer muskets."

He seemed to ponder the answer as he led them back into his carpeted reception area. He took his place beneath the canopy, then turned to Hawksworth.

"We use muskets too. But frankly they're often more trouble than they're worth. They're cumbersome and inaccurate, and while you're reloading and priming your matchlock a Rajput archer will put half a dozen arrows through you. Infantry here normally is one-third matchlock men and two-thirds archers. If you're going to be any help to us, Captain, you'll need to learn to use a bow."

Jadar stopped and turned to look at Shirin. Her eyes were fluttering with fatigue. "But I forget my manners. *You* must have some rest while we teach the *feringhi* how to fight. Perhaps the best thing would be to clear a tent for you at the rear of the *gulal bar*, near the workshops. And the English captain can stay there too," Jadar laughed. "So I can watch him practice his bow." He glanced back at Hawksworth and his eyes froze on the pearl earring. "I see you're a khan now, as well as an ambassador. Congratulations. If Arangbar can make you a khan, I can surely make you an archer."

Jadar motioned to the eunuchs, who came forward and escorted Shirin through the rear doorway of the compound. Hawksworth was watching her leave, praying for sleep himself, when Jadar's voice brought him back.

"Let me begin by explaining our Indian bow to you, Captain. I think it's probably quite different from the English bow you described." Jadar turned to Vasant Rao and motioned toward his quiver, a flat leather case hanging from a strap over one shoulder. It was covered with gold embossing and held both his bow and his arrows. "You know we have a proverb: the sword is better than the *katar*; the spear is better than the sword; the arrow better than the spear. I've heard Muslims claim the bow and arrow were first given to Adam by the archangel Gabriel." Jadar paused while Vasant Rao took out his bow and passed it over. "Now, the first thing you need to learn is how to string this. It's more difficult than you might suppose, since a bow is reflexed, curved back around the opposite way when unstrung. It's stressed against the strung position to give it more weight on the pull." Jadar examined the bow for a moment. "In fact, you can tell how much use a bow has had by the way it's bent when unstrung. The original curve in this bow is almost gone, which means it's had a lot of use. Here hold it for a moment."

Hawksworth grasped the bow in his hand. It was some four feet long, shaped in a wide curve with the ends bent back. The grip was velvet, with a gold-embossed design on the inner side.

"You say your English bows are made of wood, but I find that difficult to believe. This one is a composite, a mango-wood core with strips of buffalo horn glued over the outside. And the outer curve is lined with catgut to give it even more force. That's why this bow had to be sealed on the outside with leather. We use leather or lacquer to protect the glue from the dampness of the monsoon. The string, by the way, is a silk skein with a crisscross binding at the center."

"How do you string it?"

Jadar grinned as he took back the bow. "It's not easy. If you have to string a bow while riding, you hook one end between the stirrup and the instep of your foot and brace it backward against your knee. But usually we bend it over our back." He took the string in his hand and slipped the bow around his waist. Then he flipped it against his back and pulled its free end over his left shoulder, inverting the curve and hooking the string in a single motion. It was done in an instant.

"There. But I've made it look easier than it is. You should practice. And it would also be well if you could learn to string a bow and shoot from horseback."

"Horseback!"

"All horsemen use a bow."

"How can you possibly hit anything from horseback?"

"Practice. A good Rajput archer can shoot as well from horseback as standing. The Uzbeks shoot better." As Jadar spoke he was extracting a heavy ring from inside his cloak. One side of the ring was a green emerald, flat and square and half an inch wide.

"This is a *zihgir*, a bow ring, to protect your thumb when you draw. It also increases your range."

He pushed the emerald ring over his thumb, notched an arrow into the string, and drew it back effortlessly, holding the thin bamboo arrow in position with a touch of his forefinger. The whole sequence had taken less than a second. Hawksworth found himself staring in admiration.

"By the way," Jadar turned to Vasant Rao, "show him how you shoot under a shield."

The Rajput turned to one of Jadar's guards, whose shield was hanging loosely from a shoulder strap. He took the shield and slipped it onto his wrist. It was circular, a quarter inch thick and about two feet in diameter, and curved like a wide bowl. The front was figured with a silver ensign and in the center were four steel nailheads, which secured the handgrips on the back.

"That shield's one of the best. It's made with cured rhino hide and toughened with lacquer. You hold it by those two straps attached inside, there in the center." Jadar pointed as Vasant Rao held out the back of the shield. "Notice the straps are large and loose. So when you want to shoot, you can slip your hand through and slide the shield up your wrist, like he's doing now. Then your hand extends out beyond the rim and you can hold the grip of the bow. But remember you'll have no protection when shooting, so you'll learn to shoot fast or you won't live long in a battle. Here, try the shield."

Hawksworth took the shield and gripped the leather thongs on the back. "It's light. How much protection does it give?"

"A buffalo-hide shield is really only effective against arrows, but a rhino-hide shield like this one will usually deflect musket fire. We'll find a rhino shield for you somewhere." Jadar rose to leave. "Incidentally, after seeing how you handle that bow, I think I'd better assign you to the guards stationed back with the *zenana*. That should keep you well out of the battle. I don't want my first English ambassador dead just yet." He fingered his long pearl necklace and studied Hawksworth. "You may be interested to know my reports say the Imperial army will reach us in two days. Tomorrow I plan to poison all the tanks and water wells within twenty *kos* east of here, forcing them to attack immediately. I hope you'll be ready."

He turned and was gone.

Hawksworth awoke at noon the following day to discover work had begun on fortification of the camp. He left Shirin sleeping and walked to the eastern perimeter, where the heavy cannon were being drawn into position. As he paused to study one of the cannon, he found himself comparing it with the European design. It looked to be a six-inch bore, with a molded iron barrel strengthened by brass hoops shrunk around the outside. It was bolted onto its own carriage, a flat base supported by four solid wooden wheels, and pulled by a team of ten white bullocks yoked in pairs. Cotton ropes almost two inches in diameter were tied around the breech, looped beneath the axles and then through a heavy iron ring on the front of the mount, extending forward to hooks on the yokes of the bullocks.

While their drivers whipped the animals forward, a crowd of moustachioed infantry in red and green tunics clustered around the gun carriages pushing. A drummer in an orange cloak sat astraddle the breech of the cannon beating cadence for the other men on two large drums strapped along

each side of the barrel. A large bull elephant trailed behind, heavy padding
on his forehead, and whenever the gun carriage bogged, the elephant would
be moved forward to shove the breech with his head.

As the cannon were rolled into position, some fifteen feet apart, they
were being linked to each other with heavy ropes of twisted bull hide the size
and strength of metal chain, to prevent cavalry from riding through and cutting down the gunners. After the hide ropes were camouflaged with brush, a
leather screen was placed behind the breech of each gun to protect the
gunners when it fired.

Hawksworth counted approximately three hundred cannon along the
camp perimeter. Firepots were being stationed behind each gun, together
with linstocks and leather barrels of powder. A few bags of dirt had been
piled between some of the cannon to provide protection for matchlock men.
Around the cannon men were assembling piles of four-sided iron claws, and
beyond, diggers with picks and wicker baskets had begun a halfhearted effort
to start construction of a trench. He studied the preparations uneasily for a
moment, sensing something was wrong, and then he froze.

There was no shot. Only stacks of iron claws.

He whirled and made his way back to the munitions depot, rows of
yellow-fringed tents. The shot was there waiting, in gauge ranging from two
inch to ten inch, but none had been moved.

He moved on to other tents and discovered several hundred more cannon. Some were the same gauge as those being deployed, others much larger.
All had been fitted with harness, ready to be moved, but now they stood in
long rows, waiting. As he moved on to another row of tents, pushing
through the swarm of men and bullocks, he discovered a vast cache of
smaller cannon, thousands, also mounted on wooden carriages but small
enough to be moved by a bullock, or even two men. These too were
harnessed and sat untouched.

Beyond these were other rows of tents, where seven-foot-long muskets—
together with powder, bags of shot, and a wooden prong to rest the barrel on
when firing—were now being broken out and distributed to the infantry. The
men were being armed, but the camp itself was practically without fortification.

Hawksworth stood brooding about the preparations, about the Rajput
horn bow he had only barely learned to use—he was finally able to hit the
todah, practice target, a mound of earth piled near Jadar's officers' tents, but
shooting under a shield seemed impossible—and the situation began to overwhelm him. Jadar's position was becoming more hopeless by the minute.

He stared around the open camp and decided he would try to requisition as many matchlocks as possible, and perhaps also try to teach Shirin to
shoot in the time remaining. If they had muskets, he told himself, perhaps

they could somehow defend themselves when the Imperial army swept through the camp.

He turned and pushed his way back toward where muskets were being issued. Men were walking past him carrying heavy matchlocks, five feet in length with a barrel of rolled steel welded together end to end. The barrel was attached to the stock by a broad steel band, and both were profusely ornamented with embossing and colored enamel. Some of the muskets had wooden tripods attached to the end of the barrel.

As he approached the munitions tent, he saw Vasant Rao standing in its center, issuing orders with an easy smile, his moustache and turban as prim as though he were on muster. Beside him was a head-high pile of muskets, each wrapped in a roll of green broadcloth. Hawksworth stared at him for a moment, then pushed forward. Through the shouting mob he finally managed to catch the Rajput's arm and pull him toward the rear of the open tent.

"Why aren't the cannon being deployed?"

"But they are, Captain." Vasant Rao stroked his moustache and looked past Hawksworth's shoulder toward the next stack of matchlocks.

"But only the medium-bore guns, and even those have no shot. Nothing else has been moved."

"By medium bore I assume you mean the *gau-kash*, the ox-drawn cannon. That's true. But these things all take time."

"You're spending what little time you have left deploying medium-bore cannon, and those with no shot! Who the *hell* is in charge?"

"Prince Jadar, of course. The *gau-kash* cannon are the key to his strategy." Vasant Rao moved past Hawksworth and barked orders for the next stack of muskets to be unstrapped. Waiting infantrymen in ragged cloaks pushed forward. "Take a musket, Captain, if you want one. They're probably of some small use. When I'm finished here, I have to check all the harness on the *fil-kash* cannon, the large guns that will be drawn into position by elephants. Then I still have to issue the *mardum-kash* guns, the small cannon that are assigned to two-man teams."

"Where will this other artillery be deployed?" Hawksworth shouted toward Vasant Rao's back.

The Rajput seemed not to hear, as he paused to speak to one of the men assisting him. Then he turned and unwrapped a musket, selected a tripod, and passed both to Hawksworth. The other man was bringing a wide velvet belt from the back of the tent, and he handed it to Hawksworth. Hanging from it were a powder flask, bullet pouch, priming horn, match cord, and flint and steel. "The prince will issue orders for deployment of the *fil-kash* and *mardum-kash* guns after they've all been harnessed."

"He'd better issue them soon. It'll start growing dark in a couple of hours, three at most."

"I'm sure he's aware of the time, Captain." Vasant Rao turned and disappeared into a circle of bearded Rajputs, barking orders.

Hawksworth watched him disappear, then turned and grabbed two more muskets. Holding them ahead of him like a prow he pushed his way back into the milling street. The air was rank with sweat and the crowds seemed more disorganized than ever. Women jostled in the streets, haggling with the merchants for clay jars of oil, while grooms moved among them leading prancing horses, each wearing a gold-fringed saddle blanket that glowed like ancient coin in the waning sun.

Hawksworth studied the crowd, searching vainly for some sense of organization, then turned to begin working his way back toward Jadar's compound and his own tent.

Shirin was still there, asleep. He stood admiring her again, her soft mouth, the olive skin of her high cheeks, her shining dark hair, and realized he loved her more than ever.

Dear God, we've only just begun to live. Jadar is a madman.

Almost without knowing why, he began to rummage through the remains of his clothing, still rolled in the carpet and lying where he had thrown it. His pulse suddenly quickened when his fingers closed around a hard round object. It was his very last bottle of brandy, miraculously entangled in the remains of his formal doublet.

If there was ever a time . . .

He ripped away the rotting cork with his teeth and pulled deeply on the brandy, twice. As always, it seemed to work at the knot in his gut. He took one more swallow, then shook Shirin.

She startled awake and stared at him wildly for a second. Then she broke into a smile . . . until she saw the brandy.

"Do you really need that now?"

"I need this and a lot more. How can you sleep? This whole God-cursed camp is going to be leveled by the Imperial army in a few hours." He stopped and stared at her. "Are you listening? Only a fraction of Jadar's cannon are deployed. Most are still waiting to be pulled into position. It's unbelievable."

Shirin pulled herself up and leaned against a bolster, examining him with weary eyes. "Then why are you here? I thought you'd decided to help Prince Jadar."

"How can anyone help him when he won't help himself?" Hawksworth took another burning mouthful of brandy and stared at his bow quiver lying on the carpet. In a fit of disgust he kicked it toward the corner of the tent.

Shirin watched the bow fall and laughed.

"Have you mastered your Rajput bow yet?"

"No, and what does it matter? You know Jadar is outnumbered three to one." Hawksworth pointed toward the muskets he had leaned against a coil of rope by the tent pole. "I've got three weapons for us. Do you think you can shoot a matchlock?"

"I can shoot a bow." She dismissed the muskets with a glance. "I sincerely hope you've learned enough to shoot one too."

A trumpet sounded from the center of the compound. Immediately it was answered by others the length of the camp.

Shirin snapped alert and rose off the bolster, pulling her gauze cloak around her waist.

"That's the signal to begin preparing the firewood. Come. At least you can help with that."

Hawksworth examined her aghast.

"Firewood! What in God's name are you talking about? Is Jadar planning to light fires? Is he worried the Imperial army won't find our camp?" He turned and walked to the doorway, rubbing his brow in disbelief. "I think there's damned small risk of that. The red tents of his *zenana* can be seen for miles."

Shirin laughed and pushed her way ahead of him, past the portiere of the tent. Servants had already begun assembling piles of logs along the center of the walkway that ran the length of the compound. Hawksworth stood at the doorway and stared in astonishment as clay jars of oil were carried from the kitchen tent and stationed near the logs. As he watched, he noticed the long shadows of dusk beginning to play across the walls of nearby tents.

He turned to retrieve the brandy, and when he emerged again from the tent, Shirin was lost among the crowd of servants bringing wood. He slipped the bottle into his jerkin and started working his way down the side of the compound, back toward the munitions tent.

Pairs of elephants had been harnessed to the larger cannon, and now they were being led out of the camp, into the dusk. Following these were camels with two-pound swivel guns mounted on their backs, together with infantry pulling the smaller guns after them on two-wheeled carriages. Bullock carts heaving with powder and shot came after.

Pyramids of firewood were scattered among the tents, and already many of the Rajputs had assembled by the unlit piles, talking and embracing. Some had seated themselves and removed their turbans, chanting verses from the Bhagavad-Gita as they began to oil and comb their long black hair. Hawksworth watched silently as they started passing around inlaid teakwood boxes, taking and eating handfuls of small brown balls.

As he stood puzzling, he recognized Vasant Rao standing among the men. The Rajput was somber now, clasping each of the men in what seemed a farewell gesture. He looked up and saw Hawksworth and smiled.

"Captain Hawksworth, I'm glad you're here. You're almost a Rajput yourself by now. Do you want to comb your hair? It's how we prepare for what may happen. Who knows which of us will see the morrow."

"I can die just as well with my hair the way it is."

"Then you're not entirely a Rajput after all. But you're still welcome to join us." He held out one of the boxes.

Hawksworth opened the box and gingerly took out one of the balls. As he rolled it under his nose, it triggered a distant memory of his first night in Surat and Mukarrab Khan's dinner party. Suddenly he stopped dead still.

It was opium.

"Jesus Christ! Have you all gone mad?" He flung the ball to the ground and whirled on Vasant Rao. "That's the *last* thing you need if you hope to fight at all. It's like eating death."

"*Affion* prepares a Rajput for battle, Captain. The more we eat, the stronger we become. It gives us the strength of lions."

"Good Jesus help us all."

Hawksworth pushed his way incredulously back through the milling crowd of infantry and mounted cavalry, feeling as though the world had collapsed. All around him Rajputs were eating handfuls of opium, combing their hair, embracing in farewell. Many had already put on their *khaftan*, the quilted vest they wore under their armor. He wondered how long it would be before they became drunk with opium and began killing each other.

God, we're all going to die. Can't Jadar stop it? Can't he at least stop them from eating opium before we're attacked? And where are they moving the cannon? Out of the camp? What the hell is happening?

He wheeled and headed for the *naqqara-khana*, the entry to Jadar's compound. When he reached it, he realized the guards were gone. Amazed, he walked through the entry and discovered all the interior partitions of the *gulal bar* were also gone. The satin tents that had held the melons, the *pan* leaves, the kitchen—all were deserted, empty.

He made his way on through the deserted *gulal bar*, feeling like a man lost. In the dark there were no guards, no troops, nothing. Ahead he heard the sound of elephants trumpeting and he felt his way forward through the semi-darkness, the ground a mosaic of flickering shadows from the still-burning camp light. His despair absolute, he reached into the pocket of his jerkin for the bottle.

A *katar* was at his throat.

"It's forbidden by death to draw a weapon in the *gulal bar*, Captain."

"I was only . . ."

There was an explosion of laughter and he turned to see the shadowed face of Jadar.

"What . . . what are you doing here?"

"Thinking, Captain Hawksworth. Do you never think before a battle at sea? Surely you must."

"I think. And I also keep my gunners sober." Hawksworth felt vaguely foolish as he finished extracting the brandy bottle. "Do you know half your men are eating handfuls of opium?"

"I'm glad to hear it. It means my Rajputs will be invincible tomorrow." Jadar flipped the *katar* in his hand and dropped it into its leather sheath. "By the way, I understand you failed to master the bow. But let's talk about something more important. Perhaps you can be of help after all. I'm sure you realize, Captain, that a commander must always understand two things. He must know his own strengths, and he must know the strengths of those who oppose him. But he can really only know one of these for sure. He can never know exactly what he will meet." Jadar paused. "Tell me, if you were Inayat Latif, how would you deploy the Imperial army tomorrow?"

"What do you mean?"

"How would you choose to attack? The position of infantry, cavalry, elephants is never exactly the same in any battle. For example, often the front line is held by rows of infantry. The first row will be men wearing plate armor—which is much heavier than the usual steel netting—forming a protective wall with special broad shields. They are always excellent archers. Behind these will be another row, wearing only helmets and breastplates, and armed with swords and pikes. The third row is infantry with swords, bows, and axes. The fourth carries lances and swords. The rows are segmented, so those behind can see ahead, and cavalry can get through."

"That deployment would mean a slow-moving attack, and a very bloody fight."

"Precisely. That's why many commanders prefer to use their cavalry as the vanguard. Horsemen can move faster, and they can more easily avoid defense barricades."

Hawksworth looked at Jadar, wishing he could see his eyes. "But cavalry can be cut to ribbons with small artillery. Is it wise to charge with your cavalry if your enemy has heavy gun emplacements?"

He heard Jadar laugh. "You may make a commander yet. You see, Inayat Latif will naturally assume our camp is heavily defended. Now although it's considered questionable manners to attack a camp at night, your manners become excusable if you attack at early dawn, even though it's still dark. I've known of attacks occurring almost half a *pahar* before dawn. What's that in European measure? An hour, an hour and a half?"

"But if it's still dark, how can you see the enemy's lines?"

"You can see them if your enemy's camp has been negligent enough to leave a few fires burning." Jadar smiled as he paused to let the words sink.

"But now let's examine the third possibility. Leading the attack with your elephants. Elephant armor is steel plate and it can withstand everything except heavy cannon. If you can entice your foe into firing his biggest artillery before you charge, then you can send a wave of war elephants and devastate his gunners before their cannon cool enough to reload. Since it can take at least half a *pahar* for a large cannon to cool, large guns are rarely fired more than once in a battle. And never after your cavalry has moved out. Leading the vanguard with war elephants always entails danger, since if they panic, they can turn around and trample your own infantry, but in this case it's probably worth the risk."

"And you think that's what Inayat Latif will try to do?" Hawksworth absently twirled the brandy bottle in his hand.

"I'm asking you."

"It sounds the most plausible. He'll position his biggest cannon to fire into the camp, and after he's drawn your fire in return, he'll stampede about a thousand war elephants right through here, crushing everything in their path. Including your opium-sotted Rajputs and their invincible bows."

"You're doing remarkably well so far, Captain." Jadar took Hawksworth's arm and guided him toward the back of the compound. "And then what would you do?"

"I'd send an infantry wave right after the war elephants, with lines so thick it would be a wall of death. And behind them I'd have cavalry, with muskets, to contain the camp and meet your own cavalry when it broke through—as it probably would eventually."

"Cavalrymen wouldn't bother with muskets, just bows, but you're still thinking very clearly. Now tell me, from what direction would you attack this particular camp?"

They were approaching the tents, where servants were beginning to soak the wood piles with oil. Hawksworth found himself astonished that Jadar would listen calmly to the strategy spelling his own destruction.

"From the east, the way we came in."

"And why that particular direction?"

"Several reasons." Hawksworth tried to remember the terrain as they came into the camp. "First, if I'd marched from the east, I'd already have my army deployed there. Second, and probably more important, it's the only direction that's really accessible. The other sides are too forested. But from the east there's a wide clearing that funnels down right into the perimeter of the camp."

"With a very clear demarcation of forest on each side, which helps keep your army grouped."

"Correct. And, also, the sun would not be in my men's eyes if I hit you from the east."

Jadar stopped and looked at him. "So that is *precisely* what you would do? Attack at dawn on the eastern perimeter. And lead with a front line of war elephants?"

"With the biggest and best I had."

Jadar sighed. "You know, it troubles me that a *feringhi* would conclude the same thing I have. But I think it's a classic problem. And that will dictate a classic solution in the mind of Inayat Latif, whose alleged brilliance does not include a flair for originality. He'll have to mount a conventional attack. What's more, because of the restricted terrain, he'll have no room to split his army into a right wing and a left wing. They'll have to be a single phalanx. That's dangerous if you ever need to retreat, but he'll not even consider that possibility. And you say you also believe he'll hold his cavalry for the third wave." Jadar paused. "That's more important here than you probably realize. Everything else depends on it. The cavalry must attack last."

"It seems best. And his cavalry is mainly Rajput. He'll not risk cutting up his finest troops by sending them in the first attack wave, when your artillery is still in place." Hawksworth hesitated, then continued bitterly. "Or should be."

Jadar laughed and looked at Hawksworth, then at his bottle.

"What's that in your hand, Captain?"

"A bottle of brandy. Spanish, I'm ashamed to admit, but it's still the best."

"May I try it?"

Jadar took the bottle and gingerly swallowed a swig. He stood motionless for a moment and then coughed violently.

"Merciful Allah! Now I understand why the Prophet forbade its use." He shoved back the bottle. "But I wanted to drink once with you, Captain. I'm told it's a European custom. You've eased my mind."

"Eased your mind! I just told you how your camp will be devastated at sunrise."

"Absolutely. I will regret losing these tents." Jadar's tone grew pensive. "You know, some of them have been with me since my first campaign in the Deccan, years ago."

"How about your Rajputs? And your women? Will you regret losing them as much as your tents?"

"I don't expect to lose them." Jadar took Hawksworth's arm and led him around the last tent. In the firelight baggage elephants were being loaded with women from the *zenana*. The elephants were covered with *pakhar* armor, steel plates around the sides of their bodies and a special steel casement for their head and trunk. The women were being helped up tall ladders and into their elephants' *howdah*, an octagonal box of heavy boards strengthened with iron plate.

"Why are you loading the women now?"

"But we're leaving, Captain."

Hawksworth stared at him speechlessly for a moment, then noticed Shirin walking toward them, carrying a bow and two quivers of arrows.

"You're leaving?"

"You just predicted this camp would be devastated. I agree with you entirely. In fact I planned it that way. So why should anyone be here when it happens? The camp will be empty by dawn, Captain. Naturally we had to wait until dark to move out. And continue work on the trenches until the very end. Inayat Latif undoubtedly has scouts all around. But by dawn there'll only be smoldering fires here. And the troops needed to man our decoy cannon across the eastern perimeter. I've loaded half the cannon with elephant barbs made in my workshops. The other half with nothing. Why waste shot? We'll fire the blank cannon to induce them to charge, and after the elephants have come inside cannon range, we'll shoot the barbs in among them. A barb in the foot of an elephant can immobilize it completely. Inayat Latif will never expect barbs. They haven't been used in India for fifty years. His war elephants should be contained right out there, unable to advance or retreat."

"But where will your army be?"

"Captain. Just when I thought you were beginning to understand tactics. My army will be waiting along both sides of the open plain on the east, behind a foliage camouflage we've been erecting over the past two weeks. After the attack force of Imperial war elephants has been funneled into the empty camp, we will open fire against them with our biggest cannon. From both sides. The medium-range cannon will fire into the infantry, as will the small artillery. All the guns should be in place just before dawn if I've timed it right."

Hawksworth turned to see keepers leading an armored elephant forward for him and Shirin. Only its ears could be seen behind the steel plate. Then he looked again at Jadar.

"But you're still outnumbered in infantry three to one."

"All things in time, Captain." He turned and embraced Shirin lightly. "This was my best *swanih-nigar*. Guard her well."

Shirin examined Hawksworth's brandy bottle with her dark eyes and laughed skeptically. "I've brought my own bow."

Hawksworth cleared his throat as he slipped the bottle back into his jerkin. "I've requisitioned a brace of muskets. It's still the weapon I prefer."

"Congratulations, Captain." Jadar's laugh was cynical. "I admire your *feringhi* initiative. But I don't want to see you harmed. Like I told you, I'm sending you with the *zenana*. They'll be moved to that hilltop there west of the camp. So at least you'll be able to watch the battle." He turned to leave. "Farewell until tomorrow, Captain. May Allah ride with you."

"And I wish you Godspeed. You're a ten times better strategist then I realized, for whatever it may be worth."

Jadar laughed. "Just save some of your foul-tasting *feringhi* brandy for our victory celebration. And perhaps I'll drink with you one more time." His eyes darkened. "If not, then tomorrow we'll be eating lamb side by side in Paradise."

CHAPTER TWENTY-EIGHT

A drum roll lifted across the dark plain, swelling in intensity like angry, caged thunder. It rose to fill the valley with a foreboding voice of death, then faded slowly to silence, gorged on its own immensity.

"That's the Imperial army's call to arms. Prince Jadar was right. Inayat Latif is attacking now, before dawn." Shirin was seated next to Hawksworth in the dark *howdah*. She rose to peer over the three-foot-high steel rim, out into the blackness. Around them were the shapes of the *zenana* guard elephants, silently swinging their trunks beneath their armor. The *zenana* waited farther back on female baggage elephants, surrounded by hundreds of bullock carts piled with clothing and utensils. "Merciful Allah, he must have a thousand war drums."

"You saw the size of the Imperial army mustering at Fatehpur." Hawksworth rose to stand beside her, grasping the side of the rocking *howdah* and inhaling the cold morning air. "The queen had begun recalling *mansabdars* and their troops from every province."

Suddenly a chorus of battle horns cut through the dark, followed by the drums again, now a steady pulse that resounded off the wooded hills, swelling in power.

"That's the signal for the men and cavalry to deploy themselves in battle array." Shirin pointed toward the sound. "The Imperial forces are almost ready."

Below them fires smoldered in Jadar's abandoned camp, a thousand specks of winking light. Although the east was beginning to hint the first tinges of light, the valley where the Imperial army had massed was still shrouded in black.

The drums suddenly ceased, mantling the valley in eerie, portentous quiet. Hawksworth felt for Shirin's hand and noticed it perspiring, even in the cold dawn air.

From the eastern edge of Jadar's abandoned camp points of cannon fire erupted, tongues of light that divulged the length and location of the camp's defenses. A few moments later—less time than Hawksworth would have wished—the sound reached them, dull pops, impotent and hollow. The firing lapsed increasingly sporadic, until the camp's weak perimeter defense seemed to exhaust itself like the last melancholy thrusts of a spent lover.

The defense perimeter of the camp had betrayed itself, and in the tense silence that ensued Hawksworth knew the Imperial guns were being set.

Suddenly a wall of flame illuminated the center of the plain below, sending rockets of fire plunging toward the empty camp.

"Jesus, they're launching fireworks with cannon. What are they?"

"I don't know. I've heard that cannon in India were once called naphtha-throwers."

A second volley followed hard after the first. Although this time no fireworks were hurtled, the impact was even more deadly. Forty-pound Imperial shot ripped wide trenches through the flaming tents of the prince's camp. In moments the *gulal bar*, where they had been standing only hours before, was devastated, an inferno of shredded cloth and billowing flame.

A harsh chant began to drift upward from the valley, swelling as voices joined in unison.

"Allah-o-Akbar! Allah-o-Akbar!" God is Great. It was the battle cry of Inayat Latif's Muslim infantry.

The plain below had grown tinged with light now, as dawn approached and the fires from Jadar's camp spread. As Hawksworth watched, nervously gripping the handle of his sword, a force of steel-armored war elephants advanced on the eastern perimeter of the camp, their polished armor plate glowing red in the firelight. Those in the vanguard bore steel-shrouded *howdahs*, through which a single heavy cannon protruded . . . probably a ten-pounder, Hawksworth told himself. The steel *howdahs* on the next rows of elephants were almost three feet high and perforated to allow their archers to shoot without rising above the open top. Sporadic cannon and matchlock fire from the few hundred men left in the camp pelted the elephants but did nothing to impede their advance. Directly behind them the Imperial infantry swept in dense, martialed ranks.

Jadar knew exactly what he was doing when he picked this terrain for the camp, Hawksworth told himself. He used it to set the terms for the battle. There's no room to maneuver. When they discover the camp is abandoned, the elephants can't retreat and regroup without crushing their own infantry.

He slipped his arm around Shirin's waist and held her next to him. They watched as the Imperial war elephants crashed through the camp's outer edge, scarcely slowing at the ditch. When the elephants were at point-blank range, the specially loaded cannon along the perimeter opened fire, spraying a rain of steel barbs among them. Even from the hilltop he could hear the clang of steel as the barbs ricocheted off their armor.

"We'll soon know if Jadar's plan has a chance. Can he contain the elephants there, or will they obliterate the camp, then regroup, and . . ."

The first row of elephants suddenly reared chaotically, lashing out with their armored trunks and dismounting some of the gunners. As barbs caught in their feet, they trumpeted in pain and started to mill randomly in angry confusion, crushing several of the men they had thrown.

Just as Jadar predicted, the deadly carpet of barbs had temporarily disrupted their advance. Their ranks were broken and their guns in disarray. Behind the elephants the infantry still marched unaware, until the confusion in the elephant ranks began to disrupt their front lines. Gradually the order in the infantry ranks completely disintegrated, as the men stopped to eye the milling war elephants ahead of them in growing fear and confusion. By a single cannon salvo Jadar's men had robbed the attack of its momentum.

"Now's Jadar's moment." Hawksworth watched in grudging admiration. "Will he use it?"

As though in answer, a blare of trumpets from the hills on both sides of the plain suddenly electrified the morning air. As they died away, the woods opened wide with a single chorus, deep and throaty and unforgiving.

RAM RAM. RAM RAM. RAM RAM.

It was the ancient Rajput war cry.

A blaze of fire from Jadar's camouflaged cannon shredded away the leafy blinds erected along the foot of the hills, sending a rain of forty-pound lead shot into the Imperial war elephants. Their disordered ranks erupted in tangled steel and blood. Seconds later, a volley by Jadar's small artillery ripped into the unsuspecting infantry massed behind the elephants, hurtling fragmented bodies and orphaned weapons spinning through the ranks. Finally came the fiery streaks of rockets, thin foot-long iron tubes filled with gunpowder and set with a lighted fuse, many with a sword blade attached to the end, which cut in a deadly wave through the Imperial troops, slashing and exploding as they flew.

A dense roll of Jadar's war drums sounded from both hillsides, and the first wave of Rajput cavalry, still bellowing their war cry, charged down on the disrupted Imperial forces, discharging volleys of arrows with mechanical precision. They wore steel-net cloaks and helmet guards, and their horses were armored with woven steel netting encased in heavy quilting—with a wide frontlet over the chest, a neck-length collar secured to the top of the bridle, and a body shroud over their sides and hindquarters emblazoned with each man's family crest. The startled infantry turned to meet them, and in moments the air darkened with opposing arrows. From the hill above came the din of supporting matchlock fire from Jadar's own infantry.

The Rajput cavalry plowed into the first rows of Imperial infantry with their long *nezah* lances held at arm's length high above their heads, thrusting downward as they rode. Veins fueled with opium, the Rajputs had forgotten all fear. They brushed aside Imperial spears and swords and slaughtered with undisguised pleasure, as though each death endowed more honor to their *dharma*. Hawksworth's stomach knotted as he watched a thousand men fall in less than a minute.

While the Rajputs attacked, the prince's division of armored war elephants had emerged from their camouflage and begun advancing across the western edge of the plain, isolating the ragged remainder of the Imperial elephants from the battlefield. Although Jadar had far fewer war elephants, they now were easily able to contain the shattered Imperial force.

Hawksworth turned to watch as yet another wave of Jadar's cavalry bore down on the plain. These rode through the tangle of Imperial infantry wielding long curved swords, killing any the first wave had missed.

"I'm not sure I believe what I'm seeing." Hawksworth peered through the dust and smoke boiling across the plain below. "Jadar has already seized the advantage. He's immobilized their war elephants, their major advantage, and he timed the counterattack perfectly."

"The battle has only just begun." Shirin took his hand for no reason at all and gripped it. "And their major advantage was not elephants, but numbers. I fear for him. Look, there." She pointed toward the east, where the red sky now illuminated a vast sea of infantry, poised as reinforcements. "The prince's Rajputs cannot stop them all. And beyond there the Imperial cavalry is waiting, mostly Rajputs themselves. Prince Jadar does not have the forces to meet them. I think he will be defeated today, badly."

"And if he dies, do we die with him?"

"Perhaps not you. But they will surely kill me. And probably Mumtaz. Most certainly they have orders to kill his son."

On the field below Jadar's cavalry fought as though possessed. Rajputs with one, two, even three arrows in their back continued to sound their war cry and take head after bearded head, until they finally slumped unconscious from the saddle. Riderless horses, many with their stomachs slashed open, could be seen running wildly through the Imperial ranks, unused arrows still rattling in their saddle quivers.

Waves of Jadar's infantry had begun pouring down from the hills, following the cavalry. The men wore heavy leather helmets and a skirt of woven steel. A hood of steel netting hung down from each man's helmet, protecting his face and neck. They advanced firing volley after volley of arrows into the Imperial infantry. When they reached the plain, they drew their long curved swords and, waving them above their heads, threw themselves into the forces of Inayat Latif. The field quickly became a vast arena of hand-to-hand combat, as inevitably happened when two Indian armies met, with Jadar's forces badly outnumbered.

Shirin watched the slaughter in silence for a time, as though tallying the dead and dying on both sides, and then she turned her face away.

"Allah preserve us. Prince Jadar's Rajputs have eaten so much *affion* I think they can fight even after they die, but their numbers are already shrinking. How long can they protect the prince?"

"Where's he now?"

She turned back and peered through the dust on the field for a long moment. Then she pointed. "He's on the field now. There, in the center. Do you see him?" She paused. "He's very courageous to take the field so early. It will inspire his men, but it's a very bad omen."

Hawksworth squinted toward the east. He could barely make out a phalanx of elephants moving across the plains, into the middle of the fiercest fighting. Several of the elephants had clusters of two-pound swivel guns mounted on their backs, a few had rocket launchers, but most carried *howdahs* filled with Rajput archers. In the center moved a large black elephant, heavily armored and bearing a steel *howdah* decorated with ornate gilding. Standing erect in the *howdah*, beneath a huge embroidered umbrella, was the figure of Prince Jadar, loosing arrows in rhythmic succession as the Imperial infantry closed around him.

"Why is it a bad sign?"

"It's unwise for the supreme commander of an army to expose himself so early in the battle." Shirin was watching Jadar, transfixed. "If he's killed, the battle will be over. All his troops will flee."

"Even his fearless Rajputs?"

"That's the way in India. If he's lost, what do they have left to fight for? They will melt into the forest. In India a commander must always be visible to his men, standing above the armor of his *howdah*, so they'll know for certain he's alive."

As the circle of elephants surrounding Jadar advanced through the field, a triple line of his Rajput infantry moved into place around him. He quickly became the focus of the battle, and the Imperial infantry massed to encircle him, like the king in a game of chess. His protective buffer of elephants was coming under increasingly heavy attack. The advantage of surprise enjoyed by his original offensive was gone. Now he was clearly on the defensive.

"I think Jadar's starting to be in serious trouble. You were right. I don't know how much longer his circle of elephants can protect him."

In the silence he slowly turned to Shirin and their eyes met. Nothing more was said because no more words were needed. She reached out and touched his lips and a lifetime seemed to flow between them. Then he drew his sword and leaned over the edge of the *howdah*.

"Yes."

With a single stroke he severed the tether rope tying their elephant. Their startled *mahout* turned and stared in disbelief. When Hawksworth shouted at him to start, he hesitated for a moment, then flung his barbed iron *ankus* into their *howdah* and plunged for the grass.

Hawksworth grabbed the *ankus*, but before he could move, the elephant lifted its trunk into the morning air and emitted a long, defiant trumpet. Then he plunged past the tethered *zenana* elephants and broke into a gallop, eastward down the hill and directly toward the battle.

Hawksworth staggered backward and grasped the side of the swaying *howdah*.

"How . . . how did he know?"

"Prince Jadar didn't give us a baggage elephant. He gave us one of his personal war elephants. To protect you. He knows where he should be now."

In only minutes their elephant reached the edge of the plain and began advancing like a dreadnought through the swarm of Imperial infantry, headed directly for Jadar. Any luckless infantryman caught in his path would be seized in his trunk and flung viciously aside, or simply crushed beneath his feet.

"But how could he know Jadar's threatened?"

"He knows. His whole life is to protect the prince."

A steel arrowhead sang off the side of the *howdah*. Then another thudded into one of the wooden beams supporting the armor. Hawksworth grabbed Shirin and shoved her down, below the steel rim. She fell sprawling and turned to grab their bows. As Hawksworth took them and began to notch the string on each one, he noticed for the first time that Jadar had given them one of his combat *howdahs*, with firing holes all around the sides.

War cries and sounds of steel on steel ranged around them as they advanced, but their elephant seemed oblivious, only beginning to slow when they approached the dense lines of Imperial infantry encircling Jadar.

Hawksworth found his bow ring and slipped it awkwardly over his right thumb. Then he strung an arrow and took aim through one of the firing holes in the side of the *howdah*. The arrow sang off his thumb and glanced harmlessly against the steel net cloak of an Imperial infantryman. The man looked up, then paused to aim an arrow at the *howdah*. It was a lethal decision. Their elephant turned and seized him as he took aim, flinging him down and crushing him under its foot with a single motion. At once the Imperial infantry again started to clear a path in front of them.

"Jesus, I see why elephants are so feared on a battlefield."

"Yes, but they cannot fight the entire battle . . ." Shirin's voice trailed off as she stared through a hole in the side of the *howdah*. Suddenly her eyes flooded with fear. "Oh, Allah! Merciful Allah! Look!"

A close-ranked formation of Imperial horsemen, perhaps fifty in number, was advancing toward them from the eastern perimeter of the plain. They wore body armor of black steel and they ignored the infantry battling around them as they charged directly for the circle of Jadar's elephants.

"Who are they?"

"I think they're Inayat Latif's special Bundella guards. I've only heard about them. His elephant must be near and he's ordered them to attack. He must realize the prince is vulnerable now. He hopes to kill Prince Jadar in a quick action and so end the battle." She stared over the side of the steel *howdah* again. "If they fail, then he will send his regular Rajput cavalry."

"What's so special about Bundellas?"

"They're from the region of Bundelkhand, and their horses are said to be specially trained against elephants. The native Bundellas . . ." She ducked down and stared wildly around the *howdah* as an arrow grazed by. "Where . . . the matchlocks!"

Hawksworth quickly pulled up one of the muskets and checked the prime. He passed it to Shirin and took a second for himself. As he looked again over the top of the *howdah*, he saw the elephants guarding Jadar start turning to face the approaching horsemen. Their own elephant had now reached the defense lines and it immediately assumed its normal place in the protective circle.

Many of the approaching Bundellas were already being cut down by the spears of the Rajput infantry, but over half managed to penetrate the outer defense perimeter and reach the circle of elephants. The horsemen immediately began firing rockets into Jadar's elephants from long bamboo tubes they carried, intending to frighten them and disrupt their ranks.

As Hawksworth watched, three of Jadar's encircling war elephants shied skittishly away from the fireworks, creating a momentary opening in the line. Before the opening could be secured, two of the Bundella cavalry dashed through the space. Once inside the defense perimeter, they parted, one riding toward either side of Jadar's elephant. One of the horsemen took careful aim with his bow and shot a barbed arrow connected to a line deep into the steel-net armor of the *mahout* seated on the neck of Jadar's elephant. The horseman quickly whipped the arrow's line around his saddle horn and reined his mount. The horse seemed to know exactly what was expected, as it instantly reared backward, unseating Jadar's *mahout* and toppling him into the dust.

As the *mahout* fell, his steel *ankus* clanged against Jadar's *howdah*, momentarily distracting the prince. When he whirled to look for his *mahout*, the other Bundella spurred his stallion alongside the elephant's rump, lifting a heavy spear above his head. But instead of hurtling the spear toward Jadar he turned and plunged it deep into the ground beside the elephant.

"Shirin, what's he doing? How can . . . ?"

The horseman twirled his long reins around the shaft in a quick motion, tethering the horse. Then he balanced himself atop the saddle, unsheathed his sword, and with an agile leap landed on the armored rump of Jadar's elephant.

He secured his balance in less than a second, then grabbed the side of Jadar's gilded *howdah*. Hawksworth stared spellbound as a rain of Rajput arrows glanced harmlessly off his black steel body armor.

"Now!" Shirin's voice was almost a scream.

As though in a dream, Hawksworth leveled the long barrel of his matchlock against the rim of the *howdah* and took aim. The stock felt alien and bulky in his grip, and its lacquer inlay smooth and cold. He saw Shirin thrust her own musket alongside his own, struggling to keep its heavy barrel balanced. As the horseman raised his sword to plunge it into Jadar's exposed back, Hawksworth squeezed the gun's inlaid trigger.

The stock kicked into his face and a burst of black smoke momentarily blinded him. Shirin's matchlock had discharged at the same moment, and he looked down as she tumbled backward against the padded side of the *howdah*, still grasping the gun's heavy stock.

Then he heard a cheer from the Rajputs and turned in time to see the Bundella spin in a half circle. Hawksworth realized one musket ball had caught him directly in the face, the other in the groin. He vainly reached to seize the side of Jadar's *howdah* to regain his balance, but his foot skidded and he slipped backward . . . into a forest of Rajput spears. The flash of a sword took his head. Jadar had never seen him.

That settles one debt, you cocky bastard.

There were shouts from the other attackers still outside the defense perimeter and two horsemen reined their mounts and charged toward Hawksworth and Shirin. As they approached, the elephant began revolving to meet them.

Hawksworth reached down and grabbed the last remaining musket and rose to fire.

As he looked up, he stopped in astonishment, for a second refusing to believe what he saw.

Both Bundelkhand horses were advancing on their hind legs, rearing and bounding toward them in high leaps. He watched transfixed as one of the Bundellas discharged his bow past the neck of his horse, directly at the *howdah*. The arrow missed Shirin's dust-covered hair by only inches.

Hawksworth lifted his matchlock and leveled it against the rim, wondering for an instant whether to aim for the man or the horse. Then the matchlock blazed and he watched the horseman buckle backward in the saddle, toppling into a circle of waiting Rajput swords.

Suddenly the *howdah* shuddered, throwing him sprawling against the side. As he pulled himself up, he realized the other horse had secured its front feet against the side of their elephant. The Bundella was staring directly in his face, pulling an arrow from his saddle quiver.

The horseman's bow was already half drawn when Hawksworth heard the sing of a bowstring beside him. As he watched, the end of a shaft suddenly appeared in the right cheek of the Bundella, buried to the feathers. The horseman's own arrow slammed into the side of the *howdah*, and he reached to claw at his face with his saddle hand, forfeiting his grip. As he slipped backward off the rearing horse, the Rajput infantrymen beheaded him in midair.

Hawksworth turned to see Shirin drop her bow onto the floor of the *howdah*. She slumped against the steel side, her eyes glazed with incredulity at what she had done.

They watched wordlessly as the perimeter of Jadar's elephants was again drawn together and secured. As the other horsemen were driven back, a coherent defense barricade of concentric circles was gradually established around the prince. The outer perimeter was a line of Rajput infantry armed with long spears. Inside their line were Rajput swordsmen, who now had linked together the skirts of their long, steel-mesh cloaks to form a solid barrier. And inside these was the last defense line, the circle of armored war elephants.

As their own elephant instinctively rejoined the line protecting Jadar, Hawksworth reached to touch Shirin's hand. As he did, he noticed her thumb was bleeding and realized for the first time she had not been supplied a bow ring.

"I think we can hold off the infantry with the elephants. But I don't know how long . . ." His voice trailed off as he looked up at her face. She was leaning against the side of the *howdah*, pointing wordlessly toward the east.

He turned to see a vast wave of the Imperial Rajput horsemen bearing down on their position. They numbered in the thousands.

"God Almighty." He reached weakly for another arrow, trying to count those remaining in the quiver and asking if he would live long enough to shoot them all. "It's over."

Their battle cry lifted above the plain as the approaching cavalry neared the edge of the massed Imperial infantry engulfing Jadar. They began advancing directly through the infantry, not slowing, headed straight for Jadar.

Hawksworth notched an arrow and rose up in the *howdah* to take aim. He drew back the string and picked the man in the lead for the first arrow.

As he sighted the Rajput's bearded face down the shaft, he suddenly froze.

The Rajput had just driven the long point of his spear into an Imperial infantryman.

Hawksworth lowered his bow in disbelief and stared as the approaching Imperial cavalry began cutting down their own infantry, taking heads as they rode toward Jadar, leaving a carpet of death in their bloody wake.

"Holy Jesus, what's happening? They're attacking their own troops! Are they sotted with opium too?"

Suddenly their chant of "Ram Ram" was taken up by the Rajputs surrounding Jadar, and they turned on the Imperial infantry nearest them with the ferocity of a wounded tiger.

"Today Allah took on the armor of a Rajput." Shirin slumped against the side of the *howdah* and dropped her bow. "I had prayed they would all one day join with the prince, but I never really believed it would happen."

Jadar's circle of war elephants began to cut their way through the remaining infantry to join the Rajput forces, swivel guns blazing from their backs. In what seemed only minutes his entourage merged with the vanguard of Rajput cavalry, and together they moved like a steel phalanx against the Imperial infantry reserves waiting in the east.

Hawksworth watched as the Imperial lines were cut, separating the infantry fighting on the plain from their reserves. Next a corps of Rajput horsemen wielding long spears overran the Imperial gun emplacements, then grouped to assault the Imperial command post. When the elephant bearing the banner of Inayat Latif started for higher ground, discipline in the Imperial ranks evaporated.

By late afternoon the outcome was no longer in question. A final attempt by the Imperial forces to regroup disintegrated into a rout, with thousands of fleeing Imperial infantry falling before the swords and spears of the Rajput cavalry. Only the merciful descent of dark enabled Inayat Lafit and his Imperial commanders to escape death at the hands of pursuing Rajput archers.

As Hawksworth rode with Jadar's entourage through the dusty, smoke-shrouded battlefield, headed back for the camp, he felt he was witnessing the gaping mouth of hell. The plain was littered with the bodies of almost forty thousand men and over ten thousand horses. The proud war cries were forgotten. Through the dusky twilight came the plaintive moans of dying men and the shrill neighing of shattered horses. Rajputs moved among the bodies, plundering the dead enemy, searching for fallen comrades, dispatching with their long swords any lingering men or horses who could not be saved.

All because of Jadar, Hawksworth thought, and his stomach sickened. Now what will happen? Jadar won the day in this valley, in the middle of nowhere, but the *Moghul* is still in Agra, and tonight he still rules India. And I think he'll still rule India, if only in name, till the day he dies. Jadar can't march against the Red Fort in Agra, not with *this* ragtag army. Even his division of Rajput defectors couldn't storm *that* fortress. I'm not sure God himself could take the Red Fort. So what now, noble Prince Jadar? So far you've merely brought death to half the fighting men in India.

The torchbearers marching four abreast at the front of their elephants were now approaching the remains of the camp. Through the flickering light emerged the vision of a burned-out ruin. Scorched furrows from the first Imperial cannonade trailed between, among, through the few remaining tents. Small clusters of wounded men, some begging for water and some for death, were being fed opium and their wounds wrapped with the shreds of ripped-apart tents.

Jadar moved through the camp, acknowledging the triumphant cheers of his men. Ahead his servants were already erecting a new chintz wall around the *gulal bar* and replacing the tents for the *zenana*. Hawksworth watched as carpets were unrolled from bullock carts and carried inside the compound.

Jadar's elephant proceeded instinctively to the very entry of the *gulal bar*, where it kneeled for him to dismount. Around him Rajputs pushed forward to cheer and *teslim*. As he stood acknowledging them, the other elephants also began to kneel. Jadar's servants rushed forward to help Hawksworth and Shirin alight.

"This was the most horrible day I've ever known." Her arms closed around his neck as her feet touched ground, and she held him for a long moment, tears staining her cheeks. "I've never before seen so much killing. I pray to Allah I never see it again."

Hawksworth returned her embrace, then looked at her sadly. "There'll be a lot more before Jadar sees Agra, if he ever does. This is just one battle, not the war. I'm not sure we want to be here to find out how it ends."

She looked back at him and smiled wistfully in silence. Then she turned and performed the *teslim* to Jadar.

The prince was scarcely recognizable. His helmet had been torn by countless arrows, or matchlock fire, and his haughty face and beard were smeared with dust and smoke. The emerald bow ring was missing from his right thumb, which was now caked with blood. Beneath his armor the torn leather of his right sleeve was stained blood-dark, where he had ripped out an arrow. As he lifted his arms to acknowledge the rising cheers, his eyes were shadowed and tired, but they betrayed no pain.

Hawksworth turned and examined Jadar's *howdah*. It was a forest of arrows and broken spear shafts. Grooms from the stables had already brought water and sugarcane for his elephant and begun extracting iron arrowheads from its legs and from a section of its right shoulder where its armor had been shot away.

As he watched the scene, Hawksworth slowly became aware of a pathway being cleared through the camp toward the east. Next, the cheers of some of Jadar's Rajputs began to swell through the smoky air. Through the encroaching dark, there slowly emerged the form of another elephant approaching. In the torchlight he could tell it was regal in size and bore a gilded *howdah* shaded by a wide brocade umbrella. There were no arrows in the side of this *howdah*, nor was there more than a trace of dust on the elephant's gilded and enameled armor. With its elaborate decoration of swinging yak tails and tinkling bells, it seemed more suited for a royal procession than for a battlefield.

Jadar watched impassively as the elephant neared the center of the clearing. While the Rajputs around him stood at attention, the elephant performed a small bow, then began to kneel with practiced dignity. Several Rajputs rushed forward to help the rider alight.

The man's jeweled turban and rows of finger rings sparkled in the torchlight. As he moved directly toward Jadar, Hawksworth suddenly recognized the walk and caught his breath.

It was Nadir Sharif.

The prime minister paused a few feet from Jadar and salaamed lightly. He did not *teslim*, nor did he speak. As he stood waiting, from out of the darkness of the *gulal bar* the figure of a woman emerged. She was veiled, surrounded by her women, and accompanied by a line of eunuchs wearing sheathed scimitars in their waist sash. She stopped and performed the *teslim* to Jadar. Then she turned to Nadir Sharif.

He stared at her for a long moment, then said something in Persian. Without a word she lifted her veil and threw it back. Next she turned and gestured to one of the servants standing behind her. The servant stepped forward with a bundle wrapped in a brocade satin blanket and carried it directly to Nadir Sharif.

The prime minister stood for a moment as though unsure whether to take it. Finally he reached out and lifted the blanket from the servant and cradled it against one arm. He stared down for a long moment, his eyes seeming to cloud, and then he pushed back part of the blanket to examine its contents more closely. With a withered finger, he reached in and stroked something inside the blanket. Then he looked up and smiled and said something to Jadar in Persian. The prince laughed and strolled to his side, taking the blanket in his own smoke-smeared hands and peering down into it with Nadir Sharif. They exchanged more words in Persian, laughed again, and then Nadir Sharif walked to the waiting woman, whose dark eyes now brimmed with joy. He stood looking at her for a long moment, then spoke to her in Persian and enfolded her in his arms.

A cheer went up again from the onlookers, as they pushed forward to watch. Hawksworth turned to Shirin.

"Is that who I think it is?"

Shirin nodded, her eyes misting. "It's Mumtaz, the first wife of Prince Jadar and the only daughter of Nadir Sharif. He told Prince Jadar he decided today he wanted to see his grandson, since he wanted to see the face of the child who would be *Moghul* himself one day. Then he told Mumtaz he will die in peace now, knowing that his blood will someday flow in the veins of the *Moghul* of India." Shirin's voice started to choke. "I can't tell you what this moment means. It's the beginning of just rule for India. Nadir Sharif knew that if Prince Jadar was defeated today, the child would be murdered by Janahara. By defecting with his Rajputs, he saved Prince Jadar, and he saved his grandson." She paused again. "And he saved us too."

"When do you think he decided to do this?"

"I don't know. I still can't believe it's true."

Hawksworth stopped for a moment, then whirled and seized her arm. "Jadar knew! By Jesus, he knew last night! The cavalry. He said the cavalry had to be held to the last. He knew they would turn on the Imperial infantry if he began to lose. He knew all along."

Shirin examined him with a curious expression. "I wonder if Mumtaz herself planned it. Perhaps she convinced Nadir Sharif to save his grandson." She paused. "This must have been the most closely guarded secret in all of Agra. Nadir Sharif somehow kept even the queen from knowing he would defect with the Rajputs or she would have surely killed him." Shirin's voice trailed off as she pondered the implications. "He's astonishing. Janahara has never entirely trusted him, but somehow he must have convinced her to let him command the Rajput cavalry. What did he do to make her finally trust him?"

Nadir Sharif embraced Mumtaz once more, then bowed lightly again to Jadar and turned to leave. As his glance swept the torchlit crowd, he noticed Hawksworth. He stopped for a second, as though not believing what he saw, then broke into a wide smile.

"By the beard of the Prophet! Can it be? My old guest?" He moved toward Hawksworth, seeming not to notice Shirin. "May Allah preserve you, Ambassador, everyone at court thinks you've fled India. For your sake I almost wish you had. What in God's name are you doing here?"

"Someone tried to murder me at Fatehpur." Hawksworth turned and took Shirin's arm. "And Shirin. It seemed like a good time to switch sides."

"Someone actually tried to kill you? I do hope you're jesting with me."

"Not at all. If Vasant Rao and his men hadn't appeared in time to help us, we'd both be dead now."

Nadir Sharif's eyes darkened and he looked away for a moment. "I must tell you that shocks even me." He turned back and smiled. "But I'm pleased to see you're still very much alive."

Hawksworth studied Nadir Sharif for a moment. "Do you have any idea who might have ordered it?"

"This world of ours is fraught with evil, Ambassador." Nadir Sharif shook his head in resignation. "I sometimes marvel any of us survive it." Then he looked back at Hawksworth and beamed. "But then I've always found you to be a man blessed with rare fortune, Ambassador. I think Allah must truly stand watch over you night and day. You seem to live on coincidences. I was always amazed that just when His Majesty ordered you out of Agra, the Portuguese decided to seize one of His Majesty's personal cargo vessels and by that imprudent folly restored you to favor. Now I hear you were attacked in the Fatehpur camp by some scurrilous hirelings . . . at the very moment the prince's Rajputs just happened to be nearby to protect you. I only wish I enjoyed a small *portion* of your luck." He smiled. "But what will you be doing now? Will you be joining with us or will you stay with the prince?"

"What do you mean?"

"I understand His Highness is striking camp tomorrow and marching west for the Rajput city of Udaipur. The new maharana there, a distinguished if somewhat renegade Rajput prince named Karan Singh, apparently has offered his lake palace as refuge for the prince."

"I don't seem to have much choice. I'm probably no more welcome in Agra right now than you are."

Nadir Sharif examined him quizzically for a moment. "I'm not sure I understand exactly what you mean." Then he broke into laughter. "Ambassador, surely you don't assume *I* had anything to do with the tragedy today. The honest truth is I used every means at my command to dissuade the Rajput cavalry from their insidious treachery. They absolutely refused to heed anything I said. In fact, I actually tried to forewarn Her Majesty something just like this might happen."

"What are you talking about!"

"Their betrayal was astonishing, and I must tell you frankly, entirely unaccountable. I intend to prepare a complete report for Her Majesty. But this is merely a temporary setback for us, never fear." He turned and bowed lightly to Shirin, acknowledging her for the first time. "I really must be leaving for the Imperial camp now. We've scheduled a war council tonight to plan our next strategy." He smiled. "I feel I should counsel you once again that you've chosen very unsavory company. Prince Jadar is a thorough disgrace to the empire." He bowed lightly once more to Hawksworth, then to Shirin, and turned to remount his elephant. "Good night, Ambassador. Perhaps someday soon we'll drink *sharbat* together again in Agra."

Even as he spoke, his elephant rose and began to move out. His last words were drowned by cheering Rajputs.

"He'll never get away with it." Hawksworth watched incredulously as the elephant began delicately picking its way through the shattered camp.

"Oh yes he will. You don't know Nadir Sharif as I do."

Hawksworth turned to stare in bewilderment at Jadar. The prince was standing next to Mumtaz, their faces expressionless. As Nadir Sharif's elephant disappeared into the dark, Mumtaz said something in Persian and gestured toward Shirin. She replied in the same language and they moved together, embracing.

"Your face is still fresh as the dawn, though your kohl is the dust of war." Mumtaz's Persian was delicate and laced with poetic allusions. She kissed Shirin, then looked down and noticed her right hand. "And what happened to your thumb?"

"I had no bow ring. You know we aren't supposed to shoot."

"Or do anything else except bear sons." Mumtaz flashed a mock frown in the direction of Jadar. "If I would let him, His Highness would treat me like some stupid Arab wet nurse instead of a Persian." She embraced Shirin again and kissed her once more. "I also know you learned to fire a matchlock today."

"How did you find out?"

"Some of the Rajputs saw you shoot a Bundella horseman who had breached their lines and reached His Highness' elephant. One of them told my eunuchs." Her voice dropped. "He said you saved His Highness' life. I want to thank you."

"It was my duty."

"No, it was your love. I'm sorry I dare not tell His Highness what you did. He must never find out. He's already worried about too many obligations. You saw what just happened tonight with father. I think he's very troubled about what price he may be asked to pay someday for what happened today."

"I must tell you the English *feringhi* also shot the Bundella who had mounted His Highness' elephant."

"Is he the one there?" Mumtaz nodded discreetly toward Hawksworth, who stood uncomprehending, his haggard face and jerkin smeared with smoke. Her voice had risen slightly and now her Persian was lilting again.

"He's the one."

Mumtaz scrutinized Hawksworth with a quick flick of her eyes, never looking up. "He's interesting. Truly as striking as I'd heard."

"I love him more than my life. I wish you could know him." Shirin's Persian was equally as genteel as that of Mumtaz.

"But is he yet a worthy lover in your bed?" Mumtaz's smile was almost hidden. "I sent your message to father about the Hindu *devadasi*."

Shirin smiled and said nothing.

"Then you must bring him with us to Udaipur."

"If His Highness will have us there."

"I will have you there." She laughed and looked again at Hawksworth. "If you'll tell me sometime what it's like to share your pillow with a *feringhi*."

"Captain Hawksworth." Jadar's martial voice rose above the assembled crowd of congratulating Rajputs. "Didn't I notice you on the field today? I thought I had assigned you to guard my *zenana*. Are you aware the punishment for disobeying orders in an army in India is immediate beheading? Or if you like, I can have you shot from a cannon, as is sometimes done. Which would you prefer?"

"Your cannon were mostly overrun. I guess you'll have to behead me, if you can find anyone left with a sword sharp enough."

Jadar roared and pulled out his own sword. There was a deep nick in the blade.

"By tomorrow I'm sure we can find one. In the meantime I'll have to confine you in the *gulal bar* to prevent your escape." He slipped the sword back into his belt. "Tell me, did you manage to hit anything today with your matchlocks?"

"Possibly. There were so many in the Imperial infantry I may have succeeded in hitting someone."

Jadar laughed again. "From the looks of her thumb, it would seem the woman in your *howdah* did most of the shooting. I'm astounded you'd permit her such liberty."

"She has a mind of her own."

"Like all Persians." Jadar reached and lowered Mumtaz's veil over her face. She let it hang for a moment, then shoved it back again. "Allah protect us." He turned and stared a moment into the dark, toward the direction Nadir Sharif had departed. "Yes, Allah protect us from all Persians and from all Persian ambition." Then he suddenly remembered himself and glanced back at Hawksworth. "So tonight we may eat lamb together after all, if there's one still to be found. But not yet in Paradise. For that you will have to wait a few days longer."

Hawksworth shifted uncomfortably. "What exactly do you mean?"

"Udaipur, Captain, tomorrow we strike camp and march for Udaipur. It's a Rajput paradise." He turned and beckoned toward the Rajput commander who had ridden from Fatehpur with them. "It's time you met my friend Mahdu Singh, brother of His Highness, Rana Karan Singh, the Maharana of Udaipur. The maharana has generously offered us his new guest palace, on his island of Jagmandir. It's on Pichola Lake, in the Rajput capital of Udaipur. He was only just building the palace when I was there before, but I seem to remember it's designed in a very interesting new style." He glanced at Mumtaz. "I think Her Highness will approve." Then he continued. "Rajputana, Captain, is beautiful. What's more, its mountains are impregnable. I led the only Moghul army ever to escape defeat by the Rajputs who live in those mountains. But today I have many loyal friends there." Mahdu Singh bowed lightly to Hawksworth while Jadar watched in satisfaction. "His Highness, the maharana, may decide to make a Rajput out of you and keep you there, if you seem worth the trouble. Who can tell?"

He turned and dismissed Mumtaz and her eunuchs with a wave. He watched fondly as she disappeared into the *gulal bar*, then turned and joined the waiting Rajputs. Together they moved out through the camp, embracing and consoling.

"Did you hear what he said?" Hawksworth turned to Shirin, who stood waiting, a light smile erasing some of the fatigue in her face. "He's planning to recruit another army of Rajputs. This war is only beginning. Good Christ, when will it end?"

"When he's *Moghul*. Nothing will stop him now." She took his hand, and together they pushed through the shattered *gulal bar* toward the remains of their tent.

CHAPTER TWENTY-NINE

The advance of Prince Jadar's army west toward the Rajput stronghold of Udaipur was like nothing Brian Hawksworth had ever seen. Jadar was marching into the heart of ancient Rajput country, and the movement of his army suddenly came to resemble a triumphant victory procession.

The heavy artillery formed the first contingent, drawn by teams of elephants and bullocks. Two thousand infantry moved in front, smoothing the ground with spades. The army's baggage animals followed the artillery, and after this came Jadar's personal treasury—camels loaded with gold and silver coin—together with his records and archives. Next in the line of march were elephants carrying the *zenana* women's jewels and a collection of ornate swords and daggers that Jadar periodically gave to his officers as presents. Then came the water camels, and finally Jadar's kitchen and provisions. The baggage was followed by the ordinary cavalry, and after them rode Jadar and his retinue of nobles. Behind him came his *zenana*. The rear of the procession was brought up by women and servants, then elephants, camels, and mules carrying the remainder of the baggage and tents.

Some of Jadar's *zenana* women traveled in gilded *chaudols* carried on the shoulders of four bearers and shaded with netting of colored embroidered silk. Others were transported in enclosed palanquins, also covered with silk nets decorated with gold fringe and tassels. Still others chose to ride in swaying litters suspended between two elephants or two strong camels. A female slave walked near each litter carrying a peacock tail to brush off dust and keep away flies.

Jadar's first and favorite wife, Mumtaz, seemed to scorn all these comforts, displaying herself regally all day long from atop her own personal elephant, riding in a gold *howdah* shaded by a vast tapestry umbrella. Her elephant was festooned with embroideries, yak tails, and large silver bells; and directly behind her, on six smaller elephants, rode the women of her immediate household. Her eunuchs rode clustered around her on horses, each carrying a wand signifying his office and sweating profusely beneath his jeweled turban. A vanguard of footmen with bamboo canes walked ahead of Mumtaz's elephant clearing a path through the crowds.

Jadar himself traveled mainly on his favorite Arabian horse—except when passing through cities, when he would switch to a conspicuously bedecked elephant—surrounded by the high-ranking nobles. Trailing out behind this first circle were the ranks of the lesser *mansabdars*, who rode in full military dress, displaying swords, bows, shields. While this procession inched along at its regal pace, Jadar and his nobles frequently paused ostentatiously to bag tiger or chase stripe-eared antelope with the prince's brace of hunting *chitahs*.

A complete set of tents for Jadar and his *zenana* traveled a day ahead, to ensure that a fully prepared camp always awaited him and his women when, at approximately three in the afternoon, the procession would stop and begin to settle for the night. Each of his larger tents could be disassembled into three separate sections, and all of these together required a full fifty baggage elephants for transport. Moving the smaller tents required almost a hundred camels. Wardrobes and kitchen utensils were carried by some fifty mules, and special porters carried by hand Jadar's personal porcelains, his gilt beds, and a few of his silk tents.

The procession was a lavish display of all the wealth and arms Jadar had remaining. And nothing about it hinted that his was an army on the run . . . which in fact it was.

Hawksworth puzzled over Jadar's extravagant pomp for several days, finding it uncharacteristic, and finally concluded it was a deliberate Indian strategy.

Jadar has to raise another army and quickly. He'll not do it if he has the look of a fugitive and loser about him. He's managed to hold the Imperial army at bay for a while, wound them enough to escape entrapment. But *he's* wounded too, and badly. The Imperial army may be shattered for the moment, but Jadar's lost half his own men. The winner will be the one who can rebuild first and attack. If Jadar doesn't make some alliances and get some men soon, Inayat Latif and the queen will chase him from one end of India to the other.

Along the way a few independent Rajput chieftains had come to his banner, but not enough. When Hawksworth asked Shirin what she thought Jadar's chances were of raising a Rajput army large enough to face Inayat Latif, she had made no effort to conceal her concern.

"The greatest Rajput nobles are waiting to see whether Maharana Karan Singh of Udaipur will decide to openly support him. He's the leader of the ranas of Mewar, which is the name for the lands of Rajputana around Udaipur, and they're the highest in rank of all the Rajput chieftains of India. If Maharana Karan Singh agrees to support him with his own army, the other ranas of Mewar may follow, and after them perhaps all of Rajputana."

"What do you mean? He's providing Jadar a place to stay, or at least to hide while he licks his wounds. That looks like support to me."

Shirin had tried to smile. "Permitting Prince Jadar to camp in Udaipur doesn't necessarily imply support. It could also be interpreted merely as traditional Rajput hospitality. It's one thing to open your guest house to a son of the *Moghul*. It's something quite different to commit your army to aid his rebellion." She drew her horse closer to Hawksworth's. "You see, Maharana Karan Singh and his father, Amar Singh, before him have had a treaty of peace with Arangbar for almost ten years, after many decades of bloody war between Mewar and the Moghuls. There are many Rajput chieftains in Mewar who do not want him to renounce that treaty. They're weary of Moghul armies invading Rajputana and burning their fields and cities. Prince Jadar will have to negotiate with Maharana Karan Singh if he's to be persuaded to help. The prince will have to offer him something in return for his aid. For the risk he'll be taking should the prince lose. That's why the other Rajputs are waiting. Everyone here knows the prince has no chance if the maharana withholds his support."

A noticeable feeling of relief swept through the long columns of Jadar's cavalry the afternoon that Maharana Karan Singh was sighted riding out on his elephant, surrounded by a retinue of his personal guard, to welcome Prince Jadar at the high stone gate leading through the walls of the mountain city of Udaipur. Throughout the ranks of Jadar's bedraggled army it was seen as a positive omen.

The army and the lesser *mansabdars* camped outside the city walls; the highest-ranking nobles were invited to stay in the maharana's city palace, set on a high cliff overlooking Pichola Lake; and Jadar, his *zenana*, and his personal guards were ferried with much pomp across to the new guest palace on Jagmandir Island, in the center of the lake. As one of Arangbar's khans and a foreign ambassador, Brian Hawksworth was installed by the maharana in a special suite in his city palace reserved for dignitaries.

In an even more auspicious gesture, the maharana invited Prince Jadar to dine with him in the palace that evening. The ancient Rajputana tradition of hospitality did not normally require dining with your guests, and the Rajput chieftains traveling with Jadar were again heartened. Late in the afternoon, an invitation also arrived requesting that Ambassador Hawksworth and Shirin, characterized as Jadar's personal aide, join the dinner.

"Why do you think he wants us?" When the maharana's servants had left, Hawksworth showed the gilded invitation to Shirin. She was on their balcony watching white-necked cranes glide across the surface of Pichola Lake, spreading out hundreds of feet below them.

"Perhaps the maharana is curious to meet a *feringhi*. I'm sure he's never seen one before." She hesitated. "Or perhaps Prince Jadar arranged for you to be there. To imply he has the support of the English king's warships."

"You know I don't speak for King James on matters of war."

"Tonight you must appear to do so. I'm sure your king would help Prince Jadar if he knew him."

"He'll support him if he becomes *Moghul*."

"Then you must help Prince Jadar tonight. So that he will."

Shirin had overseen the servants who had been sent to clean and repair Hawksworth's doublet and hose. Then a bath was brought, accompanied by barbers and manicurists. The maharana sent a vial of musk perfume to Shirin, buried in a basket of flowers. By the time they were escorted through the high scalloped archway leading into the palace banquet hall, they both were bathed, perfumed, and refreshed; and Hawksworth again looked almost like an ambassador.

Accustomed to the red sandstone of Agra, he was momentarily astounded to see a room fashioned entirely from purest white marble. The hall was long and wide, with two rows of bracketed columns its entire length. Maharana Karan Singh sat at the far end in front of a marble screen, his gold wand of office at his side, reclining against an enormous bolster of gold brocade. He appeared to be Jadar's age, with eyes that sparkled mischievously, a long Rajput moustache, glistening with wax, which curled upward at the ends, and a turban of gold brocade. He wore a long red and white striped satin skirt beneath a translucent cloak. His necklace and earrings were matching green emeralds. Seated around him, on red carpets woven with designs of fighting elephants, were his Rajput nobles, each in white with an orange turban and a gold-trimmed brocade sash at the waist. Every Rajput in the room had a gold-handled *katar*.

Jadar saw Hawksworth and Shirin enter and rose to greet them. The prince was dressed in his finest, with a cloak of gold cloth, pale green trousers, red velvet slippers, a long double string of pearls around his neck, and a pink silk turban crisscrossed with flowered brocade and secured with a large ruby. He led Hawksworth before the maharana and introduced him, in Rajasthani. Jadar then translated the introduction into Turki for Hawksworth, who was startled to learn that he was a high-ranking member of *Angrezi*—English—royalty. He looked around and realized he was easily the most shabbily attired man in the room, including the servants.

After the introduction Hawksworth took his place among Jadar's own retinue of nobles. Shirin was seated on the carpet directly behind him.

All the guests sat in a line facing a long gold-threaded cloth spread along the floor. Food was brought in on silver trays, which were placed on silver stools directly in front of each diner. Hawksworth had scarcely taken his seat before a full wine cup was placed in his hands. It was never allowed to approach dryness.

The banquet was lavish, equaling anything he had seen in Agra. It was immediately apparent that roast game was the specialty of Udaipur, as tray after tray of antelope, venison, hare, and wild duck were placed before him.

In its emphasis on roasted meats, the food could almost have been English, save it was all seasoned with spices he had never tasted in London. The centerpiece was an elaborately glazed wild boar the maharana had bagged personally from horseback with a spear. Nominal Muslim though he was, Prince Jadar downed a generous portion of the boar and praised the flavor.

The trays of meats were accompanied by spiced curds, local yogurts, and baked vegetables swimming in *ghee*. The meal concluded with dried fruits which had been sugared and perfumed, followed by mouth-freshening *pan*, the betel leaves wrapped around spiced *bhang*, currants, sweet imported coconut.

The final offering, eagerly awaited by all the Rajputs, was opium. As they popped down handfuls of the brown balls, Hawksworth discreetly signaled for more wine. After the dishes were cleared, several jeweled women in red trousers and thin billowing blouses entered, drank glasses of wine in honor of the maharana, then danced among the guests to the accompaniment of a large *sarangi*.

After the dancers had been dismissed, Prince Jadar rose and proposed a toast to the maharana. The toast was ceremonial, elaborate, and—it seemed —entirely expected by everyone.

"To His Highness, the Maharana of Udaipur: whose line flows directly from the great Kusa, son of Rama, King of Ajodhya and the noble hero of the Ramayana. Descendant of the Royal House of the Sun, whose subjects will refuse their food if neither he nor his brother the Sun are present to show their face upon it and bless it."

The maharana's reply was equally effusive, describing Jadar as the greatest Moghul warrior in all of history, the equal of his Mongol forebears Genghis Khan and Tamerlane, a worthy descendant of the early Moghul conquerors Babur and Humayun, and finally, the one Moghul whose martial skills might actually approach those of the fighting Rajputs of Mewar— an oblique reference to the fact that Jadar had led the Moghul army that subdued Mewar a decade earlier and induced its Rajputs to finally acknowledge Moghul dominance over northwest India.

Immoderate praise of one another's armies followed next. Then the maharana said something else, and Jadar turned suddenly toward Hawksworth.

"Ambassador Hawksworth. His Highness has asked to speak with you."

Hawksworth rose from the carpet and moved forward. Around him the Udaipur Rajputs studied him with open curiosity. They had listened to lavish toasts for years, but none had ever before seen a *feringhi* in a doublet. The very concept of such a phenomenon exceeded their imagination.

"His Highness has asked permission to allow his court painters to make your portrait, so that he may remember your likeness. Dressed as you are tonight. Do you have any objection?"

"Please tell His Highness I would be honored." Hawksworth found himself startled, and unsure what reply was appropriate. "Please tell him that my own father was once a painter in England."

Jadar smiled through his teeth. "You mean I should tell him there are of course many skilled artists in your noble land of England. Your own father, as we both know, was a great khan in England, not a lowly craftsman."

As Hawksworth nodded dully, Jadar turned and translated this to the maharana. Karan Singh's eyes brightened as he replied to Jadar.

"He asks if your king's painters are expert in Ragamala?"

"I'm not entirely sure what His Highness refers to." Hawksworth examined Jadar with a puzzled expression.

Jadar translated and the Rajput looked surprised. He turned and quickly said something to one of the servants, who vanished and reappeared moments later with a leatherbound folio. The maharana spoke briefly to Jadar, then passed the book.

"The maharana politely suggests that possibly your English king's painters have not yet achieved the sophistication required for Ragamala. He asks me to show you one of his personal albums." Jadar opened the book and handed it to Hawksworth.

It was filled with vibrant miniature paintings, executed on heavy sheets of paper that had been treated with a white pigment of rice water and lavishly embellished with gold leaf. They showed round-eyed young women with firm breasts and slender waists lounging in beautifully stylized gardens and courtyards, playing gilded instruments or sensuously embracing their lovers, many surrounded by doves, peacocks, tame deer, and tapestry-covered elephants. In some the blue-faced god Krishna played an instrument that looked something like a sitar, to the wistful gaze of longing doe-eyed women whose breasts swelled through their gauze wraps. The paintings imparted to Hawksworth a curious world of emotional intensity: a celebration of life, love, and devotion.

"Each Ragamala painting depicts the mood of a specific raga." Jadar pointed to one of a jeweled woman feeding a peacock which leaned down from a white marble rooftop, while her lover reached his arms to encircle her. "This is the raga named Hindol, a morning raga of love. The Ragamala paintings of Mewar are a perfect blend of music, poetry, and pure art." Jadar winked. "After the maharana has painted you in your native costume, perhaps he will have his artists paint you as the young god Krishna, enticing some milkmaids to your leafy bed."

The maharana spoke again to Jadar.

"He asks whether these are anything like the paintings your king's artists create for English ragas?"

"Tell him we don't have ragas in England. Our music is different."

Jadar tried to mask his discomfort. "Perhaps I should merely say your

English ragas are in a different style from those we have in India. He will not be impressed to learn that English music is not yet advanced enough to have developed the raga."

Jadar's reply seemed to satisfy the maharana. He turned and said something to one of the men sitting near him.

"His Highness has ordered that you be given an album of Ragamala paintings to take back to your king, so the painters at his court may try to copy them and begin to learn greatness."

"His Majesty, King James, will be deeply honored by the rana's gift." Hawksworth bowed diplomatically, deciding not to inform the maharana that King James had no painters and little taste.

The maharana beamed in satisfaction and dismissed Hawksworth with a nod.

Then the exchange of gifts began. Jadar produced a gold cloak for the maharana, a jewel-encrusted sword, a jeweled saddle, and promised to deliver an elephant with a silver *howdah*. The maharana in turn gave Jadar an emerald the size of a large walnut, a gilded shield studded with jewels, and a brace of jeweled *katars*. Each thanked the other extravagantly and laid the presents aside.

Then Jadar suddenly stood up and began removing his turban. The room fell silent at this unprecedented act.

"Tonight, in gratitude for his friendship, for his offer of an abode to one who no longer has any roof save a tent, I offer to His Highness, the Maharana of Udaipur, my own turban, that he may have a lasting token of my gratitude. That in the years ahead when, Allah willing, these dark days are past, we will neither of us forget my indebtedness on this night."

As Jadar stepped forward to present the turban, the maharana's eyes flooded with emotion. Before Jadar had moved more than a pace, Karan Singh was on his feet, ripping off his own turban. They met in the center of the room, each reverently placing his own turban on the other's head, then embracing.

Hawksworth looked around the room and saw Rajputs who would gut an enemy without a blink now near to tears. He leaned back toward Shirin.

"What's the significance of the turbans?"

"It's the rarest gift any man could present to another. I've never before heard of a Moghul or a Rajput giving his turban. The story of this will be told throughout Mewar. We have just seen the creation of a legend."

Then the maharana's voice rose. "Mewar, the abode of all that is beautiful in the world, is made even more beautiful by your presence. In years past we have stood shield to shield with you; tonight we embrace you in friendship. We wish you victory over those who would deny you your birthright, which you have earned both by blood and by deed. No other in India is more fit to reign, more just to govern, more honorable to his friends, more feared by his foes. Tonight we offer you our hand and our prayers that Lord Krishna will always stand with you."

Hawksworth turned to Shirin and whispered. "What's he saying?"

Her eyes were dark. "He's delaying his answer to the prince. Offering him prayers to Lord Krishna. Prince Jadar doesn't need prayers to Krishna. He needs Rajputs. Thousands of Rajputs. But perhaps in time the maharana can be convinced. Banquets are not the place for negotiation. They're the place for perfumed talk."

Jadar was smiling as though he had just been offered the whole of Rajputana. He managed to thank the maharana lavishly.

The maharana beamed and signaled for *pan* leaves again, signifying the evening was ended. The room emptied in moments.

"I think Jadar could be in serious trouble." Hawksworth turned to Shirin as they entered the hallway. "If he fails to get support here, what will he do?"

"I don't know. I think he may still manage an alliance before he's through. But it will be costly. Otherwise he'll probably have to move south and try to convince Malik Ambar to commit him his Maratha army. But Rajputs are better." She moved closer. "I'm suddenly so very, very tired of armies and tents and strategies. I don't know where it will end. Time is running out. For him and for us." She brushed him lightly with her body. "Will you make love to me tonight as though we'd never heard of Rajputs and Marathas? We'll look at the lake in the moonlight and forget everything, just for tonight." She opened her hand. Inside were several small brown balls. "I took some of the maharana's *affion*. Tonight we have no battles to fight."

Hawksworth sat beside Shirin watching the oarsmen strain against the locks, their orange oars flashing against the ornately gilded boat like the immense gills of some ceremonial fish. A turbaned drummer sat at one end, sounding the beat, and the tillerman stood behind him.

They were headed for Jagmandir Island, on the invitation of Prince Jadar, in a boat provided by Maharana Karan Singh. Three weeks of banquets, hunting, and oaths of lasting friendship seemed to have done little to resolve the question of the maharana's support for Jadar's rebellion. Time, Hawksworth told himself, is starting to work heavily against the prince. The Imperial army let us escape because they were too shattered to attack again. But we all know they're rebuilding. Jadar has to decide soon how much longer he can afford to stay here and listen to vague promises.

Behind them the high walls and turrets of the maharana's palace towered above the cliff, reflecting gold in the late afternoon sun. As they neared the island, Hawksworth turned back to see the thick stone walls of the city following the curve of the surrounding hilltops and finally angling down to a tall watchtower at the very edge of the lake. He realized the lake itself was actually the city's fourth defense barrier.

Ahead, the white sandstone palace on Jagmandir glistened against the water. At the front a large pavilion surounded by delicate white pillars jutted out into the lake. Its entrance was guarded by a row of life-sized stone elephants rising out of the water, their trunks raised above their heads in silent salute. As their boat neared the arched entryway of the pavilion, Hawksworth saw a veiled woman surrounded by eunuchs standing on the marble-paved dock to greet them.

"It's Her Highness, Princess Mumtaz." Shirin's voice was suddenly flooded with surprised delight. Then she turned to Hawksworth with a laugh. "Welcome to the *zenana*, Ambassador."

"What's she doing here?" Hawksworth examined the figure, whose jewels glistened in the afternoon sun, then warily studied the eunuchs.

"She's come to meet us." Shirin's voice was lilting in anticipation. "I think she's bored to frustration trapped on this island prison."

As their boat touched the dock, Mumtaz moved forward and immediately embraced Shirin. Her eyes swept Hawksworth as he bowed.

"Your Highness."

Mumtaz giggled behind her veil and turned to Shirin, speaking in Persian. "Do we have to speak barbarous Turki because of him?"

"Just for this afternoon."

"I welcome you in the name of His Highness." Mumtaz's Turki was accented but otherwise flawless. "He asked me to meet you and show you the garden and the palace."

She began chattering to Shirin in a mixture of Persian and Turki as they walked into the garden. It soon revealed itself to be a matrix of bubbling fountains and geometrical stone walkways, beside which rows of brightly colored flowers bloomed. Ahead of them the small three-story palace rose skyward like a long-stemmed lotus, its top a high dome with a sensuous curve. The ground floor was an open arcade, with light interior columns and a row of connecting quarters off each side for women and servants, screened behind marble grillwork.

Mumtaz directed them on through the garden and into the cool arcade of the palace. At one side, near the back, a stone stairway spiraled upward to the second floor. Mumtaz led the way, motioning them to follow.

At the second floor they emerged into a small chamber strewn with bolsters and carpets that seemed to be Jadar's reception room. Mumtaz ignored it as she started up the next circular staircase.

The topmost room was tiny, dazzling white, completely unfurnished. The ornate marble cupola of the dome towered some thirty feet above their heads, and around the sides were carved niches decorated with colored stone. Light beamed through the room from a wide doorway leading to a balcony, which was also bare save for an ornately carved sitar leaned against its railing.

"His Highness has taken a particular fondness for this room and refuses to allow anything to be placed in it. He sits here for hours, and on the balcony there, doing I don't know what." Mumtaz gestured toward the doorway. "He wanted me to bring you here to wait for him." She sighed. "I agree with him that this room brings a great feeling of peace. But what good is peace that cannot last? I don't know how much longer we can stay here." Mumtaz turned and hugged Shirin again. "I so miss Agra. And the Jamuna. Sometimes I wonder if we'll ever see it again."

Shirin stroked Mumtaz's dark hair, then said something to her in Persian. Mumtaz smiled and turned to Hawksworth.

"Do you really love her?"

"More than anything." Hawksworth was momentarily startled by her directness.

"Then take her with you. Away from here. Away from all the killing and death. How much longer can any of us endure it?" Her hard eyes blinked away a hint of a tear. "I've lived most of my life with His Highness in tents, bearing children. I'm so weary of it all. And now I wonder if we'll ever have a place just for ourselves."

She would have continued, but footsteps sounded on the stone stairs, and Jadar emerged beaming from the stairwell, his turban set rakishly on the side of his head. He seemed in buoyant spirits. "You're here! Let me welcome you and offer you something to banish the afternoon heat." He gave Mumtaz a quick hug. Hawksworth sensed this was not the official Jadar. This was a prince very much at his ease. "I hope Shirin will join me in having some *sharbat*. But for you, Captain, I've had a surprise prepared. I think you might even like it better than your foul brandy." He spoke quickly to a eunuch waiting at the top of the stairs, then turned back to Hawksworth and Shirin. "Have you found the maharana's palace to your liking?"

"His view of the lake and the mountains is the finest in India." Shirin performed a *teslim*. "We so thank Your Highness."

Mumtaz embraced Shirin once more, said something to her in Persian, then bowed to Jadar and disappeared down the stairwell. He watched her tenderly until she was gone before he turned back to Hawksworth and Shirin.

"Come outside with me." He walked past them through the marble doorway. "Have you seen the lake yet from the balcony? This one afternoon we will drink together and watch the sunset. Before we all leave Udaipur I wanted you to see this place. It's become very special for me. When I sit here in the cool afternoon, I seem to forget all the wounds I've ever felt in battle. For a moment nothing else exists."

"I think this palace is almost finer than the one Rana Karan Singh has."

Hawksworth stroked Shirin's thigh as they followed Jadar onto the cool balcony, impulsively wanting her in his arms. Then he cleared his throat. "I don't remember ever seeing anything quite like it in India."

"At times you can be a perceptive man, Captain. Allah may have showed his wisdom when he sent you here." Jadar smiled. "You know, I still remember my first word of your arrival, and your now-famous encounter with the Portuguese. I think that morning will someday change the history of both our lands—the morning India and England met." He looked pensively down into the garden below. "It all depends on what happens next."

"What do you think *will* happen, Highness?" Shirin moved next to Jadar at the edge of the balcony.

He squinted into the waning sun for a moment, then turned his eyes away. "It's difficult to know. Probably the Imperial army will be sent against me again, any day now."

"Will the maharana support you with his cavalry?"

Jadar fell silent, as though choosing his words carefully. Then he shrugged away discretion. "I think he might, but I still don't know. I hear that many of the other ranas of Rajputana have warned him not to side with me openly. They still remember the devastation Inayat Latif wrought here fifteen years ago, when he was sent by Arangbar to put down their rebellion. Rajputs love to battle, but not amid their own cities and fields. And that's easy to understand. Rana Karan Singh is in a difficult position. He knows if I stand here and fight, the battle could well destroy Udaipur."

"What will you do?"

"I'll probably have to move out soon, and move quickly, farther north into the mountains or back south to Burhanpur. I can't stand and fight again, not yet. That's one of the reasons I sent for you." He turned to face Hawksworth. "I think it's time you left India. No one in Agra except Nadir Sharif knows you're alive. But it's obvious you can't return there, not under the present circumstances. It's probably best that you return to England, at least until my fortunes are resolved. You must not join me in any more battles. It's not your war."

Hawksworth felt a sudden chill against his skin. "There's no reason for me to leave. And besides, I have no way to return to England now. The Company is supposed to send a voyage this autumn, but . . ."

"There's always a way to do anything, Captain." Jadar stopped and laughed. "Well, *almost* anything. Here at Udaipur you're only a few days' ride south to our port of Cambay. Like Surat, it's still free of Portuguese control. I may have very few friends left in Agra, but I do have friends in Cambay. I can arrange for your passage on an Indian trader as far as the Moluccas, where you can doubtless hail a Dutch fleet. You can leave India secretly and safely. No one in Agra need ever know you helped me."

"I am not sure I want to leave now." Hawksworth slipped his arm around Shirin's waist.

Jadar looked at him and smiled. "But Shirin has to leave with you. Her life is no safer here now than yours." He fixed them both squarely. "I hereby command her to accompany you. You can both return to India someday . . . if Allah is kind and I succeed. And you'll be first among all my ambassadors, Captain, I promise you. You'll receive my first *firman* for trade. But if I die in the days to come, your English king will not be accused someday of aiding a renegade. I hereby order you both to leave, tomorrow."

"I don't run from a fight. There's some sea dog left in me."

"I know you don't, Captain, and that's one of the things I like most about you. But I'm sending you away, ordering you to go. I'll always remember it was against your will." Jadar looked up to see a eunuch entering with a tray of cups. "Now for your drink. I ordered my kitchen to make *panch* for you—I understand the *topiwallahs* in Surat think it's called 'punch.'"

"Punch? What is it?"

"An Indian delicacy. A special blend of wine, water, sugar, lemons, and spices. Five ingredients. Actually, *panch* is just the Hindi word for 'five.' Try it."

Hawksworth tasted the perfumed red mixture, slices of lemon rind floating on its surface. It was so delicious he almost drank it off at one gulp. Jadar watched him, smiling, then lifted a cup of *sharbat* from the tray and gestured the eunuch toward Shirin. "I gather you find it acceptable."

"It's perfect to watch a sunset with."

"I thought you'd like it. You know, Captain, I've rather enjoyed seeing you grow to understand and love India. That's rare among *feringhi*. That's why I absolutely insist your king send you back as his next ambassador."

"Nothing would please me more."

"I think you mean it. And I want you to believe me when I tell you that nothing would please *me* more. Together we'll rid India of the Portuguese scourge forever." Jadar lifted his cup in a toast and Hawksworth joined him.

"And here's to ridding India of one Portuguese in particular."

Jadar paused. "Who do you mean?"

"The Viceroy, Miguel Vaijantes. I don't think I ever told you he murdered my father in Goa, many years ago."

Jadar listened in silence. "I had no idea." Then his eyes grew grim. "I know him all too well. You may or may not be aware he was once planning to arm Malik Ambar against me. Unfortunately there's very little I can do about him just now. But I have a long memory too, and someday, Allah willing, I'll put an end to his trade. Will that be justice enough for us both?"

"I'll drink to it."

"And I'll drink with you." Jadar took a deep swallow of *sharbat*. "To England and India. And now, for the other reason I asked you both here today. To see what you think about something. It's curious, but living here in this little palace, I've found myself growing obsessed by an idea. I'd like to know if you think it's mad." He drank again, then signaled the waiting eunuch to refill their cups. "If I become *Moghul* one day, I've decided to build something very special for Mumtaz, a work of beauty unlike anything India has ever seen. Staying here on Jagmandir Island has given me the idea. But first come inside and let me show you something."

Jadar rose and strolled back through the columned doorway into the domed room. "Did you happen to notice this when you came in?" He pointed to one of the two-foot-high niches in the curved walls. Hawksworth realized that each niche was decorated around its top and sides with inlays of semi-precious stones set into the marble. Each inlay was a painting of a different flower.

"Do you see what he's done here?" Jadar motioned Hawksworth and Shirin closer. "This is far more than merely a design. It's actually a painting in rare, colored stone—onyx, carnelian, jasper, agate." Jadar paused. "Think carefully. Have either of you ever seen anything like this in Agra?"

"I've never seen anything like it before, anywhere."

"Of course you haven't. This is unique. It's truly astonishing. Here on Jagmandir Island, with the design of this room, Rana Karan Singh has actually invented a new style of art. It's phenomenal. Now look up." Jadar pointed to the cupola ceiling. "Notice the sensuous curve of the dome. Like a bud just before it bursts into flower. And at the top you see more inlays of precious stone. I think it's the most magnificent thing I've ever seen. Its shape and color and purity move me almost to tears." He paused and looked at Hawksworth mischievously. "So can you guess what I've decided to do someday?"

"Build a room like this in Agra?"

Jadar exploded with laughter. "But this room is so small! What sort of gift would that be for Mumtaz? No, Captain, if I should eventually find myself ruling India, I've decided to build Mumtaz an entire palace like this, a Mahal, all of white marble and inlay. I'll surround it with a garden larger and more beautiful than anything India has ever seen. It will be a place of love and of mystery, with the strength of a Rajput warrior in the harsh sunshine, the warmth of a Persian woman in the moonlight. The outside will be covered with verses from the Quran carved in marble, and inside the walls will be a garden of jeweled flowers. Minarets will rise at each corner, calling all India to prayer, and its dome will be a cupola with the subtle, sensuous curve of a ripening bud. It will be immense, the most magnificent Mahal in the world. And it will be my gift to her." He paused, his eyes glowing. "Is the idea completely insane?"

"It's beautiful." Shirin was beaming.

"I think it's magnificent." Jadar seemed not to need encouragement, as he drank again from his *sharbat*. "So now you know the other reason I invited you here this afternoon. To tell you what you may see when you return to Agra. I haven't decided on the exact location yet, but it will be on the bank of the Jamuna, placed so Mumtaz can watch the sun set over the water, just as we do here. I wanted to tell you both, for I sense you two are among the few who could really appreciate what a bold idea this is." Jadar looked sharply at Shirin. "Now, *you* must never, never tell Mumtaz, whatever else you two Persians may chatter on about. For now let's keep it a secret among us. But someday, someday it will tell all the world how much I love her." He sighed. "You know, at times I worry I'm nothing more than a romantic Persian myself, deep inside."

He looked about the glistening walls once more, then reluctantly turned and walked out onto the balcony again.

"The peace I feel here overwhelms me sometimes. It quiets all the unrest in my soul. Perhaps I'm a fool to ever think of Agra. But Agra is my destiny. The Hindus would say it's my *dharma*."

He stopped to watch as Mumtaz and her women emerged from their quarters and gathered around the fountain in the garden below. The evening air was flooded with the women's rose attar and musk perfume. He inhaled deeply, then turned to Hawksworth.

"By the way, I've had a small farewell gift made for you, Captain. It's there beside you." He pointed to the sitar by the railing. "I understand you've started learning to play it."

Hawksworth turned, startled, and picked up the instrument. Its workmanship was fine art, with ivory inlays along both sides of the body and a neck carved as the head of a swan. He found himself stunned. "I've only just begun to learn, Highness. This is much finer than I deserve. It's worthy of an Ustad."

"Then perhaps it will inspire you to become a master yourself someday." He laughed. "And now I want to hear how you play it. The Hindus believe the sitar is a window to the soul. That the sound of the first note tells everything there is to know about a man. I want to see if you've actually understood anything since you've been here. What raga have you been studying?"

"Malkauns."

"An ambitious choice. I seem to remember that's a devotional raga. For late evening. But the sun's almost down. We'll pretend it's the moon, just rising. Let's go inside, where you can sit."

Hawksworth carried the sitar and followed numbly as Jadar led the way back into the tiny marble room. The apprehension he had momentarily felt on the balcony seemed to dissolve among the bouquets of precious stones in the inlaid walls. He slipped off his shoes and seated himself in the middle of the room. Then he quickly tested the tuning on the strings, both the upper and the lower. He could already tell the sound it produced was magnificent, with the resonance of an organ. Jadar and Shirin seated themselves opposite, speaking Persian in low voices as they watched him cradle the round body of the sitar in the curved instep of his left foot. Then they both fell expectantly silent.

He knew what they were waiting to hear. For the raga Malkauns, a master would sound the first note powerfully, yet with a sense of great subtlety—slipping his finger quickly down the string and into the note just as it was struck, then instantly pulling the string across the fret, almost in the same motion, again raising the pitch and giving the feeling the note had merely been tasted, dipped down into and out again as it quavered into existence. But it was much more than mere technique. That was the easiest part. It was a sense. A feeling. It came not from the hand, but from the heart. The note must be *felt*, not merely sounded. When done with rightness, life seemed to be created, a *prahna* in the music that the player and listener shared as one. But if the player's heart was false, regardless of how skilled he might be, then his music was hollow and dead.

He breathed deeply, trying to clear his mind, then slipped the wire plectrum over his finger and gently stroked the lower sympathetic strings once, twice, to establish the mood. The cool air was crisp and flower-scented, and the sound rose gently upward toward the marble cupola above them. As he listened he found himself looking at Shirin and Jadar, their dark eyes, delicate faces. Then his eyes moved beyond them, to the garden of inlaid stones in the marble walls. And for a moment he felt something he had never felt before. This was the India he had, until that moment, only been *in*. But here, now, he was finally part of it. He took another deep breath and struck.

The first note was perfect, encompassing. He felt it. He knew it. He sensed his hand merge with the music, the music with his own life. Shirin's eyes seemed to melt, and Jadar immediately swung his head from side to side in approval. Then he began the *alap*, the virtuoso first section of the raga, meant to be played solo and without drum accompaniment. He felt the music slowly growing around him as he found and explored note after note of the raga's structure. He found himself wanting to taste and feel each note to its essence, reluctant to move on to the next. But each time he was beckoned forward, until at last nothing but the music mattered. He played on and on, the intensity of the *alap* growing organically, almost of its own self, until it burst to completion, like a flower that had gloriously escaped the entrapment of its bud.

When the final note died into silence, Shirin slowly rose and slipped her arms around his neck. Jadar sat motionless for a moment longer, then reached out and put his hand on the strings of the sitar.

"You have earned it, Captain. I've heard what I'd hoped to hear. Your music tells me all I want to know about you." He rose and led them back out onto the balcony. "I know now you *can* understand why I also want to create something of beauty someday. A Mahal that will last as long as this music. If we cannot taste love and beauty, our hearts are dead." He smiled at Hawksworth. "There is love in your music, Captain. Your heart is as it should be. And in the end, nothing else really matters. Nothing else."

He turned and stared pensively into the twilight. "My Mahal will have it too. Because it is in my own heart."

Jadar stopped abruptly and gazed toward the darkening shore. Through the dimming light a boat could be seen approaching, rowed furiously by lines of red-cloaked oarsmen. Sitting in the center on a gilded platform was Maharana Karan Singh, wearing full battle dress. His powerful bow hung loosely from his leather quiver and his rhino-hide shield rested at his side. Jadar studied the boat for a moment and concern gathered in his eyes.

"He would never come here unannounced. Merciful Allah, has the Imperial army moved against us already? How can it be so soon? My preparations have scarcely begun."

Jadar watched as the maharana leaped from the boat almost before it touched the marble dock. The women around Mumtaz fled the courtyard, and now the eunuchs pressed forward to bow and welcome him. He brushed them aside as he moved quickly through the garden and into the lower arcade of the palace. Jadar stood listening expectantly to the quick pad of his footsteps on the stone stairs, then walked inside to greet him.

"*Nimaste*, my friend. You've already missed the best part of the sunset, but I'll have more *sharbat* sent."

The maharana glanced in surprise at Hawksworth and Shirin for a second, then turned and bowed quickly to Jadar.

"The news is very bad, Highness."

"Then we'll sweeten it with *sharbat*."

"There is no time, Highness."

"There's always time for *sharbat*. This has been a special afternoon for me."

"Highness, I came to tell you Arangbar is dead. The *Moghul* of India joined the immortals two days ago."

Jadar examined him a moment almost as though not comprehending. Then he turned and stared out through the balcony doorway, past Hawksworth and Shirin. "I would not have wished it. I sincerely would not have wished it." He turned back to Karan Singh. "How did he die? Did Janahara murder my father, as she's killed so many others?"

"No, Highness. It almost seems as though he deemed it his time to die.

Two weeks ago he was hunting and saw a beater stumble and fall over a ledge, killing himself. His Majesty grew despondent, saying he had caused the man's death. Next he began to declare it an omen of his own death. He refused food and drink. Finally even the physicians despaired. He died in his bed. Word was given out that he was still hunting, so the news was carefully kept from all of Agra until the very end."

"How did you learn?"

"Nadir Sharif sent runners. He dared not send a pigeon."

Jadar walked out onto the balcony and peered down into the darkened garden. After a long moment he spoke. "Allah. Then it's finished." He turned back to the Rajput. "Has Janahara declared Allaudin *Moghul* yet?"

"She has announced she will do so, Highness." Karan Singh moved out onto the balcony next to Jadar, hesitant to interrupt his thoughts. The cries of water birds flooded the evening air around them. Jadar studied the garden again, as though lost in some distant reverie. When he spoke his voice seemed to emanate from a bottomless void.

"Allaudin will be in the Red Fort. It can never be taken, not even with a hundred thousand Rajputs. He will never come to face me. He will never need to." He turned slowly to Karan Singh. "I've lost it all, my friend. And I've brought ignominy to your lands by my presence as your guest. For that I am truly sorry."

Karan Singh stared at Jadar. "But Highness, Allaudin may not yet be *in* Agra. You know he wanted Queen Janahara to appoint him to command the army sent against you. Naturally she refused and instead convinced Arangbar to appoint him commander of the forces to be sent against the Persian Safavis threatening the northwest fortress of Qandahar. It was obvious to everyone except Allaudin that she meant it to be merely a ceremonial appointment, an excuse to elevate his *mansab* rank to equal yours. She had carefully arranged to have him detained in Agra. But he decided on his own that he would actually go north, to prove himself a commander. Just before the hunting accident, he persuaded Arangbar to allow him to march. Arangbar was apparently drunk on wine and approved the order before Janahara discovered it. Allaudin departed Agra a week ago with twenty thousand men and a huge train of courtiers. Because of their numbers, it's thought he has traveled very slowly. But Nadir Sharif said as of the day before yesterday he still had not returned to Agra. No one knows for sure how near he may actually be."

"And where are Inayat Latif and the Imperial army?" Jadar's voice quickened.

"Of that we're not yet certain, Highness. They may be in Agra by now, holding the Red Fort for Allaudin, but we have no way to know."

Jadar turned and seized his arm. "Then I will ride. Tonight. Have you told my men?"

"Two thousand of *my* men are now in their saddles waiting, Highness. By sunup another twenty thousand will be ready to ride."

Jadar stared at him for a moment, then reached out and touched the turban the Rajput was wearing. Hawksworth realized it was Jadar's gift.

"Then give me three of your best horses. Tonight. I will rotate as I ride." Jadar turned and ordered a waiting eunuch to bring his riding cloak, his sword, and his *katar*.

"I will be riding with you too, Highness." Karan Singh stepped forward.

This time Jadar embraced Karan Singh for a long moment. Then he pulled back. "No. I will not allow it. If I am too late—and the odds are strong against me—no one who rides with me will leave Agra alive. No, my friend, this I forbid." Jadar silenced Karan Singh's gesture of protest. "Your offer is enough. I want my good friends alive."

Jadar started for the stairs, then paused and turned back to look one last time at Hawksworth and Shirin.

"So our farewell was more timely than we knew. I regret we did not have longer." He paused to take his riding cloak from the eunuch. Then he reached for Hawksworth's hand. "Remember me, my friend. And remember the Mahal. I've told no one else. If I'm still alive when you come again to Agra, I'll take you there. If I'm dead, remember what I dreamed."

He turned and disappeared down the stairwell.

A tear stained Shirin's cheek as she watched him move across the courtyard below. When he reached Mumtaz, anxiously waiting by the dock, he paused and said something to her, then embraced her closely. As he pulled away, she reached out to stop him. But he was already joining the maharana in the boat. In moments they were swallowed in the dusk.

"None of us will ever see him again. You know it's true." Shirin's voice was strangely quiet. "What does it matter where Allaudin is? Prince Jadar can never challenge the troops Janahara will have holding the Red Fort. Not with two thousand Rajputs, not with two hundred thousand Rajputs. It's impregnable. He'll never see the inside of the Red Fort again." She moved next to him and rested her head against his chest. "Will you help me remember him from tonight. And the Mahal he will never live to build?"

"I'll remember it all." He encircled her in his arms, wanting her warmth, and together they watched the last shafts of sun die in the dark waters below.

LONDON

Sir Randolph Spencer studied the leatherbound packet for a long moment, turning it apprehensively in his hand. Then he meticulously untied the wrapping and smoothed the weathered parchment against the top of his desk. Around the timbered room the Company's secretaries waited nervously, in prim wigs and doublets, watching as he quickly scanned the contents. Then he looked up, beamed, and with a loud voice began to read.

JAVA, *Port of Bantam*
the 3rd of May,

George Elkington, Chief Merchant,
to the Right Honorable Sir Randolph Spencer, Director of the Worshipful Company of the East India Merchants in London

Honorable Sir, my duty premised, etc. and expecting your Worship's favorable perusing of this letter. May it please God, the Discovery will be fully laded within the month and ready to sail. In the meanwhile I forward this letter by Capt. Otterinck of the Spiegel, bound this day for Amsterdam, to advise you of certain new Conditions affecting the Company's trade. I have inform'd you by earlier letter of our Entertainment provided the Portugals in the Surat Bay, with the two of their vessels set to fire, by which they were all consumed and between four and five hundred men slain, burnt, and drowned, and of ours (God be praised) only two and some few hurt, with all Commodity safe. I have reported also the loss of the Resolve at Surat by lamentable Circumstance. Yet I maintain great Hope that we are like to discover profitable Trade with the Country of India.

I write now to advise you the Hollanders have late brought News of a new King of that Country. Reports have reached the Moluccas that the Moghul Arangbar died suddenly some two months past, to be succeeded by one of his Sons, whose Pleasure toward England is uncertain. The full Events are not clearly known here, but this will doubtless require our new Petition for license to trade.

As is oft the way in Heathen lands, the story of the Son's succession is a marvelous convoluted Tale. There were said to be two Sons in contention, belike both Knaves, and the Hollanders have deduced that the late Arang- bar's Queen, named Janahara, favor'd one Son over the other, for reasons known best to her Self, and intrigued in his succession. They have concluded thus because the new Moghul is said to have promptly rewarded her with a large secluded Estate of her own outside of Agra, with his personal Guards to protect her, something the Dutchmen claim has never before been done for a Moorish Queen in India. The Hollanders further deduce that this Queen effected the favored Son's succession through her Prime Minister, a subtle Rogue called Sharif, who, when the Moghul Arangbar died, secretly arranged the Assassination of the other Son before he could reach Agra and make his own claim for the Throne. This said Sharif was again appointed Prime Minister by the new Moghul, doubtless a Reward for his cunning Service.

So it is His Majesty King James may now desire to dispatch another Ambas- sador to Agra, to petition this new Moghul to grant English trade. If a Peti- tion is to be sent, know that before taking the Throne this Son was called by the name Prince Jadar, though doubtless he is now to be addressed for- mally as The Moghul.

I have as yet been unable to discover whether the Mission of Capt. Hawks- worth to Agra, authorized by Your Worship in your Wisdom, met success. (Though his Mission will no longer assist the Company in any instance, since he would not be known to this new Moghul, Jadar.) However, the Hol- landers have advised that an English seaman named Hawksworth was taken from an Indian vessel off Malabar one month past, in company with a Moor- ish woman, by a Frigate of theirs that later was caught by a Storm off the same Malabar Coast. Her mainmast split in that Storm, and the vessel was lost sight of soon after, leaving the Hollanders to lament it may have sunk or gone aground on the Coast, together with over five hundred ton of their Malabar pepper. If this was our former Captain-General, he is either gone to God or is now again in India (if the vessel haply made landfall and saved the Hollanders' pepper).

In closing (for the Dutchmen advise they are preparing to hoist sail), I am content to report that Indian commodity is readily vendable at the port of Bantam, particularly fine calicoes and indigo, and I adjudge the Company would be well advis'd to dispatch a new Voyage to Surat upon receipt of this letter. The Monopoly of the Portugals holds no more, esp. after their Hu- miliation in the late engagement off Surat. On condition the Company post a Gentleman of Quality to Agra (One less susceptable to Moorish ways than

Capt. Hawksworth, and therefore, in my Judgement, like to be better respected by the new Moghul) our Subscribers stand to enjoy great Profit in the Company's Indies trade.

So desiring God to add a blessing to all endeavours tending to this business of ours and of all that may succeed us to God's glory and the Company's benefit.

Your Worship's faithful servant,
Geo. Elkington

AFTERWORD

For those curious how much of the foregoing tale is "true," perhaps it may be helpful to unmask the original inspiration for several of the characters. The *Great Moghul* Akman, his son Arangbar, and Arangbar's primary consort, Queen Janahara, had real-life counterparts in the *Great Moghul* Akbar, his successor Jahangir, and Jahangir's resourceful Persian queen, Nur Jahan. Nadir Sharif, for all his duplicity, had nothing on Jahangir's devious prime minister, Asaf Khan, the brother of Queen Nur Jahan. Similarly, Prince Jadar was no more ingenious, and no less wronged, than Asaf Khan's son-in-law, the subsequent *Moghul* and builder of the Taj Mahal, Shah Jahan. Prince Jadar's strategies and intrigues, first with and then against Queen Janahara, resemble in many ways those of Shah Jahan as he struggled to thwart the ambitions of Nur Jahan. The Shahbandar and the opium-sotted governor of Surat also had counterparts in real individuals, as did Jadar's beloved Mumtaz, his younger brother Prince Allaudin, Princess Layla, Malik Ambar, and Inayat Latif. The Sufi mystic Samad was re-created from the real-life poet Sarmad, who was admired by Shah Jahan and who was executed by a later *Moghul* for precisely the reasons given in the story. Of the Portuguese, Father Alvarez Sarmento was drawn in some part from the learned Father Jerome Xavier. It should be noted that the unofficial actions of the early Jesuits in India are remembered today primarily through the perceptions of English travelers, all of whom were all staunchly anti-Catholic. The role of Portuguese Jesuits in the preceding story was faithful in spirit to the English reports, although today these may seem mildly paranoid in their fear and suspicion.

Of the English characters, only Huyghen and Roger Symmes are beholden to single, recognizable individuals: being Jan van Linschoten and Ralph Fitch, respectively. Brian Hawksworth is largely a fictional composite, whose experiences recall in part those of William Hawkins (in India from 1608 to 1613) and in part those of other seventeenth-century European adventurers. His defeat of the four Portuguese galleons was only a slight dramatization of historic victories by severely outnumbered English frigates off Surat in 1612 and 1614 commanded by English captains Thomas Best and Nicholas Downton, both sailing for the early East India Company. Hawksworth's mercurial relationship with the *Moghul* and his experiences at the *Moghul's* court were re-created in part from the letters and diaries of William Hawkins and those of his successor, Sir Thomas Roe. As did Brian Hawksworth, William Hawkins adopted the Indian style of life in dress and diet, much to the astonishment of his European contemporaries. Brian Hawksworth's love affair with Shirin was suggested by William Hawkins' marriage to an Indian woman of noble descent, possibly a member of the *Moghul's* court, on the encouragement of Jahangir, who suspected the Jesuits of attempting to poison him and wanted his food monitored. Hawkins' wife later journeyed to London, where she caused the East India Company considerable disruption over their responsibilities toward her, and eventually she returned to India.

Although most of the early Englishmen in India resembled our George Elkington far more than they did Brian Hawksworth, there was one early traveler, Thomas Coryat, whose cultural and human sensibilities would not have clashed greatly with those of Brian Hawksworth at the end of his story.

The sudden appearance of the bubonic plague in India was taken from the court history of the *Moghul* Jahangir. Similarly, the capture of the *Moghul's* trading vessel by the Portuguese, intended to intimidate him and forestall an English trade agreement, and his retaliatory closure of Jesuit missions happened essentially as described. The Jesuits were allowed to reopen their missions a few years later, but the damage was done. There seems evidence that the Portuguese did conspire to assist the forces opposing the succession of Shah Jahan, whom they justifiably feared. The rebellion of Shah Jahan extended over several years, and did include at one point a stay on the Udaipur island of Jagmandir, where some historians now believe he first saw inlay work of the type that later became a distinguishing feature of the Taj Mahal.

For those who may wish to gain more familiarity with Moghul India, various sources can be recommended. Lively historical works on the Moghul period include Waldemar Hansen's classic panorama *The Peacock Throne* and the even more recent *Cities of Mughul India* by Gavin Hambly, to mention two of my favorites. For those still more curious, and adventurous, there are the original writings from the seventeenth century, which will require more digging but are decidedly worth the effort. Readers with access to a major library may be able to find reprinted editions of the diaries of several seventeenth-century English and European travelers in India. These are the works, with their trenchant firsthand accounts, that all students of the era find indispensable. Perhaps the most easily obtainable is a collection entitled *Early Travels in India*, William Foster, ed., which contains edited versions of the diaries of William Hawkins and several others. Following this, the most thorough account of England's early diplomacy in India is contained in the diary entitled *The Embassy of Sir Thomas Roe* (1615–1619), written by England's first real ambassador to India. Many subsequent diaries and letters of seventeenth-century European travelers have been reprinted by the Hakluyt Society, whose publications comprise a virtual bibliography of the era.

The most relevant Indian writings, also obtainable in English translation from a fine library, are the memoirs of the *Great Moghul* Jahangir, entitled the *Tuzuk-i-Jahangiri,* and an encyclopedic description of court life in late sixteenth-century India entitled the *Ain-i-Akbari,* set down by Akbar's chief adviser and close friend, Abul Fazl.

In fashioning a story such as this, a writer must necessarily be indebted far beyond his ability to acknowledge adequately. The scholar who provided the greatest assistance was Professor John Richards of the Duke University Department of History, a widely respected authority on Moghul (he might prefer it be spelled Mughal) India, who graciously consented to review the manuscript in draft and offered many corrections of fact and interpretation. He is, of course, in no way accountable for any liberties that may have remained. Thanks are similarly due Professor Gerald Berreman of the University of California at Berkeley, a knowledgeable authority on Indian caste practices, who agreed to review the relevant portions of the manuscript. I am also indebted to Waldemar Hansen, who generously provided me with the voluminous notes accumulated for his own history, *The Peacock Throne.* Historians in India who gave warmly of their time and advice include Dr. Romila Thapar, Professor P. M. Joshi, and Father John Correia-Alfonso, the preeminent Jesuit authority on the early Moghul era and a scholar whose characteristic integrity and generosity roundly revise the period depiction of his order in the story.

Thanks also are due Mrs. Devila Mitra, Director-General of the Archaeological Survey of India, for special permission to study the now-restricted *zenana* quarters beneath the Red Fort in Agra; to Nawab Mir Sultan Alam Khan of Surat, for assistance in locating obscure historical sites in that city; to Indrani Rehman, the *grande dame* of Indian classical dance, for information on the now-abolished *devadasi* caste; to Ustad Vilayat Khan, one of India's great sitar masters, for discussions concerning his art; and to my many Indian friends in New York, New Delhi, and Bombay.

I am also obliged to Miss Betty Tyres of the Indian Department of the Victoria and Albert Museum in London, who kindly provided access to the museum's extensive archives of Indian miniature paintings, and to the National Maritime Museum in Greenwich for information on early English sailing vessels.

Finally, I am most indebted to a number of tireless readers who reviewed the manuscript in its various drafts and supplied many insightful suggestions: including my editor, Lisa Drew, my agent, Virginia Barber, and my patient friends Joyce Akin, Susan Fainstein, Norman Fainstein, Ronald Miller, and Gary Prideaux. Most of all I thank Julie Hoover, for many years of assistance, encouragement, and enthusiasm.

GLOSSARY

affion—opium
aga—concentrated rose oil
akas-diya—central camp light
alap—opening section of a raga
ankus—hook used for guiding an elephant
arak—Indian liquor
areca—betel nut used in making *pan*
artha—practical, worldly "duty" in Hinduism
Asvina—Lunar month of September–October
azan—Muslim call to prayer
bhang—drink made from hemp (marijuana)
biryani—rice cooked with meat and spices
bols—specific hand strokes on the Indian drum
cartaz—Portuguese trading license
chans—cattle sheds
chapattis—unleavened fried wheat cakes
chapp—seal or stamp
charkhi—fireworks used to discipline elephants in combat
chaturanga—chess
chaudol—traveling conveyance similar to palanquin
chaugan—Indian "polo"
chauki—weekly guard duty at the Red Fort
chaupar—Indian dice game
chelas—mercenary troops beholden to single commander
chillum—clay tobacco bowl on a *hookah*
chitah—Indian leopard
dai—midwife nurse
dal—lentils
darshan—ceremonial dawn appearance of Moghul
devadasi—temple dancer, a special caste
dey—Turkish ruler
dharma—purpose or duty in life of Hindus
dhoti—loincloth

diwali—Indian New Year
Diwan-i-Am—Hall of Public Audience
Diwan-i-Khas—Hall of Private Audience
durbar—public audience
feringhi—foreigner
fil-kash—elephant-drawn cannon
firman—royal decree
frigatta—Portuguese frigate
gau-kash—ox-drawn cannon
ghee—clarified butter
ghola—blend of opium and spice
gopi—milkmaid
gulal bar—royal compound in camp
gur—unrefined cane sugar
guru—teacher
gurz—three-headed club
hal—goalposts for *chaugan*
harkara—confidential court reporters
hookah—water pipe for smoking tobacco
howdah—seat carried on back of elephant
jagir—taxable lands granted to a nobleman
kama—love, sensual pleasure
karwa—Indian seaman
katar—knife designed for thrusting
khabardar—"take heed"
khaftan—quilted vest worn under armor
kos—approximately two miles
kamar-band—ceremonial waist sash
lakh—a hundred thousand
lapsi—preparation of *gur*, *ghee*, and wheat
lila—play or sport
lor langar—chain attached to elephant's leg
lungi—long waist wrap worn by men
mahal—palace
mahout—elephant driver
maidan—public square
mansab—rank given a nobleman
mansabdar—nobleman granted estates to tax
mardum-kash—small cannon
masala—blend of spices, "curry powder"
mihaffa—wooden turret suspended between two animals
mina bazaar—mock bazaar held on Persian New Year
mirdanga—South Indian drum
mohur—gold coin
mudra—hand signs in the Indian classical dance
musallim—navigator on Indian ship

mutasaddi—chief port official
nakuda—owner-captain of Indian trading vessel
naqqara-khana—entry to royal compound
nashudani—"good-for-nothing"
nautch—suggestive dance
nezah—lance
nilgai—Indian deer
nim—plant whose root is used for cleaning teeth
nimaste—Hindi greeting, "Hello"
pahar—three hours
pakhar—steel plate elephant armor
palas—wood used for *chaugan* stick
pan—betel leaf rolled around betel nut and spices and chewed
panch—wine punch
pandit—Hindu scholar
pice—Indian "penny"
postibangh—mixture of opium and hemp extract
prahna—spirit, life force
Puranas—Hindu scriptures
qamargha—hunt using beaters to assemble game
qarawals—beaters for hunt
qazi—judge
qur—hunting enclosure containing game
rasa—aesthetic mood
rasida—"arrived"; a piece that reaches center in *chaupar* board game
sachaq—marriage present
sandali—type of eunuch
sarachah—royal platform
sarangi—Indian musical instrument, resembling violin
sari—woman's wrap
sati—immolation of Hindu wife with body of her husband
sehra—bridegroom's crown
sharbat—lemon and sugar drink
shikar—the hunt
sitkrita—intake of breath signifying female orgasm
strappado—Portuguese torture device
sum—climax of rhythmic cycle in Indian music
sutra—Hindu scripture
suwar—"horse rank" granted noblemen
swanih-nigar—special spy
tari—species of palm
tavaif—Muslim courtesan
teslim—prostrate bow to Moghul
tithi—day in the lunar calendar
todah—mound of earth for bow and arrow target practice
topiwallah—"man who wears a hat," i.e., a foreigner

tundhi—drink made from seeds and juices
varna—Aryan scriptures
wakianavis—public court reporters
wallah—man
wazir—counselor
yogi—Hindu contemplative
zat—personal rank given a nobleman
zenana—harem
zihgir—thumb ring for shooting bow